Born in 1908, W. R. D. McLaughlin spent almost fifty years of his life at sea, serving first on whalers and then later on oil tankers. His popular sea adventures have been translated into a number of languages, including French, Italian, Portuguese, Norwegian and Dutch. Now retired, he lives and writes in Portlethen in the North-east of his native Scotland

Also by W. R. D. McLaughlin

SO THIN IS THE LINE
CALL TO THE SOUTH
SYNDICATE OF EVIL

Antarctic Raider

W. R. D. McLaughlin

Mayflower

Granada Publishing Limited
Published in 1977 by Mayflower Books Ltd
Frogmore, St Albans, Herts AL2 2NF

First published in Great Britain by
George G. Harrap & Co Ltd 1960

Made and printed in Great Britain by
Cox & Wyman Ltd
London, Reading and Fakenham
Set in Intertype Plantin

To
MY WIFE

CHAPTER ONE

It was December 15th, 1940, a mean, grey, overcast day. A northerly blizzard brought the first snow of winter out of a nimbostratus sky in huge petal-like flakes that blanketed the city of Hamburg.

Dusk started to fall; the gloaming was grey, then darkness and the black-out came. War-weary workers, all-weather coats buttoned to the throat, mingled with the late-afternoon shoppers as they silently groped their way homeward through the blinding snow and darkness.

They made a strange spectacle these German people. Once they were ordinary men and women, but now they did not belong among the ordinary men and women: National Socialism had changed their lives. Now they were a subjected and regimented people, but still people, men and women, sharing the same emotions, the same fears, and the same hopes of ultimate victory.

Christmas 1940 was to be a merry one for the people of Germany. Hadn't the Führer kept all his promises? He had occupied the Rhineland. He had annexed Austria and Czechoslovakia. Poland, Norway, Denmark, Belgium, Holland, and France had been overwhelmed by the victorious armies of the Fatherland. Now these same armies had blasted their way to the shores of the English Channel. Only the British remained: soon they would have to capitulate. The War could last only a few more months; the whole of Europe was at the mercy of the Führer.

Close to the Hamburg waterfront, directly across the river from the huge camouflaged U-boat pens, and near where the river ferries were disgorging their thousands of shipyard and munition workers on the first leg of their homeward journeys, an important naval conference was taking place within a well-guarded building.

The conference room was rectangular in shape. Around its

walls, fastened at strategic heights, were numerous brass plaques, each commemorating some German naval exploit of the First World War. At the top end of the room a large Nazi flag was draped from a lofty ceiling, the red, white, and black of its bunting lending colour to the sombre surroundings. A well-worn, polished hardwood table took up most of the room's space; around its sides seven men in the uniform of the German Navy were seated, their faces grim and attentive.

The chairman of the conference, a corpulent, close-cropped Admiral, glared at his juniors, until his eyes rested exclusively upon one of the officers seated to his right. 'You have this assignment perfectly clear, then, Captain Fischer?' he asked. 'You will do your utmost to carry out your instructions. There must be no failures, no half-hearted attempts to obtain the required results. You must be completely ruthless in all your dealings, both with your own officers and men and with the crews of your captured ships. I understand that a large percentage of the crews of the Norwegian ships may not be unsympathetic to our cause. That is for you to find out.'

The four-ringed officer nodded his head. He was staring hard at the huge black swastika that formed the major part of the flag draped behind the Admiral's back.

The Admiral adjusted his heavy gold-rimmed spectacles. His eyes arrogantly swept the other officers seated round the table. 'Germany must have her quota of whale-oil from Antarctica,' he said. 'You all know how impracticable it is for us to send out our own whaling fleet. We must resort to the next best thing – the seizure of both British and Norwegian whaling vessels now operating in Antarctic waters. These ships must be captured . . . they must not be destroyed. They must be brought back to Germany with their cargoes intact. We must have this whale-oil.

There was a period of silence. The Admiral shifted his gaze to a younger officer seated at the lower end of the table, and continued with Teutonic harshness: 'The task seems formidable. I can assure you all it will be formidable, but it must be successful. Germany relies on this one operation for a whole year's supply of whale-oil. It is absolutely essential that we add to our present stocks.'

Captain Fischer frowned. He was about to say something, but the Admiral held up his hand for silence.

'The Reich requires this oil, not because of its food-value, but for the most important product that can be had through the process of extraction. Glycerine, the most important of the by-products from whale-oil, is necessary for the production of gun-powder.'

Fischer nodded again. You old fool! he thought. Why don't you get down to something constructive? We know all this. He sat straight upright in his chair and stared directly at the Admiral's bulky shoulders and thick neck.

'I have assigned to you, Captain Fischer,' came the Admiral's voice, 'as members of your crew, Lieutenant Kaltenbrunner and Lieutenant Dieter. Each has held executive rank in pre-war German whale factory-ships, and is conversant with the workings of such vessels. They will act as ice pilots for you in Antarctic waters, and both will eventually take over command of captured ships. They will be responsible for taking these vessels back to Germany. You will use them purely in an advisory capacity during the voyage south. Both are in attendance at this conference.'

There was a short pause as the Admiral consulted the notes on the table before him. 'As far as is known,' he continued, 'there are four pelagic expeditions now operating in the waters of Antarctica. They are – *Antarctica*, *Cachelot*, *Southern Isles*, and *Southern Cross*. The first two expeditions are Norwegian and are controlled by the Norwegian Government in London. The latter expeditions are under the British flag.'

He left the table and went across the room to a large map of the South Atlantic which had just been hung from the wall. His grey eyes hardened as he continued speaking. 'The sphere of operation as regards the Norwegian vessels will probably be between the meridian of Greenwich and twenty-five degrees west. The position of the British ships may be well to the westward – as far west as the South Shetlands.'

He returned to his chair and seated himself comfortably. His voice droned on. 'These ships operate along the ice-edge; consequently their latitudes may vary accordingly. No trouble should be experienced in locating their respective positions. It is assumed that they will be in constant communication, by radio or by radio-telephony, with their whale-catcher fleets. Directional bearings should be taken at every opportunity. It is imperative that your own radio silence be maintained at all times.'

There was a pause, as if the Admiral wanted this last sentence to be digested fully. Fischer now sat with his hands jammed hard in his pockets, his shoulders slightly hunched.

'Radio messages, in code, may be transmitted to your vessel at any of the times mentioned in the secret code lists. Care should be taken to maintain an efficient watch on the specified wavebands. The only time your own radio silence can be broken is when it is deemed advisable to inform us that a whale factory-ship has been captured and is actually on her way back to Germany with her cargo of whale-oil.'

'Is that advisable, sir?' interrupted Fischer.

'It is necessary,' the Admiral answered curtly.

Fischer wedged himself more firmly into his chair. Necessary! he thought. Necessary! ... I can't see it. Why can't the ships send their own signals?

The Admiral went on as if he had not been interrupted. 'There may be tanker or transport vessels in attendance upon these whale factory-ships. The presence of these ships may constitute a problem. They should be destroyed or abandoned to the waters of Antarctica, whichever is thought best at the time, provided, of course, that they contain no whale-oil and that sufficient oil-fuel remains on board the whale-ships for the voyage back to Germany. In the event of whale-oil having been already loaded to these tankers it will be necessary to have it retranshipped.

'Each expedition will have approximately twelve whale-catcher vessels in attendance. They should be destroyed after their crews have been transferred to the parent ship. It may be advisable to retain one of these vessels – use it for scouting purposes.

'That is about all, Captain. I may mention that low-powered radio-telephony has been put on board your vessel. It must be used only when you are actually in the process of taking over these whale-ships. It must not be used at any other time.'

Fischer nodded, but made no comment.

'Your command is at present lying at Kiel, and is in all respects ready for sea. It is imperative that this mission should remain a closely guarded secret – that is, until such time as you are well clear of coastal waters. All shore leave to your crew has been cancelled – has been for some considerable time. You will have detailed orders handed to you prior to your sailing. I wish you success, Captain. I wish all of you good luck in this mission.'

The Admiral gathered his papers together. He shook hands quietly with Fischer and slowly walked from the conference room.

CHAPTER TWO

Captain Leopold Fischer quietly paced the luxurious day cabin of his new command – a command which was about to take him to the outer fringes of the Southern world.

What an assignment! he thought. It seemed so very easy for the German Naval Command to issue its orders. It was going to be an entirely different matter to carry them out. True, he had what appeared to be a formidable ship, an ex-passenger motor-vessel of 14,000 tons dead weight, specially rebuilt for the job in hand. A ship of twenty knots, well armed, and fitted with every modern aid. A ship to inspire confidence . . . strong . . . safe . . . comfortable . . . But there were many complications.

It wasn't so easy for a German surface raider to roam the high seas without detection. The *Graf Spee* had found that out. One can carry on for just so long. In his own particular case it wasn't as if he had to sink or even harass enemy shipping. His vessel was to be no ocean marauder, roaming the different oceans in search of easy prey. His mission was to capture ships, and to get those ships back to Germany. The Nazi Admiral hadn't had much to say about the whale-catcher fleet that was attached to each of these expeditions. How was he to maintain radio silence among these vessels, when they were scattered round the horizons of their respective parent vessels? A leakage as to his activities, and the rôles could be reversed: the hunter would become the hunted!

He glanced through the windows that took up a large area of the forward bulkhead of his day room. The port of Kiel was held in the icy grip of winter. The harbour surface was covered with a thin layer of ice. It was snowing, had been snowing intermittently for several days.

Why had he been chosen for this assignment? He knew nothing about Antarctica, and even less about these whaling vessels. Was this a form of punishment – disciplinary measure for having been at cross-purposes with some of the Hitler stooges while he was in command of his last cruiser – or was the assignment of such importance? He was fortunate in having the services of Kaltenbrunner and Dieter. These ex-whaling officers could be a great help. He had been suitably impressed with them at the conference in Hamburg. They both knew whaling life, and both could speak fluent Norwegian. They should be an asset, especially during the early stages of the voyage.

He continued the slow pacing of his day cabin. He tapped lightly on the aneroid barometer that was fastened to the athwartship bulkhead. The pointer was falling rapidly. 'Looks like we're in for a gale,' he said to himself. 'Now is the time to go. Why don't the sailing orders come? Two or three days of this weather, and I could run any type of blockade.'

There was a sharp knock on the door, and his second-in-command, Lieutenant Wenzel, entered the room. He saluted smartly and reported: 'Everything is in order, sir. We can sail at an hour's notice.'

Fischer returned the salute, glanced keenly at his young lieutenant, and smiled pleasantly. He had insisted on this arrangement ever since he had taken over command. Wenzel had to report twice daily as to the ship's readiness for sailing.

'I was hoping that you would come to report now, Lieutenant. Please sit down.'

Wenzel removed his cap and sat lightly down in the nearest armchair. Fischer noted the well-bleached hair, yellow as corn, and the cold blue eyes. A typical specimen of Nazi youth, he thought, hard . . . arrogant . . . aggressive. He looked exactly what he was – the Prussian naval officer.

Fischer relaxed in his chair. The two men exchanged glances. 'I've wanted to get to know you unofficially,' the commanding officer said. 'I must congratulate you on the efficiency of the ship, that and what I have seen of the crew. You appear to have done an excellent job of work.'

Wenzel smiled, but did not speak.

'You must understand, Lieutenant, that it's impossible for me to disclose any of my orders until we get out to sea. The job ahead of us is going to be a tough one – how tough remains to be seen – but I'm sure you appreciate this. You've been here throughout the ship's conversion; you've seen the type of stores and equipment loaded. Even with all this knowledge, however, I think our destination will surprise you.'

Again the younger officer smiled. 'Thank you, sir,' he said. 'I appreciate what you have just said. The crew appear to be rather a mixed lot, with a very large number drawn from the reserve. They can be welded together, I should imagine, into a strong and efficient team.'

Fischer nodded in approval.

'These last four weeks have been the worst, sir,' continued Wenzel. 'All shore leave has been cancelled, and there's much speculation going on among both officers and ratings. With Christmas only a few days away, every one expects the leave ban to be lifted.'

'I'm afraid that won't happen, Lieutenant.'

Wenzel nodded wearily. 'A curious thing *has* struck me about this crew, sir. Many of the ratings have little or no idea of naval discipline. They're experienced and practical seamen, about the best on board, but they've no knowledge of naval methods. They do their work efficiently, but it must be in their own way. I've been wondering about them. I looked up many of their records, and find that they're all pre-war whalemen.'

Fischer looked at his senior officer in amazement. He cursed inwardly. The implications of Wenzel's statement could be far-reaching. Someone's blundered, he thought. Someone's blundered badly. Here, before the voyage had even started, Wenzel was already probing the edge of the truth. What if this whale talk had been carried on ashore, in dockside bars and taverns? He was experienced enough to realize that British Intelligence was just as efficient as its German counterpart. Wenzel had practically solved the secret of this assignment by the simple method of checking on the records of his crew, even though he had not realized it.

Where ignorance is bliss, mused Fischer. He thought about Kaltenbrunner and Dieter. Let them just mention the word whale, and his second-in-command need speculate no more. The secret would be out – even before they sailed. All this secret matter nearly ruined, all because of some staff officer being too damned efficient! What did he want with ex-whalemen as ratings? All that was necessary was advice from his two whaling supernumeraries. He himself could deal with all other matters.

Fischer frowned. He made a brusque gesture with his hand, as if to end the interview. He wanted the senior officer off the subject. 'We have two officers joining late this afternoon,' he said ' – Lieutenant Kaltenbrunner and Lieutenant Dieter. See that they report to me instantly on arrival. They will at all times come under my personal supervision. They will act only on my own instructions – purely in a supernumerary capacity.'

Wenzel rose from his chair and waited for a break in the discourse.

'I expect my orders at any moment,' Fischer was saying. 'Please see that all communication is now severed with the shore. Under no circumstances allow unauthorized persons to board this vessel.' He gave the younger officer a curt nod of dismissal, and Wenzel left the room.

The snow had ceased, but the sky was still leaden. Fischer watched from his windows the scene of activity on the dockside within his immediate view.

On the other side of the wharf six U-boats were moored line abreast in two separate groups. Fischer watched the crews, muffled to the eyes against the biting northerly wind, as they laboured furiously to load stores and various equipment. Huge electric cranes were constantly in action, swinging their loads crazily overhead before landing them on the decks of the U-boats with scarcely a sound. An ancient and grimy-looking steam locomotive backed and filled with snorting precision as it shunted wagonloads of stores and lethal-looking torpedoes alongside the cranes.

The U-boats were in the process of fuelling. Copper oil-hoses, coiled haphazardly around the decks, carried diesel oil from some underwater pipeline.

They don't waste much time, thought Fischer. They arrive, then there is a mad scramble to get them off to sea again. What a life! Weeks on end cruising below the convoy routes of the North Atlantic! A ruthless, remorseless job! . . .

He watched a group of young officers supervising some loading detail. Haggard and gaunt-looking young men, there were no victory smiles in this group – only a war-wearied listlessness that defied adequate description.

Fischer went to his desk and switched on a radio-set. He tuned to Berlin, and was in time to hear a short summary of the news. 'The whole of Merseyside was heavily bombed throughout the night,' said the broadcaster. 'All our aircraft returned safely to their home bases.' He glossed over the fact that Berlin had been bombed during the same period. 'Germany is massing,' the voice said, 'for an all-out air assault on London – prelude to invasion. The United Kingdom is doomed – unless they ask for an armistice.'

The same old stuff, Fischer thought. He shrugged and switched off the radio. It's part of their job. Anything to boost the morale of the people. Hadn't Hitler already proclaimed a war of total annihilation? That was six months ago – soon after Dunkirk, after the remnants of the British armies had been swept into the seas. Why hadn't the Führer exploited this colossal victory? The British were daily becoming stronger. They were beginning to hit back. They were just as strong in the air as Goering's much-vaunted Luftwaffe, much more powerful at sea, and, what was more important, they were now in the process of organizing vast land forces. Perhaps they did stand alone, but they had a united Commonwealth behind them – potential power unlimited in its resources. The broadcaster was wrong . . . definitely wrong.

His reverie was interrupted by a young steward arriving with coffee. He watched carefully as the boy went about his duties. He nodded curtly, and watched him back subserviently to the door.

A squall broke over the harbour, and hailstones danced upon the decks. He watched a group of ratings scamper for shelter. A couple of weeks on the ice-edge of Antarctica, and they won't worry about hailstones! he thought.

He was pouring his coffee when he noticed the staff car come racing along the dockside and stop opposite the gangway. A staff officer stepped out, followed by a rating, and then by Kaltenbrunner and Dieter. The staff officer and his aide hurried on board. Fischer was quick to notice that the officer carried a locked dispatch-case; the rating struggled with a large package of charts. 'At last!' he exclaimed.

Within minutes they were at his door. The rating entered first, deposited the charts on the nearest chair, and quickly left the room. Fischer closed the door.

'I have brought you your sailing orders and a list of confidential books, Captain. Will you please sign these receipts?' The staff officer nervously pulled the receipts from an inside pocket.

Fischer glanced at the list, and commenced to check the papers and books against the receipt note. They were in order. He glanced only momentarily at the list of charts.

'I trust everything is in order?'

Fischer nodded. 'Yes. Everything appears to be in order.' He lifted a pen from his desk and signed the receipt notes in triplicate, handing two copies to the staff officer and keeping one for himself.

'Thank you, sir.' The officer came to a salute and took his departure.

Fischer rechecked the list of papers and books: they agreed with the receipt notes. There were three sealed envelopes. One had to be opened on receipt, one on departure, and the third after an interval of five days. He hurriedly opened the first and began to read:

OPERATION VIKING

Arrangements have been made for your departure at 2200 hours. Everything will be done to expedite the operation.

Instructions as to your coastwise route are contained in sealed envelope No. 2. This will be opened immediately on your departure.

Pilot and tugs have been briefed for the above time.

NAVAL CONTROL, KIEL

Fischer glanced at the clock – 1600 hours. They've given us plenty of time, he thought. He carefully deposited the papers and confidential books in the ship's safe, and then sent for his senior officer.

Wenzel arrived in a hurry.

'Our immediate orders, Lieutenant.' He handed the sailing note to Wenzel, and added, 'It's self-explanatory. See that these instructions are carried out. Both Kaltenbrunner and Dieter have arrived. Send them to me – immediately.'

'They are both waiting below, sir. They've been waiting ever since the control officer was with you. I'll send them to you at once.'

Fischer smiled. The perfect Lieutenant! he thought. One can't ruffle him. Hope he hasn't been speaking to them. He'll have them weighed up in a matter of minutes. He'll know at a glance that they're not the usual type of naval officer.

There was a knock at the door: Kaltenbrunner entered first, immediately followed by Dieter. Both came to an awkward salute. Fischer ignored the salutes. He shook hands warmly with each of the supernumeraries.

'Sorry we are late, Captain. Naval Control, Hamburg, kept us busy until late this morning. We came through by car.' Kaltenbrunner had elected himself the spokesman.

Fischer nodded. 'I expected that,' he said. 'I didn't expect you to arrive until we were on the point of sailing. Take a chair.'

They sat down in the nearest chairs.

'I am pleased to see you both. Welcome to the cruiser *Viking*. It seems as if we have come to the start of our mission. We're due to sail in a few hours. I hope the weather remains as it is. It could help us in our dash to the open sea.'

'Yes, sir,' said Kaltenbrunner. 'Conditions are certainly favourable. I think they'll remain like this for a few days. According to the weather experts in Hamburg, they've been waiting for a depression like this to come along. I only hope they're right.'

Fischer smiled again. 'They can be wrong, of course. We'll hope for the best. Let us wish, for once, that the meteorological experts *are* correct.' He laughed loudly, and added, 'It's a long way to the open spaces. We can do with all the help we can get.'

Dieter noddded. He spoke for the first time. 'Yes, sir, and all the assistance after that as well. We need all the luck that's going to bring this assignment to a successful conclusion.'

'That's the pessimistic view,' growled Kaltenbrunner.

They all laughed.

They don't seem very optimistic, thought Fischer. They already see the snags.

Fischer spoke about his interview with Wenzel – of the fact that his crew included many pre-war German whalemen, and that this greatly perturbed him.

'These men,' he went on, 'have been on board this vessel for some considerable time. What if this whale talk has been carried on ashore – in all the dockside bars? Why should a large group of whalemen suddenly be turned into Navy men and sent on board an armed surface raider? If Wenzel knew you were both connected with whaling-ships he would immediately jump to his own conclusions. What he can do an enemy Intelligence agent can do a damned sight better. It is my considered opinion that the whole assignment has been jeopardized by the inclusion of these men in our crew.'

Dieter glanced at Kaltenbrunner. Surprise showed on both their faces.

'This is news to us, sir,' said Dieter. 'Bad news. We have no knowledge of this. You're right – someone's blundered.' He scowled as he tried to get the thought straight – to see it in its proper perspective. 'Do you think you should report this, Captain?'

'No!' Fischer exclaimed. 'We can't do that. Who are we to screen everyone who's sent on board this vessel? There's enough of that in the Nazi Germany of today without our practising it. It's only because Wenzel started probing around on his own that we know of it. It's too late ... far too late. The damage has been done.'

Kaltenbrunner smiled. 'If there *is* any damage. We're probably looking on the worst side of the whole matter.'

Fischer made a little grimace. 'I hope you're right, Lieutenant. Yes, I hope you're right. I've enough worries.'

Kaltenbrunner nodded. 'I guess you—'

He was interrupted by the wild and eerie wailing of the shore air-raid sirens, followed by a stampede about the decks as the ratings hurried to emergency stations. Sporadic firing commenced from shore anti-aircraft batteries, which was later augmented by more regular firing from naval ships anchored or moored in the harbour. Kiel became all noise as the darkening sky was covered by black-and-white pom-poms of smoke.

Kaltenbrunner moved as if to go out on deck.

'Sit tight, Lieutenant,' Fischer said. 'The all-clear will go in a minute.'

At once there came a sudden lull in the firing, and a few minutes later the all-clear came from the shore. 'I believe the port has been worried by a single reconnaissance aircraft every second evening for the past two weeks. He arrives just before dusk, and always manages to elude the fighter aircraft in the fading light. One of these nights they're going to come across in force. Just like Berlin and Hamburg. They're going to plaster this place.'

'Then let's get to hell out of it,' Kaltenbrunner said with a smile.

'There's something in that,' Fischer said. 'What I was going to say when we were interrupted was that I have given orders that you are not to be disturbed, that you are in no way to take part in the running or navigation of the ship. In the meantime I think it advisable for you to avoid any contact with the other officers – that is, of course, only until we're well clear of coastal waters and our plans become generally known.'

He smiled broadly, and went on: 'I feel this assignment gets much more interesting as we go along. I have to admit that at first I was annoyed at having been chosen for this command. Now I'm not so sure. I'm looking forward to the voyage, and to making a success of it.'

Both supernumerary officers nodded in approval.

'It's not going to be an easy job. You both know more about it than I do. How can we keep a vessel of this size a secret from such a conglomeration of shipping, especially in such a limited area? It just can't be done!'

Kalterbrunner frowned. His usual quietness of manner left him. He looked directly at Fischer as he spoke, and a guttural note came into his voice. 'It can be done, sir. It can be done – easily! Surprise and speed – that's the main essential. If we can run the British blockade I don't see any complications in Antarctica.'

Fischer was not going to be put off by evasions. He wanted a straight answer to the question that was now obsessing him. 'But ... these ships? Do you realize that there will be over thirty ships in each of these two areas? That's the only thing that really worries me.'

Dieter broke in. 'You're not acquainted with conditions on the ice-edge, sir. Let's get on board the first ship; the rest will be easy.'

Fischer did not take altogether kindly to this. 'I bow to your local knowledge,' he said. He made the words sound flat and final.

There was deep irony in the way the commanding officer had spoken. Kaltenbrunner remained silent, refusing to be drawn. He was prepared to be tolerant of Fischer's ignorance of whaling matters, but the last remark had stung him: it was he who had prepared the plans for the whole assignment.

Fischer smiled and raised his eyebrows. His eyes were troubled as he fingered his chin. 'What does it matter, anyway?' he said. 'The more ships there are down there the more whale-oil we'll ship home to Germany.'

They all laughed as the tension eased.

'Now, if you'll excuse me. I'm looking forward to a series of interesting talks and conferences with you in the near future. My greatest worry, meantime, is to get the *Viking* out into the open sea. After that is done the going will be easier – that is, until we get to Antarctic waters. I trust you'll both find things comfortable; there's unlimited space.'

The supernumerary officers expressed their thanks and left the room.

Fischer relaxed. Another few hours, and they would be at sea, he thought. Both Kaltenbrunner and Dieter impressed him. They certainly looked efficient, and acted efficiently. He was lucky to have such officers on this mission. And there were others – Lieutenant Wenzel, Lieutenant Linder, Lieutenant-Surgeon Reuss, all young officers recently decorated for gallantry in the invasion of Norway. Unlike Kaltenbrunner and Dieter, he knew that these officers regarded their appointments to *Viking* with a sense of frustration, that through their being with *Viking* the War was passing them by. There was a surprise coming to them.

The wind was increasing. It was now force seven – a moderate gale. Visibility was poor, had been poor throughout the day. Now and again the ship trembled violently as successive squalls forced her hard against the stone dockwall.

All was noise and bustle outside. A dead ship had suddenly come to life. Fischer knew that sea watches had now commenced; he recognized the various sounds, sounds that forced his mind momentarily away from his real thoughts.

The whole world was in a turmoil, in a process of total destruction, heading for complete disintegration, like some gigantic building being overwhelmed by termites. Even the little things had to be exploited in order to wage total war – things like destroying whole whaling fleets. Did these whalemen, thousands of miles away in the distant reaches of Antarctica, worry about the War at the present time? Definitely not. They were far too busy – busy doing what they had done down through the years – earning a living under chaotic conditions. Here he was in charge of a machine planned to capture or liquidate them ruthlessly; to grasp, like the pirates of old, that which had been so rightfully earned.

He brought his thoughts back to the immediate task. If this weather lasted he could be clear of all dangers within four days. Against this there was the thought of the extra hazards involved in running his ship at full speed in fog and poor visibility. Chances had to be taken, he knew that, but as far as he was concerned it would be full speed – whatever the conditions.

2200 hours – zero-time for departure. Captain Fischer stood on his bridge for the first time, taking an active interest in the unmooring of the vessel. The last line had been severed from the shore. Slowly the tugs hauled her into mid-channel. Towlines were cast off, the engines began to turn slowly, and the German surface raider vanished into the mist of the Baltic Sea with ever-increasing power. Operation Viking had begun.

CHAPTER THREE

It was the fifth day out: nearly 2,500 miles from the departure port of Kiel. Fischer was pleased with himself, pleased with his ship, his officers and crew, and pleased with the weather, especially the past weather. One hundred and twenty hours in which his command had ploughed her way through heavy seas, continuous squalls, intermittent snow-flurries, and blinding fog. Five days in which he had never once relaxed; but he could relax now. The *Viking* was outside the range of British coastal patrols and of reconnaissance aircraft. The wide reaches of the Atlantic lay before her. She had successfully run the British blockade.

Fischer gave a sigh of deep satisfaction; he felt a self-satisfying superiority at a job well done. It had been an arduous five days for him, he thought. First it had been the navigation, the pin-point navigation, in fog, that was required for the passage through the extensive mined areas guarding the approaches to Nazi Germany. Then there had been that northward dash, that inshore course that led along the Norwegian coast until the sixty-sixth parallel was reached. Westing had then been made to pass a hundred and fifty miles to the north of Iceland. Now they were steering in a southerly direction through the Denmark Strait.

Throughout the whole of this time they had encountered nothing – nothing but bad weather and poor visibility. They had both helped. Now the weather was changing: the barometer was rising slowly, wind and sea were moderating, and the fog had turned to a drizzling rain.

Fischer bathed and shaved. He had his steward serve the evening meal in his cabin. He promised himself a full night's rest – the first since leaving Kiel. He would open the last of his sealed orders. It was about time he told his officers and crew something of the task that lay before them. Tomorrow was Christmas Eve; he would break the news to all of them in a message over the 'blower'.

He went to the ship's safe and took out the weighted bag containing all his confidential papers and codes. He seized upon the last of the sealed envelopes, marked 'Secret and Confidential', and returned the bag to the safe. He phoned for his steward, and watched him silently clear away the last of his evening meal. Now he was alone. He turned the envelope over several times before he finally broke the seals and began to read.

OPERATION VIKING

From a position in latitude 65 degrees 00 minutes North, longitude 35 degrees 00 minutes West, a course should be followed that will take you to a position one hundred miles east of St. Paul Rocks in latitude 00 degrees 30 minutes North, longitude 27 degrees 30 minutes West. Care should be taken to pass a reasonable and safe distance westward of the Cape Verde Islands.

From the position off St. Paul Rocks you should steer directly for the meridian of Greenwich in approximately 60 degrees South, or, if the ice-edge lies to the northward, then to a position as far as practicable on the same meridian. It is expected that the Norwegian pelagic expeditions will be met within that area.

After the capture of the *Antarctica* and *Cachelot* you should proceed along the ice-edge in a westerly direction until you meet the British expeditions. The position of these vessels is expected to be approximately 35 degrees West, but, depending on whaling conditions, they may possibly be farther to the westward.

The utmost caution will be necessary when closing these British ships. Scouting whale-catcher craft should be used in order to ascertain whether there are Allied naval ships in the vicinity. Speed is essential, especially in taking over these British ships.

As far as the capture of all vessels is concerned, you should use your own judgment. It is advisable that plans be worked out in conjunction with Lieutenants Kaltenbrunner and Dieter. Each of these officers has vast experience in the ways of these ships and of conditions therein.

Boarding-parties should be frequently exercised in order that they may be familiar with the boarding procedure. It is deemed advisable that one of the above officers be in charge of the initial boarding operation.

You have our instruction to the effect that these officers take over command of two of the captured whale factory-ships. We now think it advisable that you retain Lieutenant Kaltenbrunner to the last. He should be given command of the last British ship captured. This will enable you to have the benefit of his experience throughout the mission.

After your assignment has been completed, and the whale-ships are on their way back to Germany with their cargoes of whale-oil, we have now decided that it will be necessary to divert attention from these vessels by drawing immediate attention to your own presence.

This can be done only by carrying out some swift and dramatic operation. You therefore have our orders to destroy, ruthlessly, the land-based whaling stations on the island of South Georgia.

The operation should entail no difficulty, provided, of course, that it is carried out with the utmost speed. The whaling stations, three in number, are situated in Stromness Bay. The Argentine station at Cumberland Bay should not be interfered with.

The approaches to Stromness Bay are guarded by a single gun emplacement. We enclose a plan of its approximate position. A constant watch is maintained over the entrance to this bay; we therefore advise you not to enter this area until the gun has been destroyed. We again emphasize the importance of the time factor: speed is essential. There should be little opposition to a landing-party.

In order to safeguard yourself, after completing your mission, it may be necessary for you to run to the southward to avoid the Allied naval ships that are certain to come searching for you. Again we leave this to your own judgment, but you should definitely allow a reasonable time interval to elapse before you attempt your own homeward voyage.

We wish you good luck in this mission.

Fischer gave a loud grunt and returned the envelope to the safe. Not much to go on, he thought. Not much at all. He dressed in oilskins, made his way to the navigation bridge, and took up a position close to the gyro-compass repeater. His eyes grew accustomed to the darkness, and the horizon could now be seen with comparative ease.

The *Viking* was masked in blackness. Fischer watched the silent figures of watch-keepers and look-outs as they moved closely around him. The moon, riding high in the sky, shed a sickly-looking light through an opening in an otherwise overcast sky. One moment it was there; the next, it had entirely disappeared. He groped his way to the chartroom, calling out for the senior bridge officer as he entered.

Fischer glanced at the ocean chart, studying the electric log and checking the ship's speed. He turned with a start to find Linder standing close behind him. He gave a grunt and said, 'Looks like we're in for a better night.'

'It will be a change, sir. We can do with it.'

Fischer gave a weary smile. 'We can't complain,' he said in a tired voice. 'The weather has been kind enough so far. Kind enough for our purpose.'

The young officer nodded. What purpose? he was thinking. What purpose, indeed? You tell us nothing. Well over two hundred men boxed up in the ship for over a month now, and nobody with any idea what on earth it's all about. There were the rumours, all sorts of rumours, wild and fantastic ones, at that, but it was all speculation. Only Fischer himself knew, and he hadn't said anything – yet. And who were these naval officers who arrived in the staff car just before they sailed? Fischer had interviewed them immediately – a long interview. They looked like seamen, but so far they'd had no official duties. They kept to themselves. Wenzel must know something . . .

'We'll continue on the same course during the night,' Fischer was saying. 'See that an efficient watch is maintained.' He had given the chart only a cursory glance. He folded it over and returned it to an overhead rack. 'We are too far to the northward to be in danger of falling foul of east- or west-bound convoys. Tell Lieutenant Wenzel to have crews at action stations at dawn, however. It will be an exercise, if nothing else. See that I am warned at the same time.'

Linder nodded silently in the orange light of the chartroom.

Fischer half closed one eye and looked shrewdly at the young officer. He chuckled quietly, and said, 'Don't worry, Lieutenant. Every one will know what our job is to be by tomorrow. What do you think?'

Linder shrugged and looked sheepishly at his commanding officer. 'Well, seeing that you ask me, sir, it is my opinion, now that we have come this far, that the *Viking*'s role is to be that of an ocean marauder. Something like the *Graf Spee.* A surface raider that will continually prey on any Allied shipping sailing unescorted.'

Fischer smiled. Linder was young ... enthusiastic. 'That answer is as good as any,' he said. 'Only there aren't many ships that go unescorted nowadays. No, Lieutenant, you'll have to do better than that. Don't let it worry you. We'll all know by tomorrow. I hope the news will satisfy everybody.'

Linder hid his disappointment. 'Whatever the mission is, sir,' he said, 'I know that every one will be looking forward to bringing it to a successful conclusion. It will be something to do – something worth-while – something for Germany.'

'Good night, Lieutenant. I'm off to bed.' He threw the chart dividers away from him, gave a short grunt, and left the chartroom.

These young officers were all the same, he thought. Full of enthusiasm for Hitler's war. Riding on the crest of a wave of Nazi successes – a wave of terror that had engulfed the whole of Europe. They were afraid that they were going to be left out of it all. What did it matter to him? Nothing! He'd had his successes. His failures too. He had once served under the flag of a different Germany, a proud Germany, a Germany that meant something. Not a Germany that was made up of masses of uniformed, regimented, and hysterical people, run by a more than hysterical house-painter. The Germany of today had changed ... changed for the worse.

He started to undress. He had been young himself once, full of the same enthusiasm as young Linder. Hadn't he been a sub-lieutenant at the beginning of the First World War, and officer of the cruiser *Nürnberg*, sunk off the Falkland Islands on December 8th, 1914. He'd been one of the few survivors. That had been a real naval engagement, a battle in true naval tradition. Who was to blame him for his enforced captivity during the remainder of hostilities? He had actually enjoyed being the guest of the British. Germany had been defeated, and with her defeat the proud Imperial Navy had perished for ever.

Throughout the years between the Wars promotion had come slowly to him. A smaller Navy and a much vaster Army had emerged from the past, bringing in their train unlimited power to a crowd of political fanatics. He'd been lucky; he'd been kept in small, secure appointments while others of the older regime had been axed. On the outbreak of the Second World War he'd gained command of one of the latest cruisers, only to be demoted to this lesser appointment.

His thoughts rambled on. He hadn't been happy at this appointment – not after a cruiser command. Now he wasn't so sure. Here was a chance to distinguish oneself, a chance that few naval officers would have refused. The larger ships were cooped up in the fjords of Norway – powerful units of destruction, but still afraid to oppose in battle the power of Britain's heavier ships. Only the U-boat commanders seemed to have the glory now. They were the ones to hit the headlines. The days of the surface fighting ships seemed to be over: they'd outlived their usefulness.

From his position on the bridge Fischer watched the miracle of the birth of another day. Wenzel, a shrouded, muffled figure, stood closely by his side, his eyes scanning the horizon through powerful glasses. Around them, stationed at all strategic points, were the bridge look-outs and other personnel. Gun-crews were at action stations: one moment the guns of the *Viking* would be trained upward, high in altitude, the next, they would be just as quickly depressed and swinging through the horizon for close-range firing.

'Nothing to report, sir,' said Wenzel. 'Nothing in sight.'

Fischer nodded curtly. 'You can dismiss the gun-crews.'

The order was quickly executed.

Fischer took a short turn or two along the bridge. 'This is the first time we've seen the horizon in the daytime since we left Kiel,' he said. 'It makes a difference.'

'Yes, sir. A pleasant difference.'

'Let's go inside. I've something to say to you.' Fischer turned quickly and made his way to the chartroom. The executive officer followed.

The commanding officer lit a cigarette very slowly. He reached upward and took from the overhead rack the general chart of the Atlantic Oceans. He spread it over the chart-table and lifted a pair of heavy brass dividers. 'There!' he said, pointing dramatically to 60 degrees South on the meridian of Greenwich. 'That's where we're bound for!'

Wenzel gave a low whistle.

'Until we get to that position,' Fischer went on, 'we interfere with no shipping – not even though they may be sailing unescorted. Our job is to get there without our identity being discovered. The next few days will be the worst, until we get across the convoy tracks. There's danger there, danger from the destroyer escort which may be on the outer fringes of each convoy. These sweeps, as they call them, can cover a hell of an area.'

At last the younger officer spoke. 'What are we supposed to do when we get there, sir?'

'You tell me.'

Wenzel stabbed his finger at the chart. 'I should say we're due to destroy the whole of the Allied whaling fleets now operating in these waters. At this time of the year there should be both British and Norwegians engaged.'

'Your guess is good, Lieutenant. You've made only one mistake. The ships will be captured; they will not be destroyed.' Fischer imparted a chilly tone to his remark, for some reason which he could not define.

Again Wenzel whistled softly.

'The ships will be taken back to Germany with their cargoes intact. The Reich will be the sole beneficiary from the 1940–41 whaling season. The loss of this whale-oil to Britain will be a major catastrophe.'

'It's going to be a difficult proposition.'

'How?'

'Well . . . what about all the whale-catcher vessels? How are you going to stop them running just as soon as they identify us? You can't chase them all. Within a few hours the whole world will know that a German raider is at large in the waters of Antarctica. The other whale-ships will scatter at once. All operational work will cease.'

Fischer stared at his senior officer with amusement. This has got him rattled, he thought. Aloud he said, 'You're quite right, Lieutenant. You only omit one thing – the element of surprise. That's where our advantage lies. Surprise and speed. It means all the difference between success and failure. The whaleboats won't be allowed to broadcast our identity.'

Wenzel again glanced squarely at the chart. 'I hope you are right, sir.'

'Both Lieutenant Kaltenbrunner and Lieutenant Dieter have been senior officers in pre-war German whale-ships. They know this business. I've every confidence in their ability to advise me as to the best means of bringing this mission to a successful conclusion, and, what is more, to carry out the whole series of operations with the secrecy and swiftness that are necessary.'

'How about crews to take these ships back to Germany? How—'

'There are about four hundred men in each expedition. Isn't that enough?'

'Yes, I suppose it is,' answered Wenzel. 'I see what you mean, sir. You would make their own crews take them back to Germany?'

Fischer inclined his head. 'That's the main idea. If not willingly, then with a little persuasion.'

'Then that's why these whalemen have been sent here? That's—'

The commanding officer made a brusque gesture with his hand that cut short the full spate of Wenzel's question. 'That was a bad mistake.'

'It gave us some real seamen.'

'At what cost?'

'What do you mean, sir?'

Fischer shrugged. 'You should know, Lieutenant. You found

out that they were whalemen long before we left Kiel. What if some British agent found that out too?'

The younger officer looked unhappy. 'I see what you mean – now.'

'Forget it. It's nothing . . . nothing at all.'

Wenzel nodded gravely.

Fischer carefully folded the chart and placed it in its original position. 'By the way, Lieutenant,' he said, 'when I begin my series of talks with my whaling supernumeraries I will require both you and Linder to attend. I may say that I've every confidence in your ability to take over this command should anything happen to me. I want you to know everything that's going on.'

'Thank you, sir.'

'We should be in fairly safe waters after we get south of 45 degrees latitude. Most convoys will be on the great-circle track between the United Kingdom and Halifax. The other ships we don't worry about. If everything goes to schedule there's nothing to stop us being back in Germany in just over three months' time.'

'I hope you're right, sir. This job is more than I had hoped for. It's interesting; I only hope that we *can* bring it off.'

Fischer smiled again. 'That's our job, Lieutenant. There must be no failure.'

It was 1800 hours the same evening. Fischer sat before a small microphone wired to the permanent hailers throughout the ship. The *Viking*'s personnel waited anxiously for his words. They were about to hear, from their own commanding officer, the task which had been assigned to them from the German Naval Command – the task which up to then had remained such a closely guarded secret.

Fischer rested his arm on the desk, his mouth close to the microphone. He began: 'Officers and men of the *Viking*, what I have to say to you will be brief, but I hope it will ease the tension and speculation that have prevailed on this vessel for some weeks.

'It is my privilege to command a vessel whose name will, I am sure, resound throughout the length of Germany in the very near future. I know you have all waited eagerly for news of this venture. I am now in the happy position, thanks to our successful running of the British blockade, to tell you.

'The *Viking* must not be taken for an armed surface raider – not in the true sense of the term. We are not here to roam the different oceans in search of merchantmen as victims of our wrath. The *Viking* is a surface raider with her mission already planned. We are here, you and I, merely as tools to see that it is accomplished – successfully.'

Fischer paused for a moment in the tense, expectant silence, then continued in a resolute tone. 'We are now bound for the waters of Antarctica. Our sphere of operation will be along the ice-edge of that continent, and our immediate object will be to seize the Allied whale-ships that are operating there. I emphasize the word 'seize': they will not be destroyed. They will be taken back to Germany with their whale-oil productions intact. At the present time whale-oil is essential for the successful prosecution of the War. It is imperative that the Reich obtains this oil. We must not fail!'

The commanding officer's voice rang with authority. As he spoke he enunciated each word carefully. He went on: 'Some of you may be disappointed. You may say to yourselves, "This is no death-or-glory mission. This isn't going to help in the invasion of Britain." But you will be wrong. Our success means more to the German nation than any so-called death-or-glory mission.

'I am not going into any details. Everything will be explained to you in a series of talks to be given during the passage south by Lieutenant Kaltenbrunner. The whalemen among the ship's personnel will no doubt add to your knowledge.

"There are four whaling expeditions now operating in Antarctic waters. By the time we reach them they will have produced nearly 50,000 tons between them. That is our prize – our only prize. It is up to us. May we succeed and return in time to share in the final German victory! *Heil Hitler!*'

Fischer switched off the apparatus, sat back in his chair, and brooded silently. Back to share in what final victory? Nothing was final as far as these Berlin barbarians were concerned. They had to go on and on: nothing was final. A time would come when the tide of success would cease to flow, when luck would run away just as sure as sand from an hour-glass. What then? How would the regimented masses acclaim their great Führer then? Would it still be Herr Reichsführer? *Heil Hitler!* Our Führer! The Master Race! Bah! The whole thing made him sick!

The crew messrooms were crowded. The *Viking*'s personnel had listened to their commanding officer's speech with rapt attention. There was a moment of hushed silence as Fischer concluded, then pandemonium broke loose. Scores of ratings pushed and jostled one another as they broke up into private groups to discuss the dramatic news. There was little time for a Christmas meal now!

There was a wild yell from a group of ex-whalemen. Eyes turned to stare at them. All of a sudden these men had become personalities of the voyage. They had many times made this long trip to southern waters. A crowd quickly gathered round them: they were news.

'Of course! That's why Kaltenbrunner's here! We should have known it! Why the hell didn't we guess?' The speaker was Per Becker, a fair-haired young giant, well over six feet in height, and broad in proportion. He had been deck foreman on pre-war German whale-ships. 'And I thought it was going to be Norway!'

Anton Miere, another ex-whaleman, cursed loudly. 'You and your Norway! You and your six months lying in Oslo Harbour! You and your Norwegian blondes! You won't see many blondes – not this voyage!'

Becker hadn't got over the shock, Karl Gunther, another of the group, gave him a sharp prod in the stomach. 'Miere's right,' he said. 'You won't see many females this voyage. Not unless they're bloody seals!'

Becker grinned. 'All right, Gunther. But seize the whale factory-ships! Get them back to Germany! My God, that's some job!'

'Can't it be done?'

'Sure it can be done. What the hell are we going south for? To play pinochle?'

There was a burst of laughter from the assembled group.

'Seriously, Becker,' Gunther asked, 'what do you think? Can't you see how fantastic the whole thing is?'

'I don't know about that. We can take the ships. Getting them back to Germany's a different matter.'

'How?' growled Miere. 'We've got this far. They're not sending us down there unless they think there's a reasonable chance of success. They know what they're about.'

'You're right at that,' Gunther said. 'But what about all these whaleboats? What do we do with them?'

Becker shook his head. 'Who the hell cares? Sink 'em ... leave 'em ... it makes no difference. It's the whale-oil we're after. It's the factory-ships we've to worry about.'

'And is it cold down there?' asked one of the Navy men.

'Cold!' Becker looked scornfully at his questioner. 'Cold!' he repeated loudly. 'It's cold enough to freeze a brass monkey. Hell! There's nothing but ice. Mountains of the bloody stuff! There's no water . . . only ice. Nothing but ice!'

Miere grinned. 'We'll soon know all about it. According to the old man, Lieutenant Kaltenbrunner is going to give us a series of talks about Antarctica!'

'Bah!' ejaculated Becker.

The amenities of the wardroom were also taxed to capacity. Kaltenbrunner, Dieter and Wenzel were conspicuous by their absence. Linder sat with Reuss. Fischer's speech had just finished.

'So that's the great secret?' Linder said in a disappointed voice. 'Who could have guessed? What a job!' His face wrinkled. 'I wonder if Wenzel knew all the time? He did know about the whalemen; he said they were his best seamen. Where is he, anyway?'

Reuss gave a snort of disgust. 'Whale-ships . . . whale-oil . . . Antarctica! Let's get the job over and done with. Seems simple enough to me. Just imagine being thousands of miles away from Germany when she's massing ships and men for the invasion of England! Look what we're missing!'

Linder nodded. 'And we thought we were part of the invasion fleet. It'll all be over by the time we get back. There's no chance – not now.'

'It's certainly not much of an assignment,' complained the medical officer. 'Not when one considers all the preparation and secrecy that have been attached to it.'

'Fischer doesn't seem to think so.'

'Him! You know, Linder, I don't think Fischer is a true Nazi. The things he says . . . the things he does. I may be wrong, but somehow—'

'You are wrong, Reuss. These old naval officers are all the same. They haven't had a chance – not in this war. Nobody wants a real naval battle. Not after the *Graf Spee* fiasco. That was unfortunate: she was unlucky. It took practically the whole British fleet to make her run. Then they couldn't finish her off. No, Fischer's all right. There's nothing wrong with him.'

Wenzel came beaming into the wardroom. A crowd quickly gathered round him. He made his way to Linder's table. 'What do you know?' he said exuberantly. 'What do you think of our job now?'

'Not much – not much at all,' answered Reuss. 'I was just saying to Linder that the job's simple enough. There's nothing to it.'

'Don't you believe it, Doctor. By the time this thing's over – by the time the whole assignment is completed successfully, I mean – we'll have done a job of work that will seem incredible. We're not dealing with four ships. We're dealing with whole whaling fleets. Do you realize that there will be nearly sixty ships in our operational area – ships that will have to be silenced in case they give away our identity. The capture or the sinking of these ships will be the least of our worries. Our objective is not ships, only their whale-oil productions – and we still have to get the oil back to Germany. No, sir! It'll be no easy task!'

'That's what Fischer says. He fusses like an old hen.'

Wenzel turned impatiently towards the door. 'Better tell him that,' he advised.

Linder laughed. He had been staring abstractedly at the Christmas decorations that adorned the walls of the wardroom.

He appeared to be resolving a problem in his mind. He hesitated for a moment, and asked, 'Have you known all along about this?'

Wenzel shook his head. 'No, only since this morning. Fischer explained the whole thing to me then. It bristles with difficulties.'

'Then where do Kaltenbrunner and Dieter come in? We were taking them for a couple of boffins.'

'They're the key men of the mission. It's round them that the whole thing has been planned. They're Fischer's advisers. They'll eventually take two of the ships home.'

'But there are four whale factory-ships to capture. Who takes the others?'

'That's right,' chuckled Wenzel. 'You'll probably be one of the unlucky ones. No easy job – not with four hundred hostile and violent whalemen on board, and only a score of ratings to keep them under control.' He looked sarcastically at the medical officer, and added, 'But then that should be a simple enough job; sounds easy enough to me. That should be the least of our worries.'

Linder shrugged. 'So it seems.'

CHAPTER FOUR

The *Viking* sped swiftly to tropical waters; the convoy routes to and from the United States had been crossed without incident. Except for one trivial scare, the passage, so far, had been devoid of all material danger. To Fischer the translucent and weed-strewn waters of the twentieth parallel were far removed from the nerve-racking, turbulent, and dangerous waters of the North Atlantic. There was a calmness about these seas, a peacefulness – but there was menace too.

From his position on the bridge, close by one of the loudspeakers, he had just listened to Kaltenbrunner giving one of his whaling talks to a large and somewhat boisterous deck audience.

Kaltenbrunner was popular, the commanding officer thought, as popular with the regular Navy men as he was with his own whalemen, all of whom seemed to know him. His manner was a mixture of familiarity, aggressiveness, and friendliness, an advantage he held over Dieter, who spoke with a truculence and condescension unpopular with most of the men.

The crew messrooms were crowded immediately after the talk, Becker was holding court – or so he thought. Around him a score or more of ratings were listening to him expressing his views on Lieutenant Kaltenbrunner. 'What does Kaltenbrunner know about whaleboats?' he was angrily demanding. 'He's never been in the bloody ships. He's a whale-factory man – never been anything else. A hard day's work in a whaleboat, and he'd give up whaling for good. How would he know what it's like to be holding on to half a dozen whales throughout a Southern Ocean gale, trying to snatch a lee, any sort of lee, from the smallest of icebergs, with the whale-gunner stamping and raving around as if he would rather lose his ship than lose his whales?'

Becker was shouting now. 'Me! I joined the bloody Navy to

help in the invasion of England. Look where it's going to land me! Back to the ice again! Back to Antarctica!'

'And no whale bonus either,' added Miere.

'No! You're right! We get no bonus – not this trip!'

Miere laughed. 'You only throw it away on the blondes that hang around Sankt Pauli. Look at the medals you'll get instead.'

'Medals! Who the hell wants medals!' Becker roared. 'Let Kaltenbrunner and Dieter have all the medals. Let's get back to Hamburg. What are we doing here? Let's—'

Gunther broke in. 'Pipe down!' he said. 'What are you shouting about? They can hear you all over the ship. There's nothing wrong with Kaltenbrunner. It's Dieter who's no good. Never mind . . . the War can't last for ever.'

Becker nodded. 'God!' he said. 'That will be the day! . . .'

'Do you realize,' Miere was saying, 'that most of us whalemen will be shipped on board these captured whale factory-ships? It's us who'll have to go back to Germany in them. It's going to be a hell of a job. Four hundred men watching your every move, watching and thinking what a lot of bastards we are!'

Becker chuckled. 'It won't be the first time someone's thought that of you – nor the last either.'

'Me?'

'Yes, you! But let it pass; we were arguing about Kaltenbrunner. Gunther's right. There's nothing wrong with him. He's a seaman – a good one at that. It's Dieter who's no good; he never was any good. He's a creeper. I know him. I sailed with him. If anything is going to happen, let me be with Kaltenbrunner, not Dieter.'

'You're right,' agreed Miere.

'Of course I'm right. Kaltenbrunner's different: he knows his job – especially this whaling one. If anyone can bring it off it'll be Kaltenbrunner. Fischer may be all right, but he's got a good man behind him. Kaltenbrunner's the key to the whole works. Besides, who knows the ice better than him? He's got experience behind him – that's what counts.'

'But you just said he'd no experience. Why the hell don't you make up your mind?'

Becker grinned. 'You know what I mean. He can't help but have experience – not after all these years. Just like me.'

Miere couldn't help grinning.

'What's the matter?' Becker asked, frowning. 'I can't see anything funny.'

'No?'

'No!'

Miere shook his head solemnly. 'Look, Becker,' he said, 'forget all about your experience . . . forget all about your whaling. There's a war on at present. These men' – he indicated the crowd of young Navy men standing around – 'are not impressed. Your whaling days will come again – if you're lucky. Meantime, as I've just said, there's a war on. Let's get it over.'

Becker was really upset now. He was about to start a flow of profanity when Gunther stopped him. 'Miere's right, Becker. You joined the Navy just the same as the rest of us. Because there was nothing else – unless it was the Army. You knew what you were in for. Who's to blame for you being sent to the Antarctic – nobody but yourself! Now, shut up! Shut up! You're in the Navy now!'

The blond whaleman, about to make an angry retort, changed his mind, and said comparatively gently, 'But it was a hell of a good life. Six months' hard work, plenty of whale bonus and overtime, and then the pay-off!'

'Then what happened?'

'One had a good time.'

'A good time!' Gunther exclaimed. 'You certainly did. Drunk for a month! Where was your pay-off then? What did it get you?'

Becker gave a mysterious chuckle. 'There's a hell of a lot of things,' he said, 'that you don't know about. Hidden depths, so to speak. Now, will you mind leaving me to my own bloody business!'

Gunther remained silent. The ring of sincerity in Becker's voice momentarily disarmed him. The gibe did not call for an answer. He knew, as did all of his whaling colleagues, that Becker's bark was worse than his bite. He was one of the few seamen who could depend on a whole year's employment in whale-ships. His services were as eagerly sought after during the close season as they were during the actual whaling season. He was one of the best seamen in the German whale-ships. He was popular with all his shipmates, both the young and the not so young.

'I was saying,' growled Miere, 'that it's going to be a hell of a job for those of us who have to get these ships back to Germany. Well over four hundred men watching your every move! Waiting . . . just waiting for something to happen. I'll stay on the *Viking*!'

'Me too,' said Gunther.

There was a low growl of agreement.

CHAPTER FIVE

Twilight is short in tropical waters. The sun, like a huge ball of fire, seems to poise momentarily on the western horizon before disappearing. A few minutes of violent coloured lights, and darkness engulfs the whole of the heavens. The *Viking* again faced a night of total blackness, ploughing her way southward, her stem cleaving the tropical waters with a fluorescent glow.

St Paul Rocks lay to starboard. The cruiser was on the last course that led to the ice-edge of the Antarctic continent. Nearly five hundred miles a day meant a change of latitude of over eight degrees; soon it would be necessary to reduce speed. Operation Viking was ahead of schedule.

So ran Fischer's thoughts as he quietly paced the lower bridge deck. The *Viking* was a lucky ship; fortune had favoured them on this passage. Bad weather and poor visibility had enabled them to run the British blockade without much trouble; the North Atlantic seemed to have been devoid of shipping. The voyage, so far, had been nothing – nothing but mere routine.

The commanding officer still felt that sense of elation. He had the whole of the South Atlantic Ocean before him – less chance of meeting anything there. He had much to be satisfied about. Everything was under control – or so it seemed.

Yet the wide spaces of the South Atlantic were not so deserted as Captain Fischer thought. Only 1,000 miles astern of the *Viking*, a few degrees to the westward, H.M.S. *Queen of New Zealand*, an auxiliary cruiser of 20,000 tons, was speeding her way southward towards Stanley, in the Falkland Islands.

From a bomb-scarred London orders had gone out to the cruiser to detach herself from a homebound convoy and to proceed with all possible speed to the Falklands. There were no other instructions.

Admiralty, London, had built up a strong case to prove that the auxiliary cruiser refitting at Kiel Harbour over a period of four months was at large somewhere in the Atlantic, and now believed to be heading for Antarctic waters. Intelligence reports from within Germany added to the assumption. Aerial reconnaissance reported that the surface raider had left Kiel on or about December 18th.

The cruiser was now known to have slipped through the strong sea cordon which had been immediately organized to intercept her ocean-going dash. Bad weather and poor visibility had ruined the attempt. Britain was short of ships in which to search the outer reaches of the Atlantic. There was one thing left – protection for the Allied whaling fleets that were now operating in the South.

Whitehall, London, radioed its secret instructions to the Governor of the Falkland Island Dependencies. Their Lords of the Admiralty sat back to await events.

Captain Fischer was presiding at one of his regular conferences. Besides Kaltenbrunner and Dieter, all the senior officers of the *Viking* were present. The cruiser had been slowed to twelve knots in order to keep to the estimated time schedule.

The commanding officer was in a good mood, buoyant, talkative. 'In several of our talks, Lieutenant Kaltenbrunner, I notice you always emphasize that these whale factory-ships are lying stopped most of the time. Is this correct?'

Kaltenbrunner nodded. 'Yes, sir. That is so. When these ships have whales to process they'll always be lying stopped – lying stopped and drifting, usually with the wind on the port side.'

'Why? There must be a reason for this procedure.'

'Yes, Captain. The dead whales, which are always moored at the stern of the whale-ship, sometimes as many as twenty at a time, always drift up to windward. By lying with the wind on the port side the whale slipway remains clear at all times. It's the best side for processing whale. That's the only reason.'

Fischer smiled. 'I see what you mean, Lieutenant. It all sounds so complicated. As you explain it, the parent ship always lies stopped and drifting with the wind on the port beam while processing its whales. The drift, then, must be to starboard – away from the wind.'

Kaltenbrunner nodded, wondering to himself what Fischer was getting at.

'How good are the bridge look-outs when the ship is lying stopped and drifting?'

The supernumerary smiled slightly. 'I see what you're getting at, sir. It's a good point. The bridge officers of a whale factory-ship rarely look to windward when the ship is drifting, especially during the hours of darkness. It's unnecessary. All the ice dangers lie to leeward, and that's the only bearing on which these officers will concentrate their attention. The ice that lies to windward has already been passed. No ice dangers exist on that side.'

'How about the working decks?'

'During the dark hours the ships are so brilliantly floodlit that from the whaling-deck it would be utterly impossible to see in any seaward direction for more than sixty feet. No! There would be no danger from the whaling-deck.'

With undisguised relief, Fischer said, 'Then one could send a boatload of men – say, forty men – and they could board these vessels from the port-side without much trouble. I mean, they could actually get on board without being discovered. They'd be in time to prevent any radio signals going out?'

Kaltenbrunner nodded. 'Yes, sir. Easily.'

Dieter broke in excitedly: 'You're right, Captain. That's the method to adopt. You could send a hundred men, and they wouldn't be discovered – not until it was too late – much too late.'

'Then the boarding operation should entail no difficulty,' Fischer said. 'Once on board, the rest should be easy. Twenty men could hold the whole ship.'

Again Kaltenbrunner nodded.

'That, then, will be the boarding procedure.' Fischer spoke each word with deliberate slowness.

'What about all the whale-catcher vessels?' Wenzel asked. 'What do you intend to do about them?'

The commanding officer studied his senior officer carefully.

'That's where my whaling officers will be able to help me.' He looked at Kaltenbrunner. 'What do you suggest?'

Kaltenbrunner shrugged. 'There are a few alternatives here, sir. Why not make the captain of the factory-ship recall his own catcher vessels? Use some pretext or other in order to get them alongside. We can take over from there.'

'I see what you mean.'

'Will the captain do this?' Wenzel looked straight at the whaling officer as he asked the question.

For the first time a hint of exasperation entered Kaltenbrunner's voice. 'He has no option. One does not argue when a gun is held to one's temple. One has to do as one is commanded. I can see no trouble.'

Fischer smiled. 'The idea is sound – very sound. We take them alongside – say, two at a time – and we take over from there. When they've all been seized we give orders to scuttle the entire fleet, except, of course, the two vessels we're to keep for scouting purposes.'

'No, sir. One at a time will be enough. Any more than that, and the whale-gunners are bound to become suspicious. Let's not depart from the usual routine.'

'But . . . the time factor!'

Kaltenbrunner looked straight at the commanding officer for one long second. 'After we capture the first two vessels, it will be unnecessary to take the others alongside. We can do all that is necessary from these two ships. We cruise around the entire fleet and take them over with little or no persuasion. It's an easy task – once we get the first two.'

After a few moments Fischer said, 'You can certainly make the whole thing look simple. I only hope it's as easy as you make out.'

Kaltenbrunner nodded grimly. 'It will be easy, sir. It's got to be easy. We must get all those catcher vessels . . . all of them. None must escape!'

'You can be sure of that, Lieutenant. I can blast them right out of the water if they attempt to run. We'll show no mercy.'

'We can't afford to. It's much too dangerous. Circumstances could easily upset these plans. Let's not make it a standing order. Let there be some elasticity.'

They were all staring at Kaltenbrunner – Fischer, Wenzel, the other senior officers, and his fellow whaling officer. Not a muscle of the supernumerary's face moved.

'Don't let us make any one set plan for this operation,' he said in a grating voice. 'I myself will see that they do not escape.'

Fischer nodded curtly. 'I understand what you mean, Lieutenant. I won't tie you down to any one procedure.'

'How many men do we use in the initial boarding operation?' Dieter asked.

The commanding officer thought for a moment. 'I should say about forty men. Yes, I think forty men should be sufficient.'

'More than sufficient, sir,' Dieter said smugly.

'Of course, we can't afford all those men to take the vessels back to Germany. That's where we must have co-operation – especially from the Norwegians. I should imagine there'll be quite a number of Quislings on board – or so I've been told.'

Dieter's eyes were unnaturally bright. 'We can always make them Quislings,' he said. 'After all, we have their families in Norway. It's amazing what one will do for one's family, especially with the Gestapo around.'

'There's that to be admitted,' Fischer said somewhat brusquely. He turned to Kaltenbrunner, and added, 'How much whale-oil do you estimate will be in the storage-tanks of this first factory-vessel?'

'That will depend on the past weather,' Kaltenbrunner answered without hesitation. 'The ship will have been on whaling operations for at least five weeks. I should say rather more than 60,000 barrels – roughly 10,000 tons. She'll be about due for a tanker vessel to relieve her of the oil.'

'And that's where our problems are due to start. There's no doubt about it – the presence of these ships will complicate matters. There's only one thing to do with them – sink them!'

Kaltenbrunner stared at the far wall. 'As far as the *Cachelot* and the *Antarctica* are concerned, we'll be there before any tanker vessel. I don't know about the British ships. I should imagine they'll be just about to transfer their whale-oil to one or other of these tankers.'

'Then we seize the tankers,' Fischer said dryly.

'Yes. Perhaps that would be the best,' answered the supernumerary officer. 'For myself, I would rather attempt to take a tanker back to Germany than any of these whale-ships. They're less conspicuous. It would be an easy job.'

Fischer nodded. 'I understand, Lieutenant. It may be an idea. Let's wait and see. Let's get this first part over. We'll worry about the British ships later.' He smiled, and added, 'After we get the Norwegians on their way.'

'How about armaments?' Wenzel asked. 'Are these ships armed?'

'Of course they're armed!' Fischer exclaimed. 'Like all Allied ships, they'll have the usual four-inch breech-loader mounted at the stern. It doesn't mean a thing. These whalemen are far too busy to worry about guns . . . or war . . . or anything. These men are down in the Antarctic for one thing – whale-oil! Nothing else matters.'

Kaltenbrunner grinned. 'You're right, sir. The only guns they worry about are harpoon-guns. If there was no radio they wouldn't know there was a war on.'

'War will be coming to them!'

Kaltenbrunner nodded. He spoke hesitatingly. 'Yes . . . war will be coming to them. Let's get it over and done with. Let's be homeward bound with our valuable prizes.'

The conference was interrupted by the violent ringing of alarm-bells. There was a general stampede throughout the ship; the crew went to action stations. Fischer bounded to the bridge.

'Smoke on the horizon, sir! Bearing 090 degrees,' reported an excited bridge officer.

Fischer nodded. 'Come starboard,' he ordered quietly. 'Steer 245 degrees. Full speed. Watch the bearing.'

The *Viking* swung quickly to her new course, and rapidly gathered speed – away from the danger. Fischer peered through his glasses at the thin column of smoke, which could be easily discerned on the port quarter.

Another of those damned neutrals, he thought. Probably some old and dilapidated Spanish tramp heading for the River Plate area. Better take no chances, though. So far they had been lucky; it was no use tempting fate. Even if she were a friendly ship he would still have to keep clear. His job was to keep out of sight of such ships, to remain undetected until he reached the Antarctic whaling-grounds. His presence would be known soon enough.

'Bearing altering aft, sir.'

'Good!' Fischer spoke crisply. 'Keep course and speed for another hour, and then resume as before.'

'Yes, sir.'

'Seems to be all right,' commented Wenzel. 'The bearing alters appreciably. Nothing much to worry about, sir.'

'You could be right, Lieutenant. Better to be sure than sorry. We'll remain as we are for another hour. You can dismiss action stations then.'

Wenzel nodded. He looked at his commanding officer, and added hurriedly, 'Yes, sir.'

Fischer smiled. 'Cheer up, Lieutenant. Another twelve days, and you'll be able to say that you're really doing something. We'll have got the first two ships; we'll have dispatched them on their homeward journeys. This first job should be simple. I don't think the others will be so easy.'

'I understand that, sir.'

'Bearing now 050 degrees, sir. Disappearing rapidly.' The bridge officer spoke nervously.

Fischer grunted, turned away, and made his way back to his own quarters. Yes, another twelve days, he thought, and they would be able to do something about it all. It shouldn't take long to capture a couple of ships and see them on their way back to Germany. It was these whaleboats and tanker vessels that were going to cause the trouble. The whaleboats wouldn't be so bad – Kaltenbrunner could deal with them. Dieter and Linder would have to take over command of the first two ships. It was going to be a shock for the young officer.

He smiled to himself. It was certainly going to be an experience, having to spend the next few weeks in the waters of Antarctica. That's all it would be – a few weeks. Then he would be homeward bound himself. All going well, he could arrive back even before the factory-vessels. That would be the time when he would receive his acclaim – his reward for a mission that had been carried out so swiftly and efficiently. He wanted none of those Hitler or Nazi decorations; all he wanted was the respect of his own contemporary officers – those of the older school – not these Nazi fledglings, who, with little or no sea experience, were senior to him.

His thoughts rambled on. So Dieter was one of those Nazi fanatics. He remembered his remarks about the Gestapo and one's family. Yes, he was another of those disciples of Hitlerism; one of these fools hypnotized into believing the Führer to be a man of genius, a man who could make no mistakes. The Gestapo! Always the threat of the Gestapo – the terrorists who were hauling the millions of vanquished European peoples into Germany to the labour camps. What if the day should come and Germany found herself with her back to the wall? How would these millions react then? Germany should be able to fight her wars without any Gestapo – without any Hitler. The real German people could stand up to the hard, back-breaking work, the tasteless and synthetic foods, even the regimentation and the monotony, but the corruption and the lust for power of a few beer-swilling political maniacs was a scene made for tragedy – the tragedy of mankind.

CHAPTER SIX

'Let go!' The order was quickly communicated from bridge to forecastle-head. There was momentary pause as the windlass-brake was released, then, with a dull roar, accompanied by a cloud of rust-like particles billowing from around the bows, the starboard anchor went screaming from the hawse-pipe and plunged into the greyish waters of Stanley Harbour.

One, two, three, four, five, six. Each fifteen-fathom shackle-length was instantly signalled to the navigation bridge. Slowly the vessel lost sternway. She swung her head rapidly into the wind, and then she brought up. H.M.S. *Queen of New Zealand* had arrived at her destination

Captain Michael Carmichael, D.S.O., R.N., gave a sigh of satisfaction; he grinned broadly at his navigating officer and nodded appreciatively. 'Good work, Lieutenant! You're spot on. This anchorage should do us for the present – until we find out what on earth it's all about. If we have to lie here for any length of time we'll have to shift and make a running moor. We don't want to pile up on these kelp-covered rocks.'

He surveyed the shore through powerful glasses. What a dump of a place! he thought. Nothing but clusters of scattered houses. Government House and the Cathedral stood out boldly enough, and there was the Battle Memorial, a granite monument erected to commemorate the battle of the Falkland Islands of the First World War. Apart from these landmarks, there were few others.

A motor-launch came speeding from the shore: within minutes a young naval officer attached to the Governor's staff had boarded. He was quickly taken to the bridge, where he smartly saluted Carmichael and handed him a sealed envelope.

The commanding officer quickly scrutinized the contents; he looked up at the staff officer and nodded. 'I'll be with you in just a few minutes.'

'Yes, sir.'

Carmichael turned and gave a few brief instructions to his senior navigating officer. 'I have to go ashore now,' he concluded: 'Will you inform Gower that I wish to see him.'

Lieutenant-Commander Max Gower, second-in-command of the auxiliary cruiser, quickly made his appearance. 'You sent for me, sir?' he asked.

'Yes, Commander. Yes, I did. I have to report to Government House. Look after things. I don't suppose I'll be away very long.' He smiled, and added, 'At least, I hope not.'

Gower nodded. 'Right, sir. I hope the news will be good. Let's get out of this place. Let's—'

Carmichael chuckled. 'Don't say it,' he interrupted. 'I guess you'll be right at that.' He turned to the young staff officer. 'Shall we go now?'

The diesel-driven launch bore them swiftly to the shore, to a dilapidated wharf which ran parallel to the foreshore. After a short interval Carmichael was being shown into the presence of the Governor of the Falkland Island Dependencies. He saluted smartly.

The Governor was smiling. He shook hands warmly, and said, 'Welcome to Port Stanley and to the Falkland Islands.'

'Thank you, sir,' said Carmichael. 'It's a pleasure, but don't expect us to be too enthusiastic. We were nearly home when we got the sudden switch-round. Look where it's landed us.'

The Governor was still smiling. 'Never mind, Captain. Don't let it worry you. You won't see much of the Falkland Islands – not for the present. By the looks of things you'll soon be off to sea again. But that will be for you to decide.'

Carmichael leaned back in his chair. 'Is the matter that serious? What has Hitler gone and done now?'

'It's not what he has done. It's what he's about to do – if he gets the chance.'

'What exactly is the trouble, then?' Carmichael asked. 'You mean—'

The Governor nodded consolingly 'I have your decoded messages here. There is the complete file. Suppose I give you a brief summary of the whole situation?'

'That would be better.'

'The whole crux of the matter is that a German surface

raider is at large somewhere in the waters of Antarctica – or so it is believed. The vessel left Kiel on or about December 18th, and by all accounts should be in these regions now. Admiralty, London, may be wrong, but they're most emphatic that the ship will make her appearance in these waters. An extensive cordon was drawn round the outlets from the North Sea to prevent the vessel's escape. It was unsuccessful: bad weather and fog foiled the attempt.'

Carmichael was all interest. 'But what can a surface raider do in these parts? There's nothing here!'

The Governor leaned back. 'That's where you're wrong, Captain. There's plenty that an armed raider could do in these parts. Take, for example, the whaling fleets. Between here and the meridian of Greenwich, which is no great distance in these higher latitudes, there are four pelagic expeditions now on whaling operations. The combined fleets constitute more than sixty ships. At the present moment these four expeditions will have produced nearly 50,000 tons of whale-oil between them. That could be their prize – an excellent one!'

'You mean they would try and capture these ships?'

'Yes, Captain. That is my opinion – whatever it may be worth. I don't know what they think at Whitehall, but it's my considered opinion that they'll try and capture these whale factory-ships, and try to get them back to Germany. What's the use of coming all this distance only to destroy them? That could be done much nearer home – when the time came. No, Captain. If this surface raider is in these waters, and is after these whale-ships, then they'll be captured: they won't be destroyed.'

'Yes, sir. You could be right.' Carmichael spoke gravely. 'But it's a huge undertaking; there's no doubt about that. Are there any other objectives that an armed cruiser could be interested in?'

The Governor answered hesitatingly. 'Yes, Captain. Yes, there are. Again, this is only my own opinion – nothing official. The island of South Georgia lies to the south-eastward, and there are four shore-based whaling stations located there. At the present time these stations will have produced just as much whale-oil as the pelagic expeditions. Besides this, the whaling firms keep large stocks of fuel-oil. It wouldn't take much effort to destroy all these installations completely.'

Carmichael nodded. He had been moodily watching the smoke curl from his cigarette. 'These whaling stations . . . are they all British?'

'No. There are two Norwegian stations and one belongs to Argentina. Only one station is completely British, although British money is involved in all of them.'

'I see. How many people are on the island?'

The Governor thought for a moment. 'Roughly twelve hundred. Except for the Resident Magistrate, his two assistants, and, of course, their families, all the people on the island of South Georgia are seasonal whalemen.'

Carmichael frowned. 'I suppose an armed cruiser could enter any of these harbours and with a few well-directed shells utterly destroy these stations. Are there no defences at all?'

'Strange that you ask that, Captain. There were two four-inch breech-loading guns mounted last year. Each of them commands the entrance to the two main harbours. I suppose they could give a hot reception to any hostile craft.'

'Then they keep a constant watch?'

'Yes. There are permanent gun-crews composed of whalemen. A watch over the entrances is maintained at all times. They're vigilant.'

Carmichael smiled. 'A German surface raider would not dare enter any of these harbours – not before sending a landing-party before her. They'll know all about these guns. You can be sure of that, sir.'

'Yes, I think you're right, Captain.'

'How about the Falklands? What damage could they do here?'

The Governor shrugged. 'I suppose they could do plenty of material damage, but there's nothing here – nothing of importance. But such an operation might well bring self-satisfying thoughts to the leaders of the German Reich. "German surface raider bombards the Falkland Islands." Good for the morale of the masses, if nothing else.'

Carmichael sat fingering the filed copies of the decoded messages. 'I'll have to brood over these,' he said. 'In any case, we need about a forty-hour stay to carry out some essential repairs. Perhaps I can come to a decision by tomorrow. It's a tremendous area to cover; it's a destroyer's job really – several destroyers. Have these whale factory-ships been warned?'

The Governor pursed his lips and brought up a hand to his lean jaw. 'No, Captain, they have not been warned. We must wait until we're absolutely certain that there is a raider in these parts. We must not be premature.'

Carmichael grinned. 'There's only one way to find out.' There was a note of impatience in his voice.

'How?'

'When we hear of the loss of one or more of these ships. If she is down here now . . . well . . . we'll soon know.' Carmichael's sarcasm was deceptively mild.

The Governor made no reply.

'What type of ship is she supposed to be? Is she speedy?'

'It's all in the file. As far as I can make out, the ship is no more than 14,000 tons dead weight, and is, like your own vessel, a converted passenger vessel with a speed somewhere in the region of twenty knots. Her armament will be much similar to your own.'

Carmichael grinned again. 'Then it should be an easy job. All we do is knock hell out of each other – sink each other – and then these damned whale factory-ships can complete their whaling season in comfort.'

They both laughed.

'What about your crew, Captain? We'll be very happy to entertain them should shore leave be granted.'

Carmichael shook his head. 'Thank you, sir. I think it would be inadvisable meantime. For myself, I should like to go on board now and study these reports. Can I see you tomorrow forenoon?'

The Governor chuckled. 'You certainly will. I intend to invite myself for lunch. I'll come on board about 1100 hours. How will that do?'

'You'll be very welcome,' Carmichael agreed courteously.

'Then I will excuse you. Remember that I require you to dine here tomorrow evening. Bring along your senior officer. I'll take no excuses.'

'Then I readily accept, sir. For both of us.'

'Good.'

'Then if you'll excuse me—'

Carmichael's thoughts were mixed as he was quickly taken back to his command. The *Queen of New Zealand*, lying quietly at her anchorage, looked gigantic as seen from the launch. What a target! he thought. The massive hull and superstructures, with their drab grey paint, scarred badly in places, seemed to tower high over Stanley Harbour. A formidable-looking vessel, but definitely not a fighting machine – not for the job that lay ahead. Eighteen months before the *Queen* had been one of the world's most luxurious of passenger liners. You just can't turn a ship into a fighting machine by the addition of a few coats of grey paint and a handful of guns. No, these ships, as far as fighting craft were concerned, went out with the First World War. They had their uses as hospital ships, but then, who wanted a navy composed of hospital ships? Carmichael smiled grimly as he climbed the accommodation ladder and made his way to his own quarters.

That same evening he sat in close conference with Gower. He had studied all the Whitehall messages before sending for his senior officer. 'And so you see, Commander, that's all I can tell you,' he explained. 'What we want to know is – where is this German raider going to strike? Will she definitely appear in these waters? If we knew the answers to these two questions we could at least do something. I should say it's destroyers' work. The area's too extensive to cover with this ship. Even if we do come up with this armed cruiser, what can we do? We could destroy her. Yes, but they would destroy us as well. These ships are not built to fight such battles. Look what happened to the auxiliary cruiser *Rawalpindi*. She went in, hoped for the best, and was annihilated. At least we would be equal: we would annihilate each other. I suppose their Lords of the Admiralty have realized all this.'

Gower lit a cigarette. He took refuge in an air of gruff unconcern as he said, 'But isn't there some way . . . I mean some other way . . . in which we can destroy this vessel without fighting it out bodily?'

'You go on and tell me! We still have to catch up with her.'

'You're right, sir. Why on earth couldn't they have tried to stop her at one of the strategic points? She isn't invisible!'

The commanding officer nodded in agreement. 'It's a long way to the Greenwich meridian – whatever they say. A hell of an area to cover! It can't be done efficiently – not with one ship. It's like looking for a needle in a haystack.'

'Yes, sir.'

'But we have to try. That's the point: we have to try. How long will they be with this repair?'

'There's been no change, sir. Forty hours they estimated. I'll find out.'

'Good! Inform Commander (E) that we sail just as soon as the repairs are completed. Give him a line on what I've just told you. Let it be known throughout the ship.'

Carmichael smiled. 'And, Commander.'

'Sir?'

'There will be no shore leave.'

Gower's eyes opened in mock astonishment. 'Who'd want to go ashore in this ruddy place, sir?'

'*You* don't get out of it that easy. You're dining with me at Government House tomorrow evening. I hope you'll have an enjoyable time.'

Gower nodded. He didn't reply.

A sympathetic, half-amused flicker came into Carmichael's eyes. He knew Gower hated all social activities. 'Never mind, Commander. There's one thing—'

'What, sir?'

'We'll soon be bound for the South.'

'That'll be a consolation,' Gower said dryly.

The commanding officer grunted non-committally. He was looking at some notes that he had written on a sheet of foolscap. 'Listen, Commander,' he said quietly. 'It's my intention to proceed to South Georgia and make a short visit to one of these shore-based whaling stations. Call it curiosity if you like, but I think it'll be worth the loss of time. A short stay there, and then there's only one course left open to us.'

'What do we do then, sir?'

Carmichael came out of a momentary trance. 'Why, we go to

the ice-edge. We go in an easterly direction until we hear some word, or meet up with this reputed surface raider. We'll call at each factory-ship in turn. They'll be widely scattered. It's useless to search: we must wait until she actually strikes. Whichever ship is attacked first, I only hope they're able to send out some sort of warning.'

'What about whaleboats? Can't we use some of the South Georgia vessels in the search?'

'Yes, I've thought of that. We can inquire later. I suppose we can commandeer one if necessary. As I told the Governor, this is destroyers' work. Not a job for a cumbersome bastard like this.'

Gower grinned and nodded. 'You're right, sir. In any case, it should be an experience for us all. I never thought I'd reach the Antarctic – not in wartime. Let's hope that it will be – just an experience. Let's hope she's rounded the Cape of Good Hope and is now in the Indian Ocean. Let the South Africans look after her!'

'That would be one way out, Commander. Let them do the searching, and the killing, while we enjoy the sights and experience the rigours of Antarctica.'

Gower grinned again.

'Charts!' Carmichael's words were crisp now. 'Send the navigator on shore tomorrow to round up all the Antarctic charts that he can lay his hands on. We need them. We've nothing!'

'Yes, sir. I'll see to it.' Gower rose, waiting for dismissal.

Carmichael hoisted his lean frame from the chair. 'By the way, Commander you'll meet the Governor himself at 1100 hours tomorrow. He's invited himself to lunch. Make the usual arrangements.'

Again the senior officer made a wry grimace. He said reluctantly, 'Yes, sir. I'll make the necessary arrangements.'

Carmichael chuckled as Gower left the room.

The Governor was feeling pleased. It had been an enjoyable day for him – a pleasant change. His tour of the auxiliary cruiser had been followed by an excellent lunch. He had dined and wined comfortably. And there had been this dinner at his own residence; he had enjoyed the company of his two guests. Now the day was drawing to a close. The *Queen of New Zealand* was due to sail at daybreak. Captain Carmichael and his senior officer would soon have to go back.

Carmichael was speaking. 'And that is my intention, sir. I will proceed direct to South Georgia and look over one or two of those land-based whaling stations. We will then go to the eastward – along the ice-edge – and visit each factory-vessel in turn. That's all we can really do – until something does happen. Let's hope nothing will. These ships are too widely scattered. If they were all together – operating in one place – it would simplify matters. We could assume guard duties.'

The Governor was shocked. 'You can't do that! The farther they are away from each other the better. It gives them a better chance of successful work.'

'I can appreciate that,' Carmichael said with resignation. 'I can only hope that we'll be in the near vicinity should the raider strike. We can't be with all of them – not unless they carry out whaling operations in one area.'

The Governor shook his head decisively.

'Then how do I go about taking over two or three of those whale-catcher vessels? I require them for scouting purposes.'

'Take over two or three of their whale-catchers! You'll never get away with that, Captain. These pelagic expeditions are now operating with the minimum number of whaleboats. All surplus vessels were sent home at the beginning of the War. They're being used around the coasts as patrol ships and minesweepers. Try . . . just try and take any of their catchers! Everyone will down tools! I know them. They don't want to be down here in the first place – not when there's a war on. I shouldn't do that, Captain. No . . . definitely not.'

'But it is within my power to commandeer all of them if necessary.'

'Yes, I appreciate that, Captain. But, as I have just said, don't try it. Go about the matter more diplomatically. See the Resident Magistrate in South Georgia. Between the two of you you'll be able to devise some plan to get one of the South Georgia whaleboats. You have a good chance there. Don't try the factory-vessels. In any case, these boats cover a great arc of the horizon. They steam enormous distances. They can always send warning.'

Carmichael looked crestfallen. 'I'll have to take your advice, sir,' he said resignedly. 'The whole thing gets worse and worse. What can one do with a ship like that?' He pointed dramatically through the large bay window that overlooked Stanley Harbour. 'As I said before, it's a couple of destroyers that they should have sent down. They'd soon have written finish to any raider's escapade – if there is a raider. A couple of torpedoes, slap-bang into her guts, would settle any marauder's activities. We'll be lucky if we ever get within firing-range – even if we see her.'

The Governor chuckled. 'You're a pessimist, Captain.' He hesitated momentarily, and exclaimed, 'Torpedoes! I can give you torpedoes. There is a complete unit lying around – somewhere. The whole contraption, complete with torpedoes, was dumped ashore here by a destroyer just prior to the commencement of hostilities. She ran ashore and had to discharge all heavy weights in order to refloat herself. She was towed to Montevideo, and never returned for the equipment.'

Carmichael shook his head deprecatingly. 'That's a help, sir! What would a ship like the *Queen of New Zealand* do with torpedoes? We could never get close enough to use them – if we could use them!'

'But we could still take this equipment on board, sir.' Gower was speaking with great animation. 'It could do no harm.'

Carmichael hesitated. He knew that his senior officer had specialized in torpedoes, but the whole thing was ridiculous. 'We can't waste time, Commander. We sail at 0600 hours.'

'I could still get the stuff on board by that time,' Gower prodded gently. He looked at the Governor, and added, 'If I get some co-operation.'

'It's up to you, Captain.' The Governor was sympathetic.

Carmichael frowned. He glanced at Gower, who was waiting for his answer. Oh well, he thought, what's a couple of hours? 'Carry on, Commander. Get the stuff on board. I'll delay the sailing until noon. That's the extreme limit. Go ahead and do your stuff.'

Gower rose with alacrity. He looked at the Governor expectantly.

'Right, Commander. Come to my study, and I'll give you the written authority. We'll set the wheels in motion.'

They left the room together.

The Governor returned after an interval of fifteen minutes. He sat down and grimaced. 'That senior officer of yours, Captain, he's had me wake half the Falklands. There's going to be the devil to pay tomorrow.'

'You started it, sir. He'll be just like a little boy with a new toy. What have you let me in for?'

'Then you think it's a waste of time?'

'I don't know. Gower was always a torpedo man; I knew him in destroyers. He knows what he wants, and usually gets it. He's sure to have something on his mind. I can assure you of that.'

'I hope you're right. What about your charts? I hope you got what you wanted.'

'Yes, thanks to you, we did.'

'Good! Then your first stop will be at Cumberland Bay. The South Georgia Magistrate is stationed at Grytviken. He'll deal with all formalities and will take you round what whaling stations you want to visit. I have sent him a coded message – just in case they mistake you for the German raider and open up on you with that four-inch breech-loader.'

Carmichael grinned. 'That would indeed be a catastrophe.'

'Is there anything else, Captain? Anything I can do to help?'

'No, sir. You've been very kind. I appreciate all of your help.'

'It's been a pleasure,' answered the Governor. He smiled, and added, 'I wish I was going with you.'

'It's about time I was returning. We've a lot to do tomorrow – better get some rest.'

The Governor accompanied Carmichael to the hall entrance. 'May your voyage be successful, Captain. I wish you the best of luck. I hope that I may see you on your return.'

As Carmichael boarded the ship's pinnace that was waiting at the landing-stage there was a scene of wild activity going on around a large shed that was in close proximity. A score or more of naval ratings, hauling stubbornly on rope-tackles, were in the process of removing various equipment from shed to landing-stage. There was no sign of Lieutenant-Commander Gower.

CHAPTER SEVEN

A steady drizzle fell from a leaden sky as H.M.S. *Queen of New Zealand* weighed anchor and slowly left Port Stanley behind her.

'Doesn't look good, sir. Looks like we're in for a spot of bad weather. The barometer's falling rapidly.' The navigating officer lowered his binoculars and gave a slight shiver.

'You're right, Lieutenant,' grunted Carmichael. 'A filthy day! Look at it! Rain, rain, rain! Not an auspicious start to our venture!'

'No, sir. The wind's from the wrong quarter. It won't get any better – not before it shifts to the west of south.'

A heavy, confused swell was running. Visibility was deteriorating; it was difficult to make out where the sky ended and the sea commenced.

'Yes, navigator, you're right. Looks like we're in for a really dirty night. I don't think we'll get very far in this – not in the darkness. One can take no chances here. As soon as visibility goes there's nothing to do but stop the engines. Stop and let her drift until visibility improves. One can't go barging along in these waters. There's too much ice, and it'll get a thousand times worse as we go along. That will be standing orders from now on.'

'But we haven't seen any ice yet, sir.'

'No,' Carmichael agreed, 'but we will. You can be sure of that – pretty soon too. It's going to take a lot of getting used to. None of us have ice experience.'

'But we'll learn, sir.'

'We'll jolly well have to!' Carmichael's mouth was set in a hard, firm line.

The navigating officer smiled quietly to himself. Carmichael was edgy this afternoon, he thought.

Gower came clambering up the bridge-ladder, beaming all over his face.

Carmichael frowned. 'Where have you been all day? And what are you looking so happy about?'

'I know,' Gower answered with a complacent grin. 'I was up all night. I got everything on board by 0800 hours. I had half the population of the Falklands working for me.'

'Yes. The Governor told me.'

Gower laughed. 'They did a good job.'

Carmichael shrugged his shoulders. 'And did you get everything you wanted?'

'Yes, sir.'

'In good condition?'

'In fairly good condition. They can be made workable.'

'I still don't see why you wanted all that junk on board. We can't use it. I only wish we could.'

Gower smiled secretly. 'No, sir. I agree with you. We can't use it, but a whaleboat could!' His voice boomed. 'You get me a decent whale-catcher vessel, a bunch of fitters, and I can promise you something much more lethal than a score of extra guns.'

Carmichael thought for a few moments; a smile broke gradually over his face. 'I see!' he exclaimed. 'I see what you mean! I never even thought of that. Yes, that could be the answer – the only answer. You have it, Commander,' he went on excitedly. 'You take all the time you want . . . all the men. I'll get you your whaleboat – and your fitters.'

'Right, sir.'

There was a kind of baffled admiration on Carmichael's face. He had forgotten all about the weather conditions, the poor visibility, the threat of ice. 'What on earth made you think of that?'

'I just put two and two together,' Gower said. 'The Governor was talking about torpedoes. You were arguing about whaleboats. It was simple enough.'

Carmichael laughed loudly.

'I didn't want to say anything at the time – not before the Governor,' Gower added. 'After all, it's our business. It's a simple job really. Scrap and burn away some of the top-hamper fittings and mount your torpedo-carriers. You have the perfect torpedo-boat, even though she doesn't come up to the regulation speed.'

Carmichael pondered this. He stared hard at the misty horizon. A smile of anticipation seemed to come over his face.

Gower was speaking. 'Imagine ... just imagine yourself creeping up to a stationary target in total darkness or in dense fog. Just creeping ... creeping slowly up ... close enough so that it's impossible not to miss. Two torpedoes! It would tear the innards out of any ship. We have the weapon – now!'

'You go ahead, Commander. Make it the top-priority job. Get everything ready. I'll get you that whaleboat. How about assistance? Have you any good men?'

'I have Petty Officer Watkins. He knows all about torpedoes; he was with me in destroyers.'

'Good! I'd forgotten about him,' Carmichael said warmly. 'Yes, he'll understand what you want. Between the two of you I think you'll manage to have everything ready. I feel sorry for this German raider – if you ever get close enough to him.'

'We will, sir. You can be sure about that.' Gower moved off, winked slyly to the navigator, who had been listening throughout the conversation, and made his way from the navigation bridge.

So that was what he had in mind? thought Carmichael. How did he manage to think of it? The idea was real inspiration. Yes, it could well be a lethal weapon, the only chance they had of getting close enough to this raider to do any real damage. Like themselves, she would have to stop in darkness and fog for long stretches at a time. That was when the chance would come. He's right! A couple of torpedoes – right into her guts. That was the answer ... the only answer.

Visibility was definitely deteriorating. The cold air-stream, coming from the south-east, was mingling with the warmer air from off the land. Condensation was taking place. The tendrils of the fog commenced to curl wistfully along the sides of the cruiser.

Carmichael came out of his reverie abruptly. 'Half-speed!' he ordered.

'Half-speed, sir!' A junior officer leapt at the telegraphs; he swung the handles over. The engines eased down immediately.

The commanding officer studied the revolution counter. 'Slow speed!'

The order was again quickly executed.

Slowly the cruiser commenced to lose her speed through the water. The wind seemed to have eased.

Carmichael was still watching the revolution counter. 'Forty revolutions,' he muttered to himself. One could still do a lot of damage. No, it wasn't worth the risk. Better take no chances. 'Stop engines!' He barked out the words.

The telegraphs clanged to stop. Slowly the cruiser lost steerage-way; she swung her head sharply into the wind, then she fell off and lay drifting beam on to wind and sea.

'And that,' he said, 'is that. We're here until visibility improves. It's the only thing to do; it's no use hunting trouble. Pass the word on to call me when it clears – or if required. I don't suppose it'll clear much before daylight.' He hauled off his duffle-coat, and added, 'At least, I hope not.'

'Yes, sir.'

'It will be necessary to keep a good look-out to leeward, Lieutenant. Give the orders to the watch-keepers. There's sure to be ice around.'

There's going to be a lot of this before we ever get to the northward again, thought Carmichael, as he slumped himself heavily down on the settee of his sea-cabin. Even he, with all his twenty-five years' sea experience behind him, had yet to see an iceberg. It was going to be an experience – for all of them. He tried to get the thought straight, to see it in its proper perspective as it applied to this German surface raider. Was her commanding officer just as ignorant of these waters as he was? No! The thought wouldn't adjust itself. If this vessel had been sent to Antarctic waters for one specific purpose, then there were sure to be experienced officers on board – men experienced in the ways of whale-ships, and of the waters in which they operated. The thought wasn't satisfying.

He got up suddenly and tapped lightly on the aneroid barometer: it was steady. Good! he thought. It's the rain that has sent the glass down. We could get a change of wind soon; it might be possible to get under way at daylight. It was only a two-day run to South Georgia – if they could go at maximum speed. He would spend at least a couple of days there; it was a chance to learn something of whale matters. He would get among some of these old whalemen – get talking to them. He could learn much more in that way – quicker too. He smiled quietly to himself. I'll send Gower out among them. He'll pick their brains.

He fell off into a troubled sleep. Above him watch-keepers and look-out men kept their lonely vigil. The vessel drifted.

The wind had died completely. A westerly swell, mixed with the prevailing current, drove the cruiser slowly to the eastward.

Carmichael awoke with a start; he was in a cold sweat. He jumped off the settee and dashed to the porthole: it was still dark. I can't have been sleeping long, he thought. He looked at his wrist-watch: he had been asleep less than an hour. What a nightmare! He went slowly back to the settee, closed his eyes, and tried to recall the whole of the dream. What was the nightmare?

Yes, that was it. Icebergs ... pack-ice ... raiders ... torpedoes ... they were all part of the hideous nightmare, part of the thoughts that had been lying dormant in his mind.

He saw it all now. He saw himself on the bridge of the *Queen*, conning her through near-solid ice-packs. Around them, almost in every direction, towered gigantic Southern Ocean icebergs – great tabular bergs that once had been part of the ice-shelf that rings the Antarctic continent.

The dream flowed smoothly from this point. One iceberg passed close alongside – a menacing mountain of blue-white ice. From the domed roofs of its cavernous sides at water-level, ice-pinnacles, in various shades of blue, white and green, hung as if from some tapestried ceiling – a titan fairyland!

He manoeuvred his powerful but hulking vessel through the cracks in the ice, cracks which seemed to open up before them to make small navigable channels, channels lined by a complex system of ice-pinnacles fragmented to spear-like points at their sides. To the south, and stretching as if to infinity, lay the vast wilderness of virgin white ice.

It was during the second phase of the dream that he noticed his vessel was making no headway through the ice-pack. Heavy floes had closed in all around them; he could hear the grinding of the ice-growlers as they scraped and bumped against the thin steel plating of the hull. Each jar had sent a shudder through him.

On the other side of the pack-ice, in open water, the German surface raider waited. He saw it all vividly. He saw the Nazi commanding officer, smiling to his officers, as he watched the British cruiser's futile attempts to extricate herself from the trap. He saw the German gun-crews poised and actually waiting for the order to send their shells screaming into the stationary target that was his ship. It struck him then that his crew were waiting for him to do something – something that he was incapable of. Disaster was imminent – if not from human forces, then from the forces of Nature.

He now reached the climax of the dream. He saw his ship being crushed like an eggshell between the expanding ice-floes. The Nazi cruiser commenced firing. Armour-piercing shells were bursting all around them. He saw his crew clambering over the side on to the ice as hull-plating buckled under the terrific pressures. Slowly his ship was sinking – only the superstructure remained.

It was at this point that he had been shouting for Gower to do something – to do something with his torpedoes. Then he had groaned himself into wakefulness.

Carmichael got up, lit a cigarette, and began to dress himself for the bridge. Anything in order to shake off his preoccupation with the horrible nightmare! He went outside and mounted the bridge-ladder. The watch-keepers were scattered around the bridge-spaces. He noticed the look-out men in strategic positions. He took up a position and stood silently aloof.

Dawn came, cold and grey, and there was no wind. A filtered light began to fall slowly across the sky as the sun sought altitude and tried to break through a thinning mist. The fog was burning away.

Carmichael crossed the bridge and entered the chartroom. 'Damn it!' he muttered. 'Why doesn't it clear properly?' He gave a violent thump on the aneroid: it had commenced to rise. Funny thing, he thought. I'm not unusually nervous, but I'm definitely on edge this morning. What on earth's the matter? Must have been that horrible nightmare.

He was about to return to his cabin when Lieutenant Paul

Scott, the youngest commissioned officer on board, hurriedly entered the chartroom.

'The mist is thinning, sir. It's going to clear.'

Carmichael grunted. 'I hope you're right.' He made for the door.

A light breeze had come up from the south-west. Overhead the clouds were dispersing. The mist held low for a few minutes, then, as if some huge curtain had been lifted, the horizon burst into view and stretched slowly to an immense distance.

'Full speed!' ordered Carmichael.

'Full speed, sir!' echoed Scott.

The motors fired, broke into life, and rose to a ferocious crescendo. The cruiser gathered herself and was again under way.

Carmichael scanned the horizon. 'Ice!' he exclaimed. 'There's nothing but ice!'

Scott sighted the icebergs at the same time. 'God!' he ejaculated. 'What a sight!'

The whole ocean was studded with tabular-type bergs. One large specimen was only about two miles distant. They must have been dangerously close to it as they drifted.

'Ice, sir!' said the young officer.

Carmichael nodded, but remained silent. He eventually turned and gave Scott a smile which struck the young officer as decidedly wan. 'Yes,' he answered, 'that's the first of the stuff. We can expect nothing else from now on.'

A seaman came up and offered the commanding officer a cup of coffee from an electric percolator. He looked at the grey liquid and slowly shook his head. 'No, thanks. I'll wait until later.'

The seaman moved off.

From then on they passed icebergs with monotonous regularity – bergs of all sizes and descriptions. One passed close to starboard. About three miles long on the nearest side, it rose out of the water to about eighty feet. That meant that there were at least three hundred feet below the surface. The whole thing was immense – there was no other word.

Carmichael moodily watched some of his crew's reaction as

they hurriedly came out on deck to sight the gigantic ice-mass. 'God!' he heard one of them exclaim. 'Look at the ruddy ice-cubes!'

He noticed that many of his crew were growing beards. Good idea, he thought. Funny he hadn't noticed them before. Might try one myself.

Scott came across from the other side of the bridge and handed him a news-sheet that had just come from the radio-room.

Carmichael read it over quickly. He handed it back to the younger officer, and said, 'Not much in the way of news. Another big raid on London. Thirty bombers shot down.'

'There won't be any London by the time this war is over,' answered Scott.

Carmichael studied his young officer carefully. 'And there won't be any Berlin either. You can be sure of that.' He spoke each word slowly.

'There's that too,' admitted Scott.

The commanding officer was rapidly regaining his usual good humour. 'You know, Lieutenant, I wouldn't like you to get the impression that the whole thing is futile – that hundreds of lives are being thrown away every evening for nothing, just for the sake of plastering these cities. It must mean – something!'

'I fail to see it, sir. Retaliation – that's all it really amounts to. What's the use of wiping cities off the map? It's the battlefield that counts. That's where they should fight their wars.'

Carmichael shook his head. 'No, Lieutenant, limited war will never settle anything. One can't fight a limited war – it isn't possible. It must be all or nothing. London's a battleground, Berlin's a battleground, the Antarctic's a battleground – that's why we're here.'

Scott looked at his commanding officer belligerently. 'But massive retaliation only exposes risks out of all proportion to the issues at stake,' he said bitterly.

'Perhaps it did – once. Not now. It means only the difference between surrender and suicide.'

The younger officer made no reply.

Carmichael grunted and went below to his quarters.

A steward knocked, entered the room, and closed the door before Carmichael was aware of him. 'Your coffee, sir,' he explained.

'Leave it on the desk.'

'Yes, sir.' The steward withdrew and closed the door silently.

He had been thinking about Lieutenant Scott. He was a peculiar youngster. A clever and efficient officer, but definitely neurotic. He should have been a conscientious objector, for he was certainly a pacifist. It wasn't the first time that he'd noticed this. That last convoy, when the six merchantmen had been torpedoed almost simultaneously! One of them, a tanker, had been loaded with aviation spirit. He remembered vividly how she had weaved her way through the convoy, out of control, a blazing mass, leaving a trail of flaming sea behind her. Paul Scott had been ill for days after that. Yes, he was a good watch-keeper, but not a fighting man.

Carmichael grimaced. Paternal pride, he thought. Why don't they let these youngsters choose their own occupation? The eldest son had to follow in the footsteps of his father. A soldier had to educate his son to become a soldier. A naval officer sent his son to some naval college, and then to sea. It was the same with lawyers, doctors, clergymen – the whole lot. Why should it be?

On the navigation bridge Paul Scott was deep in thought as he conned the cruiser clear of the numerous icebergs. It's all very easy for Carmichael to be preaching about total war. If there wasn't a total war he'd be out of a job. He'd be like all the rest of them – axed as soon as they got into their middle forties. It's only a war that can keep them in a job. People like Carmichael – they didn't want the War to stop. They wanted it to go on for ever! They wanted to hold on grimly to their little glory . . . their power . . . their authority . . . their uniforms . . . their campaign ribbons . . . their ego! Without war they'd be nothing.

He'd have been much better off if he'd never seen the Navy. He remembered the trouble he'd had with his parents when he'd at first refused to sit for the entry examination to naval college. It was only because it had made them so unhappy that he'd actually tried. That was pre-war – a long time ago.

What did it matter if his own father was a naval officer, and his father before him? Was it necessary that he should be sacrificed to this life all because he had to keep on a family tradition? It didn't make sense. What had his father got out of it – nothing! Axed long before he ever reached fifty! Trying to live the life of a retired naval officer on a paltry pension! It was only a few – the privileged few – who ever reached the top. His father was just the same as Carmichael – longing for a war in order to get a job. They were the greatest war-mongers of the lot – just as bad as Hitler or those other dictators.

CHAPTER EIGHT

In the office of the resident magistrate of South Georgia the light was fading slowly. The room was of a moderate size, pleasantly furnished in light varnished oak, with sparse fittings. A large bay window took up a complete side of the room. Across the harbour could be seen the Argentine whaling station, the working-lights just visible in the dying rays of the sun.

The *Queen of New Zealand* lay quietly at her anchorage in Cumberland Bay, about two miles off the headland where the small cluster of houses, which was man's last outpost of the Southern Hemisphere, was located. From a tall flagstaff on the extreme point of the headland the Union Jack flew proudly in the evening breeze.

Captain Carmichael sat slumped in the high-backed chair near the window. He sat with his chin propped up on his fist, a frown of weariness on his face, looking at the black outline of sterile rock that was South Georgia.

Sitting close to the magistrate, Gower was saying in an exasperated voice, 'An old whaleboat would do me. That's all I want – something I can improvise with. Surely there *is* such a vessel on the island? We don't want to take any of their catcher fleet.'

The magistrate wrinkled his brows. 'I think we can arrange for such a vessel. We'll go to the British whaling station tomorrow. We can do nothing here. I'm sure we can get a ship that will come up to your requirements. We can commandeer the service boat if necessary.'

Carmichael sat up quickly. 'Service boat! What is a service boat?' There was impatience in his voice.

The magistrate smiled. 'It's the station's work-boat – an old whale-catcher vessel, but still capable of twelve knots.'

Carmichael nodded. 'I see. That might suit our purpose. We don't want to take away any of their operational catchers. I understand they're working with the minimum number.'

'Yes, they are. All reserve boats were taken home soon after hostilities started.'

An Argentine whaleboat came buzzing into the harbour from seaward at full speed, towing two blue whales at her sides. Squat and formidable-looking, full of latent power, she was watched by Carmichael with interest as she came astern in a flurry of foam to deliver up her whales to a motor-boat, which towed them to a mooring-buoy close by the whale slipway. There was no delay: as soon as the whales had been cast off the whaleboat turned round and headed for the open sea.

'They don't waste much time,' Gower commented. 'It must be a hell of a life.'

'Yes. They only go alongside for stores and bunker-fuel. They don't believe in wasting time – not in good weather. It's not a good job working from the island – much better with the factory-ships.'

'How?'

'Bad weather and heavy seas most of the time. Down in the ice the waters are comparatively smooth. Not like here. These boats have to operate in the open sea all the time.'

Gower smiled. 'They seem to do all right.'

The magistrate shot a glance at Gower, returned the smile, and said, 'Just sometimes. Sometimes a whole week will pass, and they won't get a whale. Just now all the stations are busy: they've had a good season.'

Carmichael stretched himself. He glanced at his wrist-watch automatically, as if he were timing himself for some appointment, but it was a reflex movement, and the position of the hands scarcely impressed itself upon his mind. 'Look, sir,' he said, 'you know the whole story now. Just what do you think about it all? Do you think it worth while for a German surface raider to come all this distance to capture or destroy a few broken-down whale factory-ships?' He smiled slightly, and added, 'Personally, I think it's a wild-goose chase – a complete waste of time.' The words, the tone, were jocular enough, but the worry in his eyes belied them.

The magistrate sat silent for a few moments. At last he spoke. 'It all depends how you look at the matter. If the German navy doesn't want this oil to reach the United Kingdom, then she'll go to extreme lengths to prevent it. They could even send a ship down here to see that the factory-ships were destroyed. But what if they wanted the oil for themselves? It's valuable stuff – especially in war. They might attempt to capture these vessels, and they might try to get them home. Remember, these four ships are expected to obtain approximately 80,000 tons of whale-oil between them. At one stroke Germany could obtain this whole season's work for herself; she would also deprive the Allies of its use.'

'Yes, I appreciate all that. But if the raider is down here, why hasn't she struck? Why hasn't she attempted something? It seems the whale-ships are all right. There have been reports.'

'She could be lying low – waiting.'

'What! Lying down in the ice! No! The risk is too great. Once she makes the initial stroke, she'll have to go through the whole fleet in a matter of days. It's no use otherwise.'

'But inside the ice-pack is a good hiding-place.'

Carmichael shook his head. 'No, not there. Is there anywhere else?'

'Only Deception Harbour. That would be an ideal place to lie low – if they wanted to lie low. Nobody has been there, not in fifteen years.'

'Deception Harbour! Where is that?'

The magistrate looked at Carmichael and grinned. 'Deception is the most southerly natural harbour in the whole Southern Hemisphere. It's situated in the South Shetlands – a small islet in the middle of the Bransfield Strait. It could take a vessel of any draught.'

'What could they do there?'

'Nothing . . . absolutely nothing. You were asking me where a ship could hide herself. I shouldn't overlook Deception.'

Carmichael shook his head again. 'No, sir. If they are down in these waters, then they'll strike immediately. They won't seek any hiding-places.'

'I disagree with you, Captain.'

'Because?'

'Because they may be hiding there now. Because when they make their first break they'll have to go through all the ships: they can't afford to stop. Because this surface raider will be officered by experienced men – men experienced in the ways of whale-ships. Because, being experienced men, they'll know all the answers. If they want a hiding-place that's where they'll make for – Deception.'

Carmichael made no comment.

'There's another thing. I don't think these whale-ships will get a chance to send out any warnings if they're attacked. Everything will be planned. There'll be no opposition. Many of these Norwegians will be only too glad to get home to their own country. Fifty per cent of these crews will give full co-operation.'

The commanding officer frowned. He already recognized all this. He was thinking how inexperienced he himself was in the workings of these whale-ships, but he had been sent down to these Antarctic waters to do a job, and he had no other choice. If this surface raider was after the whaling-ships, then she had to be destroyed. Destroy her he would, even though it meant the end of the *Queen of New Zealand*. An occupational hazard! The Navy faced them every day. Experience! It didn't mean a thing.

He studied the magistrate's face before saying anything. 'Experience!' he exclaimed. 'That's what they said in the Falklands. We can only learn by experience!'

The magistrate shrugged. He lit his pipe, also taking his time. At last he spoke. 'Maybe you're right, Captain. Still, you've no idea how these ships are run. They're not like ordinary ships. They're a community within themselves. Work goes on twenty-four hours a day, seven days a week. As long as there are whales to process work goes on uninterrupted. They are constantly on the move; their radio transmitters, their radio-telephones, are screaming all the time. Their working-lights can be seen up to forty miles away. There's no war down there.'

'Their radio transmitters can be silenced,' Carmichael said brusquely.

'Then you might as well send them all home. Just come across to the radio-shack here, and you can listen to the British ships working. They're nearly a thousand miles away.'

The offer was declined.

'What about these tanker vessels?' Gower tried to ease the

tension. 'Are they down here yet? When do they go to the factory-ships?'

'I don't know about the Norwegian ships. They're a considerable distance to the eastward – near the Greenwich meridian. The British tanker vessels are here in South Georgia. They go south in about a week's time. They take fuel-oil down and whale-oil back. Whale-oil is stored, here on the island, until the end of the season.'

Carmichael adjusted himself to a more comfortable position. He frowned again. 'You mean that the oil that is produced in Antarctic waters comes back here for storage?'

'Yes.'

Gower whistled softly.

'Then the whale-ships are nearly loaded up?' asked Carmichael.

'That's correct.'

'Then if this raider is down here she's going to strike within the next few days. It's elementary. Everyone talks of experience. If they have any experience, then this is the time to strike – when the ships are full. Another week and they'll be empty. That means we shouldn't be here: we should be down there with them.'

'Good heavens!' The magistrate was shocked. 'I never thought of that.'

Gower sat lazily fingering his tie. He shot a glance at his commanding officer. Their eyes met, each reflecting fear and a knowledge of what the other was thinking.

'We shall have to reconsider our plans,' Carmichael said. 'We'll have to put to sea almost immediately. We can't afford to waste any time – not now! We'll have to leave the whaleboat. We can't waste time for its refitting. Pity, but—'

'Not unless you leave me here with a scratch crew. I could meet up with you in about four days' time. I'm sure it'll be worth our while.' Gower spoke solidly, his eyes pleading.

The magistrate looked completely blank. 'Refitting? How?'

'You see, sir,' Carmichael explained, 'we had plans for this whaleboat. We were to line her up with torpedo-tubes and use her for scouting. A scouting vessel with a difference. Our future strategy was based on this.'

'It's a good idea. Can't—'

'What are the facilities here for repair-work? I mean, the chances of getting this vessel converted quickly?'

'Good. Very good,' the magistrate replied without hesitation. 'The British station can deal with major repair-work. They've all the facilities. They even have a floating dry dock – for whaleboats, of course.'

'I'll accept your suggestion, Commander. Line up your crew without delay. Get this vessel here by 1000 hours tomorrow, and get your equipment on board. I will sail immediately you complete your work.' Carmichael turned to the magistrate, and added, 'You can get this vessel here by tomorrow morning?'

'Yes, easily.'

'What about the men who are running this ship? How many are in the crew? Do you think we could keep the skipper and the two engineers?'

The South Georgia magistrate smiled. 'Except for one seaman, that's the entire crew. It's a service boat, not an operational catcher vessel. I suppose you could get them. Yes, I think they would volunteer.'

'Then six of our own ratings should be enough,' said Gower. 'I intend to take Petty Officer Watkins along. He knows his torpedoes.'

'Good! Then we'll settle for that.' Carmichael turned to the magistrate. 'If this whaling manager tries to put any obstruction in your way, then you have my authority to commandeer the ship.'

'He won't put any obstruction in our way. He'll give us full co-operation. I know him.'

'Good. The refitting will have to be carried out at maximum speed. Time is vital. It will be necessary to work non-stop in order to get away as soon as possible. This whaling manager, I suppose he's British?'

The magistrate shook his head. 'The manager of the station is a Norwegian. Just the same as the managers of the two British whale-ships – they're both Norwegian.'

'What!' Carmichael ejaculated. 'You mean to say that Norwegians command British ships? It's a queer set-up, this whaling business. What about the executives? Are there no British officers?'

'There are a few – not many.'

'This whaleboat skipper, I suppose he's Norwegian too?'

'You're right,' the magistrate answered with a smile. 'But you'll get a good man. Nobody has more experience of the ice than Hans Borgen. He has spent practically his whole life down here. Norwegian! He hasn't been home in years – not to Norway. I should certainly try to keep him on board. Whaling! There's nothing he doesn't know about whaling. He knows Deception too: he worked from there once.'

'Then he ought to be an acquisition.' Carmichael turned to Gower. 'I should certainly cultivate his acquaintance. When I meet you again you'll be able to teach me all about this whaling game.'

Gower nodded. 'I will certainly try to get him,' he said.

'It might be an idea for you to go direct to Deception Island. Give the place a good look-over and rejoin me in the neighbourhood of the British factory-ships. If I can I'll try and meet you at the entrance to the Bransfield Strait – at Elephant Island. Don't wait for me. If I'm not there come direct to the whale-ships. I'll have to try and keep them together.'

'Then you'll have a job on your hands,' the magistrate said decisively.

Carmichael's eyes widened as he stared at the Government official. 'I will *make* them!' his voice boomed.

The magistrate grinned. 'They won't like that. They'll be running in all directions – away from you.'

'They won't, I can assure you of that – not while we're around.' Carmichael was obviously upset by the magistrate's remarks.

There was an awkward silence.

Gower tried to change the subject. 'I suppose this whaleboat can carry sufficient fuel?'

'Yes, sir. Provided you fuel to capacity, you'll have fuel enough for a range of approximately 3,000 miles. That is, of course, at an economical speed.'

Gower was about to reply when his commanding officer held up his hand. 'Just a minute, Commander. What is the objection, sir, to my keeping these ships in one locality? Why can't they maintain a complete radio blackout? If these ships are allowed to go gadding about the Antarctic, how can I look after them?'

The magistrate hesitated, and then said reluctantly, 'These whale factory-ships do not like to be in close proximity to one another: it means poaching on the whaling-grounds of the other. Remember, each of their catcher fleets can cover an area of roughly 2,000 square miles daily – that is, of course, provided they scatter around the full arc of the horizon. You see how difficult it is. They're down here to hunt and kill whales – nothing else matters. Yes, sir, I should handle these managers carefully.'

Carmichael's eyes gleamed.

'As regards radio silence,' the magistrate went on, 'the catcher vessels must get some sort of radio bearings. How would they find their way back to the parent ship without them? She's moving most of the time.'

'Sir, if you will forgive me for saying so, the Governor of the Falklands warned me that you would be likely to keep repeating this argument.'

The magistrate seemed hurt, but he was still very polite. He smiled thinly, and said, 'Well, sir, whether I am right or not will be for you to find out. I mean, it's your business.'

Carmichael nodded. 'You're right, sir. We'll soon find out.'

The *Queen of New Zealand* was just a smudge on the horizon as the whaleboat *Albatross* rounded the headland leading into the large bay that sheltered the British whaling station in a tiny cleft that led off the bay.

It was an ideal location for a shore-based whaling station; it was sheltered on all sides by great mountain-peaks that rose sheer out of the water and undulated far into the interior. Only from one direction was the station vulnerable. If the wind came from this bearing it blew from off a glacier that brought icy blasts as rigorous as the squalls felt far to the south.

Gower, clad in a heavy regulation duffle-coat, watched with interest as Hans Borgen conned the whaleboat in the approach to a dilapidated-looking wharf close by the whale slipway. A curious stench pervaded the whole of the area – a stench which only a whaling station can produce. A hundred feet off the whale slipway thousands of birds, squawking and fighting with one another, squatted in the water, feeding off the organic matter that was continuously being pumped from the shore. A mooring-buoy, with approximately twenty dead whales attached to it, rocked lazily at its anchors to the pull of the gigantic carcasses.

'Looks like they've been whaling heavy,' muttered the magistrate. 'You see, they have about two days' work there.'

Gower nodded. He was peering intently at the floating carcasses, some of which were over ninety feet in length. He thought how interesting the morning had been. The *Albatross* had arrived on time, and it had been but the work of a couple of hours to transfer the few ratings and to get the equipment on board. The *Queen of New Zealand* had left immediately. He was suitably impressed with the *Albatross*, and with its skipper. This Hans Borgen was all the magistrate had said: he would be an acquisition.

Borgen, small and rounded, with a cherubic grin which seemed to be permanently fixed on his face, said, 'It 'as been a good week. We should make well over 10,000 barrels for the seven days. Blue whales! I haven't seen so many in a long time. Everything's full – full up!' His English was idiomatic and fluent.

'Then you'll be making a great deal of money, Hans,' the magistrate said.

'Money! Who wants money these days? What can one do with money?' He gave a twirl to the spokes of the wheel, reached out a huge hand to the telegraph, and rang full astern. The whaleboat drew up in practically her own length and was alongside.

Gower, looking over the front of the bridge, was pleased to see his own ratings making fast.

The station manager was meeting them on the quayside; his mouth opened in astonishment as he gazed at the naval ratings and the torpedo equipment. He looked with suspicion at the Government official, who waved cheerily from the bridge.

'You leave him to me,' the magistrate said to Gower. 'You go on a tour of the station with Hans here: he makes an excellent guide. It'll give you a chance to get acquainted. Let me deal with the manager.'

He made the introduction. The manager was polite, but the bewildered expression still remained on his face.

'Commander Gower would first like to tour the station. I have delegated Hans to show him round. I hope you don't mind?'

'No, not at all. It's a good day for such a visit. Everything's going full out: we're on a full cook. Meet us at my house when you finish.'

Gower thanked him. 'We won't be more than an hour. That's all the time I can afford.' He beckoned to Watkins. 'You can bring the men along.'

The party moved off towards the whale slipway, leaving the magistrate with the whaling manager. They began to walk slowly towards the manager's quarters.

'We have an armed auxiliary cruiser in Cumberland Bay,' the Government official said, as he seated himself comfortably in one of the best chairs the room had to offer. 'Do you know what that naval officer is here for?'

'What?'

'He's going to take over one of your boats. They're going to convert one of the whaleboats into a torpedo-carrying vessel – a torpedo-boat. It seems there's a German surface raider down in the ice somewhere. You understand what that would mean?'

The manager nodded. 'Which whaleboat do they want?'

'They'll be satisfied with the *Albatross*. They don't want to deplete your catcher fleet. Even the Governor himself warned them of that. It's all been worked out – in the Falklands. They're not asking a lot – only the *Albatross* and the tradesmen to convert her to their requirements. It will be a hurried job: time is vital!'

Again the manager nodded. 'We'll give them all the help they want – and the *Albatross*.' He looked at his watch – 1300 hours. 'We'll make a start at 1500 hours. What does he want done?'

'We leave that to him: he has his own ideas. I only thought I should let you know first. That's the reason I sent him off with Borgen.'

'Why didn't you warn me of all this?'

'Warn you! How could I? I only got a personal note from the Governor. It's too risky to talk over the radio-telephone. These Argentine people listen to everything. You can't trust them.'

'I understand.'

'There's another thing.'

'What?'

'Gower seems to have taken a fancy to Borgen. He'd like him to stay on the *Albatross*. He'd like the engineers as well.'

'Then he can have them, if they're willing.' The manager spoke without hesitation.

'Hans will volunteer; I don't know about the others.'

'They'll go, I'm sure of that.'

'Good!'

'Has he sufficient men?'

'Yes, he has six ratings and the petty officer. That should make a full crew.' The magistrate sat, elbows on the sides of the chair, chin propped up on fists. He shook his head incredulously, and said, 'Who would have thought that the German Navy would come down here?'

'They can do anything.' The manager spoke resignedly.

'And so can we! You can be sure of that.'

The whaling executive made no reply.

'Phugh! What a stench!' Petty Officer Watkins exclaimed. The touring party were standing in a group close to the edge of the whale slipway.

Borgen grinned. 'There is a little,' he admitted. 'These whales have to be towed long distances before they get here. Sometimes they're fairly old before they come to be processed. Down in the ice they kill them close to the factory-ship.'

The smell of a land-operated whaling station is strong, like nothing else in the world. The whole slipway was covered in mountains of gory meat, blubber, and bone. From the roofs of two adjacent buildings, which housed the steam-pressure boilers, mechanical buckets full of flesh and infats were being emptied with regular precision. Mechanical steam-saws were in constant operation, sawing the vertebral columns and other bone into segments small enough to be fed to the gaping mouths of the boilers. Throughout it all a hundred whalemen laboured in constant repetition of dismembering the carcasses.

It must be a terribly monotonous job, thought Gower. The plant was old, dilapidated, and dangerous. Men wouldn't be allowed to work under such conditions at home. A Factory Acts inspector would condemn the whole lot. He had been unimpressed in his quick survey of the place. Watkins was right. The whole place stank – a filthy and sordid place.

He spoke of this to Borgen. The whaleboat skipper nodded in agreement. 'Who can expect anything else?' he said. 'These business interests, they take everything out and put nothing back. To them it doesn't matter what the conditions are like. They give us six whaleboats, the stores, and the equipment; then they sit back on their rumps and wait for the dividends. That's all they care about – dividends!'

Gower smiled. 'Maybe you're right.' He looked at his wristwatch. 'We'll have to get back – I said an hour. Will you walk back with me?'

'Certainly.'

'Watkins!'

'Sir!'

'You can stick around here for a while. Be at the *Albatross* at 1500 hours. We have work to do.'

'Yes, sir.'

'Good.'

On the way back to the manager's quarters Gower gave Borgen some idea of his intentions. He enumerated many of the the things he had on his mind. 'I would like you,' he concluded, 'to come with us. You and, if possible, your two engineers. It may be a dangerous job – it all depends. Consider the matter. Let me know when I come down to the *Albatross*.'

Borgen whistled softly. 'You can have your answer now.'

'What?'

'I'll be pleased to go. I accept for my two engineers as well. I know them.'

'Thanks! I *am* pleased . . . very pleased!'

They made their way to the manager's house along a winding footpath that was lined on either side by broken-down sheds of corrugated iron that housed the various workshops. They separated as they approached the residence. Borgen continued on his way towards the *Albatross*; Gower knocked and entered.

There was coffee laid out. 'We were just waiting for you,' the manager explained.

Gower nodded appreciably.

'Unless you want something stronger?'

'No, thank you. Coffee will do for me.' He smiled, and added, 'I have to keep a clear head; there's a lot to do.'

'Then you can expect maximum help from all of us here. Just let me know your needs.'

'Thanks. I appreciate everything you're doing.'

A Norwegian steward poured the coffee, and silently withdrew.

Gower sat back and fingered his tie, a habit that he could never get out of. 'I suppose you already know the idea of these torpedoes. I want them placed on the foredeck of the *Albatross*, to fire over an arc of the horizon of eight points on either side. We'll have to remove the mast and to strengthen the deck where necessary. I think it would also be advisable to have that hauling-winch removed.'

The manager nodded. His expression was tolerant and sympathetic.

'I think it's also advisable to clean boilers – less danger of smoke. A coat of grey paint will do her good. My own men can undertake that. I hope you can be as quick as possible. We have faith, great faith, in this idea. It provides us with a weapon much more formidable than what we have on an auxiliary cruiser.'

The magistrate sat silent. He was thinking how easy it was to understand and co-operate with this naval officer. He had no flamboyant ways – not like his commanding officer.

Gower was saying, 'You will, of course, have to fuel and provision us. Fuel to capacity and a week's supply of provisions should be ample. We wish to get to Deception Island without delay. I hope you can give us the essential charts.'

'We can. But what are you going to do there? There's nothing there.'

Gower smiled. 'I don't suppose there is. It's the magistrate's idea. He thinks this raider could be hiding there.'

'Could be. That's the place to hide – if she wants to hide. But it's not a hiding-place she'll be looking for: it's ships!'

'I'm of the same opinion.'

'Well, enjoy your coffee. Let me get things moving. I'll see you down at the *Albatross*. Have you spoken to Borgen?'

'Yes.'

'And?'

'He agrees.'

'I thought so. The two engineers?'

'Borgen vouches for them.'

'Good! Then I'll set everyone to work.' He rose energetically and left the room.

Twenty-two hours later Gower stood on the bridge of the *Albatross* watching the whalemen unload their tools, welding and burning gear, and the various paraphernalia connected with the conversion. It had been a tough twenty-two hours, he thought. The whaleboat was looking spick and span, with her coat of light-grey paint and the white ensign now flying at her stern. The torpedoes were in place – sleek-looking weapons of death housed in the twin tubes. Petty Officer Watkins had done a good job there. He had worked both with efficiency and with enthusiasm.

The foremast had been cut away and the whaling-winch removed. The *Albatross* now presented a sleek appearance, well camouflaged, formidable-looking – a ship of war.

Gower smiled as he watched Borgen trying to hustle the last of the whalemen ashore. With the usual grin on his face, he was taking a barrage of good-natured sarcasm.

'Where the hell is all your gold braid, Hans?' asked one tough, red-bearded whaleman. 'You're in the Navy now! You can't go around like that!'

'What about splicing the mainbrace?' queried another.

'He's saving his ruddy rum ration!'

Gower straightened his face. Better get out of here, he thought. The whalemen were merry. He had been plying them with liquor throughout the night. They had done their job – an excellent one. He had already expressed his thanks to the magistrate and manager. It was time to go.

Borgen came on the bridge. 'We're all ready, sir.'

'Good! Let's go!'

Borgen hesitated. 'Shall I take over, sir?'

Gower grinned. 'Yes, Hans. She's all yours.'

The grin on Borgen's face widened. He took up a position by the helm. 'Let go fore and aft!' he shouted. He waited a few seconds, and rang the engines to full astern. The whaleboat left the wharf in a flurry of displaced water as the whalemen cheered from the shore. The *Albatross* swung quickly to starboard; the engines were put full ahead, and they were heading for the south.

CHAPTER NINE

Lieutenant Linder was standing watch. The *Viking* had changed her parallels of latitude quickly. Through the doldrum weather of the tropics and into the south-east trades; through the trade winds and into the regions of the forties – the roaring forties, those parallels of latitude so well known to seamen of another era. On to the fifties . . .

It had been a strenuous week for all the *Viking*'s personnel. Lectures by Kaltenbrunner had been followed by a series of boarding exercises and drills. Another forty-eight hours, and they would be closing their objectives.

The two supernumerary officers had now taken over bridge duties. Kaltenbrunner spent most of his time in the radio-room. So far there had been no signals intercepted from the whale factory-ships.

Linder smiled quietly to himself. Where is the British Navy? he was thinking. It seemed incredible that they had come from Germany to this southern latitude without sighting a ship. Except for the two occasions on which they had seen smoke, the voyage had been devoid of incident.

It had been so very easy to run the Allied blockade, and to get into the wider reaches of the ocean. Once there the whole thing had been simple. It was going to be just as easy on the way back – for the *Viking*, anyway. It wouldn't be so easy for him – not if he had to command one of the captured ships. He would just have to wait and see. Fischer hadn't said anything yet.

He didn't mind commanding one of these ships: he would like the chance. It would be something to make up for missing the invasion of England. Funny it hadn't happened yet. Wonder what was the delay? When they had left Germany invasion of England seemed imminent. That was the reason why everyone was disappointed when they found out that they were bound for Antarctica. It had seemed so very futile with victory so close at hand.

Wenzel was right. It wouldn't be so easy to get these ships back to Germany. Besides their being conspicuous, the whole British Navy would be on the watch for them once they found out that they'd been captured and not destroyed, and that it was the intention to get them back to Germany.

The crew problem didn't worry him. He could handle all crew worries. A score of armed ratings could easily deal with the four hundred and odd whalemen who would comprise the homeward crew. After all, they were Germans now. Their country had been lost to them, just the same as it had been lost to those other European peoples. They were, in fact, lucky to be getting home. They would be freed immediately they got back to Germany. If there were Quislings on board, so much the better. Perhaps they would all be Quislings once the ships had been taken over. No, the crew question should present no difficulties.

Those British whale-ships would be more of a problem. You can't trust Britishers – especially the Scots. About fifty per cent of the British ships' personnel were Scots. As Kaltenbrunner said in one of his lectures, 'These Scots won't take kindly to commands, especially German commands.' There was going to be trouble there.

His thoughts ran on. He would be getting married when he got back to Germany. Why couldn't he have been married before he left? That application for leave – it had been refused. He thought of the letter he had sent his fiancée; he hoped she had understood; that it was no fault of his that his application had been turned down. How was he to know that all shore leave would be stopped a month before the vessel sailed? One couldn't explain very well in letters that were meticulously censored – not about one's private life.

He wished that it hadn't happened – now! It was on his return from the invasion of Norway, after he had been personally decorated by the Führer. They had gone off together on that mountaineering holiday. The only thing was that they hadn't done much climbing. Hell! These things happen; it was common in the Nazi Germany of today. The Führer himself actually encouraged this relationship between the sexes. A rising birth-rate would eventually bring tomorrow's soldiers –

soldiers that would be required for the policing of these subjected countries. They would need them too, once the British were subdued. He smiled to himself. You just can't go and explain all this to your girl-friend – not when you've been engaged to be married for nearly three years.

His thoughts were interrupted by Kaltenbrunner coming out of the radio-room. There was a gleam of excitement about his eyes a secret smile of anticipation on his face. 'I can hear both the Norwegian whale factory-ships talking on radio-telephony. Blue whales, blue whales, blue whales! That's all they talk about. Operations must be heavy.'

'How far do you think they are away?' Linder asked excitedly.

'About six hundred miles. Yes, just over six hundred miles. We'll manage to get directional bearings when we get closer.'

'Then they must be about twenty-seven hours distant from here?'

Kaltenbrunner made no reply. He picked up a pair of glasses and focused them to the starboard bow. 'You see that whiteness low in the sky?'

Linder nodded. 'That cloud?'

'That is no cloud, Lieutenant. That's ice! You'll see when we get there.'

The younger officer's eyes widened as he peered at the whitish blur. 'How far do you think we're off?'

'About fifty miles – maybe a shade less. That's the reflection from a line of barrier icebergs. "Ice-blink" is the word they use. One can distinguish the ice-blink even on the darkest of nights. That's what you want to look for when navigating in the dark. It's the only indication that ice is in the vicinity. All these indications that you read about in meteorological books don't mean a thing – not down here. Forget all about water-temperatures and all that rot. Look for the ice-blink.'

Linder nodded his head.

Kaltenbrunner again swept the horizon with his glasses. 'You know, Lieutenant, there's a lot to see in these waters if you keep a good look-out. You see . . . look! There's whales!'

The younger officer stared hard at the bearing indicated.

'You see them?'

'Yes, there are two.'

'That's right. Blue whales. A female and a calf.' Kaltenbrunner spoke the words with such simplicity that it produced a questioning silence from the watchkeeper. He looked round with suspicion. 'How can you tell that it's a mother and calf?'

Kaltenbrunner grinned. 'By experience, I suppose. I can see by the blast that one of them is a calf. The calf is always with the mother – just like any other animal. You realize that they're mammals?'

'Yes, I know that.'

'Do you know that a whale-gunner is not allowed to kill that mother whale. It's a milk-filled whale. That's the word they use.'

'But how can they tell?'

'Just as I have said – experience. The calf is with the mother whale, therefore the mother whale must be with milk. The whale-gunner knows that he shouldn't shoot. It's simple enough.'

'But there can be mistakes?'

'Plenty of them. But the gunners don't get paid for these mistakes. That makes a difference. It's work for nothing. It teaches them to be careful.'

'I see what you mean. How can you tell these are blue whales?'

'Again that's simple enough. Each species of whale has a different type of blast. That is what the whale-shooter looks for. For example, a blue whale's blast is broader or thicker than the blast from a fin whale. And the sperm whale's blast is different again: it rises at a different angle. To trained eyes it's easy to differentiate.'

'Just as easy as that!' Linder snapped his fingers. 'You can keep your whaling life, Lieutenant. It must be hell to be working down here!'

Kaltenbrunner smiled. 'You haven't seen anything yet. Just you wait.' He spoke half-humorously, but there was meaning behind his words. 'Now I must go and inform Captain Fischer that we can hear both factory-ships. A little over twenty hours from now, and we can go into the business of piracy – piracy on a colossal scale.'

He made his way to Fischer's accommodation, and found him studying the chart of South Georgia. The commanding officer looked up hastily as he entered.

'I can hear snatches of conversation, on radio-telephony, from both factory-vessels. They must be very close together. We can try for radio directional bearings this evening, when conditions are better. I should say they're about six hundred miles away – the extreme range of radio-telephony.'

'Good! Good! Sit down, Lieutenant.'

Kaltenbrunner took off his bridge-coat and settled down.

'I was just studying this chart of South Georgia. Must be a terrible place.'

'Yes, sir, I suppose it is. I haven't been there. The German whale factory-ships always operated to the eastward.'

Fischer nodded pleasantly. 'Then we can expect anything – now. Funny there's no ice. I thought we'd have seen something by now.'

'There are icebergs coming up ahead, sir. I should say about forty miles away. We should be up to them in about two hours' time.'

Fischer was about to rise. 'I'll have to go up and see—'

'There's plenty of time, sir,' interrupted Kaltenbrunner. 'There'll be nothing but ice from now on. These two ships will be lying right on the pack-edge. Say, about six hundred miles from this position.'

'That means the ice-edge is in about sixty-one degrees?'

'That's correct, sir.'

'Then they weren't very far out at home?'

'No, sir.'

'Well, it's up to us now, Lieutenant. Let's hope we can deal with things rapidly. Speed will mean everything. I wish we had a longer period of darkness. It gets lighter all the time. By the time tomorrow night comes and we shift our latitude another ten degrees there won't be any darkness.'

'A little over two hours, sir. Looks like we'll have to reduce speed. Either that or stop. We're going to be there much too early if we keep this speed.'

Fischer nodded. 'I'll adjust the speed later.' His face was grim – a grimness born of an endless struggle with the sea and its ways. He said mechanically, 'We'll call a final conference for this evening. I have decided to send Dieter with the *Cachelot.* Linder will command the *Antarctica.* I hope we can trust him. He's young. . . .'

'He'll manage, sir. He's an efficient officer. You can trust him – implicitly.'

'I think we can. Yes, I think we can.'

The commanding officer offered Kaltenbrunner his cigarette-case.

'No, thanks, Captain. Not just now.'

Fischer lit a cigarette, taking his time. He sat back and propped his elbows on the desk before him. 'You were saying, Lieutenant, that these two ships are very close together. What are we going to do now?'

Kaltenbrunner shrugged. 'It is unusual, sir. There must be unlimited whales. Judging by the snatches of conversation that I managed to hear, they both must be on a full production. I'll be able to learn much more this evening. Conditions will be better.'

'But isn't it going to complicate matters?'

'Not necessarily. They won't be that close; they'll be out of sight of one another. Personally, I think it'll favour us. If these ships are on full production their whaleboats will have obtained their whales during the early part of the day. They'll be lying around their parent ships doing nothing. They won't be hunting whales; they'll have got their day's quota. There's much less danger of them sighting us as we approach.'

Fischer smiled, a trifle wearily. 'I see what you mean, Lieutenant. It all sounds so complicated. I'll arrange a final conference for 1800 hours. Inform Linder that he has to attend, also that he will be in command of the *Antarctica* for the voyage home to Germany. Try and give him some idea what is needed – some help.'

Kaltenbrunner rose. 'I'll tell him immediately, sir. Better let him be prepared. There's not much time – not now.'

Fischer nodded. 'You're right, Lieutenant. We have to do our part. Let's see them on their way.'

The supernumerary returned to the navigation bridge. Linder was gazing abstractedly at several albatrosses as they glided their way past the wing of the bridge. One moment they would be right alongside, the next, they would be far astern, skimming the wave-tops in undulating flight.

'They're peculiar birds, these albatrosses,' Linder said. 'You see their eyes? They move . . . move all the time. Not like other birds.'

Kaltenbrunner smiled. 'Yes. That's what the whalemen call seamen's eyes. They're watching . . . for ever watching.'

The icebergs were closer. The whole horizon was studded with mountains of ice. Broken-up ice-growlers were now scattered about the waters. Small blue ice-lumps, they didn't look dangerous, but they were large enough to damage a ship travelling at speed.

'There you have the first of the Antarctic ice. Looks like everyone is going to be busy around here for a long time.'

Linder grimaced. 'So it seems.'

Kaltenbrunner laughed. 'You'll be all right. Captain Fischer has just informed me that you're to command the *Antarctica.* He told me to let you know. You have to attend his final conference at 1800 hours this evening.'

'Who takes the *Cachelot*?' Linder asked.

'Dieter, of course.'

'I see. It's going to be a tough job.'

'Yes, I guess it will be.' Kaltenbrunner spoke seriously. 'Don't let it get you down. I'm sure you'll handle the whole thing efficiently. I made sure that you had a good crew. You've quite a number of German whalemen in your lot. They know all the ropes about these ships. I'll point them out to you.'

'Thank you – sir.' Linder added the last word as an afterthought.

Kaltenbrunner nodded appreciatively. 'We'll have a talk after this conference. Let's see if I can help you in any way. There isn't much time left.'

'I would like to. I—'

Dr. Reuss came on to the bridge and stopped the conversation. 'Have you seen the ice?' he asked.

Kaltenbrunner looked at him coldly, as if he questioned his right to come up on the navigation bridge without permission. 'What do you think we're up here for?' he almost shouted.

Reuss remained unruffled. 'I didn't mean anything,' he said. 'I've nothing else to do. I must do something! Everyone is vulgarly healthy around here. There's no work for me.'

Linder chuckled.

'It's all very well for you, Linder. You've always something to do. Me! I've nothing. Why the hell did they send me to this damned ship? Did I have to join the Navy to do tooth extractions?'

'There's a long way to go yet, Doctor. One can never tell. You won't get many illnesses. Germs can't live down here. The climate's too healthy. Even steel doesn't rust – not in the Antarctic.' Kaltenbrunner spoke as he scanned the horizon to the southward.

There were several sharp cries of *Ca-a-a-k! Ca-a-a-k!* from somewhere close at hand. Both Linder and Reuss looked up quickly with startled faces. Linder looked anxiously around. 'What on earth's that?' he asked.

Kaltenbrunner laughed. 'Only penguins,' he answered. 'You'll see thousands of them before long. They're funny birds; amphibious and lovable characters. In the water they swim like greased lightning; on the land they waddle around like old men. But you just try and catch one. They get down on their rumps and slide along the snow or ice quicker than any-toboggan. Yes, they're very funny birds. Nobody ever harms a penguin.' He took a last look to the southward, and added, 'Well, I'd better get back to that radio-telephone. Just keep clear of all these ice-lumps.'

Linder gave a brisk nod.

'He's breaking out,' said Reuss. 'Friendly – he's even started to speak. What have you done to him?'

'There's nothing wrong with Kaltenbrunner once you get to know him. These waters must be like home to him. Probably that's why he's more talkative.'

'You mean, you actually mean, he's glad to be here!'

'Yes.'

'God! Then he's welcome! He can have the whole lot for me!'

'Do you know what he's just told me.'

'What?'

'That I'm to take over command of the *Antarctica*. That I take the vessel back to Germany.'

'Wenzel told you that before.'

'He was only joking then. This came direct from Fischer. He's been a long time making up his mind. Just imagine . . . just think of it! Another forty-eight hours, and I'll be on my way home!'

'Yes, or—' Reuss didn't finish the sentence.

Linder smiled slightly. 'You were always a pessimist.'

'I wish I was going with you just the same.' He took a last look at the nearest berg, and added, 'I'll have to go and see my one and only patient. I have an appointment. You know what's the matter with him.'

'What?'

Dr. Reuss gave a loud grunt. 'Toothache!' he answered with disgust.

CHAPTER TEN

Captain Fischer came briskly into the smokeroom and took the remaining chair at the head of a rosewood table with gleaming laminated top. Kaltenbrunner and Dieter sat on each side of the commanding officer. Next to them sat Wenzel and Linder. At the opposite end of the table, facing Fischer, sat the top executive from the engine department. There was a feeling of tenseness about the room. Fischer's manner did not improve matters.

Speed had been reduced. The *Viking* was moving through the water at a speed sufficient only to maintain steerage-way.

Fischer gave a slight cough and adjusted a pair of heavy spectacles. His manner was detached and authoritative. He ran his eyes over some papers on the table before him, then, leaning back, he said gravely, 'This will be the last conference before the capture of the Norwegian whale factory-ships *Antarctica* and *Cachelot*.'

A sudden harshness broke into his voice. He went on: 'The plan of operation for the seizure of these two vessels has been formulated by me out of the talks, both formal and informal, that I've had with my two supernumerary officers. If we are successful – which, of course, we will be – then the credit is due to them.

'It is not necessary for me to emphasize the importance of these first operations. You all know they are only the first of a whole list of such operations. We must not fail at this initial stroke. When you board these vessels you must be ruthless. Let nothing . . . nothing stand in your way.'

Fischer's manner became easier as he went on. 'Lieutenant Kaltenbrunner and Lieutenant Dieter will be in charge of this first operation. If the two vessels are so close together that we must conduct a simultaneous operation, then Lieutenant Kaltenbrunner will take over the *Cachelot* and Lieutenant Dieter the *Antarctica*. I hope that this will be unnecessary. It means splitting our forces.'

He glanced at Kaltenbrunner, and asked, 'Have you any more information?'

Kaltenbrunner shook his head. 'No. They seem to be about two hundred miles away. I have just been listening to two of the whale-gunners talking on radio-telephone.'

'Good! Then it will be a single operation?'

'It looks that way.'

'This simplifies matters considerably.'

Kaltenbrunner made no comment.

'The *Antarctica* will be our first objective, and zero-time for the boarding operation will be at 2400 hours tomorrow. We have to take advantage of the limited darkness. I will take the *Viking* as close as possible: much depends on the visibility. The rest of the journey will have to be made in two power boats – twenty men to each boat. Lieutenant Dieter, assisted by Lieutenant Linder, will be responsible for the capture of the parent vessel.'

Fischer glanced at his young officer, smiled slightly, and continued. 'Lieutenant Kaltenbrunner, with a few hand-picked men, will be responsible for the capture of all whale-catcher vessels. No specified plans for this assignment can be laid down: much depends on the weather and other working conditions. He has my authority to depart from any of the plans which we have previously discussed. I repeat, much depends on the actual conditions.'

Fischer was more relaxed still. 'I am obliged,' he said, 'to emphasize again the importance of the time factor. You all know how vital it may be. I hope to repeat the same operation exactly twenty-four hours later on the *Cachelot*. That is why I impress upon you the importance of time.

'Lieutenant Dieter will be left in charge of the *Antarctica*; he will follow us to the *Cachelot* as soon as conditions permit.' Fischer leaned forward with a decisive motion, thumped heavily on the table-top with the fist of his right hand, and spoke with sudden harshness: 'Within a period of forty-eight hours after our opening gambit I expect to see both vessels on their way back to Germany with their cargoes of whale-oil. It is up to you.

'For the voyage back to Germany Lieutenant Linder will

command the *Antarctica.* Lieutenant Dieter will take over the *Cachelot*. I hope you will both have as much luck as we experienced on the outward journey.

'After dropping the boats the *Viking* will immediately steer to the northward, and will patrol in an east and west direction just over the horizon. We will then be in a favourable position to intercept any of the whaleboats which may attempt to run to the northward. On the pre-arranged signal from you – after you have successfully dealt with the catcher fleet – we will return to the area.

'At least one of the catcher vessels should be retained in commission; the others will be destroyed. We will use this vessel as a decoy when we round up the whaleboats of the *Cachelot.* This should help matters considerably.'

Kaltenbrunner gave a slight smile. Fischer, it seemed, had everything well in hand.

'There isn't much more,' said the commanding officer. 'We have discussed the boarding operation, and crews have been exercised in its procedure: they know what to expect. I see no difficulty in taking over any of the parent vessels. It's the catchers that worry me. Lieutenant Kaltenbrunner said to me only recently, "None must escape." We must make sure that this does not happen.'

Fischer discarded his glasses, and smiled. 'Now, are there any questions? Is there any point which you want to discuss?'

Nobody spoke.

'Then we must sleep on it. That is my advice.'

Fischer left in the company of his senior officer. Dieter returned to bridge duties. The engineer executive sat for a short while, and then disappeared. Kaltenbrunner and Linder were left on their own.

Kaltenbrunner rose, stretched himself, and then settled down in one of the more luxurious armchairs. The smoke-room was large. One wall consisted entirely of plated glass, with concealed lighting effects – a relic of happier days of passenger travel. Around the walls of the room was hung a series of painted seascapes. A recent addition was a picture of the Führer.

The younger officer lit a cigarette, looked through the

windows, and then followed suit. The room had suddenly become alive with an increased sense of vibration. 'Looks like they've increased speed,' he observed.

Kaltenbrunner nodded. 'Yes. We want to get within a hundred miles of the *Antarctica*. One never knows – we may have fog tomorrow. It's better to get in closer; it's no use wallowing around here.'

Linder nodded.

'Now, is there anything you specially wanted to discuss?'

'Only this passage home. It seems a tough job for only about twenty men. And the speed. The *Antarctica*'s not the *Viking*.'

'Forget it, Lieutenant. The job only looks tough – tough on paper. Actually, I think it will be simple – especially the *Cachelot* and the *Antarctica*.'

Linder smiled thinly. He didn't say anything.

'When these men left home,' went on Kaltenbrunner, 'Norway was free and independent. Look what has happened in the interval. Their country has been invaded and lost to them – even the British let them down. Their people in Norway are making the best of the matter. These whalemen will do the same. Promise them that they'll be repatriated, that they'll be paid for their season's work, and you won't have any mutineers. If necessary, hold over them the threat to their families and homes – the threat of the Gestapo! You'll have no troubles.'

The supernumerary settled his legs over the arm of his chair. 'They'll be better off than the Norwegians on the British whale-ships. It's doubtful whether they'll get home.'

'I hope they can see it in that way.'

'Make them see it!'

'Yes. I know what you mean.'

Kaltenbrunner chuckled. 'That's the way, Lieutenant. Look at me! I have to take one of those damned British ships home. That's going to be worse . . . much worse.'

'How?'

'The British and Norwegian personnel who comprise the crews of these ships are not on the very best of terms with each other – they never have been. The *Altmark* incident of last year brought things to a head. We won't get the British to do as the Norwegians will do. There's sure to be trouble in those ships.

We won't get any collaboration there. They won't be going back to their own country. They'll have nothing to look forward to – not like the Norwegians.'

Linder sat lazily studying his finger-nails.

'You keep them working, Lieutenant. That's the best advice I can give you. Don't give them a chance to worry – keep them hard at work. Let them carry out their duties in the usual manner. Paint the ship. Paint it again – and again if necessary. Do anything – anything to keep them busy. Discipline can only be maintained by hard work. As soon as discipline deteriorates something is wrong. Usually it's the disciplinarian who's at fault – not the men.'

After a brief pause Linder said solemnly, 'I will do my best. I can't do more than that.'

'Good! You keep to that, and you won't go very far wrong. It's up to you. Impress upon them the threat to their families . . . their homes . . . their very existence. You'll find them co-operative.'

He wedged himself more firmly into the chair, and then went on: 'You know, Lieutenant, the voyage back shouldn't be so very difficult. I know your best speed will only be eleven knots, but try and keep clear of everything. That's the drill – keep clear of everything. They won't take you back to Germany. Occupied France is nearer – and safer. That's where they'll route you.'

Linder was about to reply when he was interrupted by the arrival of a bridge messenger. 'Captain Fischer's compliments, sir. Would you come to the bridge immediately?' He addressed the supernumerary.

Kaltenbrunner nodded. 'I will be there at once.' He rose nonchalantly, flashed a sympathetic smile at Linder, and followed the seaman to the bridge.

Both Fisher and Dieter were in the radio-room listening intently to the telephone receiver. There were some wild crackling noises before a voice, speaking in Norwegian, came over the air waves.

'Hello, *Antarctica*! Hello, *Antarctica*! *Antarctica 5* calling! Where shall we deliver our whales? Where shall we deliver our whales?'

There was a short pause before a voice answered, 'Hello, *Antarctica 5*! Hello, *Antarctica 5*! Factory-ship answering. Hold on to your whales. Hold on to your whales until further orders.'

Again there was a pause.

'Hello, factory! Hello, *Antarctica*! What about bunkers? *Antarctica 5* calling! What about bunkers?'

Dieter grinned. He was doing the translation for Fischer.

'*Antarctica* calling *Antarctica 5*. You are not to refuel before tomorrow. You are not to refuel before tomorrow.' The voice tapered off.

'They've been calling like that for the last half-hour,' said Dieter. 'All of them. They must be on full production. By the look of things they'll have enough whales to last them another forty hours. They're on a full cook!'

'Good! Good!' Kaltenbrunner smiled. 'That's what we thought.'

'Directional bearings put her ten degrees on the port bow. I've just altered course.'

Kaltenbrunner nodded.

'Hello, *Antarctica 2*! Hello, *Antarctica 2*! *Antarctica* calling *Antarctica 2*! Deliver your whales to buoy-boat.' The voice droned on.

'God! They must be whaling heavy!' exclaimed Dieter. 'Reminds me of the good old days.'

'Yes, the good old days,' reiterated Kaltenbrunner, 'days when there was no war, when everyone could go on their legitimate business without fear . . . or panic . . . or anything.'

Fischer smiled.

'You know, Captain, I think we're going to carry out this job very quickly. These heavy whaling conditions are in our favour. It'll only take me a couple of hours to round up the whole catcher fleet. They'll all be in the same area – the area of the parent vessel.'

They sat listening to the telephone conversations; radio-telephony was being used continuously. At last Fischer rose and made his way out to the open bridge. Kaltenbrunner followed at his heels.

The sea was smooth, blue and translucent. The sun was low

on the horizon, a huge ball of fire edged by a crimson glow. Not a cloud showed in an azure sky. The *Viking*, leaving a zigzag trail behind her, was being conned continuously in order to clear the dangerous ice-growlers that lay in her path.

The horizon seemed to stretch to infinity. Icebergs rose sheer out of the smooth waters. One passed close to starboard. Kaltenbrunner was quick to point out to his commanding officer the meaning of the different hues of whiteness on its sides – the different seasons of snowfall.

Fischer grunted. He scanned the horizon with his powerful glasses. 'These icebergs! They look like white-marble tombstones in this light. It must be a mirage.'

Kaltenbrunner laughed. 'One can make them look like anything. Tombstones, ramparted castles, glacial palaces – they are there to see, if one uses one's imagination.'

A pod of whales, six in number, sounded less than half a mile off the port bow. Kaltenbrunner pointed them out to Fischer. 'Sperm whales!' he exclaimed. 'These are the world's largest toothed animals. It's the whale from which ambergris is sometimes found.'

'Ambergris?'

'Haven't you heard of the stuff? That once fabulous substance sometimes found floating on the surface of the sea after it has been vomited from the whale?'

'I have heard of it. But what do you mean by "once fabulous"? Isn't it valuable now?'

'Not now,' said Kaltenbrunner. 'They used it in the perfume industry at one time for retaining the strength of the perfume. Perhaps I should say the smell of the perfume. Nowadays the same results can be got by synthetic means.'

Fischer smiled. 'Is there anything in the whale that they don't use?'

'Hardly anything.'

'This ambergris? It's a sort of disease?'

'Yes, that's right. It's a cancerous growth that is set up in the whale's intestines owing mainly to its diet.'

'And this diet?'

'Consists only of cuttlefish. We call them squid. Ambergris is a brown waxy substance, not unlike beeswax. It has no peculiar smell of its own.'

Fischer nodded. 'But I thought they fed on some form of plankton?'

'That's the baleen whale – not the sperm. The baleen whale obtains its food comparatively close to the surface, but the sperm-whale has to dive to great depths to get his. Another peculiar fact about these sperm whales,' Kaltenbrunner added, 'is that you only get the bull sperm down here. There are no females – not here!'

Fischer chuckled. 'Then they'll be free from all those matrimonial troubles.'

'There's that to it,' agreed the supernumerary officer.

Dieter joined them on the bridge. 'I can hear them both,' he said. 'The *Cachelot* is whaling just as heavily as the *Antarctica*. All one hears on radio-telephony is whale, whale, whale. They're making no secret of the fact.'

'Good! Then they won't be able to move and complicate matters.' Fischer spoke in a relieved tone.

The sun sank below the western horizon and left a cold, grey bleakness. What had been a few minutes before an Antarctic seascape, in brilliant tints of reds and blues and whites, was now a cheerless and icy ocean.

Fischer gave a slight shiver. 'It's cold out here without adequate clothing. I think I'll go below and get something.' He slowly crossed the bridge to speak to the senior bridge officer. Dieter returned to the radio cabin. Kaltenbrunner went below.

The dark superstructures of the foredeck presented a vague silhouette against the light from a cloudless sky as Per Becker made his way forward to relieve Gunther on the bow look-out.

There was an absolute silence about the *Viking* as she slowly drifted to wind and sea. Infinite numbers of stars shone down on the cheerless ocean. The Southern Cross rode high in the heavens; the diamond-wise formation was imposing, but not so imposing as the two stars which rode in close proximity – the Centuries.

'Here I am!' Gunther shouted, as Becker stumbled noisily around. 'Where the hell have you been? You're late!'

Becker made his way to the leeward side of a small access house, where Gunther was sheltering. 'So that's where you are!' he exclaimed. 'I've been hunting around looking for you for the last fifteen minutes. What are you hiding yourself for?'

Gunther made no reply.

'You should be happy. Why don't you cheer up? You're like me. You're not being shipped on these Norsk ships. You're to stay on the *Viking*: they can't do without you and me. But just wait till we get to those blasted British ships. That's where the hell we're going! I know it. I know what's coming. We get all the bloody work around here!'

Gunther discarded his greatcoat. 'There's two icebergs to leeward. They've both been reported. The ship has been stopped since 2200 hours. I'm off!'

Becker snorted. 'Yes, Gunther, that's what's going to happen to—'

'Look, Becker. Don't you start all that again. I had enough of it last night. You kept me here all your bloody watch. Not tonight! Definitely not tonight! I know your game. I'm wise to you – now!'

Becker commenced a slow pacing of the deck, stopping at regular intervals in order to look out to leeward. Except for two tabular bergs, about three miles away, there was nothing else visible. A lightness was apparent about the eastern horizon: soon it would be dawn.

Gunther was touchy this morning, he thought. What on earth had he done to him? This time tomorrow, and they would be on board the *Antarctica*. It was going to be an easy job – nothing to it. Pity about those whaleboats. Why had they to be destroyed? He would be in Kaltenbrunner's party; most of that work was going to fall to him. He had always been the supernumerary officer's right arm, the one person Kaltenbrunner seemed to trust. He knew that from the old days – the days on the German whale-ships. They were shipmates – and friends.

'What's that?' he muttered anxiously to himself. He peered intently to leeward. 'That white patch! Is it ice? Must be.' He made a dash to the bridge telephone, lifted the speaker, then all of a sudden halted. He looked again. 'God!' he exclaimed. 'It's the bloody moon!'

I nearly made a fool of myself, he thought. Me! An experienced whaleman, accustomed to these icy waters, reporting the moon as an iceberg! Wonder what they would have said? It had been done before – repeatedly. But to have it happen to him!

He glanced up at the bridge in the half-light. Lieutenant Linder was scanning the horizon to the south. There was some activity, and then the engines commenced to break into a powerful throb. The *Viking* swung in a half-circle and again headed towards the south.

CHAPTER ELEVEN

The whale factory-ship *Antarctica* was on full production. For a period of three weeks the daily production total had exceeded 2,000 barrels. Added to earlier production, the whale-ship now had a cargo of over 10,000 tons of pure whale-oil on board.

Captain Konrad Nilsen, manager of the *Antarctica* expedition, contemplated this with silent satisfaction as he looked down upon the whaling-deck from a vantage-point at the rear end of the navigation bridge. Smoke and steam, belching from funnels and exhaust-pipes, meant that the full cook was still in operation.

Nilsen never wearied of the all-familiar sight of a whale factory-ship working to full capacity – of the wild and bewildering scene that was enacted on the whaling-deck, of the gigantic carcasses that were constantly being dismembered, and of the bloody and gory decks that were high to the bulwarks with masses of blubber, meat and bone.

The whaling-deck resembled some huge *abattoir*, only a hundred times larger. Among the masses of slimy, smelly flesh, bone, and blubber, huge vertebral columns, many of them well over eighty feet in length, were being sawn up into segments small enough to be fed to the open maws of the steam-pressure boilers. Rivulets of coagulated blood oozed slowly through the deck-scuppers, to stain the virgin-white ice that the ship was drifting through.

Nilsen positioned himself to watch a ninety-foot blue whale being hove up the whale slipway. He could follow every sound as the various steam winches came into operation and the flensers went about their complicated work. There was a dull clang as the three-ton whale-claw dropped over the tail of the carcass, and slowly the whale was being hove up the slipway-ramp to the open deck where the flensers were waiting with their flensing-knives. As the dead whale was hove slowly past them they stuck the flensing-knives into the seven-inch layer of blubber, and, letting the steam winches do most of the work, made long, longitudinal incisions on each side and top part of the huge carcass.

As the whale came to rest on the open deck, winch-wires were attached to each strip of blubber, and, as other flensers hacked and sliced with wild abandon, the winches tore the viscous covering of fat from the sides of the whale just as easily as taking skin from a banana.

The carcass was now ready for canting. Winch-wires were made fast to each of the flukes – one over and one under the carcass. With what seemed one mighty heave by a combination of steam winches, the whale was rolled completely over, to fall with a dull and squelching sound as whalemen scrambled in all directions to avoid the steel hooks that went flying through the air as the mountain of flesh landed on the deck.

The remaining strip of blubber was quickly torn away, and the skinned whale, now a red-and-white mass of flesh, bone, and blood, was hove to the forward part of the whaling-deck, where the lemmers (the expert anatomists among the flensers) waited with their knives to dismember the whole of the carcass.

Like ants around some anthill, squads of men commenced slicing tons of red, gory meat from the hundred-ton carcass, as others dealt with the casings of ribs, infats, and other parts.

Each part of the mammal's carcass went its different way. Meat was hove to the forward part of the vessel, to be cut up and fed to a dehydrating meat-meal plant. The huge liver, measuring at least eight feet square as it lay on the deck, went to a liver plant, to be rendered down into flakes and liver-oil. Ribs were sawn into small sections and fed to the whale-boilers situated below decks. The whole of the whale's innards were torn out: only the massive backbone remained.

So the deck-work went on, carcass after carcass at half-hour or hourly intervals, depending on the species and size. An assembly-line in reverse: nothing remained when the job was completed.

Nilsen could well visualize the work that was being done below decks – an oil refinery within a ship, the men working in humid temperatures, sometimes reaching as high as 130 degrees Fahrenheit, while the outside temperature was well below freezing-point. Coffined by steel, by massive steam-pressure boilers, and by a maze of complicated pipelines of all sizes and description, these men worked in surroundings ten times more dangerous than the open whaling-decks. The constant hum of electric motors and separating machinery, mixed with the dull thuds of various vacuum pumps, made up a concerto diabolic in its tempo.

The sun was low on the horizon. Nilsen went to the wheelhouse, lifted a pair of binoculars, and swept the horizon to the south. The wind, a light breeze, was from the south-west. All the catcher fleet were in the vicinity, their day's work finished, and still holding on to the whales that they had hunted and killed in the early forenoon.

A small tabular berg lay close abeam to starboard. The manager watched his bridge officer give it a casual glance as he nonchalantly swung the engine-room telegraphs over to dead slow ahead. No sooner had the engines responded than the officer again swung the handle back to stop. The vessel moved slightly ahead, her bow swung off to port, and as she slowly resumed her original drifting position the iceberg lay safely astern.

Good whaling weather, thought Nilsen. I hope the whales will hold out. Two or three more weeks of these conditions, and the *Antarctica* could well secure a record catch. It was one of those seasons when everything went smoothly – when good weather prevailed for weeks on end, and there was an abundance of whales. The whole area was covered with plankton. Prospects were good – exceedingly good.

What he had just observed pleased him. He took it as a tribute to his native country that his ship should have produced so much whale-oil so early in the season. What a pity it was that he couldn't take his cargo back to Norway! It would have to be England again – same as last year. He remembered his last sailing from Norway: that was nearly two years ago. Time passes, and now his country was in the hands of those Nazi fanatics, those great hordes of German youth, trained from boyhood to overwhelm and master the countries of Europe. As far as Norway was concerned, they had succeeded. Only the British remained – now!

His eyes were troubled as he fingered his well-trimmed beard. It would be a long time before he ever set foot in Norway again. The British would have to be subdued first, and he didn't want that to happen. He knew that many Norwegians wished for that, not because they were Quislings, but because it was their only chance of an early return to their native land. They hoped that the War would soon be over – that the British would capitulate, and it would then be possible for them to go home. How long would it be otherwise?

Nilsen was happy at his expedition's early success. The War seemed a long way from them. They were in the isolated and frozen waters of Antarctica – nobody worried them. The ice was their only enemy. If it wasn't for the constant radio news they wouldn't know that a war was taking place. Meantime they were all earning good money – in his own particular case big money! He had plans for eventually meeting his family in neutral Sweden. It would probably take time, but he was much more fortunate than the others.

His thoughts rambled on. How was the *Cachelot* faring? She was less than a hundred miles to the eastward and hadn't moved in a week – a sure sign of favourable conditions. Was she ahead of his own ship in whale-oil production, or was she lagging behind? The British whale-ships were far to the westward: they didn't come into his calculations. A whaleboat came speeding alongside and moored directly below the fuelling-platform. The manager watched with interest as the whale-gunner skilfully manoeuvred his ship alongside.

Within minutes of making fast, oil and fresh water were flowing into the tanks of the catcher vessel; the crew began to load an assortment of whaling equipment and other stores.

The whale-gunner descended from the bridge and waved cheerily as he saw the expedition's manager watching him intently from the wing of the factory-ship's bridge.

Nilsen acknowledged the gunner's greeting, smiled, and beckoned him to come on board.

Hansen, leading gunner for the *Antarctica* expedition, quickly descended to the main deck of the whaleboat. He clambered into the loading-basket, and within seconds he was whipped high into the air by the use of winch and derrick and deposited on the fuelling-platform with scarcely a bump. He got to his feet and made his way to the whaling manager's accommodation.

Nilsen was laying out a bottle of whisky and two glasses as the expedition's ace whale-gunner entered the room. He looked up, smiled broadly, and said, 'Welcome, Hansen! How goes it with you?'

Hansen sighed with a sense of weariness and stretched himself in the best armchair the room had to offer. He was uncomfortably aware of his heavy leather knee-boots, which had been covered with blood from the whaling-deck, and which were now staining the light-green carpet of the manager's day cabin. 'Everything goes good!' he said. 'It would be a sight better if the factory could deal with some more whale.'

Nilsen smiled. It was a sore point with these whale-gunners when the factory-vessel was on full production. They were never allowed to kill more whales than were necessary. Dead whales deteriorated rapidly, and it was the job of the whaling manager to regulate the numbers killed daily.

The whale-gunner yawned, lay back in his chair, crossed his huge hands over his stomach, and transferred his attention to the whisky-bottle.

'The trouble with you people,' said Nilsen, as he poured out two stiff drinks, 'is that you make too much money. You're never satisfied. Why don't you bring in whales when we really need them? It's either a feast or a famine with you people – mostly famine.'

Hansen laughed, draining his glass outright. He refilled it immediately. It was easy to make Nilsen angry. 'What's the point of all this?' he asked.

The manager grinned. 'Nothing! Nothing at all! Where have you been today?'

The whale-gunner resumed his contemplation of the whisky-bottle. Funny, he thought, funny how drab these labels are on whisky-bottles. The better the whisky the more unpretentious the labels. Funny thing . . . very funny thing! His eyes caressed the bottle. He drank, and again reached out a grimy hand for the bottle. He filled his glass to the brim. When he spoke he enunciated each word with great care. 'You ask me, Nilsen, where have I been? I've been with the *Cachelot*'s whaleboats today. We've been hunting in the same vicinity. They're whaling like hell, only sixty miles to the eastward.'

'Are they that close?'

'That close! Their whaleboats are only over the horizon! They've been around us all day!'

'Have you been speaking with any of them?'

'Speaking! Speaking with any of them! I've been drinking with them – ever since I got my day's quota!' He took another gulp at his whisky and stared belligerently at Nilsen.

'Then you'll have gathered a lot of information?'

'Information!' scoffed Hansen. 'Information! They don't give away much information – not those people.'

'No?'

'No! But they wanted to know all about how we were getting on. How many barrels of whale-oil we had, and when our tanker vessel was due.'

Nilsen focused a distasteful eye on his leading whale-gunner. 'And I suppose you told them?'

'Like hell I did! I told them we'd done nothing – nothing until this week.' He grinned crookedly, and reached for his glass. His eyes were red and staring.

Nilsen laughed. 'You know, Hansen, you shouldn't drink so much – not with that stomach. You know what our doctor told you.'

'Told me!' barked Hansen. 'What the doctor told me! That son of a bitch! He's afraid that there'll be nothing left for him. These whaling doctors are no good. They're all the same: they wouldn't go whaling if they were any good.'

Again the whaling manager laughed. 'Never mind, Hansen. At least we know that the *Cachelot* is closing, that she's whaling just as favourably as we are. Looks like we'll soon run out of whales with twenty-four whale-catchers chasing them. When that happens one of us will have to move. I think we'll go to the westward. What do you think?'

Hansen grunted. He was looking solidly at the whisky bottle. They should make the bottles more colourful as well. They were just like the labels – drab and plain. Why don't they make them like those ornamental brandy bottles. Even the Norwegian aquavit was bottled much more stylishly. Now, that was a real drink . . . nearly as good as the best whisky. It had to be properly matured though – matured in the wood. A sea-voyage in the barrel, a double crossing of the equator – that was the drill. He grinned to himself. On whaling-ships it made only the one-way journey.

Nilsen repeated himself. 'What do *you* think, Hansen?'

The whale-gunner came out of his reverie. 'Yes . . . yes, Nilsen, you're right,' he said, a trifle unsteadily. 'This bloody place is busier than Oslo fjord. One of us will have to move. It's no use lying this close together – not when the whales get scarce.'

There was a prolonged blast from the whaleboat's steam whistle, which meant that fuelling had been completed. Hansen rose to take his departure. He had been drinking since early forenoon, but had sense enough to know that he couldn't remain alongside the factory-vessel: there were other whaleboats to follow him.

Nilsen accompanied the whale-gunner to the outside door, and watched, rather anxiously, as he made his way unsteadily down to the fuelling-platform. He was quickly thrust into the loading-basket by a group of tough, bearded whalemen, and, as he made some profane remark, which drew loud guffaws from his helpers, he was quickly hove outboard and landed once more on the deck of the whaleboat. Within minutes he was on the bridge; the moorings were cast off, and the vessel sped towards the ice-pack.

From his own navigation bridge the whaling manager watched as the whaleboat entered the broken-up ice-pack. Now, what the hell is he going into the ice-pack for? he wondered. Hope he isn't off on one of those periodic binges of his. One never knew what Hansen was going to do these days; he was becoming quite an enigma. What was the sense of taking his vessel into heavy ice during the night hours, when it would have been more comfortable to have spent the time drifting near the parent ship, as the others were doing? Nilsen shook his head in perplexity.

There was no doubt that Hansen *was* becoming a problem. Once he had been the expedition's ace whale-gunner, his services sought by all the large whaling companies, but now he lagged far behind the present leaders. There were days when he never killed a whale, days when he never attempted to do so, days when he hit the bottle – hard! His nephew, who was mate of the whaleboat, and who was being trained as a whale-gunner, did most of the hunting – and the killing. It had been reported that Hansen would stay in his cabin for days on end. The crew remained silent: they never complained. They had had their good times with Hansen; now they were taking the rough with the smooth.

There were days when the whale-gunner did go on the bridge and the whole situation quickly changed, days when he could kill as many as twelve whales in the matter of a few hours. These days were few and far between now: he soon got back into his lackadaisical ways – that and the aquavit bottle.

It was curious how the War, and especially the occupation of Norway, had affected some of his fellow-countrymen. A large percentage of the expedition's personnel were definitely neurotic. Working up to fourteen hours a day, seven days a week, there was little time for brooding, but during the off-duty hours, the hours when their minds should have been at rest, that was the time when they thought and wondered what was happening to their families and friends under the Nazi occupation. Letters from home, smuggled through neutral Sweden, only added fuel to smouldering imaginations. And there were the rumours – those small-town rumours – some startling in their ambiguity, but which never could be controlled. Who were associating with Nazi occupation troops and who were not? Who were Quislings and who were working for the various Underground movements? The whole matter was baffling – a problem far beyond the capabilities of an ordinary shipmaster.

Nilsen's thoughts ran on. It had been said, he remembered, that there was a touch of neurosis in every person. A little, like some drug, could be good, but too much was definitely dangerous. That was what was happening with the *Antarctica*'s personnel. The men, through no fault of their own, were definitely neurotic. What was going to happen when operations became slack – when days would pass and they didn't have to work a whale, when bad weather and fog stopped all operational work? Nilsen dreaded the future, but what the hell! Their problems were his own: he couldn't do much about it.

He returned to his day cabin and listened to telephone conversations between whale-gunners of both expeditions. He had already noticed that the barometer was falling. He was considering the effects of having the *Cachelot* in such close proximity. Hansen was right. The whales would soon run out now that they were being hunted by the catcher fleets of two expeditions. It was nearly time to move – but where? *Cachelot* had come from the eastward; it was no good moving in that direction. Northward meant bad weather and poor visibility. To the south lay the impregnable ice-pack. The west was the obvious choice . . . but what was the *Cachelot* going to do?

He felt sure that he was in a lucrative area, that if the whales disappeared they would be sure to return. The sea was covered in the minute, shrimp-like plankton that was the baleen-whales' only food. It was difficult to give the decision to leave such an area, but time . . . time was vital! He had to consider the effects of running away from his expected tanker vessel. Oil-fuel was becoming scarce, and space for the increasing whale-oil production had now become a vital necessity. Better to stay where he was – at least until he got clear of the tanker.

Forty miles to the eastward, on the other side of an ice peninsula that extended to the northward, the factory-vessel *Cachelot*, cooking on full production basis, was in the same favourable position as the *Antarctica*. Ever since the start of the season whales had been brought in with monotonous regularity. Twenty-four hours a day, in two watches, her crew had toiled with maximum efficiency. No *abattoir* was ever bloodier; no whaling expedition could have had better results.

Darkness was falling. Massive floodlights shone down upon the bloody and gory decks with an unearthly glow. Millions of birds squatted in the water by the drifting ship. The catcher fleet lay to windward, their day's work finished, each holding sufficient whales to keep the parent vessel working for another thirty-six hours. Only the noise of the steam winches, and steam exhausts, intermingled with the raucous squeals of bird life, disturbed the silence of the Antarctic night.

Throughout it all the *Cachelot* drifted slowly through the broken-up ice-pack.

CHAPTER TWELVE

'Then we must make it a simultaneous operation,' said Kaltenbrunner. 'It's no use adopting half-measures now. The catcher fleets of both *Cachelot* and *Antarctica* are all mixed up. Circumstances beyond our control compel us to take a chance. If we hesitate all is lost!'

Dieter nodded vigorously. He had just informed Captain Fischer that the two expeditions were converging on one another, that the whaleboats were operating in the same area, and that it was dangerous to attempt the capture of one expedition without the other.

Fischer hesitated. It was no good altering plans at the last minute, he thought, but, as Kaltenbrunner had just said, it was imperative that they go after both expeditions simultaneously. Either that or wait until they separated.

Wenzel broke in: 'Looks like we're unlucky, sir.'

'Unlucky! Unlucky!' scoffed the commanding officer. 'That sounds like a dirge! Go to it, Lieutenant. Prepare for the capture of both expeditions.'

Kaltenbrunner smiled. 'I feel that's a wise decision, sir.' He glanced at Dieter. 'We won't let you down. This time tomorrow we'll be on our way to the British ships.'

Fischer smiled for the first time. 'I only hope you're right, Lieutenant.'

Eight miles to the southward the working-lights of the whale-ship *Antarctica* glowed brilliantly in the gathering darkness. Fischer knew that it was dangerous to take the *Viking* closer, but time was less important here. It was the *Cachelot* that was his greatest worry. The Antarctic summer's night lasts for only a few hours. The *Viking* had to be taken at full speed through the darkness for at least forty miles, through waters that are the most dangerous in the world, so that Kaltenbrunner could carry out his part of the night's assignments. Daylight, Fischer seemed to think, was their greatest enemy.

'Stop engines!'

'Stop engines, sir!'

The powerful throb of the motors died instantly. The *Viking* carried her way through the water for some considerable distance before she finally became motionless. Around the dark silhouette of the vessel icebergs loomed up with menacing nearness.

'Boats away!' ordered the commanding officer.

'Boats away, sir!' repeated one of the bridge officers.

Two diesel power-boats went screaming downward from the davits and plunged into the icy waters. Commanded by Dieter and Linder, each with a complement of twenty armed men, all knew exactly what lay before them.

Kaltenbrunner stood on the wing of the bridge and watched the boats as they disappeared into the blackness. 'Good luck!' he murmured to himself. 'Good luck!'

'Boats all clear, sir.' The bridge officer repeated the message from aft.

Fischer didn't answer. He himself swung the handles of the engine-room telegraphs hard over to full speed ahead. There were a few spluttering coughs, and the engines once again roared into full power. 'Come port!' he ordered. 'Steer 070 degrees!' The *Viking* swung to her new course and settled down. Men doubled up at the various look-out posts, and the surface raider sped onward – on towards the *Cachelot.*

Kaltenbrunner himself conned the *Viking* through the ice-strewn waters. He seemed to be in his element. Whereas all personnel were muffled to the eyes against the biting southerly wind and freezing temperatures, the supernumerary stood motionless on the wing of the bridge, unaffected by either cold or environment. His eyes as sharp as a needle, he appeared to sight every ice-growler long before others using the most powerful of binoculars were aware of their presence. A swing to starboard, an alteration to port, and massive ice-growlers, large enough to damage any ship travelling at speed, slid along the *Viking*'s hull with menacing persistence.

Fischer, grim and worried-looking, joined Kaltenbrunner on the bridge-wing. He stood silent, angry at himself for being nervous – angry at his lack of ice experience. It was the first time that the *Viking* had been raced through the darkness.

'We might manage it in under the two hours,' Kaltenbrunner said.

'Yes, if you don't go and sink us first.'

The supernumerary grinned in the darkness. 'This is nothing. I only hope it remains clear, and that we don't fall foul of any pack-ice. That's what's going to slow us down. We can't take chances then.'

'Is everything ready?'

'Yes, sir. Wenzel is along there now mustering the boat-crews. Everything will be ready.'

'I wish you luck, Lieutenant. Looks like you'll need it. Another three hours, and it will be broad daylight. You haven't much time. I'll take you as close to the *Cachelot* as is possible. That may help a little. What about the whaleboats? It will be daylight before you can deal with them.'

'We won't let that worry us, sir. We'll manage somehow.'

Confident, thought Fischer, confident as hell! He's more concerned about Dieter's part in the proceedings than his own. Wonder how he's getting on? He glanced at the luminous dial of his wrist-watch – 2330 hours. Thirty minutes more, and they would be boarding the *Antarctica*.

He didn't quite know what to make of Kaltenbrunner. An enigma – there was no other word. That queer sense of frustration that seemed to pervade his whole being, his diabolic hatred of foreign whale-ships and whaling matters in general, his energy and enthusiasm for the task which they were now about to begin – above all his leadership and ability. The whole thing didn't make sense.

A ragged wisp of low cloud scudded across the clear sky. Kaltenbrunner gave a start and peered intently ahead. 'Hard port! he ordered curtly. 'Full astern port engine!'

'Hard port! Full astern port!' the bridge officer echoed nervously.

The *Viking* swung rapidly and heeled slightly to the port helm and astern power. Close ahead, and now as if running away to starboard, heavy pack-ice loomed up in front of the vessel. Kaltenbrunner cursed loudly, and barked, 'Ease helm!'

'Ease helm, sir!' The helmsman anxiously brought the wheel back to amidships.

'Steady . . . steady she goes! Full ahead both engines!'

The order was quickly executed by nervous bridge officers.

Fischer felt a sudden misgiving, a moment of uncertainty, as the vessel steadied on a northerly course in a directional line with the pack-ice. His thoughts were confused. Like the other bridge officers, he had seen nothing . . . nothing until the supernumerary's orders had been executed.

'You can be sure of one thing now, sir,' said Kaltenbrunner.

'What?'

'That the *Cachelot* is on the other side of this pack-ice. Wonder how far it runs to the northward?'

There was a kind of baffled malevolence, mixed with grudging admiration, on Fischer's face as he asked, 'What do you think?'

'Not more than ten miles,' Kaltenbrunner answered. 'I think she'll be closer than we imagine. How's the directional bearing now?'

A bridge officer spoke up. 'The bearing is 045 degrees, sir. Four points on the starboard bow.'

'Good! Good! Around the north end of this ice peninsula and then to the eastward. I'd like to bet she's no more than twenty miles away.'

'I hope you're right,' Fischer said once again, but more equably. 'The whaleboats were talking of sixty miles.'

'Bah! Those are whaleboat miles! They don't mean anything. We needn't pay any attention to them.' He turned and spoke curtly to one of the bridge officers. 'Get your look-outs higher up. They're all clustered round the bridge. Never mind the ice. I'll deal with that. Look for lights.'

Wenzel came on to the bridge. 'Everything is in readiness on the boat-deck, sir. Boat-crews are at stand-by.'

Fischer nodded. He didn't reply.

The ice-edge was running back to the eastward. Kaltenbrunner glanced through his binoculars, checked the line on the wing pelorus, and then altered twenty degrees to the eastward. He turned to Fischer. 'We should have the *Cachelot* about thirty degrees on.'

His voice was drowned by a hail from the look-out on the top bridge. 'Lights on the starboard bow, sir!'

The supernumerary swept the horizon to starboard. 'Yes ... yes, he's right. That's the *Cachelot*! We'll be there in less than an hour.'

Fischer smiled for the second time that night. 'Then you'll have nearly two hours of darkness,' he said. 'Gives me a chance to get well out of the area.'

The wind had died completely. To the south, and stretching into both quadrants, the aurora australis was in one of its most active moods. Bright streamers of bluish-green light cascaded towards the zenith in shimmering curtains, that sparkled like jewels in the freezing temperature. Corposant, glittering around masts and rigging, added to the weird effect.

'We'll have fog when the sun comes up,' Kaltenbrunner said. 'The weather's too good. We're going to have fog and bad weather. There's a south-easter coming along.'

'But the barometer hasn't fallen much,' Wenzel observed.

'No, but it will. You can be sure of that.'

Fischer nodded grimly. 'There's one thing about you, Lieutenant. I can't blame you for being pessimistic. If you say there's going to be a south-east gale I believe it. I only hope it doesn't last long.'

'They don't – not in the early summer months. It usually blows like hell for about twenty hours, and then it's all over. The seas quickly subside. Within a few hours of a Southern Ocean gale the waters are as calm as they are now.'

'How is that?' asked Wenzel.

'Due to the ice, I suppose. Ice and the freezing temperatures. It all adds up.'

The *Cachelot*'s lights had topped the horizon and were rapidly closing. The whale-catcher fleet, distinguishable by their running-lights, were scattered around the parent ship.

Fischer peered through his powerful glasses. 'Good!' he exclaimed. 'I'll take over now, Lieutenant. You'd better get ready to stand by. I'll drop you as close as possible. Good luck. I'll be waiting for your coded message.'

Kaltenbrunner hurried from the navigation bridge. Luck!

he thought. It's not luck that's wanted now – it's action.

2345 hours. Dieter's boat, followed by the one commanded by Linder, crept slowly towards the illumination of working-lights that was the *Antarctica.*

Dieter was pleased with himself, pleased about his good luck, the efficiency of his crew, and the fact that these two whaleboats had been moored together nearly four miles to the windward of the factory-vessel.

A hurried consultation with Linder, and it had been but the work of a few minutes to board the two vessels from opposite sides and take over full control. Crews had been asleep; only a token watch was being maintained.

Now for the *Antarctica,* he thought. They had never realized, or even discussed, the advantage it would have been to have captured the catcher fleet first – before attempting the seizure of the parent vessel. It had been so very easy with these two ships. The hardest part of the operation had been the routing of the men from their bunks. He smiled quietly to himself as he remembered the looks of surprise, rapidly turning to consternation, on the whalemen's faces as they realized that they were confronted by the German Navy. The sudden realization that they were now prisoners and in the hands of the Nazi armed forces had been laughable, if pitiful. But who pitied Norwegians? They were one of the subservient races.

Now for the real prize! He had left an armed guard, consisting of three men to each whaleboat, with orders that they should close the whale-ship at daybreak. Just as soon as he had assumed control of the factory-ship Linder would be able to round up the remainder of the catcher fleet. He was confident that he would at least find one of them alongside for storing purposes.

He glanced round the horizon. Yes, the whole fleet was within a radius of four miles. It was only an hour's work – maybe a little more – to round up the lot of them! As far as he was concerned, his whole assignment had been practically completed.

His watch showed five minutes to midnight. Another five minutes, and the steam whistle on the factory-vessel would sound for the midnight meal. There would be no accidental sighting of the boats then. That was the time.

The whistle sounded. The creaming bow waves of the two boats died to a gentle ripple; the throb of the heavy diesels muted to a distant murmur as they slid alongside the openings in the factory-ship's hull. Within seconds of the grappling-hooks reaching for a hold both Dieter and Linder were leading their crews into the bowels of the whale-ship. The supernumerary made straight for the open decks and the navigation bridge. Linder, hard and cold-faced, with the Iron Cross on his tunic, confined his attention to the factory and propelling spaces.

The *Viking*'s crew had been well trained. The sprinkling of whalemen in the boarding-parties made all the difference; they knew the exact layout of these special ships. Without them there would have been utter confusion in the labyrinth of passages, machinery, tanks, whale-boilers, and pipelines which are the inside features of such vessels.

Dieter quickly took over the navigation bridge and radio-room. He noted with pleasant surprise the presence of two whaleboats moored alongside, and the fact that his own men were now clambering down ropes to the decks of these vessels. The whole operation had lasted only minutes. The entire ship was in his hands. The manager of the expedition was sleeping through it all.

He turned his attention to the bridge officer. He spoke harshly in fluent Norsk. 'You will carry out your duties as before. I hold you responsible for the ship's safety. Inform the chief officer, the chief engineer, and the whaleman who is the union delegate that I require their presence in the manager's room – immediately!'

The watch-keeping officer nodded sullenly.

'Allow no person to enter the radio-room,' Dieter ordered the two ratings who had assumed guard duties. 'Two of you come with me.'

He made his way below, rapped loudly on the door leading to the manager's accommodation, entered, and switched on all the lights. He ordered the two ratings to take up position by the door.

Manager Nilsen, clad only in pyjamas, came hurriedly out of

the small bedroom. He stared in bewilderment at the seated naval lieutenant and the two armed guards standing by the door. Surprise turned to fear – that fear a shipmaster can experience when he knows his ship is in peril. He gaped at the seated officer.

'I am afraid, Captain, that your entire expedition is now in the hands of the German Navy – or will be in a matter of an hour.' Dieter couldn't keep the heavy sarcasm from his voice.

The whaling manager still seemed incredulous. He sank wearily into a chair and stared hard at the two guards. The grim reality of the whole thing had just struck him. Who could have expected this? Down here of all places – the German Navy! The whole thing was incredible . . . it wasn't true . . . it must be some sort of nightmare! He rubbed his eyes to make sure he was awake.

Dieter was speaking, again in fluent Norwegian. 'If it is any consolation to you, Captain, I may say the *Cachelot* is in the same predicament. In a very short time her Commander will be going through the same worrying time as you are. Between the two expeditions the German surface raider *Viking* lies waiting for word that you will give us your full co-operation.'

The door was thrown open by one of the naval ratings; the chief officer, the chief engineer, and a seaman whom Dieter assumed to be the union representative entered the room. He beckoned them to be seated.

Dieter took his time. He nonchalantly took a cigarette from a case and paused for a few minutes before lighting it. He relaxed in his chair and critically surveyed the room's surroundings. At last he spoke. 'You will understand by now, gentlemen, just exactly what has taken place. The German Navy is in full control of your ship – your ship and all your catcher fleet. As I have just told your Commander, the *Cachelot* expedition is having the same trouble – right at this very moment. By daylight both expeditions will be in German hands.'

Linder entered the room. 'Everything is under control. I am going to the catcher fleet.' He looked at the seated men, gave a quick smile, and quickly left the room.

'What we want from you,' Dieter went on, as if he had not been interrupted, 'is full co-operation. We haven't come all this distance in order to sink your ships, or, if I may say so, to destroy the fruits of your labours. We require this whale-oil, and it is our intention to get it back to Germany – with your help. Whether this help is given freely or not makes no difference to the final result. If full co-operation is given you will be paid for a whole season's work; you will be repatriated as free men. It is up to you.'

'What if this co-operation is not given?' Nilsen spoke for the first time.

Dieter smiled. 'Look, Captain, I am issuing no threats – not for the present – but please think this over.' He stared sternly at the seated men, and went on brusquely. 'Your name is Konrad Nilsen. You live in a house five miles outside the whaling town of Tonsberg. I may say a very nice house, one that is situated on the foreshore overlooking Tonsberg Fjord. You have a wife, two sons, and a daughter. I ask you one question, Captain. What is going to happen to them if you refuse full co-operation? It's up to you . . . to all of you!'

He rose suddenly. 'I leave you to your own deliberations. I will return for your answer in fifteen minutes.'

Returning to the navigation bridge, the supernumerary noticed that the bridge officer was maintaining an efficient watch. The radio officer was standing nervously in the chartroom. He looked at Dieter as the naval officer entered, swallowed nervously, and waited. The supernumerary, who did not speak for a few minutes, suddenly asked, 'Are all the whaleboats round the factory vessel?'

'Yes . . . yes, sir. At least, I think so.'

'Find out. Find out from the bridge officer. Get me their bearings as well.'

The radio officer hurried from the chartroom.

Dieter glanced at his watch – 0045 hours. It's been a hell of a busy forty-five minutes, he thought. 'Funny how these people seemed to fold up when one mentioned their families.' He grinned as he remembered that he hadn't even mentioned the Gestapo. He would have no trouble there. They would co-operate – willingly!

Kaltenbrunner should be nearing the *Cachelot* by now. Two whaling expeditions captured in a matter of a few hours! The whole thing seemed impossible. It was a masterpiece of timing and strategy. Only Kaltenbrunner's vast whaling experience, coupled with Fischer's enthusiasm and meticulous attention to detail, could possibly have carried this assignment to such a successful conclusion. He hadn't done so badly himself either, he thought modestly.

The bridge officer entered the chartroom and silently handed him a paper with the bearings of the whaleboats.

Dieter glanced at it casually, then looked up sharply and uneasily. 'Where is the twelfth vessel?' he asked.

'One of the whaleboats fuelled early this evening, and then went to the southward.'

'Into the ice?'

'Yes.'

'What for?'

'I don't know. The manager will be able to tell you.'

Dieter threw the radio bearings away from him. 'Blast it! Blast it to hell!' he cursed loudly. One whaleboat missing, and he was thinking they were all round the parent ship. Where was she off to? If it was on one of those scouting missions she could be away for days. He couldn't go into the ice in search of a missing whaleboat. There was only one thing to do – make the expedition's manager recall her.

He made his way quickly back to Nilsen's day room and entered without knocking. The four seated men were not conversing. Nilsen's face was sullen and taut. He was glaring balefully at his deck executive.

Dieter came straight to the point. 'What is your answer?' he demanded. The question was addressed direct to the whaling manager.

Nilsen shrugged. 'You leave us no alternative. We will carry out your orders.'

'Then you can order a resumption of work – immediately! I require all whales that are now held by the catcher fleet worked up. As each vessel delivers she will immediately come alongside and land all crew personnel, with the exception of the whale-gunner and chief engineer. The whaleboat will then be taken away from the ship and abandoned five miles to windward. I intend to destroy all of them once the crews have been landed.

The two executives and the men's representatives rose to take their departure. Dieter spoke to the deck officer. 'See that all whalemen are informed of our discussions. Inform them that they will be repatriated to Norway just as soon as we reach Germany. Inform them that they will be paid – well paid – for their season's work. Inform them that we require full co-operation – that you have agreed and that your captain has agreed. Inform them of the consequences.'

'Yes . . . yes, sir,' replied the chief officer as he backed subserviently to the door. 'We'll all obey your orders.' He scowled darkly at the whaling manager as he left the room. The others followed.

Dieter seated himself facing Nilsen. There goes the first Quisling, he thought. Kaltenbrunner was right as usual. He was sure there was a large percentage of Quislings on board these ships. This chief officer was going to be of great assistance. He would have to have a private talk with him. He didn't trust this whaling manager.

'Now that we've got everything settled, Captain, let us clear up a few minor points. How much whale-oil have you got on board?'

Nilsen scowled. 'Nearly 60,000 barrels – 10,000 tons, to be exact.'

The supernumerary smiled. 'How about fuel-oil?'

'Nearly 2,000 tons. We expect a tanker shortly.'

'When?' Dieter barked out the question.

The whaling manager tried to evade the question. He was annoyed that he had spoken so hastily. 'About ten days,' he replied. 'Maybe longer.'

Dieter laughed. 'Then your so-called Norwegian Government leaves you no margin. Your 2,000 tons of fuel-oil won't go very far. Come, Captain, I know all about your tanker vessel. We'll get her too – if we think it necessary.'

Nilsen made no comment. He sat back in his chair and stared at the two ratings who were standing by the door.

'Your No. One whaleboat, Captain, I understand she fuelled yesterday evening and then went to the scuthward. What for? Why is she not here with the other vessels?'

Nilsen had got over the initial shock. He had just come to the sombre realization that his chief officer was a Quisling of the worst type, that his chief engineer had taken sides against him, and that in a very short time the whole of the ship's personnel would know that he would have endangered all of them by refusing to co-operate. It was only because of the others that he had agreed to this Nazi officer's demands. He should have known that this chief officer of his would go crawling to the Germans. The slimy, fat Quisling! He would be off crawling to the crew now, making all sorts of ambiguous promises. That was all he was fit for – crawling. Crawling to the owners. Crawling to the men. Now, this . . .

'What for?' Dieter repeated angrily.

'How should I know!' Nilsen answered belligerently. 'I've no authority over the whaling leader. I'm not responsible for his actions. He went to the southward last night. That's all I can tell you.'

'Captain, don't try and bluff me. I know just as much about this whaling game as you do yourself. I've been down here before – many times. Why did your leading gunner go to the southward last night? Was it on a scouting mission?'

'I've told you all I know,' Nilsen answered. 'He's not far away. At least, I don't think so . . .' He broke off and shrugged.

'Then recall him immediately. Inform him that you're going to the eastward, that you want to confer with him. Get him back here. I can't waste time looking for him. I've enough worries. Recall him at once. Come with me to the radio-room.'

'Eastward!' scoffed Nilsen. 'You tell me to tell him that I'm going to the eastward! We've just come from there!'

'Tell him anything,' Dieter shouted. 'Only get him back here – quickly!'

Nilsen rose sullenly. 'I will do my best,' he said. 'You don't know my leading gunner. He has a mind of his own. He does not take kindly to instruction. You'll be lucky if he returns this evening.'

'Captain Nilsen, your attitude does not improve matters between us. It is you who does not take kindly to instruction. If you still persist in refusing me full co-operation I will deprive you of your command. I should imagine your chief officer will be only too pleased to take over.'

Nilsen remained silent. He made his way to the radio-room. Dieter followed.

The guard stood aside as they entered. Nilsen flung himself into the chair and switched on the radio-telephone. He grabbed the handset and commenced calling. 'Hello, *Antarctica 1!* Hello *Antarctica 1*! *Antarctica* calling! *Antarctica* calling *Antarctica 1*! Come over, please! Come over!'

Except for static, there was no reply.

Nilsen repeated the call several times. There was no answer.

'You won't get anything before the six-o'clock schedule,' he said. 'It's a waste of time.'

'I didn't expect a reply, Captain. I only wanted to find out for certain. You will call the whaleboat at the scheduled hour. Inform the whale-gunner that you have important orders to communicate, that it is essential that he returns to the factory-ship immediately.'

The whalemen were back at work on the whaling-deck as Dieter went back to the navigation bridge. That chief officer hasn't taken so long in getting them reorganized, he thought. Might be an idea to really give him the command. He was amenable to orders – especially German orders. Anyway, Linder was the one to decide: he was the one who had to get the ship back to Germany.

The catcher fleet were lying to windward. He noticed one whaleboat moving rapidly towards another. He smiled as he remembered that the young Lieutenant was now rounding up the remainder. He must be nearly through. Blast that whale-gunner! Why couldn't he have been with the others?

Hope he hasn't gone on a scouting mission. He could be away for days. That was the leading gunner's job, searching out the ice conditions and the prospects for better whaling. He remembered vividly one scouting expedition in which he had taken part – the penetration of the ice far to the southward, the tortuous ice-lanes that had to be navigated and the open lakes of translucent blue water that lay within. Ice conditions changed so rapidly.

His thoughts rambled on. He recalled it all – vividly. The sea-leopards and the elephant seals basking on the virgin ice like great black slugs on a bleaching tablecloth. The penguins, the majestic Emperors and the tiny Adelies. Funny and lovable creatures, with their snow-white waistcoats and their red webbed feet, waddling round the floes like old, old men in dinner-jackets. And the birds – the birds of so many species. From the mighty albatross, more royal than any eagle, down to the puniest of them all – the Wilson's petrel.

Perhaps this whale-gunner hadn't gone on a scouting expedition. They didn't go into the ice much these days. They preferred to keep to the edge of the pack – in open water.

The skies had become overcast; the gloaming was bleak and grey. The barometer was falling rapidly, and the wind was increasing from the south-east. Linder noticed all this as he stationed himself on the weather side to watch the catcher fleet. He was wondering about Kaltenbrunner. Was he just as fortunate as he himself had been, or had he run into any snags. He hadn't had much darkness.

The sun rose behind a table-topped berg on the only clear bearing of the horizon. The Lieutenant smiled as he saw the whaleboats converging on the factory-ship. Linder's got them well trained, he thought. Now we can get down to business. It's going to blow like hell before long.'

He spoke sharply to the bridge officer, and sent him hurrying to fetch the deck executive. He looked over the leeward side of the bridge, and noticed that the whaleboat moored alongside was already transferring her crew. The whale-gunner stood on the bridge, scowling.

'You sent for me, sir?' The chief officer was at his side.

Dieter turned and nodded pleasantly. 'Yes, chief. How are things going?'

The executive coughed nervously. 'Everything is nearly back to normal, sir. Everyone is back at work. Production goes on. The men will soon adapt themselves to the new order. You won't have trouble.'

'Good. Keep them busy.'

'Yes, sir.'

'Try and waste no time. Do everything you can to expedite the transfer of the catcher crews. We're going to have trouble with the weather. If it gets too bad cut adrift all the dead whales. We won't bother with them.'

'That's a good idea, sir, if you want to save time.'

Dieter smiled. 'Thank you for your collaboration. I will see that it is known in the proper quarter.'

'Thank you, sir.'

'I might as well tell you that I do not trust your Captain. I expect you to do your best – you won't be forgotten. See that the men understand that it is to their advantage that we should get back to Germany, that they will be well paid for their labours, and that they should give every assistance.'

'I have already done that, sir.'

'Good. What is your name?'

The executive paused for a moment. 'My name is Berg – Anders Berg.'

'And you come from Tonsberg?'

'Who doesn't?'

'Before you go, Berg. When is this tanker due?' Dieter smiled as he asked the question.

The chief officer replied without hesitation. 'She is due in exactly three days.'

Dieter nodded grimly. 'Thank you, Berg. You can go about your duties.'

Linder brought the whaleboat alongside in a flurry of foam. He hastened on board and came direct to the supernumerary. 'That's everything under control. There's one whaleboat unaccounted for – No. One, I believe.'

'Yes, I've already found that out. The whaling manager is to recall her at 0600 hours. That is the time of the first schedule. I think it would be advisable for you to go out and meet her – just in case.'

'How's everything here?'

Dieter laughed. 'Look around you, Lieutenant. Every one is working – working for Germany. How about you? Did everything go to plan?'

'Go to plan! Hell! We had no opposition!'

'Then it only remains for us to get the other whaleboat. We'll wait until we find her before we inform the *Viking*. I wonder how Kaltenbrunner is making out?'

Linder nodded. 'I wonder. . . .'

CHAPTER THIRTEEN

There is something about a southern ocean gale that cannot be compared to the gales experienced in the other oceans of the world. It is a gale in an ocean where the glacial period has not yet retreated, where seas rise to unequalled heights, yet quickly subside at the mere easing of the storm. It is a gale in an ocean that has been but barely surveyed, where ice hazards are more dangerous than any sea.

It comes up suddenly, a rapidly falling barometer or a weird and grotesquely beautiful sunset being the only indication. The wind begins with an ominous moan, and the skies become more leaden and grey. At first a short, rolling sea, quickly changing into a boiling white mass, making it difficult to differentiate sea from sky.

Fischer thought of all this as he conned the *Viking* through the worst of the storm – a storm which might possibly upset all his plans. It was nearly twenty-four hours since he had sent Kaltenbrunner away; Dieter had been gone longer. So far there had been no messages.

There were still three hours to dawn as Fischer relaxed wearily in the high bridge-chair. Wind and sea were moderating and a few stars were showing intermittently through the scudding clouds. The wind, which had veered to the south-west, had ended the driving and freezing sleet. Visibility was good.

I wonder how they're making out? he thought. Kaltenbrunner hadn't much of a chance – not in this gale. Dieter had had much more time. Why isn't there a message from the *Antarctica*?

Wenzel came into the wheelhouse. 'There's nothing to see, sir. No lights to the southward.'

Fischer grunted. 'We must be well over forty miles to the north. We can't expect to see them all that distance. We steamed for over two hours before we hove to. If we get no message before dawn we'll close the bearing at full speed.'

'Wenzel rubbed the backs of his fingers across eyes strained by peering into the blackness through powerful binoculars. 'Yes, sir, we must be hearing something soon. What's the matter with them? There couldn't be any complications. Everything was so well organized. Kaltenbrunner was so sure.'

Fischer smiled grimly in the darkness. 'One should take into account the forces of Nature when making plans. They're more formidable than any.'

A radio-telegraphist came quickly through the chartroom door into the wheelhouse. 'We have just received messages,' he said, 'from both of them.' He handed the commanding officer the two decoded messages.

'Good news?' Fischer asked anxiously.

'Yes, sir, very good news.'

'Good!' Fischer exclaimed. He got off the chair, and, calling for Wenzel to follow him, made his way to the chartroom.

It was a few minutes before his eyes got accustomed to the orange-coloured light of the chart-lamp. He read the messages slowly and handed them to the younger officer.

Wenzel read with care.

ANTARCTICA TO VIKING

YOU CAN NOW APPROACH ANTARCTICA. EVERYTHING ACCOUNTED FOR EXCEPTING ONE WHALEBOAT. EXPECT TO CONTACT HER AT 0600 HOURS.

DIETER

CACHELOT TO VIKING

EVERYTHING UNDER CONTROL. DO NOT ATTEMPT TO CLOSE THIS VESSEL BEFORE 1200 HOURS.

KALTENBRUNNER

Wenzel handed the messages back. 'Seems a bit of a puzzle to me, sir. What does Kaltenbrunner mean? I don't understand.'

'It means that he's only captured the whale-ship. He will be accounting for the catcher fleet at daylight. There wasn't much he could do yesterday – not in that weather. Dieter's had much more time.'

Wenzel's face fell. 'But how can he account for the catcher fleet in daylight? He always advocated darkness. Darkness, surprise and speed, that's what he preached all the way south.'

Fischer's expression told Wenzel that in querying the message he had overstepped the mark. The commanding officer broke off the conversation by walking out to the bridge. The younger officer followed.

Day was breaking to the north-east, a faint glow at first, slowly rising and stretching to the north and south.

'Well,' Fischer growled as he later sipped from a large cup of coffee, 'there's one thing we must be thankful for.'

'What's that, sir?'

Fischer chuckled, his good-humour returning with the daylight. 'That it's going to be good weather. The wind's from the south-west. What more could we wish for?'

Wenzel nodded.

'Give her full speed, Lieutenant. Let's go and find the whaleship. Let's visit the *Antarctica*.'

There were a few hurried commands, and the *Viking* once more was under full power and heading for the south.

'Steer 220 degrees!'

'220 degrees, sir!'

Fischer gave a grunt of satisfaction. 'We'll keep well to the starboard of our course until we sight the ship. I don't want to get in the way of Kaltenbrunner – not before noon, anyway.'

'No, sir,' agreed Wenzel.

Fischer glanced at the wheelhouse clock, muttered something which the younger officer did not understand, and hurried from the bridge.

Wenzel smiled. He thought it was about time that he himself went below for a spell. He had stayed on the bridge throughout the gale. Wind, sea, sleet, fog, icebergs, ice-growlers, pack-ice, every hazard that Antarctic waters had to offer, had been their lot over the last twenty-four hours. He shuddered as he remembered the several narrow escapes the *Viking* had experienced. That large barrier berg! The first they saw of it was when it appeared menacingly out of the gloom high up in front of the foremast: that's how close they'd been to the mountain of ice. Only by immediate action, coupled with good fortune, had catastrophe been averted. If they'd gone to port, instead of to starboard . . . He dreaded the thought of what might have happened.

How in hell can these whalemen endure this for months on end? he wondered. Both Kaltenbrunner and Dieter could have their whaling – all of it. He'd be glad when the job was over. Fischer could say what he liked: he still thought the whole thing ridiculous, out of all proportion to the reward for success. What were thirty or forty thousand tons of whale-oil to a country like Germany? After the invasion of England they could have all the whale-oil that was produced. It would be theirs – theirs for the taking.

How were the invasion plans coming on? Wenzel knew that was what was bothering him – the reason why he couldn't settle down to this very simple job. He hoped that they wouldn't be back in Germany to see the finish. He could already visualize the vast armada that would be required for such an operation – the invasion craft, the tankers, the destroyers, all the paraphernalia of shipping involved in such a mission. The hordes of Nazi youth being ferried across the narrow expanse of water – they would complete what their fathers before them had started in the First World War. The Master Race! *Heil* . . .

His thoughts were interrupted by the return of the commanding officer. He took up a position several paces away, silent and aloof.

Now what's the matter? Fischer was like that these days. One minute he could be talkative and pleasant, the next, and he would draw within himself. Mercurial, that was the word. Up and down – like a bloody barometer!

His eyes caught the glimpse of smoke on the horizon – a tall, thin column, rising high into the air. 'Smoke on the port bow!' he exclaimed. He turned to Fischer, but he was already searching the horizon on the same bearing.

'Steer 200 degrees!' Fischer ordered.

'200 degrees, sir!'

The new course was quickly adjusted. The *Viking* swung twenty degrees to port and settled down. The smoke was now bearing directly ahead.

'You'd better get a boat's crew ready, Lieutenant. I want you to collect a full verbal report from Lieutenant Dieter. Find out if he'll be ready to move towards the *Cachelot* by noon. Inform him that I would like to have both ships together by nightfall. Give him Lieutenant Kaltenbrunner's message.'

Wenzel was about to hurry off when the commanding officer stopped him. He smiled, and continued, 'Find out everything you can. Anything that may be of use to us. Speak to some of the whalemen. Find out their feelings – what they think about it all. Most of them speak good English.'

'It may take some time, sir.'

'I expect it will. Don't forget to come back: we need you here.'

'I won't, sir.'

'Off you go, then. Get your boat ready. It should be an interesting sight – especially if they're still working whales. And—'

'Sir?'

'Take Lieutenant Reuss with you. Give him something to do.'

A smile appeared on Wenzel's face. 'Yes, sir! You leave him to me.'

'One more thing. Inform Lieutenant Dieter that I wish to see him at the *Cachelot*. Tell Linder the same. They'll be too busy for the present.'

Wenzel gazed proudly at the *Viking* as he was quickly borne towards the whale-ship in one of the specially designed power-boats that were a feature of the surface raider.

It was the first time that the executive had sighted his ship from seaward. Drab, greyish hull and superstructures, rusty and bare in places, the *Viking* looked a formidable ship of war as she lay drifting a few hundred yards to leeward in the early-morning sunlight, with her guns trained dramatically on the whale-ship. The German ensign, the Nazi swastika flag that now dominated most of the capitals of Europe, flew lazily at the stern of both ships.

Scores of whalemen lined the bulwarks as Wenzel's boat came alongside. Silent and morose figures, they glowered at the Lieutenant as he mounted the ladder and entered the bowels of the ship through the watertight door in the hull.

Reuss, who followed, muttered angrily to himself as he looked at his gloved hands, now covered in grease and blood from the old and delapidated ladder. Not much of a reception, he thought. Why the hell had Fischer to send him on this outing? He wasn't even interested in whale-ships. There was no doubt about it: Fischer had been gunning for him lately.

Chief Officer Berg guided them through a labyrinth of passages, lined on either side by a complex system of machinery, to the open deck. Here the scores of whalemen who had watched them board were in process of washing down the bloodstained decks. Huge jets of water, mixed with steam, were battering the viscous covering of fat and blood from decks and superstructure. There was no sign of whales. A curious stench pervaded the whole ship.

'God! What a smell!' exclaimed Reuss.

Wenzel grinned.

They followed the chief officer over the slithering deck to the ladders leading to the bridge. Clustered round this area were the crew from some whaleboat which was moored alongside. He mounted the steps that led to the bridge.

Dieter was in the radio-room, standing over the whaling manager, when Wenzel located him. Nilsen, sitting hunched in a chair, was looking perplexed and worried.

Dieter nodded curtly in acknowledgment of Wenzel's greeting.

Nilsen was speaking. 'I tell you, Lieutenant, there's no answer to my calls. I don't know what's the matter with them. They don't answer.'

'Call again!' barked the supernumerary for the fourth time.

Nilsen shrugged and sighed wearily. He had been on the bridge throughout the whole of the gale. He switched on the apparatus and spoke into the handset. 'Hello, *Antarctica 1*! Hello, *Antarctica 1*! Factory-ship calling! Come over, please! Come over!'

Again there was silence.

Dieter snorted. He turned angrily to the radio officer. 'Call him in Morse!' he snapped. 'Don't try any monkey business. Your signal will be intercepted.'

The officer seated himself and sent out the call-signal for

Antarctica 1. There was a few minutes' silence, and then he exclaimed, 'Yes, he's answering!'

Dieter growled. 'Give him this message: "Manager to Gunner Hansen. Return to factory-ship immediately. Important news to communicate. I am shifting forty miles to the eastward. Nilsen".'

The officer got the message through. He looked up to Dieter, and said, 'That's all right now, sir.'

'Ask for a reply.'

'Yes, sir.'

Dieter thought, The whole thing looks transparent, but what can one do? He looked for a moment as if he were going to change his mind, but then let it go. He turned to the whaling manager, and said curtly, 'You'd better get some rest – you need it.'

Nilsen was about to get up when he changed his mind. 'I'll tell you what reply you'll get. Hansen will say he's having trouble in the ice, that he's been trying to get to the southward, that he's in difficulties. It's all happened before. He's drunk – that's what's the matter with him. He's lying drifting – doing nothing.'

Dieter scowled. He turned and barked at the radio officer. 'Is that correct?'

'Yes, sir. He's done that several times this season.'

'I believe you. Get the reply, and take a directional bearing.'

There was a wait of five minutes before the reply came through.

Dieter read the message quickly: 'Hansen to *Antarctica*. Your message received. Having trouble in the ice. Will return as soon as possible. Hansen.'

He threw the message away from him in disgust. He made a brusque gesture with his hand, and cut off what Nilsen was about to say, and then said authoritatively, 'We'll fix his ship for him. We'll send Linder.'

'The bearing is 160 degrees, sir.'

'Right!'

Wenzel smiled again. 'Captain Fischer requires a verbal report. Can we go somewhere.'

'Let's go to the manager's day-room. I'll tell you all about it.

When they were comfortably seated Wenzel handed the supernumerary the message they'd received from Kaltenbrunner.

Dieter read the note quickly. He looked up and smiled wearily. 'Seems like other people have their troubles as well.'

Wenzel lit a cigarette. He looked at Dieter, and asked casually, 'What's your trouble, Lieutenant?'

'My trouble! I've had nothing but trouble ever since I came on board!'

'How?'

'We had a gale. Perhaps you people on the *Viking* didn't know.'

Wenzel laughed loudly.

'You see those catchers lying to windward, Lieutenant. How would you like to board them, capture them, and then transfer all their personnel to this ship during that gale. That's what's been happening here during the last twenty-four hours.'

'I see.'

'Those ships are lying abandoned – ready for scuttling. It's going to take time . . . a hell of a time. Suggest to Fischer that he should sink them by gunfire.'

'That may be an idea.'

'A practical idea.'

'Captain Fischer wanted to know whether it's possible for you to move towards the *Cachelot* by noon. He'd like to have both ships in the same vicinity.'

Dieter nodded. 'I can go now – if he sinks those whaleboats for me.'

'What about this other whaleboat, this *Antarctica 1*?'

'That needn't delay us. You heard what transpired in the radio-room. It only means that Linder will have to intercept her. We can't take chances: we must account for her. It won't take him long.'

'How about bunker-oil?'

'There's enough – enough to get the ship back to Germany.'

'Whale-oil?'

Dieter smiled for the first time. 'We're lucky! There's 10,000 tons in the ship. We came at the right time. There's a tanker due in three days' time.'

Wenzel stubbed out his cigarette and lit another. 'Captain Fischer wants to see you before you hand over command to Linder. That goes for him as well.'

The supernumerary only grunted.

There was a furious battering against the starboard bulkhead. Streams of water cascaded down outside the ports in a froth deluge.

'What the hell is happening?'

Again Dieter smiled. 'You'd better not go near them,' he said. 'They also use caustic sprays. It's the only way to dislodge that grease.'

'I see. Where's all your whales? I have Reuss with me. He'll be disappointed. There's nothing but empty decks.'

Dieter shrugged. 'We cut them away in the gale. We'd no time for whales. We'd more important things to do. When you go out have a look at those Norwegians working. They're actually glad to be going home.'

'You think so?'

'Definitely.'

'The whaling manager?'

Dieter snorted. 'He counts for nothing. I think we should put him on board the *Viking*. He'll be dangerous otherwise. The chief officer is the one to trust: he's already a Quisling.'

'I'll tell Captain Fischer.'

'Good! Now if you'll excuse me. I have to get Linder away. Tell Fischer I'll be ready to move towards the *Cachelot* at noon. I'll expect a signal from you regarding these abandoned whaleboats. If the *Viking* doesn't sink them by gunfire, then I must leave a crew to scuttle them. Either way it's immaterial to me.'

'Then I'll get back to the *Viking*,' said Wenzel. 'I want to have a quick look-round first. I'd like to speak to some of the whalemen.'

'Then get that chief officer to show you round. He won't be far away. I bet he's waiting.'

Dieter was right. As Wenzel made his way below Berg stood at the bottom of the ladder, waiting.

'You're going, sir?' he asked subserviently.

Wenzel looked at the portly officer, and nodded. 'Presently,' he said. 'I'd first like to take a walk round your ship. I haven't time for anything else. Have you seen the other Lieutenant?'

'Yes, sir. He wanted to see the hospital and surgery. I sent him, along with one of my men, to the doctor's accommodation.'

'Good! Then we can start immediately. Lead on. I'll follow.'

Berg led the way down to the forward factory spaces, where whalemen were still tending some of the huge pressure boilers that still contained boiling whale-oil. 'These are bone pressure boilers. They work on the ordinary pressure system at a working pressure of eighty pounds. As the bone is cooked out the oil rises to the top and is drawn off at these different levels.' He indicated the different levels to the naval officer by waving pudgy hands.

'I see,' murmured Wenzel.

Many of the boiler-doors were open. He watched with interest the work of several whalemen as they shovelled bone residue from the bottoms of the boilers on to moving belts, which quickly conveyed it overboard.

'They're cleaned out after every cooking,' Berg explained.

Wenzel nodded. 'Seems a waste to me. All that stuff going to the sea. Why don't they turn it into bone-meal – or something? We would use that in Germany.'

I agree, sir. It is a waste – we know that. We still couldn't use it. Space here is vital.'

There were many men employed in cleaning duties. Whole gangs were methodically scraping the grease and dry residue adhering to bulkheads and machinery.

'We've just begun the cleaning-up process,' commented the chief officer. 'It takes time – a lot of time.'

'And you think these men will be glad to get back to Norway?'

'Yes, sir. Definitely.'

'I'd like to speak to a few of them. Get me a few who can speak English.'

Berg went hurriedly over to a small group who were working in the near vicinity. There was a rapid conversation, punctuated by many gesticulations on the part of the executive, and the whole group came forward to where Wenzel was standing.

The Lieutenant smiled pleasantly. 'I am sorry this had to happen, but it's the fortunes of war. We came down here with the sole purpose of seizing all whale-ships. So far we have succeeded; only the British ships remain now.'

The men kept silent.

'You're lucky. You'll be paid handsomely for your season's work; you'll be repatriated just as soon as we reach Germany. The British won't be so fortunate. Neither will your own countrymen who are employed in those ships. We'll need much more collaboration before they receive the same treatment as you'll receive.'

'How do we know that these promises will be honoured?' one of the whalemen asked.

There was a hushed silence. Berg fidgeted uneasily.

Wenzel smiled – again pleasantly. 'You don't! You have to take our word for it. You've no other choice.'

Berg nodded vigorously.

'These ships will be taken back to Germany irrespective of what attitude you may care to adopt. We were told to inform you that you would be paid and would be repatriated if we received your full co-operation. There's nothing more to say. It's up to you – all of you.'

Again the men were quiet.

'Have you nothing to say?' Wenzel asked with studied exasperation. 'Have you no comments?'

At last the same whaleman spoke up. 'I can't speak for everyone,' he said, 'but most of us will be glad to take the ship back to Germany. We want to get back to our own country . . . to our homes . . . to our families . . . to everything that Norway means to us. We only hope that you will honour your promises. You don't sometimes.'

'You people are different. Why, we're all one happy family. Look what's happening in Norway at present. Everyone has work; everyone is content. Yes, it's just one happy family.' He turned to Berg, and said, 'Shall we move on?'

The whalemen watched as they moved towards the separator-room. The one who had spoken snorted in disgust. He spat on the deck where they both had stood. 'Bastards!' he exclaimed. 'Both of them!'

The other whalemen nodded in approval.

'This is the whale-oil separating-room,' said Berg, as they entered a wire-meshed room that took up half the beam of the ship. 'This is where the oil is separated after it comes from the settling-tanks.' He indicated a group of cylindrical tanks near by.

Wenzel looked at the ten centrifugal separators that were ranged athwartship in two lines. Only two of the machines were working.

Berg lifted a cup-shaped ladle and scooped some of the oily fluid from one of the spouts. He lifted it high, and then let the oil run slowly back into the machine. 'That's very dark oil,' he said. 'The whales were old before they were worked up; it's inferior quality. The best oil is very light in colour.'

'It's hot in here!'

'Not just now, sir. Sometimes the temperature in this room is over 130 degrees Fahrenheit, when all separators are going.'

The Lieutenant watched the two separator-men as they silently cleaned the non-running machinery. He was about to make some remark, changed his mind, and turned away through the door.

Berg followed.

'What's down here?'

'This's the tank-deck,' answered the chief officer. 'Each tank holds approximately 750 tons of any type of oil. At present we have over 10,000 tons of whale-oil stowed there. The value must be well over a million pounds!'

'Bah! Money values mean nothing. It's the material value we're after. Money means nothing to Germany. It's the glycerine we want. Glycerine for gunpowder.'

'I understand, sir,' Berg said hastily.

Wenzel looked straight at the chief officer. 'Lieutenant Dieter informs me that you've promised him full collaboration. We expect you, not Nilsen, to see that we have no trouble.' He smiled, and added, 'Material facts are true whether one believes, them or not. This ship is ours, and she'll be taken back to Germany. There's nothing more certain!'

'Yes, sir. You can be assured of my full co-operation.'

'Good! I will see that it's reported to the proper quarter.'

'Thank you, sir.'

They now made a non-stop tour of the remainder of the factory spaces. Wenzel saw the meat and liver dehydrating plants, the massive revolving boilers that dealt with the blubber and infats, and the various paraphernalia of machinery and equipment required for the production of whale-oil. He visited all the trade workshops, where men were carrying out repairs and other duties as if nothing out of the ordinary had taken place. It seemed as if a visit from a German surface raider was an everyday occurrence. One of their own transport vessels would have created no more curiosity. The whole thing amazed him.

Fischer will be pleased, he thought. These men were actually glad that the German Navy had come. All they wanted was a chance to get back to their own country, back to their families and friends, back to their homes. Nothing else mattered.

'Do you want to see the engine spaces?'

'I have no time – not now. I must get back – quickly. The whole thing has been interesting. I wish I'd seen you working some of these whales. Take me to find my colleague. You said he was visiting your medical officer.'

They made their way to the ship's surgery, and found Reuss in earnest conversation with the expedition's doctor.

'Come, Lieutenant,' said Wenzel, 'it's time for us to be getting back to the *Viking*.' He looked around the immaculate surgery, nodded to the medical officer, and walked behind Berg, who led the way to the waiting boat.

Reuss followed hurriedly.

'I didn't see you take much interest in the workings of the whale-ship,' said Wenzel, as they were quickly borne towards the *Viking*. 'Did you see anything?'

Reuss grinned. 'Hardly anything. I was much more interested in the medical officer. He speaks fluent German. Quite a character.'

'What the hell did you get to talk about?'

'We were arguing about the relative merits of whale and steer steaks. He maintains that the nutritive value of a whale steak, properly cooked, of course, is much greater than the best cut from a steer.'

Wenzel grinned. 'What conclusion did you come to?'

'None, until I taste the steak. You spoiled the whole thing: he was just about to grill me one.'

'You wait until I tell Captain Fischer!'

Fischer handed his senior officer a decoded message that he had just received from Kaltenbrunner after he had finished listening to the report. Using low-powered radio-telephony apparatus, both vessels had been in communication with each other for the last hour.

Wenzel read carefully.

KALTENBRUNNER TO VIKING

EVERYTHING HERE UNDER CONTROL. FACTORY-SHIP AND COMPLETE CATCHER FLEET NOW ACCOUNTED FOR. CLOSE AS SOON AS POSSIBLE.

KALTENBRUNNER

'That's good, sir. Now we can go to the *Cachelot*!'

'You're right, Lieutenant. But first we must finish off these whaleboats. You say Dieter wants us to sink them?'

'Yes, sir.'

Fischer glanced at his watch – 1000 hours. 'Right!' he exclaimed. 'We'll give the gun-crews some practice. Sound action stations! Full speed! Hard starboard!' He barked out the orders rapidly.

Alarm-bells clanged throughout the *Viking*. Gun-crews were augmented as ratings raced to take up their stations. The engines increased to full power.

'Inquire whether all is clear!' snapped the commanding officer.

The message was sent across by Aldis lamp.

There was a few minutes' delay before the all-clear signal came back. The cruiser was racing towards the abandoned catcher vessels at full speed.

'Good!' Fischer grinned as he received the all-clear message. 'We'll make two runs across the targets. It will give all gun-crews a chance. Their firing had better be good. Give her half speed! Hard port!'

'Half speed, sir! Hard port!'

The *Viking* turned in a half-circle, was steadied, and commenced her first run across the ten whaleboats that were drifting to windward at a range of less than 600 yards.

'Slow speed!'

'Slow speed, sir!'

Gun-crews waited expectantly. The boats were derelict, but they were real targets – something that would sink quickly, if the gunnery was good.

There was a sense of inevitability now in everything that happened. Fischer took up a position on the wing of the bridge, a tall, recently bearded figure in a heavy duffle-coat, with glasses slung round his neck. 'Commence firing!' he ordered.

The order was instantly relayed to the control officer.

There was a momentary hesitation – a slight pause before the guns opened up. Shell after shell, at point-blank range, went screaming into the hulls of the drifting whaleboats as the *Viking* passed slowly down the line of bearing. Within a few minutes of the bombardment the whole of the derelict fleet was on fire and in a sinking condition.

The commanding officer smiled grimly. 'Good!' he exclaimed. 'Cease fire! Now we come round and give the port guns a chance.'

Wenzel, still at Fischer's side, silently acquiesced.

'Hard starboard! Full astern starboard engine!'

The cruiser swung round, nearly in her own length, and was steaded on the reciprocal bearing.

'Slow speed both!'

'Slow speed both, sir!'

'Commence firing!' Fischer gave the order as he peered through his glasses. 'You see,' he exclaimed, 'there go the first two!'

Wenzel nodded. 'Looks like they've had enough, sir.'

'More than enough. Cease fire!' He turned quickly to one of the bridge officers, and said, 'Make the following signal to the *Antarctica*.' He thought for a moment, and then went on. ' "*Viking* to *Antarctica*. Follow me to the *Cachelot* as soon as possible." '

'Yes, sir.' The officer hurried off to the signalman.

Fischer went straight to the wheelhouse and glanced at the gyro repeater. 'What was the last bearing of the *Cachelot*?' he asked.

One of the watch-keepers spoke up promptly. 'The last bearing, sir, was 085 degrees.'

'Then steer 070 degrees. Give her full speed.' He turned to Wenzel, and said, 'You can dismiss gun-crews, Lieutenant. They can have further practice at the *Cachelot*.' He smiled as he turned away.

The *Viking*'s engines again pulsed under full power. Her stem cleaved the icy water as she sped towards her second victim.

Captain Nilsen watched the vicious bombardment from a position on the lower bridge-deck. Below him, on the main whaling-deck, groups of whalemen downed tools and broke up into small groups to watch with awe the complete annihilation of the *Antarctica*'s catcher fleet. The surface raider, her work completed, was speeding towards the east.

It was a moment of the most poignant feeling. Nilsen tried to master himself as the tears came slowly to his eyes. He became mute, overcome with emotion as he watched the ships slowly sink below the icy water. 'The bastards!' he murmured brokenly. 'The Nazi bastards!'

How very futile the whole thing was! Nilsen thought this over for a while. Why couldn't they have just left the whaleboats alone, left them to drift aimlessly in the ice-strewn ocean. They wouldn't have lasted long: the ice would have got them. But they would have died a death much more fitting than the one just dealt out to them. He thought of the many whaling seasons in which these same whaleboats had served the *Antarctica*. The good seasons – seasons when their luck had been good, and they had made fortunes for the vested interests whose property they were. The bad seasons – seasons when everything seemed to go wrong, when bad weather and fog hampered whaling operations for long periods at a time. These were the seasons when every one lost money, when the whalemen had little to show for six months' hard work in weather which is the most rigorous in the world.

His thoughts ran on. Each of these whaleboats, as she went to her icy grave, struck some chord in the memory of the past. There was the *Antarctica 2*, just going down in a flaming mass, racked by the explosions from the gunpowder which she carried for the harpoon-gun. He remembered the day when she struck the underwater ice-shelf as she chased a blue whale between two icebergs. He remembered how she looked as she was towed in to the *Antarctica*, a torn, twisted mass of steel, for emergency repairs, before beginning that long voyage, at the end of a tow-line, to South Africa.

And there was the *Antarctica 4*, lying with her bows grotesquely in the air. She was going down stern first, with her stem reaching for the sky. He remembered clearly that day she had to fight off the maddened bull sperm, when the hunted mammal turned on its pursuers and lunged with its bullet-shaped spermaceti head at the turning propeller. He remembered the whale-gunner's discomfiture as he described the scene here on board the *Antarctica*. It was another long towing job – it happened every season.

There goes *Antarctica 6*. She was the newest of the fleet – her first season in the ice. He remembered the other *Antarctica 6*, and how she went down with all hands as she chased a gigantic blue whale. They had never got to the bottom of that business: there were no survivors.

Almost physically, Nilsen forced his mind away from the picture these sinking ships presented. He looked down upon the whaling-deck, and watched with tired eyes the various groups of whalemen as they angrily muttered among themselves at the destructiveness that had just been enacted.

Berg passed him on his way to find the German Lieutenant. He eyed the chief officer coldly, making no attempt to conceal the look of loathing and contempt that came over his features. The whole thing was involuntary. His eyes narrowed to slits; a boiling hatred surged up within him at the sight of the portly officer. He tried to bar his way to the bridge, but Berg pushed his way past. 'You . . . you Nazi bastard!' he exclaimed. 'You—' The rest of the words lacked articulation.

Dieter watched the complete annihilation of the catcher fleet with little concern. He smiled as he saw the whaling manager stride with great agitation on the deck below. What the hell were a few whaleboats, he thought, if they stood in one's way? Why couldn't the *Antarctica 1* have been among that lot? He would have had all of them – just like Kaltenbrunner. It was just his luck that the whale leader had been missing.

He thought about Linder, now on his way southward in the *Antarctica 3*. He would soon locate the missing whaleboat, and would sink her on the spot. He had orders to that effect. Another five hours, and they would be at the *Cachelot*; another twelve hours, and both factory-ships could be on their way back to Germany. Twenty thousand tons of whale-oil taken in a matter of thirty-six hours was good hunting. They had only to get the stuff back to Germany, an easy task now that Britain had her back to the wall. There would be no opposition.

Berg came on to the bridge, his face white and strained, as if he had been in trouble. 'Everything is ready below, sir. We can get under way whenever you like.'

Dieter nodded sourly. 'Anything the matter?'

'No, sir, nothing at all. Just a few words I had with the whaling manager.'

'I see. We'll soon fix him. Another few hours, and he'll be transferred to the *Viking*. He's going to be sorry.'

Berg made no reply.

Dieter turned and spoke curtly to the bridge officer. 'Get your quartermaster to the wheel. Give her full speed. Follow the *Viking*.'

CHAPTER FOURTEEN

Lieutenant Linder wore a worried look as he stood on the small bridge of the *Antarctica 3*, watching the whale-gunner manoeuvre his vessel through the cracks in the ice. Open lanes led to the southward, lanes that opened up before them like wide boulevards lined on either side by ice-pinnacles of fantastic form and size. To the eastward the ice seemed impregnable – a desert of blue-white ice, hard as granite at its core.

Linder was more tolerant of these Norwegians than either of the other officers. His manner was pleasant as he addressed the whale-gunner. 'You don't seem to be getting much to the eastward, Captain?'

The gunner shook his head. 'Looks like it's going to be a job, sir. I don't think we can reach the *Antarctica 1*. We should have gone to the eastward, in open water, before we headed south.' He waved his hand towards the heavy ice. 'We can't go through that!'

Linder nodded glumly.

'I think we should go back, sir. It's getting dangerous.'

'But we can't go back. We have to find the *Antarctica 1* somehow.'

The whale-gunner smiled. 'Then we must go back and start again – either that or walk. The *Antarctica 1* is bearing three points on our port bow. It's impossible to head in that direction. If we don't turn back now it means spending the night in this dangerous ice. We can't move in the darkness – not here!'

'I see what you mean. Can't you get them on the radio-telephone? Tell them we've something important to communicate. Tell them to come and meet us.'

'I've already tried – repeatedly. They just don't seem to answer.'

Linder looked at his watch – 2000 hours. They had been steering in a southerly direction for more than nine hours. The whale-gunner was right: it was no use going any farther, he thought. Best to turn round and go back. Meet her in the morning. He scanned the horizon to the south, then said suddenly, 'Right, Captain, turn round and get back into open water. It's hopeless.'

He watched with interest as the gunner tried to bring the whaleboat round on the reciprocal bearing. It wasn't so easy. Half an hour elapsed before the whaleboat was heading in the right direction.

A blue whale sounded close off the starboard bow, leaving a scintillating aqueous vapour hanging momentarily in the air as it submerged beneath the clear icy water. Linder stood fascinated, staring hard at the rippled waters and the oily slick – all that remained.

The whale-gunner smiled. 'He's also trying to get out of the ice. We're both in the same plight.'

'Yes, but he won't get into trouble. I have a commanding officer to face.'

Heavy floes brushed against the vessel's hull as they picked up speed and sought to the northward. Swarms of penguins waddled around on the ice; they seemed to look up at the bridge, questioning the right of mere man to invade this icy domain. Scores of elephant seals lay basking on the floes, their droppings staining the whiteness of the ice.

As twilight passed it was becoming much more difficult to keep to the free channels. At last the whale-gunner spoke. 'I think we'd better stop now, sir. It's no use going on until daylight.'

Linder agreed without enthusiasm.

Captain Fischer lay back, stretched himself luxuriously, and smiled broadly at his two supernumeraries. 'Well done!' he exclaimed. 'I must congratulate you both on a very excellent job. It's taken you no time at all. I never thought it would be so easy. There's nothing to it.'

Kaltenbrunner and Dieter sat facing their commanding officer in the smokeroom of the *Viking*. Their work had been completed; both factory-vessels lay drifting to windward, all ready to begin their homeward voyage. They waited for the arrival of Linder on the *Antarctica 3*.

Kaltenbrunner chuckled in spite of his weariness. 'Don't be too sure, Captain. These ships were easy. The British whale-ships won't be so simple. I wish they'd been first. Still, 20,000 tons of whale-oil at one go is good going. Let's hope we'll be as lucky to the westward.'

Dieter nodded. 'I wish I was going with you,' he growled. 'It seems as if we've only just started.'

Fischer grinned. 'And I'll be sorry to see you go, Lieutenant. But we must obey orders.'

'It's a pity that Linder didn't get hold of that whaleboat,' Wenzel said. 'He'll manage at daylight, though.'

Fischer shrugged. 'It can't be helped, I suppose. We can't afford the time – not now! We've recalled the *Antarctica 3*.'

'Recalled the *Antarctica 3*! What about the *Antarctica 1*?'

'There will be no *Antarctica 1*. We've decided to leave her.'

'Leave her?' queried Wenzel.

Kaltenbrunner broke in. 'Yes, Lieutenant, we've decided to leave her . . . leave her behind. She won't get very far – not without fuel-oil.'

'But she has fuel-oil! She bunkered recently!'

The supernumarary looked tolerantly at the younger officer. 'When these whaleboats are whaling they carry the minimum amount of fuel-oil. She can't get very far.'

'I see. But she could report us.'

'Let her. We can't keep this mission a secret for ever. We've been fortunate so far. The tankers will be here in a few days. The disappearance of the Norwegian whale-ships will soon be known. London will put two and two together. They'll soon realize that the German Navy has been in Antarctic waters.'

'But not to capture,' said Dieter. 'They can only guess.'

'You're right,' agreed Fischer. 'That's why we must get to the westward at once. We must strike again before it's known – before they can get organized and come searching. It's only about 1800 miles to the British ships. We can get there in less than four days, if we can keep going at full speed. It's worth the chance.'

'I agree with you, sir,' said Kaltenbrunner. 'If we go a little to the north, clear of the worst of the ice, there's no reason why we shouldn't go full speed – day or night.'

'It would help,' said Fischer.

'Enormously,' added Dieter.

'Another thing that I've just thought about. When both whale-ships begin their homeward voyages, why not send out bogus messages to these tankers? Tell them that the ships are proceeding to the westward. Tell them to follow. That should delay them at least four days before they get suspicious.'

'Splendid!' exclaimed Fischer. 'And in the meantime we can be at the British ships. They won't have a clue.'

'What about whaleboats? Are you taking any with you?' For once Wenzel asked his question cautiously.

'We won't take any,' Fischer answered. 'What's the use? They would be hundreds of miles astern at the end of four days. Figure it out for yourself.'

'The homeward journey?' queried Dieter.

Fischer smiled. 'I will leave you to put Lieutenant Linder wise to everything. You should proceed independently after reaching the parallel of 40 degrees South. It's no use issuing hard-and-fast rules. Each of you is in command of his own ship. You know what's best. Remember to sink the remaining whale-boats before you leave.'

'Yes, sir.'

Kaltenbrunner went outside and gazed at the two whale-ships. They were drifting close together, arc-lights ablaze, and headed in opposite directions. A whaleboat was still ferrying naval personnel to and from the captured vessels. Baggage and other paraphernalia were strewn around the decks.

He lit a cigarette and returned to the smokeroom.

Wenzel was speaking. 'We were just saying that you did a quick job on the *Cachelot*'s whaleboats. We missed our practice.'

'What practice?'

'The sinking of the catcher fleet by the guns of the *Viking*.'

'Oh, that.' He took refuge in an air of unconcern. 'Seaman Becker fixed that.'

'That hobo!' spluttered Dieter. 'That—'

Kaltenbrunner smiled. He knew that Dieter detested Becker. For that matter, Becker detested Dieter. It was amusing – to him.

Wenzel would not be put off. 'How did you manage so quickly?'

Again Kaltenbrunner smiled. He lit another, less stimulating cigarette, and answered, 'When we got on board the *Cachelot* the gale was just beginning; the catcher fleet were running for the shelter of the ice. I could do nothing – nothing until daylight this morning. We found the manager, the officers, even the crew, most co-operative. They couldn't do enough to help us. At daylight I called all whaleboats in to pick up their own dead whales. I had cast them adrift during the night. It was an excuse to get the boats alongside. We took over from there. Becker did the rest.'

'How?'

'Becker is useful when it comes to using gunpowder. A light charge close to the sea injection, another at the collision bulkhead close to the shell plating, a couple of time-fuses, and in a few minutes there were holes large enough to sink the *Viking*.'

'Where did you get the gunpowder?'

'From the harpoon-gun charges.'

'And we used all that ammunition!' Wenzel said untactfully.

Dieter glowered at the Lieutenant.

Fischer grinned. 'But we did have some real firing practice. They wanted it badly.'

Trying to change the subject, Kaltenbrunner said, 'What about this Nilsen? Is he on board?'

Dieter nodded. 'Yes, he is,' he said coldly. 'He came on board about an hour ago. He's better here.'

A steward came into the smokeroom to serve coffee.

'We must have some brandy with this coffee,' said Fischer. 'It's an occasion.' He motioned to the steward, who went out and returned with a bottle of brandy.

Fischer lifted his glass. He glanced at Dieter, and said smilingly, 'To you, Lieutenant, and to Lieutenant Linder. I wish you both a safe journey home.'

'And to you, sir. To all of you. May you have continued success.'

All of them drained their glasses.

'Come on, you no-good whalemen! Where the hell have you

been? Have you just got back from the Ross Sea?' roared the voice of Per Becker as he watched his two mates boarding the *Viking* from the *Cachelot 2* with a bunch of other ratings.

'Where have we been!' echoed Anton Miere. 'We've just captured the *Antarctica* – haven't you heard?' He turned to Gunther, who was directly behind. 'He's asking us where we've been! Can't he see we're the returning heroes? Look . . . look at the reception!'

Becker looked around the silent and deserted decks. Only the look-outs and skeleton gun-crews were on duty. A few of the bridge ratings were tending the boarding-nets. 'Hell!' he exclaimed. 'I've been back more than two hours. I went and captured the *Cachelot*!' He grinned, and added, 'Kaltenbrunner gave me a hand.'

'You were lucky,' retorted Miere. 'Dieter went and made the usual balls-up of things.'

'Did you expect anything else? Let's go below.'

They went below to their three-berth cabin – a cabin they had zealously guarded throughout the voyage. Around the walls various pictures of half-clad female film stars were prominently arranged. Although there was a war on, their taste was cosmopolitan. American and British brunettes vied with German blondes for the best bulkhead positions.

Becker went to a metal wardrobe, grabbed inside, and deposited two bottles of the best Scotch whisky on the table in the middle of the room.

There was a hushed silence. At last Gunther spoke. 'Where the hell did you get these?'

'Oh, that! I got them from Kaltenbrunner,' Becker said cheerfully.

'Where did he get them? There's no Scotch whisky on board here.'

'From the manager of the *Cachelot*, I guess. They were just like a pair of old whaling pals – thick as thieves. He very nearly put down the red carpet for us. We could do nothing wrong. How did you get on?'

Gunther shrugged. 'Not good.'

Miere went, foraged, and came back with three Carlsberg beer-glasses that had been snatched from some dockside tavern in Kiel. He reached for the first bottle, and filled the glasses to the brim – or nearly so.

'What about water?' asked Becker.

'Water! Who the hell wants water?'

There was a stony silence

At last Gunther spoke. 'Well, here's to you, Becker. Here's to the capture of the next factory-ship. Maybe you'll get another two bottles.'

They drank to that.

Becker smacked his lips, sat back on his bunk, and repeated himself. 'How did *you* get on?'

Miere raised a quizzical eyebrow, brought a hand up to stroke his lean, bearded chin, and said sadly, 'Not so good. No, not so good. Dieter went out to antagonize everyone. The manager tried to thwart him at every turn. Only the mate would collaborate, but he was a fat, slimy son of a bitch. "No, sir. Yes, sir." That was all Dieter ever got out of him. He liked it, too.'

Becker got off his bunk, reached for the bottle, and refilled the glasses. 'That's the first dead body,' he said. He peered through its neck, a movement more involuntary than intentional, and then slung it into the far corner of the room.

Miere lifted his glass, belched noisily, and grinned. 'Why the hell don't you keep it as an ornament? It'll be a long time before we get another.'

Becker took his whisky and drank it without speaking.

'Did you see the whaling manager come on board?' Gunther asked.

'Yes, I did. About an hour ago. I admired his guts. Why couldn't they have let him stay on his own ship?'

'Because Dieter wanted to show his authority, because he was the big noise around the place. That's all. He's a—'

'He's what?' Becker prompted.

'He's a bastard! I'd like to tell him so!'

'Why don't you?'

Gunther grunted. 'I told you before. This job is only temporary. The War can't last for ever. Just wait . . . wait until it finishes!'

'Then you'll go back to whaling. Dieter will still be the boss.'

'If he doesn't get his before!' Gunther said savagely. 'I hope a British destroyer gets after him – and gets him. "Get the *Viking* to sink the catcher fleet by gunfire," he tells Wenzel. Just like that! "Get the *Viking* to sink them by gunfire." The—'

Becker chuckled. 'What about you, Miere?'

'Me! I don't care. It's all the bloody same to me. I only wish I was going home. Either of them would do.'

'I told you.'

'You told me what?'

'That we're going to be shanghaied on the British ships. They won't be so easy! No, sir! Not those ships! There'll be no collaboration there. Trouble . . . there's sure to be trouble!' He lifted his glass and drained it at one draught.

Gunther reached for the second bottle. 'Another?'

'Yes! We like it,' answered Miere.

'What the hell!' roared Becker. 'Take it easy!'

Gunther smiled. He studied Becker's leathery face and corn-coloured hair. 'Something tells me that you're going to be difficult about this.'

'You're damn-well right! I'll do the opening this time – and the filling. We've got to make it last. These Scots on the British ships won't give away their whisky – not even to Kaltenbrunner.'

There was a noise outside, a scuffling of running feet as the *Cachelot 2* came alongside with a scraping jar. Gunther went out to investigate.

The last group of ratings was about to board. Fischer was standing, along with Kaltenbrunner and Wenzel, bidding farewell to Dieter as his gear, along with Linder's, was being loaded on to the whaleboat.

Fischer was speaking. 'Be sure you sink the whaleboats. Stay for a few hours when Linder gets back. Give him a chance to get acclimatized. The *Antarctica 1* may turn up in the interval. If you think the whale-gunner is on the way in, delay your departure for a few hours. It may be worth the trouble.'

Dieter rubbed his chin in a familiar gesture. He nodded in assent.

'Stay together until you get to the parallel of 40 degrees South, then act on your own. I'll advise Germany by coded message.' He thumped the Lieutenant on the shoulder. 'Good luck – a successful passage!'

Lieutenant Dieter boarded the *Cachelot 2.*

Gunther swung himself away from the bulwark-rail and returned to the cabin. 'That's the last of the men away – Dieter as well,' he said gleefully. 'I think we must be going to move.'

'How?' Becker questioned.

'Fischer said something about sinking the whaleboats, and that he, Dieter, should wait a few hours to see if the *Antarctica 1* turned up. Kaltenbrunner seemed quite happy with himself. I was watching him.'

'You shouldn't take notice of these things,' Becker said primly. He filled the glasses, and added, 'This is for the road. We have to be up early. What's the time now?'

'Nearly midnight.'

Miere looked caressingly at his glass. 'Well,' he said, 'if you say so.'

Dawn was breaking – a slow light in the east. Captain Fischer, wrapped in a heavy bridge coat, smiled at the senior bridge officer, who was standing by his side. 'Right!' he said. 'Give her full speed!'

'Full speed, sir!'

The *Viking* turned in a half-circle to the commanding officer's order, and slowly commenced her westing.

Fischer peered through his glasses at the drifting whale factory-ships. 'Give them three blasts,' he said. 'Let them know we're off.'

The signal was acknowledged by both ships.

CHAPTER FIFTEEN

It was eerie lying there in the darkness amid the whiteness of the glacial ice-pack. The planet Venus, low on the horizon, beamed with the brightness of a young moon over the grotesque silhouettes of the floebergs.

Linder waited for the coming of the dawn. He was really confused about the whole matter, and the time that had been wasted on the unsuccessful attempt to reach the *Antarctica 1*. Now there had been that coded message ordering his recall. What was going to happen about the missing whaleboat? Had she returned – or what was happening?

He clicked his tongue gloomily, shaking his head at the realization that it was he who might have upset all his commanding officer's plans by not reaching the vessel.

How could he have reached the whaleboat when there was about twenty miles of solid ice between the two ships? It was Dieter's fault. He had followed the supernumerary's instructions and had ignored the whale-gunner's advice.

He looked at the eastern horizon. 'How long yet?' he asked.

'It won't be so long now,' answered the whale-gunner of *Antarctica 3*. 'Another half-hour and we'll be able to move. Two hours, and we'll be in open water. He waved his hands around as if to take in the whole of the ice. 'Another three hours, and we'll be alongside the factory.'

'Good!'

'Excuse me, sir, but are we to believe what Chief Officer Berg has told us?'

Linder frowned. 'What do you mean, Captain?'

The whale-gunner turned his eyes from the horizon, cleared his throat, and said weightily, 'Well . . . that the *Antarctica*'s personnel will be repatriated to Norway when she arrives back in Germany. Is that right?'

'It is correct.'

'You mean—'

'What?'

'That it's not just made up? That it will actually happen?'

'Have no worry, Captain. I can assure you – all of you – that Norwegian personnel will be repatriated. I know. I am to command the *Antarctica*.'

'I thought it was the other officer?'

'No! He takes the *Cachelot*.'

'Then you can rest assured that you will receive every assistance.'

'Good!'

Dawn was breaking; light was now faintly discernible. The whale-gunner glanced at the compass, then at the horizon to the north-west. 'I think we can try now,' he said. 'I think we'll try to the north-west.' He pushed over the telegraph to slow speed, and took the helm himself.

For the next two hours Linder watched with intelligent fascination as the gunner extricated his tiny vessel out of the ice-pack into open water. It was a superb exhibition of specialized skill; only years of experience enabled him to emerge into open water without damaging the whaleboat.

He smiled for the first time when they reached the northerly limit of the pack. The factory-ships were drifting together eight miles to the north-east. There was no sign of the ***Viking***. A solitary whaleboat drifted close to the *Cachelot*.

'That must be the *Antarctica 1*!' Linder exclaimed. 'She's already here!'

The portly gunner shook his head. 'No, sir. That's one of the *Cachelot*'s boats. That's *Cachelot 2*, I think.

'Then let's make for the *Cachelot*. Let's find out what *is* happening.'

'And so, you see, we can't wait any longer. We've orders to sail as soon as possible. We leave the *Antarctica 1*.'

'What about these two whaleboats?'

'I have a squad of men ready to scuttle them. They can start immediately.'

'Then there's nothing more to do?'

'Nothing at all.'

The younger officer considered this for a moment. 'Then I

think I'll go on board the *Antarctica*. You say the manager has been transferred to the *Viking*?'

'Yes. He started to be awkward. We thought it best to put him where he could make no trouble. You'll find the chief officer most co-operative.'

Linder smiled. 'He'll have to be.'

The supernumerary glanced at his watch – 0600 hours. Say we start off at 0900. How will that do?'

'Fine.'

'We've orders to keep together until the fortieth parallel. We then separate and go independently.'

'I still think we should have waited to get this *Antarctica 1*. It doesn't look right to me – somehow.'

'Those are our orders,' Dieter said curtly.

'Yes, I know that. But—'

'That will be his worry. It won't interfere with us.'

'How about fuel-oil? I hope there's enough?'

'That's been checked. There's sufficient on both vessels to see them back to Germany.'

'Then there's nothing more,' said Linder. 'We keep in sight of one another until we reach 40 degrees South.' He grinned, and added, 'I'll be watching for you in Hamburg. We must celebrate – when we get there.'

Dieter chuckled. 'You bet we will!'

It was a few minutes after 0900 hours when the *Antarctica* turned her bows towards the north and silently stole away.

Dieter, from the bridge of the *Cachelot*, watched the *Cachelot 2* and *Cachelot 3* as they slowly sank beneath the calm, icy waters. It's no use waiting, he thought. They won't last much longer. He turned to the bridge officer and said, 'Give her full speed. Follow the *Antarctica*.'

The *Cachelot* swung through an arc of ninety degrees, picked up speed, and followed in the wake of the *Antarctica*.

The voyage to Germany had begun.

CHAPTER SIXTEEN

The mate of the whaleboat *Antarctica 1* cursed loudly to himself as he surveyed the glacial surroundings. What on earth are we doing in here? he thought. There's no open water to the south. They wouldn't get any blue whales – not in here. What's the matter with Hansen? Why doesn't he pull himself together? Do his job! He'd said they were going south on a scouting expedition. That was when they'd left the parent ship. He hadn't seen him since.

He had decided that morning to steam back to the northward. It was no good waiting for the whale-gunner to issue orders. He would have to get over this latest hangover first. Get to the northward, into open water, and do some whale-hunting. It was the only way to get the gunner back on his feet. The *Antarctica* had been screaming out for them, over the radio-telephone, ever since early morning. They couldn't reply: the transmitter was out of order. Everything seemed to go wrong. Better that they should get a whale, deliver it up to the factory-ship, and see what was happening.

One of these days they were going to land up in trouble. That gale yesterday! It had got him into several dangerous situations. They'd been lucky to get out of the heavy ice and into an area that was much more broken up, where it had been possible to lie in the lee of a large tabular berg. What help had he got from Hansen? None!

He turned to the fair-haired seaman who had just taken over the helm. 'Any sign of Hansen down there?' he asked.

The seaman chuckled to himself. 'Yes. He just poked his head out of his cabin-door. He asked me the time.'

'You told him?'

'Yes. But not the day! He wouldn't know.'

The mate nodded glumly. 'Look after things,' he said. He indicated the ice and the bow of the ship with a wave of his hand. 'I'll go and see if I can get any sense into him.' He turned and went below to the whale-gunner's cabin directly beneath the bridge.

He knocked loudly on the door and entered. Hansen was sitting hunched up on the cabin settee, his large hands covering the front of his face.

He looked up as the mate approached. 'God!' he exclaimed. 'Have I got a headache! What's the time?'

'Time? It's just gone eight. Get washed up and have some coffee. You look like death warmed up. Get some coffee – it'll do you good.'

Hansen nodded. 'Eight o'clock. Morning?'

The whaleboat mate smiled for the first time. 'Yes, morning,' he snorted derisively. 'It's forty hours since we left the *Antarctica.* They've been screaming out for us on the radio-telephone. We can't answer. Our transmitter is out of order.'

'What do they want?'

'I don't know. "Come in immediately. Important news to communicate." That's all they say. Nothing else.'

Hansen groaned. 'Then we'd better get to the northward, get a couple of whales, and take them in.'

'That's what I'm trying to do. It's going to take us another two or three hours to get out of this bloody stuff. We've had a hell of a night.'

'Get me some coffee. I'll be on the bridge straight away.'

The mate swept his eyes round the room. He reached down and gathered the empty aquavit bottles off the floor, opened the cabin-door, and hurled them over the side. He pulled back the curtains, hooked back the cabin-door, and allowed the icy breeze to enter the room. 'The coffee will be up immediately. Get washed and freshened up. Let's get a few whales and take them in. We'll ask for radio repairs. It's a good enough excuse.'

Hansen got shakily to his feet, went to the washbasin, and doused his face liberally in the cold water. He rubbed briskly with a hand-towel. 'That's better,' he groaned to himself. 'What the hell's been happening?'

He looked into the mirror, groaned again at the hangover look on his face, and thought. It must have been those *Cachelot* whale-gunners that started me off. What were they poaching near the *Antarctica* for? It wasn't done. They should have moved off – gone on their way to the westward. That was the direction in which they were moving. He tried to recall his visit to the *Antarctica,* and to the talk he had with the whaling manager. God! He must have had a load on! He couldn't even remember leaving the parent ship. He shook his head in disgust.

The coffee arrived. 'Get me some more, son,' he said to the young deckboy. 'Get me a real big jug!'

He got into his bridge coat, looked round the cabin, and picked up several broken glasses that were lying on the floor. He tidied the room a little, throwing out the glasses and a heap of cigarette ash and butts that were littered about. He got outside and climbed shakily to the bridge.

The mate was again at the wheel, dour, unsmiling, and weary-looking.

Hansen glanced up at the look-out barrel. A seaman of the watch was there, scanning the horizon with intelligent eyes. Routine goes on, he thought, irrespective of what's happening.

'You go and get some rest,' he told the mate. 'I'll take over. We may run into whales. I feel like I'm going to have a big day.'

The mate only grunted. He relinquished the helm to Hansen, and then went below. Big day! he thought. That was just like Hansen. He could do it, too. He had the luck, and the skill, to kill in a few hours what another whale-gunner would kill in the same number of days.

The icy air, blowing from the south-west, brought exhilaration to the whale-gunner. He took a few deep breaths, banged the telegraph hard over to full speed, and spoke to himself. 'God! This is better . . . much better!'

The deckboy brought him the extra coffee. He placed it on a small portable table by the side of the wheel. The small, round face, with its curly mop of unruly fair hair, looked up at Hansen, and said, 'No whales yet, sir?'

'Whales!' he roared. 'Not yet, son! But soon . . . very soon!'

The youngster went off smiling.

Now they were steaming through large lakes of open water. He whistled for one of the seamen, and gave him the helm. 'Keep her as she goes,' he ordered. He scanned the horizon ahead, altered a little to the eastward, then spoke into the voice-pipe that led to the look-out barrel. 'Keep a good look-out for whales,' he ordered briskly.

'Aye, sir,' the voice answered. 'There's open water abeam to port.'

'Right!' He gave a double ring on the telegraph, which meant full chasing speed. The propeller increased its revolutions, and the engine throbbed with a new power. The *Antarctica 1* leapt through the water, her stem cutting the pancake ice before her.

Funny that none of the whaleboats are about, he thought. They must be all to the westward. And there's no sign of the factory-ship. He considered this seriously for a moment. Wonder should I go to the east?

His thoughts were interrupted by a loud hail from the barrel. 'Whaleblast! Starboard bow! Two points on the starboard bow!'

Hansen peered at the indicated bearing. 'Yes,' he exclaimed, 'He's right! Blue whales! Come starboard!'

The helmsman put the wheel over. *Antarctica 1* swung to starboard.

'Midships! Steady she goes!' Hansen barked out the orders. The excitement now obsessed him: he had become the hunter. Everything was forgotten in the lure of this death-stalk.

He looked over the front part of the bridge: the mate, once more on his feet, was forward at the harpoon-gun checking over the charge and whalelines. Crew members were already at stations. The young deckboy, jumping about wildly, was making his own survey of the proceedings.

The whales were closer. Course was altered to bring them ahead. The mate came on the bridge; Hansen, without speaking, darted along the catwalk that led to the harpoon-gun. He conned the vessel from this new position.

Now began a chase – a chase to the death for one or both of the mammals. The whales surfaced close under the bow, too close for the whale-gunner to bring the gun to bear. He cursed loudly, signalled for the engines to be put full astern, then stood waiting for the animals to reappear.

The throb of the engines, intermingled with the screw-race and the displaced waters, frightened the animals. They sounded together, and darted off in a single direction. The catcher vessel pursued them ruthlessly.

All the odds were with Hansen. The greater speed of the *Antarctica 1* slowly began to tell. The mammals sounded much more frequently, and for greater periods at a time. The gunner stood waiting by his gun . . . waiting for a chance. He took it!

The harpoon flew from the gun's muzzle and embedded itself in the nearest whale's back close abaft the dorsal fin. The barbs of the harpoon opened up as the weight came on the line. There was a momentary silence, and then the time-fuse functioned and fragmented the shrapnel-pointed head. The huge mammal was thrashing the water a hundred feet off the starboard bow.

'Slack away! Full astern!' Hansen snapped out the orders as he scampered back to the bridge. The whaleboat drew up in a froth of displaced water. The whaleline went screaming from the line-locker, at first slowly, then with a wild rush. The whale sounded.

Half a mile of six-inch whaleline had been run out when the gunner called a halt. The mammal was on the end of a taut line, still fighting madly on the surface. As it writhed in its death struggle it exhaled masses of vaporized blood. Gradually, a little at a time, like playing a salmon on rod and line, the blue whale was hove backward towards the whaleboat. The engines were used to advantage.

The whale-gunner, again poised behind the reloaded gun, watched anxiously as the mammal was hove back into range. Another shot, he thought. Another shot will finish him off. He sighted and compressed the trigger. *Boom*! The gun roared for the second time. The harpoon went flying through the air, and buried itself somewhere within the whale's vitals. There was a momentary silence – a dull, muffled explosion. The time-fuse functioned and fragmented the grenade. The whale died instantly.

Hansen laughed exuberantly. 'We'll put it in flag!' he shouted. 'We'll go after the other!'

The ninety-foot carcass was quickly hove alongside, and the whaleboat's crew went to work. Compressed air was blown into the carcass to provide buoyancy. A small cork buoy, with long line attachment, was made fast to the tail, to facilitate the work of picking up, and, finally, a square red flag, attached to a long spear, and bearing the whaleboat's number, was plunged into the carcass to prove that it belonged to *Antarctica 1*.

Throughout all these proceedings Hansen was searching the horizon for sight of the other whale. Although it could not now be seen, its exact bearing had been noted, and within minutes of cutting the dead whale adrift the gunner was driving his vessel in that direction. He soon came up with the second whale.

This one was wary: every time it sounded it came up in another direction – sometimes abeam, sometimes far astern. Hansen tried every ruse to make it run in any one direction. He was unsuccessful. The blue whale made for the ice-pack; Hansen followed.

Now began a chase that lasted well over two hours, a chase that was successfully completed thirty miles from the original sighting position.

The mammal had no chance. For over two hours it strove desperately to elude its remorseless pursuers. It was to no avail. Hansen waited for a chance: he didn't miss!

This second whale proved to be a female, even more gigantic than the male blue whale previously killed. It mattered nothing to Hansen, or his crew, that these two whales had been roaming the icy ocean a few hours before as king and queen of all animals. To them they were just so many calculated blue-whale feet, and a potential six hundred barrels of whale-oil for the factory's boosting production.

The whale-gunner looked at the dead whale with satisfaction. 'Good! Good! Now we'll go to the *Antarctica* and fix the radio. The tow-boat will bring the other. What's the bearing of the *Antarctica*?'

'There's no bearing,' answered the mate. 'She's not even working now.'

'What! You mean they're not working? That there are no signals?'

'Nothing! the radio officer has been listening all morning. They've missed both schedules; she's been working none of the whaleboats. Everything's silent.'

'That's queer. They must have kept the first schedule.'

The mate shook his head violently. 'No, they didn't. Neither did the *Cachelot*. Something's wrong. Something's definitely wrong. Where are all the other whaleboats? We haven't seen any.'

'This is the approximate position where we left her. She couldn't have shifted – not without us. Let's try to the north-east.'

The mate agreed.

Hansen rang for full speed. The *Antarctica 1* settled down on the new course. He ordered a seaman back into the look-out barrel. 'Never mind whales,' he said. 'Look for the *Antarctica*. We have to find the *Antarctica*!'

The deckboy brought coffee. Hansen looked at the stuff and turned away. 'Not just now – later.' Where the hell has the factory got to? he wondered. Why hadn't they sighted some of the other whaleboats?

There was a whistle from aloft. He hurried to the voice-pipe. 'You see something?'

'Yes, there's some black objects floating on the water about four points on the port bow. Looks like dead whales.'

Hansen altered course and peered intently ahead. 'Dead whales!' he ejaculated. 'Yes . . . yes! He could be right!' He commenced to count the objects.

'They're dead whales all right,' the mate said. 'There's no doubt about that. What on earth's the matter? What's happened?'

The catcher vessel closed the bearing rapidly. The dead whales, sea-eaten, battered, anonymous-looking things were covered in fuel-oil and were swollen to gigantic proportions, owing to the compressed air setting up gases within the bodies.

Hansen looked closely at the carcasses. 'You see,' he said excitedly, 'they still have the towing-wires on them. They must have been cast adrift intentionally.'

The mate shook his head in perplexity. 'What on earth for?'

Most of the whaleboat's crew had now gathered on the deck. They sensed that something was wrong. Why were these whales floating about? Where was the parent ship?

The deckboy pointed excitedly out to starboard. 'Look!' he shouted. 'There's something!'

A broken, battered-looking, half-sunken lifeboat drifted lazily about a mile away. Hansen focused his glasses, and said suddenly, 'There's a lot of stuff there. Let's go and see.'

Lifejackets, lifebuoys, wood, and various floatable objects were strewn over a wide area. The waters were covered in fuel-oil. The whale-gunner, now on the deck with the crew, scrutinized every object as it was hauled on board. There was no need for conjectures – not now! Something terrible had happened to the *Antarctic*'s catcher fleet – all of them.

'Must have been the gale,' muttered one of the seamen.

'Gale! Gale!' scoffed Hansen. He kicked over a burnt lifebuoy. 'There's no fire with a gale.'

'Then there must have been a fire.' The seaman indicated several burned planks of flotsam. 'Something like that!'

'Don't talk nonsense. How the hell can the whole fleet have been on fire? There's stuff here from six different whaleboats. Where's the *Antarctica*?'

Another lifeboat, gunwales awash, holed in several places, floated on her air-tanks less than a hundred yards away. The mate lifted binoculars to his eyes and noted the name. 'It's the *Antarctica 7*,' he muttered. 'What does it all mean? What do you think?'

'I'm afraid there's only one thing to think.'

'What?'

'That a Nazi raiding vessel has been down here. That they've either captured or sunk the *Antarctica*. They've definitely destroyed the catcher fleet. The *Cachelot*'s gone the same way. That's why there were no signals. It all adds up.'

The mate nodded grimly. 'You're right. That's the only solution. But what about the men? Even the Germans wouldn't be so callous as to wipe out the crews.'

'No. You're right. They wouldn't harm the crews. They need them. They need them to get the ships back to Germany, or whichever port they intend to make for. They wouldn't wait. There's nothing to wait for.'

One of the seamen spoke up. 'What are you going to do? It's no good waiting here. They may be already searching for us. You have to decide – quickly!'

'Yes, we have to decide something. There's only one thing to decide. We have to go west – to the British ships.'

'Why?'

'Because that's the only thing we can do. Because that's all the distance we can go with the fuel we have. Because we couldn't reach Cape Town, or South Georgia, or anywhere. That's our only hope.'

CHAPTER SEVENTEEN

From the bridge of the *Albatross* Lieutenant-Commander Gower looked at the scene of desolation and ruin that was Deception. What a place! he thought. Who would be fool enough to make for here? Not a German raider! There wasn't a chance. Not unless it was necessary to lie low to carry out essential repairs. Nobody has been here lately – not in years.

The *Albatross* was anchored close inshore in four fathoms of kelp-covered water. The entire harbour was covered in kelp – great masses of seaweed that reached out from the bottom in huge stalks that covered the whole surface of the water in umbrella-like leaves, forming a natural breakwater to an incoming swell. Not that there was a swell: the whole of the Bransfield Strait was covered in ice.

Along the rocky foreshore, broken at intervals by coarse sandy beaches, hundreds of elephant seals lay basking in the low, sickly-looking sun. The waters abounded with life: the shrieks of the penguins, mingling with the cries of the gulls and other bird life, made the whole place a bedlam. And yet throughout it all there was a queer and ghostly silence, a silence that comes to a place whose peoples move on.

It's hardly worth going ashore, thought Gower. No vessel the size of an auxiliary cruiser would ever dare enter this harbour – not without local knowledge. It was well named – Deception. The whole expanse of a large natural harbour was obscured in the narrow entrance.

He watched with interest as Borgen, assisted by several of the ratings, went about the lowering of the ship's lifeboat.

Well, better get it over with, he thought. Better see what the place looks like from the shore. There was no time to lose. The *Queen of New Zealand* would be waiting for them at the entrance to the Bransfield Strait – at Elephant Island. It's a waste of time, but . . .

'The boat is nearly ready, sir,' interrupted Petty Officer Watkins. 'Are we going now?'

Gower grinned. 'I'm going. You're not. Just give me four men to handle the boat. I'll take Borgen along. We won't be long. There's nothing here.'

'No, sir?'

'Damn it, even you, Watkins, should know that. There's been nothing here in twenty years. German surface raider! Bosh! It's a waste of time. They'll be striking somewhere while we're fooling about here.'

'Yes, sir.'

'And, Watkins.'

'Sir!'

'Inform the ratings, and Borgen, that they're to take no matches or cigarettes with them. Take nothing. We don't want to leave anything lying about these beaches that could be found. We can't be too careful. This raider, it could still come.'

'Yes, sir.'

'That goes for galley refuse as well. Better make sure of that.'

'Yes, sir. Anything else?'

'No. I'll be ready in a moment. Have the boat stand by for me.'

'Better take a gun with you, sir.'

'A gun?'

'Yes, sir.' He pointed to the foreshore. 'There's a lot of fresh meat there, sir.'

Gower laughed. 'Seal-meat is no good, Watkins. At least, I don't think so. I'll ask Borgen.'

Watkins snorted derisively. 'It's no good asking him, sir. He was brought up on the stuff. That and red whale-meat. He washes the stuff down with whisky.'

Gower chuckled. Watkins didn't like any of his Norwegian allies – least of all Hans Borgen. He made no bones about the matter. In his opinion only Britain and the Commonwealth were really in the fight against Hitlerism. The rest of them – the French, the Poles, the Dutch, the Norwegians, those who were carrying on the fight – were in England only on sufferance.

Gower thought that he would have to say something to his

petty officer about the matter. He remembered some of the quips. That one about the *Altmark* and the prisoners from the *Graf Spee*. About how they had been rescued from the tanker in Norwegian territorial waters after the Norwegian Government had stated there were no prisoners on board and how Watkins had gone on, at length and in Borgen's hearing, about the prisoners being rescued by the Navy – the British Navy!

Yes, Gower thought, I'll have to speak to him. There's nothing wrong with Hans Borgen. He's just as much British as Watkins is.

Later, as he stood on the beach with the whaleboat skipper, surveying the scene of desolation and ruin, he asked, 'And you say this harbour was used at one time as a shore base for different pelagic expeditions?'

'That's right. Before the days of the whale slipway the factory-ships used this harbour for shelter, and for the working up and processing of their whales. They were flensed outboard in those days.' The whaleboat skipper indicated the foreshore. 'They used to moor stern on to those rocks. Look! You can still see some of the moorings. They moored, as I say, stern on to those rocks with both anchors out ahead. The catcher fleets went out and scoured the whole of the Bransfield Strait for whales. They killed them, and they brought them back here for processing. They could work in any type of weather: there was shelter here.' He smiled, and added, 'That was in the good old days – before all these modern whale factory-ships. A whaling season lasted a whole year. Not like now. They're overworked after a season of twelve weeks!'

'But they did go down into the ice?'

'Of course they did. One manager would suddenly decide to go to sea, and the whole lot of them would be following him within twenty-four hours. It's the same today. They won't risk anything. There's no initiative. They're scared of a bad season: it means the sack. These whaling companies! They're no bloody good!'

Old machinery parts, steel tanks, wooden barrels, and aged whale-digesters were strewn along the foreshore. A few old boats were piled high up on the beach, their wooden planks aged and crumbling. The whole shore was littered in whale-bone, whiter than the most virgin of snow.

The naval officer pointed this out to the skipper.

Borgen nodded. 'In those days fresh water was the bugbear to all the whale-ships. We always had to come back here for fresh water. You see those boats? That's what we used to run the water in. To and from. To and from. It was a hell of a job.'

'Couldn't you have used ice?'

'You just try and collect it. It's not so easy. One can't just go and break up icebergs for a freshwater supply. The other stuff is sea-ice: it's no good. Look at that machinery. Those old whale-cookers. You see! Nothing rusts down here. Every one knows that. It just crumbles away – just like these rocks.'

'This whalebone. I suppose that's what it is?'

'Yes. The whale-ships in those days didn't worry about the carcasses. All they took was the blubber and the head. They let the blubberless carcasses drift away. That's the reason the bone lies along the foreshore. Nowadays everything is used – everything! There's no waste.'

They were passing between several groups of elephant seals that were basking on the coarse, pebbly beach. Gower stopped and stared. Borgen, smiling slightly, picked up a handful of pebbles and began to throw them lightly at one of the animals. The mammal, its eyes staring out of its head in a bovine expression, strove desperately to get up on its haunches as it opened its mouth and emitted a harsh, gurgling sound. It backed silently and awkwardly into the water.

The naval officer laughed. 'Seems like he's afraid of you. Petty Officer Watkins wanted some fresh meat. Any good?'

'Good enough for him. For nobody else.'

'Then you don't recommend seal-meat?'

'No. Perhaps we can get a sea-leopard. The liver's good . . . very good. It's the only fur-bearing seal left in Antarctica. Perhaps we can kill one, and I'll cure the skin for you. I know a good place.' He laughed, and added, 'But that was nearly twenty years ago! However, we can try.'

They made their way along the rocky foreshore, over some treacherous-looking rocks that were covered in masses of sea-weed, to the small headland the skipper had in mind.

He halted the naval officer as they closed the vicinity. 'You see? There's a sea-leopard! Don't make a noise. Careful.'

Gower gazed at the slumbering animal. It had greyish fur with several black streaks running across the body, and was spotted in places, and it looked the incarnation of fierceness and strength, with its long neck and ferocious-looking toothed mouth.

Borgen was saying, 'It's a good thing you brought a gun. One can't approach a sea-leopard in safety – not even on land. They can rip the skin from a penguin just like that.' He gave a quick snap of the fingers to emphasize the point. 'They wait patiently beneath the ice-floes for the birds to enter the water. One bird is just a morsel to them. They go for anything.'

Gower had drawn his revolver. 'This will make a job of him.'

'No! Not yet! Give the gun to me. I'll do the killing. It'll be necessary to go close up. We don't want to spoil the skin. It's got to have it right in the neck.'

The naval officer grinned as he gave the gun to the whaleboat skipper. 'Careful,' he said. 'It's at the ready.'

Borgen nodded carelessly. He walked silently up to the sleeping animal, like some slaughterman about to use a humane killer, and, placing the firearm close to the mammal's neck, pressed the trigger. The sea-leopard shuddered, tried vainly to reach the water, but managed only a few convulsive shakes, and then there was blood on the snow. It was dead.

'You're a dead shot, Borgen.' Gower grinned as he approached the animal. 'You couldn't have gone any closer. I thought you said they were dangerous?'

'This one was asleep. I didn't want to spoil the skin. It'll be a souvenir for you – a souvenir of the South, if nothing else.'

'Thanks a lot. How do you go about skinning it?'

'I can manage. I have a knife – a sharp knife.' He pulled a sheath-knife from his belt, and waved it in front of Gower's face. 'You see? Just like this!' He pushed the animal over on to its back with the aid of his foot, knelt down, and made a long incision from the lower part of the throat along the stomach to the tail-fin. He looked up at the naval officer and grinned. 'Now we take off the coat.'

With a few expert strokes of the razor-edged knife he

separated the skin from the carcass. 'There ... there's your leopard-pelt. It's a beauty!'

Gower nodded. 'How about all that blubber? How do you get that off?'

'We deal with that part later. We have to get it back on board. It's a messy job. We leave it here and send the boat.' As he spoke he was cutting out the liver and hacking at a large hunk of flesh. He looked up and smiled. 'That should please our petty officer.'

'I hope he enjoys it – all of it.'

They made their way back to the boat and the waiting seamen, their steps crunching in unison over the pebbly foreshore. 'When I get the pelt on board,' said Borgen, 'I'll cut the blubber away and put the skin on a stretching-board. Alum and the atmosphere do the rest. Keep it stretched – that's the secret.' He smiled, and added, 'It's a prize – a prize for any hunter.'

Gower was about to walk inland when the whale-gunner stopped him. 'Keep to the foreshore,' he said. 'Don't disturb the snow. It'll leave marks for weeks to come. It defeats your own purpose.'

The naval officer felt a sense of embarrassment. He muttered angrily to himself, 'Blast it! And I was giving out orders about cigarettes and matches! Thanks, Borgen. One forgets.'

Borgen grinned widely. 'I've done worse.'

'How?'

'I've just slaughtered a sea-leopard. There's blood enough on that rock to make one believe Jack the Ripper's been here! We'll get it cleaned up before we leave.'

'I don't suppose they'll come here, anyway,' Gower said with resignation. 'Our scouting mission has been a flop. Is there anywhere else?'

Borgen shook his head.

They returned to the boat. Gower enumerated all that had to be done. 'We'll wait for you here,' he concluded.

The men made off in the boat to collect the skin and offal.

Gower commenced pacing the foreshore. Borgen seated himself on a large boulder.

'What are those sticking out of the snow?'

The skipper glanced at the direction of Gower's outstretched hand. 'What? You mean those wooden crosses?'

'Yes.'

'That's the cemetery. There's a helluva lot of whalemen lying there. Funny that the crosses still stand up. It's a long time.' There was a kind of baffled expression on his face.

Gower nodded solemnly.

'Yes, sir. Those were men who died with their boots on. There were many accidents in those days. Bad, ugly accidents.'

'I can believe you.'

'Yes, those were the days all right. I saw some of those men killed. We had to get them buried quickly. There's no sympathy when whaling. After we got the grave dug we had to put a hand-pump on to keep the grave dry until we got the guy buried. Glacial water seeped into the grave all the time. Pump, pump, pump! Pump like hell – all through the burial service!' He grinned, and added, 'I suppose those bodies are just as fresh today as on the day they were buried. The glacial water, the frozen soil – just like a ruddy icebox!'

Gower listened to the grisly tale with amusement.

An Adelie penguin leapt out of the water and waddled its way up the beach. It gazed nonchalantly at the strangers. Borgen tried to grab it, but the bird easily evaded his outstretched hands. It reached the snow, and slid with amazing swiftness to safety.

A skua gull hovered directly overhead, peering down upon them with beady eyes.

'You see that bird? Do you know what she's watching?'

'No.'

'She's watching us. She's just hovering there, waiting for us to approach her nest. It won't be very far away – not when she's watching. If we go anywhere near the nest she'll come zooming at us like a dive-bomber. I know – I've experienced them.'

Gower laughed. 'Do you know, Borgen, what I was told back there in South Georgia?'

'What?'

'I was told you were once a rum-runner.'

Borgen's grin broadened. He put fat, stumpy fingers up to

his chin and commenced to massage slowly. 'Who told you that?' he asked.

'The magistrate.'

'I thought it would have been him. Yes, I was a rum-runner – once. I enjoyed it. I made a hell of a lot of money, but lost it all again when I retired from the business. I was broke. I came back whaling.'

'What happened?'

'I was caught. They stuck me in gaol and took all my money. I thought it was time I got away from it all, so I came back whaling. I have been in Norway only once since. I'm to stay here until the War's over. If Germany wins the War, then I stay here for keeps.'

'When were you away from South Georgia last?'

'Away! Away from South Georgia last! I was in Scotland nine months ago. Do you know what happened?'

'What?'

'The ship I went home with was torpedoed off the Mull of Kintyre. I spent the next three months in hospital. Do you call that a vacation? No, sir. This is less exciting . . . safer.'

Gower's eyes twinkled with amusement. 'This rum-running. I suppose that was exciting enough?'

'We had our moments.'

'Such as?'

'Oh, when the ruddy coastguard got after us.'

'What did you do?'

'We took evasive action. Our boat was just as speedy. They rarely got proof. If we were chased into the fjord we used to jettison our cargo on certain bearings – always in shallow water. We nearly always recovered the stuff later. Sometimes we were lucky enough to cripple the coastguard cutter. They got wise to us later.'

'In what way?'

Borgen smiled. 'We used to tow a two-hundred-fathom length of three-inch coir rope behind us. It stayed on the surface of the water, and, as we zigzagged across the bows of the pursuing craft the rope always got foul of their propellers.' He laughed, and added, 'They used to get into a hell of a tangle.

We had to be ready to cut adrift just as soon as we got the strain. They got wise to us in the end.'

'How did they get you?'

'Nabbed us as we entered the fjord with a full load. It wasn't fair. They had four boats waiting for us. We didn't have a chance.'

'So they put you in clink?'

'But not before they took all my money.'

The boat came back, picked them up, and quickly bore them to the *Albatross*. Gower went on board; the whaleboat skipper made off with the boat's crew to erase the marks made in the killing of the sea-leopard.

Petty Officer Watkins was examining the pelt. 'What am I going to do with this, sir?' He indicated the sea-leopard-skin and the quantity of meat and offal.

Gower grunted. 'Leave the skin where it is for the time being. Borgen will deal with that. You asked for seal-meat. Do what you like with it. See that the liver is cooked for the evening meal.'

'Yes, sir.'

'And, Watkins!'

'Sir?'

'Heave up the anchor just as soon as you see the boat coming back. We've wasted enough time in this place.'

'Looks like Captain Carmichael is not going to keep the rendezvous,' Gower said impatiently. 'We'll wait until dawn to see whether they intend to show up. If they're not here by daylight we'll go towards the factory-ships. They shouldn't be so very far away.'

Borgen nodded. 'You said that before, sir.' He grinned, and added, 'Thirty-five degrees west. That's their favourite hunting-ground. They only come in this direction towards the end of the season. If we keep to the ice-edge we can't miss them.'

The *Albatross* was drifting close to Elephant Island. Around them, on every bearing, were hundreds of barrier icebergs. Massive ice-growlers studded the open water.

'There's plenty of ice,' commented Borgen. 'It's always the same around these parts.'

Gower grimaced. 'Wonder how the *Queen of New Zealand* is getting on. I don't envy Carmichael his job – not in these waters.'

'Why?'

'Well, the *Queen* is nearly seven hundred feet long. Who wants to handle a clumsy thing like that?'

'But they handle the whale-ships easily enough. They're six hundred feet in length. There's no steam to handle them very often. All the steam goes to the whale-boilers.'

'How can they manage then?'

'They're lying stopped most of the time. They only get out of the way of icebergs when they're practically on top of them. A kick on one engine is sufficient.'

'And the pack-ice?'

'Just drift through it. Sometimes they're miles within the pack-ice.'

'You say there are no natural harbours where this ship could hide?'

'No.'

'Then where on earth can she be?'

Borgen smiled. 'Let's try and put ourselves in the position of this raider's commanding officer.'

'Right!'

'Good. Then you have run the British blockade and got into the Atlantic. You have the whole ocean before you. What are you going to do?'

Gower said instantly, 'I'm going to keep right in the middle. Try and keep clear of all shipping.'

'You're right. But once you get south of the equator you have to make up your mind where you're going – what your destination is to be. You have to steer direct for that destination.'

'Yes. You're perfectly right,' Gower admitted.

'Then the whole thing is simple. This raider is either a myth or she's at the Norwegian whale-ships. We know the British ships are all right: South Georgia can vouch for that.'

'It's a reasonable deduction, but—'

'There should be no buts. It's the only reasonable and logical conclusion.' Borgen's voice boomed. 'This surface raider, if there is a raider, went to the Norwegian ships. She should have been there by now. Is her work completed? Where does she intend to strike next? Is she coming to the westward?' He fired each question non-stop.

Gower shrugged, and said reluctantly, 'You could be right!'

'Of course I'm right. I'm perfectly right. The Southern ships are nearly full up of whale-oil. They'll be discharging into tankers in a few days' time. Now is the time for this ocean marauder to put in an appearance. If she is to the westward, then she's going to strike – now!'

'What do we do?'

'Just as you said. Let's get to hell out of this. Let's get to the British ships.'

Petty Officer Watkins came on the bridge with two steaming mugs of tea. He addressed the naval officer, ignoring the whaleboat skipper entirely. 'Just been made, sir.' He pointed in the direction of the crockery and left the bridge.

'Looks like Watkins and I are becoming friendly. He's even making me tea. I must do the same for him – some time!'

'You two will become friends yet,' Gower answered with resignation.

'Yes. Perhaps when we sink this German raider. He's a good seaman, though. I've watched him – repeatedly. He knows his job.'

They stood drinking their tea and talking. Gower enumerated many of the things he had already told the whaleboat skipper. He dealt with his life in the Navy, and with the officers who were now serving in the *Queen of New Zealand*. He talked of the convoys which they had been guarding lately, and of the losses sustained.

Time passed quickly. Dawn broke cold and grey-looking. There was no sign of the British cruiser. 'I think we'll go now,' Gower said mechanically. 'There's sufficient light. Carmichael's not coming.'

Elephant Island looked much closer in the early light. Ice-covered and bleak-looking, the homogeneous islet of sterile rock was only two miles distant.

'It's worse than Deception,' he muttered. 'The name . . . it seems familiar. Wasn't this—'

Borgen nodded. 'Yes, I know what you're about to say. This

was the island from which Sir Ernest Shackleton made his historic open-boat voyage to South Georgia – the voyage, one of the greatest epics in the history of mankind, that he made to bring help to the crew of his *Endurance* marooned here on Elephant Island. I was in South Georgia when he arrived there, when he crossed the island on foot after landing on the wrong side. When we saw him – him and his companions – we thought they were some unknown inhabitants from the interior. He's buried in South Georgia – right across the harbour from the magistrate's house. He died in South Georgia on his next expedition – the *Quest*.'

Gower nodded solemnly. 'Yes, I know that.'

Light came quickly now. The naval officer looked over the front of the bridge. He lit a cigarette and watched Petty Officer Watkins swing his torpedo-tubes over a full arc of the horizon. The gear was greased to perfection. He noticed for the first time the names painted on the twin torpedoes – Moby Dick 1, Moby Dick 2. He smiled and wondered who the wag was. He was proud of the *Albatross* – proud of her crew. He hoped that Carmichael would keep him here, but it was doubtful – very doubtful. He sighed lightly and pushed the engine-room telegraph over to full ahead. The engines responded. 'Steer south-east!' he ordered.

CHAPTER EIGHTEEN

'What ship? What ship? What ship?' The Aldis lamp flickered repeatedly as H.M.S. *Queen of New Zealand* closed the *Southern Cross* in the early light of dawn.

On the bridge of the whale-ship, to which the manager and chief officer had already been summoned, the watch-keeping officer hurriedly tried to get the signalling-lamp ready for operation.

'What ship? What ship?' The light relentlessly flickered its question.

'You'd better answer her,' the manager said nervously. 'I don't know who she is, or where she comes from, but you'd better answer – quickly.'

The bridge officer got the Aldis working to satisfaction. He raised it to his right eye, focused, and commenced the answering signal: 'British whale factory-ship – *Southern Cross.*'

The light from the cruiser again flickered: 'Received.'

'They're calling again,' growled the chief officer, a red-bearded Scot. 'They're calling again.'

'I'm going to board you at 0600 hours. Is it permissible for me to send a squad of ratings for a tour of your vessel?'

'Yes . . . yes!' exclaimed the Norwegian manager. 'Tell them it's all right.'

Again the chief officer growled. 'Ask them their name first. Funny message to send without giving their name. She could be anything. That's what the Germans would do. What does it matter, anyway? She's close enough now to blow us right out of the water. Ask them their name.'

'They're flying the white ensign. She's British.'

'Nazi ships have been known to fly the white ensign. I won't be satisfied – not until I can see them and hear them.'

'Ask them their name,' the manager said with reluctance.

'What ship? What ship?' the bridge officer signalled.

'H.M.S. *Queen of New Zealand*. Repeat. Is it permissible

for me to send a squad of ratings for a tour of inspection?'

'Tell them it's all right. Ask them if they want a whaleboat for transport.'

'What the hell's the matter with these people? Can't they signal?' Carmichael was stamping round the bridge of the cruiser, trying to keep warm.

'Probably they haven't got over the shock of us creeping up on them, sir,' said Scott. 'We could have gone right alongside, and they wouldn't have known a thing.'

'Yes. They don't stand much chance against any raider. I mean for sending out any warning.'

'I'm afraid not. They're far too busy.'

The cruiser stopped less than a mile to windward of the whale-ship. Carmichael was peering through his glasses at the ship's whaling-deck. 'Peugh!' he exclaimed. 'One can smell her even to windward!'

The crew had stopped work: they were standing in groups, pointing and gesticulating towards the cruiser. Around the decks four blue-whale carcasses were in various stages of dismembering. Smoke and steam, belching from funnels and exhaust-pipes, meant that the whale-ship was on full production. At the stern a dozen or more dead whales were moored. Slightly to windward, and astern of the factory-vessel, six whaleboats were drifting in the near-freezing sea.

The commanding officer noticed all this as he ordered, 'Call them again, signalman!'

'They're answering now, sir!'

'We expect you at 0600 hours. Do you require a whaleboat for transport?'

Carmichael was reading the message himself. Before the signalman could speak he said, 'Tell them we'll use our own boats.'

'Yes, sir.'

'And, signalman.'

'Sir?'

'Inform them that we'll be sending fifty men on this tour of inspection.'

'Yes, sir.'

'Lieutenant Scott.'

'Sir!'

'Detail fifty men off. You'll be in charge of the party. Perhaps there'll be a chance for the others later.'

'Yes, sir.'

'Inform the navigator that I wish to see him.'

He focused his glasses on the *Southern Cross*. The crews on the deck were back at work. The arrival of the cruiser had been forgotten.

The navigator arrived. 'You sent for me, sir?'

'Yes, Lieutenant. Yes, I did. I myself will be boarding the *Southern Cross*. You will remain in charge here.' He smiled, and added, 'I have a lot to discuss with this whaling manager.'

The navigating officer chuckled. 'Seems like you'll have a job on your hands, sir, judging by what you've already told us.'

'I can make trouble too!' the commanding officer said ruthlessly. 'He won't get it all his own way. Well, I'd better get below. Get shaved and make myself thoroughly respectable. The brass will scare them.' He threw the last words back over his shoulder.

In his room he surveyed himself in the mirror. He was thinking about Gower and the whaleboat. Wonder how he's getting along? It would be another three days before he could arrive at the factory-vessels. Hope everything has gone all right, that he got the right assistance in the conversion. He should be well on his way to Deception by now – perhaps on the way back.

He glanced at his watch – 0500 hours. Another hour, and he would be visiting this manager of the *Southern Cross*. First of all he would have to put a stop to all this radio-telephony talk. All that was necessary was radio bearings – perhaps three times a day. Everything else must be stopped.

There was the question of Gower. He couldn't allow his senior officer to remain on the *Albatross*. He wanted him here; it was essential that he should be here. One of the officers would have to take his place. Whom could he send? Was young Scott dependable enough? Could he rely on him to handle this thing if the chance came along? It was a risk that had to be taken. He was still doubtful of Paul Scott.

He started to get dressed. What if this surface raider wasn't down here at all? What if all this wild rush was for nothing?

According to the time factor, she should have been down here days ago. She must have gone to the eastward – to the Norwegian ships. What was he going to do now? He would have to decide once he'd had this conference with the manager of the *Southern Cross*.

He would have to ask about fresh water: they'd had no time in South Georgia. Both whale-ships were fitted with large evaporating plants. It shouldn't be much trouble for them to supply.

Instructions would have to be given that all whaleboats should keep a thorough look-out for any strange ships. They covered a tremendous area in a day's operational work. It would be just as easy searching for a ship as it would be for whales. Easier. He smiled quietly to himself, and went on with his dressing.

On board the *Southern Cross* things were soon back to normal. The whalemen went about their work uninterested in the fact that an armed auxiliary cruiser lay close to port, and that she was about to send a boarding-party. The gun's crew, now aware of the fact that the four-inch breech-loader had been covered in grease and canvas ever since the beginning of whaling operations, were frantically trying to introduce a semblance of order. As the chief officer had just told them, 'You'd better see that the bloody thing looks as if it can at least fire. You never know these naval people. They could report us.'

On the navigation bridge the whaling manager wore a worried look. The chief officer, standing close by his side, was saying, 'I still say it's a funny way to send a message. "Can I send a squad of men to tour your vessel?" Bah! Sending that even before they send their name – and we had to ask for their name. That's the Navy for you – the British Navy! They're lucky we didn't put a shell into them. If the gun had been working,' he added.

'What do you think they want?' the manager asked, a note of impatience in his voice.

'You can be sure they're not down here for nothing. We haven't had a visit from them before – not even in peace-time. You can be sure – there's something!'

'We'll soon find out. Here they come.'

Two boats were leaving the cruiser – about thirty men to each boat. They came slowly, taking a long time to reduce the 3,000 yards that separated the two vessels.

'What kind of boats are they using?' exclaimed the watch-keeping officer. 'They're not motor-boats. They're not using oars.'

'Hand-propelled,' the mate answered curtly. 'They have them in a lot of these armed cruisers. Specially made for the Wavy Navy! You use a handle – just the same as if you were drawing a pint of beer. The action of the handle drives the propeller. God! What's the British Navy coming to?'

'I thought you said it could be the German Navy?' the manager questioned dryly.

The chief officer grinned. 'No, I've changed my mind – now.'

'You'd better get down and welcome them on board. Have you detailed anyone to show them round? We don't want them falling into any of the whale-boilers.'

'The deck foreman has been detailed off to show the ratings round. I'll deal with the others.'

'Good! Then you can put down the red carpet.'

'Red carpet! I only hope they're not in their best clothes. They'll get a shock.'

'There's another boat coming, sir!' the bridge officer exclaimed. 'A fast motor-boat!'

'That'll be the big shot himself. I'll go and meet him.'

The chief officer went off chuckling.

Carmichael's boat came alongside in a flurry of foam. He stood in the stern alongside Scott. There was a short delay as the boat was made fast and held. Carmichael boarded first, and was immediately followed by the younger officer.

The chief officer smiled and made himself known. They shook hands warmly. Carmichael's manner was pleasant and easy. He looked around him in astonishment. There was steam, noise, and the paraphernalia of dangerous whirling machinery. The temperature was at least eighty degrees higher than in the open air.

'I never realized it was like this in the guts of a whale-ship,' Carmichael said blandly. His eyes widened as he looked around him. 'Is it always like this?'

'Yes. During the actual whaling season we prefer it this way. Sometimes we run out of luck, and it can get as cold as hell.'

Carmichael chuckled. 'I see what you mean. The more whales the hotter it becomes.'

'That's right, sir.'

'My men . . . they're coming behind me. I hope I'm not inconveniencing you?'

'They'll be taken care of, sir.' He beckoned to the deck foreman, who was standing near. 'You will conduct the naval party round the ship. Take all the time that's available.'

'Yes, sir.'

Carmichael nodded in appreciation.

'Now, if you will follow me, sir. Watch for your heads!'

Again the commanding officer nodded. He beckoned to Scott, and they began to follow on the heels of the executive officer.

Along a labyrinth of passages, up and down steel ladders, the officer led them through a whole system of complex valuable machinery to a door that led to the whaling-deck. Around them a dozen or more steam winches synchronized in a concerto diabolic in its sound. The doorway and surrounding deck were covered in a thick coating of coagulated blood. Steel hooks, lethal-looking steel claws, and snake-like wires were flying through the air. The chief officer halted the work in the immediate vicinity as they made their way round a mountain of flesh and infats. Two whalemen stepped forward and guided them to the ladder leading to the bridge-deck.

Carmichael gave a sigh of relief. 'Well, that was a difficult operation. How do these men manage to keep their feet?'

The executive grinned. 'They wear spikes on their heels. They couldn't work otherwise.'

'I see.'

The manager met them on the lower bridge. His face had a wooden expression, but he shook hands cordially. The chief officer made the introductions. He was about to move away when the manager halted him. 'If you will all follow me,' he said.

They moved into the accommodation spaces, and made their way to the manager's day room, a luxurious, saloon-like cabin situated immediately below the navigation bridge.

Carmichael looked around him with interest. 'They do you well, sir,' he said genially. 'I didn't know what to expect after coming across that whaling-deck.'

The manager smiled. He was edgy. His usual exuberant manner had left him.

They made themselves comfortable.

Carmichael lit a cigarette from a box which the whaling manager handed round. Scott refused: he was a non-smoker.

'Now we can get down to business,' Carmichael said with a quiet smile. 'I suppose you wonder what has brought me down here? Suppose I give you a résumé of what's going on.'

The whaling manager smiled broadly for the first time. 'I don't think it's going to be anything good. According to my senior officer, it isn't going to be good at all.' His English was slow, but precise.

'And he's right.'

'Tell me. Is there—'

'We've been sent down here to look after the whaling fleets. It's no precautionary measure. It's known that a German raiding vessel left Germany some time ago to come to these waters. Where she is or what she's doing we do not know. Time will tell.'

'How does that affect us?'

Carmichael ignored the question. 'Indications are that she must have gone to the eastward – to the Norwegian ships – but this is only surmise on my part. If she'd been coming direct to this position she should have been here now. There have been no signs.'

'You mean you have nothing definite.'

'Nothing.'

'There have been no signs here.'

'There won't be any signs, sir. Not until she actually strikes. Why, we lay on your head this morning for over three hours and were unnoticed.'

'We don't look for naval vessels – of any nationality.'

'Admitted,' Carmichael said. 'But from now on *we* do! I have my orders, Captain. I'm responsible for the safety of the whaling fleet – all of them.'

The manager shrugged. The frosty grey eyes hardened.

'I have drafted a short communiqué to each of your whale-boats. All my orders must be obeyed. I don't want to interfere with your work, but from now on all these telephone conversations must stop.'

'It's impossible to operate without radio-telephony,' the manager said hotly. 'You might just as well order us to go home.'

'I'm of a different opinion, Captain. Radio directional bearings are all they require. That's all they'll get in future.' Carmichael's manner had suddenly become brusque.

'The whale-gunners are going to kick.'

'Let them kick! Let them complain as much as they like! The order will still stand. You will send out radio bearings three times a day – nothing more. Make your own specified times.'

'But—'

'Look, Captain, the season is nearly half-way through. It will be my job to escort you to the United Kingdom. It seems this whale-oil is of grave concern to the British Government. They're not concerned about you, or me, or any of your whale-gunners, or anyone connected with these expeditions. All they're after is the whale-oil. We're here to help you safeguard it. Do you think that they would send a valuable ship like the *Queen of New Zealand* down here for a picnic? No, sir! We're down here to see that you complete your season in safety. I hope we're able to do it.'

The chief officer, who had sat in silence throughout the whole of the proceedings, nodded his head vigorously. 'You are quite right, sir! Absolutely right! In any case, these whale-gunners – they talk too much!'

The simple words cleared the atmosphere. They all laughed.

'What about the *Southern Isles*?' the manager asked. 'Does she come under the same orders?'

'Yes, sir. Absolutely the same! It will be necessary for you to work in collaboration with each other. You must use the same operational area.'

'But . . . how can two expeditions operate that close?'

'How far are they away?'

'About fifty miles.'

Carmichael smiled. 'That's what I mean by the same operational area. Fifty miles ... a hundred miles ... a distance respectable enough for me to maintain a guard over both ships. If this raider does appear, then you both run like hell. I go in and hope for the best.' The words, the tone in which they were spoken, were jocular enough, but he meant every single word.

The whaling manager sat back in his chair. 'I understand,' he said more complacently.

'If you can keep a distance like that we can work together – all of us. I don't want you to get in each other's way, but you see the difficulties ... the dangers.'

The chief officer's face was interested and sympathetic. 'And you have come from?'

Carmichael lit another cigarette. 'We have come from the Falklands and South Georgia. We were nearly home when they turned us round to come down here. You see how important they seem to think it is. I have now to consider whether it's advisable for me to go to the eastward, to see if those Norwegian ships are all right. I don't think it is meantime. I would much rather safeguard these western expeditions – that is, until you get your oil into the tankers and it's safely delivered to South Georgia.'

'Then you intend to stay here – here in this vicinity?' the manager broke in sharply.

'For the present – yes!'

The whole bridge shook with vibration as somewhere some huge hauling-winch came into operation. Both whaling men were impervious to the unearthly racket.

'Good heavens!' Carmichael exclaimed. 'What on earth's that?'

The chief officer grinned. 'It's only a heavy blue whale being hove forward. That happens every hour. We count the carcasses as we sleep.'

'It's a wonder you sleep at all!'

'We manage all right. One gets used to anything.'

'You know the whaleboat *Albatross*?' Carmichael put the question to the whaling manager.

'You mean the service boat that serves the British station at South Georgia?'

'Yes.'

'We know her.'

'We're having her converted, and intend to use her as a scouting vessel. She's being fitted up with twin torpedoes, and she'll use them – if she gets a chance. We commandeered her with this object in view; also, if I may say so, so that it would be unnecessary to interfere with any of your vessels. I understand that you're now operating with the minimum number.'

'That's correct.'

'She'll be here in less than three days. Meantime she's having a look at Deception Island. One can never tell.'

He's got it all worked out, the chief officer thought. There are no flies about this bloke. He knows his business. The *Albatross*! What could that old rattletrap do? Still, fitted with torpedoes, she could be dangerous enough. H.M.S. *Albatross* . . . that was funny!

Carmichael was saying, 'Both the magistrate and the manager at South Georgia advised me to have a look at Deception. I had no time to wait; I came direct here. I left my executive officer in charge. He was to search in that direction before coming here.'

The manager's mood was more conciliatory now. He knew he couldn't browbeat this naval officer. He would have to take the bad with the good. Well, if there was a surface raider about, better that this cruiser should be near. She would be a buffer, a breakwater, between the *Southern Cross* and any Nazi marauder. As this commanding officer had just said, 'If this raider does appear then you both run like hell; I go in and hope for the best.' That was good enough logic . . . good enough for him. That was what the Navy was there for. They were paid for that sort of business. Yes, he could get along with this Captain – just as long as he didn't interfere too much with the *Southern Cross* expedition.

'You say the *Southern Isles* is about fifty miles away?' Carmichael's question interrupted his thoughts.

'Yes, sir. About fifty miles to the south-west. The ice-pack from here runs in a south-westerly direction. She's lying in this bay. She hasn't moved – not in two weeks. Operations have been good – very good.'

Carmichael nodded. 'I hope your good luck continues, Captain. Don't let it be said that we brought you bad luck. Get your whales – and your whale-oil. Let's get back to the United Kingdom!'

The manager smiled and nodded.

'We require fresh water, Captain. Could you supply us with about two hundred tons of drinking-water? We left South Georgia in such a hurry. If the *Albatross* was here she could have ferried it over. Perhaps one of your whaleboats . . .' Carmichael was mildly apologetic.

'I'm afraid a whaleboat would be awkward. You are high out of the water. It may be . . .'

'We'll manage somehow. If it comes to the worst we can bale the damned stuff out.'

'Why don't you bring your vessel alongside? We could pump it direct,' the manager said. 'It won't be a big job.'

Carmichael knew what the whaling manager was thinking. He wasn't backing out. 'Right!' he answered without hesitation. 'Which side do you want to use? Shall we moor up, or shall we steam along together, with the hose between?'

'We'll moor you alongside the port side. 'That's the side we take our tankers. We can give you as much water as you need.'

'Thanks. What, may I ask, do you use for fenders?'

The whaling manager chuckled, his good-humour returning at last. 'We supply the fenders,' he said. 'We use dead whales! They make excellent fenders. Four carcasses placed along the side make the best fenders in the world. We always use that.'

'Good! Then just as soon as I get back on board I can bring my ship alongside. We'll come for our own water. It's good of you to supply the stuff.'

The chief officer smiled quietly to himself. He thought, What the hell has he let us in for? Of all the things, taking a twenty-thousand-ton ship alongside for a drop of water! The whaleboat, as this commanding officer had just said, could have managed – somehow.

Carmichael rose. 'I hope I can see more of your interesting vessel when we come alongside.' He turned to Scott, and added, 'Inform the men that we'll pick them up when we come alongside. Better not break up their sightseeing tour.'

The whaling manager nodded. 'You'll wait for our signal. It takes a little time to prepare these fenders.'

'Right, sir! Now, if you'll excuse me?' He again shook hands with the manager, and accompanied by Scott and the senior officer, left the room.

They made their way through the same labyrinth of smelly passages to the waiting boat. The chief officer sent a whaleman off to notify the touring party that they shouldn't return until the cruiser was alongside. 'It's better that way,' he said. 'They'll take a hell of a rounding-up.'

'I believe you,' Carmichael said agreeably. 'I look forward to my next visit. I hope we're not inconveniencing you?'

'It will be a pleasure,' the executive retorted.

'Good! Your Captain, he did say the port side?'

'Yes, sir. That's correct. The usual procedure is for us to steam slowly into the wind. If you come slowly up from the stern, gradually overhauling us, you won't have any trouble. We have all the ropes and springs ready. All you require is a good rope at each end. That's the first line we use. Leave the rest to us.'

Carmichael grinned. 'Good! Now I know all about it. I wouldn't ask your Captain.'

They were quickly taken back to the cruiser. Carmichael gave Scott a list of orders to attend to. 'Let me know when they're ready for us,' he concluded.

He had his breakfast served in his cabin. He sat over it, brooding, taking his time. Was it worth it, he thought, going all that way to the eastward to see if those Norwegian vessels were safe? It meant leaving the British ships wide open to attack. How was it possible for him to be in two places at once when they were over a thousand miles apart? No! It couldn't be done!

His thoughts were confused. Another six weeks at least down here. Six weeks, the manager had said, and the season would be finished. The tankers would be here in less than a week. Once the oil was back in South Georgia, then he could go to the eastward. He could combine a visit to those ships with a long search for this phantom raider. One could cover a pretty good distance in a week. He sat back and lit a cigarette, his mind more at rest.

There was a knock at the door, and a young officer entered. 'We have just received a message from the *Southern Cross*, sir.' He handed Carmichael a pencilled note, written on the usual naval message-form.

They don't waste much time, he thought. He put on a duffle-coat, threw a scarf round his neck, and went up to the bridge. The boats were being hoisted, creeping up the high sides of the cruiser on falls operated by electric winches. He watched as the two blocks came together and the boats themselves commenced their inboard swing to the housing-platforms.

'Right! Now we can stand by fore and aft. Give her slow ahead on both.'

'Slow ahead both engines, sir!'

'Hard starboard!'

'Hard starboard, sir!'

The cruiser began a slow swing to starboard. Carmichael steadied her as soon as the whale factory-ship was bearing directly ahead. The *Southern Cross* was steaming into the eye of the wind at dead-slow speed. Three miles ahead of the whale-ship the ice-pack swept to the westward in a continuous solid mass. The open water was punctuated by scattered ice-floes.

'Steady as she goes!' Carmichael ordered sharply.

'Steady as she goes, sir!'

They were closing the factory-ship quickly. Directly ahead her propellers were churning the water, which formed itself into a straight, broad wake owing to the whales she was towing.

Carmichael nodded appreciatively. These people knew their business, he thought. They should: they've done it often enough. So have we. He remembered the many times that he had actually fuelled at sea – even when they were under way. That was a much more difficult operation: both ships actually steaming at full speed.

'Down ten revolutions!' he ordered.

'Down ten revolutions, sir!'

Gradually the distance between the two vessels lessened. The whale slipway, a massive hole cut away in the whale-ship's stern, loomed high up before them.

'Watch the hole!' Carmichael said humorously.

The navigator made no reply.

'Port ten degrees!'

'Port ten degrees, sir!'

The bow swung slowly to port and was steadied. Along the hull of the whale-ship four blue whale carcasses, moored fore and aft in the most strategic of positions, looked like huge barrage balloons. Their blubber-encased bodies, more resilient to shocks than the finest of rubber, were far superior to any fenders that could ever be devised by man.

'Steady so!' Carmichael said confidently.

'Steady so, sir!'

'Stop engines!'

'Stop engines, sir!'

Slowly the two ships ran parallel to each other. A rocket-line was fired from the whale-ship across the bows of the cruiser; the light eight-inch mooring hawser was quickly run between the two bows, and, as it tautened, the two ships came together with hardly a tremor. Springs and additional head and stern ropes were put out, the engines were stopped, and both ships fell off from the wind and lay drifting.

'That's a really good job, navigator,' said Carmichael. 'Even though I say it myself. Their tanker vessels couldn't have done it any better.' He looked down upon the whaling-deck from the high bridge of the cruiser. Gory and blood-splattered, with inches of solidified fat adhering to all of the superstructure, it was butchery on a colossal scale.

The navigator stood watching with amazement. Right abreast of him a gang of lemmers were slicing tons of flesh from the back of one of the carcasses, while other gangs were heaving vast quantities into the open maws of boilers. Casings of ribs hung from the derrick-heads, directly above two tough, bearded whalemen, who were dissecting them with long-handled knives with total disregard of the dangers from flying hooks and wires that encompassed them. Three steam saws, snorting and belching, but with fingertip contol, were slamming back and forth into huge vertebral columns. The innards were being hauled out. The navigator watched with interest as a small group of men slung a small wire round the intestines and hove the whole lot over the side between the two vessels. There was a mighty splash; water and blood flew up as high as the cruiser's bridge.

Carmichael laughed loudly. 'God!' he exclaimed. 'It's a good job Gower isn't here! Look! Look at his ship's side! Look at his clean decks! What a mess!'

The navigator still looked on with amazement. 'Does this butcher's shop ever close down?'

'Hardly ever,' answered Carmichael. He was watching, with appreciation, a group of whalemen breaking out new fire-hoses. A line snaked on board. Within a few minutes the end of the hose was being hauled across. There was a short delay – five minutes at the most – then fresh water began to flow from the whale-ship into the tanks of the *Queen of New Zealand*.

'Good show!' Carmichael commented. He turned to the navigator, and added, 'We'll go just as soon as they complete. We can't interfere with their work. This disrupts their routine. How would you like to go and visit?'

'It would be interesting – seeing the inside.'

'Good! Then go and fetch Commander (E). I know he wanted to go. There may not be another chance. Another two hours, and we head to the south-west, to the *Southern Isles*.'

Five hundred miles to the eastward the *Antarctica 1* was steaming at economical speed along the ice-edge to the operational area of the British ships. The weather was good, with calm seas and clear visibility. There had been no sign of a marauding vessel. The whole ocean was devoid of ships – or so it seemed.

CHAPTER NINETEEN

In his own room on the *Viking* Fischer sat facing the late whaling manager of the *Antarctica*. 'You are a brave man, Captain Nilsen,' he said, 'but rather a foolish one. I admire a brave man; I detest a foolish one. You are both. Why did you go against the wishes of my Lieutenant? Why did you attempt to stop him in the execution of his duties?'

Nilsen sat silent.

'Is it worth your while trying to be at cross-purposes with us? Where does it get you in the end? You are here. The *Antarctica* is on her way to Germany. You could still have been in command. All your officers and men will be repatriated to Norway. They have our promise.'

'I hope they never get back,' Nilsen said bitterly. 'You speak of promises! What promises have your Government ever kept? Promises!' he scoffed. 'You dare speak of promises! Who would trust the promises of your Nazi masters? They have only one aim – subjection or annihilation for the peoples of Europe. Promises! Your Nazi thugs would tear the guts out of one another just as we tear the innards from the whales we work with – if they got the chance. You speak of promises!'

Fischer smiled. 'You realize where we are bound for?'

'Yes, I do! You may think you'll capture the British ships just as easily as you did the *Antarctica* and *Cachelot*. You will be wrong, Captain. Let me tell you, you will be wrong. It won't be so easy – not any more. Go back to Germany – now! The best of them has to fall. Your great pocket battleship didn't get back. What chance have you? The British will be waiting for you. They'll get you in the end!'

Kaltenbrunner, who was in attendance, lay back in his chair, morose and silent. The *Viking* was lying stopped – stopped and drifting in a dense fog which had prevailed for over forty hours. They were well behind schedule. He was impatient at this long delay – impatient at this interview with Nilsen. In his opinion it didn't mean a thing.

Fischer was saying, 'Captain, I admire your courage, but I deplore your lack of commonsense. You not only hurt yourself; you hurt your family back in Norway. I do not mention this as a threat. Imagine . . . just imagine your wife's feelings when your officers and crew are returned to their own homes, and you are not among them. These whaling ports are small places: everyone knows the other's business. They won't speak of you as being a hero – a martyr. No, sir! They'll speak of you as one who tried to threaten their whole family life – their very existence.'

'I am no collaborator,' Nilsen said quietly. 'I am no Quisling. I would do the same – even at home in Norway.'

'You may go, Captain. I can only do my best for you in my written report.'

Nilsen rose stiffly. 'I thank you,' he said resignedly as he walked from the room.

'You know, Lieutenant, I'm of the opinion that Dieter made a mistake. That man would have made no trouble. Dieter lacks the sense of handling men. It's an art – one that has to be cultivated. You yourself admitted that you were welcomed on board the *Cachelot* with open arms. Why? Because you have that sense. I admire this man's spirit. I will do my best for him.'

'But the *Antarctica 1*! She could have upset all our plans!'

'You can't blame Nilsen for that. He tried to recall the vessel. He did his best. The whaleboat would have returned – if we'd waited. I take the blame for that. It was my mistake. Success . . . it came much too easily.'

Kaltenbrunner shrugged. 'I take the blame as well,' he said. 'It was also my idea to come to the northward. Look what has happened.'

'The fortunes of war. We didn't expect to run into this fog. Do you think we should run to the south if the weather clears?'

'I was hoping you'd say that, sir. It'll be better to get back to the ice-edge – less chance of the fog persisting. This route was all right, if it had remained clear.'

'Then do that. You say you heard the British ships working?'

'Yes, sir. They seem to be working close together. Same as the *Antarctica* and *Cachelot*.'

Fischer smiled. 'That is what you're hoping for. Surely it isn't going to be that easy?'

'I hope so. We could carry out the same routine. Wenzel take one, I the other.' Kaltenbrunner smiled in grim anticipation.

'If only this blasted weather would clear!' Fischer said. 'It's only about a thirty-six hours' run from this position.'

The supernumerary left the room to go on to the navigation bridge. He stood on the lower bridge peering to windward before he climbed to the bridge proper. Looks like it's going to clear, he thought. Visibility of a mile would do us. Enough to get out of this dead spot.

Fischer sat back in his chair and made himself more comfortable. He looked around the now familiar room and sighed contentedly. This was better than being cooped up in the fjords of Norway, or in the harbours of Kiel or Hamburg. Here, right on the fringe of the Antarctic Circle, he had a job to do – something that was meant to be done. He thought about his interview with Nilsen: the whole thing disturbed him. It was the first time they'd met, and he had liked him. He liked his spirit, his defiance of everything that was Nazi. He hadn't thought much of the promises that had been made to the crews of the whale-ships – about their being repatriated to Norway. He was wrong there: they would be repatriated. They would even be welcomed when they arrived in Germany.

He lit his pipe and stretched out luxuriously. He had been dismayed at these threats the manager had been making – these prophetic utterances about the British Navy waiting for them, that they would never get back to Germany. The whole thing was bluster on Nilsen's part, yet he was sorry that they'd been made. He would have to write a full report about the matter. If Kaltenbrunner hadn't been there he could have forgotten about the whole thing, but . . .

His pipe had gone out. He struck a match and tried to relight the damp tobacco. He got it going to his satisfaction, and returned to his thoughts. Everything had been so very simple up to now – mere routine. The running of the blockade, the voyage south, the capture of the first two vessels, it had been all too simple. He gave a quick, taut smile. Blast that Nilsen! He felt a sudden misgiving, a sort of premonition. He had felt it ever since the whaling manager had left the room.

He rose and went to the window: the fog still held. It seemed a very long time since he had looked through this same window at the U-boats in Kiel Harbour. He began slowly pacing the room, trying to force his thoughts away from his interview with Nilsen. He thought about the *Antarctica* and *Cachelot.* They would be out of these leaden waters now – into the forties. They would find their way home all right. Germany would have her whale-oil.

He thought about Linder. It was peculiar how he had changed his opinion of that young officer. He remembered the first time that he'd met him – in Kiel. He had met him as he'd stepped on board the *Viking* for the first time, a hard-looking, arrogant young Lieutenant with the Iron Cross new on his uniform. This feeling of dislike had turned to one of sufferance, and then to one of admiration. Linder was capable, efficient, strong. He had that happy knack of welding a crew together. Yes, Linder would get home.

He looked at the open chart on the desk before him. The South Sandwich Islands – a string of volcanic islands running in a north and south direction – lay just ahead of them. Yes, he thought, we should have gone well to the south of them – as far south as it was possible to get. He lifted the dividers and measured off a few distances. He scrutinized the sailing directions, and read the pages that dealt with the South Sandwich group. He noticed, with interest, that most of them had been discovered by Russian navigators. He made a grimace. Imagine Russians having been down here so very long ago! It was hardly credible.

He went back to his chair and thought this over. Russia! Russia! That's where Germany's war should be – Russia. They were the menace to the whole of the world – not Germany. If Hitler and his gang were out of the way Germany could live with the rest of the world. All except Russia. Why couldn't the British see this? Germany and Britain were alike – more alike than any two nations. Why should they always have to be at war with each other?

His thoughts were interrupted by the changing of the electric telegraphs. He looked through the window and saw that it had cleared slightly: the fog was lifting. He hurried to the bridge, to find Kaltenbrunner conning the ship through a wide sweep of the compass to the south-west. Visibility was up to about two miles.

The supernumerary noticed his commanding officer. He said, 'Looks like it's going to clear, sir.'

'That will be a surprise – a big surprise!' Fischer spoke drily. 'I only hope you're right.'

The fog was lifting quickly. Small, scattered patches, their tendrils billowing over the greyish waters, were gradually disappearing. Low on the horizon a few clear patches were opening up in the sky. The sun, close to its meridianal altitude, was showing thinly through the near-overcast sky. A light air was coming from the south.

'A little breeze, a shift to the south-west, and it'll be as clear as a bell,' the supernumerary said with a smile. 'Shall I give her full speed?'

Fischer nodded cheerfully. 'Yes, Lieutenant. Give her all the speed you can get. Let's make up for lost time!'

Kaltenbrunner smiled. He swung the telegraphs over. The bridge officers and look-outs hastily took up new positions. Once again the engines throbbed under full power.

'What kind of radio apparatus have we got on this bloody ship?' roared Hansen across the bridge of the *Antarctica 1*. The whale-gunner was stamping and raving at his radio officer. 'You mean to tell me that you can't hear the "Southern" ships? That you can't hear any signals? What kind of a radio officer are you? I know your transmitter is on the bum, but hell, your receiver should be all right! You say you can hear no signals – nothing?'

'There's nothing wrong with the radio receiver,' the radio officer said angrily. 'It's just that I can't hear them. The whole Antarctic is dead! If the *Southern Cross* and the *Southern Isles* are close, then they're not using any of their radio apparatus.'

The whale-gunner turned to the mate, who had just come on to the bridge to relieve him. 'Do you hear what he said? He can't hear any of the "Southern" ships! What can you make of that?'

The mate shook his head in perplexity. 'Looks like this raider, or whatever it may be, has been here before us. Looks like they've carried out the same thing as they did to the *Antarctica.* Let's get to hell out of this area!'

The *Antarctica 1* had made a speedy westing. Good weather and clear visibility had enabled them to maintain a speed of fourteen knots even at a lower consumption of fuel-oil. Keeping to the ice-edge, they had experienced a calm sea. There had been no sighting of any strange ship. They should have been coming up with the British ships.

Hansen nodded glumly. He turned to the radio officer, and said, 'Are you sure about this radio receiver? It is working properly?'

The officer scowled. 'How can it be otherwise? I can hear London, I can hear Berlin, I can hear New York! Surely I would hear the "Southern" boats if they're working? They aren't!'

'That's short-wave. What about the other wave-bands?'

'Well, I can hear the Falklands. I can hear South Georgia. That's close enough.'

The whale-gunner frowned. 'I'll take your word for it,' he said dully.

'What are you going to do?' The mate spoke anxiously.

'What can we do? We haven't enough oil to reach South Georgia. If we strike north for there we'll have to finish the passage in the lifeboats. On the other hand, we could continue to the westward. The "Southern" expeditions may be much farther west.'

'But what if they aren't? It would mean twice the distance in the open boats. Surely if they were working they would be using radio transmitters? I can understand them not using radio-telephony, but—'

'You have it!' Hansen exclaimed excitedly. He glared balefully at his radio officer. 'You go back to your radio-shack and listen carefully. I mean carefully. Try and find if they are transmitting on spark. Listen for any directional signals. It may be that they have stopped all communication. They must send out their bearings. The boats would be lost otherwise. You can't carry out whaling operations without radio bearings. If we don't hear anything by 2000 hours we'll strike north for South Georgia.'

The radio officer left the bridge sullenly.

'I hope you're right. This raider may be around here. We'd better be careful. We don't—'

'Careful! We could see a raider long before she ever spotted us. We would soon turn round and get out of her way.'

'The *Antarctica* and her boats didn't. It was only by good luck that we were so far into the ice that we were overlooked. We could have gone the same way.'

The whale-gunner made no reply. He thought, Go on, why don't you say it? The whale-gunner was tight, and he was taking a couple of days off! Aloud he said, 'They weren't looking for a raider. We're different: we keep a good look-out. Don't say anything to the men – not yet.'

The mate was not convinced. 'It may be that they're much farther west. They could be as far west as the South Shetlands.'

Hansen shook his head. 'No, not at this time of the season. The season's only half-way through. What would they be doing at the South Shetlands?'

'It's been done before. They could even have gone into the Weddell Sea. I know it isn't likely, but you can never tell the orders that these British whale-ships get. It's the owners themselves who run the expeditions. They don't want managers in these ships. All they want is labourers. Do this! Do that! They know all the answers. That's the way they carry on.'

Hansen was thinking, You could well be right. It may be that they have found a clearance into the Weddell Sea. It seemed incredible, but one never knew what the ice conditions were going to be like. No two seasons were the same – not in Antarctica!

'I think we should go to the northward. Let's not take chances.'

The whale-gunner nodded. 'We'll wait for the four hours. If we don't hear anything by 2000 we'll turn to the north for South Georgia.'

'I think that's a wise decision.'

An albatross swooped low over the water close by the bridge, rose, circled the stern, and was back alongside the bridge all in a matter of seconds. Hansen gave the bird a momentary glance as it undulated over the slight swell. He searched the horizon to the north and west.

The whaleboat was steering less than half a mile off the main pack-ice; the sea was clear to the northward, and there were no icebergs in the immediate vicinity. The ice to the south stretched as far as the eye could see – a wilderness of ice stretching to the barrier and the polar plateau of Antarctica.

The waters teemed with marine life. Hansen, with the true whale-gunner's instinct, born from many years' experience of these same waters, noticed the intermittent blasts from a pod of sperm whale to the northward. He studied the bearing and noted the direction in which they were heading. Another pod, of killer whales – the so-called vultures of Southern waters – sounded close under the port bow. He watched as they slid below the surface, their triangular-shaped fins scarcely rippling the surface of the water.

The mate altered course to clear an ice promontory that came up ahead. He cleared the point, and brought the whaleboat back to her course.

'I think I'll go along and see what that radio officer is doing,' Hansen said with a touch of malice. 'Keep her going west.'

He made his way aft, and entered the tiny radio-shack. The officer was seated before the receiver. 'Are there any signals?' he asked patiently.

The radio officer raised his eyebrows and shook his head solemnly. 'Not a damned thing! The whole place is dead!'

Hansen sat down on the desk-top, his legs not reaching the floor. He looked at the clock fastened on the forward bulkhead: it showed Greenwich time. 'You know, Sparks, I should listen carefully on the hour. If they send out directional bearings it'll be on the hour. I'm nearly sure about that.'

'I was thinking about that.'

They waited anxiously until the minute-hand had passed the hour – 2300. There were no signals. 'Looks pretty hopeless,' Hansen said. 'We'll wait until midnight Greenwich, and then clear away to the northward. There's nothing else to do.'

'There are definitely no signals!'

'I can bloody well see that!' Hansen answered angrily.

He returned to his own room and settled himself down on the settee. It's no good, he thought. Something has happened to them. Same as the *Antarctica.* Same as the *Cachelot.* It's no use wasting any more time. He would have to try to reach South Georgia. Perhaps if they went at slow speed they could manage.

He got up, returned to the bridge, and was just in time to share the mate's tea. He glanced at the small clock that was fastened close to the binnacle – 2200 hours. 'That's midnight Greenwich,' he said. 'It's no use waiting any longer. Bring her round on the course to South Georgia. Steer 340 degrees.'

There was a wild yell from aft; the radio officer came shouting on the bridge. 'What the hell are you trying to do?' he roared. 'I was just taking bearings when you swung off to starboard. I can hear them! I can hear them both! They were practically ahead before you altered course. They were close – bloody close! They can't be far away.'

'You're sure?'

'Sure I'm sure – certain!'

'Good!' The whale-gunner turned to the helmsman, who was standing with mouth agape. 'Bring her back!' he ordered curtly. 'Bring her back to west!'

CHAPTER TWENTY

Carmichael looked through powerful glasses at the unfamiliar-looking whaleboat that was closing them fast from the westward. 'Good heavens!' he exclaimed. 'It's the *Albatross*!' He grinned as he noted the camouflaged silhouette of the ambiguous-looking naval craft. Squat, even powerful-looking, low in the water, her foremast and other deck-fittings cut away, the *Albatross* blended into the gathering dusk in perfect harmony. He noted with satisfaction the twin torpedoes housed in their tubes on the foredeck. The white ensign flew proudly aft.

An Aldis lamp flickered from the whaleboat's bridge. 'H.M.S. *Albatross* reporting for operational duty. Have you any orders for me?'

Carmichael smiled as he read the signal. He turned to the signalman, and said, 'Send the following signal: "Officer commanding *Albatross* to report on board here for immediate conference." '

The message was sent and was acknowledged.

He's even managed to scrounge an Aldis lamp, Carmichael thought. I won't send a boat. I'll wait and see what happens.

The *Albatross* drew up in a flurry of foam close under the starboard quarter. Gower must have read his commanding officer's thoughts, for within a few minutes of losing headway a lifeboat, with Gower himself at the tiller, and manned by four ratings, was alongside the high starboard side of the cruiser.

He was received on board in formal fashion. He winked slyly at Scott, who was standing close by, and made his way to Carmichael's accommodation. The commanding officer was waiting.

'Where on earth have you been?' Carmichael demanded. 'I've been all over the Antarctic looking for you.'

Gower grinned. 'Then we must have missed each other, sir. Seems to me as if I've been all over the place myself. Deception Island . . . Elephant Island . . . Joinville . . . part of the South

Shetlands. There certainly isn't any German surface raider about – not to the westward.'

Carmichael laughed. 'You could do with a shave, Commander. You could even use a bath. Have you had a good time?'

'Yes, sir. I've had a splendid time! We did as you said. From South Georgia we went direct to Deception. There's been nobody there – not in years. It's just the same as it was years ago – when the whalemen left.'

Carmichael nodded. He didn't speak.

'We left Deception, and went to keep our rendezvous with you. I waited, but you didn't turn up, so I decided to go south to Joinville in the South Shetlands. There was nothing there. I came eastward along the ice-edge to this position. It was an interesting trip, but there's nothing – absolutely no sign of any strange vessel.'

'You must have had a tough time. What did you do for engineers?'

'I got the old skipper himself, along with his two engineers: they volunteered. The engineers are British. I don't know what Borgen is – he could be anything. He was Norwegian – once. He must know more about these waters than anyone alive today.'

'He must be good,' said Carmichael. 'You make him sound as if he will be a valuable man.'

'He *is* a valuable man,' Gower said enthusiastically.

'I'd like to meet this – this whaleman.'

'Then send the boat for him, sir. I think you should have a talk with him yourself.'

Carmichael summoned his messenger and gave the necessary order. He offered his executive a cigarette, and they both lit up. 'What about a drink?' he said.

'No, thank you. Not just now.'

Carmichael shrugged, and said, 'Everything has been quiet here. I found both managers very helpful. I've even been alongside the *Southern Cross* for fresh water. They're both on full production, and are nearly full up with whale-oil. They expect the tankers in about five days' time. It seems the stuff isn't shipped home until the end of the season.'

'I saw the tankers in South Georgia. Seems like they could lift a hell of a lot of cargo. I notice all radio is stopped on the whale-ships.'

'I had a job there.'

'Borgen picked up the directional bearings once he tumbled to the times. We zoned here from two or three hundred miles away. It was easy – far too easy. They might as well use their telephony, for all the difference it makes.'

'I was afraid of that.'

'What do you intend to do now, sir?' Gower asked the question anxiously.

'Wait until the ships have transferred their oil to the tankers. We go eastward then – to the Norwegians.'

'And the *Albatross*?'

'We'll keep her with us. Scott will take over tonight.'

'Well . . . I . . . Do you think he'll be all right, sir?'

Carmichael grinned. 'Look, Commander. Let us understand one another. Getting the *Albatross* fixed up was one thing; running her is another matter. I need you here. I can't do without you. I'm not going to do without you. Scott will take over the *Albatross*. I've already given him his instructions. He knows what is expected of him.'

Gower shook his head sadly. 'But—'

The conversation was interrupted by the arrival of the whaleboat skipper. He appeared in the doorway, cap in hand, apparently awed by the luxurious surroundings and the way he had been received on board. 'You sent for me, sir?' He ignored the commanding officer and spoke directly to Gower.

The executive officer smiled. 'This is Captain Carmichael. He wanted to meet you badly.'

Carmichael shook hands warmly. 'Let's sit down again. What about that drink now?'

'Yes. I will have one now. I'm sure Borgen here could do with one.'

'That's as good an excuse as any,' Carmichael said. 'We'd all like one.'

Hans Borgen was looking round the room with great interest. Except for acknowledging the commanding officer's greeting, he had not spoken.

Carmichael poured the drinks himself. Borgen sat back more relaxed. Gower was thinking about what Carmichael had just said. 'Blast it!' he muttered to himself. 'Blast it to hell!'

Carmichael was saying, 'Commander Gower gives me a glowing account of you, Captain. I thank you for volunteering for this job. Your help and knowledge will be of great assistance.'

Borgen beamed, his cherubic countenance breaking out into one expansive smile. 'It's nothing, sir. I'm only too glad to help. That goes for my engineers as well. I only hope we meet up with this raider.'

'I hope you will, Captain. You'll be getting a new commanding officer. Lieutenant Scott will be taking over the command.'

Borgen's face fell, but he made no comment.

'As I will have to stay around here until the whale-ships transfer their oil, I think it will be advisable if the *Albatross* takes a sweep to the eastward. You have sufficient fuel. Provision for a week, but be back within a period of four days. It's no use the two of us lying here.'

'No, sir.'

'Then leave at daybreak, Captain. Scott has already got his orders. Break radio silence if you sight anything. I wish you good luck.'

Gower accompanied the whaleboat skipper to the ladder. 'Good luck, Hans. Watch Lieutenant Scott. He's all right – but trust Watkins. The two of you – you'll get this raider!'

'Damn!' Fischer exclaimed savagely as he threw his gloves on the chartroom table. The *Viking* was again stopped – stopped by pack-ice, darkness, and now this fog. She had made good speed from the South Sandwich Islands. Reaching the ice-edge, she had followed the contour of the pack until the ice, coming up ahead and away to starboard, had forced them to stop until daylight. Now there had come this fog, and ice was closing in around them – scattered packs, to be sure, but scattered packs had a habit of forming into hard, complex masses, or so Fischer seemed to think.

Kaltenbrunner entered the chartroom on his way to the radio

cabin. Fischer was leaning over the table, his head close to the orange-coloured light. His eyes were red and staring.

'I thought you'd gone below, sir. You should have a rest. It's no good staying on the bridge for so long.'

Fischer smiled thinly. 'No, Lieutenant, I don't think I could lie down. Curse this delay! A few hours earlier, and we could have been at those British ships. They can't be far away – not by the sound of the bearings. They're bursting one's eardrums.'

'But there's ice between them and us. It means we have to get to the northward and around the ice. We can try if you like. The ice runs due north – a sort of promontory. The whale-ships are on the other side.'

'No, Lieutenant. Let's wait until we get some visibility. We'll only get ourselves into trouble – it's bad enough.'

The *Viking* jarred heavily – a hard scraping and grinding noise. The telegraphs clanged. Both Fischer and the supernumerary rushed out to the navigation bridge: the engines were turning dead slow ahead. The senior bridge officer was out on the leeward bridge-wing, staring down at the hard-looking ice. An extra-large growler, dark and menacing-looking, bumped and scraped against the *Viking*'s hull as it disappeared round the quarter. There was nothing but heavy ice out to leeward.

The bridge officer turned, and found his commanding officer staring hard over his shoulder. 'The ice is getting heavier, sir,' he said nervously. 'I just gave her slow ahead to clear that heavy one.'

Kaltenbrunner swung the telegraphs back to stop. 'Just clear the ice!' he said angrily. 'Don't go steaming round the whole Antarctic!'

Fischer nodded in approval. It's no use, he thought. We must keep on the bridge with these inexperienced officers. There's more danger here than if the whole of the British Navy were after us. He looked at the luminous dial of his watch – 0100 hours. Another two hours to dawn. The fog would persist. The wind was rising from the north-east – the worst weather.

They must be less than twenty miles from the whale-ships, and here was a whole day lost. If it was to clear they would have to get out of the way in case they were seen. Funny about this radio business. First they had been using telephony, and now it was all stopped. They were using only radio directional bearings now. What was happening?

His thoughts were interrupted by Kaltenbrunner. 'I think it's advisable to turn round, sir. Every time we move the engines it's driving her harder into the ice-pack. The wind's using our superstructure like a big sail. We're drifting like hell!' he added.

Fischer nodded wearily. 'Hard port!' he ordered brusquely, without answering the supernumerary officer. 'Slow ahead starboard engine!'

'Hard port, sir! Slow ahead starboard engine!' The order was quickly executed.

The cruiser swung slowly to port, pushing the ice away with her bows.

'Slow astern port engine!' Again Fischer's voice rapped out.

The cruiser's bows passed the direction of the wind, and fell away quickly to port.

'Stop engines! Amidships the helm!'

'Stop engines, sir! Amidships the helm!'

Fischer moved uneasily around the bridge. He glared at the gyro repeater. The *Viking* was lying on the reciprocal bearing.

'This looks better, sir. Makes one feel more comfortable. Every time we move the engines now it's keeping us away from the main pack.'

Fischer only grunted.

The blanket of fog lifted, but only momentarily; it curled in thicker than ever. There was ice all round them, hard, virgin ice, its size and thickness magnified by the poor visibility.

A tabular berg towered high over their stern – less than a hundred feet away. One of the bridge officers switched on the searchlight and stabbed the gloom: the berg was close and menacing.

Fischer grimaced. 'We must have been practically alongside that one when we turned round!'

'Looks better ahead, sir.'

Again Fischer grimaced. 'We'd better get out of this at daylight. It's always better in daylight. I don't know why. I suppose visibility is the same in fog, but daylight always seems to give one confidence.'

Kaltenbrunner was thinking, If we'd only taken one of the *Antarctica*'s whaleboats with us we could have captured those whale-ships tonight. They wouldn't have had a chance – not in this weather. Everything seemed to have gone wrong since they'd left the Norwegian ships. It had been so very easy up to then. Aloud he said, 'I was just thinking how we could have used one of those whaleboats we sank. That's what we miss now – a whaleboat. We made a mistake there. If we'd only known—'

'I've been thinking about the same thing,' Fischer said absently. 'I went against my official orders. That's what worries me.'

'We'll have all the whaleboats we want this time tomorrow. I shouldn't let it worry you, sir. Another forty-eight hours, and we'll have another two ships homeward bound to Germany!'

Fischer smiled for the first time – a forced smile. 'You live up to your reputation, Lieutenant. As I told you before, you're always the optimist.'

'There is just one thing, sir.'

'What?'

'I don't like this radio silence that's been going on. Three days ago I heard them use radio-telephony – unintelligible, I know, but they were using it. Why should they stop now? Why should they be sending directional bearings only?'

'Now you're being pessimistic, Lieutenant. It might be that they've not used radio-telephony throughout the whole of the season. You were probably mistaken. It could have been South Georgia that you heard.'

'That could be the only explanation, sir. Yet it doesn't seem right.'

The wind had increased to a fresh gale. Owing to the ice there was no swell. Kaltenbrunner crossed to the weather side and checked the drift. He returned to Fischer's side, and said, 'This is definitely better, sir. We're drifting with a forward movement – away from the main pack.'

'Iceberg right ahead, sir!' The voice came through the loudspeaker from forward.

Fischer slammed the telegraphs over to half-astern himself. The astern movement of the engines halted the forward momentum of the drift. The *Viking* drifted past the danger.

The searchlight again stabbed the gloom, playing on the sheer sides of the mountain of ice.

'Don't use that searchlight so much!' Fischer roared. 'That's the third time it's been on in the last ten minutes. Don't use it – not unless it's absolutely necessary!'

The *Queen of New Zealand* was now on patrol between the two whale-ships. Carmichael had found the manager of the *Southern Isles* just as co-operative. Everything was now organized; the tankers would be alongside in three days to receive their cargoes for transport to South Georgia. Another five days, and the *Queen of New Zealand* would be on her way to the eastward.

'Blast this weather!' Carmichael exclaimed. 'I don't mind the wind, but this fog! That's what gets me down. How these people can stand it I don't know.'

Gower smiled in the darkness. He had come on to the bridge to have a few words with the commanding officer before retiring for the night.

The *Queen of New Zealand* was drifting to a strong north-east gale. There had been few icebergs in the vicinity at dusk. Carmichael was taking advantage of this: every hour he was steaming the *Queen of New Zealand* up to windward for ten minutes to counteract the drift. He wanted to remain in the same position.

Daylight would be no more than a vague promise. As long as the wind came from the north-east there would be fog. There would be no whaling operations today.

He was thinking of this as he sheltered with Gower on the wing of the bridge. 'You know, Commander,' he said, 'I think this is a complete waste of time. Imagine ... just imagine having to come all this distance to try and fight a war! There's nothing going to happen down here. It's a waste of time. Those Lords of the Admiralty! What the hell are they doing just now? I bet they've forgotten all about us. The—'

'Whaleboat coming up from the stern, sir!' a bridge officer reported.

'A whaleboat! What does a whaleboat want with us in this weather?'

The catcher vessel circled them, blinking away with an Aldis lamp.

'He wants to come alongside, sir. Important news to communicate. That's what he's sending.'

'It's a good job somebody can read him: we can't.'

'What can he want?' Gower asked. 'It must be something important!'

'Tell him to come alongside.'

'Which side, sir?' the bridge officer asked.

'Any side! Just tell him to come alongside. Better go down, Commander. See what they want.'

The catcher came speeding alongside the starboard side, and drew up amidships. There was a whale moored to her port side, which acted as a fender between the two vessels. A ladder was quickly lowered to the deck of the whaleboat. A seaman separated himself from a group standing on the foredeck. He began his climb.

What on earth is all this? Carmichael thought, as he watched the climber enter the ship. Funny way to deliver a message. Why can't they send it on board in a written message?

Gower came up on to the bridge. 'I have put him in your room, sir. He's the whale-gunner from the *Antarctica I*. He reports that a German raider either sank or captured both of the Norwegian whale-ships.'

'Come!' Carmichael went below with alacrity, the executive officer following at his heels.

The whale-gunner was standing in the middle of the room as they entered. Carmichael shook hands immediately, and said, 'Please take a chair, Captain. You say that both expeditions were destroyed or captured?'

'Yes, sir.'

'Give us your whole story, Captain Hansen. It's much better than if I questioned you.' He glanced at Gower. 'Give it to us in your own words – that will be better.'

Hansen went on to enumerate all the facts that led him to seek to the westward until he finally came up with the *Southern Cross*. 'As soon as I reached the *Southern Cross*,' he said, 'and knew that you were here, the manager decided I should report to you immediately. That's why I'm here in this weather.'

Carmichael had listened in silence throughout the whole of the story. He said, 'You never actually saw this raider?'

'No, sir.'

'So we don't know if they were actually sunk or captured. We've only the flotsam as evidence.'

'That's correct, sir.'

'You're right, Captain. That's what they've done. They sank the catcher fleets and captured the whale-ships. They'll be on their way back to Germany – now!'

Gower agreed.

'Right, Captain Hansen. You get back to the *Southern Cross*. Join up with her expedition for the present. All we can do is to assume guard duty. That's what we try to do now. This raider will come here. We are waiting....'

CHAPTER TWENTY-ONE

'What the hell's that?' Borgen said hoarsely.

'What?'

'That light I just saw. To the south. Looked like a searchlight – something like that.'

Petty Officer Watkins grinned. 'You can't see any distance in this. Must be your imagination. That's what it is – imagination. You've been too long at that wheel. Why don't you take some rest?'

The whaleboat skipper shook his head vigorously. 'No, Watkins, it wasn't imagination. There was definitely . . . Look! There! In that direction!'

Watkins probed with his glasses at the indicated bearing. 'Yes, Hans, there is something. Must be one of the whaleboats. It couldn't be anything else.'

The *Albatross* was patrolling the north and eastern areas of the bay where the British whale-ships were operating. The weather had been clear, and they had noticed the long ice promontory that jutted to the northward. Now the barometer was falling: wind and sea were increasing, and there was driving sleet and poor visibility.

Borgen had advised Scott against sheltering in the lee of the pack-ice. He knew that if the raider were to come from the eastward, then she would fetch up to the south and on the wrong side of the promontory. Before she got to the whaleships she would have to round this point–the ice was too thick otherwise.

'No, Watkins, that was no whaleboat. I don't know what it is, but it's no whaleboat. What whaleboat would lie on the windward side of this pack on a night like this? The whale-gunners look for comfort in bad weather. Besides, they're on rationed operations. They're all round the factory-ships. You'd better call Scott. You'd better get him up here.'

'Right, Hans, if you say so.' The Petty Officer rushed from the bridge.

The *Albatross* was rolling and pitching heavily to a confused sea and swell. There were many icebergs in the vicinity. Hundreds of ice-growlers, calved from some barrier berg, were drifting menacingly around. From the bridge of the whaleboat, a ship that could practically turn in her own length, the area looked dangerous.

I wish Gower were here, thought the whaleboat skipper. It isn't the same – not with Scott in command. He's all right, but . . . There seemed to be something about him. Watkins felt the same way. It had brought them closer together: they had even become friends.

Scott came on to the bridge. He lifted his glasses and probed the darkness ahead. 'It must be a whaleboat. What large ship would come into this stuff? There's more danger here on a night like this than any man-made danger. You must be mistaken.'

Borgen shrugged in the darkness. 'It's much easier to get into this stuff than out of it. I know . . . I've experienced it.'

'There's nothing – now.'

'No. But there was before.'

'What shall we do?'

'Let's go and see.' He reached out a hand and put the telegraph to slow ahead.

'Yes, let's go and see.'

Borgen smiled in the darkness. He wiped the sleet and wetness from his eyes: they were red and strained. He was at the helm himself; he wouldn't allow any of the naval ratings to take over.

Again the light probed the blackness, sweeping faintly in a wide arc of the horizon. The look-out men reported it immediately.

'Has a whaleboat got a light like that? No, sir!' Borgen answered his own question. 'You'd better get the crew to action stations, sir.'

Scott gave the order. Again Watkins hurried from the bridge.

'What else could it be?' scoffed the whaleboat skipper. 'It's the Nazi bastard all right. We'll steer up to windward – less chance of them spotting us.'

'What if it isn't this raider? We have to be careful. We can't fire torpedoes into something we can't identify.'

'My God! We can't go and ask her name! What else could it be? This is our chance – our only chance. Take it, man . . . take it!'

The searchlight snaked out again, it's light probing the darkness before it petered out in a faint glow. Borgen sprang from the helm to the compass and took a bearing. 'We're not far off now.'

Scott nodded silently.

The sea and swell had gone down. They were pushing through scattered pack-ice that was forming a natural breakwater between the open sea and the whaleboat. The wind still raged and clamoured around them. They slid past a large iceberg dangerously close to starboard, its cavernous sides gapingly open and close in the darkness.

The young officer coughed nervously. 'If this is the raider, then she's got herself into a hell of a tangle.'

Borgen grinned in the darkness. 'It is the raider! Can't be anything else!'

'We'd better make sure.'

'We will be sure. Before we can fire those torpedoes in this ice we'll have to go practically alongside. You can't miss!'

Watkins was down on the foredeck already checking torpedoes and mechanism; his crew were clustered around him. They could be heard as they moved about in the darkness.

The ice was heavier. The whaleboat skipper kept the engines at slow speed as he conned the *Albatross* up to windward, always swinging her bows away to clear most of the dangerous ice-growlers.

'We could never fire our torpedoes in this ice,' Scott said morosely. 'We must have open water.'

'We'll have open water all right – good open water. The ship herself is making open water. As she drifts through this ice she's leaving a trail of open water behind her. That's what we're after – open water to windward of her. You can plant those two torpedoes right into her guts! She won't know what's hit her.'

'We'd better make sure!' Again the young officer repeated himself.

The dark silhouette of a large berg slipped along the port side. Scott gave a startled gasp as he thought it was the unknown vessel. Borgen grinned, and looked at the compass. He altered two points to starboard, and said, 'She's about four points on the starboard bow. We keep her going for a little. See if we can make anything out.'

'We must be close – very close. Watch—'

'I know where the bastard is!' Borgen spoke in a hoarse whisper, as if to himself.

The wet sleet had stopped, and fog came billowing in from the north-east. Scott looked over the front of the bridge: the bows were hardly visible.

Again the whaleboat skipper went to starboard. 'Look for a streak of open water,' he said. 'That'll be our quarry. She leaves the open water behind her. We must cross it if we keep going to starboard. That's our only guide – now!'

Scott nodded. He had completely forgotten about the hidden ice dangers that lay around them in the blackness in this death-stalk after a stationary but hidden enemy. The whaleboat struck some heavy ice with considerable violence without either of the men paying attention.

'Dead slow speed!' Borgen spoke into the voice-pipe that led to the engine-room. He wasn't using the telegraph now. 'These torpedoes may be going off any minute. I hope you know what to expect – what's happening.'

'Yes!' The voice came back up the voice-pipe.

'Good! Then watch that funnel – no sparks!'

'Right! See that you get the Nazi bastards! Don't fire those torpedoes the way you used to fire the harpoon-gun. You're sure to miss her!'

Borgen grunted, but made no reply.

The creaming bow wave of the *Albatross* died away to a gentle ripple as Borgen ordered the engines to be stopped; the throb of the heavy steam-engine melted to a far-off sound as they slipped quietly across the last bearing of the searchlight.

The whaleboat skipper froze to immobility. 'There! There! There is open water! . . .'

'Another hour, and we should get some light,' Fischer said.

'We'll try and move to the northward – out of this ice. I don't like it here, Lieutenant. No, I don't like it here. There's danger here. We don't want to see the *Viking* wrecked, not before we get to those whale-ships.'

Kaltenbrunner smiled to himself in the darkness. Fischer's nerves were getting the better of him, he thought. This was nothing. The whale-ships experienced this many times during the course of a whaling season. Sometimes they were lucky if they ever saw open water. The ice didn't scare them. Aloud he said, 'We can move out of this at daybreak. It won't be any clearer, but, as you say, daylight always makes a difference. Yes, sir, we'll move out of this at daylight.'

Fischer nodded. He was far beyond weariness. At intervals, which could have been a minute, an hour, or a day, he would peer into the darkness from both sides of the bridge. What he was looking for he didn't know. Could have been ice; could have been the whale-ships; could have been whaleboats. His eyes were dark and brooding as he stared silently into the forbidding darkness.

Wenzel came out of the chartroom. 'The glass is still falling, sir. Looks as if it's going to continue.'

Fischer didn't say anything. The voice had startled him. At last he said, 'Your gun-crews, Lieutenant, they're on stand-by?'

'Yes, sir. You said last night to keep a skeleton crew at action stations. The guns are all manned.'

'Good! Then we're safe from the prying eyes of any whaleboat that may come across us?'

'Yes, sir.'

'Good! Then shoot to destroy. Don't let any boat get away that may accidentally sight us. We must not be discovered.'

'That's where she's drifting – down that open lane.' Borgen left the wheel and joined the Lieutenant, who was peering over the front of the bridge. 'She's not far away – about half a mile. Creep . . . creep down slowly! That's what we'll do. Creep down slowly! Go down now, sir. I'll take you to this raider.'

Scott nodded, and went to join Watkins and his crew on the foredeck.

Borgen spoke softly into the voice-pipe. 'Just keep her turning – that's enough! Watch her ... we're close!' He adjusted the helm. There was a grimness about him – a grimness born of a life at sea in small ships. He was speaking to himself now. 'Steady she goes. Steady she goes. Down this line of bearing. She's lying there ... lying there drifting. Two torpedoes – right in the guts. When she goes she'll just disappear, like a moth with burned wings. Steady she goes. There! There she is!' The grin expanded into a beaming smile.

The *Viking* was like some ghost ship as she lay drifting in the glacial seascape. Swirls of fog, curling in from the north-east, hung around her like some shroud. Except for the narrow expanse of water, which she herself was making as she drifted through the pack, she was completely surrounded by great masses of ice.

The searchlight stabbed the darkness, swung around the horizon, missing the *Albatross*, and pin-pointed a barrier berg dangerously close to the head. Its sides, catacombed by countless gaping caverns, rose sheer out of the water no more than a hundred feet ahead of the cruiser.

The *Albatross* was closing – closing fast. The engineers could hear Borgen's voice as he droned on: 'Easy does it. Not so fast. Just easy. Now come to port. Port easy. Stop engines!'

The engines stopped instantly.

'Wait ... wait!' The whaleboat skipper again spoke to himself as he adjusted the helm. 'Now! Now! Let the Nazi bastards have it! Now! Now!' His voice rose in a swelling chord.

The proximity of danger does strange things to men. Lieutenant Scott, unsure of himself, uncertain of which ship he was about to torpedo – perhaps because it was against his principles, his way of life, to cause unwanton slaughter – hesitated. He peered uncertainly into the gloom.

'Wait!' he muttered. 'Wait!'

Petty Officer Watkins, his eyes trained on the sights, his fingers reaching for the firing mechanism, was shouting, 'It's time to fire, sir! We can't get any closer ! It's time to fire!' He could hardly recognize his own voice. This Lieutenant didn't seem to understand!

Again the searchlight probed the darkness. It swung from the icebergs slowly to windward, and caught and held the *Albatross* in its powerful rays. Alarm-bells rang. The *Viking*'s guns commenced firing. . . .

Borgen came screaming from the bridge. 'Fire! Fire, you stupid fools!'

Petty Officer Watkins pressed the trigger. . . .

The torpedoes couldn't miss. Both struck the *Viking* amidships as tracer shells swept the decks of the whaleboat. There was one great roar as a magazine exploded. A series of explosions followed. . . . Flying debris told the rest of the story.

The *Albatross*, men dying about her decks, drifted slowly through the ice. . . .

CHAPTER TWENTY-TWO

'How many survivors were there?' The Governor asked.

'Only three – Petty Officer Watkins and the two engineers. We picked them up in the morning. The *Albatross* didn't sink.'

'How long was it before the *Viking* went?'

'She practically disintegrated. The torpedoes struck her amidships; she broke in two and slid below the surface. Within a short time the ice closed in, and there was nothing to be seen. The ice was her Valhalla.'

'You can't blame yourself for the loss of life on the *Albatross*, Captain. You brought your mission to a successful conclusion. You did what you were sent down to do.'

'Yes, I did. But if I'd left Gower in command there would have been no loss of life. That was my fault, my fault entirely. I knew that young Scott was unstable. I should never have sent him on the *Albatross*. I should have taken Gower's advice. If I had, then Borgen would have been alive today; the others would have been alive.'

'That's the fortune of war, Captain. Anything could have happened. If it hadn't been for the weather, and that the *Albatross* found the *Viking* like a sitting duck, she couldn't have sunk her. No, sir! You are wrong – definitely wrong.'

Carmichael shrugged. He was looking through the window at the *Queen of New Zealand* anchored in Stanley roadstead.

'What do you do now?'

'I wait until the end of the whaling season, and then escort both whale-ships and tankers to Freetown. They go in convoy from there. We return home on our own. I won't be sorry.'

The Governor grinned. 'Let me fix a couple of drinks. We have something to celebrate. Something good!' He went to a cabinet and took out a bottle of whisky and a siphon of soda. He filled the glasses and handed one to Carmichael.

'Thanks. I don't think there is very much to celebrate, sir.'

'Here, Captain. This should cheer you up.' He turned over a

message that was lying on his desk and handed it to Carmichael. 'It came last night,' he said. 'It's been decoded.'

Captain Carmichael read the message.

ADMIRALTY TO GOVERNOR FALKLAND ISLAND DEPENDENCIES.

INFORM COMMANDING OFFICER QUEEN OF NEW ZEALAND NORWEGIAN WHALESHIPS ANTARCTICA AND CACHELOT INTERCEPTED BY BRITISH CRUISER OFF THE AZORES. SHIPS RECAPTURED AND MEN FREED.

They both drank.

THE END

G. F. Newman has already achieved popular recognition and a firm reputation as one of Britain's leading writers of tough, authentic police thrillers. His most famous best-selling novels include, *Sir, You Bastard, You Nice Bastard, The Player and the Guest, Three Professional Ladies* and *Billy*. London born, he now divides his time between Ireland, where he keeps bees and horses, and Soho, where he keeps mainly bad company.

'Mr Newman has a well-earned reputation for his wickedly funny, tough British police stories, where the cops are usually supposed to be on "earners" as soon as they get into plain clothes and the crooks are real low-lifes. In *The Guvnor*, the principal is a detective chief superintendent, ambitious, ruthless, young for his rank, more interested in results than rules. But he goes a bit far when he condones a jail-break to nail the top man in a crime syndicate. A lot of action takes place in Scotland ... there's an excellent Starsky and Hutch-style chase scene, and some fine salty language. Love interest well handled, too.
The Scotsman

Also by G. F. Newman

Sir, You Bastard
Billy
You Nice Bastard
The Player and the Guest
The Split
Three Professional Ladies
The Price
Law and Order (series)

G. F. Newman

The Guvnor

PANTHER
GRANADA PUBLISHING
London Toronto Sydney New York

Published by Granada Publishing
in Panther Books 1978

ISBN 0 586 04327 6

First published in Great Britain by Hart-Davis,
MacGibbon Ltd 1977

Granada Publishing Limited
Frogmore, St Albans, Herts AL2 2NF
and
3 Upper James Street, London W1R 4BP
1221 Avenue of the Americas, New York, NY 10020, USA
117 York Street, Syndey, NSW 2000, Australia
100 Skyway Avenue, Toronto, Ontario, Canada M9W 3A6
Trio City, Coventry Street, Johannesburg 2001, South Africa
CML Centre, Queen & Wyndham, Auckland 1, New Zealand

Made and printed in Great Britain by
Richard Clay (The Chaucer Press) Ltd
Bungay, Suffolk
Set in Linotype Times

All characters, names, crimes and incidents contained herein have been invented. Any similarities to persons living or dead are coincidental. Offices have been named solely for the sake of locale and the book is in no way intended to reflect attitudes or opinions of those persons holding such offices.

Part of this book previously appeared in the form of a screenplay by Troy Kennedy Martin and G. F. Newman.

Prologue

'The lousy bastards,' Daniel Rochester said for no one's benefit. The words were quiet, their bitterness lost.

The site clerk in the parked mobile office glanced across at the resident engineer, but didn't comment. His boss was cracking up. Minor things were getting past him nowadays, things that at one time Rochester wouldn't have allowed. The current building project was in its early stages, barely two months old; how the RE would shape up when pressures on the contract began to get heavy, he didn't speculate.

He had been with Rochester for three years, since the start of the Bermondsey hi-lo-rise housing estate. The project had run as smoothly as a Rolls-Royce motor car, the unavoidable snags and hold-ups dealt with swiftly and competently. His boss hadn't been boozing then, nor preoccupied to a point where things not directly related to his problem – whatever it was – got past him. The clerk was pissed off. Daniel Rochester would make trouble for everyone in the long run. The usual inevitable snags would cause delays without firm action and instant decisions from the resident engineer; the whole project would get behind, run into penalty time. Then no one would earn anything worthwhile, neither in bonuses nor those bent numbers to be had around a large, well organised building project.

From the confusion of paperwork on his desk, the clerk selected a wad of delivery advice notes. He leafed through them quickly, his right hand dropping with easy, co-ordinated movements onto the keys of an electronic calculator.

There was a sickening, despairing anger churning over in Rochester's stomach; it brought the taste of gin and an acid bile to the back of his throat. He almost wished he could be sick, rid himself of his problems in one cathartic fountain of vomit. But an easy end to those problems was nowhere in sight. What *was* in sight was a worsening mess.

The bastards! The lousy bastards. The expression ran on

a loop through his mind. He hadn't believed they would do it – they had promised. Alex Jacobs, that time he had managed to see him, had given his emphatic assurance. But watching the four articulated lorries wind along the cinder service road, Rochester felt himself grow numb. At first he thought his lunchtime gin intake was the cause. He read the name on the sides of the cream-coloured lorries. *Frank O'Connor & Son.* Nothing very surprising in that. O'Connors were the main contractors. His eyes moved across the twenty-foot iron sections of the two tower cranes chained on the lorries. They were the same cream colour, with the same bold red lettering. He sought out the red legends on various lattice-work sections trying to tell himself it was a mistake. But even in his alcohol-dulled state he couldn't begin to convince himself. The two tower cranes belonged to O'Connors, were part of the whole fleet of machinery they were moving onto the site. They weren't the two Rochire Plant tower cranes that they had agreed to use for the duration, along with most of the other plant that Rochester's own company now had standing idle.

Until those four lorries rolled on to the site Rochester had been able to delude himself that his plant would be used, even though logic told him otherwise – no one from O'Connors had been on to his company to agree long-term hire prices, or exchange contracts. Now the last delusive veneer was stripped away, and Rochester knew the kind of financial trouble his company was heading into. It was already way out of its depth – and so was he. He had tried to run with the big boys and make a killing, instead of being satisfied with that steady, untaxed, untraceable money from O'Connors that weekly had almost doubled his official income from the GLC. Why hadn't he been satisfied? God, why had he ever let them talk him into forming a plant hire company? A turmoil of figures swirled around in his head as he listened to the calculator across the office. All those thousands the bank had lent him to finance the business; with zero income, the majority of his plant lying idle, he couldn't even service the initial loan. The bankers Duckett, Reinhardt, who had been so co-operative at the start of the venture, offering all sorts of assistance after O'Connors' recommendation, were no longer very helpful. They wanted their interest and weren't about to advance more capital for yard rentals, wage bills or to tide Rochire Plant over so that they could re-enter the market with cut-throat rates.

In the face of these mounting problems, Alex Jacobs, contracts director at O'Connors, and co-director of Rochire Plant, seemed unperturbed – and, for all Rochester knew, was, for he rarely managed to reach Jacobs these days. At the height of the Bermondsey contract they had lived in each other's pocket. It was futile wishing they were back at Bermondsey. Padding specifications so that the bills of quantities were far in excess of actual requirements, then telling whoever one wanted the contract to go to just what price to tender; that, along with recommending the same outfit for all untendered work once on site, and passing work which ordinarily wouldn't get passed, that was the area of corruption on building contracts which Rochester understood and with which he could cope.

The combined hi-lo-rise housing project at Bermondsey was about nine months along and ahead of schedule, something which happened infrequently. It was known to be due in large part to Daniel Rochester's efficiency.

Rochester had been to one of his familiar Friday lunches with Alex Jacobs, during which he had collected his monthly ex gratia salary of two hundred pounds. It was then that the contracts director had mooted the proposition of their going into the plant hire business.

Straight faced Rochester said, 'But it's illegal for GLC employees to enter into those kind of business ventures. It might mean at some time that I would be hiring plant to myself, Alex. They discourage that sort of vested interest.'

The large, dark eyes of the man across the table locked on Rochester's expression, his calculating mind considering whether he could have read him incorrectly after all this while.

'Quite right,' Jacobs said with a wry smile. 'Perish the

thought of a public employee taking advantage of his position to enter into such a profitable enterprise.' He knew now that the RE wasn't serious.

Rochester needed little selling on the idea. 'How profitable do you imagine such a venture might prove, Alex?'

'That would depend on a number of factors. Certainly we're talking about a lot more money than you're drawing at present.' He pulled out a silver pencil and scribbled sums on the napkin. 'On this site alone there's something like four thousand pounds per week in plant. On average we can expect a twenty-five per cent profit margin over two years. Plus, of course, one comes out having paid off the initial loan.'

'What about continuity of hire?' That was Rochester's only real doubt.

'No problem, Daniel. O'Connors would guarantee continual hire of all the plant, provided of course that our association goes on as happily. You were able to help us get the contracts to keep the plant working.'

The details were easily worked out. Rochester's wife, Mavis, would be the company secretary, with Rochester and Jacobs as directors. Alex Jacobs knew all the roads to the bank, the plant manufacturers and the yards from which to operate; he simply steered Rochester.

At that point, not even in his wildest nightmares did Rochester predict that in just over two years he would be inextricably involved in a company which was in hock to the tune of ninety thousand pounds; that he personally would be in for another sixteen thousand, with a second mortgage taken on his house by the bank in addition.

Quite what had gone wrong, and how, he wasn't sure. The slump in building due to the general recession was the most apparent reason. But O'Connors had remained active, and after that first good year, Rochester couldn't make out why things began falling apart, why his plant wasn't working. He had fulfilled his side of the bargain. It was his active participation which had helped secure O'Connors the Mazehill high-rise housing project in Battersea, the biggest contract he had so far undertaken. But all they gave on their side was empty promises. Now, instead of having his machinery on site for two years plus, he watched their lorries bring in *their* plant.

The bastards!

Daily, as things got further beyond the control that had once ordered his life, Rochester grew more and more determined not to sink alone. If they let him go under, he would do everything in his power to bring them down. He had an awful lot of information about O'Connors and how they operated. He wasn't the only public employee to have taken their money; the network was vast, and Rochester couldn't begin to speculate what tens of thousands, even hundreds of thousands of pounds the various pay-offs all over the country amounted to.

As yet the resident engineer hadn't taken to keeping a bottle in the office to answer his need. And his need at that moment was quite intense; a vague, ill-defined pain that only a drink would ease.

Flipping back his cuff he saw that it was turned two-thirty – barely time for another drink before the pub closed at three, which meant going to Gladys's. She ran a drinking club where, reputedly, one could get a drink at any time. Rochester didn't doubt it. Gladys's had been open whenever he'd been there, or had opened at a rap on the door. It was probably as well not to go to the pub next to the site; the solitary remaining building in the whole acreage that had not been devastated by bulldozers, it stood like some obelisk marking a vanished epoch, and anyone approaching it was identifiable a mile off.

The clerk glanced up as his boss pulled on his heavy sheepskin and went out. He didn't comment, but guessed where the RE was going, and knew where he would be if he was wanted urgently. Likely as not there wouldn't be anything cropping up that he couldn't handle himself.

'Put another one in there, Glad,' Rochester said, shoving his glass across the table at the club-owner as she moved around collecting empties. His words were becoming slurred, his manner truculent, but none of the other nine customers took much notice. Either they were at the same place he was, or had been at some time.

'D'you want any tonic water with this one?' the large woman with henna-dyed hair asked, without removing the cigarette from her lips. The last three she had served him had been straight. She didn't mind one way or the other, only some men preferred pacing themselves to oblivion.

'What's your problem then, darlin'?' she said, not unkindly, as she fetched a bottle. She splashed gin into Rochester's glass and, easing her excess weight on to a chair at the table, carefully recapped the bottle. She waited while the man tilted the glass against his lips and swallowed. Gladys shuddered. She could drink almost anything that was set before her, but gin was the exception. From the general make-up of customers passing through her bar the woman figured she knew something about drunks; most of it she didn't want to know. The texture of his face told her the man hadn't been boozing this heavily for long; he had been using her club for about two months, but before now she had had no real inclination to talk to him. He had always seemed a bit standoffish, unlike most drunks.

Rochester took another pull at his glass and finished the gin, making no attempt to communicate with her. She poured some more.

'You really are giving it some stick, aren't you? Like you meant it. That bad?'

A vacuous expression fell over the RE's face as he wrestled helplessly with his problems. They wouldn't go away. All he had to do was dig through the alcohol-deadened layers.

'The bastards,' he said quietly. Then, to reinforce it, 'Fucking bastards!'

The violence in the words startled Gladys. She reached out to him in a calming manner, something she rarely did. Drunks couldn't distinguish between friend and foe. Rochester knocked her arm away.

'Just take it easy, darlin'. You're among friends here.'

'They really think they've found a prize chump. That's what. Well, they haven't. Let me tell you. They haven't.'

He caught hold of the woman to press home his point. His words were indistinct but Gladys could decipher the most incoherent conversation. The others around the club weren't even listening, for most of them had heard it all before. Rochester was sounding off about O'Connors, what they had done to him and what he was going to do to them.

Seeing how one-sided this was going to be, Gladys decided the man was best left alone. A couple of customers who had just walked in provided the excuse. The woman topped up his drink, then rose, taking the bottle back to the bar.

He would call Alex Jacobs, that's what he would do, Rochester decided. Tell him just what he intended doing about O'Connors and the whole corrupt show. Or had he done that? He couldn't remember clearly, but had some recollection of having called and told that stuck-up secretary of Jacobs' just what he intended. Maybe he hadn't. He would go to their Millbank offices, demand to see him, have it out.

Tipping his glass back, Rochester's watery gaze fell on David Champion, who was sitting at the far end of the bar with a colleague. Champion was one of O'Connors' senior quantity surveyors and frequently visited the site, though lately he'd seen less and less of the RE. Rochester realised why: he was in league with Jacobs, and knew just what was going on.

Champion reacted too slowly to avoid a confrontation with the figure lurching across the club. On entering he hadn't seen Rochester or he wouldn't have stayed. The man fell across him as he pulled away from the wild, disconnected punch. Champion fell off the bar stool and the RE crashed to the floor on top of him, swearing and hitting out at him.

'Hey, what's going on?'

Gladys came round the bar protesting. The man with

Champion tried to pull Rochester off him.

'Come on. D'you want me closed down? Nice goings on.'

'Are you mad?' Champion said, scrabbling away. No one else moved to assist either party.

'Making a bloody fool outta me ... you tell Mr Alex Jacobs and Sir bloody Frank O'Connor that they won't get away ...' Again he swung at Champion, his arm stopping abruptly against Gladys's solid mass.

'Enough of it. Or you'll have to leave.'

'You're drunk,' Champion said, getting to his feet. 'You don't know what you're saying.'

'I'll get you all put away. Crooked bastards ...' For the first time he noticed the woman, who was physically supporting him. 'Give me a gin, Glad.'

'Only if you're a good boy and behave yourself.' She didn't need help getting the man into a chair.

Champion and his colleague left, after an apprehensive glance in Rochester's direction. Both knew there was danger in him. At the moment, like the times before, he was drunk, and no one paid serious attention to what drunks said. But if he started making his allegations when sober, people might begin to take notice.

Making a right-hand signal, the grey saloon car swept across Falcon Road in front of an oncoming bus and pulled up outside Gladys's club. The driver, a thick-necked man with a Gannex raincoat that was too tight across his broad shoulders, slid from behind the wheel and moved into the narrow entrance of the club. There was a ritual for gaining admittance and the man observed it, even though he wasn't a member and hadn't been there before.

At the bar he ordered a drink from the fat lady, whom he knew was Gladys, and exchanged a few words in a casual, familiar way that would neither get him noticed nor remembered. His glance swept the club, looking for Daniel Rochester. This was one of the four places he had been given where the RE might be. The site office was one, but he hadn't been there. The resident engineer's office, like the site itself, had been in darkness. Rochester wasn't here, unless he was taking a leak. The man finished half his drink, set the glass down, then moved out to the toilet. Rochester wasn't there either. The man didn't return to the bar.

The pub along the road was the third place he tried. He found Rochester there, with a load on and shooting his mouth off, as he had so thoughtlessly done many times before. The man in the Gannex went directly up to him.

'Mr Rochester? Daniel Rochester?' he said in a quiet, firm tone. There wasn't any doubt. He put out a steadying hand, as though in anticipation of what he was about to tell him. 'Got some bad news for you, old son.' He pitched his voice so that no one else would hear. 'It's your wife ...' he paused. 'Afraid she's met with an accident.'

'Mavis? What?' Awareness instantly started piercing the confusion caused by uncounted gins. 'Accident? What's happened? Where is she?'

'Hammersmith. I'll take you. My car's outside.'

Instinctively Rochester started out with the man, assuming he was from either the police or the hospital, not stopping to question. Hammersmith worried him as they drove. What was his wife doing there? They lived in Dulwich. He groped for one clear thought, but his mind was full of cotton wool. She didn't have any relatives in Hammersmith; her only sister lived in Kent. No friends there. Did she? The channel that had begun to clear immediately filled with more cotton wool. The man driving told him to prepare himself for a shock, then, in his next breath, to try not to worry. He thought of Mavis being hit by that bus; lying under its front wheels. Was that what had happened? Or was it the bus overtaking them around Shepherd's Bush Green which had jumped into his mind? Poor Mavis. He felt culpable, and was overwhelmed with remorse.

The grey Volvo turned north into Wood Lane and travelled past the television centre. Before reaching Du Cane Road to make a left turn for Hammersmith Hospital, as Rochester expected, the car swung across the road and up the ramp to the site of the Westway motorway construction. The cotton wool intervened again. No longer were they going to his wife in hospital; but he was paying a visit to the Westway project to check something out, even though the job wasn't in his district.

The car bounced along the uneven surface of the railway-sleeper track, heading for a single arc light. The low whirr and rattle of a premixed concrete lorry could be heard. As the car drew closer the RE saw the lorry parked on the ramps, the arc light on the back of it. The Volvo stopped and the driver got out and moved around, passing between the car and the concrete lorry.

Mavis.

The image of his wife hit him. He was supposed to see her in hospital. What was he doing on the Westway site? Who was the man who had driven him? Why was there no one else around?

'Look here, what's going on?' Rochester demanded, starting from the car. 'What's happened to my wife?'

'Ah, suddenly sober, Mr Bigmouth, are you?'

'What . . .?'

Rochester didn't see the second man who approached from behind, he only felt the pain as he was struck across the back of the head. It was more intense than sitting up sharply with the worst hangover, except for the certain knowledge that he wouldn't recover. His leg muscles had lost their stiffening; he was floundering, the cotton wool filling his head again; his arms flailed as he went down, his fingers catching on something, a button, but it didn't support his falling weight.

Chapter 1

Rain slanted down steadily, occasionally thrown off course by gusts of wind. The canopy formed by the Westway fly-over offered little protection to the five men. Traffic crawled monotonously past, tyres throwing up dirty rainwater which caught on the gusts and added to the discomfort. The men weren't in danger from passing traffic, but the local uniformed police should have been called in to give them a clear lane; that, though, would have meant more policemen knowing what they were about. The fewer people who knew the better.

Fordham had had word passed to Hammersmith police station that they were up to something along the Westway; he hadn't spoken to the local chief superintendent himself. One of his detective chief inspectors, who had once been stationed there, had called, and had been purposely vague. There were no objections, but the call simply covered them should a radio car show up and the uniforms inside not take the hint when told to piss off. The CID in general didn't waste much time explaining their moves to the uniform branch, and the Squad wasted even less.

Fordham's gaze turned from the slow stream of cars and met Frank Borroughs's eyes. The big DCI pulled a face. It wasn't the best day for this type of operation and he'd sooner have been back in his office at the Yard. Why either of them were here, Fordham wasn't too sure. He didn't often get involved personally in this end of enquiries. There were too many detectives under him to send out in the rain. He guessed it was the lack of progress on the case, which had now been going on for fifteen months, that had caused his initial reaction. The Westway was a digression, but it had looked worthwhile.

The third detective present was Inspector Leslie Norman, who ran one of the ten squads within the umbrella of the Squad. He had received information that a key witness they had been seeking all this time was concreted into one of the stanchions along the elevated section of the motorway. 'Wouldn't that be just our fucking luck,' had been Fordham's reaction.

'What do you think, Les?' he now asked flatly.

The DI shrugged, trying to keep a low profile. His information might have been wrong. 'The man didn't say which stanchion, guv. Only this section.' Fordham didn't reply, and the DI glanced at Frank Borroughs, as if for support.

'How reliable d'you reckon his information was, Les?' Borroughs asked, wiping the rain from his face. He would happily have quit then. If the man they were after was tucked up in the column he wasn't going any place. But he understood why the guvnor was pursuing the matter in this way.

'Who can say? I mean, he's not going to earn anything, is he? A punch in the mouth, if he fucks us around.'

Rare indeed would be the occasion when Fordham wasn't prepared to back the judgment of detectives like Norman. The DIs were often the men with their ears closest to the ground. If ever the time arrived when he felt he couldn't back a man, then it meant that he was no longer wanted on the Squad. That day certainly hadn't arrived for Les Norman.

Casually Fordham glanced the length of the Westway, feeling slightly depressed at the thought of examining all the pillars on this elevated section. The huge concrete boles seemed to stretch through the rain into infinity: to Acton westwards and Holland Park in the opposite direction. He hadn't counted, but there were a lot of stanchions.

The two scientists from the forensic lab weren't happy about being out in this weather with their sophisticated infra-red photographic apparatus. Both were far more concerned with keeping that dry than they were about themselves. Neither had any appreciation of Fordham's need for secrecy, and he hadn't enlightened them. He had simply told them what he wanted and asked if they could and would do it. Had they refused, he would have found another way around the problem. Fordham was very resourceful.

The infra-red camera on its telescopic hydraulic lift finished the slow descent of the seventh column. The result was negative. The two men looked beseechingly towards Fordham, before winding off the wheel-locks and proceeding to the next pillar. Norman went to help; Fordham and Borroughs stayed put.

'I'd go and sit in the car,' Fordham said, 'but I'm sure they'd quit on us if I did.'

'Think you'll lose them before long anyway, if their machine gets rained on much more.' Borroughs cleared the catarrh from his throat and spat into the passing traffic. 'D'you think it really works?'

'They've had a couple of results.' Fordham only knew what he'd read about the recently developed camera in the *Police Review*. At first it had read like something out of a science-fiction comic; but forensic science seemed increasingly to be moving into that area. It was useful in establishing evidence and helping to secure convictions, but it wasn't much use when it came to capturing villains. You had to think and react like a criminal for that. That was where detectives like Fordham scored.

Through the noise of traffic and the rain the buzz of excitement from the three men at the concrete pillar was clearly defined. It was reflected in their movements – the numbed listlessness of a wet February afternoon was gone. Fordham felt the prickles of anticipation as Norman came striding over to him.

'Think we've got something, guv.'

The two scientists had stopped their camera half way down the column, some nine or ten feet from the ground, and were adjusting the intensity dials, creating a concentrated field of penetration with the infra-red arc.

'What do you think?' Fordham asked in a low expectant tone.

'Difficult to say, sir,' replied Colmain, the senior of the lab men. 'There's something here. Quite definitely. It's a large substance. And would appear to have less specific gravity than concrete.'

'D'you want to hazard a guess at it?' Borroughs prompted.

'Not really, Chief Inspector. For the present I'd rather leave that to you.'

It took about forty minutes of close examination of the pillar, moving the camera up and down, with corresponding lateral movements, before the two men would commit themselves with any degree of certainty to there being an adult body entombed in the column.

'That's it, then,' Fordham said with an air of finality that surprised the two scientists. 'Thanks for your help.' He turned away.

'Chief Superintendent!' The senior man started after Fordham. 'What about our report, sir?' That was standard.

Fordham paused and regarded Colmain, his steel-grey eyes measuring him. He was deciding whether or not to take this man into his confidence. He decided not to. 'You've told me all I need to know. I don't want to see your report. In fact I don't want you to write a report.'

The man hesitated. 'It isn't usual, you know.'

Fordham nodded slowly. 'Do it as a favour, Mr Colmain. Any problems, refer them to me. Do you need any help with your gear?'

Again the scientist hesitated, still uncertain. Finally he said they could manage. Fordham watched him rejoin his colleague; then motioned the others to follow his precarious path through the grinding traffic. His car was parked on the opposite side of the road.

Fleetingly Fordham wondered about the two lab men and the possibility of their writing a report anyway. Such a document might cause him problems. Tearing down the stanchion was likely to prove expensive, but that wasn't why Fordham chose to keep quiet about the discovery. The man inside the concrete wasn't going to be of any use to them as a material witness in their wide-ranging enquiries, but revealing who they thought he was and the fact that he was there would probably take their enquiries off at another tangent, one that he mightn't be able to control. Leaving the man where he was would, for the moment, give them an advantage over the people they suspected were responsible. Fordham wasn't ready to move against them, and the way things were shaping he wondered if he ever would be.

'Musn't inconvenience the poor motorist,' Fordham said, as Borroughs climbed into the rear of car. DI Norman slid in next to the driver.

'Wouldn't do at all.' Borroughs smiled wryly. 'Fucking handy turn-up.' He sounded disgusted.

'It might have been worse. He might have been tucked up in the South of France, or Mexico. Which would have meant a trip out there.' Fordham's sarcasm wasn't lost on either detective.

Inconvenient as it was to have had a potentially valuable witness taken out of the case, the fact of his removal did indicate that he was important and that someone had felt threatened by him. Fordham read the question in the thin, pointed face of the DI, who was turning in the front seat.

'Stay with this end of the enquiry, Les. Rochester, we assume, was about to blow the whistle. Might help if we can establish why. Maybe you'll come up with someone else who's willing to make a deal.'

'Given another fifteen months.'

'We might get lucky. Perhaps whoever it is will wind up in concrete too. How long's this been open?'

'About a year. Be about right for his disappearance eighteen months ago. This wasn't one of O'Connors' contracts.'

'No. Why would they shit on their own doorstep?' Fordham was silent for a moment. 'Don't worry about being quite so discreet with your enquiries, Les. See if we can't poke a few holes in O'Connors' respectable façade.'

'You want me on this exclusively?'

'Not unless you've got everything else cleared up.'

'Some chance of that, guv.' Norman, like most other detectives, took every opportunity to bemoan his workload. 'If you put everyone on it instead of just my ten we might make some show between now and next Christmas.'

Fordham readily acknowledged his detectives' problems, and wasn't unsympathetic. But few detectives, particularly on the Squad, had the luxury of working exclusively on one case. Things came in the whole time, and wouldn't stand in line until someone could cope.

'You'll be wanting to go on holiday next, Les,' Borroughs said.

'I was called back off the last bastard if I remember,' the DI said.

'You blokes are always fucking moaning. Think of the poor miners on strike again.' Few senior detectives could get away with talking like that to their men, but John Fordham could. He had a well established rapport with them; he didn't simply stand off and throw them shitty orders. 'All right, Syd, let's go and do some work.'

The driver put the Austin 2200 in gear and swung out into the traffic with the same peremptory assumption of right as a marked radio car.

Up on the fourth floor of the Yard nothing had stood patiently in line awaiting Fordham's return.

'John!' Detective Superintendent Winkle, glancing up through his open door, saw Fordham go past. He didn't come back, so Winkle rose from his desk and moved out of the small office after him. He was next door, hanging up his damp coat. 'How d'you get on?'

'Nothing. I think whoever stuck that one up was trying something.'

'What a sod.' The detective sounded disappointed. 'Maybe he got his location wrong.'

Fordham moved behind his desk and removed a bottle of scotch and a paper cup from a drawer. 'Who cares? Some of this, Willy?' He poured a short measure and replaced the bottle when the man shook his head.

It wasn't that Fordham didn't trust Winkle, or any of the other Ds on the Squad. He just thought it better that as few as possible knew about Rochester. There was less chance of the wrong people getting to hear about it, and of anyone being hauled before the Disciplinary Board.

'Bingham's been on again. Personally this time. They really want to interview you up there.'

'So it would seem.' He swallowed his drink and crushed the cup. 'S'pect I'll get to him sooner or later. When I've got time.'

Winkle regarded the younger man, feeling inclined to advise him to proceed cautiously. Angus Bingham wasn't just some minor policeman out of the uniform branch whom Fordham was wilfully blanking, but a very senior member of a currently very prominent branch. He was one of the two commanders who ran A10, and the sort of person who, if Fordham fell, he would fall foul of. However, John Fordham was the boss and Winkle figured he knew what he was doing.

'I think it might have to be sooner rather than later, John. His patience sounds as though it's about run out.'

'Nothing else to do, that's the problem. If A10 got off their asses and did some proper coppering – Anything else, Willy?'

'A number of calls. I think Bill Senior put the list on your desk.' He watched Fordham lift the fresh pile of paperwork from his In tray. He started back to his own office.

'Thanks, Willy . . .' He glanced up suddenly from the reports. 'How did Jack get on with that barge-load of copper?' Jack Owen was the other detective superintendent on the Squad and shared the office with Winkle.

'He's convinced it's all down to the security guard. He put the thieves in, and took the beating. Trying to allay suspicion. He's gone back to see him now.'

'Not surprised,' was all Fordham said as he sat at his desk. He would get the details from Owen's report. Winkle went out, leaving the door open.

Fordham picked up the list of people who had called, Detective Inspector Senior's neat, back-sloping hand, was an indication of a quirk of personality, quite what he couldn't remember; he'd have to ask Kika, she was into all that.

Probably meant that Senior was a pervert, but then everyone knew that: if it moved Senior would try to stiff it.

Commander Bingham was at the top of the list. Below his name A10, with Bingham's name in closed brackets, which meant his secretary had called also. Fordham glanced down the other twelve names. Most would call back, for the telephone wasn't a compulsive habit of his. Kika was on the list. She had probably called to say she'd be late at rehearsals. Being an actress was a bit like being a detective, the hours weren't always regular. He couldn't recall whether they had anything planned for that evening where either of them being late would make any difference. He didn't call her. Putting the list aside, Fordham considered a pile of reports that had been placed on his desk while he was out. No sooner had he started through them when the phone rang. He lifted the receiver, still reading. It was Superintendent Nester from C11. His name was on the list. He wanted to know if Fordham had time to see him.

'Sure, Stanley. You'll have to make it soon, though, I'm leaving shortly.' Nester said he'd be over directly. He hadn't far to come. He was on the same floor. Criminal Intelligence had their offices on the opposite side of the corridor to the Squad. Their offices were easily identified; the doors were always closed and locked; doors of the Squad offices, from Fordham's on down, were invariably left open, inviting anyone in.

Fordham had scan-read and initialled six reports by the time Nester arrived. He closed the door firmly, from habit. He was a tall man with a pronounced stoop and a melancholy expression, as if he carried all the troubles of the Metropolitan police force around on his shoulders. Fordham couldn't recall ever having seen the man laugh.

'What's on your mind, Stanley?'

'That.' He passed over a thin manilla folder. The report inside ran to a page and a half. It didn't warrant a folder, but the DCS assumed C11 expected to collect more information. 'Got it this morning. A big post office in Wimbledon. A lot of potential. We think it could be connected with the series of robberies you've got.' He paused while Fordham finished reading the report. 'What do you think?'

'Seems like the sort of thing they've been going after. S'this all you have?'

'We're working on it.'

'Is Wimbledon CID involved?'

'Not yet. I thought you'd like first look – maybe you'd care to take it over?'

'Not really, Stanley – unless you can't cope.'

'We're coping. Just about.'

'It looks like a prospect for us. Be nice to get in on the ground floor with something like this.' He returned the folder. 'Give it to Willy, will you? Keep us in touch with whatever you get.'

Fordham dealt briskly with the routine of his office: telephone calls, and reports which needed his attention or signature, or both; he read most of the Crime Reports he signed, gleaning all the salient facts. Most of the people on his telephone list got back to him; Kika and Bingham didn't. He wondered briefly about the commander in A10; mainly just how patient he really was. Not very, from what he knew of the man, although that seemed to be contradicted by the fact that he had held off screaming and demanding his presence up in his office for so long.

Being one rank above Fordham, Bingham could in theory come down and insist that he accompany him to his office for the much-requested interview. In practice that didn't happen with senior ranks; the rare occasions when it did usually meant that the policeman involved would be either suspended or arrested. Neither prospect was likely as far as he was concerned, Fordham told himself.

But then his predecessor, Peter Walsh, had thought that. There had only been minor infractions which he could come unstuck on, and they would have had to want him out of the office pretty badly to cut him down on those, he had confidently told Fordham, who had been a detective superintendent at the time. Fordham had been close to Walsh, and because of it had been surprised when he was made

DCS after his governor's suspension. Fordham had been involved in almost all of Walsh's ramps – but then they were both practical policemen. He had been about to quit himself after Walsh's suspension, but then the DCS had been allowed to resign ahead of the pending charges – the final straw had been his holiday at the villa in Spain belonging to a known criminal. Such an association was considered highly undesirable; the edict which was issued shortly after meant in effect that no detective, senior or otherwise, should associate with known criminals.

In their towering offices the hierarchy seemed to lose touch with the realities of capturing villains to such an extent that one might almost believe they'd never themselves put any away, nor earned off any of them. In their wisdom they had decided that almost all CID work could or should be conducted within the precincts of police stations. Nothing was further from being practicable, not if they wanted the clear-up rate maintained.

Fordham knew in part the reason for their reaction. It was a combination of the sudden accessibility and vulnerability of the police to the news media; plus the hierarchy's reluctance to admit that policemen, like most people, were susceptible. The public image of the police seemed to those administrators almost as important as results. Taking the argument to its logical conclusion, Fordham foresaw the day when it wouldn't matter if they didn't arrest anyone, just as long as they did their fat nothing without consorting with criminals.

The pressure on the Squad had slackened somewhat since Walsh's departure, but a cloud still tended to hang over it. Especially when A10 started investigating any of them. It had been Walsh who persuaded Fordham not to resign. His argument was pretty convincing: Fordham hadn't been named in any aspects of corruption, and no allegations of malpractice had been laid against him, but if he resigned he might draw a lot of unnecessary attention to himself, especially as he had been made operational head of the Squad. Fordham had thought at the time that Walsh ought to have been given more support from both the commander of the Squad and the Assistant Commissioner—Crime. He doubted that he himself would get much backing from either in the event of a straightener with Bingham, except perhaps tacit support from the Commander, Gerald Pope.

After two years in his current office it was possible that A10 had come up with something substantial against him. Fordham guessed he had upset enough people in his time. Briefly he wondered if this new pressure on him had any connection with the area into which this O'Connors investigation was taking him. Doubtless he was touching a few raw nerves. Fordham leaned back from his desk and considered that, then dismissed it as signs of paranoia. A10 were simply making themselves busy, trying to justify their farcical existence. Well, they'd have to try harder. He had no intention of calling them. He was going to go home and get out of his damp clothes.

Chapter 2

Reaching out, Fordham brushed the woman's breast with his knuckles. He didn't speak. She made no sound, and he wondered if she had gone to sleep. He had frequently fallen asleep on her. He turned his hand over and touched her nipple, which was tense and erect. With the planes of his fingers he caressed her nipple and she responded; then he stopped.

'You build a girl up, then quit.' She sighed exaggeratedly.

'These little attentions, Kika. Next you'll expect marriage.'

'Don't you believe it. I'm going to marry a movie star.' There was a resonance to her voice that made hearing easy.

They fell silent, and Fordham rubbed her nipple again. More and more of late he had considered the possibility of marriage, but his feelings remained ambivalent. So many policemen's marriages went wrong. The job put an enormous strain on them, and in most cases either one or both parties couldn't cope. He saw no reason why Kika and himself should be any different. Certainly if their relationship ceased working to a convenient or tolerable degree neither of them would hang together for very long; not for old-time's sake, out of laziness, or any other reason; they were both far too independent. But if it stopped working the reason would almost certainly be that one of them had found someone else they liked being with more. Neither had trouble sustaining themselves during the periods they were on their own. But Fordham loved the woman despite the problems she had had in reconciling herself to a relationship with a policeman. He knew she believed it made her something of a contradiction in terms.

Kika Martin was an actress and a pretty good one. She wasn't a movie star, but she didn't really want to be. She had a three-year contract with the National Theatre which left little time for films. She seemed not to have much time for anything else now, not the splinter union groups nor the International Marxists nor left-wing protests with the Redgraves. But she never truly knew whether this was because she could no longer fit them into her schedule or because she was living with a high-ranking policeman; she denied the latter possibility. In fact she quite frequently denied Fordham altogether.

Instinctively she urged herself to adhere to the principles which had once governed her existence, and reject the policeman for all that he represented. Only she couldn't. He would have delighted her parents if they'd met him; they'd have thought him a wonderful match. Her parents had a great regard for law and order. Some of her friends would have been wary of him had they known what he did, particularly the less successful ones, for success tended to dissolve one's fear of the police. Kika sometimes felt ashamed of the reluctance she experienced about having Fordham meet her friends. She got nervous when he called around at the National for her, especially when his car and driver were left waiting outside. They had more rows over this than anything. After one such row, Fordham had called for her the next day in a radio car with a uniformed driver. She never met any of his friends, only other detectives. At times she wondered if policemen had friends.

'What are you thinking?' the woman asked.

Fordham made a noise in his throat which either meant he wasn't going to tell her or that he was thinking about work. Asking his thoughts was something she frequently did. It resulted in a sort of question-evasion game.

'Where do you keep getting coal from?'

'I have to scour half of London for it. That little place near the theatre's run out. The man was so apologetic about it. He doesn't know when he'll be getting any more.'

'Crocodile tears. You must have kept him alive.'

'He was a perfectly sweet old man.'

'Did you let him feel these?' He raised his index finger under her breast.

'Anticipating your screwing me, I was able to resist.' She

laughed. It was a deep, sensual laugh.

They were both naked in front of the open coal fire on a cow-hide rug which she had fetched back from a tour in the United States. They had made love earlier. The woman preferred to make love wherever she was turned on – once it was in the kitchen against the stove. For his part, Fordham would have left their love-making to bed at night, but there was never any guarantee that he would get to bed at night. If he did, he might not have been there for the two previous nights, which meant he would have been in not fit state for anything but sleep. Though he had to admit that the rug in front of the fire on a wet February evening had a lot to recommend it. An open coal fire! They were surely the only people in Chelsea, probably the whole of central London, who lit a coal fire. Then Kika was like that. She would sneak her bags of coal past the hall porter. A coal fire contravened both the Clean Air Act and his lease. The fireplace had been blocked off when he had moved in, and opened up and restored by Kika when she arrived.

The woman rolled on to her hip and traced her slender fingers around Fordham's profile, pausing at his lips, which she had too often seen turn down in a cynical smile. They yielded now and he bit her finger. She smiled. Her hand moved on down his throat and across his chest, which was deep and the sparse flesh there soft. Too much energy was expended in too many hours for him to be fat, although he gave that impression. His stomach was paunching, but not unattractively. She liked stomachs on men, provided they didn't reflect excesses; that was where a man's strength lay. His belly was quite firm. She slapped it.

'It wants feeding,' Fordham said.

'Unlucky. You should have called back. I wanted you to pick up some food.' Her hand clenched into a fist, trapping pubic hair. 'You're too fat. You're getting like that disgusting Mr Borroughs.'

'Frank? – he thought you a pretty good actress, too.'

She was surprised. 'You mean he actually went to the theatre and saw something?'

'He caught an old movie you were in on TV.'

'It figures.'

Fordham smiled. 'He said he hadn't realised you were that old.'

She saw the smile – 'You bastard! For that I'm going to tear this off.' Kika grasped his penis.

'For what good it'll be to me for about another three weeks.' He smiled as Kika stroked him back to life.

'Do I get a prize?' She leant over and kissed him, leaving his mast reaching.

'How do you know that's really an erection? How do you know it isn't acting?'

'I'll take a chance, my love.' She kissed him again, then slid on top of him. 'Do you want it this way?' she asked, planting tiny kisses around his prickly neck.

'I'm not doing anything. Just lying here waiting for my dinner.'

Fordham wasn't able to maintain his sense of detachment.

The woman was asleep on top of him and Fordham was comfortable; the fire was giving off a nice heat. He didn't want to answer the phone but he knew it would ring on. He reached out towards the bell, only it wasn't that easy. The instrument was up on an armchair. Finally Kika woke.

'Sorry, love.' He eased her off himself and got the phone. 'Fordham.' There was no one on the other end. Whoever it was had laid the phone down and gone off to do something else. He waited, scratching his scrotum.

'Caught something from one of your other ladies?'

'From you, more than likely. Hello?'

DCI Dyce, the duty officer, identified himself.

'Something's turned up might interest you, guv. That accountant we've been looking for. He walked into Barnet police station a short while ago. Gave himself up.'

'Of his own accord, Malcolm?'

'Apparently. Said he couldn't take the strain. What do you want done with him? Do you want to see him this evening? Or will I have him fetched down to Cannon Row for the morning?'

'That's no way to reward such enthusiasm. A night in a cell might give him second thoughts about what he's got for us.'

The interlude Kika had provided was over. He was functioning as a policeman again. He had Dyce send his car, and locate DI Stephen Peacock, who had handled the original investigation.

'Would you like something to eat before you go?'

'Thought you hadn't got any food?'

'It'll only be a yoghurt sandwich, my love.'

His car had arrived by the time he had showered and dressed. Kika made him an omelette, which he took time to eat, keeping his driver and the DI waiting.

At times like these Fordham regretted his profession. He would have preferred to spend the night in with Kika. He wasn't a zealot, and knew few policemen who were, but the suspect he was going to see up at Barnet could prove a vital witness, and might open up a whole new area in their investigation.

He became a policeman by chance. There was no such tradition in his lower-middle-class family. His mother would have approved, believing, like countless other people, that God was an Englishman where the police were concerned. Fordham wouldn't have disillusioned her. His dad had been slightly prejudiced, having been busted for reckless driving. Fordham had decided on an impulse to join the force after his parents had died in a car crash. He had been impressed by the way in which the young constable in charge of the case had conducted himself. His authority had brought calm to the confusion that inevitably pervaded fatal road accidents.

At the time Fordham had been reading sociology at Reading University. When he applied to join the police the question of his completing his degree course was raised at a high level. The academic qualifications he subsequently achieved held him in good stead. He was put on an inspector's course, after which he had gravitated, like most of the brighter policemen, to the CID. Unlike the majority he had shown exceptional aptitude. He was promoted quickly, then seconded to the Squad at a time when they had peremptory right to the best from division. His promotion, two years ago, at thirty-seven, to operational head of the Squad made him the youngest in office.

The Austin was parked on the forecourt of the block opposite the River Thames. Peacock sat in the back.

'Did you have one to meet, Syd?' Fordham said to the driver holding the door for him: the man was frequently called out to drive his governor at all hours. The price of being a driver to the head of Squad; though Fordham's hours showed some semblance of regularity compared to those of a lot of detectives.

'Only watching the telly, guv. Same old rubbish.' As a Squad driver Syd Worker carried the rank of constable, but wasn't required to wear a uniform or do any coppering. He stayed with the car and drove; occasionally he might be called upon to assist Fordham in making an arrest, but DCSs rarely got into those situations. The drivers saw a lot of what went on around the Squad; but all they were required to do was drive.

On the journey north across London Fordham and the DI broached various subjects, most of them connected with other investigations.

'What's happening on that robbery in Walthamstow, Stephen? S'there a nicking imminent?'

'I think the local CID were just trying to lighten their load, calling us in.' He sounded put out. 'There's a couple we could pull. They were involved. The evidence isn't there, though. They'd probably get it chucked if we went to court.' He hesitated and glanced at the DCS. 'The only way to nick them is to fit them.'

Fordham wasn't perturbed by such practices when they were deemed necessary, particularly not when the detective involved was a good as Peacock. He simply said, 'Checks and balances, Stephen.'

If a policeman was certain that a villain had committed a

crime for which he couldn't be arrested, then it didn't really matter if he went away for another crime, even one he didn't commit. That was part of the game which the CID and felony played. Both knew the rules – though neither were exactly happy when the other scored points.

Barnet police station was of the old red brick type that resembled Victorian school-houses. When turning oneself in, those stations were best avoided, as their accommodation left a lot to be desired. The facilities were usually old and inefficient, from the typewriters in the CID room to the lavatories in the cells. The latter often didn't flush and had a tendency to stink. A night inside such a cell usually gave criminals a foretaste of prison, if they weren't already acquainted.

Harold Stonehall seemed relieved to be brought up from the cells. They could have interviewed him there, but Fordham had no intention of doing so when there were more comfortable places. He was offered an interview room, in keeping with the ruling that all suspects must remain within the close vicinity of the front office until charged. The accountant hadn't yet been charged, but Fordham wasn't concerned about those rules. He took Stonehall upstairs to the CID room, where he used the local DI's office. The inspector had gone home three hours earlier. Judging by the lack of activity in the CID room, most of the other detectives had gone too. Coming to stations like this, Fordham never doubted why the Squad was kept so busy. An overweight detective whom Fordham figured as a sergeant, looked up from the keys of a typewriter as the three men came into the room. Fordham stopped by his desk and let Peacock and Stonehall go on into the office.

'Have one of your lads fetch chummy a cup of tea, will you, skip?'

The DS knew instinctively that the man before him was a senior detective, had probably even guessed what rank. 'Just one cup, guv?'

Fordham nodded. He could imagine what the local tea was like.

'Make yourself comfortable, Harold,' Fordham said in an easy, friendly manner as he came in and closed the door. 'Might be a long session. No need to make it seem longer.' He yawned and moved behind the desk.

The office was about the size of his own, some twelve feet by ten, and about as untidy. There were a dozen or more bulldog clips on nails on the wall behind the desk, each with a large wad of reports crammed into it. Fordham let his eyes run uninterestedly over them: action taken; to be taken; results achieved; insoluble! The local governor, like most people who ran CID offices, had his own unfathomable filing system. The DCS wondered fleetingly what his clear-up rate was. Removing his brown herringbone coat, he laid it across the basket on top of the filing cabinet and turned to Stonehall.

'You gave us a bit of a run. We'd about given up on you.'

Stonehall didn't say anything, but shrugged sheepishly.

'We're pleased you turned up, though, aren't we, Stephen?' Peacock concurred. 'That's Inspector Peacock – he's the man you caused all the work for. But he's not one to bear a grudge. Right?'

'Depends on what he gives us now, I suppose.'

'I've got a feeling he's going to prove very helpful. Right, Harold?'

Stonehall nodded. 'I'll try and be as helpful as I can. I don't wish to cause more inconvenience.'

'I think we're going to get along very well.' Fordham sat. The chair was comfortable, the sort of chair a man who enjoyed sitting on his ass would have. 'What we want you to do, Harold, is go right back to the beginning. Tell us why and how you got involved.'

Leaning back, Fordham regarded the man, whose face bore a pensive, distressed expression as if he were digging into memories of things he'd rather have left buried. This could be the break they'd been waiting for; the accountant, if he proved to have held the position they hoped he did, could be the key to a lot of doors. But looking at him, Fordham began to have doubts. Aside from the suntan which put him apart from the general February public there was nothing about Stonehall to suggest he was a foundation of any kind. Had they found him without his being the apparently willing party the DCS didn't doubt that they would have easily cracked him.

'I don't know where to begin,' the accountant said in a subdued tone. 'It's difficult to know just how one gets caught up. It's as if one wakes on a certain morning in one's life to find oneself completely embroiled.' He stopped and stared down at his neat hands.

There was a rap on the door. Peacock opened it and took the cup of tea from the policeman outside. 'There you are, Mr Stonehall – keep the throat lubricated, is all about.'

Casually Fordham began searching the drawers in the desk. He found what he was looking for, a half-full bottle of scotch. Most detectives who had their own desk kept a bottle; not because they were alcoholics, although a drink was necessary at times, but to celebrate a worthwhile result, or someone's promotion – they were the excuses anyway. The DCS uncapped the bottle and extended it towards Stonehall, who hesitated, then accepted some in his tea.

'Could I trouble you for a cigarette ...? I came without any.'

Fordham didn't smoke, but glanced at Peacock, who, like most detectives on the Squad, resisted smoking in his company. He produced a heavy silver case. Stonehall got a cigarette and a light. He coughed.

'I don't often ... just felt a need, you know.'

'Who first approached you, Harold?' Fordham asked, getting the interview back in the right direction.

'A man calling himself Richardson. Maurice Richardson. Though I suspect that wasn't his real name. Don't know why. Just an impression I had.'

Ponderously, Harold Stonehall told how the man had approached him, saying that a mutual acquaintance, Clive Jacobson, had recommended him and thought perhaps he'd consider taking on some private accountancy. At first Stonehall wasn't interested as he had quite enough work as senior accountant with an electronics manufacturing corporation. But Richardson called on him again to pursue the matter and spoke of all the extra, tax-free cash he could earn. It was on this visit that Stonehall realised that the man had something else on his mind. He referred to Stonehall's past involvement with a small overseas investment bank which had cheated the Bank of England out of one and a quarter million pounds.

It was a complicated affair, or had appeared so to Fordham from the details he had got from the Fraud Squad. Stonehall now offered an over-simplification. The fringe bankers were called Wisbech and Jacobson, who handled foreign investments for clients. British residents who bought foreign shares were compelled to buy special investment dollars on which there was a premium payable to the Bank of England. When shares were subsequently sold, the premium element was divided seventy-five / twenty-five between the investor and the Bank respectively. In a complicated maze of bogus foreign share transactions, Wisbech and Jacobson created the one and a quarter million which, they claimed, was due under the seventy-five / twenty-five per cent split, and this the Bank of England duly paid. The bankers were confidently setting up another similar fraud, only on a much larger scale, when the Treasury moved against them with summonses under the Exchange Control Act. Clive Jacobson and Jack Wisbech had quickly departed the country, leaving Stonehall as the next most senior remaining member of the firm, to carry the can. In his defence Stonehall claimed that he was merely an employee, but the Treasury weren't impressed and the money he had on deposit both here and in Switzerland didn't lend credence to his argument. He was tried and convicted, fined ten thousand pounds and made bankrupt for his assets. The banking firm was fined a total of seven hundred thousand pounds, but in assets wasn't found to be worth even seven thousand. The accountant told of Maurice Richardson's blackmail; how he was sure his current employers didn't know about his past.

'I confess,' Stonehall said, nervously interlacing his damp

hands, 'I acceded readily to his suggestions. As you know we had very large shipments of cash for wages. The company was forever trying to arrange payment by cheque, but the unions resisted. Occasionally these shipments were almost doubled by production bonuses, profit participation, things like that. Richardson simply wanted details on the next big shipment.'

'Which you gave him?' Peacock said, matter-of-factly.

'Yes – I mean, no. I had those details, of course. Any I didn't have weren't difficult to get. But he didn't want them. He sent another man to see me. This man took the details. He gave his name as Percival, I don't know whether that was correct. It all seemed so easy. I wasn't going to be involved. But after the robbery had taken place and that guard was hurt. Well, you caught some of the robbers. I was convinced it was only a matter of time before you got Richardson, then me. My nerves couldn't stand the uncertainty. I just had to get out, so I went to Spain.' He glanced apologetically at Peacock. 'That's when I heard you were looking for me – the newspapers. Being over there didn't seem half bad at first, not even after you began looking for me. But finally it was too big a price. The thought of forever being on the run, giving up everything here. I just had to come back.' He sighed heavily, regretfully.

After a pause Fordham said, 'That wasn't why you went to Spain. You were sent to supervise the sale of the money – you used a bent passport and moved throughout Europe. Germany, Switzerland, through France, back into Spain.'

That completely surprised Stonehall. He stammered out his denial. 'It's not true. Really it's not. Honestly.'

'Do you really think we're going to accept that you were just a minor informant in a single robbery?'

Actually, Fordham was now convinced of just that. With Stonehall's knowledge of foreign money markets they had originally cast him as the exchange rate supervisor, not just for the job he had been involved on, but for the eight other interconnected jobs that had taken place over the past fifteen months. But that was wishful thinking now.

Listening to the accountant's denials with only a part of his mind as Peacock pursued the line, the DCS considered other aspects of the case. There was no doubt in his mind that this robbery was connected to the central aspects of his overall investigation. Clive Jacobson had been a director of Frank O'Connor and Son, the building and civil engineering contracting monolith. O'Connors were an important foundation stone, on which a lot of empire building with bent money had taken place; another director of that apparently august company, and a foundation stone in his own right, was Anthony Duckett. As yet Fordham had as much chance of moving against him as of pissing on the moon. He was way out of reach; but Fordham was building a set of steps, if exceeding slow. He had the bottom treads: some of the cowboys they had captured, the villains with the guns who did the actual robbing; he knew the whereabouts of the people at the top; it was that middle strata, the cadre of professionals whom he needed in order to fix it all up. One man, he knew, was most important of all: Charlie Ryman.

'Describe the man who first came to see you – Richardson. Can you, Harold?'

'Well, I'm not too sure, to be perfectly honest.'

'It would go a long way in helping us believe your story,' Peacock said. 'As I've told you, if you want us to help you, which we're willing to do, the more assistance you render the better we'll appreciate it.' The DI glanced at Fordham as though uncertain about this being confirmed. Fordham didn't comment.

'He was, oh, I don't know. Late forties, I suppose. I'm never very good at ages. He looked comfortably off, his clothes were quite expensive, I'd say.' He hesitated, his mind's eye trailing back. 'He had a fullish face, fair complexion – that's what made his age so difficult, I think.'

'Brownish, sand-colour hair,' Fordham said, filling in the gaps. 'Blue eyes; heavy build, heavier than me, perhaps a little taller. Five-nine or ten.' The accountant's expression said that they were talking about the same man. It was Charlie Ryman. 'If we showed you some photographs, do you think you'd recognise the man again?' He thought he would. 'But more important, Harold, when the time's right, would you be prepared to ID him?' When the man hesitated, the DCS added, 'That's how you get all the help you're going to need – by helping us.'

Stonehall was completely committed to the police. He trusted them. He had no reason to do otherwise. He wasn't a criminal with any experience of the CID and didn't know how treacherous they could be at times. He was less positive about the other man than he had been about Richardson, and the policeman didn't have a candidate to offer him. They knew what the second man was – he was the draftsman – but not *who* he was. He could have been any one of about six, but Stonehall wasn't even sure that he would be able to identify him from a photograph.

'What we're going to do, Harold, is take you out of here, down to Cannon Row, and have you charged. Then I want you to go through all this again with Inspector Peacock, and sign a statement. What we'll do first is take you back to your house and let you collect any bits and pieces, toothbrush, cigarettes, couple of books – just to show you some goodwill.' Fordham had a witness who was cooperating; he wanted to keep him that way. The fact that they would take time out to search his house might have had no bearing on the gesture.

By making the moves he had made, Stonehall had now become a police witness. Whether he ultimately went down the road for his part in the robbery would depend largely upon just how helpful his information proved, and through it how high Fordham managed to reach. He had no doubt that he could arrest Charlie Ryman, and get a conviction, but in the event that would only get him Charlie Ryman in the bag. It wouldn't get anyone higher, because through the one charge he wouldn't be able to get enough pressure on him to make a trade-off and so prise the whole of the iceberg up. Ryman was a curiously old-fashioned villain in some respects, though because of vested interests rather than any perverse sense of loyalty. He would take one himself rather than trade the people above him, and Fordham wasn't that concerned about those below him. There had to be something very concrete threatening Charlie Ryman, something more than a probable ten-stretch for conspiring to rob – from which he would be paroled after about four years – before he gave Fordham all he needed.

Chapter 3

The Jaguar XJ6 had a lot of power. The potential acceleration was reassuring, Ryman found. It could get one out of all kinds of trouble. He had been used to big cars, ever since his first. However, most of his previous vehicles had been owned by the finance company. Not this one. The Jaguar he had paid for outright. He had been in that sort of position for a few years now; comfortable, well set up, able to weigh on. It was a nice situation. He wouldn't like to go back to the way things used to be. A smile etched into Ryman's fleshy face as he thought about the early days. He had pulled some outrageous strokes then; a case of having to.

The early afternoon traffic was tolerable across South London, and Ryman felt no sense of frustration as he manoeuvred the car down through Mitcham. A watery sun strained an appearance between intermittent cloud and made him feel good. He was heading out into the country, and that pleased him. Instinct told him he should move to the countryside, as he always responded well to it. He had been born in London and had lived there all his life. Maybe it was just the prospect of where he was going that gave him his lift.

A heavy TIR lorry heading for the channel ferry swerved across Ryman's car, throwing specks of mud over the brightly polished paint. He thought about pounding the horn, but realised how futile that would be. The mud would wash off and the lorry was well ahead now. It was better not to bring attention to himself; not that there were problems in doing so these days, but it was a sound principle. Billy Holford leapt to mind – a villain cursed more than usually with the trait of drawing attention to himself. He had got into a row with another driver while in a stolen car on his way to make one. A couple of wollies had nicked him.

Where the A25 cut across the A23 at Redhill, there was a

girl hitching. Ryman spotted her far enough back to stop, but was undecided about doing so. He hesitated, foot hovering over the brake pedal; he glanced in his rear-view mirror; there was traffic up his daily. He had left the decision too late. He studied the girl as he sailed past. She had that expectant, hopeful look of hitchhikers, that look which turned sour on drawing a blank. She was pretty, in her early twenties. It was a long time since he had screwed something like that, and he knew he would probably regret not stopping, for a while at least. He was placated by telling himself that she wouldn't have been going his way, as he would be turning on to the A21 down through Kent.

Once clear of the massive urban sprawl of south London and Surrey, the road was quickly eaten up. He had set out in good time, and was in no hurry, so he had avoided the motorway. He liked the winding A21, passing through little towns and villages. He wasn't unfamiliar with the route, having made the trip a number of times.

Ryman was going to see Anthony Duckett out at his house at Benenden. He assumed that the purpose of this trip was business; it usually was, when he got the sort of call he had received from Duckett.

When he had first approached Duckett he hadn't been sure how deeply his involvement went. He had known the man now for about ten years; they had been very beneficial years, and not only financially. Ryman had gained a lot more than money by the association. Having always believed that the Establishment orders were corrupt, Charlie Ryman had had little first-hand experience of it before encountering Duckett – apart from the police of course, but then everyone knew they were bent, and they only worked for the Establishment anyway. He had been not much better than a tearaway in those days, specialising in long-firm frauds, and only occasionally getting involved in anything heavier, which he had once taken one for.

Like his father Charlie Ryman was a criminal. But having seen his old man go in and out of prison, he decided that wasn't to be his fate. After the three-stretch he did for being an accessory to a robbery he was determined that that would be his one and only sentence. Looking around, he identified the truly successful criminals – those who kept both what they earned and their liberty – as either policemen or the Establishment, or those who, because of their manoeuvring or what they had to offer, had been adopted by it; people in the City, in government offices, people who because of their positions had never been suspected, much less challenged. Ryman had had a choice of either aligning himself with the police, which would have meant grassing to survive, or with the established orders of corrupt commerce. He chose the latter.

He had watched young Ralaigh O'Reilly operate, getting finance from the City to fund his long-firms, on a scale which most villains would neither have had the credentials to float nor the front to carry off. In O'Reilly he had recognised a rare talent, and decided to stick close, though without losing touch with the villains actually pulling the strokes. Shortly he had found himself occupying some safe middle ground. He wasn't untouchable like O'Reilly, for whom he fronted, but he was a lot less vulnerable than those he employed in front of him. What made him so safe was his choice of men. Because of the way in which he recruited them, they couldn't trade him to Old Bill any more than he could have traded O'Reilly. His previous single mistake in his choice of associates had cost him three years, had made him careful.

When the bottom had fallen out of the long-firm business and O'Reilly had speedily decamped to Switzerland, he had done so without owing Ryman anything, and had left him with some worthwhile contacts. All Charlie had to do was step up the ladder.

He felt very secure in the way in which he operated now. Again, not quite as safe as the man above him, but then Anthony Duckett was born with the Establishment endorsing each move. Ryman had every intention of staying in his present respectable position, aligned with the most solid elements of society. There were too many cowboys around for the use of, without his having to take chances.

He tried to anticipate what Duckett had in mind for this meeting, what kind of earner. The more jobs he put together from information the banker gave him, the more intrigued he became. What made a man like that tick as he did? A merchant banker, involved in the capitalisation, and with seats on the boards, of some of the major companies currently quoted on the Stock Exchange, even a local JP. Yet he had been instrumental in initiating robberies which accumulatively ran into hundreds of thousands, possibly even a million pounds. There was never any breath of robbery mentioned at their meetings. He had no wish to be informed on any details, not when or how it would be concluded. Everything was left to Ryman, including that final detail, the amount of money which passed from Ryman into the strange machinations of Messrs Duckett, Reinhardt, merchant bankers. What happened to it then he wasn't supposed to know, but he had made careful enquiries, kept his ear close to the ground, filled in the gaps with intelligent speculation. He believed that through the bank the money was funnelled out of the country for laundering in foreign exchange dealings. Duckett was in the ideal position for such transactions, and must have got full value on the bent cash, unlike most money fences. Why Duckett was into this sort of operation had puzzled Ryman. After all he couldn't need the money; it was doubtful that he had ever been in need in his life. How much money Duckett was worth personally Ryman couldn't guess. That wasn't the sort of question one asked a man like Duckett; only the new-rich answered those questions. But somewhere there was a need of cash, an enormous cash-flow without black and whites; so he assumed that the money must be used for paying bribes. Who was being bribed and what for he hadn't discovered, but he'd decided it had to be an enormous enterprise to take so much money. Then he had heard a whisper about the GLC resident engineer who had disappeared off of one of O'Connors' sites; it had given his speculation a definite direction. Idly he wondered what the return might be in relation to the outlay. Millions, probably. But then such figures were part of Duckett's daily bread, and doubtless their gain or loss neither excited nor disturbed him.

Ryman thought how it must give one a good feeling to be that well set up. He'd once had ambitions of being rich, but they had been tempered by the pragmatism he had found over the past ten years. He didn't envy Anthony Duckett as most people in the 'us and them' situation might have, but respected and admired him. But that wasn't something Ryman would openly admit.

The road Ryman turned on to to reach Duckett's house was quite narrow and twisted. Trees overhung the road so low in places that the ends of branches were bruised from passing vans. The few houses there had mostly been set way back, and those that hadn't had lots of trees and shrubs in the garden. Seclusion seemed to be the keynote of this part of the countryside. Attractive as it all was, it wasn't at its best. Given a month or so when buds and green shoots began appearing on trees and from the ground, that's when it would really look something. Although he had seen the place in autumn when the leaves were turning, it was terrific then; autumn made the cities particularly shitty. That was the time he'd move to the country, if ever. He wouldn't mind getting a house down this way, something more modest than Duckett's place. Clara, his old lady, would probably like that. Perhaps he would bring her out for a drive at the weekend.

From the point where Ryman had turned off the A21, the green Mini-Cooper which had been following him dropped back to reduce the possibility of his sussing out the tail. He obviously had no idea he was being followed, though, or he would have taken evasive action. The first sign and DC Alan Mason would have let go and returned to the Yard. Those were the instructions from his governor, DI Garmonsway. They hadn't wanted to make a big production of keeping observation on Charlie Ryman, which was why only one car had been used. Normally six or more would be employed in rotation when making a good tail.

When Ryman had turned south on the A21 they had anticipated where he was going. Not why, of course. DC Mason and the detective constable in the car with him weren't fully in the picture, only the senior detectives saw the overall plan, but sometimes they wondered about that. The investigation they were on didn't even seem to be full time. They were pulled off and put back at whatever whim seemed to take Mr Fordham, though they knew it had to be more than that which determined the guvnor's actions, for he was too calculating to act merely on whim.

'Looks like he got there,' Mason said, uninterestedly.

They watched the Jaguar make a left-hand signal and turn on to a driveway between two red-brick gate pillars.

'I suppose we'd better phone in.'

They were too far away for the r/t fitted below the dashboard. There was a phone box on the road past the gateway. DC Mason pulled over. He let DC Trafford get out and call in about Ryman's destination.

Chapter 4

There was a clear view of the upper paddock from the study window, where Duckett stood and watched with pride as his daughter Carolyn took her pony over the jumps. She had a natural seat and would be as good as if not better than her mother. Jane was still a fine horsewoman, although no longer up to competition standard. Duckett could see a close resemblance to his ex-wife in his daughter where she sat her strawberry roan. And just as he had been so pleased to watch Jane ride, he found as much pleasure in watching Carolyn.

Carolyn was on holiday, and as arranged by mutual consent at the divorce Jane and he divided their only child's holidays between them. Such arrangements had been arrived at amicably, but then he would have been surprised had they not. They were both reasonable people. He hadn't regretted the divorce; an irretrievable breakdown in the marriage was a convenient euphemism, and spared them the messy alternatives. Duckett had known the judge, they went back as far as Eton together; that had made the whole process less painful for both Jane and himself. There might have been serious ethical problems had there been a property dispute or child custody suit. But the chances were that he wouldn't have had to go far before he ran across a judge he knew or had some connection with. Being a JP threw him further into legal circles.

Jane had agreed that their daughter could stay with him for the whole of her half-term holiday; it suited her as much as him, she was off to Innsbrück skiing. Some trips she would take Carolyn with her, when he allowed her back the extra days she had given him.

A smile crossed his long, pulpy face as his eleven-year-old daughter pushed the pony into a canter and cleared the parallel rails, which stood at four feet, with a four-foot spread; a considerable jump. Duckett's attention was caught briefly by the car which pulled round the drive, identifying the owner by its colour. He couldn't imagine anyone else driving a puce car. The vehicle stopped alongside the split-rail fence and Duckett watched as the girl trotted her pony over to it. Duckett knew she would engage Ryman in conversation as easily as her mother might have done.

He had a genuine feeling for Charles Ryman, rough diamond that he was. The man had tried to develop finer tastes and a more discreet life-style, and possibly those better acquainted with him would have considered that he had achieved it, but basically there was no disguising his antecedents.

Charles Ryman had a lot of spunk, and always proved very accommodating, Duckett had found. What had endeared him to the man was the manner in which, at the start of their association, he had helped extricate him from an unwise business venture with the entrepreneur Ralaigh O'Reilly. The net result hadn't been particularly profitable; however, Duckett was not only spared financial embarrassment, but considerable embarrassment with the government whose support he had successfully solicited for a huge components deal in North Africa.

Ryman had originally been brought into the picture by O'Reilly, who had had a profit-sharing arrangement with two top government officials in North Africa. The electrical components were to be manufactured by a company O'Reilly had recently acquired, financed jointly by Duckett's bank and the British Government, which had been attracted by the vast export order. The major drawback was, as a closer look at the figures revealed, that to produce the component stock at such low cost meant producing at a loss. That was fine, if the goods weren't delivered, and that was the plan O'Reilly had hatched with the two government ministers. After the initial shipment the North African electrification programme was to be shelved; the full order, by then – according to the false paperwork – having been fulfilled, would be left to corrode or be stolen. The one enormous fly in the ointment was a sudden violent change of government out there. The new incumbents were very much in favour of mass electrification, only they weren't prepared to pay the new price quoted after Ryman had arranged the burning to the ground of the warehouse where some of the loss-cost manufactured components were stored. The Arabs and the British Government both lost money, but the latter was prepared for that, provided it kept face; the insurance company lost money too.

Duckett wouldn't have been aware that arson was involved had Ryman not come to him for the balance of his fee after O'Reilly's departure. Certainly no one else had been aware of the felony, apart from whoever Ryman had do the deed. For some reason Duckett assumed he had never struck the match himself, but neither of them had spoken of the matter since that day.

He didn't regret the departure of Mr O'Reilly, but was pleased to have retained Ryman. At first he had been apprehensive about the connection, feeling he might leave himself open to blackmail. Quite obviously nothing had been farther from Ryman's mind. Duckett hadn't found him brash or offensive, as he suspected so many of his ilk were. And as their relationship progressed he came to consider Ryman less and less as a criminal. They were business associates. Ryman sought his advice about investments, and to judge by some of the quotations he came along with, he listened in the right quarters. There were still a few sound investments to be made for a prudent man.

The butler entered without rapping at the door.

'Mr Ryman is here, sir,' the man said. He had a precise, stiff appearance, more like a hotel manager in his neat grey suit. Some American clients who came to the house sometimes seemed disappointed that the man didn't have the traditional Edwardian appearance of an English butler.

'Thank you, Clifford. Ask him to come through.'

The telephone on the desk rang and Duckett answered it. The butler made no attempt to. Any of the other phones in the house he would have answered, but this one was an unlisted number which few people had. Down the line was

Duckett's secretary, with a Japanese banker on another connection. The man was returning to Japan in the morning and wanted to know if it was possible to have dinner that evening. Most appointments his secretary could cope with, but when Duckett sat on the bench at the local magistrates' court she was out of touch with his day.

He didn't want to drag into town this evening, but to spend as much time as possible alone with Carolyn. Normally he might have asked his partner, Herman Reinhardt, to meet the man, but Reinhardt was in New York.

Reluctantly he said, 'Ask Mr Mifune if he would care to have dinner here. Arrange to have him collected in the Daimler.' Had the meeting been potentially more important he would have sent the Rolls. 'Seven-thirty for eight.' When he replaced the receiver Ryman was in the room, standing by a large Adam fireplace. They were neither formal nor intimate in their greeting.

'A drink, Charles?'

'Eh, no. I don't think so. It's a bit early.'

'Perhaps some tea. I'm going to have some.' He found Clifford in the hall. 'Do sit, Charles,' he said when he returned.

Ryman took one of the leather wing-chairs on either side of the fireplace. Duckett placed himself opposite.

'Good run down?'

'Not too bad. I used the old road.' There was a pause. Ryman's glance swept the book-lined room. He didn't know why, but his attempts to duplicate this room at his Wimbledon house, and other rooms which he admired, were just not successful. His gaze settled briefly on the regular features of the man opposite, then moved to the window.

'She rides that horse pretty good, doesn't she.'

Duckett didn't look towards the window. 'She rides at school, of course.'

'She's grown since I last saw her. On holiday?' He guessed she was, having seen other kids. 'It's nice to meet a properly brought up kid. Most of the little bastards nowadays – right tearaways. Don't take any notice of their parents, teachers; no one.'

'The problem of vandalism in schools is becoming rather serious. They're being brought before the bench in increasing numbers. There were two cases this morning.'

'Lock 'em up. That's the only thing to do. Give them a taste of Borstal.'

Duckett resisted a smile. They had placed each of the boys before them this morning on probation. In one incident they had broken up a classroom and terrorized the teacher, but even so he had seen some vestige of hope in them. Approved School would merely have brutalized and destroyed them.

On the bench Anthony Duckett was by no means a limp-handed liberal. Quite the reverse. He believed in the punishment fitting the crime. A lot of people thought him callous, uncharitable; some called him as much, and worse, after sentencing. But he never allowed that to deter him. He had implicit belief in the efficacy of his actions. If a man committed a crime and it was subsequently proven, then punishment was a natural consequence. However, he took no pleasure in sentencing miscreants; it was part of the duty which he performed for society as best he could. He recognised that from birth he had had far more of life's advantages, the privileges which set men apart, far more than could ever be hoped for by most of those who appeared before him on that one day a week he gave to public service. But he tried not to let that influence him. A man wasn't necessarily a rogue because he was poor; it simply gave him more reason for being one.

'It's a problem that we must take firmly in hand before it grows beyond manageable proportions.'

'I don't know what's happening with kids today, straight I don't. I suppose it's the parents. They've no control over them. Kids do as they like.'

'I'm sure you might be right, Charles.'

A stoutish woman with grey hair and wearing an apron fetched in a tea trolley. The cook, stepping into the breach on the maid's day off.

'Thank you, Edwina.' The woman left after pouring their tea. 'You care for milk or sugar? Help yourself.'

Ryman took both in his tea, and a piece of the cake. He was momentarily in a slight dilemma over how to eat the cake. Normally he would have picked it up, but he saw the dessert forks and finally used one. In Duckett's presence he tried to behave perfectly correctly. 'This is good cake.'

'Yes. I'm very fortunate with Edwina.'

His wife had found the cook, and he had expected her to take the woman after the divorce. Possibly she had felt that a cook was an unnecessary extravagance – not that she had previously concerned herself over such matters.

'I'm not entirely sure that we should blame the parents. Any more than one can blame television, football hooliganism, or a woolly-minded government. Doubtless all factors contribute to the problem.'

With a mouthful of cake, 'I still think they should be cracked down on. Worse day's work ever when corporal punishment was abolished.' Ryman, like a lot of his contemporaries, believed it.

Duckett rose with the cup and saucer and went to the window. His daughter was still exercising her pony. His wealth, the position he held in society, the kind of existence he led, all served to make him an isolationist; Duckett wondered what the future held for Carolyn, whether there was any hope of her comfortable insularity being preserved as his had.

Fifty-eight years ago the birth of Anthony Irving Alexander Duckett had been recorded on the front page of *The Times*. He was the first son of the banker Henry Duckett, who was at one time Chancellor of the Exchequer; he was also related by marriage to Edward VII. Henry Duckett's excursion into politics had been brief, and his son had no aspirations there. But like his father he had understood the essential nexus between banker and politician, and for that reason had cultivated friendships with members on both sides of the House. Anthony Duckett hadn't merely inherited a position at the top of the family banking business, he had earned it, along with the respect of his peers. Theirs had been old money, staid, safe, faithful to the institutions of banking; Anthony Duckett energized it, formed alliances with new money. A number of traditionalists in the City believed, incorrectly, that they were rash misalliances. The newest partner in the bank had undoubtedly been the most energetic, yet at the same time exercised a fine degree of prudence. He not only acknowledged the ethical code of banking, but also the family ethic, which consisted of religious feeling, hard work and the recognition that every pound in the family bank implied a responsibility, every client a duty.

The streak of piety that persisted in their banking habits did so up until the death of Henry Duckett. By that time Anthony Duckett had earned a good deal of the bank's equities; his father left him his entire stock, with a stipulation that he provide for his mother and two brothers. The one major difference between Anthony and Henry Duckett in their banking attitude was that the father would never entertain anyone lacking impeccable credentials; the son would listen to anyone's proposition, regardless of who or where he came from, then subsequently commit or not solely on the merits of the case. In addition to the securities, interest or whatever else was needed to cause them to commit the bank's resources, a seat on the borrower's board was usually required. That way Duckett felt he would have some control over the destiny of the bank's finances. Between them, his partner, the other three bank directors and himself held hundreds of directorships, though they rarely took any active part or attended board meetings unless the fortunes of a particular company were ailing. Almost certainly the old boy wouldn't have approved of the partnership he had formed twelve years ago with Reinhardt, but fortunately he didn't have to.

He turned, came back to the trolley and put down his cup. 'What do you know of Glasgow, Charles?'

'Not a lot. It's a tough city, or always was. Plenty of vandalism there, I think.'

'I'm sure. And insufficient policemen to cope with that sort of problem.' He poured himself more tea.

Ryman watched him attentively. The face, with its even, pink, wax-like complexion and crow's-feet around the eyes, gave nothing away. Then Ryman never expected it to.

'Why do you ask?' He knew there'd be a reason.

'Do you know, Charles, that in spite of what was known as the Great Train Robbery, money is still shipped out of Glasgow in the same fashion?'

'No. That surprises me. You'd have thought they'd have made some other arrangements after that one.'

'Apparently they did at first. But the arrangements they had originally were the most economic and viable. After all, Glasgow airport could prove as vulnerable as a railway hi-jacking.'

'That's incredible. Exactly the same method?'

'With one or two refinements. They have Securicor guards on the train,' conversationally. 'The money from the Scottish clearing banks goes in smaller batches, and more frequently.'

'Amazing. What sort of parcels do they ship at a time?'

'Around two hundred thousand pounds.'

'I bet the lads tucked up inside would be interested to hear about that.'

Duckett glanced over at the man and wondered. He couldn't see how the information would make the slightest difference to those criminals. But such meaningless statements were simply a characteristic of Ryman's. Resuming his seat by the fire, Duckett gave his visitor the rest of the details he had about the money shipments. This was limited, as he never researched the information which he sometimes received; there was never any need. Not once did he offer to reveal how he came by his information, and Ryman never asked.

The conversation shortly moved away from the subject they had met specifically to discuss. They speculated on the weather; the possibility of snow was still present, though Duckett hoped they wouldn't get it, as his farm manager was experimenting with advanced spring sowing.

Carolyn looked in; ate a piece of chocolate cake through telling how her pony was coming on; then went to bathe.

'You don't have children, Charles, do you?'

'No. We've a couple of poodles.'

That was a strange juxtaposition, Duckett thought, but didn't pursue it. There was a pause. He rose decisively, indicating that their meeting was over.

'Well, I suppose I'd better be getting back.'

At the main door Ryman extended his hand. Here again, as throughout their meeting, he avoided addressing him by name, Duckett noticed. At the onset of their relationship Ryman had called him Mr Duckett. He had dropped that as they became less formal, but rarely addressed him by his Christian name. He supposed that was as it should be; each remaining within his clearly defined area.

Chapter 5

More and more frequently Kellan had found himself walking the cold, windswept streets of Glasgow, trying to absorb the last vestiges of the city he knew and loved and hated; trying to suck in its last undistilled essences before the little of the original that remained disappeared beneath the plethora of redevelopment. This change was odious to Kellan, and like most changes, he resisted it. With all its faults he preferred the old order; the past, of which he had been an active part, had lived and breathed. The new, towering office blocks, and those flyovers which simply got you to the next traffic jam quicker, were conspiring to force him out.

He was very possessive about Glasgow. It had its problems; he had lived with them on the streets throughout his thirty-four years as a policeman. But somehow in the past they had always been in proportion, manageable, whether it was drunken rivals at the Celtic-Rangers matches or hardened criminal gangs like the Liberty Boys from Southside, San Toy from Calton, the Beehive gang from the Gorbals. Most had been broken, forced on the line, sent down; their familiar spawning grounds crumbled before bulldozers. Now there was a whole new set of criminals – though that description elevated them to an undeserved status. They weren't criminals as Kellan had known them: tough, hard men who did their crime and their time; they had been almost heroic figures by comparison, and had reasons within Kellan's comprehension for turning to crime. Their background, its inherent lack of opportunity, left little alternative. But today's criminals were nothing more than thugs, tearaways. Their crimes were invariably accompanied by waves of senseless violence, untold vandalism, defying logic. There was no need for them to be villains; they lived in a spoon-fed society crammed full of opportunity, and if you didn't want to take advantage of it, no one said, Too bad, laddie! The government were happy to support any idleness. He had heard arguments put up by defence lawyers and psychiatrists about how these tearaways were alienated by their new concrete and glass boxes – he could believe that; how their brains had become softened with boredom – that he could believe also; no one had to think for himself any more. But as far as he was concerned the arguments carried no weight. He would lock the lot of the bastards up and throw away the key. Keep them in cages for the rest of their lives, like animals, for that's what they were.

Criminals, cossetted by the very society whose property they destroyed, whose lives and happiness they threatened, defended by psychiatrists who never had the misfortune to encounter them on the streets: Kellan could no longer relate to them. Not like the old days, when you could admire a good professional job.

Kellan shivered convulsively, though he didn't feel cold, and forced his hands deeper into the pockets of his sheepskin coat. The night was raw, even for a Glaswegian February. Too cold for snow, everyone said. He hoped they were right. This sort of weather was good for Glasgow. It left the city dry underfoot and gave the air a crispness, a freshness for having killed off the filth which had built up over the months. It also tended to kill off the winos who fell in the street, those who had had enough booze to collapse but not enough to keep out the biting cold through those lonely hours until daylight. They were probably better off dead, Kellan had decided a long time ago.

From the elevation where he stood on St Vincent Street, his gaze moved vacantly across the skyline of the city. The night air was clear and the city fairly still. It had got so that these days he didn't notice the scrape and grind of everyday traffic. The occasional lorry that was arriving into the markets either too late or too early was the only reminder of it now. The pubs weren't chucking out yet, so the evening's spate of drunken disturbances hadn't reached its pitch. An hour or so and radio cars would be answering calls for help from publicans in trouble where customers decided they wanted to drink after hours.

A tug boat sounded its horn for some reason on a down-river stretch of the Clyde. The sound echoed a forlornness which made Kellan shiver again. It might have been a death knell for himself or the city, or both, for he often felt they were inseparable. He had been part of Glasgow for a long time, fifty-three years. They had stolen pieces of the city from him, changing its shape while his back was turned, but he had hung on regardless, refusing to slacken his grip. He had recognised a growing sense of futility in his actions; the old orders were going to the wall in spite of him. He stared down towards the Clyde. He could not see it because of a new office block. The area below had been redeveloped out of its comfortable squalor, beyond the needs of the people. There were certifiable cretins working in City Hall; no one else would ever have willingly been a party to what was happening, unless they were earning a lot of money in bribes. Perhaps they were. Kellan didn't pursue that though. Shaking his head despondently, he moved away along the street; his car was parked on the other side of the block, and it would have been quicker to turn the opposite way to police HQ.

The strident wail of a klaxon immediately took Kellan's attention. Every time he encountered it unexpectedly it caused a stirring of excitement in him, an inclination to speed after the noise, to investigate. He did that rarely. He would probably see the resulting police report, especially if the cause subsequently proved to be anything at all worthwhile.

As head of Strathclyde CID, Detective Chief Superintendent Kellan got copies of all major Crime Reports as a matter of course. Reports were made in triplicate; one copy remained in the book, one went to the front office for the uniform branch and the other continued through channels to Kellan. That way all who needed informing were informed. Some senior officers didn't read the reports, but just glanced through them or automatically added their signature. Kellan made a point of reading every report which came across his desk, and made sure that every report did come before him, rather than leaving them for his superintendents or chief inspectors. This procedure helped him keep his finger on every pulse, kept him in touch with what was going on in his city. Kellan rarely delegated responsibility. It wasn't that he believed the men under him to be incompetent, but rather that he knew they weren't. He was afraid that the younger detectives around him were crowding him out of his job, just as he felt he was being crowded out of his city.

The divisional HQ on Pitt Street, where Kellan had his office, was a sprawling four-storey, red-brick building. It had been a telephone exchange, but now it was one of the most modern computerized police headquarters in Europe. The place had an inviting look, despite the heavy steel-reinforced riot door and shutters on ground-floor windows. But it didn't fool the locals, most of whom wouldn't have gone there to report the loss of a dog, much less get involved any deeper with the police.

Kellan drove his car into the compound at the back. He had a car and driver at his disposal twenty-four hours a day, but rarely called his man out when he made an impromptu visit like this. Not infrequently he returned in the evening, and kept to no regular time. He expected to catch his men off guard, and did. But that wasn't the only reason for returning.

Subconsciously he was afraid. The possibility that things would run as smoothly in his absence as in his presence was his secret fear. Unknown to himself, Kellan was striving to create such a degree of dependence upon him around HQ, in all matters, that they wouldn't be able to let him retire when his time arrived. He wouldn't retire willingly. He would go on for as long as he was able. Kellan would be compelled to retire in two years, on his fifty-fifth birthday, unless the system decided otherwise. He might fail his next medical. But he tried not to think about the future. He had been entitled to retire on half-pay nine years ago, but had decided to go on; an extra five years qualified him for another ten sixtieths of his pay as a pension. Only that wasn't the reason; Kellan wasn't short of a few quid, having salted some away over his career. He was one of those policemen who didn't know what to do off duty. He had no interests outside police work. His wife had often urged him to find something else, but his excuse had always been that he never had time. The woman cooked his meals, washed his clothes, kept his house tidy; they shared the same bed still, but the passion had gone out of their marriage. There had been little enough in the first place.

Kellan took the lift to the third floor and went along to the control room to check the duty log. The room was very warm with the dry heat from electronic equipment constantly running, and things had the appearance of being slack and lethargic there. Three uniformed policemen sitting around a steel map-table, half-full mugs of tea within easy reach, stiffened perceptibly one after another as each became aware of Kellan's presence. The duty sergeant appeared out of one of the side offices. He was a portly man with a red face from too much booze. He wasn't as tall as Kellan, or as heavy. He saluted.

'Good evening, sir.'

The DCS let his glance fall on the three men at the table. Again, they were the uniform branch and as long as they always did what was required of them in relation to assisting the CID, that was all Kellan cared about, although he would doubtless mention the slackness to Superintendent McWhirter when next he saw him.

'Pretty slack this evening, sergeant,' Kellan said brusquely and moved on to the table where the huge duty log was kept. The sergeant fell in alongside him.

'Aye, quieter than a kirk social, sir. One or two wee things were passed downstairs.'

The DCS wasn't listening. He was running his fingernail down the entries, checking what was written there, his finger traversing the page as he read items that had been passed to the CID. There was a breaking reported; one more suspected, nothing much else.

Kellan raised his eyes, met the duty sergeant's apprehensive look, then briefly swept the room, taking in most things at a glance. The alarms board circuit was quiet; the r/t receiver made a faint crackle, indicating life in it; the computers hummed but, like the teleprinters, were quite still. A distant telephone rang in an office somewhere and was answered. Another rang in this large office. One of the policemen answered it promptly.

'There's some kind of disturbance on Sauchiehall Street, Sarge,' the constable said in a heavy Glaswegian accent. Having informed the duty sergeant, he turned his attention back to the caller for further details.

The sergeant told one of the other constables to find a car in the vicinity and get it down there.

Kellan moved out, satisfied that some kind of activity had started, however insignificant.

Sergeant McTovey watched the large frame of the DCS disappear. He suspected that he was on his way along to the CID squad-room to see if they were any busier. He reckoned the man ought to stay downstairs. He had no inclination to ring ahead and warn the detectives that Kellan was on his way. They no longer had that kind of relationship.

Kellan's office was on the second floor, along with the Chief Constable's office and those of the four Assistant Chief Constables, plus their secretaries. Although the Chief Constable and his deputies wore uniforms, all dealt mainly with administrative matters; that included the Assistant Chief Constable with responsibility for crime. Kellan didn't resent that, in fact he preferred it, as it meant in effect that there was no one in the constabulary actively to interfere with him. The CC or the Assistant Chief Constable would sometimes visit the scenes of major crimes, and have a few words with the press, but neither stuck his oar in much beyond that.

The offices were in darkness as the lift stopped and the gates slid open. The light from behind Kellan cast an enormous shadow along the narrow corridor. There was no need to reach for the light switch, the lift would remain with the doors open until called. The floor was so familiar to Kellan that he could have found his way as easily in the pitch dark.

Kellan's office was large, with a lot of window space, and arguably the best view. He faced south-east towards the Clyde; the stretch of river he could see was little compensation for the squalor beyond it. At night it could almost be described as picturesque, even with the harsh sodium lights which had proliferated in Glasgow quicker than any strain of VD. Kellan much preferred the gas lamps which had popped and spluttered where the glass was so often broken. There weren't many gas lamps left now, and those that remained were almost permanently broken. The tall concrete standards made the orange street lights less accessible, and their heads were of toughened glass; but weren't infallible.

Easing off his coat, he laid it on one of the two cracked leather armchairs, then lowered himself into the heavily padded chair behind the desk. Kellan liked sitting behind his desk, it reassured him of his power. Still he didn't put the light on. His eyes had adjusted to the darkness and he let his gaze wander around the office, moving over the framed photographs which lined the walls, as easily crossing the thresholds of memory. There was a picture of him with the previous Chief Constable, another with the present man; one when he met the Queen; numerous pictures at the scenes of crimes he had been particularly successful in cracking. Most of the photographs came from the press, including those early ones of his grandfather, and later his father, who had been shot dead while on duty. 'The Glasgow Gangbuster' was how the captions heralded Kellan. More than any other man he had cleaned up the streets of Glasgow, removed the canker of hardened criminal gangs which had given the city its notorious reputation. The Gangbuster. He had liked that name a lot. His gaze settled on a shadow-enshrouded photograph, and although he couldn't define the images he knew the picture as well as his hand. It was his triumphant departure from court after seeing the four top members of the Hamilton gang sent down for twenty-five years. Podgie Hamilton and his two brothers had been real basses. No one was going to put his picture in the newspaper for capturing the bits of thugs who ran wild nowadays.

The fact that there were no longer any real, hardened criminal gangs left, headline-catching gangs, Kellan perversely took as an insult rather than a compliment to his personal efficiency and the effectiveness of his detectives.

His eyes moved on to another photograph, his gaze falling into the middle distance as thoughts trailed back. At such times Kellan, like most men with an infinitely greater past than they could anticipate a future, relived his glory, those moments when he was the single identifiable hard man. Those moments were his. No one could take them away, they were etched into his brain with the freshness of that evening's Glasgow *Evening Times*, only with greater clarity. At that point Ian Kellan wasn't the senior policeman confronted with the daunting, inexorable approach of compulsory retirement, he was a detective in full stride, one who couldn't be stopped, whom no one but those he was operating against would want to stop.

Time slipped away from Kellan when he was in such a reflective mood. He was startled by the phone. DS Tarelton informed him that they had picked up two suspects for the mugging on Sauchiehall Street. They were being brought in – a couple of kids.

The DCS received this last piece of information with reluctant resignation. He flicked on his desk lamp after replacing the phone, but didn't glance beyond the pool of light now to the photographs and memories which lay out there. He decided he would stay around a while longer, having little enough reason to go home. He reached over for the pile of reports that had been put into his 'posts' tray. Regardless of how major or minor the villain was, the paperwork never stopped.

Chapter 6

Janet Bothwell wouldn't have had her husband within a mile of a telephone when he was off duty. But she understood how Stuart felt about his job. It meant a lot to him and she knew he did it well. Whenever the phone rang at that time of evening they both knew where the call would be coming from.

'It's Sergeant McTovey – full of apologies as usual,' she said, returning to the living-room. She had prevented him rising to the phone, as though her answering it would put off his inevitable return to work. She didn't blame Sergeant McTovey. From what she knew of the man he wasn't the type to call unnecessarily. Mac was generally someone who coped.

'Tell him I cannae come. I'm in front of ma fire wi' ma feet up watching TV.' He was rising.

'I already told him that. But your man will not be put off. Will I make some cocoa?'

'I'd say coffee'd be more like it, hen.' He went out into the small entrance hall. His wife went to the kitchen.

'Mac,' Bothwell said into the phone. 'What's the trouble?'

McTovey told him about the two lads, Billy Stevenson and Tim Duffy, who had been brought in. They were thirteen and fourteen years old, and were being interrogated by the CID. That was a problem for the boys, but not one that McTovey would normally call on Bothwell with at that time of night. As duty sergeant and assistant to Chief Inspector Bothwell, who ran Community Involvement, McTovey was in the ideal position to handle the arrest of two minors. The problem which had arisen, and it was serious in that it negated his authority, was the presence of DCS Kellan. Kellan was known for his lack of sympathy in that area; he had even less time for Community Involvement, where minors in trouble with the police were taken before a panel of three members of the public rather than the courts. Kel-

Ian's main bone of contention, shared by most detectives, was that kids so dealt with were rarely sent to Approved School, but released on probation to commit the same crimes over again.

'I'll be in directly, Mac. Just hold the fort.'

Bothwell was proud of the uniform he wore. He wasn't like some of his colleagues, who couldn't wait to get out and were only staying on for their pensions. His job gave him a great sense of purpose, which he complemented with effort. Earlier that evening he had been out visiting over in Springboig, trying to help a couple of kids who had got into trouble. Sometimes a visit by a uniformed policeman could do more harm than good. The trust he was building up was tentative, and could easily have been lost if the lads had been subjected to neighbours' scorn by having the police to them, other than in the form of a raid.

He had three uniforms. One was away at the cleaners; one was kept hanging in a polythene bag; the third, which he wore, was always neat, no breakfast stains down the front or dandruff across the shoulders. He wasn't a martinet about neatness, it was simply a question of personal choice. He put on a clean shirt. A crumpled appearance would, he felt, put him at a disadvantage if he came to any kind of confrontation with DCS Kellen.

Before leaving for work Bothwell went through a ritual of kissing each of his four daughters goodbye. They were a close family, and he enjoyed their displays of affection. A lot of policemen had abysmal family lives and simply blamed the unsocial aspects of the job. But Bothwell thought that a poor excuse, suspecting that a lot of them didn't care for people, least of all children. They were losers for that, he believed. His daughters were aged from eleven to four. They were all soundly asleep save the youngest. She put her arms around her father's neck as he stooped over her bunk to kiss her. She tried a ploy. 'Can I get in with you? This bed, it's cold. I catch cold.'

'Let me feel.' He slid his hand into the bed and tickled her. 'You wee monkey, you're as warm as toast.' He straightened the covers and kissed her again. 'You can get in wi' us in the morning. Night night.'

She entreated him to stay, but Bothwell went out.

Collecting his peaked cap off the hall stand, he moved along the hall to the kitchen. His wife had made him tea and he swallowed some.

'Will I wait up for you?' Janet Bothwell asked, making an unnecessary adjustment to the knot in his tie.

Bothwell smiled at the implied offer. 'You get to bed, hen. I should no be too long, but . . .' he didn't need to finish the sentence.

There was a taste of cocoa at her mouth when he kissed her goodbye. He thought about it as he reversed the car out of the garage, and waved to his wife where she stood watching his departure from the tiny half-glazed porch. A familiar soft yearning welled up inside the man when he saw her standing there. The feeling he had was as strong each time. Bothwell was still very much in love with the woman, as she was with him; it was something they frequently talked about, were still able to talk about. Without Janet's active support Bothwell knew he wouldn't have been the sort of policeman he was; certainly he wouldn't have taken on that extra area of work in Community Involvement, and enjoyed it as he did.

DC Kevin Daly was large, florid, intolerant. He disliked queers, especially the kind they now had there. The nancy was pear-shaped and had on too much scent, and Daly would as soon have given him some stick as the two kids. But he had made the complaint, and that made the difference.

'Noo, Rory,' Daly said, cajolingly, 'I wan' ya to walk past the door there and tell me if they were two of those who worked you over. Understand?'

The homosexual offered a hesitant smile. The detective gripped his arm and steered him towards the door. The two boys were sitting in an interrogation room up in the CID office. They were bored rather than scared. They had been arrested before. Rory walked past, taking a hard look. He didn't need to come past again.

That was how most IDs were made, unofficially. Identity parades weren't convenient at the best of times, but at eleven o'clock at night with kids they were impossible. Without short cuts the CID could never have coped with half their load. Officially all parades should have been conducted by the uniform branch and conducted within the precincts of the front office, the idea being to eliminate the kind of unfair practice to which the two boys had been subjected. But even then it didn't work out that way. When the police wanted someone, the witness was given every advantage, whether or not there were eight others lined up with the suspect.

'There're two of them. Absolutely no doubt, officer.' The pear-shaped man shuddered.

Although he felt no sympathy for him, Daly guessed his ordeal had been real enough.

'That's good. If you like to go along wi' ma friend Roy here, you can fix up your statement. We'll get them to gi' us the other little basses.'

Roy Neal was younger than Daly and hadn't been in the CID as long. He turned away to hide his smile at the DC taking the piss out of the queer.

'C'mon then, mister.'

Moving into the interrogation room, Daly stood and grinned menacingly at the two boys. 'You wee basses. Thought you'd tek yersel' a few bob off yon poof, did you?'

They scowled at him, neither attempting to speak. Theirs were the hard, burred faces of street kids, sensibility bred out of them long ago. They knew how to survive where survival was dictated by fleetness of foot and hardness of fist. Advantages of innate intelligence were used to think up more cunning ploys rather than to get out of the vicious circle of street-level existence.

'We gotcha cold, so you might as well cop. Gi' us the other two wi' ya.' He waited, growing impatient at their insolent silence. 'What ha'e ya to say, Billy Stevenson?'

The elder of the two boys raised his scrawny shoulders. He was wearing a dark blue windcheater with a large C on the breast. Asked by a policeman what it stood for, he had replied 'Cunt'. The remark had earned him a clout around the head. He had known it would.

'We dinnae touch the fat queer, did we, Tim?'

The second boy, who was thinner and had on enormous combat boots, was quick to agree.

Daly knew he'd progress faster if he separated them. He gave them a cold, measured stare.

'You fancy your chances wi' me, then?' He could have beaten holy shit out of them and half a dozen more besides.

Taking Billy Stevenson into the main squad-room, Daly left him under the watchful eye of DS Tarelton; back across the corridor he purposefully shut the door.

'You gonna beat me up, sur?' the younger boy asked.

Daly had been a detective long enough to know that you didn't let suspects dictate the terms, certainly not wee kids, though he felt like slapping him a bit to take the lip out of of him. 'I'm a policeman, lad. Dinnae your Ma tell you to respect policemen and answer them truthfully?' There was nothing kids like this detested more than being talked down to, unless it was being talked at in that way in front of other kids.

'Tol' me what a lot o' thieving basses you were.'

'Aye, well, we all gotta get a living, Tim.' The lad was getting under his skin, and going the right way for a bashing. 'Where's your Ma? On the streets? Or is she over the wall?'

'She ain't fucking neither!' The denial was angry.

Sitting on the edge of the scarred table, Daly looked the boy slowly up and down. 'I bet you're right handy in the crowd down Ibrox Park. Stand up, Tim, tek your boots off.'

'What?' – it emerged as a cry of alarm.

'You heard. Tek 'em off, or I will! Move, you little fooker.'

Seeing that the detective meant business, he quickly unlaced his boots and pulled them off.

When Daly inspected them he found that large metal studs had been driven in the front part of the soles. Inside the toecaps there were wads of cotton wool, both to reduce the impact from kicking and to make the boots, which had to be three sizes too big, fit better. The boy was reduced in status without them, and became subdued.

'Why did you attack yon fat queer? After his poke, were ya?'

'We dinnae touch him.'

'He's identified you. Who d'you think the sheriff's gonna believe when you get ta court?' – it was wishful thinking.

'Och, he can go fook hissel'.'

'Aye, I daresay he's tried 'fore now.'

That drew a smile; the boy had found a common enemy with the cop. Not all the polis liked the judges and court sheriffs.

'Ah, the old fat lad probably had it coming. Out to do a bit of queer-bashing, were you?'

'Never saw him before in m' life.'

Daly turned the boots over, wondering whether scrutiny in the forensic lab would show fibre traces from the man's clothes.

'D'you usually go around wi'oot any boots on?' He let the boy puzzle over the question, then said, 'Unless you tell me about the jumping I'll burn these.'

'They're ma boots. Ya cannae burn them.' The prospect distressed him. Without his boots he had no identity.

'You wanna bet? I'll tek the fooking things down to the icinerator. You can ha'e 'em back if ya tell me about yon queer.' He placed the boots on the table.

The boy looked from the boots to the unremitting detective, then back to the boots. He was having problems over the choice, but finally made it.

'Fooking burn 'em,' Stevenson responded to the threat to *his* boots. 'Plenty more where they come from.'

His patience spent, the larger, more senior DC hit the boy, sending him sprawling. The blow left a red weal across his face. That sort of treatment he had come to expect; kids with less experience of the police didn't always need the hard treatment, they were often tricked by the soft promises of the second detective. Billy Stevenson immediately recognised what it was they were doing. He was determined not to yield, and didn't even mind if they beat him up; that was sometimes an advantage when appearing before the Panel.

'We don't need you to tell us a thing, laddie, your wee haufer has told us all about the other two.'

'Ach, Timmy dinnae ken whit he's talking on.'

A smile spread across Daly's booze-broken face. He had the boy worried. 'Enough to get you a bit in the housey. You won't have your boots and fags there.'

At that stage Daly knew he could break the lad, and would have done, had Chief Inspector Bothwell not pushed into the room.

With little love lost between the CID and the uniform branch, situations like this only made matters worse.

From the information he had so far received Bothwell knew that the two detectives were guilty of serious malpractice. Pursuing the matter to the Disciplinary Board would depend on whether he felt the position the two boys had been taken to was irreconcilable. He had no wish to exacerbate the bad relations with the CID, but at the same time wouldn't turn a blind eye to such infractions solely for the sake of peace.

The detectives and the man in uniform regarded one another, the boy between them clearly puzzled, his small brain working at the angles; the intervention of a third polis, senior and in uniform was, he thought, a new version of the old hard–soft routine.

'Has the lad been charged?' Bothwell asked pointedly, knowing that he hadn't, nor would be.

'Not yet, sur.'

'I see. A word please, Mr Daly.'

Bothwell stepped out into the corridor. The DC followed without shutting the door. The chief inspector reached over and pulled the door to. Rebuking officers in front of subordinates or suspects was something Bothwell always avoided. He took no pleasure in another man's humiliation.

'Well, mister?'

'Just having a chat, sur, a friendly wee chat.' His tone was insolent.

'You know better than to have him up here like a hardened criminal.'

'With respect, sur, that's what the bass is. A hardened criminal. They mugged yon big soft bender.'

'Aye, maybe they did,' Bothwell said ponderously. 'Or maybe they were protecting themselves from his homosexual advances. Did you think on that?'

Anger was rising through DC Daly. He resisted replying but the blood disappeared from his lips where they tightened against each other.

The two policemen were about the same age, late thirties. One was successful and could cope with his job, the other one couldn't and had to take short cuts. Daly had known that the two young suspects would be protected once they entered the official channels of police procedure. He would have got away with the stroke he tried had one of the other uniformed sergeants been the duty officer instead of McTovey.

'We'll have them both along in my office and interview them there. With their parents. Meanwhile run a check on the victim and see if he's a record for importuning. Wee boys or otherwise.'

A uniform man telling a detective how to do his job, the difference in rank notwithstanding, was hard to swallow. 'I already have, sur. I'm waiting for the report now.'

'Good,' Bothwell said generously.

The two boys were taken out of the CID offices. Ensconced in Bothwell's office, given tea and shown friendship, they were completely disorientated. It was a trick, every instinct told them so.

Neither of the boys' parents had phones, so a wireless car had to be sent to contact them; the pubs were out, so there was a good chance they would be at home. Bothwell casually chatted to the lads, who were both Rangers supporters, proud of it and of the damage they managed to inflict on the traditional enemy, Celtic supporters.

It sometimes amazed Sergeant McTovey how his chief managed to get such a response from kids. For his own part he didn't mind assisting him in Community Involvement administration work, but knew his contribution was slight compared to Bothwell's. The chief inspector had a great empathy with, an unflagging tolerance of Glasgow's riot of destructive youth. Most officers would simply have locked them up after a beating, but Bothwell seemed to understand every combination of circumstances which made kids behave as they did. Many lads had been saved from the 'Grove or Borstal because of his intervention – a particularly aggravating point with the CID. Bothwell wasn't overly concerned that the CID weren't having their results confirmed with convictions. There were times when Bothwell appeared out of touch with the reality of the situation. Quite often McTovey recognised that some of the more wily youths, along with their parents, were trading on his good nature. But the man had frequently said he would rather that, if it meant helping just one lad who was genuine. He even took kids to his home when their parents couldn't be located, rather than have them spend the night at the police office or a remand home.

The front office was getting busy now the pubs had shut. There were complaints of fights, broken windows, disturbances; people were fetched in for charging; other incidents merely required the presence of a uniformed policeman. All in varying degrees required McTovey's attention. It was during this activity that he saw DCS Kellan's approach. His appearance didn't augur well for Chief Inspector Bothwell, whose office he was making for. McTovey had no opportunity of either heading the DCS off or of warning his chief.

Throwing open the door, Kellan let it bang against the stop, catching it on the rebound. The sight confronting him enraged him more. Bothwell and the two youths were having a cosy little tea party.

'Just what the hell do you think you're aboot, laddie?' Kellan demanded. 'Coming on like some bloody fairy Godfather, taking prisoners off the CID.'

Bothwell looked at the two suddenly bewildered children, the rapport he had established vanishing with this new threat. He looked at the DCS, wondering whether to invite him into the next office. But he hadn't designed the scene.

'They should no' ha'e been in wi' the CID, sir. They're minors.'

'Aye. But they're also vicious wee criminals who can do as much damage as their big brothers and fathers.'

All Bothwell could do was quote the script when arguing with officers like Kellan. 'The ruling is very precise, sir. Minors should not be taken beyond the front office.'

'Don't tell me! I was breaking those sort o' regulations before you considered becoming a copper. I do no' care if you are the officer with overall responsibility for Community Involvement. That does no' put a magic wand in your mitt. These buggers are going to be charged with the vicious assault they committed. Now you can get their parents here; solicitors; their Aunt Marys on the Panel, too. But they're going to be interrogated by the arresting officers. Are you reading me, Mr Bothwell?'

'I am, sir.' The prompt, mild response surprised Kellan.

The DCS gave the two boys a withering look, then turned his stare on the chief inspector before wheeling out.

There was a pause before Billy Stevenson said, 'Ha'e we gotta go back down the corridor, sur?'

Bothwell glanced at the boy, wondering when he had last called anyone sir of his own accord.

'I think not, Billy. But it depends on what you tell me noo.'

He offered the boys more tea. He had some ground to win back.

Chapter 7

Armed with the details of the potential blag in Glasgow, Charles Ryman was now committed to finding the right draftsman for the job. Someone to do all the planning on the ground; reconnoitre the proposed scene of the robbery, work out whether the robbery was practicable; put a stop-watch to all moving elements, get out the road maps and surveyor's maps; discover the ways in and out of the blag, the city and, if necessary, the country. On some jobs the draftsman also had to find out exactly what it was worth, how much it would yield from the fence; find the fence and arrange delivery to him. Also he had to get the villains, negotiate what they would receive and how. The draftsman was a technician of the highest order, and the number of men in that specialised profession was limited. Ryman knew of only six, and of those he had first-hand experience of three.

First choice was Michael Trippet. He had done several jobs for Ryman, including his last, which had gone without a hitch. No draftsman ever worked exclusively for one firm, any more than they ever exclusively employed one team; so there was never any guarantee that Ryman would be able to get the man he wanted when he needed him. Trippet had given him no indication of his availability, but the world wouldn't exactly stop if he couldn't make it. Ryman had arranged to meet him at the Castle in Camberwell. This particular draftsman didn't like moving off his manor, and for that reason Ryman suspected he might turn him down. It would mean a trip to Glasgow, and also spending time there setting things up. Their previous jobs together had all been in London.

Around Camberwell Green the traffic was solid. A bus had broken down, which wasn't helping matters. The puce-coloured Jaguar filtered slowly right and eventually turned left into Camberwell Church Street. Ryman guessed correctly that he wouldn't find a place to park legally. He was already late, despite having left in plenty of time. Searching out a meter to park on wouldn't only make him later still, he might miss Trippet altogether. Avoiding illegal parking and the accompanying risk of tickets was almost like a religion to Ryman. It was not that he couldn't afford the fines; but a parking ticket established that he was in a certain place at a certain time; something he would rather not have established. Today he took a chance and parked in a restricted zone, hoping the traffic wardens were making themselves busy elsewhere.

The detective constable driving the ice-blue Rover 3500 had no less a problem finding a place to park, though a parking ticket would be taken care of internally. It was made easier for the DC by the presence of Detective Sergeant Brian 'Hawkeye' Lemon. No one was too sure where his nickname originated, some said he got it because he was the best there was at this sort of detail. He could follow a suspect for days without the person ever knowing.

DS Lemon slid out of the car, leaving his colleague to park somewhere convenient in case they had to take off in a hurry. He pushed into the same bar Ryman had entered. The likelihood of his being IDd wasn't great. Dressed in a scarred, worn sheepskin, jeans and boots, he looked more like a street trader than CID, and merged with the pub clientele.

Ryman bought himself a gin and tonic and found a quiet table. The bar was overhung with the stale smell of cigarette smoke and booze. Why Michael Trippet used this class of pub Ryman didn't know. It wouldn't have been *his* choice.

Shortly Trippet detached himself from the company he was in and joined Ryman. 'How are you, Charles? – Can I get you another drink before he shouts "Time"?'

'No, I'm all right.'

Ryman ran his eyes carefully over the other customers. They all looked harmless enough, except one. A woman sitting near the door, who looked like she might give you a little touch of something nasty.

They didn't talk about business straight off. Trippet admired the double-breasted beige wool suit Ryman had on, and was offered his tailor. His top coat was a brushed pigskin. Discretion, which wasn't reflected in Trippet's choice of pub, was something he did otherwise display. He avoided delicate subjects; he didn't ask about the attractive young woman he had once seen in Ryman's car. He didn't talk about past jobs, nor about villains, unless in direct relation to a proposed job. He knew Ryman preferred being called Charles, though the man through whom they had originally met always called him Charlie.

Fifteen minutes passed in idle, safe talk. The publican called 'Time' and set about emptying the bar. The customers finished their drinks and left unhurriedly. The soapy woman by the door was the last to depart, leaving Trippet and Ryman. The landlord made no move to turn them out.

'There's something that looks like coming up pretty soon,' Ryman said in a low voice, glancing towards the landlord and barman, who were clearing up. 'Worth around two hundred, it's estimated. It's a little bit out of the way's the only problem.'

The draftsman was still listening.

'Glasgow.'

Trippet didn't recoil. He thoughtfully raised his glass and emptied it. 'When, exactly?'

'Immediately.' That meant as soon as it could be arranged. 'What's your availability?' He might have been a film producer seeking an actor for a part. But then, that was how most robberies tended to be organised, leastwise the successful ones executed by professionals. Cowboys operated spur-of-the-moment hold-ups.

'To be perfectly truthful, Charles, I don't think I'd be able to help you. Not immediately.'

'How soon do you reckon?' Ryman was already thinking about his alternatives.

'Can't say without putting you on a promise. I've got a couple of things at the moment. Don't think it would be fair to my clients if I was to take on something else. Especially out of town. If it could be put back?'

Ryman grinned. 'The way inflation is, Michael, there wouldn't be enough out of it to pay you, even.'

'Sure, it's best done as soon as possible. All the while one person knows about something there's a chance somebody else might. If you're interested there's someone who might be able to help you out.'

Ryman would explore his own alternatives first, but recommendations were always worth having for future reference. Ryman didn't know the man he was offered, and took his phone number.

'Sorry I can't do anything on this one,' Trippet said. 'Another time. But give him a call.'

Ryman slid his address book away and rose.

Camden Town was his next stop. He had a man there who might help him out. He ought to have tried him first; he didn't relish having to drive across town. He'd hit the rush-hour traffic both ways.

There was a white parking ticket in a plastic envelope under his windscreen wiper. He retrieved it, feeling irrationally depressed. He glanced up and down the street, but the warden had vanished. A whole line of cars had been hit, but that didn't placate him at all.

Things just weren't going his way that afternoon. Then when he pulled off into a side street to turn his car around, he found another car up his daily. Ryman opened his window and waved the car past. After a moment's hesitation it eased through the gap.

'Think he's tumbled us, skip?' the Squad detective driving the car asked, as though DSs were infallible.

'Shouldn't think so. He's was turning. My fucking fault – should've realised. Look a bit lively, Alan,' he said, leaning around to watch Ryman. 'Up there, take a left. We'll catch him at Camberwell Green.'

They were in time to see Ryman's car shoot the lights and go away towards Central London. The unmarked police car was jammed in traffic.

No matter how good the detective on the observation detail was, there were times when several cars were needed so he could radio ahead for someone else to pick up the tail.

Ryman wasn't exactly running clear, though. Traffic impeded his progress, and he was wearying of it, wondering irritably just why he paid road tax. As the car edged towards the Oval the red, white and blue sign of the underground station loomed large. He hit on the idea of parking his car and taking the train across town. But looking around, he saw the immediate parking situation was hopeless. A gap appeared ahead of him; he took a chance and made an illegal right turn into Kennington Road, planning to take the tube train from Kennington station.

'Fucking traffic!' DS Lemon punched the padded dashboard angrily. 'Here, this gap!' He shoved his arm out of the window to signal changing lanes.

The car cut in front of another, advancing them by about twenty feet. Hawkeye wrenched open the door and stood on the sill, trying to look over the traffic. 'Keep it coming, Alan.'

He stood down, slammed the door and stepped through the traffic and along the pavement, searching for the puce-coloured Jaguar, moving faster than the vehicles. The heavy, exhaust-laden air hung in the back of his throat, obliterating the taste of the scotch he had drunk earlier.

A feeling of elation leapt through him when he spotted Ryman's car. He watched its slow progress for a few moments, then sprinted back to his own car, which had gained the filter lights, and got impatient blasts from cars behind when it stopped. They swung off to the right.

The large, blackened Victorian houses flanking the road looked as though they had severe headaches from the constant throb of low-revving internal combustion engines. As the traffic had grown to its present level, local residents began to quit. Now a number of the once-splendid houses were empty, desolate, boarded up, awaiting the urban planners' next move. An eight-lane flyover would make life much more pleasant in that part of the city.

Both Charlie Ryman and Brian Lemon would have thought it an improvement just then.

'There can't be a fucking green light in the whole of South London.'

The car the two detectives were in had just ground to another halt. Lemon opened the door and stood on the sill again, but there was no sign of Ryman.

Why the order had remained for such a lightweight tailing detail Lemon didn't know; they weren't that short. The guvnor had to have some reason for not getting too heavy. Possibly he wasn't sure that Ryman could give him anything, so he didn't want to waste manpower.

'We lost him?' the DC asked as Lemon climbed back in.

'We? You. You lost him, Alan. You're driving.'

The car ran forward for a hundred yards. The traffic lights in front of Kennington Underground stayed green. As the Rover passed the junction Lemon shouted to the driver to stop. He had seen Ryman go into the station. Leaping from the car, the DS danced through the stream of vehicles. There were four people queueing at the ticket window. Ryman wasn't one of them. A lift had just descended. The DS crashed the barrier and ran down the stairs, ignoring the ticket collector.

The rush of air which preceded a train could be heard as he reached the bottom of the stairs. The tunnels leading to the platforms seemed endless. He headed for the northbound platform, as that was the way Ryman had been driving, and reached it in time to see the train doors close. He sprinted across to the train and hit the emergency button between the last and second to last carriage. The doors immediately slid open. DS Lemon climbed aboard, making sure his party didn't get off.

Bell-pushes lined both sides of the door without order. Most of them appeared to be broken, or had the names of previous tenants scratched out and their successors drawn in. Ryman pushed Alan Day's again, longer this time, and listened for the bell sounding somewhere in the house. He only imagined he heard it. The bell-push was unmarked, and gave no indication of who it belonged to or what floor it sounded on. That was in keeping with Alan Day, who was an enigma. Ryman knew him as a criminal draftsman and a good one, had employed him in that capacity, but much beyond that he didn't know. Sometimes it was far better not to know.

Perhaps he had decided the arrangement was too vague and had gone out. But he had definitely said he would be in all afternoon. Ryman was beginning to feel annoyed for having travelled across town, especially on a train with all those soapy commutors.

Hitting the bell-push once more, he spun away, but hesitated on the top of the steps. His glance traversed the street. The houses were crumbling. A few had been done up, mostly in bright colours; obviously they belonged to spades. The rest were probably rented in flatlets or rooms to sitting tenants; the landlord, unable to raise the rents, would see no profit in putting the houses in good repair.

Ryman was about to quit when the door was opened by a fairly attractive young woman. She appeared nervous and stammered when she tried to speak.

Finally she managed, 'Go up . . . He said for you to go up.'

Awkwardly she launched herself through the doorway. Her jerky movements made Ryman watch as she descended the steps. The woman had a severe limp, and he thought that perhaps she had an artificial leg under her trousers. She glanced back, showing the sort of anxiety which suggested she believed he was going to hurl something at her.

There had been rumours about Day liking cripples, and now Ryman figured there must have been some truth in them. He shuddered, and entered the dark hallway to be met by the smell of putrefaction.

Day lived in two rooms on the second floor. There was a sink and a small stove in one, a bed and wardrobe in the other. A couple of chairs and a cantilever table were the only other substantial items of furniture, yet the rooms had the impression of being full; they were a shambles of drawing materials, maps, timetables, catalogues, stopwatches, clockwork, books and magazines. It looked as though Day resisted ever throwing anything away.

Evident in Ryman's face was his distaste for the squalor in which Day lived. 'I don't know how you stand this, Alan. I should've thought you earned well enough to get yourself somewhere a bit nicer.'

Ryman picked his way through the room to check that there wasn't anyone in the bedroom.

'It does me, Charlie. I don't earn a fortune.'

There was a secret smile on Day's face. He was a man with a lot of secrets. The one that caused the smile was his house in the country, which only he knew about. The house in east Hertfordshire wasn't large, or particularly isolated, but it was safe and secretive, and made Day feel secure. If problems ever arose he could lie up there for as long as necessary.

'Do you want some tea?'

'Only if I get a clean cup.' He turned back to Day. 'Did you stiff that?' – disgust in his tone.

Day's incredibly pointed face remained expressionless. 'She came in to wash the teacups.'

His eyes were dark, close-set like a crocodile's, his hair was iron-grey and clung to his skull like a bathing cap. He wasn't good-looking, in fact he was a bit like the photokit picture outside Wimbledon police station of a flasher seen on the Common; but he had to be holding money, so getting a normal woman shouldn't have been too difficult for him. Ryman was tempted to ask about the woman he had seen, whether she had an artificial leg. But Day's manner didn't invite such questions.

'At least you look as though you're busy, Alan.'

'Mustn't complain. Bits and pieces going on most times.'

'Not too busy, I hope.' Reluctantly Ryman sat on a chair. He might have resisted had he not had to stand on the train.

'Never too busy to listen to anything you have.'

Draftsmen worked for a set fee, usually small in relation to the gross yield; but then the risks they took were relatively small. They never went on the blags, and always kept themselves at the safest possible distance. As a rule they talked only to the man whom they employed to run the job, but sometimes it was necessary to talk to others if there were specific or complicated instructions for them. They could be nicked for conspiring to rob, but only if they were careless either in their contacts or in their own conduct.

Day listened with interest as Ryman told him about Glasgow.

After considering the prospects briefly the draftsman gave a commitment to the job. He thought that robbing the Glasgow-to-London Royal Mail train might present a big problem in that there was bound to be a lot of tight security. But he would look into it, check the potential problem and subsequent feasibility of the blag.

That pleased Ryman. He felt that he had got the proposition moving forward. Day was nothing less than brilliant at making this sort of job work. Money in transit was his speciality. He was probably better in that area than Trippet, Ryman decided. It would be precision detailing all the way, nothing left to chance. Even the matter of his weakness for cripples was almost acceptable now.

'Who do you plan to use? If it's on, that is.'

Day poured some tea. He avoided looking at Ryman. 'I think it's a bit early to say yet.' It wasn't, of course. Names had immediately sprung to mind, and he guessed Ryman suspected as much. He wasn't compelled to give details, it was merely a courtesy. 'There's a couple of people. Don't know if you know them. Brian Connell, if he fancies it.' Ryman inclined his head. The gesture might either have meant that he knew him or that he approved. 'He'd be ideal to run things if the blag was in London. But as it's Glasgow, it needs a local man. Someone like Donald Brodie.'

'Brodie?' The name struck a chord, but he couldn't place him.

'He was on Barclay's Bank, in Houndsditch. About three years ago.' Day knew precisely, it had been one of his jobs, and not a complete success. 'The only slight problem is that he's down on the Moor, doing twelve.'

'A slight problem,' Ryman echoed. 'I don't think it'll wait that long, Alan. Is Brodie essential?'

'I'll have to check who's available.'

Rarely was anyone indispensable. But Brodie was a native of Glasgow and had contacts there that could help Day considerably when setting up the job. And besides, it was after the Houndsditch blag that he had been arrested. That represented failure to Day who, out of professionalism, would like to redeem himself and recompense Brodie. Even though Brodie wasn't the most stable of personalities, running a blag in Glasgow would be the perfect excuse for having him sprung. He would arrange to visit him in Dartmoor and get whatever introductions in Glasgow he could. Especially someone who might be able to help him penetrate the GPO network. Day had contacts in the Post Office in London; they were well bent and could possibly help.

The potential robbery in Glasgow was now actively engaging his thinking capacity. He would make it work.

Chapter 8

'I expect you to vote with me at this afternoon's board meeting, Jeffrey,' Sir Frank said to the man across the lunch-table. It wasn't a request, rather a behest, delivered in the charming, direct manner which left a lot of people believing they did have the option.

As he spoke, Sir Frank O'Connor turned to dismiss the waiter offering him more sauce. They were in Prunier's. Sir Frank frequently ate lunch there, though rarely dinner; by that time he was usually across town. He had a house on the edge of Hampstead Heath.

Jeffrey Stebbings always openly agreed with the chairman and managing director, and would continue to do so while he was on the board of O'Connor's; however, his present thoughts followed a different tack. He was afraid of what was going on, and wanted some means to get out from under. He was also scared of Sir Frank. Stebbings had a soft, fleshy face with large jowls and a slender chin, which made him look like a foxhound. He hadn't always been scared. There had been a time when he had stood up to people, had resigned rather than capitulated to their demands. But nowadays directorships weren't exactly abundant in the City, and his talents weren't such that people created vacancies for him. His feelings towards Sir Frank were ambivalent. He despised him for a contemptible bully, yet admired him as a very astute businessman. His only fault in business, if it could be considered one, was his scorn for the resources upon which wealth and power were founded. Stebbings knew that Sir Frank, like most of his contemporaries, considered the resources infinite. Perhaps his own age, and its accompanying fear for the future, caused him to begin to doubt this most fundamental tenet of his forty years in business, Stebbings thought. Certainly his young boss had no such doubts.

At thirty-eight Sir Frank O'Connor was one of the most

powerful men in the British building industry.

He had started with a few advantages. In 1910 his grandfather had left the rural decline of West Cork and come to London with another man, Frank Keegan. All they had had was a talent for building and as much again for hard work. James O'Connor had been the brightest of eleven sons, always showing an eye to the main chance, even in a land then decidedly lacking in opportunity. In a country of seemingly endless prospects, he wasn't found wanting. Hard work had made them prosper and grow; then O'Connor had despotically halved their profits and put them to work where they had done most good. He had made gifts to those who most counted in local government offices, resident engineers, building inspectors; to architects who, through means of their own, had dominated whole areas of public works. They had grown bigger; that had been inevitable. Only one thing held them back, and that had been Frank Keegan's conscience. When in 1921 it had taken him back to Ireland to help build the new Irish Free State, James O'Connor didn't look back. He forged upwards, building a personal empire, aided in the late twenties by his son Frank, who had proved an apt pupil. What was endowed to Frank's son, also called Frank, who enjoyed what neither he nor his father had had, was a formal education, the best there was. He hadn't the background for the diplomatic corps or the government, so his only alternative was to become one of the Eton mafia. His passage through Eton and Cambridge, with all their social and business contacts, plus the distillation of the sound business instincts of two generations, made him the ideal candidate to take the helm of O'Connor's when his father died. The company had recently gone public. The family had owned twenty-six per cent of the equity and Frank O'Connor was thirty-four years old. The Labour Government gave him his knighthood for his immense contribution to British industry. Financial contributions were made to both major political parties, but his affinity was pro-Tory.

Stebbings picked disinterestedly at his crêpes. He hadn't

finished his lobsters, either. He wasn't generally a fussy eater. 'Do you anticipate any trouble?' He was thinking about the reason behind the board meeting.

'I shouldn't think it likely.' Sir Frank smiled winsomely. 'We'll sue the bastards,' he added lightly.

The meeting of the board of O'Connor and Son was a formality, the result a foregone conclusion. It had been called especially to endorse a course of action for dealing with the current rumours of bribery in obtaining lucrative national and local government contracts. Sir Frank knew what substance the rumours had; in varying degrees all but two of the board knew also. There was, and always had been, a long tradition in the industry of bribery for contracts, of insiders and padded bills of quantities; of privately negotiating contracts before putting them out to tender. Sir Frank resented the fact that it was his company running into this persistent flak. It had begun about a year and a half ago, then had stopped, then started again. He wanted it stopped again.

Later that afternoon, glancing up from the papers his secretary had fetched him, Sir Frank's eyes met those of Alex Jacobs. The contracts director was seated half way down the long polished table. Sir Frank knew there was no likelihood of dissent from Jacobs who, apart from himself and Anthony Duckett – who wasn't present but whose proxy he held – knew most about the way contracts were secured. Neither Jacobs nor Duckett, despite their close involvement, had the total picture, but doubtless both were well able to speculate on it.

Like Stebbings, Sir Peter Walton, another director present, would support whatever decision Sir Frank O'Connor made.

The only two directors who might resist and press for a full enquiry, as they had indicated at separate meetings, were Horace Thwaytes and Lord Richard Emms. They were the least informed, and had no notion what a bag of hellions they could turn loose. Sir Frank believed threats of prosecution the best course, and if such action was embarked upon then a united front was essential.

The chairman called the board to order. As this was a specially convened meeting, the minutes were read only where they related to the rumours. The matter had been raised before by Lord Emms in 'any other business'.

'Do you have anything further to add, Dick?'

'Well, I regret not,' Emms began in his ponderous tone. 'Unfortunately I'm not a sleuth of any worth. I did try to track the source of these confounded rumours. But it was rather like trying to find the source of the swirling mists on Dartmoor when one is in the midst of it. It won't go away. But there's no smoke without fire, is what they say. That's something I can't confess to enjoying.'

Thwaytes nodded in agreement, but only his voluminous chins seemed to move.

'That's not quite true, Richard,' Jacobs said authoritatively. 'Friction causes smoke.' He paused and looked around the table. 'Without doubt O'Connor's is one of the most successful contractors in the British Isles, if not Europe. I think that fact causes a great deal of smoke from our rivals.'

Jeffrey Stebbings glanced to the head of the table, then said, 'Here, here!'

'If there was substance to the rumours, then I think I would have been the first to know.' No one leapt in with concurrence. 'It is smoke without fire, in my opinion. But none the less irritating for all that. We must locate the source, then take the appropriate action.'

The debate ranged around the table. Everyone said what he wanted to say, but that still left Horace Thwaytes and Lord Richard Emms uneasy.

Sir Frank O'Connor regarded the two possible dissenters, while Sir Peter Walton concluded by emphasising the need for unity among the board.

Peter Walton had at one time been leader of the Tory controlled Greater London Council and, although he had resigned, he still had a great deal of useful influence there. When in office he had made some shrewd investments in the companies GLC redevelopment contracts were going to, not least of all O'Connors. He had a fine appreciation of the specific value of the pressure and influence that could be brought to bear in business. That didn't seem to be the case with Thwaytes and Emms, who had both served in local government.

Briefly Sir Frank wondered if he shouldn't instigate some move to get these two off the board. Anthony Duckett had advised against such a move; he thought their prudence and moderation a valuable asset, and they were both well regarded in the City. Duckett wasn't infallible, of course.

Sir Frank considered the other piece of advice the banker had ventured in order to placate the two men; to ask where they supposed all the money these rumoured pay-offs came from. Thwaytes was a traditional City money man, who sat on the board of the National Westminster Bank, and on the board of Duckett's bank. He understood about money, in particular the scarcity of cash. Yet O'Connor's books were impeccable.

When Sir Frank raised the question, Thwaytes conceded the point immediately.

'Perhaps Alex is responsible,' he said. 'He's paying these people out of his salary.' That brought mirth to the table.

How much simpler life would be, Sir Frank reflected, if everyone present knew all there was to know, instead of varying degrees of tactic knowledge.

Even he himself only knew in vague terms that it was the proceeds of robberies which had been turned into untraceable cash through Duckett, Reinhardt. His relationship with Duckett was simple: the available cash of one adequately filled a need of the other.

That was how the business association had started. Shortly after taking control of the company, Sir Frank had found that he was paying out so much cash in bribes that it could no longer be disguised. He had taken the problem to Duckett. Being a very secure contractor, O'Connors could raise money for the initial financing of new development anywhere, and at competitive rates. But instead they dealt exclusively with Duckett's bank at his slightly higher rates. Sir Frank had never had any problems selling that to either the board or the shareholders. The company was profitable, after all. Through the illicit cash that Duckett supplied, Sir Frank O'Connor was coming nearer to fulfilling his single ambition, to own all the company's equity, so that he alone would profit from his talents.

Despite Thwaytes and Emms conceding the improbability of the company producing this huge illicit cash flow, Sir Frank saw that they weren't entirely satisfied. He decided to upstage them.

'Perhaps we should have an enquiry. Quite independent of the board. That should scotch any rumours once and for all.' There were murmurs of agreement, mostly from Thwaytes and Emms.

Alarm didn't seize Alex Jacobs by the throat; he realised that his boss wouldn't make a move that left any part of them exposed.

'The proposal is, then, gentlemen, that we set in motion a full, rigorous enquiry. Is it seconded?'

Thwaytes seconded the motion with alacrity.

'Perhaps you'd deal with the press, Jeffrey?'

Stebbings said he would.

A charming smile spread across Sir Frank's bland face, as though he had brought some business to a satisfactory end. He had nothing whatsoever to fear from an enquiry; after all, he would be paying the enquirers, and if for no other reason they would be as biased as he wished.

Then the conclusion would be absolute, he was sure.

Chapter 9

The Tate Gallery was an impressive piece of architecture. There were some pretty impressive paintings hung inside too, although Detective Inspector Garmonsway, who used the Tate quite often, spent little of his time there in serious appraisal of art. Some of it he simply didn't like; some he didn't understand; some of the pictures he thought pretty. He used the Tate to meet one or other of the informers he ran: the gallery was as safe as anywhere that was mutually convenient, for neither was likely to run into anyone they wouldn't want to meet.

They would stand and regard canvases while they talked, moving on when someone else came up. But all they ever saw before them were textured colours.

Garmonsway was on the ground floor in the Impressionist room, considering a work by a painter whose name wasn't even vaguely familiar. It was nicely coloured but childlike and he wouldn't have wanted it on his wall.

Hearing footfalls, the DI decided that they belonged to the party he was meeting, but didn't look round.

The grass came and stood by him. That meant the meeting was safe, for few people approached a detective more carefully than an informant.

'Morning, guv,' he said in a low, cautious manner. 'Sorry I'm late. Fucking underground gets worse.'

'S'all right, Ivor – plenty to occupy me.' He inclined his head at the line of paintings.

Ivor Hopper scoffed.

'Fucking wicked waste of public money' – he had probably never paid tax in his life – 'You see what them silly bastards paid for that picture outta Southeby's the other day? Four hundred grand – and people starving in the world. S'wicked.'

They moved on. The time was just turned ten and the gallery was quiet. There wasn't anyone else in room twenty-one. The willowy figure of Garmonsway stood about eight inches taller than the informer, and Hopper wasn't noticeably short. Both men had pronounced stoops, but one had a relaxed, detached look; the other furtive and edgy.

The DI ran three grasses, which was about as many as any detective could run, to be able to give them the close attention that would net worthwhile information. Informing was a desperately lonely, often dangerous occupation, and although the DI didn't admire his grasses, he showed them compassion, and gave them what comfort he could. They chose their profession – if sometimes through police pressure – placed themselves in isolation; but that was no reason to deny them when they reached out, desperate to make contact. Whatever time grasses phoned him, day or night, Garmonsway tried to make some positive response. Sometimes they called simply because the pressures in that channel in which they lived had got too much, and at subsequent meetings offered nothing more than idle, worthless gossip, or information on ramps they had pulled themselves. Grasses were compulsive people, it didn't matter on what or whom they informed, even themselves, just as long as they told someone.

Hopper had been giving him stuff for about two years. How much longer he could continue was anyone's guess, though the DI suspected his time was about up. The careers of grasses weren't usually long. When they came on top, they frequently had to be locked away to save them the inevitable beating, not that that was any guarantee.

Previously Hopper had been a blagger, but he was now past his best. Occasionally he had it off with small jobs, which Garmonsway purposely did nothing about. That was the way most detectives rewarded their informers, working on the theory that no one was going to come across with dangerous and valuable information for the sort of money they earned out of the Informers' Fund. The odd twenty pounds for incidental expenses was all the DI ever gave Hopper; and those infrequent insurance rewards couldn't be relied on.

'What's the news, then?'

'Something a bit tasty. But I dunno if it's in your province, Mr Garmonsway. They're gonna spring one from Dartmoor. For a blag in Glasgow.' He shrugged apologetically. 'S'what I heard, guv.'

'Who's doing the springing?'

That Hopper didn't know, nor when.

'I think it's imminent, 'cos of this one in Glasgow.'

Two women entered and the grass clammed up instantly. The women moved along the opposite line of pictures. Hopper's glance continually checked their progress, and he continued in a whisper.

'The geezer going out's Donald Brodie. A right vicious bastard. But don't tell him I told you.' Hopper grinned.

He hadn't got what the job was, nor who was putting it together. The only other information he had was that Brodie's brother-in-law, Ronnie Haston, was involved. Also a hard man called Brian Connell.

When Ned Garmonsway praised the grass the man physically took on greater stature, momentarily losing his stoop. He laid four five-pound notes on him, telling him to keep listening.

Fordham, along with DCI Borroughs, listened with interest to all Ned Garmonsway had to say, but was disappointed to learn where the robbery was to take place. He had dealt briefly in the past with the head of Strathclyde CID, and anticipated that getting his cooperation on this wouldn't be a simple matter.

'Can't get them to change it to Birmingham, Ned, can you?' he joked.

He was at a meeting in the DCIs' office, two doors along from his own. He sometimes preferred using their office: it was more comfortable, especially the old, broken-down chair tucked between the filing cabinets. He had considered taking that chair, but wouldn't have used it in his own office.

Also present was Chief Inspector Trevor Corrigan, a good

anchorman and sounding-board, but a detective who rarely produced spectacular results any more. He had only one ear to the conversation, and continued with the routine of the office. There was a stream of traffic in and out, plus a flow of information by telephone. Everything was dealt with by Corrigan, with odd contributions being made by the DCS or Borroughs.

From the information, Fordham decided that they might get in on the ground floor with the blag in Scotland – despite possible local CID difficulties – and subsequently get some good levers under the right sort of people. If they nicked Donald Brodie and Brian Connell in favourable circumstances, they might provide the leverage to prise up the draftsman, and through him get Charlie Ryman, whom they suspected was putting it together, on a second, more serious charge; then, hopefully, on to those people at the top. But first they needed something substantial. They could pull Ryman, and most of the draftsmen known to be active, and get them to court; but it was doubtful whether they would get a conviction, other than for conspiracy – that would get them about three years each, and give Fordham nothing to trade with. He was growing more and more determined to reach up and topple those higher echelons. He was pissed off with the four- and five-hundred-page reports by his superintendents, spelling out in embarrassing detail just how unsuccessful the Squad's investigations into the major robberies had been. When they did get a result there was no need to elaborately justify the efforts, so all that was required then was a ten- or twelve-page report for the Director of Public Prosecutions.

Pensively Fordham flicked the edges of the CRO files resting on his knee. These contained the full antecedents of Brodie, Connell and Haston. DI Garmonsway had fetched them. 'What's your grass doing now, Ned?'

'Punting around, guv. Keeping his ears open.'

'Is he earning anything?'

The DI hesitated. He knew that Fordham knew how informers worked, the DCS wasn't trying to entrap him. But even so that wasn't the sort of admission one made to a senior detective on principle.

'Keep him clear,' Fordham went on. 'Apply for some money out of the Fund. I'll recommend it. Rather than him scratching around and maybe getting himself nicked. Think he'll come up with anything more?'

Non-committally Garmonsway said, 'He's been a good 'un, Guv.'

Fordham leant forward and passed the CRO files to Borroughs, who was resting his bulk against his desk. Borroughs was the detective most involved on the case, apart from Fordham.

'What have we got to date that's anything worth a fuck?' Fordham glanced at a DS who came in to talk to Corrigan about a case. 'A huge need of an untraceable, untaxed cash-flow, for O'Connor's to pay out in bribes to local government officials – that's unsubstantiated of course. Rochester, out best potential witness, is head deep in concrete . . .'

'Les Norman thinks he's on to someone else,' Borroughs put in.

'Good as Rochester might have proved?'

'Wouldn't have thought so.'

Fordham went on, 'We have a strong link between O'Connor's and our suspect banker – though not a proven criminal link. Possibly Duckett is supplying the money to O'Connors; possibly he's financing the robberies – what else are bankers for?'

'Did you see the statement in the *Financial Times* about O'Connor's?' Corrigan broke off from his conversation about pornography and blackmail with the DS.

'Don't read it, Trevor. Haven't got your sort of dough tucked away.'

'The board dismissed the rumours about bribery, and announced an independent enquiry. End of statement.'

'Oh, that'll save us a lot of work,' Fordham said sarcastically. 'Would you fancy trying for Duckett at this point, Frank?'

'What for, speeding?'

Those present were all too aware that people like Anthony Duckett were too powerful, had too many important connections for the police to go after them without having met with the DPP. Because of the way the DPP was appointed, and the ranks from which he was selected, they also knew that he would blank such moves against the Establishment, or one of its pillars.

'I wouldn't even fancy trying for Charlie Ryman. Not to guarantee it.'

Ryman was safe at the moment. However, not for the reasons he doubtless thought, the past deals he had made with the CID, Fordham included. When his time came, the DCS wouldn't let those influence him. Few detectives ever did. That was part of the game; the CID wrote the rules.

'Below Ryman things fan out. There's Trippet. A noteworthy suspect, that. He almost certainly designed the Rushy Green bank blag; and there's a good chance the Putney post office raid was down to him. But we might as well pull ourselves off as pull him. Same goes for Alan Day.' Fordham paused and considered the serious faces in the room. Another detective came in to speak to Corrigan, who was now talking on one of the phones. 'On the ground we have nine major robberies. All almost certainly connected by a common denominator – hopefully more than by the fact that we haven't captured anyone significant. All we have are a number of cowboys, none of whom want to or are in a position to trade. A pretty dismal return for over a million pounds stolen to date.' And on a lighter note, 'I'm beginning to sound like the ACC. Maybe I'll get his job.'

Borroughs shifted his weight uneasily on the desk, though the burden of responsibility for lack of progress wasn't entirely his. For a moment everyone in the room switched their attention to Corrigan's one-sided conversation. He was giving details of some charges.

A phone on Borroughs's desk rang. He turned and answered it, dealing brusquely with the caller. Another detective entered. The phone on Malcolm Dyce's desk began ringing. The DCIs' office frequently got like that.

The DCS took Brodie's file back from Borroughs and opened it, glancing through the copious notes.

'What do you want done about Brodie?' Borroughs asked, replacing the phone. It rang again and he had one of the waiting Ds take a message.

'He's about the best we've got. I think we'd better let him have a taste.'

'Do you want me to get on to Prison Liaison for the governor's cooperation?'

Fordham didn't answer. He rose, and inclined his head, indicating Borroughs and Garmonsway to follow him.

In his own office the DCS said deliberately, 'Whoever's doing all the arranging is good enough to get him out. They might fuck up. But I'd sooner take that chance than have some bent bastard in the prison service tipping him off.'

That wasn't the kind of statement he made for whoever happened to be within earshot.

From remarks in Brodie's file Fordham saw he was a violence specialist. He even had a conviction for hitting his wife. That interested him.

'Is Brodie still married, Ned?'

The DI didn't know. The record said he was, but the last entry was his conviction three years ago. The DCS had Garmonsway make some enquiries. There was an idea shaping in Fordham's mind. He figured that if he primed Brodie right, then they wouldn't need to try and follow him if and when he made his escape. All they would have to do was first make sure to keep the local police away from his wife's house, and wait until he showed up.

Chapter 10

Sound and smell were the two things you were most conscious of in prison. Ever since the bell for lights-out last night, Brodie had been lying on his cot, staring at the ceiling, listening to the prison, and smelling his two cellmates. He had been doing that for three years, with the depressing prospect of another nine. It didn't seem possible that it was going to end that morning. Tension came with anticipation, and he tried to exclude both. He resumed listening.

At night in Dartmoor the most consistent noise was what sounded like dripping water. Where it came from Brodie had never discovered. The place was cold, damp, bleak. Worse than that stone bastard up in Peterhead, Aberdeenshire, where he had done some; more depressing than Broadmoor, where he had also had a taste.

With morning the sounds changed to the more frequent footfalls of screws; the familiar coughs of cons. You could set a watch by them. The raucous cough starting up a couple of cells along echoed through D wing, always beating the bell.

At seven o'clock the clanging bell erupted, followed by a crackling rendition of 'Onward Christian Soldiers'; then a whole cacophony of distorted noise rose through the tall stone wing, rattling coughs, banging doors; shouts of abuse from screws, muted protests from prisoners. This was something Brodie had known from a very early age, having suffered such institutions and their abuses all his life.

A runt child born thirty-six years ago in the Gorbals – the most notorious district of Glasgow – had little chance of surviving. But Donald Brodie did. His father was a drunk who never worked, but hadn't the wit to be a professional criminal. All he had ever done time for was violence and the destruction of other people's property while drunk. Never once was he prosecuted for beating up his wife or kids. All the children had left home as soon as they could, usually beating up the old man before they did.

By the time Brodie had reached his twelfth birthday, his mother, who had barely been clinging to existence, finally gave up. Brodie and his immediate sister, who was ten months older, had been the only two left at home. The father had got himself arrested on the day of the funeral, which none of the children had returned for. Brodie's sister went to live with an aunt, who wouldn't take him; Brodie had been given to the tender mercies of State care. At fifteen he had been taken in by a married sister, but only because of the job he had got himself.

The first identity Brodie had found had been in a gang that ran on the streets of Govan. In Care he had grown stronger for three meals a day and his own bed to sleep in, but he still remained a runt. On the streets he had learned to steal and run; fight and run; then fight and stand his ground. Because of his size he had to work hard, prove himself twice, thrice over; he had done this through an exaggerated streak of violence. So furious were his attacks that lads twice his size had been leary of him. His first conviction had resulted in Borstal, which only served to harden him further. There he had earned the name of Wee Fury. On release two years later he had picked up where he had left off. By then he had achieved his full height of five feet three, was a man and a fully-fledged criminal. Prison had followed, for cutting a rival gang member. Normally the police wouldn't have bothered, but he was wanted for some breakings, which they hadn't been able to get him for. Released from prison, he had been yet more knowledgeable in both the ways of crime and the police. He had had a good run at robbery with violence, then ducked down to London for an even better run. Until his last job.

Three fucking years. Again Brodie's thoughts found the prospect that awaited him outside, and he tensed. His palms were wet and sweat broke out along his spine. What if he got the day wrong? Or some other piece of information? If the whole thing aborted? Doubts sickened him; they were what had kept him awake the whole night. He was too close to fuck up now.

Brodie was hardly aware of his cellmates rising. The screw who slammed open the door came abruptly into focus. Still Brodie didn't move.

'C'mon, Brodie,' the uniform screeched. 'What do you think this is, a holiday camp? Up. Before I have you on Report.' The man moved on to the next cell.

Brodie rose, letting the three thin covers fall to the floor. Being on Governor's Report wasn't something that normally worried Brodie, it meant a few days banged up in solitary, with loss of remission for more serious infractions. But having to go up on the mat this morning was the last thing he wanted.

Thoughts of his wife suddenly crowded him, and he immediately felt angry. Those thoughts he could do without or he was a stone ginger to flare up at someone and so ruin himself for the outside working party. But there was no way he could stop his anger when he considered that dirty whore. He was going to give her such a hiding.

Preparing to slop out didn't take Brodie long, as he was already dressed. He hadn't bothered removing his clothes last night, only his boots. He folded the two blankets.

'Down to you to slop out, my son,' said his Cockney cellmate.

Brodie nodded. They took turns to empty and rinse the bucket. After about the third prisoner had been to the recess the place began to stink worse than the public toilets on Sauchiehall Street on a Saturday night, especially as some of the dirty fuckers shat in their piss-pots.

'Don't envy you, Jock. Be colder than enough out on the rock pile this morning.'

Brodie didn't reply as the queue of pot-carriers shuffled into the recess.

Everything in prison was done noisily. Doors were slammed; boots stamped; pots banged into the sluice. All the noise conjoined, making hearing difficult. This wasn't why Brodie didn't respond; he was trying to keep a low profile. If he didn't make the work detail he wouldn't get to escape.

The planners had been quite explicit about his staying on the quarry working party.

He had only been on that detail for a week, and didn't know how they had arranged it. Quarry work was something prisoners were put on prior to official release, to get them into shape and acclimatised to work on the outside – as if any prisoner ever went from a stretch on the Moor to such work.

Although he had never tried for quarry work before, Brodie had sought other outside working parties, only had been considered a security risk. He would've had it away the first opportunity. He wondered which screws had been bent; the PO? the deputy governor? He didn't doubt their susceptibility. They were all at it.

Never in his life could Donald Brodie remember praying. But now as he went through the waking-to-working routine, fragments of prayer formed between his apprehension and the angry thoughts of what he would do to his old woman. He thought not at all about the real reason why he was being sprung. Silent imprecations to God not to let anything go wrong did nothing to reassure him. His guts twisted into tense knots, making it impossible for him to eat breakfast. Had he forced down that porridge or hard fried egg he'd have thrown it up. The young con who was the third man in the cell ate Brodie's breakfast.

Every glance, every approach of a screw was, Brodie imagined, to call him out, tell him to stand down from the work detail; to have him up for some minor infraction. He'd murder the fucking screw who did that to him now. He meant it.

Outside working parties mustered at the main gate, prisoners escorted from various parts of the building. Virtually all movement required an escort.

That walk with a second prisoner across the open courtyard was one of the longest Brodie had ever taken. At any moment he expected to be called out. He was tense, his ears straining for the sound. He wiped the beads of sweat from his sunken top lip, but didn't relax at all.

There were eleven others on the detail. Names were checked off by the gate screw, who looked up as he read each one. His first glance at Brodie was no less casual, but caused him to look again. 'You feeling all right, Brodie? Do you want to report to sick bay?'

This was it. Normally screws wouldn't notice a prisoner's condition if he was dead on his feet. Now this slag wanted to send him to sick bay.

One of the escort said, 'He's all right. A bit of fresh air'll do him good.'

A prisoner going sick would mean a delay, inconvenience. Brodie was never more grateful to the uncaring attitude, and wondered briefly if the screw hadn't simply been straightened.

The route to the quarry was via a series of paths and tunnels, designed to prevent prisoners having contact with the public. Where the path ran through open moorland it was fenced, and crossing roads it went underground, with the approach completely enclosed in chain-link fencing.

Approaching the second tunnel a fight broke out between two prisoners. Brodie, who was at the rear, hardly noticed it at first, he was too intent on searching for the hole in the fence. By the eighth post on the left they had said. When he couldn't immediately find it, Brodie believed he had miscounted. His apprehension increased as he glanced back, trying to make a rapid calculation of the posts. Suddenly he saw what he was looking for. The links had been cut down the side of the post to a height of about four feet and were held with clips.

Brodie became aware of the fight in the mouth of the tunnel when the screw from the rear ran to assist his colleague. Brodie didn't need telling, he pulled open the chain-link and quickly worked himself through. His tunic snagged and he yanked at it, pulling free. He raced across the open ground to the retaining wall by the road, the distorted sounds of the fight from the tunnel pursuing him. You could always rely on someone in prison. The thought stopped abruptly. Stretching as hard as he could, the best height

Brodie could reach was seven feet, while the top of the wall was about nine feet high. He felt deflated, angry, frustrated. He glanced back, considering whether he would have time to take a run at it. Another con was through the wire. He ran across to Brodie.

'Cannae reach the fooking top!' Brodie screeched, emotional stress making his Glaswegian accent barely understandable. 'Gi' us a lift.'

'You fucking Scotch midget,' the bigger man mocked, and unquestioningly cupped his hands. He straightened up, lifting Brodie within reach of the top of the wall.

Brodie's hard fingers gripped, and he pulled himself effortlessly on to the flat ledge, those hours of weightlifting and press-ups, put in out of boredom, paying off. He paused on the shelf for a second, savouring his first exquisite taste of freedom. Looking down, he saw the other prisoner reaching for his hand. But Brodie didn't respond. Instead he pushed himself up, turned and ran up the short incline to the road.

'You dirty fucking Scotch bastard!'

Brodie paid the words no heed. He searched the road for the car that was supposed to be there to pick him up.

A car appeared and he felt an enormous sense of relief, until he identified it as a police car. He assumed he had been grassed somehow by someone; he'd top him if he found whoever it was.

He ran, zig-zagging crazily as if to prevent his ultimate arrest. When the car drew alongside, he ran down the short bank to the retaining wall.

The policeman in the front passenger seat opened the window. 'Brodie! What are you pissing about at? Get in here, for fuck sake!'

Brodie spun round. That wasn't Old Bill. He hesitated, then ran to the car, and wrenching open the rear door, threw himself in.

The car accelerated away before the screws had disengaged themselves and raised the alarm.

The rest of Brodie's escape was executed as efficiently. He had clothes in the car, a police uniform like those of the two felons helping him, in case they ran into snags. They didn't. He was driven to a quay outside Exmouth, put aboard a boat and taken up the coast to Portsmouth. On the trip he was dressed as a crewman, though didn't do any crewing. For one thing he felt too ill. Donald Brodie was a landlubber, and boat trips on the calmest areas of water were something he avoided. The sickness was a small price to pay for freedom, but didn't stop his complaining. The ten-hour trip was without incident. His journey by car up the A3 to London was equally uneventful. Brodie was relieved to be back on dry land, and in a form of transport more to his liking. He was now dressed as a silk – that amused him. His stiff collar almost choked him, he wore the club tie, black jacket and pin-stripes. Next to him on the back seat of the Daimler a black homburg and briefcase completed the barrister image.

The face driving was unknown to Brodie, as were those he had so far encountered. He was impressed by their efficiency. He knew that Alan Day, who had arranged things, had one going off where his services were required, his escape was part of the price. The details he didn't know, but the job wasn't a priority with Brodie now they were approaching London. He was thinking about his wife, the whacking she had coming.

'Where we going?' Brodie said.

The driver glanced through the mirror. 'Gotta take you to a place in Battersea, 'in' I.'

'Who's there, d'you ken?'

'What? Oh. No, I dunno. They just gimme the driving job, didn't they. S'pect Bri' will be. S'his place.' When Brodie didn't respond, the driver said, 'Brian Connell, you know?'

Again he didn't respond. He knew Connell vaguely via his brother-in-law; he had heard he was a tearaway. He wondered who else he might be put in with.

'What's the address?'

The driver hesitated, then gave the address of the flat in a mansion block in Prince of Wales Drive.

'Good. I want you to drop me off somewhere.'

That surprised the driver, who had his instructions, which didn't allow for dropping Brodie off. He told him so.

Brodie was insistent. He knew this was his best, probably his only chance of seeing his wife. Once they had him tucked away they weren't likely to let him go until after the job. That would have meant June getting away with her strokes. Brodie believed the woman had taken a wicked fucking liberty, and wasn't about to let her get away with it.

He told the driver to forget Battersea. He wanted dropping in Hammersmith. Being officially separated, Brodie doubted that the police would be watching his wife's place. He'd take a chance anyway.

'Look, what'll I do? Wait?' The driver was unhappy as he pulled up at a junction off Hammersmith Road.

'Don't bother – I'll make ma own way over there.'

He checked the address again; then straightened his hat, before moving warily along the street.

An otherwise great evening had been spoiled for June Brodie by the news earlier that day. She had heard of her husband's escape on the radio. She had been tense, had been unable to relax, not even when they finally had supper. She felt awful about the man spending his money on her when she wasn't giving her best. But despite everything she was sorry it was coming to an end.

The car turned off Hammersmith Road into Rowan Road. The man looked over at her.

'Everything all right, love?' He was feeling tense, and imagined that the apprehension he sensed in her was for the same reason. 'Which one is it now?' He searched for the house.

'Oh, by the next lamp-post.'

Pulling into a space in the car-crowded street, the man put on the handbrake and switched off the engine and lights. He leaned back in his seat.

Neither said anything.

The woman was thirty-three, the man thirty-nine; both

were as hesitant as would-be lovers half their age, and less daring.

He was wondering whether he would make it inside.

She was considering whether to invite him in, but it was late. She wouldn't let a man make love to her after only one proper date, but hoped he would want to see her again. After the second or third date it would be more fitting, although tonight she felt a need to be with someone, and was tempted, if only to be reassured by his presence. She still hurt a little from a previous relationship, which had ended a few months ago. Believing it was the real thing, she had committed herself, only to discover after two years that the man hadn't felt as she had. How could you know someone that long and not know him?

Self-consciously the man slid his hand across the seat and on to her shoulder. At first he met resistance when he tried pulling the woman towards him. Then she yielded.

'A million he makes it inside,' a voice said in subdued tones from the dark interior of a van parked unobtrusively further along Rowan Road.

No one would have suspected that the vehicle was a Squad observation van. It had the beaten-up look of a scrap dealer's van, and the road fund licence was out of date. But the outside belied the inside, which was skilfully maintained by the mechanics who kept the whole fleet of Squad vehicles running. The back of the van was fitted out so that detectives weren't too uncomfortable during long periods on watch. The two detectives had currently been in the van six hours.

'He'll get a nasty surprise if he does,' the second man replied. 'Bet he doesn't get it in tonight.'

He grinned and reached under the seat for the box holding a flask and sandwiches his old lady made him, like she always did when he had observation watch. Often the food was wasted, though he never told her that. Tonight he was grateful for it.

'Want a sandwich, Tom?'

The first detective reached out, without taking his eyes off the car. 'What are they?'

'Ham, I s'pect.'

'I don't think there's any need for chummy to go inside. He's having it right there. Got her tits out, he has . . . reaching down, hand up her skirt . . . pushing his finger into her pants . . . Now he's slipping his finger into her . . .' He took a bite of his sandwich.

'Leave off, I'm getting a hard-on' – despite knowing his colleague was merely doing a number.

'Now, the lucky bastard's going down on her. He gets a taste; I get one of your old lady's ham sandwiches, Skip. There's no fucking justice.'

There was a short silence.

'I once nicked a couple for screwing in a car – I was in uniform.'

'Did you?' He sounded surprised.

It wasn't something he had told anyone on the Squad about, he wasn't proud of it now. 'Seemed right at the time. Dead jealous, I was. I had an erection while I was nicking them.' The thought amused him. 'Look up!' the DC said suddenly. 'He didn't make it.'

There was a muffled sound of the car starting.

June Brodie stooped at the window. 'Thanks again for a wonderful evening – see you Saturday, then.' She tried to suggest some intimate promise.

'I'll look forward to it.'

Impulsively she kissed him again, then hurried up the path. At the door she waved as the car drew away.

Letting herself into the house, June felt prickles of apprehension. A sixth-sense forewarned her as she switched the light on. There was only a second between sensing and seeing, but long enough for her to stifle her cry. 'Donald . . . !'

Brodie was sitting on the stairs in the narrow hallway.

'Tha' ya fancy man, is it?' He was unable to keep anger out of his voice. 'Did he no wanna come in and beef ya tonight?'

An involuntary trembling started through the woman as the man rose. 'Donald, I can explain . . . I thought . . .' Panic caused the words to jumble in her brain.

'Aye, I bet ya can, ya wee fooking hooar. And when ya done? Fooking every bass wi' a cock between his legs. Fooking explain that, you dirty hooar.'

He felt no desire for this woman, other than to hurt her, and so offset his anger and hatred.

'Donald,' she began on an intake of breath. There wasn't anything to explain. The marriage hadn't worked, but her husband would never have yielded to reason, would never have let her go.

'Well, ya fooking cunt?' the man demanded, closing on her.

Panic completely enveloped her when she saw the club-hammer in his hand. She knew her husband, and the worst possibilities sprang to mind.

Brodie's right fist smashed into the woman's face in a succession of short jabbing blows. She collapsed against the door. As she fell he kicked her; then again on the floor. She lay in a crumpled, whimpering heap, blood streaming from her mouth. It wasn't enough; Brodie intended fulfilling his promise to himself. Pulling her legs from under her, he raised the club-hammer, catching the look in her pain-dulled eyes. She understood what he was going to do.

The woman's scream rented the street, piercing the sound-proofed police van like tissue paper.

'Fucking hell!' the DS exclaimed. 'Sounds like he's done her in.'

'What'll we do, call the police?'

The detectives' smiles stopped as Brodie emerged from the house. He checked in both directions, then moved off. A couple of lights went on in response to the scream, but there were no further signs of concern from neighbours.

'You'd better call in for an ambulance. Perhaps the local police as well.'

It wasn't within their brief to display such charity, and they might even get a bollocking if and when their governor found out. But knowing what they did about Brodie, it was likely that he had killed the woman.

The younger detective reached for the radio, as the DS cautiously opened the small door into the cab. He climbed through and started the van. They would be in more trouble if, having made contact with Brodie, they went and lost him.

Chapter 11

Curled around the small of his back, Kika reached over and scratched sleepily at the mat of hair on the man's stomach. Had she known Fordham less well she might have fondled his cock, but even a goodbye kiss taxed his limited capacity for morning affection.

Fordham didn't need his girl-friend's prompting. He had heard the door buzzer. His driver would have been on time, nine-fifteen. He was never a minute earlier or later than the time Fordham told him to pick him up, regardless of the hour he had dropped him the previous night.

Easing himself reluctantly from beneath the warm duvet, he sat on the edge of the bed and massaged his face, then turned for his bathrobe. Only Kika's lay within reach, so he pulled that on. Showering, shaving and dressing wasn't an elaborate ritual, but the start to his day, the process by which he became alert and presentable.

Living with an actress meant, for various reasons, that existence was generally disorganised. And although Kika would remember to fetch coal, she would forget food. There was rarely anything in for breakfast. All the fridge held was seven pots of yoghurt and half a grapefruit which, typically, hadn't been cut into segments. He squeezed the juice into his mouth, and took two cartons of yoghurt and a spoon. He didn't bother with tea as there was only jasmine.

'Morning, Syd.' His driver held the door.

Normally Fordham would travel in front, but Detective Inspector Bill Senior was in the rear of the car. He climbed in next to him.

'Bill.'

'Morning, guv.' Senior saw the yoghurt. 'No breakfast again?'

'Chance would be nice.' He opened one of the cartons.

'They say it's good for virility.'

'I wouldn't know. The last time I got it up it gave me a

blinding headache.'

The driver grinned as he started the car.

The CID in general were horny, and would stiff anything that moved; the Squad were hornier still. Even detectives like Senior, who ought to have known better, if only on account of his age – he was forty-six – entered into the chase. Fordham's high office excluded him. It wasn't done for the governor to go whoring with the lads, and since his relationship with Kika he had had no inclination.

'Brodie turned up at his old woman's last night. As you figured he would.' The DI fiddled distractedly with the catch on his black, standard-issue briefcase.

Fordham nodded, as if there could have been no doubt.

'Gave her a right good hiding.' Senior hesitated. 'Broke both her legs. Wicked fucker.'

That wasn't something Fordham had anticipated, though the woman receiving a beating had been a possibility. He listened to the details unemotionally, continuing to eat his yoghurt. Rolling down the window, he dropped the first empty pot out – that kind of pollution was someone else's problem.

'Where is she?' He was told Hammersmith Hospital. A superfluous piece of information. Maybe he'd send some flowers. Haston, her brother, might appreciate that. 'Where's Brodie now?'

'Prince of Wales Drive.'

'Connell's place?' It didn't need confirming. 'Who's on watch, Bill? After going to all this trouble.'

'Ronson's down there. He knows the score.'

Fordham nodded, finished as much of the second yoghurt as he wanted, and disposed of it. He licked the spoon and put it in his pocket. He thought about Brodie being sprung. It meant the blag in Glasgow was going ahead. Although the DCS had played no active part in Brodie's escape, because of his prior knowledge he felt slightly relieved that it had gone off without problems. Not informing the Prison Liaison department or the Home Office, and permitting the escape to go forward, could have let him in for serious disciplinary action, especially if things had gone wrong. But that was the way he operated. He wasn't interested in capturing cowboys, not as the single end product. He would want them in the net when he eventually pulled the string, along with all those big fish who had hitherto gone untouched because they had too much respectable front, too many privileged friends. Fordham wasn't bitter about the situation, he viewed it pragmatically, handling it the best he could.

'Is there a phone in the flat?'

Anticipating his governor, Senior passed him a sheaf of forms. 'It's included with the other applications.'

Fordham glanced over the top copy, skim-reading the information on Brian Connell. Finally he approved the warrant application, which DCI Malcolm Dyce had prepared, and added his signature.

'Be nice if we got them all, guv.'

'Some chance,' Fordham said. 'Still, worth a try.' He looked through the other four applications, then handed them back.

Unlike most of the DIs on the Squad, Bill Senior didn't have his own unit. Someone was needed to ease the burden of procedural back-up, and Senior doubled in this capacity with that of aide to the DCS.

There was a lot of over-heated, snarling traffic crawling along Millbank. The detectives were travelling east, their first stop Whitehall and the Home Office, where they would present their applications. But their car, unlike wireless cars, had no special magic for getting them through the traffic. They inched into the jam on the northside roundabout junction at Lambeth Bridge.

Fordham stared at the solid lines of vehicles. London's congestion depressed him. They were completely hemmed in.

'You did well there, Syd.'

The driver accepted the censure with a shrug; a minute later he made a left turn into Horseferry Road, then, taking a liberty with the oncoming traffic, cut down into Smith

Square, completely redeeming himself.

The Home Office, which was situated in a splendid bust-adorned building at the bottom of Whitehall, looked particularly impressive for the recent stone cleaning. There had lately been an urgent rethink on the building's security. Like the police having their cars stolen, the Home Office being bombed would have been too embarrassing.

'Mr Johnson-Iles,' Fordham said to the uniformed man encased in the booth in the entrance hall.

'S'he expecting you, sir?'

Fordham said he was, gave his name and was given directions to room H on the second floor, though he knew the way.

Compared with his own cramped surroundings, the wasted space here always struck the DCS forcefully. The corridor was wide, the ceiling high; had this been for CID use there would have been a grey-painted steel partition erected down the centre and one half subdivided into a labyrinth of offices.

Room H had lost its original eighteenth-century splendour, the front area having been partitioned to accommodate the secretary of the Under-Secretary. She was a tall lady with butterfly-shaped glasses.

'Would you take a seat, gentlemen? Mr Johnson-Iles won't keep you long.'

Fordham ignored the leather chairs against the wall. 'We'll stand if it's all the same.'

He disliked sitting in those circumstances, it gave him a psychological disadvantage. Probably Johnson-Iles wasn't even in yet, despite their nine-forty appointment. It was nine-forty-five.

'You have the applications, chief superintendent?' The woman had retreated behind her desk.

The DI opened his briefcase and pulled out the five forms. He passed them to Fordham, who shuffled them, separated three and gave the remaining two to butterfly eyes. The others he handed back to Senior.

'Just the two?'

'They'll do.' Fordham watched her go to the door behind the desk. She rapped once, then entered.

The DCS wanted to tap the phones in all five applications, but the two he had offered, Duckett and Ryman, were the most important, also the most likely to be blanked. If they were granted, Fordham would quickly offer the others, as they would certainly be no problem. They concerned known members of the criminal fraternity, who had few recognisable rights.

As he waited, Fordham's eyes passed swiftly over the office, taking in details like a moving picture camera. Filing cabinet indexes, the obligatory plants; headings of papers on the desk. Despite his high office he hadn't forgotten his street-level training; detailed observation distinguished detectives. A lot of CID became slack when they reached mainly administrative offices. Fordham didn't allow himself to. He preferred to stay in touch, if not actively involved, with most levels of investigation, to know that he was capable of getting actively involved.

At thirty-nine John Fordham was not only the youngest detective to hold the office he held, but also the most progressive. He cut corners, took chances that most detectives, even his immediate predecessor, would never have considered. Sometimes he got away with his strokes, sometimes not. The Commander from A10 who wanted to interview him flashed into his thoughts. Maybe he had already come unstuck.

'What do you think, guv?' DI Senior asked, standing in a businesslike fashion, feet apart, hands clenched on his briefcase.

Fordham shrugged. 'Be useful if we can get one on Duckett's phones.'

The door from the Under-Secretary's office opened and the woman reappeared. She smiled thinly.

'Mr Johnson-Iles will be with you shortly.'

The wait didn't auger well for their applications. Normally Home Office warrants for telephone interceptions were just a formality. Officially the Home Secretary approved every application, but it was doubtful whether he saw a fraction of them. That was what Under-Secretaries existed for. Possibly the Home Secretary was going to see these. It might have been better had Fordham given them to his opposite number in the Special Branch and had him put them in. Then there'd have been no problem. In the past he had slipped dodgy ones through like that. But favours needed returning, and owing the Branch one wasn't something Fordham cared for.

The phone on the desk buzzed and the secretary picked it up. 'Yes, Mr Johnson-Iles. Right away, sir.' She replaced the handset and rose. 'The Under-Secretary will see you now.'

Henry Johnson-Iles was a sauve looking man in an expensively tailored grey chalk-stripe suit. He had a thin, bony face accentuated by his sleek hair. His eyes lifted from his large mahogany desk, and acknowledged the detectives with a slightly deprecating look. He was one who, through a lifetime of privilege, had the facility of effortlessly dismissing the most important people with a glance.

Fordham refused to be intimidated.

'Chief superintendent. I trust you're not serious with these applications?' The sarcasm was very apparent. 'Anthony Duckett is a highly respected banker. He has a hitherto impeccable reputation ...'

Cutting in on the man, Fordham said flatly, 'He's a crook. He's financing large-scale robberies.'

'Oh, are you submitting evidence to support your claim? You don't seem to have offered any here.'

'That's what we expect to get with intercepts.' This was lost, Fordham realised, before he saw the man behind the desk shake his head.

'It's not on, I'm afraid. It would amount to a gross invasion of privacy. Had there been a question of national security it might have been a different matter.'

'All I need is a forty-eight-hour warrant –' Fordham regretted the move immediately.

'The applications are denied, chief superintendent.' Then,

as if anticipating the DCS, 'Do you have any others you wish to go before the Home Secretary?'

Fordham glanced at Senior, then shook his head. 'No, sir,' he said with laboured politeness. The interview was over.

Cars were no longer allowed to park outside the Home Office. Even the most respectable vehicles had parking difficulties in Whitehall. As Fordham waited on the steps of the Home Office for his car to arrive, he smarted.

'Fucking bureaucrats. About all he's any use for is screwing his secretary on the floor in the lunch hour. He gets about ten grand a year for that.'

Senior nodded solemnly. 'What about these others, guv?'

'Blank them. We'll take a chance and bend a few more, Bill. Time is not on our side.'

Fordham moved away to his car as it drew into the kerb.

The DI seemed to take on a more pronounced stoop at the prospect. The thought of using illegal wire-taps didn't inspire him. His pension was at risk as well as his governor's. But he guessed the DCS knew what he was doing out on those dangerously thin limbs. At least he hoped the man did.

What routine Peter Walsh kept now, Fordham couldn't say. They had lost close touch with each other. That was always the way after someone left office, regardless of whether or not the departure was under a cloud. Since he had ceased being a policeman Peter Walsh had fallen nicely on his feet as head of security on the telephone section of the GPO. He looked well on it at their lunchtime meet in Holborn.

'The life must be easy, Peter,' Fordham said as the Italian waiter showed them to their seats. 'You never looked this good on the firm.'

'I mustn't complain, John.' He turned to the waiter. 'Whisky-sour. And, scotch?' – looking back at his guest. Fordham nodded. Another waiter gave them menus. 'Putting on a bit of weight. Sitting around in a comfortable office. I miss the life, I do that.' There was regret in his voice. 'Peter Goodfellow still full of shit?'

'Don't see much of him. Apart from the meetings we avoid each other like we've both got the pox.'

'He has, John. The dirty fucker.'

They were talking about the Assistant Commissioner—Crime who, ultimately, was every Metropolitan detective's boss. There was no one higher than Peter Goodfellow directly responsible for the CID. Fordham had inherited his predecessor's dislike of the man, but hadn't realised before that Walsh hated him. Possibly the feeling was justified, for there was nothing he had enjoyed more than coppering, unless it was running the Squad. The AC—Crime had stopped him doing both. Without doubt power corrupted, and Peter Walsh and Peter Goodfellow had both been corrupted by their absolute power. Goodfellow had been the new broom of the new Commissioner of Police. Walsh had run foul of him.

Peter Walsh was smallish, only an inch taller than Fordham's sixty-eight and a half inches – the half was important, it placed him above the minimum height requirement. Walsh had a very round face that seemed to belong on a much heavier body, and round, intelligent eyes which were capable of burning into people, stripping away falsehood. Behind them was a sense of loss, yearning for the past.

Maybe that was something he was simply reading into the face, Fordham thought.

Over their pasta they swapped reminiscences; regrets; the results of their brief contact during the past two years when either one had called the other offering or seeking information. They touched generally the enquiry Fordham was endeavouring to work up. The DCS was instinctively cautious about putting out information. With Walsh there were always wheels within wheels.

'To be honest, John. I think you're going to have a lot of problems trying to get anyone much above the man in the middle. There are always too many vested interests – including our old friend Peter Goodfellow.'

Fordham didn't say anything.

'I heard he has the job of head of security at O'Connors'

earmarked.' His shrug suggested that either way the rumour was immaterial to him.

Fordham accepted that there was probably some truth in it. It wasn't the sort of thing the man was likely to invent. Peter Goodfellow had about a year to go before retiring; understandably he would be shopping around. However, Fordham couldn't help thinking what a bad choice the man had made if it was true. But possibly he hadn't such information as Fordham upon which to make a judgment. The AC—Crime's intention might well affect his reaction to the direction of Fordham's present enquiries; he could stop those cold. While the DCS just might survive a straightener with the Commander of A10, he certainly wouldn't with the AC—Crime. However, he didn't tell Walsh that he had neglected to inform his bosses of the full extent of his enquiries. The ex-Squad man would have appreciated that.

During the muddy, bitter coffee, Walsh stared across at the younger man. 'Well, John. You didn't make the meet simply to talk about old times. What is it you think I can do for you?'

A smile spread across Fordham's face. 'I want some taps put on a number of phones.'

'Bent intercepts?' Walsh said flatly. 'S'that all?'

'We couldn't get warrants. They're a bit dodgy. You'll have to be slippery, Peter.'

'They won't exactly be the first, son. Whose phones?'

Fordham offered him the five names.

'The only one there might be problems with is Duckett's home – his bank's all right. He lives in Kent. Outside my area. A bit of luck, I'll find someone down there to oblige me. Wheels within wheels, John.' He finished his coffee and flapped his hand for the bill, which he paid for with plastic.

Briefly Fordham remembered some of the meals they had had on bent credit cards taken off fraudsmen. It still went on.

'Might take a day or two. Don't have the peremptory right of the CID.'

His smile said they could take more liberties than the

official intercepts department out at Chelsea. Most of their information went through C11.

At the Yard Fordham's driver took him into the bowels of the building where the carpark was; bays were marked with rank and office, as the names changed too frequently. Syd Worker dropped him by the lifts.

Waiting for the lift, Fordham thought about his meeting with Peter Walsh and was pleased with what he had achieved. He was sure the phone-taps would yield something, and he had no misgivings about their illegality. There were probably more intercepts made illegally than ever with Home Office approval.

It was ironical that Commander Bingham should have been in the lift; Fordham had been initiating just the sort of stroke that A10 would investigate.

The two men stared across the threshold at one another, neither making any move in or out. The Commander was silver-haired and had a high, broad forehead and spiky grey eyebrows; he was around fifty, but he looked older, despite his erect carriage.

'Chief superintendent,' Bingham said in a distant manner, his Scottish accent barely noticeable.

Ford responded in the same way.

Both were reluctant to give an inch or allow anything that had gone before to be negated, not by word or gesture.

'You're a very difficult man to get to.'

They passed each other through the lift entrance, Fordham taking over holding the gate.

'Been rather busy, Commander.'

'Aye, thinking up ways of stalling us. For over a week now you've been fobbing us off. Do you intend keeping it up? Just so that I'll know how to arrange my week.'

Fordham had no answer to the sarcasm, none he could get away with. He simply withdrew his hand and let the gate close.

Chapter 12

Rising early was an entrenched habit with Brodie, even though Connell's flat was far more comfortable than his past surroundings.

But the three rooms soon closed in on him. Moving around in the half-light of six-thirty a.m., he tried to outpace his frustration, feeling more like a caged animal than he had in prison. He was conscious of the presence of Connell's girl-friend, Maureen Hoyle. Brodie had been a long time without a woman – the benders on the Moor offered only limited relief. He resented Connell and his woman, felt jealous of them. They had something he didn't, something he wondered if he would ever have. He thought about his wife again, and pockets of anger exploded in his head. Despite having given her what she deserved, he now felt less than satisfied. That beating hadn't alleviated his humiliation, nor his suffering at the hands of others throughout his life.

There were noises from Connell's bedroom, sounds which emanated from Maureen Hoyle. The dirty wee whore. Connell was beefing her. They were probably doing it purposely to wind him up. He felt his cock begin to stand. Prostitutes were his only alternative to masturbation – unless he had Maureen Hoyle. He considered Connell, whether the man might be able to stop him. He didn't know any prostitutes, or even if there were any who'd oblige at that time of the morning. He would have crossed the water into Soho, but the lazy slags there didn't start before midday.

With the idea implanted in his brain, Brodie decided to venture outside. He had been cooped up for thirty hours and needed to get out. The impulse overwhelmed him: to test his option of walking unchallenged through the street door into the unrestricted world beyond.

Through Connell he had been instructed by Alan Day to stay inside the flat. But Brodie suspected that it was Connell's idea alone, that he was simply trying to exert his authority. The Scotsman had decided that Connell had no authority. If he wanted to chance his luck he'd get a good hiding.

The entrance of the mansion block was deserted. Brodie waited for a moment, then moved along the dimly lit passageway. There was a mixture of smells, lavender wax and what Brodie took to be kippers; it was so long since he had smelt kippers. Whatever the smell, it was a whole load better than anything on the Moor.

London air tasted fresh, nice at that hour. Prince of Wales Drive had the double advantage of Battersea Park right across the street, and the river beyond that.

Brodie hesitated in the doorway recess, almost afraid of the freedom before him. He checked both directions, his deep-brown eyes seeking anything that might represent a threat. But there was no Old Bill lurking behind newspapers, no suspicious-looking vehicles, only a woman in a fur coat walking a poodle. She was probably a brass just home from work. He watched her turn through the broken gateway into the park.

Starting after her, Brodie was almost knocked down as he stepped out between parked cars. He swore quietly as the vehicle continued without even slowing down. His next attempt was more cautious.

Walking in the park was nice. Pleasure swamped over him like relief after prolonged discomfort, and he relaxed, briefly forgetting who and what he was. He wandered through the crisp, frost-encrusted grass, unaware of potential danger. For the first time in a long while Brodie felt glad to be alive. He wanted the feeling to stay with him.

He firmly resolved at that point never to go back to prison. He wouldn't allow himself to be taken back.

Wakened by a shrill noise in the street, Connell sat up with a start. He checked his watch. It was ten o'clock. He immediately remembered Brodie, and wondered what he was doing. He didn't like the Scotsman, and would sooner he wasn't staying there; but it was only for a couple of days.

With an effort Connell got himself up off the bed. His back ached from the base of the spine to the top of his shoulders. He groaned as he reached round, pushing his pudgy fingers into the thick flesh. He found little relief.

'Give my back a bit of a massage, will you, Mo?' He lay down again and she pushed her hands against his spine in a tired fashion. 'That ain't no fucking good. Do it properly,' he exhorted, causing her to work with more enthusiasm.

When he finally prised himself off the bed he felt no better. Maureen Hoyle told him to see a doctor. He suggested going to a masseuse for an assisted shower. The woman didn't respond. And as Connell turned from his morning ritual of checking the street through a chink in the curtains, he said, 'C'mon, Mo. You gonna get up? I want some breakfast.'

The thought of cooking his own breakfast, or doing anything domestic, no longer occurred to him since she had moved in.

Brian Connell was large and fleshy. He weighed around two hundred pounds, but wasn't disproportionately fat. He was in his mid-thirties, but had a plump, boyish face and mop of black curly hair.

In the bathroom he regarded himself in the mirror for a long while before shaving. He liked the physical image, the image he believed others had of him. He thought he led an enviable life. He worked infrequently, and always had plenty of money. It was immaterial that he was a criminal and occasionally paid for it with prison sentences. The last, for armed robbery, had been two years ago. He had earned plenty since then. He had only been nicked the last time because the filth had reneged and arrested him despite the bribe they had taken.

Connell had been a criminal ever since he could remember. As a kid he had gone hoisting in Woolworth's, quite why he never knew. It wasn't from need; half the stuff was no use anyway, and he had given most of it away. There had been no material need in his life; his parents hadn't been well off, but they weren't destitute like some of his friends, who'd never had a spare shilling in their house. Without his realising it, his childhood had been disturbed; his parents had constantly been on the verge of splitting up. Rows had been rare, but there had been a continual atmosphere in the house. A lot of it was due to his father being a small-time sub-contractor, whose fortunes had frequent peaks and troughs. That was what a prison psychologist had told him.

Inevitably Connell had gone on to real crime. He specialised in armed robbery now. A gun in his hand tended to complement the image he had of himself.

Finishing with his electric razor, Connell listened to the silence of his flat, sensing something missing. It came to him in a flash: Brodie. His waking hours the previous day had been spent restlessly pacing around.

Connell wrenched open the bathroom door and moved along the passageway, searching the rooms. Brodie's departure was conclusive, for reaching the front door he found both the mortice unlocked and the latch snib off.

He felt very angry. The little cunt! He'd smash his face in. Going out like that he was risking everything, putting everybody in jeopardy. But more importantly, he was endangering Brian Connell. Brodie had been given strict instructions not to so much as stick his head outside the door.

'S'that the way it's going to be with the little cunt, Alan?' Connell vented his anger on the phone at the draftsman. 'S'that how he's going to shape? Putting us all at risk? Not doing as he's told?'

'I expect he just felt a bit closed in there,' Day said, trying to placate the villain without increasing the tension by openly condoning Brodie's move.

'Oh great. I mean, how fucking hard's that? Staying banged up here, after all the bird he's done?' He paced the bedroom with the phone, pausing frequently to peer through the curtains. 'How's he going to do what he's told when he gets up the road?'

Day said, 'He's all right, I promise you. I wouldn't give you a wrong 'un.' He listened to the man's angry snorting. He knew what Connell's problem was; he was feeling threatened, seeing his authority challenged. That was the drawback of using two men like Brodie and Connell on the same job. Each felt he should have been running things.

'Where is he now? Any idea?'

'How the fuck do I know? Probably up the hospital breaking his old lady's arms!'

That incident hadn't pleased Connell. Not because it was too drastic or the woman hadn't deserved it, but because Brodie had flouted instructions in order to put himself about.

He glanced through the window again, and felt tension claw at him as he saw Brodie. 'Hold up, Alan. He's just shown.'

'Is he clear?' There was an apprehensive note in his voice.

'Far as I can tell,' he said grudgingly. 'The cunt. He wants a good whacking.'

'Well, no harm's done. Look, I'll come over, do the briefing this morning. I'll have a word with him.'

When Connell replaced the phone, he saw Maureen Hoyle looking at him. She was sitting up in bed, her large breasts hanging over the covers.

Without make-up her complexion had a dense paleness resembling putty, her features too were dull, but her smile redeemed her: it was warm, especially when she was amused by something the man she loved did.

'First you were pissed off with him here. Then with him leaving.'

'Well . . . he should do what he's told, shouldn't he.'

Maureen Hoyle agreed. She invariably did.

'Where the fuck you been?' Connell demanded when he admitted the small Scotsman.

'The fook's it to do wi' you, man?' Brodie retorted.

'Sure it has. You were s'posed to stay here. Not fucking taking silly chances for no reason.'

'There wis a reason. An' d'you think me a bairn, that I cannae go out wi'oot getting in trouble?'

The two men looked at one another with hard, unflinching stares. Both were tense and prepared to hit out. But it didn't come to that. Connell backed off.

Alan Day was on edge when he arrived, uncertain what he might run into: a fight, of which he would have to be arbitrator; Old Bill, whom Brodie might have led to them. There was neither, only a heavy atmosphere.

Even though Maureen Hoyle was now a part of things, especially in Connell's arrival and departure from Glasgow, Alan Day indicated that he wasn't about to talk in front of her. The woman, who was in her dressing-gown, went back to bed when Connell told her to quit the kitchen.

'She's all right, Alan. You don't have to worry.' Connell hadn't defended the woman's presence before.

'I don't doubt it. But as far as anyone other than you two know, I don't exist.'

That wasn't quite true. The people he had contacted in Glasgow in setting up the job knew he existed, but not as Alan Day. He had used the name Percival; grown a moustache and worn glasses.

'What about the other fella?' Connell said.

Alan Day shot him a look. The first thing Connell had asked when propositioned was who it was funding the blag. Brodie, on the other hand, hadn't asked at all, and remained in ignorance of Charlie Ryman. Nor did he raise the question now as Alan Day turned his glance to him. It seemed almost inconceivable that someone as small as Brodie would be able to pull off this blag. But the draftsman knew what he was capable of.

'Well, it's all set for Friday. By Saturday we should all be a little richer, and a lot safer – you'll both be out of the country. That do anything for you, Donald?'

'Ask me when I'm away. Then I'll tell ya.'

'What local talent d'you come up with, Alan?'

'Some very worthwhile people. Joey McDonald. Ian Gordon. And Scotch Pat, he'll do the main driving.' With each name he looked towards Brodie, expecting him to approve.

The Scotsman indicated neither approval nor disapproval.

'You'll have no problems there. I liked the way they

shaped up. They've some good recommendations.'

Now Connell looked at Brodie, dismissing out of hand his part in that. The Jocks would have to prove themselves to his satisfaction. 'Be better if we had a few more lads from down here. I'd feel happier.'

'There'll be enough resistance from the police, without getting it from local villains.'

'What are they? Old mugs, that's all.'

'They'll put you away any time,' Brodie said evenly. 'Any fooking time you want.'

'They're grasses, that's why,' Connell said, winding him up. 'All Jocks are.'

Brodie sprang out of his chair, fetching it round over his head to hit Connell. 'Right, you gallous bass, I'm no' feart o' ya.'

'Any time, Jock!'

The threats might have become blows but for Day. 'Leave it out, will you? We've a job to do. What's the matter with you?'

'He don't do as he's told – that's the fucking nause.'

'Aye, who's man enough to tell me?' Brodie wanted to know.

'I'm telling you both. Fucking well leave it out. Understand?' The firmness surprised Day as much as Brodie and Connell.

A pause followed. Both antagonists backed down.

'There'll be a couple going up from here. Syd Haimes. And Ronnie, of course.'

'S'he still going?'

'He'd better. I haven't made alternative arrangements.' Day completely disregarded what Brodie had done, and thought Haston should do the same. That was after all simply a marital breakdown.

'I shouldn't be too sure, Alan. If some cunt broke my sister's legs, I'd fucking shoot him.'

'The dirty hooar had it coming. She should no ha'e fooked around while I wis banged up.' There was a frightening air of menace in the man.

Connell didn't pursue the tack. He knew there was justification for what Brodie had done. A man didn't want his old woman screwing around while he was locked up.

'Well, he's counted in. You better tell him when he calls, Brian. He's in trouble if he tries to drop out.'

He gave Connell the schedules for getting Brodie, Haston, Haimes and himself to Glasgow, along with Maureen Hoyle – they were flying to Spain afterwards. Day had made those arrangements too. The draftsman's responsibilities didn't start and finish with the blag. In order to provide an alibi a couple resembling Connell and his girl-friend had flown out two days ago using their passports. Connell and Maureen Hoyle would go out on bent passports, eventually return on their own, the entry visas proving that they weren't in the country at the time of the blag.

Using diagrams, he took them through the job. The three Scotsmen who were involved in Glasgow had been over as much with Day as he had been prepared to give them; they would get the final briefing from Brodie on the night before the job. That was all they needed. Elaborate rehearsal was neither necessary nor practical. The only part that could be rehearsed was the escape route after the blag, but that was pointless, for a traffic jam could throw out everything.

Despite its complicated appearance, the design Day had got out was relatively simple; the raid on the morning special Royal Mail would work if the plan was adhered to. He went through it a couple of times, Brodie and Connell getting the details firmly implanted in their heads.

The way out for Brodie after the job was another boat trip, travelling with the money to Liverpool. There he would be met and relieved of his burden before taking the ferry to Dublin. Haston was supposed to go with him as far as Liverpool, but Day wondered now if that wasn't a mistake.

When Day had covered all the ground there was one vital piece of information that Brodie wanted.

'Ma passport, man? When do I git that?'

'I hoped to have it before you went north. But there's a bit of delay.' He saw the man's suspicion. 'Not a real problem, Donald. I want something a bit near the mark for you. I could get you half a dozen dodgy ones. What good?' He was apologizing again, and wondered why. He had made up for his last arrest; he had had him sprung, at no little expense and effort. 'You'll have it at the latest when you reach Liverpool. I promise you.'

Then the debt, if it had ever existed, would be paid.

The warm, antiseptic atmosphere of the hospital corridor where Haston paced had combined with anxiety and dried out his throat and mouth. He had tried the tea in the hospital cafeteria but that hadn't helped.

Haston was awaiting news of his sister, who was in the operating theatre, having the third operation on her legs. The first two had been emergency holding efforts, according to the young Indian doctor he had spoken to. The one she was having now was to try and put her bones together so that she would be able to walk again. They had the top man doing that. From what the nursing sister told him, Haston liked the sound of the man; he didn't have any faith in the Indian and Chinese doctors he saw around. He couldn't understand most of them, their English was so bad

Each time he turned in the corridor to walk in the opposite direction he increased the distance. Soon he would reach the end of the corridor where the section in which the operating theatre was situated joined another.

He was angry and tense over what had happened to his baby sister; depressed and frustrated because he was powerless to go after Brodie. He was scared of Donald Brodie, as all sensible people were scared of maniacs. The only way to go after him was with a shotgun, do the job properly. Only that frightened him also. They were supposed to be making one together, but Haston couldn't see it now. He wanted nothing to do with him, apart from hurting him, making him suffer, more than he had made poor little June suffer.

Turning, he saw one of the schwartzer doctors emerge from a door. He tried to call to him, but got no more than a squeak from his dry larynx. He quickened his pace and caught the white-coated doctor before he turned into another room.

'Doctor . . .' he couldn't remember his foreign name. The man waited. 'What's the word, doctor? Have you heard?'

'I'm afraid I haven't, Mr Brodie . . .'

'Haston. It's Haston. I'm her brother. Brodie's the bastard who done it. Didn't you find out?'

'We do not know until the surgeon has finished. It could be two, three hours yet. Why do you not go home? We will telephone you.'

Haston looked into the brown, unsympathetic face and felt annoyed. Black fucker! What did he care what a white man's sister was going through? 'I'll wait.'

He turned, blanking him, and resumed pacing. When finally he reached the corridor at the end of where it ran at a right-angle, he saw a wall telephone with a dome-shaped canopy.

He stepped down to the phone and called Connell.

Chapter 13

'Bri'? S'Ronnie. Thought I'd give you a bell.'

'Hello, son. How's your sister?'

'Fucking wicked mess, 'in't she. He took a fucking wicked liberty there. Know what I mean?'

'Fucking right. The cunt was well out of order. Hope she goes all right. I mean that. If there's anything I can do.'

'Yeah, well, thanks . . .'

Both men sounded embarrassed.

There was a pause.

'Everything's on. It's all confirmed. Confirmed it today, he did. All right?'

'Well, I dunno, Bri', do I. I mean, this fucking little turn-out. I didn't expect this, did I.'

'Sure. I know you didn't. But it's family, 'in't it. I mean, you can't let it interfere with business.'

'Fucking hell! How would you feel if it was your sister? Then you was s'posed to make one with the cunt what did it. I mean, how would you feel?'

'Like topping him, I s'pose. But you gotta do it afterwards. You can't fuck the job.'

There was a long silence.

'Ronnie? You still there?'

'Yeah. I was just thinking.'

'I tell you, son, a lot of people'll be very upset you try and pull out . . .'

'Myself included,' Fordham interjected, his thoughts actively scheming.

'A lot of work's been done. You'd better stay in. Look, can you get over here?'

'No. I wanna stick around the hospital, see how June comes out of her op. I'll see you later.'

'Make sure you do.'

There was a click, then a heavy burr on the line. The detective in Battersea telephone exchange came on after he had taken the tape off telephone relay.

'Do you want it played again, guv?'

'That's fine. Just get it up here when you're relieved.'

He replaced the phone and stared pensively through the half-glazed partition of the radio room where he was with DCI Borroughs and DI Senior.

The radio room was located next to the Squad office on the fourth floor of the Yard. It was for the exclusive use of the Squad, who had their own r/t equipment and frequencies, teleprinter and telex machines.

'Looks like we're getting something,' Borroughs observed. 'If Haston doesn't screw it all up.'

'Mind you, understandable that he might want to,' Senior added.

'I can understand it, Bill. But it mustn't happen. The way Ronnie Haston's feeling, I think he'll prove very useful. We'd better have a word. Have a couple of lads pick him up, Frank. We'll see how he shapes.'

'Do you want to see him?'

'Not really – well, if he's brought somewhere handy. Are we still using that flat along the road?'

They were. It belonged to a body who owed them a favour; he repaid it by letting them use his flat to meet people they couldn't or didn't want to fetch to the Yard.

'Give me a call when they have him.'

Not having spent much of his career in a general CID room, the noise and apparent confusion there with more than two detectives working on different cases always surprised Fordham. Some two dozen detectives were now working in an area forty feet by thirty, an area which already seemed over-crowded with desks and filing cabinets. As one detective raised his voice to make himself heard, so the next had to speak louder. The only volumes that didn't rise were those of typewriters deftly hammered by Ds, and telephones, which had the same decibel persistency.

Outside there was a freezing east wind, so it wasn't difficult to understand why so many were in the office working.

Fordham considered the constant motion of bodies, the

continuous exchange of information. Words reached him and became separated; fragments of cases on which he read reports were recognisable. '... I'm saying that if they're assuming what there was in those safe-deposits, then where's the missing sixty per cent ... it's a ramp ...' 'You're paid fifty quid a week to sit on your ass in a car and watch that factory, that's all ...' It sometimes amazed the DCS that cases ever emerged with a single identity, much less a result.

Back in his own office Fordham took a call from Stanley Nester. Criminal Intelligence had picked up information on the Glasgow blag. They had heard it might be the Tate and Lyle factory that was being hit.

'This investigation is one of yours, isn't it?' the superintendent wanted to know.

'In a manner of speaking.'

'The thing is, do you wish us to pass this information to Strathclyde CID? Or are you liaising directly?'

'We're handling it, Stanley. And anything else you might pick up.'

It was likely that C11, which had its own means of gathering information, would come up with something more on the Glasgow raid. But they were generally obliging to the Squad.

Detective Superintendent Winkle brought the DCS a piece of information he could have done without.

'I had a meeting with Bill Pritchard down at Croydon this morning. About the post office raid. But he casually let it go that he was ready to nick Charlie Ryman.'

Fordham leant back in his chair.

'Didn't you have an interest?' Playing some things as close as Fordham did meant that sometimes senior officers weren't sure who he was after.

'What's he got on him, Willy?'

'His early long-firm activities. He reckons he's about due. I mean, I couldn't say anything.' That was a faint plea for more information.

Such a move by the Croydon CID, if allowed to go forward, could throw Fordham's plans completely. If Ryman was nicked down there, then Fordham might as well arrest those going up to Glasgow on conspiracy charges without reaching any higher.

'What sort of case has Pritchard got?' If it was strong, and Bill Pritchard proved amenable, then he might be able to use that in a trade-off with Ryman for the people above him. He wasn't keen to let the Glasgow job go forward. Because of both its location and the nature of the CID involved, he wouldn't have the same control as he would had it been going off nearer home.

He telephoned Pritchard to try and arrange a meeting, but couldn't reach the man. He left a message for him to call back.

Haston was picked up at the hospital and taken to the flat in Great Smith Street, where Borroughs was waiting. The DCI called Fordham, who was less than five minutes away. The owner of the flat had been in when Borroughs arrived, but obligingly stepped out.

As they waited for Fordham, Borroughs offered the felon a drink, which was refused.

The DCI found Haston a nervous animal. He paced a lot, and whined, wanting to know, not unreasonably, why he had been brought there. Borroughs simply told him his governor wanted a word, which made him more nervous. In the past he had only ever dealt with the lower ranks of CID; now heavy filth had taken an interest, and that he didn't like one bit.

Haston had dark hair and distinctive dark eyes set wide apart. Half way across the top of the right eye the lashes changed to snow white. Just one eye and one lid. Though not tall he was sturdily built, and could probably have done a lot of damage in a fight, if he had the front, but Haston was definitely without an asshole.

When Fordham arrived he treated the suspect like an old friend, and Haston immediately responded to the DCS's easy charm.

'How's your sister shaping, Ronnie? The hospital, they don't give you much, do they?'

'She's past the worst of it. But she's gonna be in plaster six months.'

'Is that right?' Dismay and concern showed in his voice. 'That's wicked. That fucker wants hurting badly. Brodie's a nutter, of course.'

'Oh, a fucking maniac, Mr Fordham.'

'Still, she was having it off, wasn't she? With half the street.'

Haston looked askance at the detective, uncertain how he knew about his family. 'But getting out just to break your wife's legs. It's a bit strong.'

'That wasn't the reason, was it?' He glanced at the DCI leaning his rump against the window-sill. 'He was sprung for this blag.'

'What blag?' Haston became alert, struggling through the subterfuge of apparent concern he had been offered.

'That one you and Brian Connell are making on Friday.' He watched Haston as the colour drained from his face. He looked suddenly ill. 'Glasgow. That's where it's planned to go off.' Casually Fordham gave the impression that he knew more than he did.

'I don't know what you're talking about, guv. Straight I don't.'

'I'm not looking for you, Ronnie. Not especially. And the job itself, well . . . It's the firm I'm interested in. The people putting you in.'

'I don't know, Mr Fordham.'

'Oh, I believe you. We know who they are; what they're earning; what jobs they've been responsible for. What was your take-home pay from the last one you made, Ronnie? A couple of grand? Much as that?'

Haston didn't reply.

'They earned a lot more, believe me.'

'It cost more than what you earn to spring Brodie,' Boroughs put in. 'That's how well you're thought of.'

'Look, you got it wrong. I don't know nothing. All I

know was that my brother-in-law made one off the Moor, then gave my sister some stick. That's all.'

There was a pause. Fordham slowly shook his head.

'As of this moment, Ronnie, I have enough on you to get you banged up for ten.'

Desperation pulled at Haston. 'Look, why don't you just go and nick 'em if you know?'

'If I could, Ronnie, I wouldn't bother about Glasgow. Or getting you to help me.'

'All right. One was put up to me. It happens all the time, guv. But after what Brodie did. I mean, well, you know. I couldn't have none of it, could I.'

'Oh but you will, Ronnie. You do want to weigh off Brodie for the stroke he pulled. I'm going to give you the opportunity' – as though doing him a favour.

'I ain't having any of it. I told you, Mr Fordham. You know, I said I wasn't.'

'You're not listening, are you. I told you different. You're committed, and you're going to stay that way right to the end.'

'People are relying on you, Ronnie,' Borroughs said. 'You can't let them down.'

'If it goes off you'll nick me.' There was panic in his voice.

'I'll nick you anyway, Ronnie. So why not help me and help yourself at the same time. And settle with Brodie in the process. Being locked up hurts him more than ever shooting his legs would. And without risk to yourself.'

The words were reaching into Haston like dulled barbs. He knew he was hooked. You had little chance against the ordinary CID when they had you; with the Squad you had even less. The thought of settling with Brodie in that way was appealing; perhaps not as satisfying as shooting him, but then he knew he hadn't the front for that. But whatever way he booked it or tried to justify it, what the filth was asking him to do was become a grass. That held no appeal.

'What is it you want from me, Mr Fordham?' Haston was being obtuse.

Spelling it out, Fordham said, 'The firm who are putting you into Glasgow. You're going to be my inside man up there. If anything goes wrong, I'll see you're okay.' He paused. 'When and how are you travelling north?'

Haston didn't reply immediately. Finally he said, 'I was s'posed to go up tomorrow on the train, twelve-forty-five out of Euston. Unless things have been changed.'

He didn't know what the job was, nor when it was going off, nor where. He didn't know where he would be staying either, only that he was being met off the train.

Fordham believed him, guessing that Haston had, albeit reluctantly, accepted his new role.

The felon made one last appeal, 'I don't want to go, Mr Fordham. I mean, I don't want to be involved.'

The detective was unmoved. 'You'll go, Ronnie. Even if I have to put you on that fucking train personally.'

Chapter 14

Wrapped in a heavy sheepskin coat a size too large for him, Donald Brodie stepped briskly from the entrance of the mansion block. As he moved to the waiting car, his eyes searched left, then right through the late afternoon gloom. The street looked safe enough.

'We're gonna be a bit tight for that train, my ol' son,' Haimes said, hunched behind the wheel.

'Aye. That's better than hanging around on the fooking station and getting masel' recognised.'

Haimes let in the clutch and eased into the traffic towards Albert Bridge Road.

The van that the Ds were on watch in was facing in the wrong direction. It started away and proceeded past Connell's flat before DC Tony Young, who was driving, executed a neat U-turn and went after Brodie's car. The Squad detectives kept a good distance as the car went over the bridge and headed north through Chelsea, Kensington, Knightsbridge. Cutting through Hyde Park, they found they were getting too close. There wasn't much traffic here.

'Drop back a bit,' DS Smith said. 'You'll be up his daily in a minute.'

The DC halted for some horses emerging from the park. A girl on the last horse turned and waved, thanking them. DC Young waved back, grinning like a Cheshire cat.

'Will you look. Has she got some form!'

'Yeah, not bad. Wouldn't mind giving it one.'

The van edged past the horses, and both detectives watched the girl. She was extremely pretty, and quite young.

'That would get you nicked.'

'A bit young, skip. But I'd take a chance.'

'We'd better look lively, 'fore we lose Brodie.'

They saw the car turn on to the one-way system around the Lancaster Hotel. Traffic was heavier, their distance more difficult to maintain. Along Marylebone Road the traffic was dense and they got into trouble. The van driver took a couple of liberties and managed to close the gap. Then the car Haimes was driving accelerated and opened it again.

'Do you think he has sussed us, skip?'

'Could be,' the DS replied. 'Look sharp, he's done the light.'

The felon's car passed through the green lights at the junction of Albany Street and Euston Road. The four cars immediately behind did also, the fourth making it on amber and red. The van tried to scrape through, and would have done but for the acceleration of the sports car sitting on the opposite light, engine revving. The front nearside wing smashed into the rear bumper of the van, becoming hooked up. It remained that way when the two vehicles came to halt.

Both detectives leapt out. Young to check the damage, Smith to keep sight of Brodie's vehicle.

'You're supposed to stop at red lights. You blasted fool,' the sports car driver screamed. 'Look at my car. Just look...'

DC Young wasn't listening to the man's ranting, but was figuring how to get the vehicles unhooked so they could get on their way; that was his sole priority. He wrenched at the bumper, causing a rending of metal, and a louder scream from the car owner.

'Stop! Stop it, you're ruining my car.'

'Get in and back it off, will you?'

'I want the police called. I'm not going anywhere. I want your driving licence and insurance...'

'Fuck off!'

He wrestled further with the tangled bumpers. DS Smith came to help. They lifted and rocked it, as the car owner ran to the uniformed constable, who came towards them through the traffic that was building up.

'Try it, skip, will you?'

The DS jumped behind the wheel of the van, snatching it off the sports car with more tearing metal.

Mistaking the move for a getaway, the uniformed constable ran to the van and reached in, grabbing the wheel.

'Just one moment, sir.'

The DS briskly produced his ID. 'We're in a hurry, son. Following a suspect. Straighten chummy out. He jumped the lights.'

The uniformed policeman proved very obliging. He moved back and began berating the sports car owner. The van drew away.

The delay had been too long for them to catch Brodie's car. But they tried. Going in that direction they had three logical options, three of London's eight major railway stations: Euston, St Pancras and King's Cross. They took the first. Had they known Brodie's ultimate destination they'd have realised it was the only choice.

By the time Haimes had got the car parked where it could be left, they had only minutes to catch the four-forty-five Inter-City to Glasgow.

It wasn't simply luck that the two detectives saw Brodie and the other man pass the barrier on to platform four, but the methodical process by which most detectives survived. The indicator showed the Glasgow train as the first out; so having chosen Euston, and, based on the not unreasonable assumption that the felons would be catching a train, the first to depart was the first they checked.

There was a meeting of senior detectives scheduled for ten-thirty the next morning. These meetings were fairly infrequent, about every three or four months. Most detectives with the rank of chief inspector and above attended. General CID matters were discussed; problem areas, where and how improvements might be made; policy was touched on and how it related to their jobs. The more outspoken bitched at the idiocy of some policy, despite the occasional presence of the AC—Crime, one of the policy-makers. Rarely did the bitching result in direct changes. If it proved sufficiently persistent and voluminous, then there was a gradual shifting of ground until the policy fell into disuse. Never a complete reversal or immediate abandonment.

The meetings as such were no problem for Fordham,

other than that there was always something else in which his energies would be better employed. And it did mean he had to clear any back-log of incoming reports. He read them for information, as aspects of various cases were often raised. That was all right; what DCS Fordham resisted was imparting details of those cases which he was playing close, such as that involving Duckett, O'Connor and Ryman. There was a problem arising out of its proportions now. The bigger it got the more difficult it was to keep the lid on. It had caused a few awkward moments at the last meeting. The matter was bound to be raised again; only Fordham wouldn't be able to dismiss it so lightly, if he was able to dismiss it at all. Peter Goodfellow would probably start asking for reports, full reports, especially in view of what Walsh had said about his retirement expectations. Too many detectives on the Squad were holding too many ends of the investigation to disguise it now.

Scrawling his name on a report, he slid it off the pile and into his Out tray. His eyes moved swiftly across the immaculately typed lines of the next one. It contained details of a robbery in Walthamstow. A villain called Billy Gray had been arrested, made a court appearance and been given bail. Fordham's eyes ran back over the words to make sure he had read them correctly. There was no mistake: the arresting officer, DI Stephen Peacock, had not only raised no objection to bail, but had also allayed the magistrate's doubts. At first glance it looked as though Peacock was earning. That was always a possibility, but if it was the case Fordham wished the DI had proceeded more discreetly.

Detective Superintendent Jack Owen had countersigned the report; so it was to him Fordham went rather than undermining his authority by going to Peacock.

Owen wasn't in his office, only Superintendent Winkle was there. 'Jack around?' Fordham asked.

'Gone home, John. His cold was getting worse.'

The information alone would have sufficed. Fordham didn't require an account of his officers minute by minute.

They were entitled to decide how long their day should be.

Fordham went along the corridor to the DIs' office. There were only two of them in. One was Peacock, who knew what the DCS wanted.

'Does seem a bit strong, guv. Billy Gray's looking for some help. He wouldn't be able to get anything to trade with if he's shut away. I thought it worth a go. He won't be too difficult to pick up if he tries to have it away.'

'You believe he'll come up with something, Stephen?'

'A good chance. He's desperate enough. He knows he can get a five-stretch instead of fifteen if he weighs in with something.'

That was reason enough for the DI's action, but it wouldn't go on record.

The operator in the r/t room saw Fordham step from the DIs' office, and beckoned him. Detective Sergeant Smith was on the radio from Euston, and told him about Brodie and the other man catching the Glasgow train. Fordham thanked him and told him to check back with Reggie Howe, the DI whose squad he was in.

The radio message was recorded in the log. Fordham glanced down the entries in the quasi-shorthand the police used, and read off the last one. It hung ominously on the page. He wished it hadn't been recorded, for if anything went wrong and Brodie wasn't in the bag at the end of the operation, that message might cause him trouble.

The information now having been committed to the system, Fordham officially acted on it. He had Bill Senior send it up to Strathclyde CID, via C11, with the attached instructions 'Observe and Advise', suspecting the DCS up there would be unwilling to cooperate if he knew who was involved. If he realised this was a Squad operation, with any subsequent glory going their way, Kellan would probably arrest Brodie on sight. Certainly he wouldn't allow the blag to go forward to the point where Fordham would have something substantial on Ryman. With Criminal Intelligence as the apparent source, he might just get away with what he was trying.

Chapter 15

Scottish detectives were positioned throughout Glasgow Central Station. Around ten o'clock the station was becoming deserted enough for them to stand out like a third tit on a lassie's chest if they weren't discreet. They were being discreet, DCI Alan Crombie decided, as his eyes swept the arrivals hall. He had eleven detectives there, almost the entire night squad, and he had made a point about the caution they should employ with Brodie. Each had a copy of the photograph which had been sent up on the teleprinter. They had only the description of the other man, but it was enough.

The decision to commit the night squad had been made by Crombie; Chief Superintendent Kellan had already gone home for the evening when the details had arrived from London. Crombie had hesitated, undecided whether to call his boss. But he had resisted, realising that he had been calling upon the DCS to make the most trivial decisions. He was at liberty to commit detectives. As duty officer, assuming a more senior officer couldn't be contacted, he was temporarily with as much authority as the head of CID, and could commit the entire Strathclyde CID to an operation; that was the theory. He hoped there were no problems. He didn't foresee any. Brodie and the other man were there for some reason and they had been requested to observe and advise Scotland Yard. However, Crombie wondered briefly if twelve detectives wasn't an over-reaction.

Checking his wristwatch, the DCI looked over at the clock above the train indicators. 'A couple o' minutes I make it, Andy,' he said to DS Galbraith, who was standing in the entrance of the buffet with him. Each had a plastic British Rail tea cup with scotch in it.

The four-forty-five from London arrived two minutes late, which didn't surprise those who noticed. Some railway officials and the detectives were the only ones aware of that delay. The train had been held up by a red signal down the line, just beyond Cambuslang.

The barrier from number two platform had been restricted to allow passengers through singly. DCI Crombie thought it better to risk arousing Brodie's suspicions than have an open gate which he could slip through in a crowd.

Twelve pairs of trained eyes scrutinised the faces of the disembarking passengers. None of them were Brodie, nor fitted the description of the other man. They waited as the stream slackened to a trickle. Crombie was anxious. Mr Kellan's probable reaction was in the forefront of his thoughts. The trickle of passengers disappeared completely.

'How ha'e we missed the sods?' DS Galbraith asked, surprised.

'I don't know, Andy. I cannae tell you.'

The tall detective with the clipped moustache felt disappointed. It was as though he had let Mr Kellan down. He had the DS search through the train with some detectives. Only after that proved negative would Crombie know what he only suspected, that Brodie hadn't been on the train when it came into Glasgow, if at all.

For a man with only three fang-like, brown tombstone teeth hanging on spindly threads from his gums, Joe McDonald laughed altogether too uninhibitedly. His mood was buoyant, ebullient, like someone on a coach trip with a crateful of booze. Nothing was further from the truth. He was cold sober, driving through the Glasgow suburbs to a hotel in Cambuslang. The reason for his mood wasn't simply that he had just picked up Donald Brodie and Syd Haimes from along the railway line, rather that the Englishman who had planned this had said the pick-up would work, and it had. It boded well for the job itself.

'He wis a queer hawk, man, and no mistake. Wan' he, Pat?'

Scotch Pat, a less demonstrative villain – except behind the wheel of a car – agreed, but hadn't anything to add.

'You coulda knocked me doon wi' a feather when he said

he had one planned wi' ya. I knew where you were, man.' McDonald glanced in the mirror at the two men, their faces lit occasionally by the glare of the overhead sodium lights. 'At first I thoat he wis fae the polis. We thoat he wis crazy, some of the ideas he had. Dinno' think it'd work.'

'He's fooking good, Joe. You can rely on what he says'll work.' Despite his prison sentence Brodie had great faith in Alan Day.

'I believe it noo. Never thoat you'd be there tonight. Did we, Pat?' Scotch Pat concurred. 'He hid some right weird taste in lassies, he did. He liked them to ha'e something wrong wi' 'em. We fixed him up wi' yon' gimpy Sheila. Couldna believe her luck, could she. She's no had a wee cock inside her since we all fooked her as kids. She wasn't able to run as fast as the other girls,' he explained for Haimes. 'On account of her leg-iron.' He laughed at the recollection.

The third felon whom Alan Day had recruited in Glasgow was waiting at the hotel, a crumbling house that stood within walking distance of the station, shaking whenever a train went through. It had a rank smell, seeds of stale sweat hanging in tired, unlaundered clothes, entombed in the house tightly sealed against the northern winters. Day had selected the hotel for them, so one thing above all else to recommend the place was that it would be safe.

Neither the three Glaswegian villains nor Haimes knew what the blag was, for the proposition had been put to them in a way sufficient for them to commit, but not to endanger it if they didn't. There was no surprise or alarm when Brodie told them. A blag was a blag, and if someone as good as the draftsman said it would work, it made no difference whether it was the Royal Mail train or the royal household at Balmoral.

'You say we're doin' it in a day, Donald?' Gordon questioned. 'But the postie goes in the evening, do it no'?'

'Aye. But they've laid on a day special,' Brodie informed him.

After going over the basic details of the plan, Brodie left

with Scotch Pat to make a couple of telephone calls. He called the man who was getting the shooters for them; then the man supplying the vehicles. Both told him there were no problems, they had all they had been asked for. He arranged to meet them separately early in the morning. The calls were purposely brusque as he felt very exposed in the lighted phone box – but safer than he would have felt phoning from the hotel.

Stepping from the box, Brodie moved quickly to the car and climbed in. Scotch Pat started away immediately. Two men in a stationary car were more suspect than two driving.

'Where to now, Donald? A bit of relaxation?'

Brodie didn't reply, but waited to see what he might suggest.

'Annie's is no' from here. S'always worth a visit, you ken.'

'S'that old hag still in fooking business?'

'Aye. A loot of tit down there. You wanna try it?' Scotch Pat felt good being out with Brodie. It was like being with an elder brother who was a celebrity, he wanted to go where he was known, show him off. He had never worked with Donald Brodie before, but knew about him.

The offer was tempting. A few drinks and maybe one of Annie's lassies would do him good. But common sense prevailed. He also blanked Scotch Pat's next suggestion, about calling a couple of girls. When he was safely away and in Spain he could have all the women he wanted.

The hotel made no difference to Brodie's sleeping and waking habits. He rose early and woke Scotch Pat, who was in the same room.

They had breakfast in a café a short drive from the hotel. No one gave them a second glance. They called on the man who was supplying the vehicles. He gave Brodie the addresses where they were, including their getaway and back-up cars. All the vehicles were stolen, with rung number plates, but safe for the short-term use they would get.

Wilfrid Gullane, the guns dealer, was reluctant to have Brodie come either to his house or his greengrocery shop, even though he conducted his arms business at both places. Brodie wasn't prepared to risk a carpark meeting, which the man favoured, and Gullane finally yielded, telling him to come to his house on his own. So Brodie had Scotch Pat drop him along the road and wait. The business didn't take long. Brodie was simply given the location of the guns in exchange for the balance of money due. Wilf Gullane had dealt in guns for a good while, and stayed in business by being reliable. The guns would be in the boot of the parked car, exactly as he said.

Afterwards, Brodie made one more stop which he told no one about. This one for insurance. Again he had Scotch Pat drop him off and wait. Brodie walked around the corner out of sight and into a car rental company, where he hired a Volkswagen, saying he would collect it the next morning. That was no problem. The paperwork was made out against Brodie's bent driving licence. He signed the forms and paid in advance. If anything went wrong tomorrow, Brodie wanted an alternative way out. Lack of one was why he had been nicked on his last blag. Now he was all set.

Slowly, methodically, Kellan pulled the razor down his face, the careful strokes leaving the skin glistening. He was reluctant to finish, for this morning he was not looking forward to going to his office. Stuart Bothwell had arranged for local school kids to visit the police HQ. In theory it was useful PR, but Kellan knew that in practice it wouldn't make them any less belligerent towards the police as adults. Probably it wouldn't even make them any less belligerent as kids. But he had agreed to say a few words, why he didn't know, nor what he would say to them. I have every expectation of nicking most of you before you're very much older! The thought caused Kellan to smile. As his face muscles slackened the razor cut him. He swore.

Bloody kids!

His mood was even worse when he arrived at his office, having gone through the police HQ making his usual checks; duty log, charge sheets, questioning detectives in response to their greetings, and was finally confronted with the report about Donald Brodie. Had it told how they had arrested Brodie, things might have been different.

His grey, flecked eyes with their yellowing whites lifted from the page to Dougie Douglas. The DI was in the office waiting to start their morning routine of checking reports and referring back to the officers concerned. Kellan dealt this way with all reports.

'If Alan Crombie's still on duty, I'd like a word.'

DCI Crombie was still in the building, as he had a court appearance later that morning. He had expected the DCS to pick up on the incident.

'What happened, Alan?' Kellan asked in a moderate tone.

'If Brodie went on the train in London, he got off again. For he no' came off at Central.'

'Where did the train stop? Did you check?'

Such questions irritated Crombie. Of course he had checked. The two scheduled stops had been Preston and Carlisle.

'This information sent up by Criminal Intelligence is no' good enough, Dougie. Get on to them. I want to know where they received this and how. What meks them sure he's here? Also I want to know who gave this order "Observe and Advise". What do they think we are? Remind them that Brodie's a dangerous escapee. If he's on my pitch he's gonna be arrested.'

With a conscious effort Kellan managed to establish his routine and get through a lot of work before the kids' visit. One of the reports concerned a GPO mail van that had been stolen. There had been no trace of the mail, nor had the van been carrying registered packets.

'That's curious, Dougie. I'd like to see more action on that.'

DI Douglas made a note, but they got no further. The babble of young voices rose in the corridor. Why they wanted to come and see him, Kellan didn't know. The uniform branch's way of annoying him, he suspected.

There was a rap at the door. Douglas opened it to Sergeant McTovey and about forty kids. He turned back into the room, hiding the smile. 'They're here, chief.'

'Aye,' Kellan said grudgingly.

McTovey was half-driven into the office by the kids, a lot of whom couldn't get in because the ones at the front seemed reluctant to get too close. McTovey, referring to his clipboard notes as though not sure who Kellan was, read the introduction.

'This is Chief Superintendent Kellan, who is the most senior and most important detective in all Strathclyde. Perhaps the whole of Scotland. Decorated by the Queen for bravery, he was known throughout the city as the Gangbuster, the man who cleared Glasgow of its thugs and hoodlums . . .'

The man who arrested your big brothers and your dads, Kellan was thinking as he stared across his vast desk. He missed his cue, and there was an awkward silence.

'Next you'll be having them think I'm God, Mac.'

An unidentified voice said, 'God's a protestant!'

Giggling followed, but stopped when Kellan said, 'So am I, lad. So am I.'

There was another silence.

The kids regarded Kellan with a mixture of curiosity and mistrust, as he sat like granite, his cold, suspicious eyes boring into them.

'Well, boys and girls,' Kellan started, his expression yielding slightly.

Kids began to fidget.

Neither party fooled the other for a moment.

Chapter 16

The number and value of the grasses a detective ran was usually a measure of his worth. In his present high office John Fordham saw little of the grasses he had once employed. Most of them had either been passed to other detectives – a move that frequently didn't work – or abandoned. However, he didn't blank his erstwhile informers out of hand when they called him, certainly not those who had been as good as Eddie Russell. Inconvenient as it was, Fordham went to see Russell, who was now caretaker of an office block in Hatton Garden. Most of the companies in the block were diamond merchants. The reason Russell called was because he had been approached by a firm who were looking to blag every company in the block.

Although Russell was probably better off now than ever he had been as a grass, Fordham still felt sorry for him in his small basement flat. He was a forgotten man, a has-been trying to stage a come-back. But for the obvious potential in the information the DCS might have been inclined to view the man's call as a pathetic attempt to resurrect the past. With the ease of yesteryear Fordham gave him all the reassurances, the words of caution and goodwill he would have given the man at the height of his activities. He also gave him ten pounds and the promise of any reward money, but Russell was disappointed that Fordham wouldn't be handling the investigation personally.

Moving out of the lift and down the long, neon-lit corridor, abstractedly greeting other policemen, Fordham considered whom he might put on the investigation. It was a decision easily left to one of his three DCIs. Maybe one of them would even care to step outside the Yard, and see the changing world. It had been so long since they had felt a collar that, like himself, they'd probably forgotten how.

Work in the CID was often allocated on a hit-and-miss basis, to whoever answered the phone when something came in, the idea being that whoever had time to spend around the office answering phones had time to take on another case. Things worked not too dissimilarly in the Squad, only there it was usually whoever was around when senior detectives allocated the jobs. Normally the Squad was called in by the divisions or other police forces around the country when they had a difficult or abstruse case which they couldn't crack.

'Morning, Roy,' Fordham said as Inspector Jackson passed him. The man returned his greeting.

The problem was solved. Spinning round, 'Roy!'

The DI came back.

'What are you on?' He had a vague idea.

Jackson reminded him about the missing lorry-load of stereo equipment he was investigating. Fordham added the possible Hatton Garden raid to his work-load.

Jackson's squad was one of the four not involved with the investigation that was increasingly occupying Fordham. However none of the other six were on it exclusively. They all had other cases, and possibilities they were pursuing.

Most CID were over-stretched, and none of them believed the police would ever be brought up to strength. They were coping undermanned, or liked to think they were; so at strength, or overmanned, there might logically follow a degree of zeal which would terrify the liberals. The shortage of manpower could almost have been the result of a tacit deal struck with the radical, disruptive elements to keep a relatively low profile vis-à-vis the police in return for permanent undermanning. It was as if the Home Office merely paid lip-service to achieving strength.

Detective Inspector Norman phoned Fordham, and came along to see him directly.

Continuing his enquiries around O'Connors, Norman had discovered that the missing resident engineer, Daniel Rochester, was joint director of a plant hire company with O'Connors' contracts director. The firm had ceased trading and Messrs Duckett, Reinhardt had entered liquidation proceedings through the High Court for forty thousand of a ninety-thousand-pound plant mortgage, plus compound interest. The DI had got his information from a Board of Trade investigator who had been put in by the Official Receiver.

'That's first-rate, Les. Looks like you're opening it up. Keep with it. Give me a shout if your other stuff becomes a problem. What we want is another malcontent. Someone with a grudge who might be prepared to split it wide open.'

'There's someone I'm working on.'

A call from Superintendent Pritchard ended the meeting with Norman. He told Fordham that he thought his case against Ryman for his long-firm activities was good, but not one hundred per cent.

From the brief details, Fordham decided that with the sort of lawyer Charlie Ryman could afford he would either get the case chucked or get a conditional discharge. What it amounted to, as far as Fordham was concerned, was that there wouldn't be enough pressure on Ryman for him to use in a trade-off. He asked the detective from Croydon if he would hold back. Pritchard agreed, albeit reluctantly.

The telex from Glasgow CID in response to his information about Brodie didn't really surprise Superintendent Nester. Nor did John Fordham's reaction when he phoned him. The DCS was out on a limb, Nester felt, even further than usual. Something was going off in Glasgow, something that only Fordham knew about, and about which, for his own reasons, he was informing neither Glasgow nor C11. The Squad had a peremptory right of operation, and weren't obliged to inform anyone; to do so was merely a courtesy. As far as he knew it was the Tate and Lyle refinery that was to be robbed. Nester wondered if, instead of stalling Glasgow as Fordham had requested, he shouldn't send up that information. But who would it benefit? Glasgow? – possibly giving them one brief flurry of glory. It might ruin some overall plan of the Squad's. Such action could easily be justified by arguing that Fordham ought to have kept C11 in the picture. The way things were at present, all their resources were needed simply to keep pace with the Squad. Perhaps the best thing would be to raise the matter at the senior detectives' meeting later that morning.

Fordham didn't want their illegal tapes to be played in the radio booth with all its casual traffic. Finding a spare room anywhere in the building, let alone on the fourth floor, was impossible, he believed. But his aide proved resourceful. Bill Senior found a room, and on their floor. It was the one used by women detectives on the Squad as a rest-cum-work-room. Senior moved them into the general squad-room.

'Put them all on a promise, guv,' he explained to Fordham with a wry smile. The DCS wouldn't have been surprised how many of them Senior was stiffing.

The room could have been requested officially, but that meant black-and-whites, people knowing the reason.

A DS and three DCs had been assigned to the tapes. They did the monitoring and delivered the tapes, bringing items of special importance to the attention of either Fordham or Borroughs.

Calls across the tapped phones were pedestrian, none offering Fordham any kind of leverage. There were calls between Duckett and Sir Frank O'Connor discussing a board meeting; advice about a share issue; an invitation to a property speculation in Corfu. There were a few on Day's phone, but revealed nothing, apart from the fact that he was trying to make a woman called Celia, who sounded as though she was in an iron lung. There were dozens on Ryman's phones, one between Ryman and Duckett, which DS Neville Spears, who was running the tapes, seemed embarrassed about.

Duckett, who had called on a clear phone, asked if Ryman knew Fordham.

'Little bloke over at the Yard? Dark hair?'

'*He'll* have to be nicked,' Fordham put in humorously.

'I'm not concerned with what he looks like,' Duckett was saying. 'What does concern me is his recent visit to the

Home Office. He tried to obtain a warrant to intercept my phone calls. So a friend recently informed me at my club.'

There were noises of dismay from Ryman.

Also from Frank Borroughs in the small room. 'What fucking chance have you got?'

'Is he venal?' Duckett asked.

'Oh, well bent. Like all CID. Show me a detective and I'll show you one at it.'

'Chance would be a nice thing, Charlie,' Fordham said.

'Did you want me to go into him with anything?'

'I don't think that will be necessary. But it's useful to know, Charles. The need might arise; some form of pressure may have to be exerted.'

'There's no chance that they got to your phone?'

'I think not. I had a friend in a senior position in the GPO check that out.'

That move caused Fordham a bout of anxiety.

'Mr Walsh covered it, guv. Duckett's friend checked with security at Maidstone, who got straight on. Mr Walsh told him to pull the plug, to be on the safe side.'

Fordham nodded ponderously. 'He's not going to give us anything now. How about the others, Nev?'

'A lot across Connell's phone. Two of interest.'

He ran the tape. One was a short conversation with Alan Day. Connell was asking about shooters, whether the arrangements were all right left to Brodie. The second call was from Haston, trying to persuade Connell to cancel the job, saying he thought they'd all be nicked. But without saying why. Connell got heavy with him.

'Sounds like his bottle's well gone.'

'Doesn't it. Have him picked up, Frank. Make sure he catches that train. Lean on him a bit, in case he decides to jump off.'

'You want anyone to ride up with him?'

'No. It might not please Kellan if it got out.'

'What are you going to tell Glasgow?' Borroughs asked.

'Enough to cover ourselves, in case there's a fuck-up. But only just enough, Frank.'

'Guv,' Bill Senior said as Fordham came into his office, 'that bod from the Home Office looked in. Wanted to know if you can spare him some time. I told him you were at the meeting.'

Fordham checked his watch. 'I'm supposed to be. Ten minutes ago.'

In the corridor Fordham met Arthur Maulding, the Home Office admin. officer who was making a projection of the Squad's material requirements for the next two years. Fordham simply told him to double everything on the last projection. Spending a morning with the man would be a waste. No notice was ever taken of the projection, for what the Squad received bore little relation to what they sought. The fact that Maulding was looking for him during a scheduled meeting epitomised the impracticality of it all.

The meeting, which took place in the briefing room on the first floor, was under way by the time Fordham arrived. He slipped in and found a place at the back. As one of the heads of one of the most important branches in the CID he was obliged to put in an appearance, but Gerald Pope, the Commander, was perfectly able to present the Squad's case, as and when it became necessary. He was conversant with most of what went on. The only matter that he wasn't sufficiently informed to answer on was the extent of the Squad's investigation into areas involving Sir Frank O'Connor and Anthony Duckett, and for what was happening in Glasgow; he had been given only limited information about those enquiries.

DCS Fordham was hoping such questions wouldn't arise, and was jolted out of his drowsy, bored position when one was raised by Superintendent Akerman from C11. Commander Pope referred it to Fordham.

The DCS rose slowly, considering how best to answer. Most of the eighty or so detectives present were looking in his direction. How many collective years of police detection had these men between them, he wondered. He noticed the keen interest the ACC, who was chairing the meeting, was now taking. His cold, disdainful eyes were fixed on him expectantly.

What was Freddy Akerman fucking about at asking that question.

'We are making enquiries in those areas, Superintendent,' Fordham said formally to Akerman. 'There isn't any question of our not being open, but an urgent need for discretion. Some important and influential people might be involved, people whom we'd want to cause as little embarrassment as possible. As for Glasgow, something's going on up there, but I'm afraid we're as much in the dark as C11.'

There was a ripple of amusement, though Fordham wasn't trying to put the man down.

'How long have these enquiries been going on?'

The voice of Peter Goodfellow sounded clear as a bell across the room. Fordham only hoped it wouldn't prove to be a death knell.

'Not very long, sir. About a week or so.'

The ACC nodded, apparently satisfied, and the meeting moved on.

But Fordham suspected that the ACC was far from satisfied. He could read him like a book. The man was doubtless wondering why he hadn't seen any reports, and why, if important people were involved, it hadn't been referred to him for a directive. He would appreciate as well as Fordham that there, with a room full of detectives, wasn't the time or place to discuss the matter. Peter Goodfellow was too subtle, too much of a politician to commit such a tactical error. He would first ask for reports, probably via Gerald Pope; then proceed as he saw fit.

Fortunately Fordham had a report for every aspect of the investigation, apart from the illegal ones – these he had simply held up, instead of passing through for his superiors. Even so, that didn't exactly put him in the clear. Especially not now that Peter Goodfellow had the bit between his teeth.

Chapter 17

They might have been three friends moving through the conjestion at Euston Station, rather than two Squad officers taking Ronnie Haston under escort to his train. It was waiting in the platform, only minutes to the off. They walked unhurriedly to the first-class section. One of the detectives, DS Lessing, opened the carriage door.

'Here you are, Ronnie. Delivered safe and sound.'

'Mind the step, sir,' the other CID said mockingly, helping him into the carriage like an invalid. 'Got your toothbrush and your tartan pyjamas?'

Haston stared out at the two men with a forlorn expression, hoping they would relent. Missing that particular train might have resolved all his problems.

'Don't get jumping off, Ronnie. There's a couple going aboard to make sure you get there.'

Actually, Lessing couldn't make out why Mr Fordham *wasn't* sending someone, but accepted that the DCS knew what he was doing, as he had frequently proved. Like many other detectives, Lessing was sometimes amazed by the strokes Fordham pulled and got away with. His predecessor had taken liberties, but had come unstuck. Fordham could leave him cold, and would doubtless stay the course.

The whistle was blown. People seeing passengers off stepped back with hurried parting words.

'Don't forget to call Mr Fordham. By nine oclock tonight.' He stuffed a slip of paper in the pocket of Haston's double-breasted camelhair coat. 'His numbers at the Yard and home.'

The two detectives stepped back, leaving a distressed picture of Ronnie Haston at the window. As the train jolted into motion the second detective raised his hand in a mocking farewell wave.

The second teleprint from Scotland Yard, concerning the

arrival in Glasgow of another felon, angered Kellan more than the first. Along with details and photographs of Haston was again the instruction, 'observe and advise'. The words jumped off the page and jabbed at Kellan like painful spikes. What made it worse for him was the originator's name: DCS Fordham.

If there was one detective who epitomised the threat Kellan felt to his position it was Chief Superintendent John Fordham. He had met him in Brighton the previous year at the superintendents' conference. He had listened to Fordham debate Law and Order as though achieving that state was an intellectual exercise, rather than a dedicated and dangerous job demanding twenty-four hours a day of practice. He had instantly disliked the smooth-talking young know-all, who hadn't been in the job five minutes, yet had people treating him as though he had the answer. Most of all Ian Kellan resented the fact that, by some means other than putting in his time – he suspected connivance on the part of those corrupt bastards down south – Fordham had at the age of thirty-seven reached the rank it had taken himself over thirty years to achieve.

Criminals were invading his city, and now he had not only a London detective, but that particular one, trying to tell him how to proceed. No one did that to him, least of all some wet-behind-the-ears upstart.

'Get some photos run off, Dougie. Then tek two squads to Central Station and pick up Haston. Mek sure you cover every way off the train. I want this one. Through him we'll find the others, that's if they're in my city' – about which Kellan had his doubts. He thrust the teleprinted details back at DI Douglas. 'I'm not playing any cat-and-mouse games for Mr Fordham's benefit.'

His decision was final.

He should have got off at Preston or Carlisle, taken a chance with the CID on board. What had he to lose? He was going to be nicked anyway. The tension in his stomach was making him feel sick, and the couple of beers he had drunk in the bar weren't helping.

The train was on its last leg to Glasgow. He had missed his chance now to jump out and blank the blag. The threat Fordham represented had caused him to hesitate; it weighed heavily, almost physically held him in his seat. That wasn't the sort of filth to have looking for you, not if you valued your liberty. His thoughts moved on to consider his chances if he did as Fordham asked. If he called him and was helped after all the others had been nicked, it was a stone ginger he would be booked as a grass. But if he didn't call he would probably be in more trouble. Faced with the prospect of certain arrest but the option of a hard or a comparatively light sentence, Haston favoured the easier of the two. It would be better if he could get them to abandon the blag. Maybe if he put up a story about how he thought Old Bill was following him. But if not, then his problem would be how to contact Fordham safely.

Within the space of five minutes Haston turned his cuff back to check his wristwatch not less than half a dozen times. The repeated gesture caused the man opposite to glance up. Haston's eyes met his, and he wondered briefly if he could be one of the Old Bill. The man had taken his seat at Preston, he recalled, but that meant nothing, as he hadn't actually seen him board. It was only minutes away from jumping off point, if the train was on time, and if it stopped where Brian Connell told him it would. Haston had little faith in the arrangement.

As he was about to rise, Haston saw a man go along the corridor. He was wearing a short raincoat and a felt hat, and seemed to take an uncommon interest in the occupants of his compartment. He was the filth, Haston decided. He waited in his seat to see if the man came back, anxiously checking his watch. The train seemed to be going much too fast to stop so soon. Not that it mattered, he wouldn't be able to jump with Old Bill around.

The man didn't return. Maybe he wasn't the filth. Haston knew he had to go then if he was going to be ready. Cautiously checking that the corridor was clear, Haston stepped out, shutting the door. He moved up the train in the direction the other man had taken, towards the lavatory and the communicating doors. The sign on the lavatory door flipped to 'vacant' as Haston drew level, startling him. The man in the raincoat and felt hat emerged and went away without giving Haston a second glance. Haston watched him go, then moved around the corner to the door.

The train began to slow. Outside, the suburbs of Glasgow sprawled untidily beneath garish lights. Haston lowered the window and reached out for the door handle. He eased the door open as the train came to a halt. Stepping on the running board, he carefully shut the door, checked round, then jumped on to the track. Remaining crouched, he looked along the train to the guard's van; then in the opposite direction. A red signal was showing, just as Connell predicted. Amazing.

Light from the train picked out his camelhair coat as he moved in a crouch off the track – he'd been told to wear something dark. He reached a line engineer's shack and raised himself.

What seemed like an hour passed before the train started. Haston had begun to think it never would. The guard's van slid by, gathering speed. No one else had disembarked. He was still amazed that it had worked, but getting off the track wasn't as easy as getting off the train. There was a chain-link fence topped with barbed wire, which he had to climb, and to do so brought him out on to the road. He swore as he snagged his coat on the wire, putting a neat right-angled tear in it.

Haston moved briskly away from where he had climbed the fence. A man from a boarded shop doorway said,

'Ha'e ya a light, Jock?'

'What?' Haston spun round. The man emerged. 'You McDonald?' He was. 'Fucking hell, you might have helped anyone. Look what I done to my fucking coat. I fucking bought this to go again, didn't I. Some fucking chance now.'

McDonald looked at him as though not understanding a word. 'I got a car parked up the road.'

He turned and started away. Haston followed, resigning himself to his dismal future.

Pockets of fury exploded in Kellan at the negative response from Central Station, making him incapable of dialling Fordham's number at the Yard. He seemed to have six thumbs on his hand, and each was too big to fit the dial. He crashed the handset back on the rest and depressed the button on the brown bakelite intercom.

'Jean!'

There was no reply. His secretary had left for the day. Releasing the button, he lifted the phone again and had the switchboard get Fordham's number.

Expending his wrath immediately the phone was answered, Kellan felt foolish to find that he had reached Fordham's aide.

'What sort of information is this, laddie?' Kellan demanded when he eventually got Fordham. 'There was no sign of your man on that train.'

'What are you telling me, chief superintendent?' Fordham said with the restraint becoming a senior policeman, 'that you've lost him?'

'Lost him? Of course we no lost him. He wasn't on the train.'

He was surprised to find Fordham at his office at this hour, expecting him to be a nine-to-five policeman, unlike himself – because of developments he would probably have to stay there most of the evening.

'How definite is your information? Is there a robbery on or not?'

'I'd think it almost certain now. You'd better try and locate a man called Brian Connell. We'll send up some details. He should be arriving by plane this evening.' He knew that from an illegal intercept; which flight they would only know if his Ds followed him to the airport successfully. 'I can't be more definite. Unless you want my men to get on the plane and deliver him personally.'

'I don't need any of your lot setting foot in my city.' Kellan said it as though their presence would soil the place, then, like a man who wasn't listening to the whole of the conversation, pressed for information on the blag.

Fordham hesitated, wondering if, in view of what had occurred at the senior detectives' meeting, he shouldn't give Kellan all he had. Finally he decided not to, anticipating how the man would react; it would put them back to square one. He would wait and see if the C11 rumour about the Tate and Lyle factory was firmed. If he got the information he wanted then he could move detectives into Glasgow with the Squad's peremptory right in such operations.

With a promise to contact Kellan if and when he got further details, Fordham rang off.

Rising, he checked the time. It was too early for Haston to come through, but he wondered briefly if he would; the man had no practical alternative. He was curious to know how he had avoided the Scottish detectives. Perhaps he should have put a couple of Ds on the train. It wasn't impossible that Haston had jumped off, but unlikely, he concluded. Collecting up a sheaf of reports, Fordham went along to the DCIs' office.

Malcolm Dyce was there, the other two DCIs having left. Dyce was gaunt and wiry, and his suit looked like he was hoping it would come back into fashion. Fordham didn't care how his Ds dressed, and most chose clothes to suit the job they were on; but he preferred Dyce's lack of style to some of the pricks who floated around looking like would-be fashion models with wide lapelled-jackets, belled trousers and sculptured hair.

'It seems like Davy Houghton's squad might be on to something worthwhile with that drugs info', Malcolm,' the DCS said, sliding the reports on to the desk.

'Oh, could be a right good 'un, a bit of luck.'

'That's all any of us need.' He told the DCI about Haston. 'Get on to the railway, see whether the train stopped anywhere between Carlisle and Glasgow. If only for a signal.'

British Rail was a nine-to-five-thirty organisation as far as that sort of information went, and nine o'clock the next morning would probably be too late, especially if Haston didn't come through. But Dyce was resourceful.

Bill Senior found Fordham back in his office. He wanted to know if he had anything else planned that evening.

'Got one to meet, Bill?'

'Like to have. Taking the old woman out. S'her birthday.' He lifted Fordham's phone as it rang. 'Chief Superintendent Fordham ... yes, sir. He is.' He extended the phone. 'Commander Pope.'

The commander wanted to see him.

Fordham knocked on Gerald Pope's door before entering; he was in the habit of knocking on any office doors that were kept closed.

'Evening, John. Glad I caught you. Wanted a word.'

Gerald Pope looked as if he had a lot on his mind and was reluctant to say most of it. He had a fleshy face with a slightly supercilious expression, caused by his large, turned-down mouth and uninterested gaze. However, he was neither haughty nor contemptuous. His big frame wasn't easily disguised behind his desk.

Fordham didn't say anything. He leaned against a filing cabinet. The position was more comfortable than standing in front of the desk. He had a good idea what the commander wanted.

'A10, John. You'd better find time for them.' He didn't look at Fordham. 'Commander Bingham was on to the ACC, who came straight on to me. He said, "He won't capture many worthwhile villains directing traffic out at Bromley".' Pope looked embarrassed. 'His words, John.'

'I've been meaning to get to them.' He nodded thoughtfully. 'But we've got this other business coming to a head. I think we're about to prise it right open. Unfortunately finding time for A10, there are only twenty-four hours in the day.'

It wasn't that he feared being interviewed by the Rubber Heels, but putting off such things was a part of John Fordham's character; he wouldn't see a dentist until a toothache forced him to.

'How's it going? Anything worth putting up? The ACC was wanting a look.'

'Tomorrow should see us with something. I hope.'

'Good.' He paused. 'Accommodate them, John.' He might have been talking about A10 or the hierarchy in general. The underlying threat in Pope's voice was as heavy as he ever got with his senior officers. He would no more treat them like children than he would show disloyalty to his superiors. He was that sort of man.

His unpleasant duty done, Commander Pope rose cumbersomely, showing a collusive smile. 'Let's have a quick one in the Tank, shall we?'

Fordham grimaced and opened the door for him.

The Tank was the ground-floor bar, used by the police and civilian personnel who worked in the building. It was a drab, uninviting place, which observed strict licencing laws – policemen who wanted to drink late had to use the after-hours pub along the road. There was tubular furniture, and linoleum covering the floor.

After Pope had left, Fordham stayed for a second drink, bought by Ernie Jenkins, a Regional Crime Squad DCS who had been in for the senior detectives' meeting. Jenkins was big and not very bright and had got his job by succession; he wasn't Fordham's choice as a drinking partner, but such people were in constant liaison with his office, so he didn't purposely avoid them socially.

'What's this I hear about you finding one tucked up along the road?' Jenkins asked in a quiet voice.

A number of policemen and policewomen were in the bar.

Fordham looked over the rim of his glass, then swallowed some scotch. 'Where did you hear that, Ernie?'

'I've probably got more spies out than you have.' He winked exaggeratedly. 'S'not Ginger Marks you've come across?'

'They would have to have dug him up and replanted him. Along the Westway.'

'Oh. I heard it was the Hammersmith section of the M4. My mistake.' He immediately lost interest.

Fordham had heard the rumours about Ginger Marks, the villain who went missing all those years ago, being buried in the M4 motorway. He was dead, there was no doubt, nor any that those responsible had little connection with the building trade, which would have been essential for a concrete grave. Marks had been cut up and fed to pigs, that was what Fordham believed.

DCI Dyce appeared at the door, searching for Fordham, and made his way over.

'Kellan's been back on. Complaining there was no sign of Connell. He wants to talk to you.'

'What the fuck does he want, his hand held?'

'Connell checked in for the Glasgow flight at Heathrow, but didn't board.'

That caused Fordham some concern. Maybe Haston warned them off after all. 'Check the other flights to Scotland, Malcolm. See if he'd have had time to make either the Edinburgh or Dundee plane.'

'Incidentally, Haston's train stopped for a red signal outside Cambuslang.'

Fordham smiled. 'That's where they probably are. I'd say it was going ahead to plan.'

'Do you want me to inform Kellan?'

'I don't think so. Call him back, say you can't find me. But advise him to hold the night relief for a possible contingency tomorrow morning. We might need them. We'll try and get back to him.'

'Something big breaking north of the border, John?' Jenkins asked conspiratorially.

Fordham looked askance at the DCS with the red complexion. 'Ask me this time tomorrow.'

'After I read it in the papers?' He grinned.

Most detectives were protective towards their cases, especially if they looked big. It would be the same with Fordham, so Jenkins didn't pursue it.

Considering the situation now shaping in Glasgow, Fordham recognised that he would like the job actually to take place, and so have total, inextricable commitment on the part of all those involved. The instincts which made him a policeman told him he should prevent the raid. However, both options were based on the assumption that he would get the vital information he required.

The hotel room was soapy to begin with, and during the evening it became progressively worse with seven men and a woman sitting around smoking and drinking and eating. The window was closed tight against the freezing night. Any suggestion to open it was immediately decried. All but two of them were at the heavy-legged dining table, which typified the oddity of the furniture in the bedroom. They were playing napoleon, and the amount of money in some of the pots was reaching fifty pounds.

Neither Maureen Hoyle nor Haston were playing. Bored, the woman sprawled on the bed like she was waiting to be stiffed. She flipped distractedly through a copy of *Cosmopolitan*, stopping at cartoons and adverts. Low in a dilapidated armchair, Haston appeared to be hiding. His hands were thrust in his pockets to stop him fiddling, as Brodie, on a losing streak, had shouted at him. Others had done likewise. Haston could not have felt more of an outsider. When earlier he had complained about the job going forward, he was called a hex by the Jocks. They weren't about to listen. Even Brian Connell, who was usually disturbed by bad feelings, maintained the attitude he displayed in London. The blag was going forward.

Anxiety tore at Haston's stomach, and he made frequent visits to the lavatory. The bathroom was situated off the bedroom, the door scraped the worn lino; it was difficult to open and more difficult to close; the cistern wouldn't flush properly, and Haston was very conscious of the noise irritating the others. Occasionally a thin reed of bile crept up the back of his throat and into his nostrils, making his eyes smart. Haston's conviction that the others were suspicious of him grew by the minute. Every glance in his direction from one of them only increased it. They were watching him. They knew that he wanted to get to a phone. Fucking

Donald Brodie, he could fucking well read minds!

Trying to find an excuse for getting out to phone Fordham as his future depended on it, Haston had announced his intention of going for a walk. Brodie insisted McDonald go too.

'In case he gets hi'sel' lost and has to ask a polis the way back here.'

The other laughed.

The words meant only one thing, Haston reflected. He didn't know what he could do to stop the job. But he felt he had to try something.

Chapter 18

Nine o'clock came and went. Fordham, working in his office, hardly noticed. He finished reading the last Crime Report and placed it on the pile in his Out tray; tomorrow there would be another pile in the In tray. Swallowing scotch from a paper cup, he rose decisively, as though once up from his desk he couldn't be entrapped by more paperwork. He stretched, and only then realised the significance of the hour. Haston not phoning irritated him, but he accepted that he should have contrived greater control of the circumstances which enabled Haston to give him the information.

'That's one villain who's going to be nicked,' he told Dyce, who was at his desk in a single pool of light.

'He might come through yet,' the DCI said optimistically.

'It will leave things a bit late for us now. Especially if it goes off early in the morning.'

He decided to visit Charlie Ryman, in the hope that he might spring something for him. He told the DCI where to reach him if Haston came through.

Ryman was at home, and surprised to be opening the door to the DCS.

'Servants' night off, Charlie?' Fordham said as the man stepped aside to admit him.

The man's tastes were improving, Fordham noted as he was led through the entrance hall. The garish purple carpet he'd seen on his last visit had been removed, revealing the original Victorian glazed tiles. Fordham didn't comment.

In the large, comfortable sitting-room Ryman had been watching *Come Dancing* on the huge colour TV with his wife and two toy poodles. One dog was on the couch next to the woman, the other on a chair. Neither moved for Fordham.

'Evening, Mrs Ryman,' Fordham said, like a canvassing politician.

'You remember Mr Fordham, Clara?'

She did, for what good it did her. She was obliged to leave them, quitting her comfortable niche opposite the television.

'A drink or a cup of tea, Mr Fordham?' the woman asked, lifting her thickening forty-odd-year-old rump off the couch. She had two grown-up, married daughters from a previous marriage. But her new babies were too comfortable to move.

Fordham declined her offer.

'Charles?'

'Tea's not a bad idea.'

The woman went.

Ryman's attention turned back to the TV where figures in tails and yards of sequinned organdie glided around.

'They haven't got a lot of chance,' Ryman said, his face a picture of seriousness. 'Number nineteen earlier on. Fantastic. Like Fred Astaire and Ginger Rogers, they were. If they don't go through to the semi-finals, then I don't know anything about *Come Dancing*.' It was his favourite programme.

'Sit down, John, take your coat off. Come on, Fleur, make a bit of room there.'

The dog lifted its tiny head and looked, then tucked it back into its body. Fordham took the vacant armchair, but didn't remove his coat. His glance went to the picture above the fireplace; it was a Tretchikoff.

'Busy?' Ryman asked.

'Busy enough, Charlie. It doesn't slow down at all. You?'

'Can't complain. Some people still like clean washing, pleased to say.'

Part of Ryman's legitimate enterprises were launderettes throughout South-West London.

'What brings you this way? Business?'

'I wasn't exactly passing the door.'

'No, somehow I didn't think you were.' He held Fordham's look, trying to divine his thoughts. Then diverted his eyes to the TV. 'That's how Clara and I were once. Perhaps not quite as good.' He turned back to Fordham. 'Still seeing that schoolteacher?'

'Actress,' Fordham said with a smile, thinking about Charlie and Clara Ryman on the dance floor. Anyone on a dance floor struck Fordham as comical.

'I thought it was discipline you went in for.'

'This one wouldn't know the meaning. Left wing; women's lib, you name it.'

'No accounting for taste,' Ryman said. 'Incidentally, how did it go with Charlton House? Do you any good?'

'Not bad at all.'

Fordham had been given favoured inside information about an imminent takeover, which it transpired Duckett's bank had been financing. Fordham had got some shares in the Charlton House Group at a very reasonable price before they rocketed.

'Terrible, wasn't it,' Ryman said with mock sympathy. 'That's the sort of earner worth having.'

'Talking of favours, I can do you one.' Fordham paused for effect; suddenly Ryman was no longer even aware of the TV. 'There's a Superintendent Pritchard out at Croydon looking to nick you.'

'Bill Pritchard?' He sounded genuinely amazed. 'Nice bastard – he's had more than enough in his time.'

'Doesn't mean a thing in the final analysis.'

Few criminals truly understood that. Contrary to what so many believed, the money they paid to detectives never gave them absolute immunity.

The man's expression told Fordham that deeds being resurrected were things Ryman thought safely buried.

'A long time ago,' Ryman said quietly.

'Long-firms can be pretty complicated investigations, Charlie,' he offered like a fact of life.

'Why you warning me? Looking for something yourself?'

Fordham shook his head. 'Peter Walsh's bit of bother proved that there's no one safe any more,' he said ambiguously. Then smiled broadly. 'I expect to nick you myself, Charlie. For something more substantial than long-firms.'

Ryman's high pitched chuckle indicated that he thought Fordham was joking. 'What's the other fellow got?'

'Nothing I can't blank, for now.'

'Well, it would be very civil if you would have a word with him.'

'I've had a word. Favours don't come cheaply nowadays.'

There was a pause while Ryman considered this. Fordham pushed up out of his chair and helped himself to some scotch. Then switched off the TV. 'Take it as read that number nineteen won.' Both poodles suddenly snapped at Fordham. 'They don't agree with the decision. Here's to your continued freedom.' He swallowed some scotch.

'What is it you heard?'

'That there's one you're responsible for going off in Glasgow tomorrow.'

'That's a bit far north, isn't it?'

'A long way. You know Donald Brodie?' Fordham doubted that he did personally. 'He comes from Glasgow.'

'I thought the papers said Dartmoor.'

'Whoever's putting it together had him sprung. How much would it have cost? Five, six grand?'

'From the Moor? And the rest. Inflation hits everything.'

'Must be something special, wouldn't you think?'

'Laying out that sort of money for one man. I'd have thought so.' Ryman lifted the white, pink-eyed poodle on to his lap. 'Isn't it a bit early to be worrying about something like that? It might never happen.'

'By my calculations it's too late to stop.'

Ryman shrugged philosophically. 'So a few villains get put away. Who'll ever miss them?'

'You won't, Charlie. They'll take you with them.'

'Ah, now what sort of talk is that?'

The detective's words were making a disturbing chink. Until now Ryman had been taking this conversation in the spirit he believed it was intended, one of camaraderie.

'You're an ambitious man, John. Leastwise I always thought you were. You're not interested in a punter like me. What I'm involved in nowadays isn't worth the attention of the newest recruit to the Squad, let alone the head of the outfit. You're up reaching for people in high places, if I know anything.' He tried to make his last remark sound casual.

Fordham was amused, and felt like mentioning the intercepted Ryman/Duckett call; it was from this that he had obviously drawn his conclusion. But he didn't moot the subject.

'Let's just say that for a while I have an interest in your staying loose.'

Ryman nodded, misunderstanding Fordham's motives, thinking they were self-interest.

'A close associate put me on to a nice share that's going to do a lot. Celtgas. Territories in the Irish Sea that are being developed. I'll have a few put by for you. Nothing spectacular.'

'Make sure they're safe,' Fordham said, setting his glass down. He glanced towards the door. 'She must've gone to Ceylon for your tea.'

'Slid up to the bedroom, I suppose; watching the television there.'

Fordham went home.

After Fordham's departure Ryman instinctively bolted and locked the door as if to protect himself from the threat looming on the horizon. When he returned to the sitting-room he didn't switch the TV back on. Cher, the other poodle, leapt up at him, and he sat stroking her pensively.

Even though he wasn't actively involved and couldn't be tied in with it directly, Ryman wondered if he shouldn't call off the robbery; after all, he didn't want to see men go to prison for no reason. Better they lived to fight another day. But he wondered if he was able to call the job off. Possibly if he phoned Alan Day.

Taking Cher with him, he went to the telephone and began to dial Day's number. He didn't finish it. Cancelling things would mean wasting a substantial investment in both time and money. John Fordham obviously had nothing, he argued, or he wouldn't have come fishing. He tried to work out the psychology behind the detective's move: Fordham would know that if he was involved he wouldn't have been about to give him anything; maybe the visit was a warning for old-time's sake. But that wasn't likely.

Whatever the detective's thinking, Ryman decided the job would stand. But he thought he might have to do something about Bill Pritchard. Either by putting some more money into the superintendent, or making a contingency plan.

Half expecting Kika to be at the flat, Fordham was disappointed when she wasn't. There were times when he actually yearned for her company, which had nothing at all to do with the prospect of making love to her. He assumed she was at the theatre, and tried to recall whether she had mentioned it. Working in the repertory at the National, Fordham was never really certain which evenings she was appearing. Had he realised he would have met her there.

Alone in the flat, Fordham allowed thoughts of the Glasgow robbery down into the conscious areas of his mind. Contrary to what he had hoped, they had failed to get control of the circumstances of the robbery. Certainly they could have no physical control with the Squad in London and the blag going off in Glasgow, where DCS Kellan was. The only thing to do was to attempt to abort it, and try for another lever at some unknown date in the future. Maybe it would take another fifteen months. Maybe he'd have a lot of pressure from the ACC long before then; he was sure he would, feeling he was already getting it. Possibly it was coincidence that not six hours after the senior detectives' meeting he should get noises from Peter Goodfellow via the commander to accommodate A10.

Had there been word from Ronnie Haston, Fordham would have heard. The duty officer would have contacted him. But he checked with Dyce all the same.

'Send them a telex, Malcolm. Have them pick up Brodie, Haston and Brian Connell, who's believed to be in the company of an unidentified woman. Plus other unidentified suspects. They're to be held pending escort to London, where they'll be charged with conspiracy to rob.' There would be other charges. but that would do for now. 'Tell them they should concentrate their search in the Cambuslang area.'

'What about the possible target, guv?' Dyce asked.

'Yes, give them that. Tate and Lyle refinery in Shawfield. You can put my name on it.'

One of the other telephones rang persistently while Dyce was scribbling the details of the telex. Replacing his own phone, he stretched awkwardly across to DCI Corrigan's desk and lifted the other.

'CID. Duty officer.'

The caller was DS Roger Green, who was in Houghton's squad. His voice was controlled, but excited.

'We've hit pay-dirt, guv. The dealers are on the move.'

'That's good news. Compliments to Davy Houghton – tell him to shoot the fuckers if necessary – I'll tell him myself. I'll get him on the radio.'

'Jesus Christ!' The exclamation came out of the phone like a cold slap. 'They've just gone past doing a hundred and ten.'

The phone went dead. Dyce didn't bother trying to get the DS back. He rose and moved out of his office.

In the radio booth the operator raised Houghton's wavelength. Dyce followed the chase there. It went on for a long time. The dealers were lost momentarily. Then contact was made again; a shooting incident followed. No one was hit, certainly no policemen were; that was all that mattered to Dyce.

The chase ended at Leytonstone. There the dealers' car was forced to a halt by the local police, who tried to arrest both felons and detectives for speeding. The two dealers were taken to the local nick, where there were further consultations with Dyce by phone. Others were arrested at the house in Islington, where the dealers had started out. All were eventually taken to Cannon Row police station and charged.

By the time Dyce got around to sending the telex to Glasgow it was the small hours of the morning.

Manpower was at its lowest ebb when the telex clattered routinely out of one of the three machines in the control room of Strathclyde Police Headquarters. The warm, dry atmosphere created by the computer tended to make operators lethargic, especially at that hour. It was a little after half-past five, and the night relief changed at six o'clock; policemen avoided getting too involved at that hour, especially with anything that might delay them getting off duty. None of the three men rushed forward for the message. Finally one of them gave it his attention. An acknowledgement should have been sent back to the Yard, but wasn't. Perhaps because of the animosity existing between uniform branch and CID, or possibly because of the hour, the telex was simply processed through normal channels, rather than given the priority it called for.

Chapter 19

Dawn seemed reluctant to break over the city, to light up the crumbling, decaying buildings and the disorientating new ones.

The three men emerging warily from the hotel doorway in Cambuslang shivered and pulled their coats tighter about themselves. Shut outside from the warmth, there was no point in not going forward. They moved off towards the parked car, their white breath streaming before them in the cold air. None of them had wanted to rise when Brodie had woken them; none of them were used to rising early.

'Och it's colder than a witch's tit,' Ian Gordon said.

Scotch Pat agreed with him and fell silent again. Syd Haimes wasn't sure what either had said.

Traffic was light as they drove across Glasgow. Conversation in the car was almost nil. This was the start of the blag, and each was alone with his thoughts, wondering how he would come out of it, and if he would; trying not to let anxiety have any affect.

Their first stop was at a shed on Prince's Dock along the Clyde, where a pantechnicon was parked with a Dormobile inside it. The tailboard was lowered to form a ramp; Scotch Pat reversed the Dormobile out. Gordon drove the pantechnicon out of the lock-up.

The three vehicles followed one another through the Clyde Tunnel and headed east on the expressway to the centre of Glasgow. The large van was parked at the end of Fox Street, a quiet road of warehouses and not far from Central Station. Ian Gordon was staying with it until the others showed up after the robbery, when he would simply raise the ramp and drive away.

Haimes, driving the car, followed the Dormobile back across the Clyde and down into Gorbals.

The former slum area was largely redeveloped, but huge scars remained where bulldozers had ploughed down the tenements and nothing had been put in their place. There were old buildings still standing, a cinema, a school, odd and incongruous; roads remained that no longer served anyone, not even the new towering blocks. Half-streets were left standing, dark and bleak. People who were reluctant to be parted from their dwellings and familiar neighbourhood, no matter how squalid they had become or how close the wreckers got, had been reprieved. Houses still showed signs of occupancy among the boarded-up dwellings. The people in the remnants of Gorbals were safe for a while, the redevelopment having been arrested for whatever reason; the blocks began to fester and show signs of people alienated by and unhappy in their new environment.

Scotch Pat parked the Dormobile on the service road between two blocks off Cumberland Street. Leaving any vehicle unattended was a risky thing to do in most parts of Glasgow – in Gorbals it would have been madness to do so a few years ago – but hopefully they wouldn't need the Dormobile. It was a back-up vehicle.

After parking the van, Scotch Pat put the keys in the petrol filler housing and closed the lid. That was about the safest place for them. He knew of cases where fast getaways had been stymied by keys being misplaced.

A young lad delivering newspapers in one of the blocks of flats stopped in the entrance and watched with interest. Especially when he saw Scotch Pat climb into the car which had been turning. Having delivered his last paper, he waited for the car to get out of sight. Excitement was building up in him, causing a slight trembling. He hurried over to the van and was delighted to find that it was the keys he had seen being put in the petrol filler housing. Knowing about a parked van with keys – which he took – would give him a certain amount of power in his gang; the knowledge would in turn give the gang more power.

Scotch Pat's next stop was St Enoch's Station, which was awaiting redevelopment and now functioned solely as a car-park. The platforms had been levelled to facilitate parking over the entire area. There weren't too many cars there yet, but it would soon fill as people arrived for work. Scotch Pat had no problem locating the car they wanted. It was parked under the large square sign marking where number nine platform had been. The key which Scotch Pat had been given unlocked the boot, where there were two parcels. One was brown, the other a green Marks and Spencer carrier bag. Both contained guns. The brown one was for Scotch Pat. In it were three sawn-off shotguns and shells. He was tempted to take the other bag, knowing it contained two five-shot Smith and Wesson .38s in addition to shotguns. He would have preferred one of those handguns. He didn't see why he needed a shotgun in the van; a tool like the .38 would have been more useful. But he left the other parcel, as instructed.

From a lock-up in Govanhill Scotch Pat collected a very hot car, a Jaguar which hadn't been rung. He was wary of driving it over to the Tate and Lyle refinery, especially with one of the shotguns on the back seat. Parking within sight of the refinery, Scotch Pat walked away with no small sense of relief.

Their final stop was back at the Prince's Dock shed. In the lock-up next door was a red thirty-hundredweight GPO van. Its plates had been switched to make it safe to be driven to Central Station. Scotch Pat placed the two remaining shotguns in the van, climbed in and turned the engine, making sure it started. Locking the warehouse after them, they went to find a phone.

It was now daylight.

The freezing temperature had barely risen when Brodie left the hotel and drove into town with McDonald. They collected the second parcel of guns from St Enoch's Station. There were many more cars parked now and they had difficulty in locating the one they wanted.

A blue and white Panda patrol car with two policemen in it turned through the carpark barrier and along the road towards Brodie's car. McDonald, sitting behind the wheel with the engine running, didn't immediately see the police car. He saw it through the driving mirror as it turned at the end of the double line of parked cars on their road. He called to Brodie, who was lifting the Marks and Spencer bag out.

They didn't wait to explain or to try and bluff their way out. McDonald gunned the car as soon as Brodie's feet were off the ground. The Panda car accelerated after it.

The attendant couldn't even have been hopeful about being paid the parking fee.

The brown Rover that McDonald and Brodie were in cornered hard into St Enoch's Square, forcefully joining the traffic with a squeal of rubber and a lot of honking. It gained the junction of Argyle Street before the police car appeared; the driver obviously wasn't as desperate, he had the advantage of a radio-telephone.

The traffic along Buchanan Street was heavy and hampered the Rover. The Panda closed the gap. Brodie reached into the bag and fetched out a .38. His fingers scrabbed in the bottom of the bag for some bullets and pushed them into the chamber.

A gap appeared between two vehicles.

'There!' Brodie shouted.

McDonald accelerated through a controlled crossing where traffic had stopped. Pedestrians shrank back: then again when the police car came through.

'Fooking hell, the polis basses gonna get us.'

'I'll shoot the fookers first,' Brodie said, wrenching round.

He was very calm and knew they had to lose them soon or be boxed in by other police cars that would be called up.

A car changing lanes where the road forked had its front off-side smashed in, gouging the near-side of the Rover when it veered left into Cowcaddens Street. McDonald hit another car on the same side, but didn't stop.

The police car was close behind now, taking advantage of the path the Rover was clearing.

A street-cleaning truck was proceeding noisily along Cowcaddens Street.

'Mek a left, man,' Brodie said as they approached the truck, confusing McDonald slightly. 'Up the pavement, on the inside!'

The Rover mounted the kerb, McDonald blasting the

horn at the somnambulant pedestrians. The car bounced off the pavement on the inside of the sweeping truck and raced away, ironically, along Hope Street.

The Panda didn't try the same trick, was too late to make a left turn and overshot the turning. By the time the driver had reversed against the traffic and turned into the street, Brodie and McDonald were long gone. The only hope was that other police cars being directed to the area would head them off.

Looking like two unenthusiastic workers with their bag of lunch or overalls, Brodie and McDonald boarded a bus to Glasgow Central. There they picked up a cab out to Cambuslang.

McDonald was full of the story.

'I tell ya, man, it was better'n a fooking James Bond film. I'm a telling ya.'

The only person to show interest was Maureen Hoyle. Her sleep-filled eyes came alive.

Connell remained purposely unimpressed; anyone could give the local Old Bill the slip. He told Brodie that Scotch Pat had phoned to say they were all set.

Haston, who had lain awake all night worrying, was literally scared sick. Having already vomited once, he managed to get in another warning about the police being on to them before rushing to the bathroom. He didn't have time to close the door, but threw himself on his knees before the WC and retched. With nothing inside his stomach, it was a dry raucous sound that he made.

The three men and the woman glanced at one another, then avoided each other's eyes, embarrassed.

When finally Haston stopped, McDonald said, 'Wha' about some breakfast, man?'

Brodie looked at Connell. 'Get Maureen to slip across to the cafe fur a few bacon and egg sandwiches.'

'Good idea. Plenty of sauce on mine, Mo.' He glanced at Haston, who staggered from the bathroom. 'What about you, Ronnie?'

Haston shook his head. 'They're on to us. Argue any way you like,' he said feebly. 'Call it off, tell 'em. We'll all be nicked.'

The others weren't interested. They had had this all morning. McDonald produced a bottle of scotch and offered it to Connell.

'You want some of this?' He uncapped the bottle.

'I have these.' He opened his hand to reveal some reds, which he popped.

'Ya fooking drug addict,' McDonald said in disgust.

'I got this feeling. I just know they're on to us,' Haston continued ineffectually.

'In three fooking hours they're going to be on to us, that's fooking well when.' Brodie was growing angry. He reached for McDonald's bottle. 'Gee us a pull on, Joe.'

Haston switched his appeal to Connell. 'Call London, Brian, call 'em. We're gonna be nicked.'

'Leave it out, for fucksake, will you. Leave off.'

There was a pause.

'Perhaps we'd better leave him behind,' Connell said as Brodie produced one of the handguns.

'I'll le'e the cunt behind wi' a fooking bullet in his skull. That's how. He can tek his choice.'

A menacing atmosphere fell across the room. It was a serious choice. Every trace of colour drained from Haston's face, and a cheek muscle twitched convulsively.

'It's all right for youse lot,' Brodie said. 'Call off the joab and youse just go back to your fooking pits. But I'm on the run. I'm responsible to those who put this up. Sprung me specially for it.' His eyes swung from face to face, challengingly. 'All I want's ma fooking passport. And I'll tell youse something for nothing. I'm not goaney go back to that fooking brig. Not if I ha'e to shoot him or half the polis in Glesga. Another nine fooking years of that. That's nine of fooking pillows and yon benders. Nine fooking years of bastard screws. I been learning Spanish for three fooking years, thirty-six fooking months of that. I ha'e no poked a woman in three fooking years. This joab holds no terror for me. I tell ya, it's fooking well on and stays on.'

Brodie's violence suddenly slackened. But it left none of the four people in the room in any doubt that he meant what he said.

Chapter 20

Collected at eight o'clock from his house in the residential area of Milngavie, north of the city, Kellan followed his Friday morning routine. Visiting the markets and a number of shops, he picked up his weekly supply of groceries, meat, fish, fruit, drink, all of which his driver stacked in the boot of the car. He wasn't by any means greedy, but he and his wife lived well. Kellan no longer bothered with offering to pay for the goods; the storekeepers and stallholders wouldn't accept his money. Gifts received in this way weren't corruption, leastwise Kellan didn't consider it so. This was a simple form of homage, a way of saying thank you for making the city a bit safer.

Arriving at his office, Kellan was presented with Fordham's telex by DI Douglas, upon whose desk it had routinely landed not half an hour before. The delay made Kellan explosive. He told his secretary to get Fordham on the phone, and had her find Superintendent Muirhead, who was uniform branch and would receive most of Kellan's anger over the delay. Kellan demanded to know why the message took so long to reach the CID from the control room. From Fordham he would demand all sorts of things, not least the reason why the message was not sent until five-seventeen.

'Call a planning meeting, immediately. I'll want all senior officers. Uniform branch included.' The phone rang and Kellan snatched it up. His secretary informed him that Fordham couldn't be reached. 'What do you mean, cannae be reached? If he's in a meeting, interrupt. If he's no' in the building, keep trying until he arrives. I want to speak to that man, Jean.' He slammed the phone down. 'Recall all detectives off duty. It'll be too late for those on leave.' There wasn't any great delay in the DI's reaction, but Kellan was in a mood for shouting. 'Move yourself, Dougie.'

'You're to attend a planning meeting wi' CID,' McTovey

told Chief Inspector Bothwell as he came on duty.

'Sure he wants me, Mac?' Bothwell removed his hat.

'All senior officers. Some kind of flap on. Had Mr Muirhead in and gave him a right bollocking.' He explained about the delayed telex.

Whatever the result of the delay, Bothwell was philosophical about the failing which caused it. 'They're only human, Mac. Policeman, like everyone else, are subject to error. Thank God.'

His interest moved on. The planning meeting wasn't his greatest priority. 'You've an appearance at the sheriff's court this morning, Mac.'

'Three, to be precise,' McTovey replied.

'Aye, it's the two lads involved in the taking and driving away the car I'm interested in. Give them what help you can.' He anticipated the sergeant. 'I ken they broke probation. But Dermont's a wee tyrant, and wi'oot someone speaking for them he'll refer them back to the advisory board, who'll recommend Approved School. They deserve another chance.'

McTovey nodded. It went without saying that Chief Inspector Bothwell thought everyone under the age of sixteen deserved a second chance, no matter what they did, nor how often.

In his office Bothwell stood idly sifting through reports, still in his greatcoat, unconcerned about getting to the meeting, knowing he would have little to contribute.

He was pulling out of his coat when he got a call from a woman who lived in a new block of flats by Gorbals Cross. She was worried about her ten-year-old son, who was on probation; he was off school and had money which she believed he had stolen.

The telephone call excited Bothwell. It represented a step forward, an immense achievement in what he was attempting as head of Community Involvement. People like Mrs Proctor breaking those closed-mouthed traditions to seek help for her son, rather than simply resisting the interference of just another polis bastard, showed the measure of trust and respect he and his divisional officers were getting. Bothwell could have referred her to the Community Involvement officer at the local police office, but instead told her he personally would be out to see her directly. Then he remembered the planning meeting.

'I'll ha'e to make it around eleven o'clock, Mrs Proctor. Try and keep Marlon there.'

When he rang off Bothwell felt like calling his wife to tell of this breakthrough. But he went to the briefing instead.

There was a distinct separation of detectives and uniformed men in the large briefing room. They sat and stood around like children listening to the headmaster at a school assembly. Kellan was at the top of the room by a blackboard. He was flanked by his two closest allies, DCI Robert McFageon and Dougie Douglas. Bothwell felt like a schoolboy arriving late for morning assembly. Kellan was speaking in a loud, authoritative voice that invited no response.

'... Tate and Lyle. Our prime target. It's Friday and they ha'e a large wage bill. But it's only rumoured, so we're marking down other possible targets; the larger banks, money in transit. Superintendent Stalker will be assigning units to various locations. If we've got some unwelcome visitors, then I want them behind lock and key across the road.' The cells of the adjacent police office served the HQ.

'The question of arms, sir,' a detective asked. 'Are they being issued?'

'We don't know that we ha'e any robbers here, let alone armed.'

As if in answer to Kellan's uncertainty the telephone rang on the desk in front of the blackboard. Douglas lifted the handset, scribbled some details and handed them to Kellan. The DCS read ponderously, then looked up.

'The car your lads lost this morning, Mr Muirhead,' Kellan said, 'It's confirmed that Donald Brodie was one of the occupants. His finger prints were found. It would seem that we ha'e definitely got visitors. We've every reason to believe they'd be armed.'

That offended Ian Kellan far more than merely having

intruders coming to his city to rob its institutions.

Further information was relayed to him during the planning meeting. Someone had phoned about seeing a shotgun in a car parked near Tate and Lyle's. Subsequent investigation revealed that the car had been stolen. If this was part of the planned robbery, it didn't indicate a high degree of professionalism, but then nothing said that robbers had to be professional. Kellan had DCI McFageon liaise with the refinery management; he put a concentration of detectives in and around the factory. Every other policeman throughout the city was placed on full alert.

Having been informed both about the robbers and the robbery, Kellan knew that, despite the lack of hard facts he had received from the Yard, he would be embarrassed and compromised if the job went off.

'Superintendent McWhirter, concentrate on the Cambuslang area. Check out all hotels and boarding houses, Sally Army. Anywhere our visitors might stay. Better we pick them up before they get near what they're here for.'

From the type of information received Kellan inferred that DCS Fordham knew a lot more about the job than he was telling. The fact that he had telexed instructions about where to concentrate their search confirmed this, he thought. What reason Fordham could have for holding out on him Kellan didn't know, but he was determined to speak to Fordham and find out.

Commander Bingham's office on the seventeenth floor of the tower was relatively imposing, and suggested the man had either a large ego or thought his job important, or both. Bill Senior's call to A10 to arrange an appointment for his chief to be interviewed had thrown the Rubber Heels. But they made a quick recovery, and the interview was arranged immediately.

Although Fordham would never exactly find it convenient to accommodate A10, this was as close as he would get. Pressure in his office had slackened, freeing a part of his brain, which could now be employed to fence with A10.

Fordham could think with just a fraction of his brain.

A10 kept him waiting. That was expected and Fordham didn't let it irritate him. He rarely sat on these occasions, but he did now, as if in defiance of some contrary order. Slouched in the chair, legs crossed, Bingham recognised the contempt in his attitude on opening the office door to invite him in.

When interviewing a policeman in connection with possible offences it was done by another at least one rank his senior. In Fordham's case, Bingham, as head of A10, interviewed him personally. Normally he might have been aided by an inspector or a sergeant, but for this interview Bingham had the support of a chief superintendent. Both men were ex-uniform, and wore dour expressions which looked in danger of fracturing.

They covered the early part of Fordham's career in general terms. Fordham knew there was nothing there that he was at this stage going to be brought to book for, not unless A10 had done an excessive amount of work, in which event they wouldn't have politely sought to interview him but would have arrested him.

On the large oak desk across which they faced him was an array of papers for reference. There was a pile of slim files, their titles discreetly concealed. It was from these that Bingham opened one that brought them more up to date.

'Denis Marples.' Bingham said it like a *fait accompli*. 'You recall the name?'

It had been one of the last cases Fordham had worked on with Peter Walsh, and one of the least damaging. He guessed Bingham was saving the worst till last.

'One of Peter Walsh's successes. Marples went down for about ten years.'

'There were allegations made in court of dubious practices by the police . . .'

'With the greatest respect, sir,' Fordham said laboriously. 'Such allegations are standard with villains nowadays.'

Bingham wasn't impressed. 'Namely that there were illegal telephone intercepts used.' He paused. 'Tell me, chief superintendent, is that also standard?'

Fleetingly Fordham wondered if the man had any word of his current bent intercepts. He looked at the man directly. 'Not in the Squad. If the Home Office won't grant a warrant, we resort to other means.'

'We'd be interested to hear about those methods, Mr Fordham. In the Platts-Oates case for instance.' He finished the sentence abruptly.

Another case Fordham had been involved in with Walsh. He almost smiled at the man's predictability.

'There was nothing untoward in the methods employed, that I remember.' Out of context even the simple expedient of pressurising a suspect could seem untoward. 'The prosecution of Trevor Platts-Oates was successful. The DPP commended Mr Walsh.'

'Nothing is ever so successful that it can't be challenged. Platts-Oates's solicitor claims you employed a detective as an agent provocateur.'

Fordham smiled blandly. 'Not to my knowledge. I doubt that Peter Walsh would have needed to.'

'You were quite close to Walsh?' the A10 chief superintendent said.

His name was Dudley Fishburn. He was a man who had originally been attracted to the power of a uniform, and ideally suited in A10, where he policed policemen of lower rank.

Without losing his blandness, Fordham said, 'About as close as you must be to Mr Bingham.'

Both men seemed embarrassed, as though even implied closeness wasn't permitted in the office.

'Were you privy to all his investigations?'

'He conducted himself quite openly. Where practicable all senior officers on the Squad were kept in touch with what was going on. As they are now.'

'Are they, Mr Fordham?'

'All the information is on file. If they have time to read the reports.'

'Is it not true that you've been conducting a major investigation in what amounts to a highly secretive manner? With no more than a handful of Squad officers? An investigation that is so close, means so much to you, that it might be described as a personal crusade?'

'I wouldn't have thought I'd have the time.'

'You seem to find the time, chief superintendent.'

'Presumably a credit to my efficiency. The work that comes in gets dealt with.'

'But it's how it's dealt with that concerns us. Are you saying that you're not conducting a vendetta against a certain merchant banker and one of his fellow company directors?'

'If you're talking about Anthony Duckett and Sir Frank O'Connor, the answer's no. There is an investigation in which both of them are involved. Whether they're finally charged is another matter.'

'Have you resorted to telephone intercepting devices during the course of this investigation?'

'The Home Office refused the applications.'

'You didn't employ illegal means?'

Fordham thought, what pricks this pair were if they really expected him to answer yes to that. Even when you were bang to rights you still denied all allegations. That was standard.

'No, of course we didn't.'

'You're quite sure?'

There was a pause. Bingham measured him with a look, then slowly, as though producing the most damning evidence to the contrary, he opened a folder. It was a trick most detectives used at times. The delay was to rattle the suspect, cause him to panic and retract his statement.

Fordham wasn't the rattling kind.

'You were heavily connected with the case involving Bennie Griffiths?'

Fordham didn't deny it. He had known it was only a matter of time before they got to this. Griffiths was the villain at whose villa Walsh had holidayed. 'I was part of the team that arrested him.'

'Only that, chief superintendent? Griffiths had a surprisingly long run. Somewhat longer than the average criminal, whose activities were so far ranging.'

'Some are more difficult to take than others.'

'Did you not have several deals with Griffiths?'

'I don't know that I understand the question,' Fordham replied evenly.

'Come now, chief superintendent,' Fishburn put in. 'You understand perfectly.'

'Is it a question or an allegation? I have deals all the time with criminals, informants; people who trade something I need for something they think I can give them.'

'Such as their liberty?'

'I can't give anyone that, only a judge and jury can.'

'Isn't it true that you were making trade-offs with Bennie Griffiths? Extending his liberty?'

'We were building a case. In the process of getting information from him we allowed him to believe we would extend his liberty indefinitely.'

That was the line Fordham had taken when questioned by A10 at the time of Walsh's trouble. He didn't deviate as these two men probed deeper and wider in that area. Finally, realising that their questions weren't moving them forward at all, they changed their tack. But still Fordham didn't give them anything that wasn't already on record.

Maybe it was strains of paranoia working through, but as the interview progressed Fordham increasingly felt there was something other than the possibility of malpractices on his part that had brought this attention. Certainly it wasn't a specific complaint against him personally. Peter Goodfellow crept obliquely into his thoughts. He sensed the ACC's influence, as though his hand was guiding A10; they kept on returning to the Duckett/O'Connor investigation. If the ACC had more knowledge of that investigation than he let on, why would he operate at this distance? He had the authority to move in on any enquiry, redirect it, or stop it completely. Or did he think Fordham just perverse enough to open the thing right up despite any directive to the contrary? It was a possibility. He would wait and see what developed beyond this interview.

'… Newman's lawyers claimed that you intimidated defence witnesses.'

'Was there a direct complaint from any of them? Newman was against the wall. When felons complain about the Squad, it means we're winning more than them.'

'It's not only the felonry,' Bingham said tersely. 'There are also the regional constabularies. One in particular from Sussex concerning a trade-off.'

'You're referring to Norman Saunders?'

'Vital evidence they had gathered on activities of a London criminal was conveniently lost. This, they say, you did as a favour to a man called Ryman.'

Fordham didn't bat an eyelid. Ryman had been kept clear at that time; however, he didn't tell A10 that the action would be vindicated when Charlie Ryman fell with the others.

'I don't know. Saunders is doing five years somewhere, I believe.'

'Sussex said he would have gone away for fifteen had that evidence not been lost.'

'Length of sentence isn't my concern. My relationship with regional forces has always been excellent.'

Bingham gave him a frosty look.

Fishburn raised the phone as it rang. He listened, looked at Fordham, then at his boss. 'Glasgow CID for Chief Superintendent Fordham. It's urgent.'

Bingham nodded. Fordham took the phone.

'Fordham.' He waited for DCS Kellan. 'What's your problem, chief superintendent?'

'Where are those bloody neds you have so much information on?' Kellan's voice boomed angrily out of the phone.

'You're telling me you've lost them?'

Fordham put the worst interpretation forward, knowing Bingham was listening with interest because a fellow countryman was on the line.

'Lost them? We've had but one positive contact. Fingerprints in a stolen car. We have Tate and Lyle staked out, but Securicor delivered their payroll half an hour ago. I want more information from you, laddie.'

'You've had all we can give you. You've had names, antecedents, photographs, times of their arrival. You were advised that they were there to commit robbery, even given the probable location. There's nothing more I can do, Kellan, save come up there and do the job for you.'

Kellan started to protest, but Fordham put the phone down. Turning his attention back to Bingham, he saw that the short conversation hadn't exactly endeared him.

'I think we were discussing my relationship with provincial forces,' Fordham said insolently, almost causing the commander to suffer apoplexy.

For Fordham the interview was over. All questions would be answered negatively, as that part of his brain which he had freed to deal with A10 was re-engaged with the fuck-up he was sure was taking place in Glasgow.

Chapter 21

The third police car in minutes went down the street and Connell, who was standing behind the greying net curtains at the window said, 'What d'you think?' for the third time.

Brodie, who was also at the window, didn't answer.

'You think it's all right?' Connell repeated, an edge of uncertainty in his voice.

'Hoo the fook do I know?' Brodie snapped. 'Sure it's aw right. What do ya expect, all the polis to go on holiday? There's probably been an accident or something.' He looked around at the four anxious faces. They were not convinced. 'C'mon, polis or no, we ha'e a train to catch.'

Haston and McDonald left the house first, each with a heavy grip. One carried a small oxygen cylinder, the other an acetylene tank, burning gun and a few tools. From the window Brodie and Connell watched their progress towards the station, both ready to make a break if Old Bill pounced. The short walk was unimpeded.

Nor were there any setbacks when Brodie and Connell walked up to Cambuslang Station with their bags. The only problem was the one that the porter presented them with.

'S'running a wee bit late,' he said, and huddled deeper into his greatcoat against the cold. 'There's a wee bit of ice on the points.'

'How late?' Brodie asked, trying to keep anxiety out of his voice.

Timing was vital, and although Day had given them safety margins, these were limited. If they were delayed too long it would mean Scotch Pat and Haimes were at extra risk in the stolen van.

'Aboot ten minutes. They're all running late.'

That was of no consolation, nor was the glowing fire in the waiting-room. Brodie strode up the windswept platform towards the other two, who were standing, stamping their feet. Connell didn't follow, but went in by the fire.

*

A wave of steam escaped from the café as Scotch Pat and Haimes pushed out. Both shivered convulsively. Neither of them had eaten much breakfast; their stomachs churned with nerves, and they had only picked at their greasy eggs and bacon. They were running ahead of time, but couldn't sit in the café any longer, having been in there over an hour.

Returning to the shed where the GPO van was parked, they slowly pulled into their post office greys. Haimes climbed into the back of the van, with a shotgun. The rear doors had been fixed to open and close from the inside.

'All right, Jock?' Scotch Pat asked from outside. Haimes banged in reply.

Cautiously checking the road along the dock, Scotch Pat opened the lock-up, then quickly climbed into the van. They were still running a fraction early, but nothing to worry about. The engine turned easily. The thought of pushing battery-flattened vehicles on cold mornings flashed through his head. His hand touched the loaded shotgun by his seat. He had forgotten something, he was sure. Gloves! He reached into his pocket and found a thin pair of leather gloves, noticing that his palms were sweating, despite the cold.

Shoving the van into gear, he eased in the clutch. The road was still clear when he nosed out; he gunned the engine and headed away from the Clyde Tunnel.

He was going too fast, and told himself to slow down; the last thing he wanted was a pull for speeding. His eyes scanned the road, searching out possible dangers. He was tense and apprehensive, yet excited; he wouldn't have seen anything threatening had it leapt up and bitten him.

Traffic along the expressway was light, as if so planned to get him to Central Station ahead of time. All he could do was drive to the speed of the traffic; going too slowly would be as risky as driving too fast. He would simply have to make a couple of turns around the block when he arrived.

Stop and start, start and stop; that was all the train from Cambuslang did once Brodie and the others were aboard. At the rate they were travelling they'd lose their connection.

It would be ironical, Brodie thought as he checked the time again, if this special Royal Mail train was saved from robbery by the inefficiency of British Rail.

The train halted for a red light outside Central Station. Brodie rose and wrenched down the window. The light on the signal bridge sat unmoving as if in silent mockery.

'Fooking light!' Brodie said angrily. He would have smashed it had it been in reach; then gone on and smashed up the railway carriage.

'Shut the window, Jock,' Connell said. 'I'm freezing my balls off here.' He pulled his sheepskin closer.

Alarm suddenly swept through Brodie. The reason was that the track up the left-hand side of the train was empty, when in fact the mail train should have been there.

'We're coming in on the wrong platform,' he said. 'It's the wrong fooking platform, the cunts!'

Springing to their feet, Connell and McDonald leaned out of the window as if not believing Brodie. They saw the empty track where it curved to the left into Central Station.

The red light changed and the train lurched forward. It didn't travel far before it hit a set of points and veered off sharply to the left, crossing the empty tracks and moving into platform ten. Standing in platform eleven was the reassuring sight of the special Royal Mail train. The three men at the window restrained their delight.

Haston's spirits, lightening at the prospect of the job falling to pieces, sank again.

'Hoo about that fur planning, man?' Brodie said.

Not only had the local train pulled in right alongside the mail train, the compartment at the rear where Day had told them to board was directly opposite their access.

Half a dozen or so commuters got off the train, the few braving the cold to come into the city to spend what little money they had.

Brodie and his team didn't disembark on to the platform, but climbed cautiously out between the two trains and crouched below the windows on the running board. After looks, first at Brodie, then Connell, amounting to a final unheeded appeal, Haston dropped between the trains. He was handed a tool bag, and slid under the mail train with it. It took him less than two minutes to locate the alarm system and break the circuit. About as long as it took the others to pull on masks.

Two turns around the station block and Scotch Pat was still ahead of schedule. He wondered how long it might be before someone noticed the van. He decided to go in early, take a chance; couldn't do any harm, and he had his shotgun to get him out of trouble. Emerging from the entrance tunnel off Hope Street, he saw by the station clock that it was eleven-twelve. He was three minutes ahead, his arrival being timed for ten minutes after that of the train from Cambuslang. He decided to hold back after all, and stopped on the road near the barrier access to the carpark between platforms eleven and twelve. He slid out of the van and casually walked to a kiosk for a pack of tobacco.

Vans with mail going on trains other than the London special turned on to the exit ramp and dropped the sacks just ahead of the taxi rank. The stationary van near platform eleven puzzled Andrew Frazier, the GPO supervisor. He knew what vans to expect, and he wasn't expecting another for an hour. Certainly there weren't any more due for the London postie. When he saw the driver return he was about to dismiss the matter. Leaving a van unattended was a reprimandable offence; that was doubtless how that van came to be stolen the other day. He decided to take the number and report the driver. It was only then that he realised what he was looking at. The vehicle registration meant nothing to him, but the post office identification number on the side door did. Instinctively he ran to a telephone to call the police.

The van started through the barrier and cruised along the road between the platforms. Cars were parked both sides, with the mail loading area left clear. The van described an arc away from the train and stopped. Scotch Pat slammed the gear shift into reverse and backed over the small kerb and across the fifteen-foot wide platform.

Two GPO workers, who were sitting on an empty truck reading a paper, were puzzled.

'I thoat we'd done the last, Jimmy. You ken?'

'Aye. Me too.' Leaving his workmate, he rose and ambled across to the van. He wished he hadn't. Scotch Pat had the shotgun on his lap, the muzzle upwards in a position to take the man's head off.

'Hold it right there, Jock,' Scotch Pat ordered. 'Just act natural, like.'

Haimes threw open the van doors, and waited for the mail car to open. It didn't. Something had gone wrong. All that driving around, the Scotchman had fucked up the timing. He banged the door with the butt of his shotgun.

Inside the sixty-foot car four GPO sorters were at work pigeon-holing mail which was spread on the ledge before them. They each had on a grey nylon overall, and all wore spectacles. A fifth post office worker was being admitted through the end of the carriage by one of the two guards, while the other guard checked out the hammering, putting his eye to the security viewer.

'S'nother van,' he said ingenuously. Then, 'He's got a gun!' He stabbed at the dead alarm button.

As Brodie gripped the handle of the door on the other side of the train, for the second time in living memory a vague prayer began forming in his mind. He was praying that the inside man Day had got had done his stuff. He turned the handle and pushed, but the door didn't yield. Immediately he remembered that they opened outwards. He tried again. Brodie's timing couldn't have been finer. He sprang inside, shotgun in his hand, the other two close behind. Haston held back, making sure that everything was under control.

'Stop or I'll shoot!' Brodie screeched at the sorter who was just entering.

The man believed him.

Brodie ran to the sorter and guard and slammed the door shut, then hustled them along to the others, pushing open the door to Haimes.

'Fucking hell! I thought we'd got the wrong train.'

'Don't give us no trouble and you won't get none,' Connell was saying, his words distorted through his mask. The shotgun waved like an extension of his arm. 'Face the bench, put your hands and head on it. Move!'

'You won't get away with it. The others didn't . . .' one of the guards stuttered.

'You an' all. Unless you wanna be a dead hero.'

The guard whom Brodie hustled from the end of the truck tried to resist as he was made to lean on the bench. Brodie hit with the shotgun.

The sacks Brodie was interested in were in a high-tensile steel cage at the end of the car. The gate was secured with two large locks, and each sack had a sealed lock.

With the cutting equipment McDonald lamped through the quarter-inch steel rods and swung the gate open.

Tensely Scotch Pat watched both the area at the top of the platform and the post office worker, flicking his eyes between the two. Not that he thought the little Glaswegian, whose skin was the colour of his grey overalls, would try anything. As his eyes darted back to the man he saw he was looking hard at him. He'll identify me! The thought made him jumpy. Maybe he should shoot him. Nobody ever looks at the driver, that was what he had been told.

'Dinnae look at me! Dinnae look,' he said irrationally, and felt relieved when the man averted his eyes.

The post office workers remained quite passive until the sacks from the cage began leaving the mail car. Then there was a curious, illogical chain reaction of resistance, one that frequently occurred when people found themselves in positions of responsibility for other people's property, which they felt compelled to protect. The post office foreman fell upon one of the bags that McDonald was heaving out. Another sorter and one of the guards tried to prevent others going.

'I'm responsible,' the post office foreman was saying, 'it's my job . . .'

The resistance cost the villains valuable time. They had yet to deal with the sorters and guards according to plan. Connell and Haimes, who were in the rear of the van sprang across to assist in subduing them. Connell swung his shotgun effectively as a club. Haston tried pulling a sack clear of one of the men who had been beaten down and who, despite a bleeding head, held firm.

'Let go! Let go, for Christsake. S'not your money, you silly bastard.' Haston made an impassioned plea. He was terrified that someone was going to wind up shot.

First to answer Andrew Frazier's telephone call was a police Panda car. It stopped at the top of the entrance tunnel where the GPO supervisor was waiting. The driver was immediately directed towards the London mail train.

The policeman inside the blue and white Vauxhall had only been mobile a week; before that he had patrolled a much smaller beat on foot. He was tense and alert, like most policeman in Glasgow, awaiting that big crime they had all been warned to look out for.

For a moment Scotch Pat thought he'd imagined the police car among the constant motion of people and vehicles. Then he tried to convince himself that it was merely another car coming to park. When finally he shouted to the others, barely a squeak emerged from his tense, dry throat. They heard his second attempt. The bellowed warning seemed momentarily to deaden the noise under the station canopy. Scotch Pat anxiously raced the engine and violently engaged the gear, not noticing the post office worker duck away.

The job had started to go wrong from the late arrival of the Cumbuslang train. Now it continued inexorably on that course. The six villains scrambled from the mail car and into the post office van. Brodie, the only one in a state remotely resembling calm, took the last of the sacks with him. The squeal of tyres caused heads to turn as Scotch Pat gunned the van across the platform and up the road. That was the only way out.

This wasn't how they were supposed to make their getaway. They were to tie up the post office workers; then transfer back into the Cambuslang train just before it pulled out. All except Connell, who was to have taken Haimes's place in the van.

The Panda car reduced speed, the policeman galvanized with surprise that it was he who had stumbled upon the big job. Fear made him slightly nauseous. He wouldn't be able to do much on his own. But he was a policeman, some sort of action was expected. He remembered his radio. Other vehicles would be in the area answering that emergency call. He wished one of those had arrived first as he unhooked his phone.

Instinct common to most policemen carried him forward, but no further than the point prior to impact with the GPO van, when the survival instinct caused him to wrench the wheel over. The Panda car avoided the van and buried its nose in the line of parked cars.

The GPO van careered on, braking violently as the car-park attendant dropped the single pole barrier. The van didn't pull up in time but hit the pole, which bowed and broke, the fractured end shattering the windscreen. The van went out of control, mounting the kerb towards the booking hall. Scotch Pat wrestled with the wheel, bringing it back under control. He had no need to blast the horn, everyone around was watching his progress. The van bounced back off the kerb and down the exit ramp. A cab eased out in front of it.

'Get out the fooking way!' Scotch Pat screamed.

The van smashed the taxi back in line. It was going too fast for Scotch Pat to brake for the sharp left turn through the arch on to Hope Street; it mounted the kerb and went straight through the pedestrian arch, running down a woman struggling with two cases. The van ran across the pavement, barely missing the round cast iron stanchion supporting the forecourt awning, and bounced down the last kerb.

The felons were clear of Central Station, with no sign of

other police vehicles. As the GPO van swung along Gordon Street, above the midday roar of traffic the wail of police klaxons could be heard. Scotch Pat wove the van in and out of other vehicles, scraped between two city buses and made a right turn against the lights into Union Street, causing chaos as vehicles braked and others ran into them. The lights on the junction of Argyle Street favoured them, but not the next set on Jamaica Street; making a fast left-hand turn into Howard Street, without any kind of signal, Scotch Pat put the van up on its two nearside wheels. The five men in the back were violently thrown about. They made a right-hand turn into Maxwell then left into Fox Street where the pantechnicon was parked down near St Andrew's Cathedral.

Seeing the van turn into the street, Gordon immediately lowered the tail ramp. But at that speed he knew even if it made the ramp it couldn't stop within the length of the van, but would crash through the cab. Something had gone wrong. He had sensed it when they had started over-running. At that point he had considered skipping. Now he wished he had.

Approaching the ramp, Scotch Pat stood on the brake, but too late. The van skidded, the front nearside wheel missed the ramp and hit the kerb; the offside front wheel ran up the ramp and the van tilted. Scotch Pat thought it was going to topple over, and it might have but for hitting the warehouse wall.

Speeding along Clyde Street in response to the all-car directive to Central Station, the police Rover cut across traffic, which had frozen for it, and on through Dixon Square. As the car raced across the T-junction of Fox Street, a plain-clothes observer in the rear shouted, 'There!'

The driver braked hard but the car overshot the junction. The observer had seen the post office van manoeuvring into the larger van.

Scotch Pat jumped from the ramp, ran along the pantechnicon and wrenched himself into the cab, where Gordon should have been. He raced the engine and pulled away as fast as possible, leaving behind a surprised Haimes and Gordon who were trying to get the locking pins into the tailboard. Neither side was secured and the huge van didn't go ten yards before the tailboard crashed and dragged with a grating, screeching noise along the road. Haimes and Gordon ran after the vehicle but had no chance of catching it, less of having Scotch Pat stop.

The police car swooped past the two men, ignoring them as they ran back. The policeman in the front with the driver was issuing urgent information into the radio. Within minutes the area would be jammed with police and vehicles and the maroon pantechnicon wouldn't get far. Accelerating after the van as it turned into Fox Lane alongside the Cathedral, the police car slid past in the narrow street and tried to get across it. It was a mistake; Scotch Pat rammed him.

'Fook you, Jock!' the uniform on the nearside said to the driver at the impact.

Steering contact was lost as the van bulldozed the police car out of its path, into oncoming traffic on Clyde Street. A lorry ploughed into it. Another swerved into the opposite lane of traffic along the Clyde. The pantechnicon swung out regardless, turning west. There was a gap in the disarray of vehicles, and Scotch Pat shot for it, unconcerned that it wasn't big enough to accommodate his vehicle; he had the weight to push through, and he did.

Two police cars wove at speed through the traffic, heading towards the van; a third came from behind. It could almost have mounted the dragging ramp.

Four vehicles were crushed as the pantechnicon made a left-hand turn against the lights on to Glasgow Bridge. The van rocked dangerously. In the rear panic was rising among the felons.

'He'll kill us all! The cunt's gonna kill us . . .'

'We're all nicked . . . Jesus fucking Christ . . .'

All four had something to say, none of it constructive. McDonald made imprecations to God, whose fault it was that he was in this situation.

As two police cars came on to the bridge after them Brodie hit on an idea. 'Gi's a hand wi' this,' he said, pulling some sacks from the GPO van. Then releasing the handbrake, 'Push the fooker out. Push it, man!'

The van rolled easily with the pull of the moving pantechnicon, and would have shot clear had not Scotch Pat braked. The red van raced forward, smashing into the back wall. It was wrenched clear as Scotch Pat accelerated. The GPO van bounced on the bridge and slewed across the road, tipping over on its side. One of the police cars stopped, the other mounted the kerb, scraping between van and parapet. It continued on the pavement, overtaking a vehicle which the huge van had passed. The police car went up on the pantechnicon's nearside. Scotch Pat saw it and swung in. The radio car went into the side of the bridge, the heavy stone parapet preventing it from taking a dive.

The radio car which had positioned itself on Carlton Place at the far end of Glasgow Bridge had no chance. The ripped and smashed pantechnicon continued to run, and bowled along like a tank, shoving the white Jaguar aside. It ran on across Carlton Place and along Bridge Street.

Scotch Pat was endeavouring to reach the parked Dormobile, as though that faster, smaller van guaranteed escape. Had he been thinking logically he would have known there was no escape, not even with the help of the shotgun he still had. The only practical thing he could do was slam on the brakes and give himself up. Things could only get worse now, more desperate. But villains like Scotch Pat were rarely logical or practical.

Chapter 22

Small wonder crime was so rife, considering the circumstances in which people were compelled to live. Bothwell thought the same each time he visited blocks of flats like the one where Mrs Proctor lived with her kids. He would like to have forced some of the smug city fathers to live in such projects, then ask them if they believed they were meeting the housing needs of the people; ask what chance they really thought they were giving those families whom they so wantonly handicapped. The blocks were spiritually cold, emotionally disorienting, physically alienating. They were breeding grounds for discontent and the chaos of lawlessness. Most people felt they had put something over on life just by surviving there without cracking up.

Young Marlon Proctor wouldn't have to go before the advisory panel this time, though not simply on account of Bothwell's visit. The lad had had three pounds on him which his mother had been worried about. Reluctantly Marlon had revealed how he came by it. Instead of attending school he had collected scrap with a friend and sold it. Bothwell believed the boy, had wanted to. As a matter of procedure he would check with the scrap dealer, for what good that would do; his sort tended to deny everything on principle.

Emerging from the flats, Bothwell noticed the hostile looks of women in hairnets and carpet slippers as they shuffled along to the local shops. It was the uniform which so many of them resented, always assuming that the reason for its presence was to put one away.

'A lot of activity this way, sir,' Bothwell's driver said. Information was issuing from the radio.

Bothwell listened. It wasn't often that there was so much traffic on the air. Control was continually giving the direction of the pursued vehicle, breaking off to direct cars to anticipated points of interception, and to ask police in other vehicles their positions.

'Delta-Foxtrot-4. Are you reading me, Delta-Foxtrot-4? State your position.'

That was the identfying call of Bothwell's own car. Control knew he was in the area, for when out visiting he booked on the air, the same as all other police vehicles. That was in case they received a diversionary call.

'Delta-Foxtrot-4 to control. We are stationary at the service access north end of Crown Street. Looks like they're heading this way. Over.'

'Control to Delta-Foxtrot-4. Proceed south along Crown Street for possible interception at Cumberland Street. Switch to Channel five, Delta-Foxtrot-4, for car to car link up.'

The car was travelling now, heading fast towards Cumberland Street. Bothwell glanced at the young constable behind the wheel, his face showing excitement mingled with apprehension. Not enough apprehension, Bothwell thought. The lad was new to the job.

The pantechnicon van, its aluminium bodywork gouged and torn, trundled along the derelict streets beside the new housing projects like a huge wounded beast with wild dogs after it. Police cars were closing now, as if sensing there was no fight left in it. That was a mistake. As one accelerated to overtake, Brodie fired his shotgun, shattering its windscreen. The car swerved across the road. Two others following braked hard: one stopped to check out the policemen in the first car; the other mounted the kerb to avoid a collision.

'You mad fucker!' Haston screamed hysterically at Brodie, who clung on to the side of the van for balance while fitting two more shells into the breech. 'You'll kill 'em, you will.'

Scotch Pat saw the police car ahead on Cumberland Street. But the service road where the Dormobile was parked was nearer. Still he clung to that one hope of escape. He swung the van on to the service road and trundled towards the Dormobile. Visions of himself free and running clear danced in his inner eye. Slamming on the brakes, he leaped from the pantechnicon before it had come to a halt and, like a sprinter, ran towards the Dormobile. Only then did he see what had happened. He stopped, dismay and disbelief overwhelming him. Half the Dormobile was missing, including two of the wheels and the seats. What could that fucking Sassenach draftsman know about the tearaways on the streets of Glasgow? He sat on the step of the van, the shotgun across his knees. He was close to tears.

The other four felons scattered from the rear of the pantechnicon. Brodie ran along the road the way they had been heading, taking with him one of the sacks. McDonald ran back towards a group of boys who were sitting astride bicycles, watching the proceedings. Haston ran across the adjacent waste ground where dwellings had once stood, and turf some day might be laid. Fear and frustration brought tears to his eyes. Connell followed Haston, not out of any faith in his judgment, but because it was the only unimpeded means of escape: until a police car mounted the pavement from the far side and sped across the ground, tossing on the cement remnants and hummocks. When the car reached a point where it cut them off, Connell turned back. But Haston, heart racing and lungs almost bursting, swerved off course. The police pursued him.

Connell started after Brodie. Assuming now that the tiny Scotsman had some secret way out, Connell was angry at not following him in the first place. Or maybe McDonald was better off. Feeling increasingly desperate that one of the others might get clear while he was captured, Connell ran harder, his weight dragging on him, his breath short, his chest heaving painfully.

Running flat out along the side street, McDonald's efforts were made to look puny by kids who came swooping after him on bicycles with eight-speed gears. Mockingly, they urged him to run faster and cut sharply in front of him, ignoring the klaxon of the approaching police car.

Panic swelled through Connell as Brodie suddenly swung round, started back, then dashed across the road. A police car from the road beyond the flats was coming towards them through the children's play area. Bothwell and the constable climbed from the car that was now blocking their retreat.

Brodie ran into the block as Bothwell started towards them. Connell didn't intend being left behind. Brodie had something in mind and he was going to be part of it.

They both charged into the hallway, its walls scarred by aerosol graffiti, sounds of their running feet echoing up the stairwell. Brodie crashed through a door at the end, and Connell, catching it on the rebound, found himself in a communal laundry. There the noise was jarring; large machines, some with worn drum bearings, competed with a baby howling, a radio disc jockey and the conversations six women carried on at a shouted pitch. The talk, which no one could possibly have understood, was the only thing to stop as Brodie and Connell charged through. The latter slipped on the wet floor and, floundering, scattered a pile of folded washing.

This he proceeded to run through, having got his balance back. Abuse chased Connell as he followed Brodie out of the opposite door.

The yard, formed by blocks of twenty-three storeys on one side and a low-rise housing complex on the other, was about forty feet by a hundred. There was a wall at either end, with a gate, and dozens of ill-assorted lines between posts strung with washing. Built on to walls at various points were sheds housing inadequate, overspilling communal rubbish bins.

Emerging from the laundry, Brodie turned and ran towards the top of the yard. He seemed without direction, like a man lost in a world that had changed in his absence. Connell, who had got his second wind, was close behind. Both men had to duck beneath the lines of washing, sheets dipping towards the ground obscured their view.

The gate at the end of the yard was not only locked, but nails had been driven into the frame to prevent it ever being opened, other than with great force; certainly not by the casual vandals who had frequented the yard. The force that Brodie threw against the gate wasn't enough, nor when Connell gave it some shoulder.

Both felons spun round and saw Bothwell – his young

colleague was still in the laundry untangling himself from the washing. Connell turned and smashed at the gate. He glanced back at Bothwell, who had shortened his step now, faced with Brodie's shotgun. Brodie was motionless, but Bothwell came on cautiously.

'Shoot the fucker!' Connell screamed. 'Shoot him!' Forgetting the .38 in his belt.

Still Brodie made no move.

Bothwell reached out. 'Come on, you cannae go anywhere,' he said, calmly and reasonably. He moved closer, feeling confident and with no awareness of fear.

'Stay back. You'd better stay back, man...'

'Put up the gun, laddie. It'll do you no good the now.' His advance continued.

'I said shoot him!'

Connell snatched the shotgun as Bothwell sprang forward. The first barrel exploded with a deafening retort, the lead tearing open the chief inspector's chest. The second barrel peppered the face and chest of the constable who came weaving through the sheets. He was bowled backwards.

Neither Brodie nor Connell could quite comprehend it. The two separate explosions rang in their ears. Instinctively both turned and hit the gate with such blind fury that it split, bursting the nails out.

Parked on the road beyond was a bakery van. The startled driver stood with a basket of bread and pies on his arm. Brodie hesitated briefly before jumping into the cab. The delivery man hadn't the sense to remain motionless; he was responsible for the firm's van. He started forward to stop what was happening. His protest ended when Connell shot him with the .38. Loaves and pies spilled on to the pavement as the man was thrust backwards.

Connell clambered into the van, which sped off.

The wounded constable staggered through the gate, his face streaming with blood. All he was in time to see was a ludicrous icecream van painted with icecream-eating animals. He heard its equally ludicrous jingle before he collapsed.

Chapter 23

Fourteen police cars arrived within minutes of each other, on the service road where the pantechnicon and Dormobile were. The policemen inside were mainly uniform branch. Other vehicles appeared, carrying detectives, most of them armed. Their guns weren't necessary.

Haston, McDonald and Scotch Pat had been picked up without resistance, Scotch Pat quietly relinquishing the shotgun.

Other policemen had gone through and found Bothwell, the wounded constable and the dead bread delivery man. Word quickly spread among the uniforms; tension and anger mounted, and they loomed threateningly over the three felons, who were bewildered until they too learned what had happened. Then they were distressed, and terribly afraid. Ronnie Haston cried. This was his worst nightmare come true. He retched, but his tension-knotted stomach was empty.

Kellan wasn't long arriving from Pitt Street with DI Douglas. He had received the brunt of the news over the car radio: two policemen had been shot, one was dead. A uniformed inspector, Alex Ingrams, briefed him. The wounded constable's name meant nothing to the DCS, but he was a colleague, notwithstanding how recently attested.

Betrayal was what Kellan felt most strongly when he went through to inspect Stuart Bothwell's body. Despite past conflict he regretted his death no less than he would have regretted the death of any policeman. But the information he had been given was in the first place inadequate, and the second, incorrect. The robbery wasn't supposed to have happened at Central Station. The uniform branch shouldn't have been involved, least of all Stuart Bothwell. Had it happened at the Tate and Lyle refinery then his detectives would have been waiting to intercept the murderers. Chief Inspector Bothwell wouldn't have been within a mile. Kellan swiftly concluded that John Fordham was in part responsible for the death of this senior officer.

Bothwell's body had been covered with a sheet, through which blood had spread like red ink through blotting paper. Up and down the dwellings people were peering from windows. Others who had gathered in small groups in the yard just beyond the last washing line, stared in fear and fascination. The gaping public in situations like this offended policemen, but there wasn't much they could do, apart from keeping them away from the immediate vicinity. The Scenes of Crime officer, portly Sergeant Twining, with his meticulous eye for detail, noted everything from the angle of the body to the items of washing on the nearby line. These details were noted in addition to the dozens of photographs, not instead of them.

'How long?' Kellan asked brusquely, catching Sergeant Twining's eye.

Scenes of Crime wasn't something that gave value for haste, though here the job was a formality. They knew who had done the shooting. 'Want those bastards through yon building to tek a look at the result o' their handiwork.'

'I'll no be long, sir.'

Twining wasn't thrown by the DCS's impatience. He didn't envy him his job, and wouldn't delay him getting on with it. He asked the inspector to get the spectators back and arrange to have some proper barriers erected; also to get the area beyond the gate cordoned off. Regardless of rank, the Scenes of Crime officer had absolute charge until his task was completed.

The three felons were reluctant to go through to view the body, but knew instinctively that the tense, angry policemen surrounding them only needed an excuse. Scotch Pat went first, then Haston. McDonald held back, suspecting treachery, believing that the police merely wanted to get them off the public street and out of sight. He was mistaken. Such discretion hadn't even occurred to the uniforms. About half a dozen set upon McDonald for refusing to respond to the order. They threw wild furious punches at him in the hope of relieving the terrible sense of loss and inadequacy they felt over the death of Stuart Bothwell. Also they were hitting out at their own fears, the possibility that some criminal or violently disruptive element of a crumbling society might one day murder them, knowing they would be equally helpless to prevent it.

McDonald crumpled to the pavement, where they kicked him, the hard, glossy toecaps of their boots striking home on the yielding body. The beating ceased as abruptly as it had started, and strong hands pulled the limp, bleeding suspect to his feet.

'When we gi' an order, you wee bass, obey it,' the burly, red-bearded sergeant said, leaning menacingly close to McDonald.

When McDonald tried to speak no words emerged, only his broken threads of teeth on a spool of blood.

Kellan didn't bat an eyelid at this bloodied, swollen-faced villain. He knew each of them was going to get a lot worse before his men were through. Even if he had any inclination to stop such beatings he wouldn't have been able to. The suspects were liable to fall down stairs, get their hands crushed in cell doors, have mugs of scalding tea spilt in their faces. All accidents, and unavoidable.

Haston wept and retched further at the sight of the policeman with the hole in the side of his chest from which white ends of broken rib poked out, along with fragments of mashed lung and heart. His distress was acute. '. . . I didn't want this to happen, honest to God I didn't.' The words were almost incoherent.

'You fooking murdering bastards,' Kellan said as he viewed the three men, unable to disguise his loathing. 'Get on back wi' 'em, Alan, and mek a start.'

DCI Crombie, who was as numbed as any policeman present, stirred into action.

'Has a call gone out for the baker's van, Dougie?' It had. 'I want every available man looking for it. They'll no' get far. Recall everyone who's off duty . . .'

'We did for the alert this morning,' Douglas reminded him.

'Then get everyone back off leave,' Kellan snapped. 'I don't care where these murdering fookers are, I want them. And quickly.'

Inspector Ingrams, who was organising things in the street, came and informed Kellan that the press were showing up.

'Keep them out until Sergeant Twining's finished. Then I'll see them through here.'

He had good relations with the news media; they understood how difficult his job was, and for that he didn't prevent them doing theirs. He would let them have all this, let the public see just what sort of violent animals they were dealing with. Know why they had to be stopped; caught; caged.

Even a moron would have known the bread van would within minutes be the hottest vehicle in Scotland. And minutes were all that Brodie and Connell employed. Clear of Gorbals they headed south for Hutcheson Town. There on the industrial estate they picked up a car from a factory carpark. Jumping the fuses to short-circuit the ignition was an easy job for Connell.

From behind the steering wheel Brodie watched the man lower the bonnet; he considered gunning the car away and ditching Connell, but decided against it. He didn't want this car becoming too hot before he got to where he was going. Both men wanted to get back to Cambuslang. Brodie knew Connell's reason: the stupid wee whore at the hotel, if she hadn't already been picked up. He doubted Connell knew his reason for heading in that direction. He was going to pick up his hire car before road-blocks were set up.

Brodie glanced over at the post office sack and the shotgun tucked down between the front and back seats, reassuring himself about their presence as Connell climbed in. The murdering cowboy would get a ride out of the carpark, but one thing was certain, he wouldn't be going far with him.

Neither spoke much as they turned east, not wanting to speak of what was dominating their thoughts.

Suspicion flashed through Brodie's mind when Connell said, 'Hadn't we better call London? Day or someone?'

He wondered if Connell was planning the same thing as himself. But nothing was further from his thoughts. The man was simply afraid, and could only relate to what he knew and trusted. At the moment that was Brodie. If they had spoken further he might have proposed sticking together.

Cautiously Brodie slid from behind the wheel, leaving the engine of the Jaguar running outside the phone box. He watched Brian Connell through the mirror in the box as he dialled Alan Day's number, and only started to relax when the man concentrated on watching the road, making no move to jump into the driving seat. It was then that he saw the means of dropping Connell.

Day's number rang a few times before the draftsman answered. He was a little surprised when Brodie identified himself; there should have been no contact between them again.

'What a fook-up,' the Scotsman said, before Day could ask how it went. 'Biggest fook-up since Culloden. He went and shot Old Bill just lek it were a film . . .'

The phone immediately went dead.

'Alan?' Brodie said quietly, alarm spreading through him. He didn't need the force of a hammer to get the message. No one would want to know them now.

He glanced at Connell, who was watching him, then said into the mouthpiece, as though continuing a conversation, 'Yeah, hold on, I'll git him.'

He left the handset dangling. Climbing into the car, he said, 'He wants to talk to you. Mek it quick, we cannae hang around.'

As Connell reached for the dead handset he heard the car engine race and the tyres squeal and he knew he had been had over. He burst out of the box and sprinted hopelessly after the accelerating car.

He felt desolate, desperate; thought about firing after the Jaguar; then remembered Maureen Hoyle. She would have to hire a car and pick him up. She was his single hope of getting away. He knew he could rely on her.

Chapter 24

With a tight closing of ranks the murder hunt moved into gear. Past friction between the CID and uniform branch dissolved instantly: one of their own had been shot dead; not a uniform man, not a detective, but a policeman.

Certain that the two murderers were tightly boxed up, the police set about finding them in earnest. Road blocks were set up to cover every route out of the city. Doubtless the proverbial mouse could have squeezed through, but it wasn't thought likely that either Brodie or Connell could, unless they knew the city a lot better than the policemen covering the exits. Watches were put on bus and train stations, the airport and the docks; police made visits to long-distance haulage firms and car-hire companies. This fell mainly to the uniform branch, with the CID directing things. Detective Superintendent Ross Stalker was in over-all charge. This job he did exceptionally well, being an experienced, slow, meticulous policeman who never missed a detail.

Haston, Haimes, Gordon, Scotch Pat and McDonald, all safely ensconced in cells and interview rooms at the police office across from headquarters, began to get the treatment. This varied from intensive questioning to straightforward beatings. Not one of them had arrived at the station unmarked. A policeman with knowledge of first-aid saw McDonald and said he ought to be in hospital. A faint ray of hope appeared across McDonald's swollen, blood congealed face before DCI McFageon said, 'That will no' be possible. This laddie's gotta answer some questions.'

That indicated to the other four prisoners what they could expect. It left each with a sinking, sickening feeling of fear in his stomach.

The three detectives who interrogated Syd Haimes were all over six foot and thirteen stone. Glaswegians tended to be small, until it came to police. Haimes started like so many felons when the whole firm hadn't been captured, foolishly not knowing anything. It wasn't a game to these CID, and they weren't about to observe those rules which often governed relations of police and villains. Information, such as Haimes had, began rattling out of him in staccato jolts each time he hit the wall. He hit the wall a lot.

Detective Inspector Andy Duncan did most of the questioning, his two colleagues did the throwing.

'Who supplied the guns to you, Haimes ...?'

'I dunno ...' Haimes stopped like he'd bitten his tongue.

The two detectives slammed him against the wall. One said, 'Mr Duncan does no' accept that kind of answer.'

'Brodie got them with Scotch Pat. They got them. They didn't say where from.'

'Who organised the job in London?'

'I dun ... Connell. He brought me in, sir. I swear that's all. It's all I know, it's all, it is.'

Duncan slowly shook his head. 'That's no a quarter o' it, laddie.'

There were four others like Duncan interviewing the other prisoners. He felt in competition with them over who would extract the most information, fastest. Duncan wanted to win the competition.

'Fur Christsake hold him up, will ya?' the DS said as McDonald sagged like a sack of smashed eggs. He was mumbling, his words almost inaudible. 'What the fook's he saying?'

'... Hail Mary, full of grace, the Lord is with thee ...'

'He's praying, boss. Sounds like a few Hail Marys,' the detective kneeling over McDonald said.

'Fooking Catholic bass, he needs to pray.'

That detective didn't win the competition. McDonald passed out on them and finally had to be taken to hospital.

Scotch Pat fell down the fourteen stone basement steps on his way to the interview room. The detectives escorting him helped him back up. Scotch Pat whimpered. He didn't want to fall down again. In the interview room he was chatty, but then the detective conducting the interrogation was quite friendly. DI Waterman had an easy manner. He sat against the table opposite Scotch Pat and smoked his pipe. He talked in a low, even voice which belied the sudden violence he was capable of.

'I'm aware you were no' heavily involved, Graham. You were just a driver. But you drove Brodie when he went to see the gunsmith, so you know him . . .'

'I don't. I dinnae go in wi' him . . .'

'Lemme finish. You know the gunsmith,' he said quietly, 'and unless I get him, we're going to open your legs and kick your balls.'

Instinctively Scotch Pat closed his legs. 'Honest, sur. Please don't. Please. I only drove Brodie where I tol' ya. I dinnae go wi' him. I dinnae, please. Please. Please believe me . . .'

Scotch Pat glanced desperately between the other detectives in the small grey-and-blue-painted room, as if soliciting their support. He missed Harold Waterman's signal.

Scotch Pat screamed as the detectives grabbed him, but not as loud as when they actually held him for the DI to kick him. Having been wound up, knowing the Ds were capable of it, the actual kick wasn't necessary. But it seemed Waterman didn't want to disappoint the man. Scotch Pat writhed breathlessly on the floor, clasping his genitals. No other acts of violence against him were needed. Threats alone achieved everything. Scotch Pat wasn't able to give them the gun-dealer, but he grassed everyone else he could think of, regardless of whether or not they were connected with the mail train robbery or murder. All Scotch Pat wanted was the promise that he wouldn't be kicked again.

Ian Gordon was least able of the five felons to give the detectives any information and, curiously, the least pressed. The Ds believed him, simply taking details of the man who had recruited him. The felon who had done him this service was called Kenny Eastlake; the man for whom he'd recruited him being Alan Percival.

Detectives were despatched to pick up Eastlake.

Of the five, the most informative was Ronnie Haston, or as he was quickly nicknamed, the cry-bairn. McFageon drew him. At seventeen stone the DCI was formidable, and people thought twice before offering him wrong answers. He never thought twice about hitting people.

The interrogation started with McFageon informing the felon that he was a murdering bastard.

Haston didn't respond.

'What are you? I want to hear the words, laddie!'

When still Haston failed to respond the DCI kicked the chair, skidding it sideways. Haston crashed to the floor, cowering and covering his head as though expecting to be kicked – he had seen it happen to McDonald. The two Ds with McFageon lifted Haston to his feet.

'C'mon, let's hear you. I am a murdering bastard.'

'I didn't want no Old Bill shot. I didn't . . .'

'Away on, laddie, let's hear it. What are you?'

'What are you, Haston?' another detective chipped in. 'A fooking murderer. That's right.'

'No, it's not. It ain't . . . I didn't . . .'

McFageon started casually past the suspect as if quitting, as he did so he punched him in the stomach; then turned with surprising grace for a man of his size and hit Haston in the kidneys.

'Noo let's hear it. I-am-a-murdering-bastard.'

It might have been a precondition of truthfulness.

'Yes,' Haston whispered painfully. 'I am . . . a murdering . . . bastard.'

'We know it, mister. Now depending how helpful ya are to us in tekking the other two is how much of a beating you tek. You can walk into court, or we'll carry you on a stretcher. It meks no difference to us.'

Hoisted back into the chair, Haston whimpered, 'I wouldn't shoot no policeman, straight I wouldn't . . .'

'Course you wouldn't. You dinnae ken it was gonna happen. You just took the guns to keep yourselves amused.'

'Brodie done it. He's a fucking maniac, broke m' sister's legs, he did. A fucking nutter. I wouldn't shoot no one. Ask Mr Fordham, he put us on the train. He knows. He put us on the train.'

Hamish Archibald was tall and elegant and looked well in uniform. Uniforms suited him. He had worn them all his life, having previously been a professional soldier. Born in India, the son of a soldier, Archibald had gained an early taste for both uniforms and discipline. His mother had come from Edinburgh, which he considered his spiritual home, and he had retired there until his appointment as Chief Constable of Strathclyde. His accent was noticeably different from those around him. It had the softer Midlothian vowel sounds. His lean face slightly resembled a rat's, although he never indulged the nickname Ratface, by which he was sometimes known. The half-moon glasses perched on the end of his nose curiously accentuated the impression.

Archibald had cut short his leave, though he hadn't been far away, at Killermont golf course. He hadn't come directly, but first returned home to get into uniform, without which he felt ill at ease around police headquarters. Also, on this grave occasion he considered it would have been inappropriate to be incorrectly dressed, especially as he would have to see Bothwell's widow and doubtless appear before the press.

Kellan briefed the man, along with Vincent Reid, one of the four assistant chief constables who had over-all responsibility for crime. Reid was barrel-chested, always immaculately dressed, and although the closer of the two to Kellan in his area of administration, like the chief constable he rarely interfered. Kellan gave them as full a picture as he was able about the raid, its execution and the subsequent shooting. No complete account of what happened at the gate could be drawn until either Brodie and Connell were captured, or the wounded policeman had regained consciousness after his operation. Kellan doubted even then whether it would be complete.

'How long before the raid had you the information, Ian?' the assistant chief constable asked, seeking a clear line through the plethora of details.

'We did no' ha'e it at all. I think Fordham held information back, for reasons best known to himself. I suspect he was looking to mek an eleventh-hour deal with the neds,' Kellan speculated, glancing at Archibald's passive expression.

'If that proves so, then Mr Fordham will be a very sorry policeman. I do not care how highly thought of he is in London. His head will roll if he's found to be in any way culpable,' Hamish Archibald assured him.

Kellan knew the chief constable meant it. There was a direct, no-nonsense manner about the man to which he responded. He had welcomed him for that when ordinarily he might have resented him as an outsider. One such policy that had earned him the DCS's respect concerned the homosexual problem in the city. The CC had them picked up – by policemen, escorted to Central Station and put aboard the first London train with a warning not to come back.

'I'd gi' ma pension to know just how involved the man was.'

'Let's hope he's an adequate explanation. It's never pleasant pursuing a fellow policeman, especially when the result's so tragic. How did Bothwell's widow take it?'

'Badly. Very badly. Superintendent McWhirter broke the news. He and Bothwell were close.'

'Aye,' he said ponderously, not wanting the next step to arrive. 'Well, I must away and see the poor lass. I wish I had some crumbs of comfort for her, like the arrest of the two who shot him.'

There was a brief pause. The assistant chief constable looked at Kellan.

'I no' think it'll be long. I'm asking the press to hold their front pages so they can run photographs of each as soon as the latest arrive from London.'

They had requested better photos of Connell and Brodie, but if need be they would run those they had in the newspapers and on TV.

'Jesus, what a fuck-up.'

That was Fordham's reaction when he got the news via Malcolm Dyce. It was the only sign of emotion he allowed.

He regretted that a policeman had been shot, but breaking his heart wouldn't alter the fact. Death in the line of duty was for a policeman, if to a lesser degree in Britain than most other countries, an occupational hazard. Fordham was able to accept it, especially when the policeman was unknown to him.

'Send them up everything we have on Brodie and Connell. Were there any better photographs?'

'Not on Brodie. We're getting something on Connell and the girl.'

'Is Frank in the office? . . . Ask him to step along here.'

Things couldn't have gone more wrong in Glasgow. Perhaps the gods were conspiring to protect Duckett. As an indirect result Fordham foresaw what might happen: instead of giving impetus to his enquiries, the murder could have the opposite effect, and take the pressure off the people at the top. It was illogical, but then the police thought a great deal of their own, and when they were gunned down almost everything was sacrificed to capturing the killer.

'A bastard,' Fordham said as Borroughs appeared.

'A right fuck-up and no mistake.' His manner was subdued, as if Bothwell had been a friend.

'I want something to tie Charlie Ryman in to Glasgow, no ifs and buts now, Frank. See what's on the intercepts – I think we'll take a chance and pick Day up. But see if those tapes give us anything first.'

The detectives bristled with anticipation when they heard Brodie's voice telling Alan Day about the shooting.

Borroughs despatched DI Roger Edwards and three other detectives to get the draftsman. Each was issued with a Smith and Wesson .38 and twelve bullets. This was done out of habit by Dyce; momentarily forgotten in the excitement was his promotion to superintendent; it wasn't yet effective, but already he was easing himself out of his familiar duties as DCI, one of which was armourer. Whoever replaced Dyce would get that job, as firearms were kept in the metal cupboard nearest Dyce's desk.

Two detectives went round the back of the house where

Day had his flat, while Edwards and DC Thompson entered through the front door. There was no practical rear exit; only a long drop from a window and several garden fences to climb.

The landlady who admitted the Ds was an inquisitive soul, and wasn't prepared to answer questions unless she got about half a dozen of her own answered. Edwards was usually accommodating but had neither the time nor the inclination then. He told her in no uncertain terms to get back in her own room and stay there. The woman retired in alarm at the sight of their guns.

There was no answer at Day's door. The Yale lock was old and sprung easily when the DI jiggled a Harold Lloyd around the doorstop. Day was gone, but there was a burnt smell in the room. This they tracked down to the kettle, whose element had recently burnt out.

'He's not long gone, guv,' DC Thompson said.

'I wouldn't have thought so. From the look of this he must have thought the house was on fire.'

The two rooms had been abandoned in a hurry. Papers and books spilled where things had been hastily grabbed; a trail of clothes from cupboard to bed; making of tea uncompleted. Edwards gazed round the room.

'Give the other two a shout, Peter,' he said as he picked up the phone to call in.

Borroughs told him to hang on until he got there.

'Go over the place with a fine comb, Frank,' Fordham instructed. 'Fetch everything that's anything. And leave someone on watch there in case Day comes back.'

'I wouldn't have thought there was much chance.'

'No. Fuck it!' The words burst out angrily. 'I should've foreseen Day's importance and had someone at his place before. Make him a priority. Airports, seaports, usual stuff. He might not be out yet. He's got to be nicked if we're ever going upwards.'

Chapter 25

The magistrates' court was specially convened for Saturday afternoon. It would have been possible for the police to have brought Haston, Haimes, McDonald, Scotch Pat and Gordon before the bench the day before, but their interrogation had gone on all day and throughout the night. With the weekend intervening the rule governing the time prisoners could officially be held prior to appearing in court didn't apply. But holding them until Monday would have made it seem to the outside world that the police were inactive.

None of the five had been allowed to sleep during the periods they weren't being interrogated; policemen weren't getting any sleep, so they had no intention of allowing any to those responsible for that situation to. Prisoners lost all resistance from lack of sleep. There was no prospect of them getting any in the near future, either; the police hadn't finished their interrogation.

The suspects were assisted from the van in the yard at the rear of the court, each with a blanket over his head. Press cameras clicked rapidly from the gate, getting pictures of five hooded figures amidst a cordon of uniforms. Photographs of the suspects uncovered wouldn't have been publishable; having been charged they were now sub judice. Actually, most editors would have refrained from publishing pictures showing prisoners in the condition of these five men; the press tend to support the police and uphold virtues of law and order – apart from the underground press, but they had no reporters present.

There was only one magistrate on the bench, and the fact that the five prisoners were uniformly marked caused him no comment. He was a dour, crablike Scotsman called Appin-Hamilton, and the police couldn't have brought their suspects in front of a man more likely to support them.

Standing in the well of the court, Kellan formally asked for the prisoners to be remanded in police cells. This procedure, rather than a remand to the local gaol, gave the police easy access to the prisoners.

Appin-Hamilton granted the remand without question. The only point he raised was whether or not the prisoners were legally represented.

'They have been given the opportunity to seek representation, sir, but have so far declined,' Kellan replied.

The magistrate nodded solemnly. 'Then I think you should use your influence, Mr Kellan, and persuade them.' He smiled grimly as if he had made a joke.

The five men were taken back to police headquarters under heavy escort.

Reporters were beginning to annoy DCS Kellan with their persistent questions. They reminded him of childhood geese on his aunt's farm when she went out with their pail of food. They gobbled around her, tugging at her long skirts. He had always been a little afraid, thinking them unpredictable. The press flocked around, firing greedy questions as though they believed he was holding out on them. He was in fact giving them everything just as soon as it was prudent to do so, but they did not seem to appreciate that.

'How long was the remand, chief superintendent . . .?'

'Are you any nearer the others, Mr Kellan . . .?'

'Why was it in police cells?'

'Do they know the whereabouts of the others?'

'Is an arrest imminent, sir?'

'Could you say if there'll be an arrest soon?'

He could feel their beaks pulling at his coat.

A reporter from *The Scotsman* said, 'Is there any possibility that the murderers are by this time out of the city?'

The question brought Kellan up sharply. Until then the thought had merely lain in the back of his mind, it hadn't been mooted, much less considered. Kellan wasn't about to admit the possibility.

'There's absolutely no' a snowball's chance in hell, Allen. Unless they're bloody invisible. They're out there; someone is helping them. And their time is fast running out.'

'Does that mean there's to be some arrests imminently?'

The Times man asked.

Having committed himself this far, Kellan had to go on. He responded brusquely, saying there would be, then pushed through them, ignoring their gobbling. Both the chief constable and the assistant chief constable gave up their Saturday afternoon golf as their contribution to bringing Bothwell's killers to justice. The thought that the detective in charge had to interrupt his concentration in order to brief them, and so set things back, might never have occurred to them.

The briefing took place in Hamish Archibald's well appointed office, which was littered with cups and shields of constabulary achievements. There was little progress to report, nothing of significance to add. A lot of work had been done by a lot of policemen, but they hadn't taken Brodie, Connell and Maureen Hoyle, which was all anyone wanted to hear.

'Do you think the underworld is hiding them, Ian?' Vincent Reid asked.

Kellan didn't even want to admit that there was an underworld in Glasgow. He had, after all, spent over thirty years fighting it.

'I'll let you know after we've finished raiding everyone with any connection.'

There was a brief, awkward silence. It was as though the two uniformed men were so far from their familiar Saturday afternoon routine that they had lost the ability to carry on a fluent conversation.

The chief constable raised the matter of Bothwell's funeral. This wasn't really Kellan's province, but as he was the most active senior policeman in Strathclyde the CC chose to involve him.

'There'll be a coroner's hearing first. That's scheduled for Tuesday morning. It would be appropriate, capturing Brodie and Connell in time for the funeral.'

'It will be a big production, Ian,' Reid added. 'Something in keeping with the officer's rank; a tribute to his achievement. Full honours.'

'Aye,' Kellan said reflectively, 'he deserves no less. A good man; a great loss to the force.' Kellan believed every word.

The CC glanced at Reid in a slightly conspiratorial way. 'I've decided to promote him posthumously. No reason why he should not have been made a superintendent. The pension. It'll help Janet Bothwell. There are four bairns, you know?'

Kellan didn't know. He guessed Bothwell would have had a family. He never imagined the chief constable could be so thoughtful, or so practical as to secure a bigger pension for his widow. The chief constable of the day hadn't been so thoughtful of Kellan's mother when his father had been shot. Janet Bothwell was juxtaposed in his thoughts with reflections of his widowed mother. He thought perhaps he should go and see the woman. He didn't know what he would say to her, but felt he had to make the gesture.

Police activity remained intense throughout Saturday and Sunday. Not only was every known felon being turned over, so was everyone he knew. Detectives didn't go to bed, but snatched cat-naps in chairs, and ate only odds and ends of food. The canteen was in the basement of police headquarters and a trip down there seemed too much of a detour, a deflection from their purpose. No one felt much like sitting down and eating a proper meal, anyway.

No detective was pushing himself harder than Ian Kellan. He matched the hardest working detective hour for hour, interrogation for interrogation, and in addition made all the decisions. He had the most to lose in personal esteem; he felt compelled to prove he was not merely as good as, but better than the next detective. He was determined not to let two snivelling murderers best him.

Although the intense police onslaught seemed to bring Brodie and Connell no closer to capture, it did turn up numerous other felons and their crimes; things that Ds would sooner not have come upon at that point. Getting involved with them, once they had found that they couldn't use the details as levers in securing what they were really after, only delayed them.

Armed detectives raided the house in Renfrew of a villain whose name they had been given by another previously raided; the hope being that it would get the pressure off himself. The villain in Renfrew had too many items in his house that he was unable to account for; but even so the detectives wouldn't have bothered proceeding further, only they found hidden beneath a floorboard in the cupboard under the stairs a sawn off shotgun. Any other kind of weapon and they might have listened to the man's explanations more sympathetically. As it happened they didn't listen at all.

Sergeant Galbraith punched the man, cutting his knuckles as he broke his front teeth. That didn't stop him hitting him again.

'I think we found ourselves another fooker involved in the murder,' Galbraith announced.

The felon's mouth hurt too much for him to protest verbally, and he knew better than to do so physically against armed detectives. The mood they were in they'd likely shoot him. Dunning's wife, who stood at the top of the stairs clutching her three wailing kids, hurled herself in defence of her husband.

Avoiding her flailing arms with a skill that indicated an earlier boxing career, DC Daly hit her, sending her sprawling.

Dunning didn't spring to his wife's aid.

At the police office the felon proved to the satisfaction of senior detectives that he wasn't involved with Brodie. Being in possession of a shotgun illegally was one thing, and a number of reasons, if barely plausible, could have been put up; however, there was only ever one reason for possessing a sawn off shotgun, and the way the Ds handled him Dunning didn't last long. He admitted being part of a planned robbery on Barclay's Bank in George Street. It had been postponed in view of what had happened on Friday, he had added, as if that made everything all right again.

No felon ever made a statement with a view to helping the

police. Dunning gave the names of the other four people involved, and that of the man who had supplied the guns. The name itself didn't mean anything to Detective Superintendent Stalker when it was passed to him. But the gun-dealer's address did. It was in the same street as the dealer who had supplied Brodie. They had to be one and the same. So far the police had failed to identify the gun-dealer, and short of searching every building in the street, which would have been counter-productive, they were unlikely to. It was a lucky break.

After despatching detectives to get the gun-dealer, the tension which had kept Stalker awake and functioning for such a long, unrelieved period slackened, and with his head resting against a hand and elbow on his desk he nodded. Phones rang almost continuously in the squad-room on the third floor as both the well-meaning, and not so well-meaning called in with 'sightings' and information about Brodie and Connell, all of which had to be checked. Detectives shuffled around, some of them more somnolent than others; policemen and women in uniform bustled in and out, bringing the latest reports from patrols and road blocks; typewriters clacked irregularly; voices rose and dipped. In his odd snatches of sleep Ross Stalker was oblivious to it all.

'Ross,' Kellan said kindly, grasping his shoulder.

The detective superintendent came awake with a start and blinked several times. 'God, for a minute, Ian, I thought you were my old woman.'

A thin smile parted the DCS's lips. It was the first time he had smiled in a long while.

'Why don't you get off, get a few hours sleep? Alan Crombie can tek over here.'

'Aye, I'll not say no.' Stalker knew his limitations. He wasn't a superman, able to function without sleep. He was aware that he was no longer giving his best. 'What about yourself? You've no' had any sleep.'

Kellan's moment of weakness passed. He stiffened at the implication of his fallibility. 'I've a comfortable chair.' He didn't say whether he would use it.

Kellan was determined to push himself until he either dropped or caught the two murderers.

'The Glasgow police murder, and that of the bread delivery man,' said the ITN newscaster who wore a wig that looked like a dead rat. He glanced at his notes. He gave a résumé of the robbery and murders and details of police searches throughout the city and roadblocks, with accompanying film; and reminded viewers of who was being sought. The details were endless, it seemed.

The scene shifted to an unobtrusive semi-detached house in the Craigton district, and Mrs Bothwell and her four children.

The man watching the television stiffened perceptibly. He listened as the reporter sketched in background, told of the growing feeling in the city in favour of the reintroduction of the death penalty for police murders; he felt deeply for the woman in her distress, and was gratified to hear of the flood of messages of sympathy and support.

Lord Basingstoke was impressed by the widow. Her apparent forbearance and dedication to her family in time of tragic loss, indicated that she had the right mettle.

Putting off the TV set as the news broadcast moved on to more mundane items, Lord Basingstoke paused, standing very erect, thinking about the policeman's murder. Despite his feelings for the widow, he saw the slaying as the answer to his prayers. It had the sympathy of the entire nation, and through it he believed this time he could find support for the reintroduction of capital punishment. The nation would cry out as one.

Crossing to his roll-top desk, he sat to write Janet Bothwell the letter he had been composing since the tragic news had broken. He would appear in person close on its heels. As he set pen to paper he prayed that this mission would not prove fruitless. The nation needed the return of the hemp for the good of its soul, its very salvation depended upon it, it represented the status quo; hanging was the single act which redeemed a murderer and returned him to God.

No psychiatrist or gaolor could do that.

'... To be hanged by the neck until you are dead. And may the Lord have mercy on your soul.' The words had a purity about them. Lord Basingstoke yearned for the day when he could sit in any court in the land and hear them pronounced by God-fearing judges, without having some weak-kneed Home Secretary subsequently rescind the sentence.

The gutter press sometimes referred to him as Lord 'The Hemp' Basingstoke, and vilified his dedication. Some said he was obsessed. But that wasn't true. It was God's work he was doing, and with God's help he ...

Before retiring Lord Basingstoke had two rituals. One was to kneel by his bed and pray for the strength he needed to succeed in his mission. When that was done he went to the locked right-hand drawer of his dressing-table. Inside were hemp nooses. Some had been used on the most infamous necks. He had the noose taken from Dr Crippen's neck, and Christie's. The rope was only ever used once. Under a microscope could be seen fibres of the sack that was placed over the murderer's head. The rope was never allowed to touch the neck.

A message formed in Lord Basingstoke's mind as he relocked the drawer. He would achieve his goal this time, it was as though God had spoken to him.

Chapter 26

The coroner's court wasn't far from police headquarters, but DCS Kellan still managed to arrive late. His presence wasn't actually needed; he hadn't been with Bothwell when he was shot; he couldn't enlighten the coroner in any related area; in fact he wasn't being called to give evidence. But he felt he ought to be there; both Hamish Archibald and Vincent Reid were present.

The court was packed, and Kellan could barely squeeze in. He stood at the back and listened to the proceedings as though they were about to throw new light on the murders. They didn't. The hearing served to stir consciences, if nothing else.

Kellan's watery, bloodshot eyes trailed over the backs of people in the court, and he wondered briefly what they were doing there. Morbid curiosity. Those from the news media were there to serve the morbid curiosity of all those who couldn't make it. His gaze settled on Janet Bothwell, at the front of the court. Dressed in black, she was sitting quite erect. Occasionally her shoulders heaved with a disconsolate sob, and she raised a handkerchief to her face. Kellan was curious about the elderly, silver-haired, fleshy-faced man comforting her. As the man turned to her he got a better view, and recognised him from a recent newspaper photograph. It was Lord Basingstoke. Kellan knew about the English peer's dedication to the restoration of capital punishment, and hoped he succeeded. Those who murdered Bothwell deserved nothing less. The coroner seemed to agree.

The verdict of the court was that Superintendent Stuart Bothwell was wilfully murdered during the execution of his duty. The coroner praised Bothwell's immense service to the community, his great courage. 'His one fault, possibly, was that he was too courageous; he was a man almost born out of his time.' He condemned his murder as an act of incomparable barbarism, and appealed to those giving the killers succour to turn them in.

The murder of the bread delivery man might not have happened.

After the hearing the press showed no interest in Kellan, but clamoured to interview Mrs Bothwell, who was making her first public appearance since her husband's death. With the aid of uniformed constables Lord Basingstoke steered the woman through the crush. He directed her every response, and at the same time parried the welter of questions in his reedy, well-bred voice.

Inevitably, 'Are you in favour of the death penalty for the murder of a policeman, Mrs Bothwell?'

Both Kellan and the assistant chief constable had their cars there. But the latter's offer of a lift wasn't merely politeness, Kellan realised.

In his car Vincent Reid removed from his briefcase a copy of a report that Fordham had made to the Assistant Commissioner—Crime concerning the Squad's connection with the mail-train robbery. Goodfellow had sent him a copy. It was a complete vindication of the Squad, stating how they had sent up adequate information for the arrest of Brodie's entire team before the robbery, much less the killing of a policeman, ever took place.

'That's a lot o' bollocks!' Kellan exploded.

The report was long, as they tended to be when there was little success. But the gist of it enraged Kellan, who could only begin to justify his own position by attacking Fordham.

'From the very beginning there's been duplicity, underhandedness on the part o' Fordham. Information he's sent us has been inadequate, incomplete; at times even misleading. I think that bastard is involved in something way over his wee heid, and's noo trying to pull himself clear. Well he'll no' do it at my expense, Vincent. If he wants to drop bombshells, there's one that'll blow him up. Haston's statement. In it he said he gave Fordham all the information he asked for; then Fordham subsequently had him put on the

Glasgow train. Wi' two detectives to mek sure he stayed aboard. Let's see how he'll wriggle out of that.'

The assistant chief constable nodded pensively. 'Aye, we'll ha'e to show them, Ian, they can no' make fools of us.'

It was a grey, wet day, clouds pressed low in the sky. It was a day for dying and for burying; the day reflected what most people felt. The cold March rain earlier that morning had made being on the streets miserable, yet people had turned out; shops had closed along the route of the procession, and some of the nearby factories so that employees could pay their last respects. This was the silent majority who supported law and order, who respected those men dedicated to enforcing it, and mourned their passing in circumstances as tragic as those in which Bothwell had died.

Almost the entire police representation in Glasgow turned out. The cortège wound slowly through the streets, led by the Glasgow police pipe band, who played traditional Scottish airs which alone were enough to make their countrymen weep. The chief constable had promised a funeral in keeping with the esteem in which their brother officer had been held, but even he was surprised at both the immensity and spontaneity of public support. There were barely enough black vehicles in Glasgow to carry the wreaths which flooded in. There was one from every constabulary in the country, most of whom were also represented in person.

The largest gathering was outside the church on Corkerhill Road, Mosspark, where the Bothwells had worshipped on an irregular basis. The church itself, which normally got no more than a couple of dozen worshippers, was packed. TV news cameras and lights added to the flock's discomfort.

In front of the camera the pastor, who conducted the service as he had countless times before, but without heed or appreciation being paid, seized his opportunity. He was being lifted from the rut of disregarded local pastor, and projected into the homes of millions of people across the country. He vilified all criminals as the canker of society, to be purged by the most astringent means that it might make the body whole again.

'... Courageous; fearless; dedicated, these are the words that spring to mind when recalling Stuart Bothwell. A man who never thought too little of his fellow, not even degenerates such as those who killed him; a man for whom no task was too much, no effort too great. A man who feared God and loved his fellows; a man who had a purpose in life. His purpose was to make this country a better, safer place. He made the supreme sacrifice, he gave his life attempting to stem the vile tide of crime that is breaching the dykes of society, threatening to engulf us all. Let him not have died in vain. Let us take up his staff, pray for his strength that we might rid ourselves of those evil parasites ...'

The tone of the service was taken from Lord Basingstoke at a meeting the pastor had had with him and Mrs Bothwell. There had been offers from prominent church figures to conduct the service, but Janet Bothwell had been guided by Lord Basingstoke. He knew from experience that the humble local man better suited his purpose than those turgid, self-opinionated church leaders.

Led by Sergeant McTovey, six police cadets, serving as pallbearers, carried the coffin along the police-flanked road at the head of the cortège. Like an endless snake it moved through the gates of Cardonald cemetery and wound between the headstones to the open hole in the ground.

Standing by the grave while the pastor recited prayers, Kellan remembered his own father's funeral. It had been a far quieter affair. But that wasn't significant. Within hours his father's murderer had been caught, and, after due process, hanged. They had yet to catch Brodie and Connell, and when they were caught they wouldn't hang, even if the cries now coming from Mrs Bothwell eventually moved Parliament to reinstate the death penalty. Watching the coffin disappear into the ground only hardened Kellan's determination to bring the two murderers in, whatever the cost. They had violated his territory. That was the unforgivable sin.

When he got clear of the crowds and across to his car Kellan's driver was missing. He should have stayed with the car. Understandably he had gone to the service, but at that moment Kellan wasn't about to understand. When he showed up he would get a rocket, despite his wife's presence. Kellan didn't have a key and paced agitatedly outside the car.

'Be still, Ian, for goodness sake. Your man'll be here soon enough,' Alice Kellan said patiently.

'Aye. I've only two murderers to catch.'

The woman wasn't impressed.

Kellan turned away to avoid her look; then he noticed the car. There was a deep scratch on the front nearside wing and a mirror had been snapped off. He tensed. The fact that his car couldn't even be left without being vandalised only accentuated the sense of impotence he was currently experiencing. He had to capture Brodie and Connell. That was the only way to redress the balance.

'I think they are now out of the city.'

Kellan made the admission with great reluctance, for it meant he had failed; not only failed to come up to the expectations others had of him, but failed to come up to those he had of himself.

The assistant chief constable had arrived at the same conclusion. He had been seeing the reports indicating the intensity of the manhunt. Detectives had left no stone unturned; no one, especially not two fugitives as vulnerable as Brodie and Connell, could have stayed at large. He nodded, but didn't say anything, waiting instead for Kellan.

'London's their most obvious destination. It's where their contacts are; where their organisation is. They must ha'e got out wi'in minutes of the shooting. That means sharp organizing. This lad Alan Percival we got from both the gun-dealer and the inside man at the GPO.' He paused and looked into the face in uniform, wondering what he was thinking. He wasn't reacting and Kellan felt that the ground was slipping from under him, that he was losing Reid's support. 'I can no' rely on cooperation from London. There's no satisfaction from telexes and telephone messages. I think it right for Glasgow detectives to mek the arrests, not ha'e some London policeman glory in it. I want to tek ma investigation down there, mek sure of them.'

'I doubt they'll welcome you, Ian.'

'Aye, but they'll no' resist me if I'm there.'

Anxiety crept into Kellan's face as he awaited the man's reply. Likely this would be his last and biggest case before retirement. He was desperate not to fail or lose it to foreign detectives.

'What about your work here?'

'Ross Stalker can hold the fort.'

'Good. Then pick your squad. I'll call London and make the arrangements. You're right, of course, it is important that we make the arrests, no matter where the murderers are.'

Kellan felt a huge sense of relief.

Chapter 27

Ordinarily Peter Goodfellow might have resisted such a move as that proposed by the assistant chief constable of Strathclyde. His own detectives were more than capable, should Brodie or Connell be in the London area, and wouldn't need a gang of Glaswegians to assist them. But he had readily agreed to the visit. He saw it as a means of taking the heat out of the Squad's surprisingly far-reaching enquiry into the affairs of O'Connor's, with its ramifications for the Establishment, which were now proving slightly embarrassing for him. This gave him the means of steering Fordham out of those areas without having to declare a vested interest.

Officially blocking an investigation wasn't particularly difficult for him; he had all the authority. Any number of investigations leading into areas similar to those Fordham was reaching had been abruptly terminated in the past, without subsequent questions. But on each of those occasions it had been done with the active consent of the Commissioner, the DPP and sometimes the Attorney-General. He himself had no interest other than that of most senior policemen: maintaining the status quo.

Leaning back in the leather chair in his comfortable office, Goodfellow considered his future as he waited for the Squad Commander to arrive. He wondered if the position as head of security with the O'Connor group was essential to him. As a job per se he suspected not, but for all else it represented it was important. There would be other lucrative jobs on retirement; the Post Office, insurance companies, banks, security firms; but none carrying the same status. He would have security, comfort, the opportunity to travel to check their operations abroad, but most of all the position carried an associate directorship in the parent company. That pleased his wife greatly. He was a policeman who had no intention of retiring simply to write his memoirs.

The brushed stainless steel intercom on his desk buzzed. 'Commander Pope is here, sir,' his secretary said.

'Have him come in. And no calls, Ruth.'

When informed of the Scotsmen's imminent arrival Gerald Pope wasn't pleased. Then the ACC never imagined he would be. Policemen got very possessive about fields of operation.

'They're not needed, I wouldn't have thought. John Fordham's handling this end all right.' Pope's argument was reasonable, but not forceful.

'Tell him to leave all other aspects of the case for now. I can't see that he's making any progress. Personally I doubt there's anything resembling a case.'

'He feels the whole thing's about to crack open.'

Mild interest was all the ACC allowed. He waited for the commander to elaborate, and when he didn't, 'Doubtless he's felt that for the past fifteen months, Gerald. Full marks for effort and perseverence.'

'Wouldn't it be better to let Mr Kellan work with the Regional or Serious Crime Squads, leaving my Squad free?' Pope suggested. But his boss wasn't buying it.

'Your lads have been on this from the start. Better it stays in their court. Kellan will be based out at Tintagel House. It's the only place there's room.'

'How many are coming down?'

'In the region of thirty, I believe.'

'Sounds like a sheriff's posse.'

The ACC smiled at the thought. 'Have John Fordham concentrate his energy on the murder hunt. I mean *all* his energy. That's the Squad's priority. I think perhaps we ought to let it be seen that we don't really need a posse to do our job. But at the same time, Kellan should get all the cooperation the Squad would themselves expect in Glasgow.' There was no awareness of the irony of what he said.

Fordham screamed when he got the news. 'What the fuck.' It wasn't a question. 'I'd say a gang of Jocks is about the last thing we need, Gerald.'

'My sentiments entirely,' Pope responded in his imperturbable manner.

'Any good my seeing the old man?'

Shaking his head, Pope said, 'None at all. He didn't leave any opportunity for argument. His decision's made. They're on their way.'

Recalling the information about the ACC's retirement aspirations, Fordham wondered if they had any bearing, or whether he was simply becoming paranoid. The ramifications of the case were enough to make him uneasy, for the tendrils of corruption spread, not merely through the police hierarchy, but through local and national government offices as well. Fordham considered where, if the need arose, he might finally turn in confidence, with three of the five main institutions involved, namely government, police and commerce. There was only the church and the media left. He wasn't so sure about the latter, and wasn't likely to turn to the church.

Paranoia or not, he had no intention of letting go his over-all enquiry, especially not after they had got so far. Nor could he guarantee the sort of help Kellan would receive.

Returning to his office to get things organized, Fordham found the fourth floor more deserted than it should have been for that time of evening. He remembered the party to celebrate Malcolm Dyce's promotion.

The party was being held in a small club off Victoria Street. It was the sort of place where policemen felt comfortable. It was neither smart nor fashionable; the prices weren't too far over the odds and the women working there got fucked without charging. The Squad held functions there whenever they had anything worth celebrating, and almost anything could be blown up to afford them the excuse. One detective did most of the organizing, Sergeant Mark Howell. He booked the club, got the rates for booze, arranged the entertainment; sometimes comics, strippers, blue films or a combination. He knew a lot of people in show business, got to see most shows in the West End. He saw everything at the National; Fordham didn't even see things Kika was in.

Fordham was expected to put in an appearance, though he didn't feel much like it. However, he had no choice, as he wanted some work done in readiness for Kellan, and that was where his men were.

The club was L-shaped but not large. Along the main stroke of the L was a bar, at the bottom of the short stroke a small stage with a proscenium arch. The room was smoky and noisy and reeked of booze. Waitresses in bathing costumes and fishnet tights wove through the hundred odd Ds who had jammed the place, serving drinks without spilling one, despite frequently being groped.

Fordham didn't remove his coat, but got a drink and, locating the newly promoted superintendent, toasted his future. Dyce, like many of the detectives, had had a lot to drink.

'You missed the best act, guv,' Dyce shouted. 'A pair of strippers; talk about form. They did everything, including plating each other.' He laughed.

Fordham's eyes turned instinctively towards the stage to the little fat comic there. It took him a moment to tune to his heavy Brummie accent. His face seemed vaguely familiar. He was bald on the top of his head, but around the sides hair grew exceeding long; the effect was very comical. His name was Laurie James. Another of DS Howell's curious friends; the comic would have come expensive to hire straight. His general appearance didn't suggest homosexuality, only occasional intonation and butterfly mannerisms. His patter was endless, some of it made Fordham laugh.

'... I've heard about captive audiences, but this is ridiculous – captive comedian. I don't have to be here, you know. I could've been busted instead.' His ring-adorned fingers flicked his hair while policemen laughed. As they quietened, DCI Borroughs belched. 'Ooh,' James intoned, 'ask her if she's got a friend, will you? That brought hoots of laughter. 'Did you see the terrible two earlier? Frightened the life out of me when they took those costumes off – they're fellas.' He singled out a detective. 'We all make mistakes, son ... Two lads, Bill and Ben. The foulest mouthed kids you ever heard. Never, "Where's m' clean pants please, Mum?" But, "Where's m' fucking pants, you old bitch?" Anyway, their parents, so fed up with this, decide that the only way to stop their swearing is to beat fuck out of them the next time either one swore. Next morning Bill's mother asks what he'd like for breakfast. "Some fucking cornflakes." Before the words are out of his mouth, Dad's up from his chair, punching and kicking him, pounding him into a horrible bloody mess. Sitting back at the table, the father asked Ben want he wants for breakfast. Ben shrugs, "Well, I'd be a cunt to ask for cornflakes."'

The entire club erupted. The comic waited, glorying in it. The laughter took a long while to fade.

As the patter continued, Fordham edged his way over to where Borroughs and Corrigan were sitting. Conversation was difficult and Fordham didn't want to shout. He put his hand over Burroughs's glass.

'Make it the last here, Frank. Trevor.'

He caught the eye of the tall stooped figure of Ned Garmonsway, and told him to come along also.

Fordham made his apologies to Dyce, and departed with Bill Senior, leaving the others to make their own way.

The four detectives were collectively pissed off about the arrival of the Jocks, especially for the fact that it was the Squad who had to accommodate them.

Up in his office Fordham removed his bottle of scotch and paper cups. 'Sorry I haven't got any strippers.'

'Did you see them, guv? I bet there were a few cockstands there tonight,' Trevor Corrigan commented. He was short and round, and easily marked by his mannerisms and style of dressing. The most striking feature of Corrigan were his brown eyes, which were unusual as his hair and complexion were fair.

'You know me, Trevor. Doesn't cut much ice. My only interest's work.' Some might have believed him, despite his smile. 'Talking of which, we've a lot to get through. Let's hope Kellan doesn't want briefing the second he arrives.'

'When's he getting in?' Borroughs asked.

'Any time now. So let's make a start. Every piece of information in any way connected with what we've been investigating has got to be sifted, evaluated, then either given to the Jocks or put aside for our exclusive use. Ideally I want them to have nothing that doesn't relate directly to the Glasgow blag.'

'I mean, what the fuck are they coming down for, precisely?' Borroughs asked.

Fordham looked at him, wondering how much he had had to drink, whether he would last the night.

'Specifically to capture Brodie and Connell.'

'Why don't they leave it to us?' Garmonsway said. 'We'll find them a lot quicker.'

'Because they fucked up in Glasgow, and Kellan knows it. What they're doing is trying to redeem themselves. My bet is they won't give a shit who or what they wreck in the process. That's why I don't want them getting any of the wrong stuff. The two names essential to keep from them are Day and Ryman. I don't want the Jocks getting lucky and nicking them so that finally we can't make any trade-off for Duckett. A lot of work for you, Trevor.'

'Whenever hasn't there been?'

'I want you as briefing officer. Also to act as collator on all information that comes in. Make sure you separate what's for us and what's all right for them to see.'

'What about Jack Owen and Willy Winkle?' he asked, in deference to the two superintendents.

'They'll have to cope with all the other stuff we've got. It's not going to stop just because some Jocks are in town.'

'Our priority is actually Brodie and Connell?'

'They murdered a policeman, Ned,' Fordham replied ambiguously. 'But like I said, everything doesn't stop. I'm not letting go all the inroads we've made.' He turned to Senior. 'Bill, get some reliable Squad drivers for them, rather than the drivers they'll be allocated. That way we'll know what they're up to. Also you'd better have some of our lads standing by to work with them.'

'You think he'll want to use them?'

'Not for a moment, but we're cooperating. So let Kellan say he doesn't want them.'

He anticipated Kellan crossing his lines and screwing up all manner of things, unless he employed every possible safeguard. 'Have Brian Lemon report to me in the morning.'

That would provide one more safeguard. He would have Hawkeye Lemon follow the Scottish DCS constantly, just in case he tried to steal a march.

Fordham capped the scotch bottle.

'Shall we get some work done, then?'

Chapter 28

The Glasgow train slid into platform five at Euston, the noise of the air-brakes reaching a crescendo. From the rear door in the fourth carriage stepped Ian Kellan, carrying a large, over-stuffed briefcase and a grip. Thirty other detectives disembarked, all similarly equipped. The briefcase and overnight bag might have been standard. The men formed into two bunches as they moved off. Detective Inspector Murray and DS Gallbraith broke off when they reached the front of the train. They had to ensure that the four filing cabinets, full of case papers, got unloaded safely.

Up on the main concourse a uniformed chief inspector waited. He moved forward as the Scotsmen came through the barrier, recognizing Kellan from his recent newspaper photographs. He saluted.

'Chief superintendent. Welcome to London, sir. My name is Hollis. I'm to escort you and your men to your office and living quarters.'

Kellan gave him a measured look, then simply handed him his grip. The move surprised Hollis, but he recovered himself and led the way downstairs to where the green single-decker bus was parked.

'We've had to accommodate you out at Wandsworth, sir,' Hollis was saying in the easy manner of a PR man.

'Where's that, laddie?' He had only a vague geography of London from infrequent visits.

'Five miles south-west of Tintagel House.'

'A long way in London traffic, chief,' Douglas said as they reached the bus.

'The only place we could put you all together.'

'We ha'e no' need to hold each other's hands. Find somewhere closer, even if it means a hotel.' Kellan was determined not to give an inch.

'We have a van for your filing cabinets.'

There were just two vehicles. The bus and the black

fifteen-hundredweight police van.

'Where's Mr Kellan's car?' Douglas asked as detectives boarded the bus.

'There isn't one,' Hollis said, adding ingenuously, 'It was thought he'd prefer to travel with his men.'

He glanced apologetically at Kellan, who stood bristling. The chief inspector realised the error.

'The inference being that I might get lost on ma own,' Kellan said tartly. 'S'that it?'

The chief inspector began to apologize, but Kellan wasn't interested. He stepped up into the bus, allowing London that point. It was the only one he was going to give them. He might have resisted, made an issue over the car, had he not been impatient to get on.

Tintagel House is a tall, fairly modern police administration building, situated along Albert Embankment on the south side of the Thames between Lambeth and Vauxhall Bridges. Like most purpose-built buildings, certainly those used by the police, it had swiftly become too small for its purpose. In addition to administration, several operational squads use it as their headquarters.

The three offices to which Kellan was assigned might have comfortably accommodated three detectives. The Scottish DCS surveyed them with evident displeasure. Not only were the interjoining rooms small, the half-glass partitions dividing them provided Kellan with no separate office. This was another way of seeking to crush and confound him. He knew existence in London would be a constant struggle for survival.

'A briefing has been called for ten o'clock tomorrow morning, sir,' Hollis informed him. 'That'll be in the briefing room on the third floor. If there is anything else I can be of assistance with . . .'

'Aye,' He glanced disdainfully at the two telephones on the table at the far end of the largest office. 'There's no' enough telephones. I want two more out there. Two in here, one there. At least three direct-dial lines. Also we'll want a telex machine. Now transport. What ha'e you – or are we supposed to travel *en masse* in that bus?'

'Transport's being arranged, sir. Six cars will . . .'

'S'no' enough. I've got thirty men here. I'll no' want more than four of them in these offices. That means a dozen cars, not less. Ten o'clock briefing you say? What is it youse work here, a nine to five day? Are you no' aware a policeman has been murdered?' Kellan was irritated and becoming more so. He dismissed Hollis before he could offer more excuses. 'Just mek those arrangements, laddie, that's all.'

'We're gonna survive down here, Dougie. That I guarantee,' he said after Hollis had departed.

Kellan lifted his briefcase and carried it into the smaller of the three partitioned offices. Douglas followed, as other detectives continued to drift in, opening drawers, lifting telephones, complaining about the lack of space, which was reduced further by the four filing cabinets.

Having slept a couple of hours on the train, Kellan felt refreshed and was impatient to get started. He accepted that for various reasons it wasn't practical to get going immediately.

'Tell the lads to get a good night's sleep, Dougie. It might be their last for a while. And tell them no' to drink too much. I'll no' want them showing up tomorrow looking and smelling like something from the Sunday-morning gutters. We'll show these Sassenach bastards we mean business.'

He had always taken a pride in his nationalism, but now he felt excessively jingoistic.

When he saw the briefing room next day Kellan immediately decided he would try and commandeer it as his operations room. It would be ideal, its size more in keeping with the importance of his investigation.

The Scottish detectives were first to assemble, some of the more senior sitting at the oblong table in the centre of the room. Others arranged themselves against windowsills and on the edges of side tables.

The first of the Squad detectives to arrive took up positions on the opposite side of the room. Inevitably the rest followed suit, so that by the time Fordham got there, coincidentally with the ACC, whom he met in the lift, there was a distinct division, the centre of the table being the line of demarcation.

Kellan immediately saw treachery in Goodfellow's and Fordham's arrival together. Twice he had rung the DCS this morning, only to be told he wasn't in. He should have tried the ACC's office.

Goodfellow moved around the table to greet the head of Strathclyde CID. Kellan, like all the detectives who had been sitting, stood at the ACC's entrance.

'Pleased to meet you, Mr Kellan,' the ACC said, shaking his hand perfunctorily. It wasn't that he believed Kellan had brought some virulent disease with him from Scotland, just that Goodfellow wasn't a tactile person. 'Let's hope your visit is a first rate success.'

'Let's hope so, sir,' Kellan replied brusquely, and glanced at Fordham, who stood on the opposite side of the table. 'Chief superintendent,' he said grudgingly.

'Chief superintendent,' Fordham responded.

The two senior detectives held each other's look, and most of the other detectives' attention. Sparks were expected.

'Sit down, gentlemen,' the ACC said, taking his place at the head of the table, where his aide had been arranging papers. Goodfellow studied his notes during the scraping and adjusting of chairs. He looked up.

'Commander Pope not attending?'

The question was directed at Fordham, but DCI Corrigan, who was distributing notes, answered.

'Sends his apologies, sir. Said he would be a few minutes late. Traffic.'

The ACC's preliminary remarks were brief. He welcomed the Scots detectives, reiterated why they were there, said they would be rendered every cooperation in fulfilling their task, and extended to them the full resources of the Metropolitan police. He then called upon Fordham to open the briefing.

The Squad DCS didn't attempt to rise. He had little to

say, having decided it was better to let Corrigan do most of the talking.

Leaning back in his chair, Fordham said, 'I've made Chief Inspector Corrigan the collator. He will liaise between our two groups and continue to process all the information and put it into priority categories. As I'm sure you'll appreciate a lot of the stuff we're getting is from cranks – Trevor Corrigan has a particularly good nose for sorting them out. Their information still has to be investigated, but not with the urgency of that with a higher grading. So, unless Mr Kellan's any objections, I'll let DCI Corrigan précis the main points.'

There was no objection. There was none Kellan could reasonably make to Corrigan's position as collator. Even to suggest that one of his own men sort it out with him was to imply mistrust.

As Corrigan rose, Commander Pope arrived. He apologized for his lateness and took a chair at the table, helping himself to copies of the xeroxed notes.

'From the most recent reports we've had,' Corrigan began, 'there now seems no doubt about Connell and Brodie being in the London area. Also they have split up. Both men would appear to have been abandoned by their organization though we can't be sure . . .'

'What makes you think so?' McFageon asked.

'You are?' the ACC enquired.

'McFageon, sir. Chief inspector.'

'They're both foot-loose, so to speak. We've had a couple of close misses with them. They seem to be running scared. Panicky. This doesn't suggest the efficiency that planned the robbery.' He waited, but McFageon didn't come back.

'Perhaps when asking questions you'd identify yourselves so that we get to know each other a lot quicker,' the ACC said. 'Carry on, Corrigan.'

'However, this same abandonment can't be said for the underworld in general. At least, not in Brodie's case. Then this is probably due both to the forty thousand pounds he got away with, and the belief that it was Connell who did the shooting.'

'We have statements to the contrary,' Kellan said. 'Brodie had the shotgun when they ran through the laundry.'

The Squad were purposely trying to lower Brodie's profile in order to mitigate their part in his involvement.

Corrigan said, 'It's our opinion, chief superintendent, that this kind of violence wasn't in Brodie's character . . .'

'He broke his wife's legs. Is that not so? After escaping from prison.'

'A personal matter,' Fordham said dismissively.

'Personal? Breaking a woman's legs?' There was contempt in his tone. 'An animal like that would no' think anything of shooting a policeman about to arrest him.'

'He was a professional criminal. As such, less likely to have used the gun in panic. It's only an opinion.'

That left Kellan no room to manoeuvre.

The two DCSs stared at each other, then back at Corrigan.

'You have in front of you, or should have, a number of reports. From these you will see that the investigation has been two-pronged. The search for Brodie has been concentrated in West London, where most of his time here has been spent. It's rumoured that he has the forty thousand. Which makes the search for Connell a very different kettle of fish, particularly as he has Maureen Hoyle with him . . .'

After Fordham had departed to his bed all too few hours ago, Corrigan and Ned Garmonsway had stayed on and put a lot more work into the sifted material, knocking it into intelligible and intelligent order so that there weren't too many holes apparent. There were reams of information for the Jocks to work through. Most of it Fordham had either checked out or dismissed as it neither cut the corners he wanted to cut, nor took him in the direction he wanted to go. Nevertheless in there were the names of some good villains and some potential crimes worth pursuing, had the Squad's priorities not been elsewhere.

When it was Kellan's turn to speak, he chose to stand. He had had his plan of operation mapped out before ever coming to the briefing. The London underworld was hiding Brodie and Connell, and would offer them up if handled right. He knew just how the underworld was being handled by the Squad, with favours and trade-offs, though wasn't prepared to reveal his hand by saying so at this meeting.

'I do no' believe in the efficacy of molly-coddling violent criminals, or soliciting their active cooperation and so putting myself in their debt.' He glanced casually at Fordham. 'The only way to handle them is to recognize 'em for what they are; scum, parasites, blots on society. They should be pressured so that breathing the same air as you and me is difficult; pushed so hard that they ha'e to deliver the goods.' He paused for effect. 'And believe me they will.'

Fordham tapped his thumb thoughtfully with a pencil in the silence that followed.

'As a general principle,' Fordham began, politely, 'what the chief superintendent says makes sense. Blitzing the London underworld might get what we're after a little quicker, I don't know. But it would certainly upset a lot of delicate relationships that are proving immensely valuable in over-all police terms.'

Seeing the means and direction he wanted things to go in, Peter Goodfellow said, 'Let us not forget that a policeman has been murdered. Every assistance should be rendered to Chief Superintendent Kellan to bring the two murderers in with the greatest speed.'

The urge rose in Fordham to remind the ACC that other major crimes were being committed and would have to be solved after the inevitable arrest of Connell and Brodie. He resisted. He saw through the man, and accepted his move for what it was.

Having been given *carte-blanche* by the ACC, Kellan immediately proceeded to crash the underworld, arresting anyone who looked remotely like a suspect. There was little Fordham could do to prevent him bruising villains and souring hitherto productive relations, so simply allowed him to get on with it, deploying the bulk of the Squad's energies elsewhere.

The names which the Squad had given the Jocks were only a starting point. After interrogating them other names inevitably went on offer; that was thc only way Kellan's men were letting even a fraction of pressure off.

McFageon and eight armed detectives raided a drinking club in Ealing. They weren't admitted politely, nor asked to sign the guest book.

'Everybody who's in here, Murdock,' McFageon said to one of the DSs. He moved out through the club with two other detectives.

In the passageway a man wearing a loud check sports-jacket, with a lady, was hurriedly trying to open the rusty locks on the back door.

'Frank Simpson?'

'One minute, friend!'

The heavy-set barman, who had followed the DCI, caught his arm. McFageon reached up one of the beer bottles over-spilling the crates stacked in the passage and, turning, crashed it across the barman's head. He didn't have anything else to say, but sank to his knees, blood tipping down his forehead.

'He's done – assaulting a police officer.' He turned back to Simpson, who offered no resistance. His girl-friend was screaming. 'Shut the wee hooar up, or she'll get some.'

All those present in the club were taken to the local police station for questioning.

Curtains twitched in Shepherd's Bush Road as a black man was dragged unceremoniously by the feet from the house by two Scottish detectives. He clutched desperately at the doorframe. The third detective, DS Andrews, kicked his fingers. There was a small scuffle getting him into the car. The black man didn't want to go with the nice detectives!

The darkness of the bedsitter felt oppressive to DI Murry as he waited with DC Daly. He wondered if the man calling himself Denis Tyson would show. Possibly someone had warned him. Whether he would, in fact, prove to be Brodie was another matter.

The DI had grown accustomed to the smell of the place, and was hardly aware of it. How people lived like this he didn't know. The old poof who had tipped them off seemed to live in even worse squalor in the room next door. He had viewed fat Kevin Daly with a disgusting yearning when they had checked out his place. Daly would have put a fist in his mouth had he seen the look.

His personal radio crackled. 'He's away in,' a voice said.

Murry acknowledged brusquely.

He tensed when a key scraped the lock. The door swung open. His lads in the street had remained well concealed.

Throwing on the light and seeing the two men, Tyson knew immediately what they were. He ran, but didn't make the first half-landing before Daly's fist hit him squarely between the shoulder blades.

Had it been Brodie they might have shot him. He was taken back to the room.

'What did you run for?' asked Murry, lighting the cigarette he had resisted for the past hour.

'Remembered I had one to meet,' the man said sarcastically, his Scots accent barely detectable.

'That was no' polite after we'd waited. Who are you? Whit's your name?'

'I might ask the fucking same of you?'

Murry smiled. 'I dinnae think you need to.' He pushed the radio on. 'It's no' Brodie, but I'd say he wis a candidate for something. We'll bring him down.'

'Now wait. I ain't done nothing. What are you taking me in for?'

'People who ha'e no' done anything dinnae run from police officers.'

'How was I to know?' the man tried.

Murry shook his head solemnly. The man would be taken to Notting Hill police station, printed, identified, interrogated. There was doubtless something about him that wouldn't bear police scrutiny. But whether he could give them either Brodie or Connell . . .

'You practise inna dark, don't you?' The question suddenly thrown in by Sergeant Gallbraith confused the suspect.

'What?'

'Practise in the dark, don't you?'

'I dunno what you're talking about.'

'Of course ya do. You practise in the dark, don't you? Don't you? Practise in the dark?'

It wasn't perversity that caused the DS to ask the apparently nonsensical question, or for him to repeat it over and over. It was designed to wear the suspect down. Having him admit that he practised in the dark, as he eventually would, was the point in the interrogation from which everything could go the detective's way.

Maurice Royston was another suspect who wasn't able to give them either Brodie or Connell, but he was involved in other areas, which caused his discomfort.

Graves-Charlton had been hearing a lot about the aggravation those Scots detectives had been causing over the past forty-eight hours. It seemed no one was safe. He was just a pop record distributor, and bent nothing out of the way; even so he didn't want any truck with the filth, not if it meant the sort of hassles one-time associates on shadier deals were now getting. He wondered about the call from Balham nick he had on the line as he waited for John Clerides to be connected. Perhaps he should just hang up and make himself scarce, not get involved. Why the fuck Clerides had called him and not his silk he couldn't think.

There was a click and Clerides came on in his whining, broken English, explaining how he had been picked up. He sounded subdued, but Graves-Charlton assumed that that was because there were probably policemen around.

'Look, don't take nothing from them, son, no shit. Know what I mean? They've got nothing on you, John. I'll call your brief, and see what he's got to say.'

John Clerides, a portly Greek-Cypriot, stood in the ground-floor charge room in Balham police station, naked but for a blanket that smelled of disinfectant. A uniformed sergeant of about the same stamp as Clerides leant on the tall desk which, apart from one wooden bench against a wall, was the sole item of furniture, and watched the man with disdain. Two Glaswegian detectives watched also, making sure Clerides said no more than they'd agreed.

'Is not me dey wan', is dat other fuckers, Connell and his mate. Why don't someone give dem? Den I get dese fuckers off me back?'

'Stand on what I tell you, John. You've nothing to worry about, son. Leave it to me.'

Graves-Charlton put the phone down. He wasn't getting involved further. In fact he was going to take a holiday, leaving his answering service to cope. Lock his one-room office on the corner of Oxford and Berwick Streets, with its framed signed photos of pop stars, and let the Jocks take London apart.

Not having a secretary, visitors knocked on the door and, if he was inclined, Graves-Charlton opened it. DCI Crombie didn't knock. He just walked in with another detective.

'Who the fuck are you?'

'Let's no' do this the hard way now, Mr Charlton.'

Common sense prevailed. Graves-Charlton didn't, after all, know where Brian Connell was, and only knew him via business associates.

McFageon was growing increasingly frustrated. Not at the time his detectives were taking. It was the sense of futility in all their efforts. They seemed to be getting nowhere. His men were feeling the same way, at some cost to morale.

He watched as Franklyn was brought out of the converted house and hustled into the car next to him. The DCI had a dull ache at the back of his neck, and a prickling sensation in his eyes. He wanted simply to get pissed and then sleep for about twenty-four hours.

'Where are they, Franklyn?' he asked routinely.

'You've got to be kidding me. Like I told laughing boy, I wouldn't have anything to do with those jokers.'

'S'no' whit we heard. Your name was given us.'

'Well, any old mug can go and stick up a few names, can't he. Who was it? Some slag.'

'Why don't you try us wi' a few?'

'Not my game, friend, is it. I'm no grass.'

'Extortion's your game. S'what we heard. Whit we've got on you . . . It's gonna cost you plenty.'

Franklyn looked at the DCI, then at the Ds who had remained outside the car. He realised now why they had stayed outside. He smiled.

'I knew you Jocks could be as sensible as the London filth. How much we talking about?'

'We're not. No' this time, laddie. I wis referring to whit you could get for this wee extortion . . . involving one Albert Wilder.'

'What the fu . . .?' He choked off his surprise. 'There's got to be some give and take here. Know what I mean, friend?'

'Gi' us Brodie then,' McFageon said bluntly.

'You think I wouldn't to get out of this?'

'Who can ya gi' us then?' McFageon wasn't looking to trade, he intended having the local CID charge him anyway.

The man hesitated. 'Have a word with Jackie Roach.'

Roach ran a pub in Hammersmith; his wife held the licence, as Roach had form. Not wanting a scene in the crowded bar room, McFageon waited in the outside toilet while two Ds invited Roach out. The car would have done, but the DCI needed to shed the poisonous hot dogs and meat pies he had consumed over the past couple of days. He emerged from the single WC in the now rather evil-smelling toilets as Roach entered the urinal area.

The publican reacted with distaste to the smell.

'I suppose yourn comes out lek roses.'

'They said you wanted a word. What's wrong with inside?'

'This place is more apt. Brodie. We were told you could

deliver him.'

'Who?' – he tried.

The detective didn't respond.

'No, not likely. You're out of luck there, pal. Don't know the fella.'

'He's around somewhere. You ha'e the run o' the manor, so I've been told. A wee sparrow cannae fart wi'oot your knowing.'

'Whoever told you that's having a game with you, pal. All I do is run a pub. You've got the wrong name . . .'

The man's sneering attitude angered McFageon; so he hit him, knocking him back against the urinal wall. The blow surprised and angered Roach.

'Look, if some Scotch wolly chooses to run into a shotgun . . .' He didn't finish.

The DCI hit the man with a series of stunning blows. He crashed against the wall again, only this time his legs buckled. McFageon kicked him, then motioned the two detectives from the entrance.

'Search him.'

Searching Roach's pain-racked body where he lay with his shoulder in the half-filled trough of urine and cigarette butts, the detectives found a wallet, change, keys, a penknife; then, as if by the merest chance, a pair of brass knuckles which would get him charged.

'Fucking filth . . .' Roach muttered.

'Pick him up.'

They did, and McFageon hit the man some more.

Kellan's eyes were sore from the reports he had read over the past three days. He rarely wore the spectacles he had been prescribed, as though to do so was an admission of age. His head buzzed from the interrogations he had conducted himself. He felt dejected, demoralized; more so than any of his men, because he was expected to produce the results, therefore it was his name that was synonymous with failure. But that wasn't all. The more reports he read, the more interviews he conducted, the greater the feeling he got of incompleteness, that he had been taken for a ride.

'We're busting a lot o' heids, Dougie,' he said despondently, pushing out of the chair at the small desk. 'But that's all. There are no real patterns, no ladders, only bloody circles. They are peripheral characters who lead us nowhere.'

Douglas leant back from the report covered desk, without attempting to interrupt. He figured his boss would crack-up if he didn't either ease off or get a result soon.

'I know we're teking a lot o' neds in. But I've got the feeling someone has always been there aheid of us wi' some other kind of proposition, or if they ha'e no', could ha'e been and do no' care whether we get there.' He paused and rubbed his head, pulling a face that indicated pain. 'Get me Fordham onna phone, Dougie.'

Kellan returned to the paperwork.

Both prongs of the investigation under DCIs McFageon and Crombie were achieving almost identical results. Such consistency couldn't be coincidence alone, Kellan was certain.

Douglas covered the mouthpiece of the phone, having been told by Bill Senior that Fordham was in a meeting. The DCS flared up at this information.

'Gi' us that.' He snatched the receiver. 'You tell Mr Bloody Fordham that I'm coming to see him, and by God he'd better be there.'

He allowed no reply, but smashed the handset back, causing detectives in the other two offices to look round. They had known a showdown was coming, and as far as most of them were concerned it wasn't a moment too soon.

Kellan's large strides carried him swiftly along the fourth-floor corridor at Scotland Yard. Douglas had to put in extra steps to keep pace. The two Glaswegian detectives received strange looks from Squad Ds. Douglas stopped at the doorway as Kellan banged on into the DCS's office. Fordham was at his desk. His aide was present also.

'Oot!' Kellan said to the DI, jerking his thumb at the door.

Senior glanced at his governor, who nodded.

'You tricky wee man. Just whit the fuck do you think you're playing at?'

Fordham's professed innocence had a sound ring. 'What are you talking about? What's the problem that brings you in here like a screaming lunatic?'

'Screaming lunatic, is it?' Kellan bore down on his opposite number, thumping the desk as though about to heave it aside. 'You took us fur a load o' idiots, wi' all that rubbish you put us on to, while you try and steal the glory.'

'Glory, who needs that? I heard you were getting results.'

'Aye. Wasting our time while Brodie and Connell get farther from us, man.'

'That was all we came up with. We're passing on everything we get as we get it.' He was beginning to feel uncomfortable with Kellan's bearing down on him, and rose from his desk.

'You know better. You ken a lot more than you're letting on, laddie.'

'You're not thinking logically, Kellan. There's no reason I wouldn't want those bastards brought in...'

'Aye, by your men alone.'

Fordham shook his head, in dismay rather than denial.

'Go back to Scotland. We'll find your killers.'

'Course you will. You put those neds on the train in the first place.'

'I expected you to take them off.'

Kellan bristled, but didn't have an immediate answer. 'There's but one way I'm going back. That's wi' Brodie and Connell.'

'Then stay the fuck out of my way,' Fordham said, 'and I'll find them for you.'

'Whit if I don't, laddie? Whit'll you do, punch me in the kneecaps?'

It was a possibility, Kellan being five and a half inches taller. Fordham almost laughed. He suspected the man was a borderline paranoid; doubtless his feelings were made worse by the Squad's conduct. But John Fordham was a realist, who had to stay afloat, getting results after Kellan's eventual departure.

Shutting a door to shut in a row within the precincts of Scotland Yard was pointless. The walls were thin, and what had gone on between Kellan and Fordham soon permeated the entire building.

Despite the straightener, possibly because of it, the situation didn't improve for Kellan. He continued to struggle forward into more significant areas of the underworld, his feelings of frustration becoming increasingly random. Instead of blasting detectives as they turned in results which fetched them no closer to the two fugitives, he found himself apologizing, making excuses.

The following morning he received a call from Angus Bingham, who had heard that Kellan was having problems. They arranged to meet for lunch at St Ermin's Hotel, just along the road from the Yard. Kellan felt he could ill afford the time, but had an urgent need to talk to someone who wasn't intensely involved. He knew Bingham from when he had been a uniformed chief superintendent with the Ayrshire constabulary. He could never understand why the man had wanted to come south, even with promotion.

'You don't change, Ian,' Bingham said, rising from the table as Kellan joined him.

'The life does no' seem to be treating you so bad. You've put on a bit. Too many fancy meals.'

'Aye, I dare say. I dare say. Well, sit you down, and have a drink.'

Kellan looked carefully around the restaurant as he sat. It was a place senior policemen from the Yard used, and he didn't particularly want to run into Fordham.

Both men selected simple, inexpensive dishes, as though each believed the other was his guest, and drank beer with the meal.

Throughout the lunch they avoided the topic that was preoccupying them, reminiscing instead about their past, the good old days, when it was relatively easy to define the role of a policeman.

'He's a canny wee bass, Ian, and no mistake,' Bingham said, apropos of nothing that had gone before.

Kellan knew immediately to whom he was referring.

'Aye, so I'm discovering. He's given us a lot o' stuff that's got us nowhere. And knew just where it would get us. But what I cannae understand is *why*. Damn it, he's a policeman, the same as you and me.'

'Vested interest. I've no' been able to get to the bottom of all he's been up to. But given time . . .' He saw Kellan's puzzled expression. 'Did you no' ken he was being investigated?'

'I'm no' surprised, Angus.'

'The way that man operates, everything and anything's expedient provided the result is right. I'd no' be surprised if he does no' have some knowledge where those two murderers are, and's simply waiting his most favourable moment.' He paused and studied Kellan's look which took on an intensity that had been absent throughout lunch. 'He's a great one for making deals, Ian, wi' bastards we wouldn't waste our breath on. Trade-offs he calls them. Checks and balances. Corruption by another name.'

'Is there no way your department can move?'

The two senior policemen, having started on a common enemy, didn't stop. Lunch crept away into afternoon tea. Anticipating Fordham's come-down from his exalted position made the two men cheerful. Before departing, the A10 commander gave Kellan the names of various felons he had come upon during his investigation. Included on the list was the name Charles Ryman; just a name, indicating a peripheral character of no particular importance.

There was new heart in Kellan when he got back to his office. He was almost cheerful.

'Run a check on all of these, Dougie,' he said, handing his DI Bingham's list. 'I want them all interviewed – most of them have records over at CRO.'

There were still two murderers to capture.

Chapter 29

Working on the names Bingham had supplied, Kellan started a new blitz, hitting all suspects with any kind of connection that led back to Fordham. From each he demanded at least one name before he would even consider any alternative, and the villains produced the names, trying to get pressure off themselves and on to someone else.

Progress was made. Alan Day's name came up as a possible for the draftsman. The address the Jocks got was the only one anybody had: Camden Town. It was raided, but there was no sign of Day nor any evidence which tied him into the Glasgow robbery.

The raid was witnessed by the Squad detective on watch at the house, and reported back to Fordham.

'The landlady was pretty helpful,' DI Murry told Kellan back at the office. 'She said that Day disappeared shortly before the other policemen with guns raided his place.'

'Who were they? Fordham's lot?'

'They dinnae identify themselves, boss. But it was the same day as Superintendent Bothwell was shot.'

DI Douglas came into the office. 'There's no CRO file on Day, but C11 had a file which they passed to Fordham two weeks ago. They're sending over a copy. These are the main points.'

Kellan studied the handwritten sheet. At length he said, 'There's getting to be less doubt about it. Alan Percival and Alan Day, they're almost certainly one and the same. If we can locate this laddie ... Get on to the Squad, Dougie. I want all they've got on Day, and I'll not tek no for an answer. If they want to argue, then it'll be in the ACC's office.' The phone rang and he let Douglas answer it. Turning to Murry, he said, 'Get on to all those even suspected of being involved with Day. Possibly Criminal Intelligence can improve on this.' He glanced at his aide.

'S'your lad on again,' Douglas said.

Kellan hesitated, about to dismiss the boy; then impulsively reached for the phone. Douglas went out after his colleague, shutting the door.

'Kellan,' the man said, sounding from habit like a detective rather than a father. He hardly recognized his son's voice. There was little trace of an accent. That instantly rankled.

'What is it you want, David?' Kellan asked coldly.

His son wanted to meet with him, and suggested the Festival Hall cafeteria.

'I'm up to my eyes. I do no' ha'e the time . . .'

'You never had time, did you,' the young man said angrily. 'I'll be there whether you make it or not.'

The line went dead. Kellan did not move for a moment, wondering whether it was conceivably his fault that his son had turned out a religious fanatic. Perhaps his constant involvement with work had been an excuse for not getting closer; he wondered, had David followed the family tradition in the police, he might have been just as disappointed in him. But David was family and as such, despite their past differences, might provide some relief, Kellan felt, some neutral ground beyond the pressure he was getting.

David Kellan was as tall as his father but half his weight. His black clothes did nothing to relieve his thinness. The colour didn't go with his pale skin and fair hair. He was surprised and pleased when his father climbed from the large grey Ford that drew up on the restricted service road.

Kellan moved directly to him in the three-quarters empty cafeteria. He stood by the table and looked at him. David stared up. It might have been a competition.

'David.' Kellan slid his bulk awkwardly into the seat.

'Dad.' He inclined his head towards the car. 'Why didn't you come in a radio car?'

'I'm pretty busy down here.'

'Yes, of course.' He tried to make it sound apologetic. 'How's it going?'

'Oh,' Kellan said ponderously. 'Well enough.'

Bravado, David instantly decided. This man had never in his life admitted defeat. As he studied the worn, haggard face, he experienced compassion for his father for the first time. No longer the tough, unyielding policeman, he was a man floundering out of his depth, unable to cope.

'Is it true? What I've read about the friction between you and the London police?'

The man was a long time answering, so David assumed it was true. His father was getting the worst of it.

'The press,' he said disgustedly. 'They need something to tart it up. S'that all you wanted?'

He noticed the rings with crosses on them on the young man's fingers. They made him angry.

'I was busted yesterday on a drugs charge.'

'That any way for a religious ... anyway to carry on?'

'A little pot. It's not exactly child-sacrifice.'

Kellan shrugged wearily. 'You shoulda used my name. Might still be worth something.'

'It is,' the young man informed him. 'Did you want some tea?' Kellan didn't. 'But Streatham CID weren't prepared to let my girl-friend go as well.'

'She ha'e religion too?' he asked bluntly.

'We share the same views.' There was a pause. 'I'd like you to use your influence.'

'Saving yourself, David, that's all that matters.' He became reflective. 'Aye, saving yourself; surviving.'

'You owe me this, Father,' he said formally.

Kellan looked at him. 'Is it a favour you're asking?'

There was no reply; to speak would be to commit in an area their past couldn't reconcile.

'Aye. maybe so. Maybe so.'

Getting his son's girl-friend pulled clear presented no problems; it simply meant Kellan making a trip to Streatham. Although her name had gone on record, it hadn't been entered in the charge book as she wouldn't be charged until the drugs found in her possession had been analysed. He had a word with the local detective superintendent, who had a word with the DS on the case. Both were reasonable men. They could either scratch her name, or leave it and switch the positive lab report for a negative one. Whichever was easiest. Either way Kellan knew she would be pulled clear.

'You dinnae tell me she was supplying other kids,' Kellan said to his son, who was in the Ford outside the station. He sounded more disgruntled than he was.

'She was giving it away.'

'That makes some difference?' Kellan shook his head dismayed. 'She's inna clear.'

There was an awkward pause, neither knowing what to say next. David opened the door.

'You want to come round the flat?'

'No time,' he said, indicating he should be getting on.

David climbed out, then stopped at the open door. 'Thanks, Dad. Bless you.'

Kellan felt embarrassed. He glanced at his driver, then at his son. 'Drop your old lady a line more often. Tek care of yourself.'

The young man stood on the kerb as the car started away. His father didn't look back.

Maybe there was hope yet for him, Kellan thought. Three years ago he had been such a blatant prig that he wouldn't have dreamt of using his influence to such effect.

The Jocks continued to delve into the underworld. As they did, more and more of the delicate negotiations, the profitable relationships Fordham had established went bust. Felons who before had always got the time of day for the DCS, either clammed up, disappeared or were languishing in the cells, smarting and totally uncommunicative.

All this only served to infuriate John Fordham, and led him to question the point of the effort he put into his office. The fact that the Scotsmen were proceeding in what could be described as a proper manner in their relationship to the underworld didn't help. Whatever worked and produced results was proper, regardless of whether or not it was by the book.

Fordham and the Squad weren't the only ones put out, and by no means the most put out. Other detectives were also complaining. But it was Fordham who bore the brunt, as the detectives whose manor Kellan was crashing around assumed he was acting in concert with the Squad.

While having a drink in the Tank with Superintendent Jack Owen, no less than three senior detectives approached Fordham, complaining. The latest was a detective superintendent up from Brixton.

'Nine months' work down the fucking pan on account of Kellan's men,' the blotchy-faced superintendent said, pausing to order Fordham and Owen another drink. 'I've been working on this guy, Alan Parker, nine months. Not a bad sort of villain, well involved. Nine months. I kid you not. Then along comes Kellan's boys. Bugger me if they don't bring him into my own nick. Now I ask you, what are you supposed to do?'

Fordham took the line of least resistance. Kellan wasn't his responsibility, and he hadn't time to debate the point with every CID put out by him.

'You have to try and be a bit philosophical, Reg. A policeman was shot. His killers have to come.'

Police officers weren't the only ones complaining.

'Everybody's cagier than enough.' The grass was especially furtive, although the flat where Borroughs had met him was safe. 'I tell you, guv, s'more difficult than enough getting a hello, how are you, out of anyone, much less worthwhile info'.'

'You do all right, Harry. You'd get the last squeak out of a dying mouse if it was any value.'

The informant responded to the compliment.

'Well, you know me, guv. I try to keep my ears open.' He smiled conspiratorially. 'Paul Simpson. Ever hear of him?'

Borroughs shook his head. He wasn't one of those storybook detectives who could put the face to any villain's name. With all the bad lads in the CRO it would be the purest coincidence if their paths had crossed.

'Nasty piece of work. Extortion and a bit of black's what he goes for. He might know about Brodie. He's flush. Word is he's drawing dough off Brodie for helping him.' He gave Borroughs details. Then, almost by way of a bonus, casually added, 'Word's out that it was Charlie Ryman who was behind the Glasgow blag. He's supposed to have put one or two nice tickles together.'

It wasn't that information which disturbed Fordham, but the fact that it had reached street-level. It meant the Jocks would get to hear of it before long.

'Have Simpson picked up, Frank. See how he shapes.'

'You going to bring the Jocks in on it?'

'Might be a gesture. See how he makes out first. I'd better have a word with Charlie Ryman.'

They met in Hyde Park.

Ryman was on one of the benches on the path above the Serpentine ride, watching young ladies trot by on horseback, the thin spring sunshine doing as much for them as it did for the daffodils along the bank.

'Wicked, isn't it,' Ryman said as Fordham joined him. 'Doesn't do my bloodpressure any good, you know.' He inclined his head after the riders.

'Well, you ought to start thinking in terms of a long rest, Charlie, regular hours. Say about twenty years.'

Ryman jerked his attention back abruptly. 'That's not even funny, Mr Fordham. Not the way all those Scotchmen are putting it about.'

'I wasn't joking.' Fordham smiled. 'Anyway, I wouldn't have thought that worried you. You're supposed to be legitimate these days. S'what you said.'

Ryman didn't reply. He watched a man canter by on a large black horse.

'What a life he must have,' he said, momentarily envying him his freedom, the apparent lack of complications in his life. 'Nothing to do but gallop around the park.' He sighed. 'Those Jocks are getting to be a pain. I even had a visit.'

That surprised Fordham. 'Where'd they get your name?'

'I don't know, I wasn't at home. I went away for a few

days, things were getting embarrassing. People are blaming me because of this pressure. Somehow they seem to think I can get it off.'

'What was the outcome?'

'Clara told them I was away on business. They said they'd call back, but they haven't.'

Fordham felt slightly relieved. It meant less of a problem than he figured, for the visit paid to Ryman could have been nothing more than routine. Had the Glaswegians seen anything special in Ryman they wouldn't have been so casual about calling again.

'I'll tell you something, Charlie. It's going to get a lot worse. With Kellan charging around, you're as vulnerable as the next.'

'Me? What do I know about some poor bastard copping it in Glasgow?' Ryman protested.

'More than I do, a lot more. Don't bullshit me. You've got problems; everyone has. The only way to make life easier is to come up with Connell and Brodie.'

'If that was only possible. Do you honestly think villains would take all this stick if they knew where those fuckers were? No one knows, I promise you.'

It made sense to the DCS. He knew that honour among thieves was just a fallacy.

'Then Alan Day knows, so I'd better have him.'

He didn't believe Day was in touch with either party, but he wanted his whereabouts. He considered Ryman's uncertain expression.

'We heard he was the draftsman you had on the Glasgow blag.'

That sort of talk made Charlie Ryman more unsettled.

'Him. He did the vanishing trick better than Houdini,' Ryman said disgruntled. 'Only wish I could do one half as good.'

'Until we get those three, Charlie, I can't nick you – not for what I want; so we can't do any trading.'

He knew he could claim the dapper Charlie Ryman any time, and the possibility of his breaking and running wasn't a serious threat. All the while he was loose there was a chance he was going to get that connection between him and Glasgow, which even Ryman would then realise was pointless denying.

'You'd better make some very active enquiries, Charlie,' Fordham said with an overtone of menace. 'Before the Jocks capture you. If that happens, there's no way you're going to get any help.'

Detective Inspector Norman was waiting for Fordham's return. With him was another DI, whom he had run across while concentrating his energies in the direction of O'Connor's. DI Tony Gateskill, who was out of Lambeth, was on a similar tack, with different objectives. He had been investigating minor crimes in the public works department at County Hall, eventually turning up a district surveyor called Bertram Worthington, who had copped. In a moment of abject remorse after he had been charged, Worthington also told of money he had received from senior employees on the staff of Frank O'Connor and Son for passing substandard work.

A vein of excitement ran through Fordham as he listened to the details.

'You think this could be it, Les?' he asked cautiously.

'It looks better than anything I've come up with to date, guv. Apart from the other fella.'

'One of those he had money from was a quantity surveyor called David Champion. I had a word. I don't think he'd be hard to break.'

'Where's chummy now?'

'On remand, guv,' the DI said. 'Two hundred pounds in his own recognizance. He comes up again on the twenty-eighth at Lambeth.'

'Will you have the case tied up by then?'

'No, nothing like. We'll get another remand.'

'Good.' Fordham became pensive. 'How would you feel, Tony, about having him dropped out? Maybe having the Squad take over your enquiry?' Fordham made it sound as though the DI had an option.

Gateskill glanced between the two Squad detectives, trying to fathom what they had in mind. There was no sense of betrayal in his expression.

'Makes little difference. The same firm.'

'Pleased to hear it.'

It made a pleasant change, Fordham found, not to have to wrestle a detective from one of the divisions. In a straight fight the DI would have lost, but Fordham wasn't being entirely straight, and nothing like above board; Gateskill could have been a nuisance. He would remember the DI, when next an opening on the Squad came up.

'I'm not saying we will drop him out. That'll depend on the information he's got, and whether we can have a deal.'

'I think you'll find him amenable, guv,' Gateskill said. 'You'll be having a word with my guvnor?'

'It's Jimmy Lowry, isn't it?'

'He's at division. At the nick it's Geoff Measham, superintendent.'

'Was there any interest from division? Special note for the DPP? It was government offices.'

'Not that I'm aware. It started as a routine matter.'

'I suppose a Crime Report went up to division?' Fordham said.

'Yes, of course. Did it myself.'

'Pity.'

A Crime Report was an extended, elaborated version of the Crime Complaint, which contained skeletal details of the offence, and immediate action taken; it was normally handwritten. The typed Crime Report, and two copies, had to be drafted within seventy-two hours of the court appearance. All this paperwork, plus the suspect's court appearance, did nothing to facilitate dropping him out, not without involving the Divisional Commander and the DPP. Although this didn't make it easy, it wasn't impossible. If things came to the worst Fordham could make Worthington large promises, then subsequently not fulfil them.

It was ten o'clock before Fordham had had enough for

one day, having briefed DI Norman after a protracted meeting with Geoff Measham; briefed both his superintendents about other activities of the Squad; had a long meeting with DCI Corrigan and been made conversant with the Jocks' activities, apart from what he had gleaned from the bitching of Ds; and caught up on his paperwork.

DS Lemon was the last to stop by his office. He didn't submit written reports on Kellan's movements. He brought the DCS up to date, telling him about Kellan pulling his son's girl-friend clear. That amused Fordham, but after consideration he decided against using it. It was, after all, the prerogative of CID to help their family and friends and friends of friends, and anyone who made an attractive offer. He told Lemon to stay with Kellan, especially now that Ryman had fallen into the man's perspective.

When he left the Yard Fordham had his driver drop him at the National Theatre. Kika had opened in something of Shakespeare's the day before. She hadn't invited him to the opening, but she never did. It was partly that she was nervous about friends being at first nights, and partly her attitude towards him as a policeman. But he didn't care about such things as first nights.

He had no problem getting into the theatre, and stood at the back of the full house for the last twenty minutes, when it was revealed that Rosalind wasn't a boy, but a girl in love with the poof playing opposite her. At the end the audience was ecstatic. Had he been an actor Fordham believed he would have found curtain calls embarrassing. Then his profile tended to be a good deal lower than most actors.

'Oh, I thought you were quite wonderful, Miss Martin,' Fordham gushed, as Kika emerged from the stage-door.

She said sternly, 'Go away, or I shall call a policeman.'

He took her bag, and put his arm through hers. 'You're supposed to simper and flutter your eyelashes.'

'Where are the flowers and chocolates?'

'Times have changed, dear. Most of us don't even have cab fare.'

The woman tensed as they reached the street, expecting to find his car and driver there.

'I sent him home.'

She smiled, 'I'm sorry.'

Fordham raised his hand for a taxi and was ignored. Kika tried successfully a few moments later.

'A sign of the times. No one takes any notice of policemen nowadays.'

On the way to Chelsea, with Fordham relaxing against her, Kika asked, 'Are you winning your much-reported struggle against the eunuchs?'

'Oh. Winning some, losing some ... I'm not infallible, least I've seen no sign of it.'

He was tired, and with Kika now, and wanted to forget work.

'No,' she said quietly, and kissed him.

Fordham was asleep when they reached the flat.

Chapter 30

Reports and pieces of information on Brodie, Connell and Maureen Hoyle, separate and together, along with the results of door-to-door enquiries conducted either by the Jocks with the help of the local uniform branch, or, less frequently, by the Squad, now numbered thousands. Most of the information came past Corrigan or the Ds assisting him, and needed action taken, but it wasn't difficult to categorise into priorities. Low priority automatically went to Tintagel House for the Scots detectives, as did most of that with a medium rating. High priority was offered first to the Squad.

Superficially low-grade information came in concerning Brodie. The extortionist Paul Simpson had been hiding him, and making him pay dearly until Brodie threatened to shoot him. The information received was about Brodie's new address. The informant was anonymous and ordinarily Corrigan might simply have passed the details to the Jocks. But as the call had come to the Yard directly – most came via local stations – and DCS Fordham, who was counting on Charlie Ryman, had warned him to expect something, he took notice.

Fordham knew instinctively that this was it, and passed the information to Borroughs who, with one of the squads, organized a raid.

Major raids were usually conducted in the early morning, around dawn. There wasn't any firm ruling, but that was the period of least resistance, when the suspect was almost certain to be at home, and probably asleep.

However, the raid Borroughs organized was at nine o'clock on a rainy evening, a fact about which all eleven of DI Roger Edwards's squad complained, particularly when they had to get out of their cars to approach the house in Bethnal Green Road.

Most of the houses in the street were narrow and situated above shops. Below the building where Brodie was supposed to be had once been a tailor's shop, for a dummy and a card advertising Tonik mohair was lying askew in one of the steel-mesh covered display windows. Access to the upstairs flats was between two shops. The tiled entrance had a rank smell where people crept in for a piss, rather than use the public lavatories at the end of the street. The building, typical of its kind, had a crumbling, decayed appearance.

There was only one logical way in and out, the front door. At the rear was a wide track of land where buildings had been pulled down for redevelopment which hadn't yet started. The three detectives in the parked car had a clear view of the house. They had no need to get out into the rain, unless Brodie tried to leave that way. The door half way up the building at one time doubtless had steps down into the yard, but these had long since rotted; the windows were high enough to break a leg jumping into that junk-littered yard.

Cramped in Borroughs's car, which was parked near the Brick Lane intersection were six other policemen sheltering from the rain as they discussed final arrangements.

'The woman who owns the building's some kind of wog,' the DCI was saying. 'Greek, I think. She'll probably scream the place down. I'll leave her to you, Peter.'

'Shove m' fist in her mouth, guv,' the young DC said.

'What about the roof?' Edwards said. 'Will we try and crawl through the lofts?'

'Be useful if we could get in above him. You reckon there might be access?' he said, turning to the only uniform, a local inspector.

'The roofs are divided about every fourth one – we had a load of Pakis kipping in other people's lofts a while back.'

The detectives were amused.

'Okay then, Roger. Try next door, get through the lofts above him. We'll go through the front door. Contact us as soon as you're in.'

There was a long pause. Edwards and the two Ds seemed reluctant to get out of the car. When at last they did, Borroughs watched them hurry through the rain and disappear into the doorway beyond the former tailor's shop. It seemed an age before there was radio contact, and then it wasn't from Edwards.

'Guv? What's happening?'

The voice belonged to DS Dick Richards, who was in the car at the back of the building. The Squad were very casual on the air, especially car to car.

'Nothing yet. Anything there?'

'No . . . Hang on. The light on the second floor's gone off.' There was a pause. 'S'all right. It's back on again.'

There weren't any Pakistanis under the tiles but a lot of dust and cobwebs, as the detectives found as they climbed among the rafters. Edwards went first; DC Benedictus who was immediately behind him stumbled and crashed into a rafter.

'Fucking hell, Dave,' the DI hissed, 'go easy.' The DC apologized.

What damage had been done they didn't know. They waited a moment, listened, then continued, almost bent double with the limited headroom. The flashlight beam showed clearly the loft ingress from the room below, but there was no sign that it had been opened in a long while. Neither easily nor silently they prised the hatch open.

'Who the fuck are you?' – was how Edwards was greeted when he lowered himself.

The goodlooking ginger-haired youth, sitting up in bed as naked as each of the two girls with him, was more stoned than brave. The DI ignored him and went directly to the door. The youth must have thought he was having a bad trip as DC Benedictus dropped in out of the ceiling.

'I'll give you one minute to get the fuck out, or I'll call the police.'

'Keep it dark, we are the police.'

Sergeant Vaughan, the third man down would sooner have stayed there. One of the girls ducked beneath the covers, the fact of their being policemen having only just reached her.

'What's she then,' Vaughan said, 'under age?' He moved

out after the other two.

'We're in position, guv.' Edwards's voice was barely audible.

Borroughs depressed the switch on the side of the microphone. 'Well done, Roger. We're going in now.' He handed the set to his driver.

As the detectives were about to climb out into the rain a taxi heading west made a right-hand signal, then a tight U-turn which brought it to a halt outside the empty tailor's shop.

'What's this then? Look lively.'

The detectives moved quickly, catching the cab driver as he went into the entrance recess.

'Hold on, pal. What d'you want?'

'What?' The cab driver was surprised. 'Jes' come ta collect a fare, haven't I. What's the madder?'

'Who is it? Where are you going?'

'Someone called Patterson. To Paddington.'

Patterson was Brodie's mother's maiden name. It was a piece of information Borroughs had stored for no good reason. He thought it touching that Brodie should remember his old mum.

'You'd better ring, then, hadn't you,' the DCI said, edging back around the doorframe.

' 'Ere, what the fuck's going on?'

'Ring the bell.'

The cab driver did as he was told, but panicked when the Squad pulled their guns. 'Fuck you – oh not you, dear,' he apologized to the huge lady with the moustache who opened the door.

The cabbie backed off, realising he was into something he hadn't bargained for.

Donald Brodie, white and unshaven, looking like he hadn't slept in a long while, came down the stairs in threes, carrying a small gripbag. He leapt past the fat lady and straight through the tiled recess, crashing into the taxi driver, bowling him over. Brodie floundered, trying to keep his balance, but pitched forward. Across the pavement he stopped himself falling by pushing against the cab. Detectives came after him.

Like a blind man Brodie launched himself off the kerb. A van hit him.

When taken to Bethnal Green police station Brodie was in one piece after his mishap with the van. His interrogation didn't leave him that way. The Ds wanted Day's whereabouts, which he was unable to give them; the beating he took in the process was by way of vindicating the Squad for his breaking his wife's legs.

'He's in a pretty bad way,' the DCI told Fordham when he called him. 'He ran out into the road. A van hit him.'

'Is he likely to give the Jocks anything?' Fordham asked disinterestedly.

'Not even the time of day.'

'Well, get him to hospital. I'll call Kellan with the good news.'

There were quite a few detectives present by the time DCS Kellan got across town to the London Hospital. A number of his men had arrived ahead of him. Also there were a few reporters floating around, and others continually turning up. Someone at Bethnal Green nick was obviously earning a few quid for tipping them off.

Brodie was unconscious on the high, plastic-covered couch in the casualty examination room. He regained consciousness in brief snatches, but not long enough to be coherent. Kellan stared at the man belligerently, hating him intensely. He wasn't listening to the Malayan casualty officer who stood about a foot and a half shorter than him.

'Fractured vertebrae; fractured collar bone; renal damage. Further tests are needed to ascertain the extent. He also has a dislocated jawbone, severe damage to the left eye. We are uncertain whether this is of a permanent nature.'

'He's alive,' Kellan said. 'When can he be moved?'

'He must not be. Not unless you want to kill him.'

'He killed one of my officers,' Kellan replied, intimating that whatever happened to him was justified. 'I want him revived, doctor. I need to interrogate him.'

'But this is impossible, sir. He has to go to the theatre.' The Malayan doctor's resistance was tenuous. He was aware of how much authority the police had, he had always been aware of it. During the Emergency in his own country they had shot suspects out of hand. Anyway, he had been on duty fourteen hours and was much too tired to resist wilfully.

'He has information we need, doctor.' Kellan pressed forward to the couch with Douglas, as Brodie began mumbling. 'Brodie? Donald Brodie. Can you hear me?'

'What . . . ? I think he's asking for water, sir.'

'Wet his lips so he can talk easier.' Kellan glanced at the doctor, expecting some protest. None was forthcoming. They were able to make out 'Day', and then 'Alan Day'. He drifted away, came back to consciousness again, and muttered some more. Then they were able to make out three names before he sank again.

Borroughs was in the corridor when Kellan and his aide emerged from the ward. 'Get anything worth the trouble, Mr Kellan?' he asked solicitously.

Kellan gave the man a withering look. He believed that the Squad had done this purposely to prevent his interrogating Brodie. Also he was furious that it was the Squad who had captured the murderer.

'You made a proper mess of him and no mistake.'

'Not us,' the DCI protested. 'That van driver ought to be nicked.'

'Aye,' Kellan said, then swung away and marched angrily out, Douglas hurrying after.

'Leave some of our lads in with him, Dougie, the whole time mind, in case he mutters. And keep the press out.'

At that point the antipathy Kellan felt towards London and Londoners reached a peak. In a bout of acute paranoia he believed that every Englishman was actively against him. Because of this feeling he made a late visit to the House of Commons, having dismissed both getting drunk and calling up Angus Bingham. He needed the reassurance, the sympathy of someone who wasn't involved.

Filling out the necessary forms to call an MP from the Chamber, Kellan handed it to an usher, who was in formal dress. He had to wait in the enormous, circular, vaulted reception area, with its mini post office and mystery-shrouded oak doors. There weren't many people around then, and he didn't know if Alistair McKindoe would be in the House. Fortunately he was and made his appearance from the large double doors, where a police constable was on duty.

McKindoe was an old acquaintance of Kellan's. As a Scottish Nationalist MP, he was quite new to the House and spent a lot of time there. A curious-looking man, with a large nose which the rest of his features seemed to crowd around as if for company.

'Ian, my dear fellow,' he said expansively. He shook his hand as though soliciting his vote. 'I heard you were in town, and wondered if you'd have time. Does this mean your task here is concluded?'

'Och, I only wished, Alistair. I only wished, man,' Kellan replied wearily.

McKindoe knitted his brows. 'Let's away upstairs. We can talk in private.'

The MP listened sympathetically to Kellan's great outpouring; he was as jingoistic, and often experienced Kellan's antipathy for the English, never having forgiven them Culloden. He said he had heard the rumours of friction between the two police factions, and pledged his support.

'I'll table a question to the Home Secretary in the House tomorrow. That'll put them on the spot. Also I'll call the Commissioner of Police personally, and leak it to the press. The police here get away wi' too much.'

'Aye. Well, it was good to talk to a friend, Alistair. I began to think there were none.'

When he left the House Kellan felt curiously lightheaded, as if he had shed an enormous burden. He didn't really care what the MP achieved; the talk he had had with him had been very beneficial.

At the press conference held at the Yard the following

morning Kellan found himself alone answering a battery of questions about the damage Brodie had sustained. He had expected Fordham to be present, but the only detective from the Squad was Roger Edwards, whom the press ignored.

The reporters had a more comprehensive list of the man's injuries than the DCS could remember being given. Doubtless they had added things for measure. All he could say was that Brodie had been hit by a speeding van while resisting arrest. He wanted to remind them of what Brodie was, what he had done; to question why they were wasting sympathy on him. But seeing the pitfalls, he refrained from doing so.

'... Hosenball, *Time Out*. Could you say, chief superintendent, how he might have sustained a severely bruised thorax from being hit by a van?'

'Mr Kellen isn't a medical expert,' the Yard PRO smoothly interjected.

'Could the rivalry between the two police factions have had any bearing on the manner in which he was arrested?' The reporter talked fast, insistently, refusing to be squashed.

The question of inter-police friction was becoming familiar now, and drew the same reaction from Kellan. It caused him to close ranks.

'We work in the closest concert. We're all working for the same end, laddie.'

Fordham had purposely blanked the press conference when the press officer had rang through. He had a prior appointment with Peter Goodfellow, and by the way he had been summoned, with Commander Pope, Fordham knew that the purpose of the meeting wasn't so that the AC—Crime could pay them his compliments.

Immediately the two men stepped inside his office Goodfellow let go. It was Fordham he was gunning for, but Gerald Pope, as his immediate superior, couldn't be let off, for he had allowed the situation to develop as it had. The man ranted about McKindoe complaining to the Commissioner.

'He's far from pleased with things. He barely managed to persuade the MP not to call for an enquiry. You've been behaving like ten-year-olds, trying to score points off each other and losing sight of your prime objective.'

'With greatest respect, sir,' Fordham began. It was a standard approach when disagreeing with a senior officer. 'As a result of the way they've been proceeding, there's not a piece of information left on the street worth having.'

'Nonsense,' he said emphatically, as though he was in touch at street-level. 'You found Brodie. Only it would have been better had you done so in a joint operation.'

'He wasn't likely to wait around at Mr Kellan's pleasure, sir,' Pope offered tentatively.

'It was low-grade information, supposedly. But the Squad's reaction suggests otherwise. This is really like some game you're playing. If it is, you're making a fool of yourself, John, and me into the bargain. You have your priorities wrong. Wrap this up, get out and find Connell, get your picture in the papers.' He paused. 'And stop wasting time in this other area. I won't tell you again.'

There was the bone of contention. The AC—Crime's reaction had little to do with the hammering the Jocks were taking. It was to do with Fordham's ongoing enquiries into areas concerning O'Connor's.

When the two men left the AC—C's office and were walking towards the lifts, Gerald Pope spoke of what was on their minds.

'Seems like he's protecting his vested interest. That's why he wants you to soft-pedal in that area.'

It was the first time Fordham had known Gerald Pope show disloyalty to a senior officer. Not that his statement was exactly a stab in the back. They walked on in silence.

'What do you think, John?'

'He's left it a bit late. It's about bursting at the seams.'

'To continue could bring a lot of unnecessary trouble,' Pope said noncommitally.

'For whom, Gerald? That's the question.'

Fordham wasn't about to heed the warning. It was becoming a personal matter between him and the AC—Crime, a contest of wills. Had he liked the man, or had any respect for him other than that which his office demanded, it might have been different. But he was a holier-than-thou hypocrite, who had accepted without a murmur the expediency in forcing Peter Walsh out for doing little more than he was doing himself.

'If he wants that area of investigation dropped, then he had better put it in writing. In triplicate!' Fordham hit the lift button.

Chapter 31

Some people said crime didn't pay. Mainly those who were earning from the socially acceptable crimes.

Tony Pepper had always indulged in the less social kind, and had found it most profitable. The farm he owned in Sussex was the proof. He didn't farm seriously; he kept a few chickens and pigs, and let most of his seventy acres. He had bought the land and buildings as an investment. But then Pepper was shrewder than most villains. He had known when to quit, or rather when to scale down his villainy so that it amounted to little more than what the average man in the street was having; a bit of bent gear he could go again on.

However, of late Pepper questioned how shrewd he was, taking in Brian Connell and Maureen Hoyle. The gesture to the woman was madness. He had been in the army with her elder brother, who was now doing five over the wall, and he had stiffed her when she was younger. None of which amounted to this sort of favour. He hadn't even known she knew where he was living. Instinct had made him take them in when they had shown up, and now he regretted that instinct which sometimes pulled certain people together and made them respond to each other.

Over the eight days they had been at his place he had watched them become like caged animals, snapping and snarling; growing more tense and nervous as they paced the confines; living from minute to minute, constantly on the edge of cracking. They had no money, no prospects, and hardly any clothes; they lived by inches, waiting for they knew not what: capture, presumably, though it wasn't a subject they easily mooted. There were moments when they almost broke and came close to giving themselves up; only knowing what would happen to Connell if they did prevented them. They had seen the news coverage of Brodie's arrest. Anyway, Pepper had some say in the matter now. At times they were suspicious of their host, especially as he spent so much time out of the house. The truth was he couldn't stand the strain of being with them, and spent most of his time in a pub in the nearby town of East Grinstead.

Whether they knew it or not, Tony Pepper was about the only friend they had, and even he had thought more than once about grassing them, only he couldn't find the means of getting sufficiently distanced to do so with any degree of safety. Despite the excellent relationship he had with some of the local CID, he wasn't about to risk trying to give them Connell.

Whenever she wanted clean underwear, Maureen Hoyle like Connell, occasionally borrowed Tony Pepper's pants and vests. But more frequently she flopped around naked beneath her raincoat while she washed and dried her own. The flimsy nylon garments dried in no time above the stove, and there was no reason why she shouldn't have dried them the same way that morning. No reason except that she was sick of being cooped up. Tony was out and Brian was sleeping fitfully. She wouldn't have dared stepping outside with either of them around. Going those few short paces across the yard to hang up her pants, bra and tights would break the monotony. It couldn't do any harm, she thought.

Standing anxiously at the line pegging the articles, she suddenly had an overwhelming feeling that someone was watching her. She spun round. Beyond the patchy beech hedge at the side of the yard a boy stood staring at her.

'Oh God!' The words came out in a helpless cry. He might have been a policeman rather than a child. Whoever or whatever made no difference. Since going on the run she had undergone intensive conditioning against encountering anyone; everyone was a potential threat. Tearing the clothes from the line, Maureen Hoyle rushed back to the house. There she started to sob convulsively, screwing the washing into her face to prevent herself. She knew she had let Brian down, put him in danger. She thought about waking him, telling him, but was afraid of what he might do. With her breath coming in short, painful snatches, she sank to the floor, there, leaning against the kitchen door she buried her face against her knees.

The boy was the kid of Pepper's nearest neighbour, who lived half a mile along the lane. When he got home he mentioned to his mum that he had seen the lady. She didn't understand what he was talking about, and hadn't the time to get involved with the fantasies of a ten-year-old.

'The lady what were in the newspaper,' the boy insisted.

The photographs of Connell and Maureen Hoyle hadn't been in the newspapers for days, but he delved into the cupboard for an old paper. The woman read of how the police had been conducting house to house searches in parts of Hertfordshire and Middlesex. It didn't say anything about Sussex.

'Are you sure it's her, Darren?' she asked, becoming drawn into the intrigue.

Along with thoughts of calling either the police or the *Daily Mirror*, she thought about having her hair done. If those people were hiding at Pepper's farm reporters and photographers would come and she'd get her own picture in the newspaper. Hesitantly she called the police in East Grinstead. They were courteous and thanked her, and said they would send someone out to see her.

Later the information was passed on to Scotland Yard for collation. It looked interesting to DCI Corrigan when the detective who processed it pushed it his way. But Fordham declined to send the Squad to Sussex, and told him to pass it to the Jocks. They decided to raid the farm, liaising directly with the Sussex constabulary. Their instructions to the local police were to keep the farm under observation, but on no account to go near it until they arrived.

In the pub which Tony Pepper used there was a barmaid he was getting to know quite well. He played with her verbally, propositioning her without serious designs. She was a divorcee, and although she had a boy-friend, he knew she wouldn't be difficult. But he couldn't even think about that until he got rid of Maureen Hoyle and Connell.

Pepper was chatting to the barmaid when Freddy Tavendale, a local CID, came in. There weren't many customers in at that time of the evening and the detective made straight for Pepper.

'Freddy. You look as if you could do with one.'

'I bloody well could, an' all. A bottle of Guinness, Carol.'

When he had got his drink the harassed-looking detective drew Pepper away. Pepper assumed the man had business to discuss. They'd had a few deals in the past on stolen property that had been recovered by the CID and not entered into the Property Found book. The DC was a sociable sort who didn't get too many opportunities for earners, not like the hungry bastards in London; Pepper liked to help him out.

'What you got on your mind, Freddy?' Pepper asked.

'A lot of bloody Scotsmen, that's what. They're on their way down here, that crew who're in London.'

Tony Pepper didn't bat an eyelid, but felt a steel band tighten around his heart; his stomach turned to water. There could only be one reason they were coming down here.

The detective was warning him about the proposed raid on his farm, not because he thought Pepper was hiding Connell, but because he thought he might have some bent gear there.

With a supreme effort of control, Pepper joked, 'Tell them not to make a mess, Freddy, will you.'

After the DC departed, Pepper rang his own number; he had devised a signal with Connell. He told him about the raid and that the placc was being watched; instructed them to go out through the pigsty, and the copse beyond it. He would park his car on the road there, and leave in it what cash he had on him, but wouldn't wait around. They were on their own.

Connell and Maureen Hoyle got clear without any trouble.

Before going to bed that night Tony Pepper worked through the house, cleaning it.

At around dawn the farm was raided by the Jocks and a lot of local police; there were also two marksmen who climbed into trees overlooking the house. All they found when they crashed in was Pepper, asleep. There was no sign of either Connell's or Maureen Hoyle's occupation, until the police dusted the place for fingerprints. Pepper hadn't been as thorough as he'd imagined. He was arrested, beaten up, then charged.

Chapter 32

For Alan Day the burden of isolation had become intolerable. Ordinarily he didn't mind being on his own, but these were not ordinary circumstances. Despite the comfort of his eighteenth-century Hertfordshire cottage, and its safety, Day felt like a prisoner; the twelve days he had spent there seemed like years. How time would hang in prison was too disturbing even to contemplate.

Since arriving, he had hardly emerged from the house, and then only as far as the refuse bin in the back garden; the garden was relatively safe as it abutted an open meadow and the River Lea. There were neighbours to his right, but they spent most of their time in London, while the old widower on his left remained totally absorbed with his greenhouse. Encountering the old man briefly, Day was offered some tomato plants. The house was well stocked with provisions, the huge freezer in the outhouse all but full. Materially he was well set up, also physically to some extent; however, resistance was fading, for on checking the road from behind the curtains, as he frequently did, he had twice seen a woman with a club foot. The first time he had lusted for her; the second time he had fallen in love with her. His mental preparation for the stay had been nil, and now his level of endurance had reached that point as well.

Finally deeming it safe to re-enter the world outside, Alan Day decided to make a brief excursion to his flat to retrieve the incriminating evidence. He bitterly regretted now that he had departed in panic. A logical person, he knew he couldn't stay in hiding for ever. He had no means of knowing if he was still being sought, for he had no contact with the underworld and none with Ryman. But just because his name wasn't appearing in news broadcasts didn't mean he was safe. He knew he had to make positive moves to pull himself clear, and the start was at his flat, where he had bent passports and cash well hidden. Keeping them there was now another cause for regret, but when making that decision he had wanted no hint of anything illicit to touch his existence in Hertfordshire.

The moment he stepped from the cab that had taken him to Camden Town from Liverpool Street station he sensed that going there was a mistake, even though he had carefully checked out the street. He almost climbed right back into the cab.

Everything incriminating that he had left behind was gone. He shifted the furniture, going from one hiding place to another. They were all empty. Floorboards had been taken up and replaced as carefully as though he had done it himself; the same with the skirting board. Even the hollowed out area behind the light switch had been emptied. He considered Ryman, the landlady and the CID, in that order. Ryman wouldn't know about the stashes; the landlady wouldn't be that thorough, and the police wouldn't be this careful. But it had to be the latter, he finally decided.

Day started violently at the rap on the door.

'You in there, Mr Day? It's me.'

Recognizing the landlady's voice, he guessed she had seen him come in. He didn't guess that she had telephoned Inspector Murry.

Two Scots heavyweights hit the door as Day opened it a fraction. The door crashed back, the edge smashing into his face, and breaking his nose.

'Thank you for your trouble, Missus.' Murry steered the woman away, as DCI Crombie and other detectives moved into the room.

When the Jocks eventually left the house with their prisoner a green Jaguar arrived and the three detectives sprang out, led by DI Edwards. The fourth Squad detective, who had been on watch, joined them.

'Jock! That's our prisoner you've got there.'

'Away wi' ya, laddie, you' no' a snowball's chance in hell,' Crombie replied, unruffled by this lower ranking officer's attitude.

'The fuck we have,' Edwards retorted. 'We're nicking him.'

Squad detectives seized Day, who instinctively shielded his tender, broken face as the other faction resisted.

'Go fook yourselves,' DS Galbraith shouted.

'Why don't you pricks go back to nicking drunks on Sauchiehall Street . . . ?'

'I'll warn you only once. This man is our fucking prisoner.' Crombie's calm exterior started to disintegrate.

The fray over who arrested Day continued until an elderly woman opened a window and said, 'If you men don't moderate your language I shall call the police.'

The situation as recounted to Fordham struck him as funny, despite its implications. If word reached the ACC, the detectives involved could expect disciplinary action. But worse, far worse, was the fact that the Jocks had Day. Fordham was pissed off about that. He didn't believe the man could give them Connell, but he knew he would almost certainly give them Ryman.

Sounding his most apologetic, Fordham telephoned DCS Kellan and made the appropriate noises about the scene that had taken place between their respective detectives. Kellan responded to the apology, but not the request for Day to be turned over to them so that he might assist them with other enquiries.

'So you can mek some deal wi' him,' Kellan retorted. 'Well, no go. This laddie's ma ticket out of here. He's gonna gi' us Connell.'

'Warn Ryman,' Fordham told Bill Senior as he replaced the phone. He didn't want to go near the man at this stage. 'Tell him the Jocks have Day. If he wants to trade now's the time. Also alert our lad listening in on his phone, and put someone on watch there. Now he's really under pressure he might start making rash moves. And, Bill,' he paused. His aide glanced at him. 'Mind how you go.'

Satisfaction spread through Ian Kellan when he thought about his conversation with Fordham. He felt he had put something over on the man by refusing even to let him be in on Day's interrogation. They must have wanted him pretty badly for the DCS to come on in sackcloth and ashes. Obviously Day was more important than they had anticipated. Kellan decided to give the interrogation the benefit of his personal attention.

Tintagel House wasn't a police station and had no facilities for coping with prisoners; there were no cells, no front office where they could be processed and charged. For this they were taken to the local police station. There were, however, rooms available on the ground floor where detectives could interview both suspects and witnesses. It was in one of these that Day was being interrogated by DCI Crombie and DS Galbraith, and quite efficiently, until their boss showed up and inhibited them.

'It seems you're a very important person, Mr Day. There's been a lot of interest in you. Is he ready to mek a statement, Alan?'

'We were just discussing that. He says he's nothing to state.'

'Is that so?' There was a latent threat in his question. 'Then we'll ha'e to show him he's mistaken.'

The detectives stood regarding Day where he sat in isolation. His face and nose were swollen, he looked white and shaken. He stared at his hands, nervously interlacing his long, elegant fingers, only occasionally having the courage to glance at the detectives.

'Where's Connell holed up, mister?'

Day carefully shook his head.

'We know he contacted you recently.'

'He didn't, I swear he didn't. I've not seen him since . . .'

'Since you sent him to Glasgow to murder one of my men.' He paused. 'I want his whereabouts, and you're going to gi' it me. Get him on his feet, I dinnae like hitting a man who's sitting down.'

The advance information did more to break Alan Day than the beating he believed would follow. He couldn't stand physical pain, but contemplating it here was even worse. He tossed his chair aside and backed into a corner, taking a protective position as the detectives advanced.

'Where's Connell? Where's the murdering bass hiding?'

'I don't know. I promise you, sir, I don't. I haven't seen him since he went north.'

'Tek a firm hold of him,' Kellan said.

Trying to scramble away, Day slid to the floor and writhed in panic. They eventually took him. His protests became a thin, reed-like whine.

'Get his legs apart,' Kellan said. 'I'm gonna kick his balls.'

That proposal in a matter-of-fact manner finished Day. He screamed and writhed when Kellen took a step towards him.

'Please don't, please. I don't know ...'

'You fooking liar. You helped him. You must ha'e. Someone's got to be helping him ...'

In his mind's eye Day anticipated the man's foot landing a vicious blow to his genitals. He felt the nauseating pain. He couldn't stand it. Telling the truth to these detectives was the only way he was going to spare himself suffering '... Ryman, ask Charles Ryman, he knows.' It got the pressure off himself.

The name immediately rang a bell. 'What happened about Ryman?'

The DS replied, 'He was away when Mr Murry called, sir.'

'He was, was he?' he said irritably, imagining some kind of slip had been made.

There was a sharp rap at the door. Douglas entered without giving Day's position a second glance.

'Word's just in, sir. A constable in Paddington spotted Pepper's car parked in a street. The woman and Connell are under our noses somewhere.'

'Good news. Nice to know someone down here's trying. Right with you, Dougie.' He turned back to Crombie. 'I want a statement from him. I don't much care what condition he ends up in getting it.'

*

The hotel room, with its crooked partitioned walls, flaking ceiling, creaking bed and dusty curtains, made Connell uneasy. The hotel was one of the many seedy, anonymous places around the Bayswater–Paddington border. They were converted terraced houses, most of them fire-traps. They were the sort of places prostitutes took clients when they didn't have a flat of their own, and where low-budget summer tourists bedded down when London filled to capacity.

The proprietor hadn't asked questions when Connell and Maureen Hoyle checked in. They had paid for two nights in advance, that was all that mattered. No comment was passed at their having no luggage. Most of the people who stayed there had none, apart from those summer tourists.

Coming here was a mistake, Connell concluded. He felt trapped. But when they had fled from Pepper's place they had done so in panic, never believing they'd get this far; then every place they had considered had been deemed too risky. He knew no one in the Paddington area who was likely to help them. Staying as long as they had in this hotel was another mistake; two nights was begging for trouble. Sending Maureen Hoyle off to give Charlie Ryman the bell was yet another mistake. He was no longer sure he could trust her. The way they had lived over the past two weeks had worn her down, she was ready to give herself up. Maybe that was what she had done now.

Connell checked his wristwatch, and went on wondering about Maureen Hoyle as he moved restlessly around the room, tensing frequently and listening to the sounds which crept through the hotel, imagining that every noise was the filth stealing up the stairs.

Perhaps Charlie Ryman was a mistake. Why should he help? Because he had put up the money for the job, that was why. Connell didn't know that he had for a fact, but he had a good idea. He had to help, he was their last hope. The forty sovs Pepper had left in his car had all but gone. They needed money if they were going to reach safety.

His thoughts stopped abruptly, he sprang to his feet,

snatching at the Smith and Wesson .38 he had got in the habit of keeping in his belt. Out in the hallway creaking floorboards warned him of someone's approach. Whoever it was went past and relative silence followed, with the distant throb of traffic on Bayswater Road.

Looking at the gun in his hand, Connell wondered vaguely what he was doing with it. How it might help him. Shafts of logic began piercing through his shroud of fear. But he wasn't capable of sufficiently long concentration to relate significantly to the hopelessness of the situation.

His thoughts returned to Ryman and Maureen Hoyle – what was taking her so long? Should he stay put?

From Lancaster Gate to Queensway along Bayswater Road Maureen Hoyle had come upon four different telephone boxes, none of which was in order. As she had progressed from each, her feeling of despair increased. Perhaps she should stop the first policeman and tell him who she was. She knew the relief would be immense. But when presented with the opportunity shortly afterwards, she demurred.

Continuing towards Notting Hill Gate, she saw three policemen standing talking in the street. Panic welled up in her, imagining they were waiting for her. She veered across the road, through the gaps in the traffic. She entered Kensington Gardens via Orme Square Gate, past the children's playground that was tucked away in the corner as though children and their play apparatus were unsightly. The children's cries of delight and discomfort reached across at her like clasping fingers, and she stopped. Never having Brian's baby was her big regret. There was still time ... the thought tailed off. She turned away, moving deeper into the gardens, heading towards Kensington High Street.

Flower beds crowded with tulips and daffodils were a riot of colour. The flowers swayed unperturbed by the March breeze. People walked dogs, flew box kites, pushed children and took short-cuts through the park. Maureen Hoyle was conscious of them all doing ordinary things, and she was envious of the most humble, wanting to be just like them, doing what they were doing.

At that point the thought of giving herself up crossed her mind again, but her feet didn't respond. Instead she found herself leaving the park and moving along Kensington High Street. The first phone box she reached was in order. She dialled the number Connell had given her and heard it ring out. It seemed to take for ever being answered.

'Mr Ryman? It's me. I mean, Maureen Hoyle . . .'

'Who . . . ?' came the voice, traces of alarm apparent. He knew, of course.

'Brian told me to call. He said you'd help . . .'

'For fuck's sake! Where are you?'

'Please, Mr Ryman. There isn't no one else.' She began to cry.

'Where is he? Where's he now?' Ryman sounded a little desperate. Suddenly he saw how to get the pressure off himself. Grassing was against his principles, but Connell had taken a wicked liberty. 'Just calm down, love. 'Course I'll help. But you have to tell me where he is.'

She hesitated, remembering what Brian had told her. 'I can't, you'll have to meet me . . .'

The detective who had put in the most paperback-reading hours out at Wimbledon telephone exchange felt a buzz of excitement as he called Fordham with their rendezvous. The Hypermarket in Kensington High Street. He had believed it would never happen.

'Do you want Ryman picked up as well?' Borroughs asked. He was at a briefing Fordham was giving the squad who were going to tail Maureen Hoyle and Ryman.

'No reason for keeping him loose, Frank. But I want him nicked along with Connell, so there're no doubts. We won't need Day then.'

The bell sounded for so long that it might have been jammed. A hammering at the door followed, as if the caller hadn't a moment to spare. Ryman stood anxiously at the end of the hall as Terry Stonehouse, his factotum, peered through the security hole. He turned back to Ryman, a surprised look on his face.

'I'd have a guess and say Old Bill.' The mannerisms he had affected were now lost.

'You'd better let them in, Terry . . .'

Before Stonehouse had the opportunity the doorframe splintered, screws tearing out of the lock where the door was kicked.

McFageon was first in, four other detectives on his heels.

'Look, what the fuck . . . ?'

'Ya should ha'e answered the door a wee bit faster. We're no' Paki' brush salesmen. You Ryman? – against the wall. And you, laddie.'

Detectives hustled Stonehouse, as one of Ryman's poodles raced out of the living-room and snapped at McFageon's feet. The DCI picked up the dog.

'Ah, ya wee beasty. You're barking at the wrong side.'

'I trust you are police officers, and that you have a warrant to come busting in here,' Ryman tried.

'We are. And we ha'e – at the office. Perhaps you'd like to accompany us there?'

The twelve detectives who were positioned around and in the Hypermarket had no problems marking Maureen Hoyle. It was a wonder no one else recognized her as she moved agitatedly from stall to stall.

Borroughs waited in the back of a cab which the Squad were using, parked along the road from the Hypermarket. Another car was positioned further back, and two more across the street.

Detective Inspector Roy Jackson came along with a shopping bag and climbed into the cab. 'She's getting very restless in there,' he said. 'I don't think chummy's going to show. Do you?'

'Doesn't look like it, Roy. Fuck it. I thought we were gonna wrap this up.' He pulled down the window and hawked into the street.

'I suppose I'd better get back in there.'

Some of the stall holders were becoming suspicious, she was sure. They were giving her funny looks. Suddenly it occurred to Maureen Hoyle that they probably thought she was a shoplifter.

The wait seemed interminable, and again she considered where Ryman might be, whether he was going to turn up, and help them. More and more she thought that he might not, and a feeling of acute distress came over her. She began to feel sick and hot and wanted to get out of there, but was afraid to in case she missed him. There was a payphone fixed to the wall and she used it to call Ryman's number.

There was a silence down the line when the phone was picked up. Maureen Hoyle waited anxiously.

'Hello?' she said. 'Is Mr Ryman there? Is he please?'

'No, he's gone out. Can I help?' the Scottish DS enquired. 'I'm a friend.'

'How long's he been gone. I was to meet him, like.'

'Where are you now, hen?'

'At the . . .' She stopped, alarm bells began ringing in her head. The man had a Scottish accent which she connected with the detectives who were looking for her and Brian. She slammed the phone down and swung round, believing the police were already there. Her eyes darted about, panic swelling through her. Oh God, what have I done? The question came on a wave of despair. She thought of how she had failed Brian, betrayed him. She considered what those detectives would do when they captured him. She couldn't bear to think about his broken, pain-torn body.

It took her a few moments to realise that policemen weren't closing on her, that there wasn't anyone paying her any particular attention. But they would be arriving soon, and she had to get away. She turned and fled the market.

Outside she stopped and searched the street, remembering Brian Connell's advice about making sure she wasn't followed. She would take evasive action. There wasn't a vacant cab in sight and the hope she felt about getting away and back to Brian began to sink.

'Look sharp,' Borroughs said to the Squad driver. 'She wants a taxi. Put your light on, pick her up.' He immediately vacated the cab.

The Squad cab plied towards Maureen Hoyle like a regular working taxi. As it did so a number of people appeared on the kerb wanting the same cab. The driver ignored them and drew up in front of the blond woman with the putty-like face. She climbed in without stating the destination. She was more interested in checking the street behind. The driver turned.

'Where d'you want to go, sweetheart?'

'Oh,' she hesitated. 'Bayswater Road.'

The cab juddered away, negotiating for the off-side lane to make a right turn into Kensington Church Street. The driver reached out and opened the r/t set, putting him on the air to other vehicles.

'Which part of Bayswater Road, sweetheart?' he asked.

After a moment Maureen Hoyle said, 'Oh, any part, it doesn't matter.'

Immediately after the cab had picked up Maureen Hoyle, one of the Squad's cars on the opposite side of the road made a U-turn and collected Borroughs. He contacted Fordham by radio telephone to tell him of developments, only to be told why Ryman hadn't shown up.

When the cab reached the top of Kensington Church Street and stopped for the traffic lights, Maureen Hoyle jumped out. Thrusting fifty pence at the driver, she ran towards the underground station, glancing over her shoulder as though suspecting she was being followed. She swung down the entrance steps.

'The prat's marked us!' Borroughs said over the radio. 'Get after her, Roy.'

The car Jackson was in swung out past Borroughs's car and the cab, and into Notting Hill Gate. Jackson and two other detectives leapt out and ran down the steps into the station.

Maureen made no attempt to reach a train. Instead she went past the booking hall and along the tunnel, turning left to exit on the north side of the road. The three detectives broke into a run.

As she emerged from the subway and hurried into Pembridge Road, Borroughs's car swept across Notting Hill Gate in front of an oncoming bus, and headed the woman off.

The DCI climbed out with another detective. When she saw them Maureen Hoyle tried to double back, only to encounter Jackson, whom she lashed out at in a final act of protest. She appealed for help from passers-by. No one offered any.

Borroughs had questioned her provisionally by the time Fordham arrived at Notting Hill Gate police station. He had threatened and cajoled and promised her the earth, but had got nowhere. Fordham's attempts got them no further.

'Give her to the Jocks, Frank. Let them beat her up. They'll get Connell's whereabouts, I guarantee it.'

He rose from the table where Maureen Hoyle sat. Jackson and a local policewoman were also present. Fordham had no further use for the woman. In the event of his taking Connell, it wouldn't commit Charlie Ryman to any greater degree. The Jocks arresting him had almost certainly put a spanner in the works. Fordham's only hope was to let them have their moment of glory, then maybe they'd return home leaving him to salvage what he could.

Turning back to the woman, Fordham said, 'You know what they'll do to him for killing one of their own?'

That was the woman's worst fear. But still she didn't yield. These were detectives too; Brian could expect no easier treatment from them.

'Give her to them.'

Despite Fordham's warning, the Scots detectives didn't touch her. Instead of hardness, Kellan showed her kindness when she was brought to Tintagel House; instead of bullying her, he was his most persuasive. The tactics worked. Slowly, tearfully she yielded ground as he plied her with questions about her relationship; her love for Connell; the future they had anticipated; the future he could expect if he remained at large.

Quite obviously from the way the woman was reacting, the point was going to come when she would impart Connell's whereabouts to the detective in the firm belief that she would be helping Brian.

Chapter 33

Connell quit the hotel, his only piece of luggage the Smith and Wesson .38. He guessed that something had gone wrong when Maureen Hoyle failed to return. He didn't stop to consider what might have happened to her; vaguely assuming some kind of betrayal, he fled instinctively, knowing that his survival depended on leaving the hotel quickly.

On foot he moved into the more fashionable part of Bayswater, harbouring ideas of stealing a car. But it was too light to risk trying for a car yet, unless he saw one with the keys in.

His eyes darted anxiously about as he walked, first one street, then another. He didn't want anyone surprising him. When he reached Bayswater Road and the park, he realized angrily that he had been going in the wrong direction, but didn't know why; he had no firm idea where he was going or what he would do when he got there. The most important thing was to keep moving, he felt, away from central areas. He would have preferred to cross the river and get back on familiar ground, even get back to his flat. But he knew he couldn't take a chance. He wouldn't have got as far as Prince of Wales Drive, much less his flat.

A number twelve bus stopped for traffic lights. Connell ran across the road for it. Buses offered a legitimate excuse for running, and he felt like running all the time; he felt too exposed when he walked, there was too much time for people to ID him.

When the black bus conductor came along the top deck collecting fares he didn't even glance at Connell. It was doubtful whether he would have recognized him anyway. One white man looked much the same as any other.

There were a few people on the bus and Connell felt edgy. He had picked the seat at the front, as opposed to one with easier access to the exit at the rear, to avoid people's looks as they disembarked. The man who vacated the seat across from him left a copy of the *Standard* behind. Connell reached for the newspaper and raised it in front of his face. But being unable to concentrate he didn't get to read a word.

Billy Gray! The villain's name came to him as the bus reached Shepherd's Bush Green. He lived in a block of flats off Goldhawk Road, or used to. Connell had been to his place a couple of times when they had worked on a blag together a few years back.

Billy Gray, a shortish, plumpish villain with a heavily lined face and, ordinarily, an easygoing manner, almost died when he opened the door of his high-rise flat and found Connell there.

'Jesus . . . fucking stroll on . . . What the fuck . . . ?'

He wrenched the man inside, and after quickly checking outside, closed the door. It was alarm which made Gray react in that way. He immediately regretted the reaction.

'I'm desperate, Billy. I had nowhere else . . .'

'Fucking hell, Bri'. I'm bang in trouble myself . . .'

Gray was working himself into a state. He was on bail to make an appearance at the Old Bailey on an armed robbery charge, and knew he could get the telegram to surrender himself any day. Connell was just what he didn't need.

'I don't wanna put you in it, but I couldn't do nothing else . . .'

'I can't afford to get involved, Bri' . . . fuck! I can't. I really . . . Jesus.' He turned away, then back, agitated, exasperated.

'Please. Just till it's dark. So I can nick a car . . .' he stopped, and stared beyond Gray into the flat. 'Where's your missus and the kids?'

'Ahh' – a noise of irritation and disgust. 'Pissed off, she has, taken 'em to her mother's, down at Portslade. Couldn't stand the life no more . . .'

Staring hard at the man opposite, Gray realised what a mess he was in. This wasn't the Brian Connell he had made one with. He had lost weight, his once full, fleshy face was now gaunt. He wasn't surprised that he had passed through the streets unrecognized; there wasn't much resemblance between him and the picture which had appeared in the newspaper.

'You look like you could do with a shave and something to eat, son,' Gray said calmly.

A trace of a smile started across Connell's face.

Reluctantly, against his better judgment, Gray agreed to help. 'I must be silly as a goat.' He led him deeper into the flat.

Bathed and shaved and fed, Connell looked a different man, though remained very tense as he moved about the flat, pausing carefully at the window to peer from the ninety-odd-foot viewpoint to see whether the police were massing on the bald, litter-strewn grass area in front of the block.

Money and a car were his immediate objectives; beyond that he couldn't think, and his host hadn't any particularly bright suggestions. Gray was holding about sixty pounds, which included two weeks' rent. He thought he could maybe borrow a bit more if he put himself about, which he agreed to do. Dragging a car wouldn't be any problem, and he even joked as he started out about what sort of car Connell fancied.

'How long d'you think you'll be, Billy?'

'I dunno, do I? However long it takes to collect what dough I can. Then nick a car.' He tried to ease the man's apprehension. 'Nobody knows you're here, right? Just keep away from the windows. Remember, I'll give three short rings, then one long 'un. Don't come near the door for any other ring. I'm not expecting anyone.'

It took Billy Gray more time than he figured to borrow the money. Working against him was his impending appearance in court. With a possible ten-, twelve- or fifteen-year sentence coming, people considered him a bad risk. Some slipped him the odd fiver for old-time's sake. It was a hopeless exercise, which would have been made worse if he'd mentioned Connell. Getting a car proved no easy matter either – it was one of those nights. As he was forcing a window, he glanced up and saw a police Panda car turn into the street. Fortunately he saw it before the driver saw him. A trickle of sweat ran down his spine as the police car passed, and it was with a sinking feeling that he realised what he had let himself in for. What chance would he have of any help in court from the CID if while on bail he was done for attempted car theft? To say nothing of his chances if word ever got out that he helped Connell. Finding himself in that situation made him very uneasy; the only possible way out that he saw made him feel even worse.

Being an armed blagger, Billy Gray knew how easily he could have been in the predicament Connell was in; he might have shot a copper on any of the bank raids he had been on. It was no good telling himself that he had more sense. It happened; you went with a gun, you had to expect it.

But his own determination to survive, and show his wife that the life wasn't all aggravation, was a stronger pull. He knew of no one, not a single villain who would blame him for turning Connell in, and many who would thank him.

Detective Inspector Peacock wasn't at his office, but then Gray wasn't surprised, at that time of night. The filth who answered the phone wanted to take a message, but the felon had Peacock's home number.

'Is it important, Billy?' the DI asked, reluctant to stir out of his comfortable position in front of the TV.

'Would I be phoning you if it wasn't, guv? I think this'll get me all the help you promised me for the right thing.'

When they met later Stephen Peacock couldn't disguise his excitement as Gray gave him Connell's whereabouts.

'He's there now? You're sure?'

'Ain't got nowhere else to go, has he,' the felon said. 'What about my help, guv? Will that do it?'

Peacock agreed with alacrity, 'I won't let you down,' though he knew he couldn't guarantee it. Only he didn't tell Gray that. He would however try and do what he could. He'd ask Mr Fordham to approach the DPP on Gray's behalf and get him help that way.

'I don't suppose you want to be there when we crash in?'

'Fuck I!' Gray exclaimed. 'Would you?'

'Here's what you do then.' He checked the time. 'Get back there. Tell Connell you've arranged to get a safe car for him. That you've got to go back for it at one. Then call this number at the Yard. That'll give us time to set things up.'

'What if he wants to go with me?'

'Tell him the fella who's supplying doesn't want to be involved. He trusts you, Billy.'

Peacock didn't expect to find Fordham at the Yard, but to have the duty officer tell him where he could be found. Martin Savory, the DCI who had replaced Dyce, said that the governor had not long left, and was on his way to Wimbledon nick to see Ryman. He told the DI to get down there; meanwhile he would send a couple of Ds to Gray's place on watch, and get two squads back for the anticipated raid.

Nothwithstanding weeks on remand in Brixton Prison, Harold Stonehall, the accountant who had given himself up at Barnet police station, looked remarkably well. Relief from the pressure of being a fugitive had made a difference in him, and on remand he had all home comforts, unlike prisoners who had been sentenced.

At Wimbledon police station Fordham greeted the man as though he were an old friend; Stonehall had arrived there first with Senior and another detective. There had been no problem getting him released into the Squad's custody for the purpose of making an identification.

'Has he had a look yet?' the DCS asked.

'No,' Senior replied. 'Thought we'd wait for you, guv.'

Stonehall had a mugful of tea, which Fordham told him to finish, and went off to find the duty sergeant to check what was happening with Ryman. He was informed that Ryman hadn't been charged, and that Scottish detectives weren't long finished interviewing him.

'Always did have a good sense of timing,' Fordham said, but didn't qualify the statement.

'We have someone down here we think you know,

Harold,' Fordham said, leading Stonehall to the cells. 'We want you to have a look through the shutter, see if you recognize him.'

Without hesitation the accountant identified Charlie Ryman as the man who, calling himself Richardson, had blackmailed him into giving details which subsequently led to the robbery at his firm.

'We'd like a new statement to that effect, Mr Stonehall. Inspector Senior will take it.' Stonehall was agreeable. 'Then take him over to Battersea, Bill, where they're holding Day. See if he can't ID him as the draftsman. I'll be here quite a while, I think.'

Ryman looked up expectantly as the cell door opened. He was both pleased and surprised when Fordham stepped inside and closed the door, but he checked his reaction, as though believing it might weaken his position.

Standing inside the doorway, Fordham considered the prisoner, then shook his head in dismay. 'All the trouble I went to trying to keep you out of here, Charlie ... You'll never know.'

'Tell that to those fucking Jocks,' Ryman began angrily, but realised Fordham was the wrong man to get angry with. He smiled. 'It's a turn up for the book, John. Me in here without my belt – as if I'd hang myself.'

'Some of them try. Have you seen your brief?'

'No. They haven't let me near a telephone. They haven't even charged me.'

'The thing is, Charlie, they don't know what to charge you with.'

'Well, just as soon as I get in touch with my mouthpiece, he'll sort them out. He'll get a writ of habeas corpus.'

'Who's your brief? Symons? He's very good – mind you, the price he charges.'

'You'd better tell *them* how good he is.'

There was a pause. Ryman watched the DCS, as if he expected him to be sufficiently impressed to spring him immediately.

'How do you and this Kellan get on?'

Fordham shook his head. 'We don't see eye to eye.'

'I'm not surprised. He seems one of the old school. You know, likes to put a lot of stick about.'

The DCS nodded. 'Especially when one of his lads gets shot.'

'Understandable. Still, there was no need to come down here and turn the world upside down. Was there? Live and let live, that's what I say.'

Fordham didn't say anything. He was happy to let Ryman talk in his quick, nervous manner, pacing and frequently hitching his trousers.

'I mean, no one wanted to see a policeman shot, did they. Doesn't matter where he comes from. Doesn't do anyone any good. A lid gets slammed down on the town while the Jocks crash around ... I don't know, I'm sure. Did I resist? 'Course not. I was the first to cooperate. You wanted some action; you conveyed your wishes to me; I had a punt around; suddenly Brodie's in the bag. We've always understood each other, John. Wouldn't you say?'

Fordham said, 'I can say that.'

'So what am I doing here? I ask as one reasonable man to another. What am I doing in this pisshole?'

Silence fell between them as Ryman awaited an answer.

'Well, Charlie, you're waiting while the Jocks consult their Procurator Fiscal to make sure the charges they lay on you stick.'

'What charges?' His anxiety was dominant.

'Starting with conspiracy in the murder of Superintendent Bothwell ...'

'What? You're not serious!'

'Never more so in my life.' He didn't, in fact, know what charges Kellan was contemplating, but conspiracy was a reasonable guess. 'Unfortunately for you, Charlie, they've nicked Alan Day. By virtue of the briefing you gave him he's put you right up there in Glasgow with the blaggers. If that wasn't enough, they also have Maureen Hoyle, who's told them how you agreed to help get her and Connell out of the country ...'

'She's a fucking liar. You know I'd have more sense – I was trying to get Connell for you.'

'I believe it, but you're not dealing with me.' He watched Ryman sink despondently on to the edge of the bed shelf to consider his prospects. To judge by his expression he knew they weren't good. 'Your team's been set for a reverse for a while now, Charlie, and you know it. You've probably taken all the precautions you could in the event of going away yourself; put your property in your wife's name; some of it in your stepdaughters' name. I 'spect most of your money's been placed too, just in case the court decided you should make restitution. You could probably have coped with a three- or four-stretch; full remission, early parole, you'd have been out in twelve months. But now we're into a different league. We're talking about twelves and fifteens, maybe even twenty years. Probably with a recommendation. That makes you what, forty-nine – sixty-nine years old before you get another taste, Charlie.'

Ryman closed his eyes, trying to deny the possibility. He nodded very slowly, as if he had aged those twenty years and was afraid to make active movements.

He looked straight at Fordham. 'Can anything be done? You know I can put plenty of dough into you, and make it safe.'

'Don't think I couldn't use it.' He appeared to make himself amenable, extend hope, only to snatch it back. 'But it isn't down to me. It's the other fella.'

'What do you think of the chances of putting an earner into him? If you made the approaches?'

'I'm sure his needs are as great as anyone's, especially as he must be nearing retirement. But then he's a proud man, and it was one of his lads who died. The fact is we don't talk civilly to one another . . .'

'Fucking Scotchmen,' Ryman said. 'If only they hadn't come crashing in, I could have had Connell for you. She was going to take me.'

'Connell?' Fordham laughed. He didn't enlighten Ryman about the plans he had had for him over Connell's arrest.

'Who the fuck wants Connell? Brodie and Connell were just sops, to get the Jocks off our backs. I don't want them. It's you I want, Charlie, and the man behind you. I want Duckett, and the man behind him; Sir Frank O'Connor, and the money behind him. I want the whole network of bent architects, resident engineers, local government officials. I want everything you know about that set-up, and everything you weren't supposed to know but speculated about and made it your business to find out. Then, and only then, we'll start talking in terms of help for you.'

Utter amazement appeared on Ryman's face. He looked at the man as though suspecting he had taken leave of his senses. He said carefully, 'But what good will it do you, Mr Fordham?'

'The proposition at this moment, Charlie, is what good will it do you?'

'But I don't see how it'll help you, knowing such things. I mean, I'm nothing. But the people involved above me, I mean, that's the Establishment. Important people. They're Cabinet Ministers, Members of Parliament working for them. People with connections to Royalty. That's the ruling class.'

Fleetingly Fordham was tempted to indulge in a piece of conceit and tell the man not to underestimate his power, but he knew that would be overestimating it. Instead he said, 'Think of me as a bank, Charlie, in which people deposit secrets rather than money. Now, you know how banks work. The bank pays the depositor interest, keeps his money safe and still makes a profit.'

There was a long, thoughtful silence.

Finally Ryman cleared his throat nervously. 'Three or four?' he asked quietly. 'Is it still a prospect, guv?'

'I'd say it was.' Fordham would promise him the moon if necessary. 'You're a million.'

The opening shots of their trade-off were fired. Now Charles Ryman was committed. Having forsaken his aspirations to move up the social ladder and join the class for whom he had such admiration, he was determined to save himself, get what help he could, get the most favourable terms. Whether or not the DCS dared to charge the people above him had become immaterial to Ryman. The relevant points were, one, that he was nicked himself, and two, those people weren't likely to get themselves involved by trying to do anything for him. In the final analysis it always ended up at what you achieved for yourself in life.

Leaving Ryman in the cell, Fordham went to the front office and made the arrangements for having him transferred to Cannon Row police station, where he would be his prisoner rather than Kellan's. He anticipated a long session before getting the statement he needed, and then probably a lot of subsequent meetings to verify points. He didn't want to have to travel out to Wimbledon each time. He telephoned Battersea police station to make arrangements to have Day transferred as well.

Fordham leant back in the duty sergeant's chair and put his feet on the desk. He yawned expansively, the tension which had been building up to this point slackening slightly. He felt tired and would like to have gone home, maybe drunk a little, even made love to Kika. But that wasn't the moment to ease off. When he had Ryman's incriminating statement carefully written and signed, plus one from Alan Day complementing it, that would be the time.

As the duty sergeant came in, fetching him a cup of tea, Fordham removed his feet from the desk; he didn't indulge his rank in that way. Stephen Peacock followed the sergeant in.

'Stephen. What brings you this way?'

The DI glanced at the uniform.

'Thanks, skip,' Fordham said, lifting the tea. The sergeant went out.

'Connell, we have him well bottled up, guv.' He couldn't keep the excitement down.

Fordham listened to the details, and about the situation with Billy Gray. Then he congratulated Peacock, and said he'd have Commander Pope approach the Director of Public

Prosecutions about getting help for Gray. But finally he blanked Peacock's request to lead his squad in after Connell.

In such a situation it was Peacock's unspoken right to make the arrest. 'With the greatest respect, guv, I'd like to be there. If it's all the same.'

'It's not, Stephen,' the DCS said simply.

He had something else in mind; he wanted the Jocks rendered amenable, tied up, made harmless, thus giving him a free run with Ryman and Day. Now he had the means.

'Let the Jocks have him, Stephen. Let them have their moment of glory. I'll see you get your credit.'

Chapter 34

The news that Fordham had transferred both Charles Ryman and Alan Day to Cannon Row made Kellan see red; it preceded the news of Fordham's arrival at Tintagel House only by minutes, thereby causing and subsequently allowing the Scottish DCS to vent his wrath.

Detectives who were gathering in the two general offices, turned their attention to Fordham as he sauntered through, disregarding the tearful Maureen Hoyle.

Kellan rose violently when Fordham reached the third office, demanding to know why he had taken it upon himself to transfer his prisoners. The door was left open this time, and none of the detectives were even pretending to involve their attention elsewhere.

'The reason,' Fordham said evenly, 'is so that they can help further with my enquiries, which you seem bent on wrecking.'

'Is that it? Or so that you can do some trading in private, laddie?'

'Same difference, Mr Kellan. Checks and balances. S'what keeps us all working. I came here to do you a favour. I thought you might like to know where Connell is.'

'Save your breath to talk yoursel' out of the mess you're in. We know where he is.'

Glancing out at Maureen Hoyle, who was also following the proceedings, then back to Kellan, Fordham smiled, neither maliciously, nor condescendingly. 'If you're mustering your men to raid that flop-house in Bayswater, you're wasting your time. That's old news. He's long gone.'

Surprise galvanized Kellan; then came the dawning that Fordham had information he wanted.

Fordham swung back to the door, clasping the edge. He stared at the Scottish Ds. 'Have you no fucking work to do?'

They responded instantly. It was the automatic response of the lower ranks to a senior officer. Fordham closed the door.

'I'm no' meking deals wi' you, Fordham.'

Fordham regarded his opposite number. 'I'm not giving you the option. I'm telling you how I want things to go.' He paused briefly. 'Perhaps you would prefer the Squad to pick up Connell as an exclusive operation? That might make people wonder what you were doing here in the first place.'

'You're talking about the vicious wee bastard who killed one of ma men. I want him.'

'It's got nothing to do with Bothwell's death, not any more. Not for you. It's your fucking star image. Your ego. You have to prove you're the front runner still. Number one.'

'You aided and abetted that robbery. From keeping the Hammersmith police away from Mrs Brodie's house while Brodie went there, to putting the villains on the train. Aside from meking deals all round wi' their accomplices. I'm going to see you broken, laddie.'

'You're going to do no such thing. You're going to have your moment of glory. Capture Connell; then collect Brodie from hospital, and take them both to Scotland. Later you might, but only might, get Ryman and Day and the men who put the job together. At the moment they're both part of an enquiry that I've spent eighteen months on. With their help it's at last coming to fruition. So that not only do they get weighed off, but also the people higher than them; those who put up the initial expenses for the Glasgow blag, along with about nine others like it.'

The two DCSs stared at each other in silence.

Then Kellan capitulated. 'Give me Connell's whereabouts.'

Fordham did. 'One final thing. Don't even think about trying for the man whose flat it is.'

Watching Fordham move out, Kellan wondered fleetingly how the man ever got into the police force. He probably lied about his age to start with. The thought caused a flicker of amusement. He crossed to the door; expectant faces of his detectives met him.

'Dougie?' he said, and turned back, indicating Douglas

to follow.

'Is the raid off, sir?'

'A change of venue, s'all. Muster the men at Shepherd's Bush police station for one o'clock. Full turn-out, Dougie. Get on to the station officer, Dougie, mek the arrangements. I'll want to speak to the local superintendent. I'll see Mr McFageon, Crombie, Murry, Waterman and yoursel' here before we leave.'

When his aide went out Kellan sat heavily. His mood was pensive but his thoughts were engaging nothing in particular, merely passing at random over events which had led him to this point. He wondered if tonight would see the end, if by daybreak they would have Connell. He hoped so, for he felt exhausted, both physically and mentally, and he knew he couldn't sustain the pressure for much longer. For the first time he admitted to himself that he wasn't the man he had been ten years ago, nor even five years ago. His gaze fell into the middle-distance, and he ceased to be aware of those around him. As he sat there a strange feeling came over him; he felt very insecure, as though he had been set adrift; the ground having been cut so often from under his feet, there no longer seemed to be anything to which he could immediately anchor himself.

Abstractedly he reached for the telephone and dialled his home number. The phone rang out for a long time before it was answered.

'S'that you, Alice?' he said. The call surprised him as much as it did his wife.

'Is there something wrong? Have you had an accident, Ian?' Normally he didn't call her.

'No. I should be back tomorrow evening, wi' luck ... I ha'e Connell, I think ...'

'I was in bed, I didn't hear the phone.'

'He's hiding out at Shepherd's Bush, West London ... I'm going to pick him up shortly.'

'Ha'e you been getting any regular sleep, Ian? I don't suppose ...'

There was a long silence, neither knowing what to say.

'I'm surprised you called,' the woman said vaguely.
'I saw the lad. He called me.'
'How is he?'
'He looked well enough, I'd say. He'll be writing.'
'Did you row again, Ian?'
'No. No . . . Look, hen, I ha'e to go. I'll see you tomorrow.'

Kellan felt a sense of relief when he replaced the phone. Talking to his wife had reassured him that nothing had changed; that there in Glasgow his familiar world was awaiting him.

Back at the Yard Fordham called Frank Borroughs and Ned Garmonsway at home and had them come in. Then he phoned Commander Pope, getting him out of bed, told him about Stephen Peacock conjuring up Connell, and made a request for some help for Billy Gray. It was always as well to get that in early, as it would have been pointless asking if they missed Connell, regardless of whether or not it was Gray's fault.

Against Fordham's advice the commander decided he would be present at the raid.

'I think the Squad ought to be represented, John,' he said, justifying his position. 'Since you're not going to be present.'

'S'up to you, Gerald, but I think we're better off out of it. I'll be down at Cannon Row, if you want me.'

Fordham stepped into the corridor, and, running into a young DC, whose name he couldn't remember, sent him to fetch some coffee. Then he moved along to the DCIs' office. Martin Savory was working in a small pool of light. Fordham gave him about a fortnight of such conscientiousness before, like most DCIs when night duty officer, he was off stiffing one within close call.

'Morning, guv. Busy night,' Savory commented cheerfully.

'Looks that way, Martin.' He found an electric shaver in Corrigan's desk, plugged it in and ran it over his scratchy beard.

'One to meet, guv?'

'Wish I had.'

He blew the razor clean, and replaced it in the drawer. He never considered getting one of his own. He didn't like electric shaving much anyway, but a shave of any kind gave him an edge at that time of the morning over someone who hadn't had the opportunity.

'When Bill Senior gets back here have him join me at Cannon Row. And I'm taking a couple of lads from the night squad with me.'

Borroughs, Garmonsway and Senior all arrived within minutes of each other. The DCS had no need to warn them that it was going to be a long night. They knew that interrogating both Charlie Ryman and Alan Day would be a mammoth task, likely to take several days, though not continuously, when they would constantly be returning to them to cross-check different aspects of their statements, which might be either contradicted or corroborated by elements from elsewhere. Fordham was going to interrogate Ryman, Borroughs would take on Day. Before they started both detainees were asked for permission for their apartments to be searched. This was done in the presence of the station officer. Both men granted their permission and weren't concerned about having anyone accompany the officers making the search. They had no worries of being planted, for they were already well stitched up; both men knew there was little at their dwellings that might do them further harm. Ryman's wife was at home to take care of his interests; however, Day wasn't anticipating the DCS.

While DI Garmonsway went out to Wimbledon to Ryman's house, Bill Senior headed for Day's two rooms, going via the Yard, where he collected all the incriminating evidence which Borroughs had previously removed. He would return it and amazingly re-discover it.

Interrogating Ryman was like breaching a dyke, Fordham found. Once a start had been made information poured out. Ryman seemed to get carried away by his self-created impetus. Every word was meticulously taken down by DS Lessing, who was in with them. While carefully probing at the information Ryman had, so as not to miss any aspect, Fordham knew that at last the case had yielded, he would get enough leverage to prise open the whole operation. This, along with all that DI Norman was now getting from David Champion, one of O'Connor's senior quantity surveyors, concerning bent architects and companies that had been set up for two ex-Cabinet Ministers to skim off the top in the guise of advisors, added together with all the other aspects of the case, including the resident engineer tucked up along the Westway. He knew it was enough to move against O'Connors, Duckett and so on. He felt very gratified, as though there was something more to his job than the games which detectives and villains seemed for ever to be playing. He was suddenly into a win-all lose-all situation, and anticipated how he would come out.

Chapter 35

Thirty-one Scottish detectives, all armed, gathered in the muster room at Shepherd's Bush police station. Most of the local CID had been recalled, and many of the uniform branch were present also. It made quite a crowd in that room. So Ian Kellan kept his briefing short. He told them why they were mustered; he didn't need to tell them why they were armed, but he told them anyway; also there was no need to speak of his determination to take Connell, but again he did.

With the assistance of local officers Kellan had worked out his plan for approaching the flat. The entire area around the block would be sealed by the uniform branch. The rest of the operation would be done by stealth. If and only if that failed, force would be employed. Police marksmen would be positioned on the balconies of a block opposite; detectives in twos and threes would go up in lifts and by the stairs, placing themselves on the floors immediately above and below Connell. McFageon, who had put his hand up for the job, would go in through the front door with DI Waterman and DC Kevin Daly. They would use the key and the bell signal they had been given.

'Whatever happens,' Kellan said, 'I don't want this bass shooting another policeman.'

The twelve cars the Jocks had, plus eight local cars and two Ford Transit vans full of uniforms, left Shepherd's Bush police station at two a.m. in a tight convoy. It was impossible to keep that sort of operation secret from the media. No matter how important in police terms, there was always someone who would give them the bell. Kellan raised no objection when they began turning up, and wouldn't, provided they stayed out of the way.

There was little other traffic as the convoy proceeded along Lime Grove and into Goldhawk Road. There were even less pedestrians. A black man, bopping along to a

Reggae beat inside his head, took fright on seeing so many police vehicles – there was no mistaking them – and quickened his pace, as if hurrying for the empty night-bus that was cruising along.

Kellan's car turned into Hammersmith Grove, then first right into Benbow Road, where it stopped. Other cars pulled up immediately behind, some staying on Hammersmith Grove; others continued along Goldhawk Road to the next two turnings. Within minutes the entire block was cordoned off. No one could pass either in or out without meeting policemen. The radios had all been switched to the same waveband and one by one each position was reported to the DCS.

Kellan turned to DCI Crombie. 'Start getting your men in, Alan.'

Crombie nodded and moved round to each group of detectives where they stood in tense, tight knots. As he did so they started away towards the block.

When the DCS's eyes met his, McFageon held Kellan's look. They were closely in tune, he thought, each clearly understanding the other's feeling. Kellan knew why the DCI had put his hand up for the job, and guessed McFageon knew he would like to have been doing it himself. But this was one occasion where Kellan had to demur.

'Good luck, Bob,' Kellan said in a low, slightly emotional voice.

'Aye,' McFageon replied, and moved off with Waterman and Daly.

There was a flurry of activity at the police cordon on Hammersmith Grove as Commander Pope arrived. The uniform sergeant there instinctively knew brass hats, and vaguely recognized the Squad Commander anyway. He saluted briskly. The press immediately waylaid Pope, throwing questions at him, most of which he wasn't able to answer. 'Was it Connell?' 'Were they confident of capturing him?' He told them to ask Mr Kellan, whose raid it was. They followed the commander through the barrier the police had set up; a few were pursued by uniforms and turned back, but some fell into step alongside Pope as though they were detectives themselves.

Displeasure was much in evidence on Kellan's face when Pope joined him; his greeting was brief, grudging.

'What's the position, chief superintendent?' Gerald Pope asked, as if oblivious to Kellan's hostility.

Kellan gave him the bare details in a tone which brooked no tactical argument. Even the press, who held back so as not to be sent away, understood this. It was Kellan's raid and it would be conducted without help or hindrance from anyone on the Squad.

Pope offered no argument. There was nothing he could suggest that would make the task of going in and fetching Connell out any safer for the detectives involved.

Word started to come through from the units in the block of flats as they got into position. The final word was from McFageon. He was on the landing to Gray's flat and about to approach the door. Kellan tensed as the radio went silent. He glanced at Pope, who seemed equally apprehensive.

'Ready, then?' McFageon said to the men with him.

There was a moment's hesitation from each. He knew how they felt. That same reluctance twisted a knot of tension in his gut. He could think of many things he'd rather be doing then, far more things he would rather contemplate than walking up to that door and running the risk of being shot; some of those things passed fleetingly through his thoughts, but he didn't even try to engage them. This was where he was, the course he had chosen; he knew what he had to do.

Launching himself off the wall, he said quietly, 'Let's get it done.' He led the way, the other two detectives close behind.

The walk was no more than fifteen yards, yet it took for ever, like one of those walks in a dream where your legs worked but you got nowhere. Their feet on the terrazzo floor combined to make a cacophony of noise, it seemed to them.

They stopped before reaching the door and each checked

his gun, making sure the safety catch was off. There was little point in going armed unless the gun could be fired.

At the door they paused. McFageon looked at the other two men. They appeared calm enough, but he guessed they were feeling no less tense than he was. He wondered if he looked as calm.

After carefully inserting the key in the lock McFageon's hand moved across to the bellpush; he hesitated, then stabbed it with three short and one long ring. A light appeared almost immediately in the darkened flat. Connell must have been sitting in the dark waiting for the signal. McFageon counted to three, giving Connell time to get into the lighted hall, then twisting the key, he threw the door open. The detectives went through the door so closely they might have been one.

For a fraction of a second Connell froze in disbelief, staring like a rabbit mesmerised in the beam of a car's headlamps. 'Oh, no, no ...!' In panic he ran towards the policemen, gun in hand.

Which of them fired first was impossible to say. But quite certain was the fact that all three detectives fired their guns and Connell died. Four bullets hit him. One through his throat, two in his chest, one in his stomach.

The silence which followed in that narrow hallway had a strange, almost eerie quality when the retorts from the shots died away, leaving only a ringing in the detectives' ears. None of them spoke as they looked down at the contorted, blood-torn body. Each in their time had been personally involved in a road accident, the immediate aftereffect the same now: a weakness in the legs; looseness of the stomach; slight trembling, partly of relief, partly out of fear. Complete awareness of what they had done wasn't yet reaching them, certainly not the full implication.

Kevin Daly began to shake. Attending scenes of violence as a uniform constable hadn't really prepared him for this.

'You all right, Kev?' McFageon heard DI Waterman enquire as he stepped forward and stooped by Connell's body to pick up his gun. Releasing the catch and checking the chamber, he discovered the gun was empty. The fact didn't mean anything to the huge DCI. He straightened up, hearing now the running feet outside; then the exclamations of the detectives who appeared in the doorway.

Automatically McFageon moved along the hallway to check the rest of the flat, to make sure there wasn't anyone else waiting with a gun.

People wouldn't forget in a hurry that Brian Connell had shot and killed a policeman.

Chapter 36

Dragging his heels like an old man to his wife's funeral, yet feeling as lightheaded as a boy on his first date, Fordham moved past the constable on duty at the back entrance of the Yard. The policeman saluted as he held the door. Acknowledging him with a flick of his eyes, Fordham continued to the lifts, the folder containing the preliminary results of the three-hour interviews with Ryman and Day held firmly under his arm. Both prisoners had signed their statements, if a little reluctantly – that final commitment to paper invariably caused villains to hesitate. It had been a long and arduous haul, but they were almost there, and Fordham felt it had been worth while.

'D'you hear the news, guv?' Martin Savory said as Fordham entered the DCIs' office. The expression on his face told the duty officer that he hadn't heard. 'Connell bought it when the Jocks went in. Shot stone dead.'

Fordham hadn't known that would happen, but he wasn't surprised, and even less concerned. 'Does that mean we'll have them hanging around for an inquest?'

'I shouldn't think so. From what I heard they can't get out of town fast enough now – Commander Pope was present.'

'Fuck his luck,' Fordham said, knowing the man would have to make the report.

His thoughts moved on. He laid the handwritten copies of the statements on Savory's desk and told him to get them typed and a copy of each sent to both the commander and the AC—Crime directly. He wanted Pope and Goodfellow to have copies waiting for them by the time they got in later that morning.

Fordham went home expecting to fall into bed and right off to sleep. But Kika awoke.

'What time is it?' she wanted to know.

'Almost ten o'clock,' he lied. 'You've a rehearsal, haven't you?'

'Mm, tomorrow.' Reaching her arms around him, she pressed her face against his chest and kissed him. 'We can't go on meeting like this, darling,' she said. 'The neighbours are beginning to talk.'

Trying to ease himself down in the bed, Fordham met resistance. Kika had no intention of letting him find a comfortable position and drift off into sleep.

'I've just come from there,' he said vaguely.

'What?'

'The neighbour's.'

She was amused. 'Is that the reason for this?' she asked, taking hold of his limp cock. It responded to her caresses, but Fordham didn't. Sleep seeped through him, saturating his mind.

The telephone rang, what seemed like only minutes later, but was in fact eleven the next morning. Commander Pope was on the other end, sounding as if he hadn't been back to bed. He informed Fordham that the ACC wanted to see him at two o'clock, and that he wasn't pleased.

On his way in to the Yard, Fordham didn't stop for a copy of the early editions of the evening papers, but he could see from the billboards that they were full of the Connell shooting. Tomorrow the national dailies would give it another going over. Doubtless the police would take a hammering.

At his office Fordham involved himself with routine matters. The Jocks had left town, and he was determined not to become embroiled in the row blowing up in their wake. He held the position that he had maintained all along, that after Kellan had finished the serious business of investigating crime would still remain. Life was going to be difficult, at least for a while.

When Bill Senior gave Fordham the list of his telephone calls, a number of which were from the press, he pointed out that Ryman's lawyer had called three times wanting the details of his client's arrest, and to know what charges, if any, had been brought. Cannon Row police station had blanked the man on instructions from Fordham, who had also told them not to let the lawyer near Ryman unless he made a specific request. The lawyer's threats to get a writ of habeas corpus didn't impress Fordham.

On his way up to see the AC—Crime at the appointed hour, Fordham looked in on Commander Pope. He was engaged in drafting the report on Connell's shooting.

'Everyone from the ACC to the Home Secretary wants the fullest details. It doesn't do to have one of the other side get shot, John.' He sounded disgruntled. 'They'll probably call for an enquiry. Mind you, I suppose it looks bad, Connell's gun being empty.'

'Did he have that information printed on his forehead?' the DCS asked.

'You were well out of it. I wish I was.' He sighed. There was a pause.

'What about the ACC? What's his problem?'

'Can't you guess? He was hopping mad about those statements. About how he told you to drop that investigation.'

'But we came up with the goods, Gerald. Didn't we.'

'You don't have to tell me. I think it's a result. I did what I could to smooth things over, but he wasn't having it, I'm afraid. That's why he wants to see you on your own.'

There was a straightener on the cards between himself and the AC—Crime, but the prospect filled Fordham with no sense of trepidation. He held a trump card. No matter how the man argued, he wouldn't be able to deny the evidence as it was stacking up.

'Evidence?' the ACC said deprecatingly from the safety of his desk. 'You're grabbing at straws in the wind, reaching for the people you're reaching for.'

Fordham was left standing, like a schoolboy up for smoking in the lavatory. He was determined not to take on the mien of that schoolboy.

'The evidence is there to bust them wide open. I have the witness who will testify.'

'Optimistic conjecture. A statement from a once-convicted criminal who currently has his neck in a noose?' He dismissed Ryman's statement contemptuously. 'That will cause

Duckett minor embarrassment, nothing more. I can assure you.'

'That's only the start,' Fordham argued, sensing the whole weight of Establishment bureaucracy moving against him, blocking him. He realized he had made a tactical error in presenting the statement this early, instead of letting it serve as a springboard. 'There are people in local government offices who are going to come as well. Some of them in key positions, who suddenly acquired blocks of shares in O'Connors and its subsidiaries just prior to their getting redevelopment contracts.' Fordham was totally committed now. There was no turning back. 'We've barely scratched the surface of O'Connors. DI Norman got a call from one of their directors, Jeffrey Stebbings. He wants to talk.'

The ACC didn't consider what Fordham had said, but shook his head before he had finished. 'This is as far as it goes, John.'

The air of finality in his words hit Fordham like a blow between the eyes.

'With the greatest respect, sir. I think the DPP should decide that.'

The ACC sighed, as if reluctant to say the words. 'He already has. He doesn't want to know any more or see any more. If he does he might be forced to act. Such a course, in the areas into which you have been delving, wouldn't be in the best interests of the country at the moment. It could cause too many people in high places a great deal of embarrassment. Not least two members of the Government, both of whom are on the board of the Duckett, Reinhardt bank. The ramifications of the scandal this sort of thing inevitably develops into have the unhappy habit of undermining confidence. You have the men responsible for organizing these robberies. You have Ryman and Day. You're to be congratulated on your diligence.' He paused. 'But beyond those two there isn't any case.'

'The fuck there isn't!' The words exploded angrily out of Fordham, but he knew immediately that his anger was as useless as his most reasoned argument.

'What's the matter with you, chief superintendent?' the AC—Crime asked calmly. 'Have you been working too hard?' He waited. 'How do you require this spelt out?'

Fordham didn't reply. The question called for either his resignation or tacit acceptance. He didn't offer to resign. He had lost this battle, maybe even lost the war, but he wasn't prepared to lie down yet.

After Fordham's departure, the ACC leant back in his chair to consider the man in relation to the area he had been probing. He wondered why Fordham was being so pugnacious about the whole matter. There was nothing in his past which suggested he was left-wing or particularly radical. But of most concern was the prospect of whether Fordham would, in fact, let go. Perhaps he'd do well to safeguard against the possibility that he would persist.

Raising the phone, the ACC called Commander Bingham at A10. 'Angus,' he began, sounding his most winsome. 'John Fordham. What's the current position with your investigation?'

'The wheels grind slowly,' Bingham said ponderously.

'But exceedingly small, I hope. Perhaps you would care to come and discuss the matter? Can you make three o'clock . . . Fine. I'll look forward to it.'

Goodfellow sat back and pursed his lips thoughtfully against his index fingers. If there was anything more than a slight justification for suspending John Fordham, pending a full investigation, the ACC wouldn't hesitate. A serious allegation of corruption was needed; the allegation alone would be enough. The integrity of the police had to be seen to be intact.

Epilogue

Drinking wasn't an entrenched habit. Fordham couldn't match his detectives drink for drink and wouldn't try. But sometimes he felt the need as he did then.

There had been no let-up for the past week, which had culminated in his appearance at Bow Street magistrates' court that morning with no less than twenty-three villains. Each had been remanded, having been picked up in a massive raid by the Squad on over forty addresses in and around London. All resulted from information received from Ryman and Day, and the way things were stacking there was a better than good chance that over ninety per cent of them would be commited for trial; they were each connected with the ten robberies for which Ryman had been responsible.

A tremendous effort, the hierarchy and the press would say. Putting villains where they belonged was a tangible result, it wasn't simply figures on a graph which showed how, despite increased police efficiency, they were losing ground.

But for Fordham the tremendous effort was quite meaningless, which was why he felt as he did. He swallowed his scotch, then signalled the barman in the James Street, Covent Garden, pub where he had gone with Frank Borroughs.

The DCI was surprised at his governor drinking like this, but comfortably emptied his own glass so as not to miss out.

The effort was meaningless to Fordham because it had been forced in a single direction: downwards from Ryman, hitting only the cowboys. Although Fordham agreed that they deserved locking away for the part they had played, he felt society wasn't even paying lip-service to justice when he was not allowed to at least try for those people up there in safe positions above Ryman.

The main reason for his depression was the knowledge

that he had capitulated. Having come so close to Duckett, O'Connor and Alex Jacobs, he had buckled under pressure. The AC—Crime and the DPP had leaned on him and he hadn't resisted. He liked his job, liked being the guvnor; he had allowed himself to become corrupted by the power he currently held. How long before he was like the hierarchy, resembling it so closely that he could no longer tell himself apart? The question, he realised, wasn't how long, rather how soon. Kika had realised something was wrong; she had told him he had stopped smiling. She didn't know what the matter was, and he was glad. He wouldn't have enjoyed her knowing he had given way. She meant that much to him. His being a policeman was something she could reluctantly accept, but his kowtowing to the Establishment would be something else. She would never have accepted that that was the single choice – he knew himself it wasn't. She was very perceptive, and he wondered how long it would be before she recognized him for what he was allowing himself to become.

'We going to have a bit of lunch, John?' Borroughs said, concerned at the way Fordham was starting his third large scotch.

'Yeah. I won't get pissed. Much as I feel like it.'

They made their way to the end of the bar where food was laid out.

As they were eating, Borroughs glanced at the DCS and said, as though anticipating the trouble, 'It is a bit of a result, John, whatever way you look at it.'

'You don't believe that, Frank, any more than I do.' He pushed some beef into his mouth. 'Even if they all get twenty years apiece, which they deserve, it's still a joke unless we at least try for the others.'

They ate without talking for a while, the noise of the pub filling the silence.

'Have you had plenty of earners in your time, Frank?' Fordham asked casually. 'Tucked enough away for when you retire?'

The big man laughed. 'What are you, A10?' He hesitated,

but knew the DCS was making a point rather than an enquiry. 'Had my share, I s'pose. No more than that. Lately, though?' – he shrugged.

'Don't really have too many opportunities at our level,' Fordham said helpfully.

'True. But the few are usually bigger. And no one looks too closely, do they. I mean, not at our rank. 'Specially not at yours. I mean, everyone believes the guvnors are straight. They think they've got to be, or there's no hope.'

'I don't know, Frank. Take Peter Walsh. He got looked at, didn't he?'

The DCI acquiesced.

'Sometimes you wonder if it's all worth while. The effort getting into that position. Oh, not because it no longer guarantees your earners. But because of the way you have to conduct yourself. It makes you conform to a pattern, do what's expected of you.' He paused. 'What do you think Peter Goodfellow's having?'

'His old lady, I suppose. I heard one or two whispers, but he's a fucking sight closer than you. But like I say, people would be very leary of him if he wasn't.'

'Did you know he was in line for a directorship with O'Connor's?'

Loud laughter burst from Borroughs, causing people in the pub to turn. Surprise more than mirth was the cause.

'Fuck a duck! No wonder he's been protecting them.' He chuckled to himself in quiet amusement. 'And here was me thinking his moves were dictated by something as noble as maintaining the status quo,' he said mockingly. 'All it is, in fact, is a nice bit of self-interest. Still, I don't suppose that's so much different from a DI somewhere doing a favour, getting a friend or someone dropped out of a charge. We've all done it.'

'Sure,' Fordham said. His opinion about policemen using their position in such a manner hadn't changed. What he objected to was the way Goodfellow had dressed up his vested interest, sought to protect it in the way he had. Had he said it wasn't in his own interest to have that area of investigation proceeded with, Fordham might have responded. But to say it wasn't in the public interest was shit – worse, it was an insult. The directors of Frank O'Connor and Son, of Duckett, Reinhardt, a couple of members of the Government, and various members of local government weren't the general public, they weren't even representative. He wondered how Goodfellow would react to the news of Daniel Rochester being tucked up along the Westway, whether his vested interest would provide strong enough glue to keep the paper stuck over that one.

'Fuck them,' Fordham said, and emptied his glass.

'Y'what, guv?' The DCI noted the change in his governor.

Fordham looked across the small marble-topped table and considered the heavy figure opposite him. The information Frank Borroughs had been given about the ACC had been absorbed, and stored in his brain, stamped 'accepted'. It was interesting, unexpected, but finally permissible. Borroughs was a good detective, knew the score. But because of his whole lifetime in the practice, and the conditioning he had received, whether or not he would openly admit it, like most of his fellows he would support the status quo; that was what he was there for. He might deviate, make a few rules for himself, but in the final analysis he would do what was expected, respond to whatever edicts the hierarchy laid down. Fordham knew himself to be different. Maybe it arose from the fact that he had taken short-cuts by coming in directly from university as an inspector and missing out on all that early conditioning. Quite definitely he was from a different mould.

'There are a few more yet to come, Frank.' The way he said it left no doubt about his moves.

Regardless of the AC—Crime's directive, Fordham made a trip to Benenden in Kent to see Anthony Duckett.

As his car swept along the driveway, Fordham was impressed. Going on reports received from his detectives, the DCS had figured Duckett lived in some style. The house was like something out of the Stately Homes of Britain, a big, square, solid-looking building of the Regency period. Yellow and green ivy grew up one side and had been carefully kept back from the windows. The gardens were meticulous, yet avoided regimentation, with large patches of daffodils growing naturally under trees. The relatively mild winter had brought plants on early, rhododendron buds were bursting pink and crimson, and cherry trees were in blossom around one side of the paddock.

'It's a bit of a gaff, guv,' Syd Worker said.

Fordham didn't reply. He was thinking how much of a punishment giving up this place would be, but to do so for prison would be murder.

'Is Mr Duckett expecting you, sir?' the butler asked, admitting Fordham.

'Well. I telephoned him ...' He didn't add that he thought he wouldn't make it as a result.

'Just one moment, sir.'

The grey-suited man moved away along the spacious entrance hall. Fordham let his gaze wonder over the paintings on the panelled walls. They weren't portraits of ancestors, but works by painters whose names one recognized, if only by the prices they fetched at Sotheby's.'

'Mr Duckett suggested you might care to join him in the conservatory. Shall I take your coat, sir?'

Fordham kept his coat on but wished he hadn't. The conservatory was very humid, plants, most of which weren't familiar to him, ranged the shelves. Attending those alone would probably have been a full-time job for a gardener. The glass construction ran the length of the house.

Rising from the cracked leather couch, Duckett came forward, shaking Fordham's hand.

'Your man seemed surprised,' the DCS said bluntly.

'Quite frankly, Mr Fordham, so am I. But I suppose there must be some independent thinking in the police.' He smiled at the joke. 'Do sit down.'

'I'll be fine standing.'

'I see. It's to be that sort of meeting, is it? Well then, let us get directly to the point. What is it you want with me?'

There was a sudden brusqueness that his previous display of charm belied.

Fordham produced a folded copy of Ryman's statement and handed it to Duckett. 'That might interest you.'

Taking the typed sheets, Duckett ran his shrewd banker's eyes over them, identifying them immediately. Their contents caused him no distress, nor the *fait accompli* presentation. He wasn't even surprised, for he had seen it before, and had read it closely. The DPP had shown it him over lunch at the Junior Carlton Club in Pall Mall earlier in the week, when he had adequately explained his relationship with Ryman, certainly to the DPP's satisfaction. Ryman was in a hole and responding to police promises with whatever idiotic speculation he could think up. Duckett wasn't in the least disturbed by it, nor embarrassed, but rather amused.

'He ought to extend this to a full-length work of fiction,' he said dismissively and returned the document. 'I'm sure it would top the bestseller lists.'

'Nothing else to add, sir?'

Duckett offered a formal smile. 'Did you expect me to prove equally verbose? I have nothing to add to what I told Sir Horace Sampson the other day.'

He précised his meeting with the DPP. The fact that the two men had met and discussed the statement embarrassed Fordham, but the banker took no pleasure in his discomfort.

'Short of perhaps implicating the DPP, and suggesting he is part of a gigantic conspiracy, I don't know what to add. In either event, I think you would come to grief. Far be it for me to tell you how to run your investigation, only I do feel you are drifting into very deep, and somewhat uncharted, waters.' He smiled again, and moved across to where a single decanter and some glasses stood on a tripod table by the end of the couch. 'Sherry? I can recommend it.'

Fordham declined the offer and watched the man fill just one of the lead crystal glasses.

'I see there is one of two options open to us. Either you bring on all of your evidence and we fight, a fight which, I hasten to add, you won't win. Or we proceed in a reasonable manner.'

There was a pause as Fordham's look measured the man. Surrounding him was a strong wall, erected through generations of privilege, and logic told Fordham that he had little chance of knocking it down to make a significant assault on the man.

'Is there another security directorship in the offing for when I retire?' he asked pleasantly.

'Unless you were to conduct yourself in a completely irrational manner, I would have thought you were a long way from retirement, Mr Fordham. However, I don't doubt that with shopping around a lucrative position could be found for a man of your talents. Even some kind of directorship.'

Fordham nodded. Those sort of moves were far safer than taking straight bribes, yet paradoxically there were less risks in taking money; then one wasn't caught in a state of uncertainty, left dangling, wondering about the probabilities of those promises, whether they would finally be fulfilled.

Finding himself at a watershed, Fordham hesitated, unable to make an instant decision about his future direction.

'Is this your interest?' he asked tangentially, indicating the greenery.

'Not really. My ex-wife had a passion for the exotic. I don't know why I keep them on. I suppose because I'm a sentimental sort of person.'

Fordham nodded, not believing it. The man was far too practical. He had arrived at the decision about which direction to take.

'I'll have that glass of sherry now.'

Possibly he only imagined it, but he thought he saw relief wash fleetingly across Duckett's face.

The weekend was on his side, but it was about the only thing that was. On Saturday and Sunday the hierarchy slept; so on those two days he could steal a march, and chance their fury on Monday when they got the report about his activities. There was going to be a fight, and Fordham was preparing himself. Quite why, he wasn't sure; possibly it was nothing more than perversity which kept one foot going on down in front of the other.

Fred Colmain was preparing to leave for the day when Fordham rang the forensic lab. He didn't seem terribly happy about the delay, but said he would hang on for the DCS. He was even less happy when Fordham arrived and told him what he wanted.

'You want us to go back to the Westway and re-examine that column?' he said incredulously. 'But what's the point, chief superintendent? We won't be able to state with any greater accuracy what we believe might be buried there.'

'The point is, this visit will be official. And you will be able to speculate with some degree of certainty that you think it's a body tucked up there . . .' He silenced the protest the forensic scientist was about to make. 'At least with enough certainty to have the column opened for a sample of what's inside for you to examine. On your official speculation, I'll have a hole drilled in the column. Now I can't do that on the non-existent report of a non-existent examination you made previously, can I? So if you would oblige me, I'd appreciate it.'

Colmain considered the situation, then nodded. He was intrigued to know what the concrete stanchion held. 'I'd better call my wife, and tell her I'll be late. Then arrange some transport.'

'It's all arranged.'

That wasn't the only thing Fordham had arranged. He had laid on builders to drill a hole in the concrete; he had been in touch with the local council to close down the overhead section of the motorway, not that the design engineer, who would be present, foresaw any resultant structural damage; Borroughs was liaising with the Hammersmith police, getting them to control traffic along Wood Lane. This was intentionally a big production, one at which the media would inevitably make an appearance. Fordham hadn't called them, but he wouldn't resist any who turned up.

A body was very tangible, especially a dead one. It would give new impetus to the investigation. Someone had placed the body there; someone on the site in an administrative position had to be involved, for you couldn't simply add a whole section to a column without someone being aware of it. Someone higher up the ladder must have employed whoever to do the deed. Fordham was confident that all roads would eventually lead to the boardroom of O'Connor's.

Because of these activities the hierarchy might find cause to suspend him for his past conduct, though more than likely they would transfer him out of the Squad to a divisional HQ, where he would be so tied up running his division that he wouldn't have time to cause trouble. But one thing was for sure: the cracks Fordham was causing wouldn't be easily plastered over. All his efforts during the past eighteen months wouldn't have been for sweet nothing.